NOT FOR SALE AT ANY PRICE

"You can't sell a galactic citizen down there," Captain Bel Thorne said, gesturing jerkily to the curve of the planet beyond the viewport. The quaddie Nicol's intense blue eyes blazed.

Ryoval turned back, feigning sudden surprise. "Why, Captain, I just realized. If you're a Betan, you must be a *genuine* genetic hermaphrodite. You possess a marketable rarity yourself. I can offer you an eye-opening employment experience at easily twice your current rate of pay. And you wouldn't even have to get shot at. I guarantee you'd be extremely popular. Group rates."

Miles swore he could see Thorne's _____ _____ ssure skyrocketing as the meaning of wh___ _____ _____ aid sunk in. Bel's face darkened, a_ _____ _____ ___hed up and grasped Bel by ___

"No?" sai_ _____ _____ _____ _____ y well for a tissue sampl__ _____

Bel's breath _____ _____ ___ body—or yours—you—you—"

Bel was so ma__ ___ ___uttering, a phenomenon Miles had never seen in seven years.

"It's time to withdraw, Bel," hissed Miles.

Fell gave Miles an approving nod.

"Thank you for your hospitality, Baron Fell," Miles said formally. "Good day, Baron Ryoval."

"Good day, Admiral," said Ryoval. "You seem a cosmopolitan sort, for a Betan. Perhaps you can visit us sometime without your moral friend, here."

"I don't think so," Miles murmured.

"What a shame," said Ryoval. "We have a dog-and-dwarf act I'm sure you'd find *fascinating*."

There was a moment's absolute silence.

"Fry 'em from orbit," Bel suggested tightly.

Baen Books by Lois McMaster Bujold

The Vorkosigan Saga:

Shards of Honor
Barrayar
The Warrior's Apprentice
The Vor Game
Cetaganda
Borders of Infinity
Brothers in Arms
Mirror Dance
Memory
Komarr
A Civil Campaign
Diplomatic Immunity

Falling Free
Ethan of Athos

Omnibus Editions:

Cordelia's Honor
Young Miles
Miles, Mystery & Mayhem
Miles Errant
Miles, Mutants & Microbes
Miles in Love

Also of Interest:

The Vorkosigan Companion,
ed. Lillian Stewart Carl and John Helfers *(forthcoming)*

MILES, MUTANTS & MICROBES

Lois McMaster Bujold

MILES, MUTANTS & MICROBES

Preface copyright © 2007 by Lois McMaster Bujold. *Falling Free* copyright © 1988 by Lois McMaster Bujold; "Labyrinth" copyright © 1989 by Lois McMaster Bujold; *Diplomatic Immunity* copyright © 2002 by Lois McMaster Bujold.

Vorkosigan® is a registered trademark of Lois McMaster Bujold.

A Baen Books Original

Baen Publishing Enterprises
P.O. Box 1403
Riverdale, NY 10471
www.baen.com

ISBN 10: 1-4165-5600-1
ISBN 13: 978-1-4165-5600-8

Cover art by Alan Pollack

First Baen paperback printing, November 2008

Distributed by Simon & Schuster
1230 Avenue of the Americas
New York, NY 10020

Library of Congress Cataloging-in-Publication Data: 2007018974

Printed in the United States

10 9 8 7 6 5 4 3 2 1

Pages by
Frank Aguirre at Hypertext Book and Journal Services
hypertext1@gmail.com

CONTENTS

Preface

My author's preface for this collection is both a history and an apologia—a word which means not an expression of regret for a fault, but a speech in defense. (What I'll be defending is my selection criteria for assembling this grouping of tales, and it will mainly be of interest to old Bujold readers.)

New readers need have no fear: dive right in! The stories here will explain themselves as they go. In this volume you will find two novels and a novella from what, due to my reluctance to coin a suitably imposing-sounding series name, its fans have eventually dubbed "the Vorkosiverse," after its most memorable and central (but far from only) character and his family. Science fiction and fantasy are the only genres I know where a series is defined by what universe it is set in (making mainstream fiction, looked at with the right squint, the world's largest shared-universe series). All the tales under this cover belong in the same "future history," if at widely divergent times.

1

What links them, mostly, are the quaddies, a race of humans bioengineered to live in zero-gravity that you will meet in the kick-off novel for this omnibus, *Falling Free*. This book falls early both in the timeline of its universe and in my career; it was the fourth novel I ever wrote and also the fourth published, and won both my first appearance in the venerable *Analog Magazine* and my first Nebula award. Taking place some two hundred years before the main body of stories, in it Barrayar (and the Vorkosigans) have not yet been discovered by the universe at large. The second tale, the novella "Labyrinth," introduces both a new quaddie character, and Miles Vorkosigan in his "Admiral Naismith" hat. (He has more than one persona, sprawling over several books, but I think you'll get enough about him in the novella to go on with; it was written to stand alone and indeed also appeared as a self-contained story in *Analog*.) The third tale, *Diplomatic Immunity*, as of this writing the most recent of my Vorkosiverse novels, brings elements of the first two tales around to meet again, in much more depth and detail.

At this point, the new reader is most welcome to stop reading this introduction and go read the real stories, which will be much more fun. You can circle back later for the "how these came to be written" part, which will then make much more sense. Anyone who still wants more orientation (though I don't think it will be needed) can have a peek at the series timeline included in the back of this volume. Don't be daunted by the accumulation; due to my decision to write all these books, though linked, as potential stand-alones, you don't have to read them in order or all at once.

Old readers will note that the novella "Labyrinth" also appears in the Baen omnibus *Miles, Mystery & Mayhem*, in its due position in a strict series timeline. Up until the novel *Memory*, the series grouped in internal-chronological order in a very tidy fashion, with two novels and a novella for each collection. (With the exception of the first, *Cordelia's Honor*, which is more the re-marriage of two halves of one intended tale, as explained in its afterword.) From *Memory* on, however, there was no way to make the books divide up evenly no matter how they were sliced. All the grouping schemes had a different defect: too much text, too little, the separation of strongly thematically linked tales that truly belonged together, and so on.

So the repackaging effort stalled out for a long time. But when the time came around on the guitar again to relicense the books, I was finally inspired to cut the Gordian knot in this fashion: the pivotal *Memory* left as a stand-alone, the Miles-and-Ekaterin sequence collected together in the upcoming *Miles in Love* (an inevitable title if ever there was one), and the quaddie-linked tales put together, here.

You are *not*—all you internet complainers, and you know who you are—being ripped off by your faithful publisher by being tricked into buying the same story twice. Due to the vagaries of tree-ware economics, this volume would have been the *exact same price* (if much less comprehensible) if the novella hadn't been included at all. It's being thrown in for free as a gift to the new readers. And it was my idea, so don't kvetch at Publisher Toni. (You can kvetch at me, I suppose; I hang out pretty regularly on Baen's Bar in the "Miles to Go" conference, so I'm not too hard to find.) This was an artistic decision, not an economic one.

So there. On to the history.

Falling Free actually came to be written as a result of a phone conversation with Jim Baen. I had written my first three science fiction novels "on spec," that is, without a

prior contract or even contact with a publisher, which is
pretty much the norm for first-time novelists. They sold on
one memorable day in October, 1985, in my very first
phone conversation with Jim, when, after reading *The Warrior's Apprentice*, he called me up and offered for all three
books. I was then faced, for the first time, with writing a
novel with a known publishing destination, and intimidating *expectations*.

I had been thinking of following up a minor character
from *The Warrior's Apprentice* named Arde Mayhew, a
jump pilot afflicted with obsolete neural implant technology who would be on a quest for a ship that would fit him.
I pictured him finding his prize among a group of people
dwelling in an asteroid belt whose ancestors were bioengineered to live in free fall, and who were eking out a living,
among other ways, as interstellar junk dealers. Jim was not
much taken with Arde, but he seemed to perk up when I
came to describe my proto-quaddies, and opined that a tale
about them might be more interesting and science fic-
tional. We all know what happens when technological
obsolescence hits the products of engineering; what would
happen if (always a key SFnal question) technological
obsolescence hit the products of bioengineering?

Taking the hint, I turned my thoughts to developing the
quaddies' world, culture, and history. It seemed to me best
to begin at the beginning, and I reasoned my way backward
to their two-hundred-years-prior genesis. I decided to
make my protagonist a welding engineer because I knew
the type—my father was a professor in the subject, and one
of my brothers had taken his degree in the specialty. This
also seemed to handily solve my technical research problems; with two small children in tow at the time, I knew I
wasn't going to be able to get very far from home to do

research, or much of anything else. This would have been early 1986.

I was about five chapters into the tale when my father died of a long-standing heart condition, in July of that year. At the timely invitation of then senior Baen editor Betsy Mitchell, I took a needed break to write my first novella— also the first work I'd ever sold before I wrote it, a scary step into a larger world for me as a writer. But "The Borders of Infinity" turned out well, and found its place in Betsy's novella collection series in *Free Lancers*, along with tales by Orson Scott Card and David Drake, which may well have served as the first introduction of this new writer Bujold to some of their readers. After a few months, I was able to return to work on *Falling Free* and, my confidence boosted, send it to contract.

I turned at that point for technical research answers to my brother and, through him, to an engineer friend of his named Wally Voreck, who sent me the fascinating material on ice die formation, which is a real industrial process. With such a cool (literally) gimmick, I reasoned my way backward to a plot development that would use it as a solution. (Writers cheat with time, you know. *We* can run it both ways.)

So the tale wended to its conclusion, or at any rate, grew long enough to qualify as a publishable book. At the time, it seemed to suggest further developments. It was clearly a kind of *Exodus* story, which implied that maybe forty years in the wilderness should be volume two, and arrival at the Promised Land volume three, a proper trilogy. But I wandered off instead to write *Brothers in Arms*, and never got back to the idea of continuing the quaddie-genesis adventure. I already knew how it would come out, after all.

But I did manage to sell the novel to *Analog Magazine* as a four-part serial, which ran from December 1987 through February 1988. This brought my work to the attention of a whole pool of new readers who might not necessarily have picked the paperback (which came out in April of 1988) off the bookstore shelves. This was the first of several happy sales to *Analog*, one of my Dad's favorites back in the '50s and '60s, and one of the first SF magazines I'd read when I was discovering the genre in my early teens. Since *Falling Free* was very much a tribute (if slyly updated) to the science fiction of that era, it felt much like coming full circle. The serial also was splendidly illustrated by Vincent di Fate; I still have five of the scratchboard originals, my first real art purchase. (He kindly adjusted his rates to my budget.)

I was always horribly conscious of being a slow writer, by some genre standards. When the time came to negotiate my next contract with Baen (Jim called me up again, come to think), I hit on a time-saving idea: to offer a novella collection of my own, rescuing "The Borders of Infinity" and adding two new tales to it to make up the weight. Looking up the contracts for that period, I see this was the triple-header including *Borders of Infinity* (the proposed novella collection), *Miles to Go* (the first of many uses of that place-holder title—the book I actually wrote was *Brothers in Arms*) and something called *Quaddies*, the proposed *Falling Free* sequel that never came to fruition—I wrote *The Vor Game* in its place. My Baen contracts were always *very* flexible.

"Labyrinth" was the last-written of the Miles-adventure novellas. With two rather dark tales already in the bag, I decided to make this one something of a comedy, for balance. The character of the quaddie Nicol, though a rather minor player, got me thinking again about the quaddies and my lost promise to complete their saga, and how their exodus might have come out. But other stories were crowding for my attention, and the impulse slipped away yet again.

It was over a decade later before I had the chance to return to these notions. The opening situation of the book that became *Diplomatic Immunity* called for Miles, in his brand-new hat as a Barrayaran Imperial Auditor (a kind of high-level troubleshooter), to become involved in straightening out an imbroglio with a Barrayaran fleet at a deep-space station. I had an entire wormhole nexus to choose from for this setting, and it occurred to me that this gave me the long-awaited chance to visit Quaddiespace and finally see—fourteen years later!—how *Falling Free* had come out. Because I rather wanted to know. It was unfinished business that still niggled, though the time and impulse for anything like a direct sequel was past and long past.

So I wrote it. And I found out. And Quaddiespace was much better than I'd ever expected, more complex and subtler.

Diplomatic Immunity has a whole 'nother level that deals with the Matter of Miles, which the new reader can take up separately and later, but several of the novel's most important precursors are found in "Labyrinth." Most especially, of course, the tale of Bel Thorne, the Betan hermaphrodite, and the quaddie Nicol, although some of the unfinished business with Bel stems most directly from the end of *Mirror Dance*. But I found a certain pleasing roundness to connecting the first tale in this universe to, if not the last, the latest.

Now all we needed was a title, which proved almost the hardest part of all. (I would say, "But you should see the ones we discarded!" except that I don't think anyone ever should. Ever, ever.) We were by this time rather stuck with having "Miles" in somewhere, to give a proper series-signal to the prospective book purchaser. After that (and eliminating a great many dreadful puns), alliteration took over. But most of all, this omnibus, haunted as it is by the ghosts of books unwritten, never to be written, collects the quaddies in all their charm.

Enjoy!

Lois McMaster Bujold
October 30, 2006

Falling Free

Chapter 1

Chapter 1

The shining rim of the planet Rodeo wheeled dizzily past the observation port of the orbital transfer station. A woman whom Leo Graf recognized as one of his fellow disembarking passengers from the jumpship stared out eagerly for a few minutes, then turned away, blinking and swallowing, to sit rather abruptly on one of the bright cushioned lounge chairs. Her eyes closed, opened, caught Leo's; she shrugged in embarrassment. Leo smiled sympathetically. Immune himself to the assorted nauseas of space travel, he moved to take her place at the crystal viewport.

Scanty cloud cover swirled in the thin atmosphere far below, barely veiling what seemed excessive quantities of red desert sand. Rodeo was a marginal world, home only to GalacTech mining and drilling operations and their support facilities. But what was he doing here? Leo wondered anew. Underground operations were hardly his field of expertise.

The planet slid from view with the rotation of the station. Leo moved to another port for a view back toward the hub of the station's wheel, noting the stress points and

wondering when they'd last been x-rayed for secretly propagating flaws. Centrifugal g-forces here at the rim where
this passenger lounge was situated seemed to be running at
about half Earth-standard, a little light perhaps. Deliberately stress-reduced, trouble anticipated in the structure?

But he was here for training, they'd said at GalacTech
headquarters on Earth, to teach quality control procedures
in free fell welding and construction. To whom? Why here,
at the end of nowhere? "The Cay Project" was a singularly
uninformative title for his assignment.

"Leo Graf?"

Leo turned. "Yes?"

The speaker was tall and dark-haired, perhaps thirty,
perhaps forty. He wore conservative-fashionable civilian
clothes, but a quiet lapel pin marked him as a company
man. Best sedentary executive type, Leo decided. The hand
he held out for Leo to shake was evenly tanned but soft.
"I'm Bruce Van Atta."

Leo's thick hand was pale but flecked with brown spots.
Crowding forty, sandy and square, Leo wore comfortable
red company coveralls by long habit, partly to blend with
the workers he supervised, mostly so that he need never
waste time and thought deciding what to put on in the
morning. "Graf," read the label printed over his left breast
pocket, eliminating all mystery.

Van Atta grinned. "Welcome to Rodeo, the armpit of the
universe."

"Thank you." Leo smiled back automatically.

"I'm head of the Cay Project now; I'll be your boss," Van
Atta amplified. "I requested you personally, y'know. You're
going to help me get this division moving at last, jack it up
and light a fire under it. You're like me, I know, got no
patience with deadheads. It was a hell of a job to have

dumped on me, trying to make *this* division profitable—but if I succeed, I'll be the Golden Boy."

"Requested me?" Cheering, to think that his reputation preceded him, but why couldn't he ever be requested by somebody at a garden spot? Ah, well . . . "They told me at HQ that I was being sent out here to give an expanded version of my short course in non-destructive testing."

"Is that all they told you?" Van Atta asked in astonishment. At Leo's affirmative shrug, he threw back his head and laughed. "Security, I suppose," Van Atta went on when he'd stopped chuckling. "Are you in for a surprise. Well, well. I won't spoil it." Van Atta's sly grin was as irritating as a familiar poke in the ribs.

Too familiar—oh, hell, Leo thought, this guy *knows* me from somewhere. And he thinks I know him. . . . Leo's polite smile became fixed in mild panic. He had met thousands of GalacTech personnel in his eighteen-year career. Perhaps Van Atta would say something soon to narrow the possibilities.

"My instructions listed a Dr. Cay as titular head of the Cay Project," Leo probed. "Will I be meeting him?"

"Old data," said Van Atta. "Dr. Cay died last year—several years past the date he should have been forcibly retired, in my opinion, but he was a vice-president and major stockholder and thoroughly entrenched—but that's blood over the damned dam, eh? I replaced him." Van Atta shook his head. "But I can't wait to see the look on your face when you see—come along. I have a private shuttle waiting."

They had the six-man personnel shuttle to themselves, but for the pilot. The passenger seat molded itself to Leo's body during the brief periods of acceleration. Quite brief periods; clearly they were not braking for planetary re-entry. Rodeo turned beneath them, falling farther away.

"Where are we going?" Leo asked Van Atta, seated beside him.

"Ah," said Van Atta. "See that speck about thirty degrees above the horizon? Watch it. It's home base for the Cay Project."

The speck grew rapidly into a far-flung chaotic structure, all angles and projections, with confetti-colored lights spangling its sharp shadows. Leo's practiced eye picked out the clues to its function, the tanks, the ports, the green-house filters winking in the sunlight, the size of the solar panels versus the estimated volume of the structure.

"An orbital habitat?"

"You got it," said Van Atta.

"It's huge."

"Indeed. How many personnel would you guess it could handle?"

"Oh—fifteen hundred."

Van Atta's eyebrows rose, in slight disappointment, per-haps, at not being able to offer a correction. "Almost exactly. Four hundred ninety-four rotating GalacTech per-sonnel and a thousand permanent inhabitants."

Leo's lips echoed the word, permanent . . . "Speaking of rotation—how are you handling null-gee deconditioning in your people? I don't—" his eyes inventoried the enor-mous structure, "I don't even see an exercise wheel. No spinning gym?"

"There's a null-gee gym. The rotating personnel get a month downside after every three-month shift."

"Expensive."

"But we put the Habitat up there for less than a quarter of the cost of the same volume of living quarters in one-gee spinners."

"But surely you'll lose what you've saved in construction costs over time in personnel transportation and medical expenses," argued Leo. "The extra shuttle trips, the long leaves—every retiree who breaks an arm or a leg until the day he dies will be suing GalacTech for the cost of it plus mental anguish, whether he had significant bone demineralization or not."

"We've solved that problem too," said Van Atta. "Whether the solution is cost-effective—well, that's what you and I are here to try to prove."

The shuttle sidled delicately into alignment with a hatch on the side of the Habitat and seated itself with a reassuringly authoritative click. The pilot shut down his systems and unbuckled himself to float past Leo and Van Atta and check the hatch seals. "Ready for disembarking, Mr. Van Atta."

"Thank you, Grant."

Leo released his seat restraints, and stretched and relaxed in the pleasurable familiarity of weightlessness. Not for him the unfortunate nauseas of null-gee that sapped the efficiency of so many employees. Leo's body was ordinary enough, downside; here, where control and practice and wit counted more than strength, he was at last an athlete. Smiling a little to himself, he followed Van Atta from hand-grip to hand-grip and through the shuttle hatch.

A pink-faced tech manned a control panel just inside the shuttle hatch corridor. He wore a red T-shirt with the GalacTech logo over his left breast. Tight blond curls cut close to his head reminded Leo of a lamb's pelt; perhaps it was an effect of his obvious youth.

"Hello there, Tony," Van Atta greeted him with cheerful familiarity.

"Good afternoon, Mr. Van Atta," the youth replied deferentially. He smiled at Leo, and cocked his head at Van Atta in a pantomime plea for an introduction. "Is this the new teacher you were telling us about?"

"Indeed he is. Leo Graf, this is Tony—he'll be among your first trainees. He's one of the habitat's *permanent* residents," Van Atta added with peculiar emphasis. "Tony is a welder and joiner, second grade—working on first, eh, Tony? Shake hands with Mr. Graf."

Van Atta was smirking. Leo had the impression that if he hadn't been in free fall, he would have been bouncing on his heels.

Tony pulled himself obediently over the control panel. He wore red shorts—

Leo blinked and caught his breath in shock. The boy had no legs. Emerging from his shorts were a second set of arms.

Functional arms, he was even now using his—his lower left hand, Leo supposed he'd have to call it—to anchor himself as he reached out to Leo. His smile was perfectly unselfconscious.

Leo had lost his own hand grip and had to fumble to retrieve it, stretching awkwardly to meet the proffered handshake. "How do you do," Leo managed to croak. It was almost impossible not to stare. Leo forced his gaze to focus on the young man's bright blue eyes.

"Hello, sir. I've been looking forward to meeting you." Tony's handshake was shy but sincere, his hand dry and strong.

"Um . . ." Leo's tongue stumbled, "um, what's your last name, uh, Tony?"

"Oh, Tony's just my nickname, sir. My full designation is TY-776-424-XG."

"I, uh—guess I'll call you Tony, then," Leo murmured, increasingly stunned. Van Atta, most unhelpfully, seemed to be thoroughly enjoying Leo's discomfiture.

"Everybody does," said Tony agreeably.

"Fetch Mr. Graf's bag, will you, Tony?" said Van Atta. "Come on, Leo, I'll show you your quarters, and then we can do the grand tour."

Leo followed his floating guide into the indicated cross-corridor, glancing back over his shoulder in renewed amazement as Tony launched himself accurately across the chamber and swung through the shuttle hatch.

"That's," Leo swallowed, "that's the most extraordinary birth defect I've ever seen. Somebody had a stroke of genius, to find him a job in free fall. He'd be a cripple, downside."

"Birth defect." Van Atta's grin had grown twisted. "Yeah, that's one way of describing it. I wish you could have seen the look on your face when he popped up like that. I congratulate you on your self-control. I about puked when I first saw one, and I was prepared. You get used to the little chimps pretty quick, though."

"There's more than one?"

Van Atta opened and closed his hands in a counting gesture. "An even one-thousand. The first generation of GalacTech's new super-workers. The name of the game, Leo, is bioengineering. And I intend to win."

Tony, with Leo's valise clutched in his lower right hand, swooped between Leo and Van Atta in the cylindrical corridor and braked to a halt in front of them with three deft touches on the passing hand-grips.

"Mr. Van Atta, can I introduce Mr. Graf to somebody on the way to Visitor's Wing? It won't be *much* out of the way—Hydroponics."

Van Atta's lips pursed, then arranged themselves in a kindly smile. "Why not? Hydroponics is on the itinerary for this afternoon anyway."

"Thank you, sir," cried Tony, and darted off with enthusiasm to open the air safety seal before them at the end of the corridor, and linger to close it again behind them on the other side.

Leo fastened his attention on his surroundings, as a less-rude alternative to surreptitiously studying the boy. The Habitat was indeed inexpensively constructed, mostly prefab units variously combined. Not the most aesthetically elegant design—a certain higgledy-piggledy randomness indicated an organic growth pattern since the Habitat's inception, units stuck on here and there to accommodate new needs. But its very dullness incorporated safety advantages Leo approved—the interchangeability of airseal systems, for example.

They passed dormitory wings, food preparation and dining areas, a workshop for small repairs—Leo paused to gaze down its length, then had to hurry to catch up with his guide. Unlike most free-fall living spaces in which Leo had worked, there was no effort here to maintain an arbitrary up-and-down to ease the visual psychology of the inhabitants. Most chambers were cylindrical in design, with work spaces and storage efficiently packing the walls and the center left free of obstruction for the passage of—well, one could hardly call them pedestrians.

En route they passed a couple of dozen of the—the four-handed people, the new model workers, Tony's folk, whatever they were called—did they have an official designation, Leo wondered? He stared covertly, breaking off his gaze whenever one looked back, which was often; they stared openly at him, and whispered among themselves.

He could see why Van Atta dubbed them chimps. They were thin-hipped, lacking the powerful gluteal locomotor muscles of people with legs. The lower set of arms tended to be more muscular than the uppers in both males and females, power-grippers, and thus appeared falsely short by comparison to the uppers: bow-legged, if he squinted them to a blur.

They were dressed mostly in the sort of comfortable, practical T-shirt and shorts that Tony wore, evidently color-coded, for Leo passed a cluster of them all in yellow hovering intently around a normal human in GalacTech coveralls who had a pump unit half-apart, lecturing on its function and repair. Leo thought of a flock of canaries, of flying squirrels, of monkeys, of spiders, of swift bright lizards of the sort that run straight up walls.

They made him want to scream, almost to weep; and yet it wasn't the arms, or the quick, too-many hands. He had almost reached Hydroponics before he was able to analyze his intense unease. It was their faces that bothered him so, Leo realized. They were the faces of children. . . .

A door marked "Hydroponics D" slid aside to reveal an antechamber and a large airy end chamber extending some fifteen meters beyond. Filtered windows on the sun side, and an array of mirrors on the dark side, filled the volume with brilliant light, softened by green plants that grew from a carefully-arranged set of grow tubes. The air was pungent with chemicals and vegetation.

A pair of the four-armed young women, both in blue, were at work in the antechamber. A plexiplastic grow tube three meters long was braced in place. They floated along its length carefully transplanting tiny seedlings from a germination box into a spiral series of holes along the tube, one plant per hole, fixing them in place with flexible sealant around each tender stalk. The roots would grow inward, becoming a tangled mat to absorb the nutritive hydroponic mist pumped through the tube, and the leaves and stems would bush out in the sunlight and eventually bear whatever fruit was their genetic destiny. In this place, probably apples with antlers, thought Leo in mild hysteria, or potatoes with eyes that really winked at you.

The dark-haired girl paused to adjust a bundle under her arm. . . . Leo's mind ground to a complete halt. The bundle was a baby.

A live baby—of course it was alive, what did he expect? Leo gibbered inwardly. It peered around its—mother's?—torso to glower suspiciously at Leo-the-stranger, and tightened its four-handed clutch on home base, taking a squishy defensive grip on one of the girl's breasts as if in fear of competition. "Ackle," it remarked aggressively.

"Ow!" The dark-haired girl laughed and spared a lower hand to pry the little fat fingers loose, without missing a beat of her upper hands patting sealant in place around a stem. She finished with a quick squirt of fixative from a tube floating conveniently beside her, just out of the infant's reach.

The girl was slim, and elfin, and wonderfully weird to Leo's unaccustomed eyes. Her short, fine hair clung close to her head, framing her face, shaped to a point at the nape of her neck. It was so thick it reminded Leo of cat fur; one might stroke it, and be soothed.

The other girl was blonde, and babyless. She looked up first, and smiled. "Company, Claire."

The dark-haired girl's face lit with pleasure. Leo flushed in the heat of it. "Tony!" she cried happily, and Leo realized he had merely received an accidental dose, as it were, of that beam of delight, as it swept over him to its true target.

The baby released three hands and waved them urgently. "Ah, ah!" The girl turned in air to face the visitors. "Ah, ah, *ah!*" the baby repeated.

"Oh, all *right*," she laughed. "You want to fly to Daddy, hm?" She unhooked a short tether from a sort of soft harness on the baby's torso to a belt around her own waist, and held the infant out. "Fly to Daddy, Andy? Fly to Daddy?"

The baby indicated enthusiasm for the proposal by waving all four hands vigorously about and squealing eagerly. She launched him toward Tony with considerably more velocity than Leo would have dared to impart. Tony, grinning cheerfully, caught him—handily, Leo thought in blitzed inanity.

"Fly to Mommy?" Tony inquired in turn. "Ah, ah," the baby agreed, and Tony hung him in air, gently pulling his arms out—like straightening out a starfish, Leo thought—and imparting a spin rolled him through the air for all the world like a wheel. The baby pulled his hands in, clenching his face in sympathetic effort, and spun faster, gurgling with laughter at the success of his effort. Conservation of angular momentum, thought Leo. Naturally . . .

Claire tossed the infant back one more time to his father—mind-boggling, to think of that blond boy as a father of anything—and followed herself to brake to a halt hand-to-hand against Tony, who proffered an automatic helping grasp for that purpose. That they continued to hold hands was clearly more than a courteous anchoring.

"Claire, this is Mr. Graf." Tony did not so much introduce as display him, like a prize. "He's going to be my

advanced welding techniques teacher. Mr. Graf, this is
Claire, and this is our son Andy." Andy had clambered
headward on his father, and was wrapping one hand in
Tony's blond hair and another around one ear, blinking
owlishly at Leo. Tony gently rescued the ear and re-directed
the clutch to the fabric of his red T-shirt. "Claire was picked
to be the very first natural mother of us," Tony went on
proudly.

"Me and four other girls," Claire corrected modestly.

"Claire used to be in Welding and Joining too, but she
can't do Outside work any more," Tony explained. "She's
been in Housekeeping, Nutrition Technology, and Hydroponics since Andy was born."

"Dr. Yei said I was a very important experiment, to see
which sorts of productivity were least compromised by my
taking care of Andy at the same time," explained Claire. "I
sort of miss going Outside—it was exciting—but I like this,
too. More variety."

GalacTech re-invents Women's Work? thought Leo
bemusedly. Are we about to put an R&D group to work on
the applications of fire, too? But oh, you are certainly an
experiment. . . . His thought was not reflected in his bland,
closed face. "Happy to meet you, Claire," he said gravely.

Claire nudged Tony and nodded toward her blonde co-
worker, who had drifted over to join the group.

"Oh—and this is Silver," Tony went on obediently. "She
works in Hydroponics most of the time."

Silver nodded. Her medium-short hair drifted in soft
platinum waves, and Leo wondered if it was the source of
her nickname. She had the sort of strong facial bones that
are sharp and unhappily awkward at thirteen, arrestingly
elegant at thirty-five, now not quite halfway through their
transition. Her blue gaze was cooler and less shy than the

busy Claire's, who was already distracted by some new demand from Andy. Claire retrieved the baby and re-attached his safety line.

"Good afternoon, Mr. Van Atta," Silver added particularly. She pirouetted in air, with eyes that cried silently, Notice me! Leo noticed that all twenty of her manicured fingernails were lacquered pink.

Van Atta's answering smile was secretive and smug. "Afternoon, Silver. How's it going?"

"We have one more tube to plant after this one. We'll be finished ahead of shift change," Silver offered.

"Fine, fine," said Van Atta jovially. "Ah—do try to remember to arrange yourself right-side-up when you're talking to a downsider, Sugarplum."

Silver inverted herself hastily to match Van Atta's orientation. Since the room was radially arranged, right-side-up was a purely Van Atta-centric direction, Leo noted dryly. Where *had* he met the man before?

"Well, carry on, girls." Van Atta led out, Leo following, Tony bringing up the rear regretfully, looking back over his shoulder.

Andy had returned his attention to his mother, his determined little hands foraging up her shirt, on which dark stains were spreading in autonomic response. Apparently that was one bit of ancient biology the company had not altered. The milk dispensers were certainly ideally pre-adapted to life in free fall, after all. And even diapers had a heroic history in the dawn of space travel, Leo had heard.

His brief amusement drained away, and he pushed off after Van Atta, silent and reflective. He held his judgment suspended, he reassured himself, not paralyzed. In the meantime, a closed mouth could not impede the inflow of data.

✦   ✦ ✦

They paused at Van Atta's Habitat office. Van Atta switched on the lights and air circulation as they entered. From the stale smell Leo guessed the office was not often used; the executive probably spent most of his time more comfortably downside. A large viewport framed a spectacular view of Rodeo.

"I've come up in the world a bit since we last met," said Van Atta, matching his gaze. The upper atmosphere along Rodeo's rim was producing some gorgeous prismatic light effects at this angle of view. "In several senses. I don't mind returning the favor. The man at the top owes it to remember how he got there, I think. Noblesse oblige and all that." The tilt of Van Atta's eyebrow invited Leo to join him in self-congratulatory satisfaction.

Remember. Quite. Leo's blank memory was getting excruciatingly uncomfortable. He smiled and seized the pause while Van Atta activated his desk comconsole to turn away and make a slow, politely-waiting-type orbit of the room, as if idly examining its contents.

A little wall plaque bearing a humorous motto caught his eye. *On the sixth day God saw He couldn't do it all*, it read, *so He created ENGINEERS.* Leo snorted, mildly amused.

"I like that too," commented Van Atta, looking up to check the cause of his chuckle. "My ex-wife gave it to me. It was about the only thing the greedy bitch didn't take back when we split."

"Were you an—" Leo began, and swallowed the words, *engineer, then?* as he finally remembered, and then wondered how he could ever have forgotten. Leo had known Van Atta as an engineering subordinate at that time, though, not as an executive superior. Was this sleek go-getter the same idiot he had kicked impatiently upstairs to Administration just to get him out from underfoot on the Morita Station project—ten, twelve years ago now? Brucie-baby. Oh, yes. Oh, hell . . .

Van Atta's comconsole disgorged a couple of data disks, which he plucked off. "You put me on the fast track. I've always thought it must give you a sense of satisfaction, since you spend so much of your time training, to see one of your old students make good."

Van Atta was no more than five years younger than Leo. Leo suppressed profound irritation—he wasn't this paper-shuffler's ninety-year-old retired Sunday school teacher, damn it. He was a working engineer, hands-on, and not afraid to get them dirty, either. His technical work was as close to perfection as his relentless conscientiousness could push it, his safety record spoke for itself. . . . He let his anger go with a sigh. Wasn't it always so? He'd seen dozens of subordinates forge ahead, often men he'd trained himself. Yeah, and trust Van Atta to make it seem a weakness and not a point of pride.

Van Atta spun the data disks across the room at him. "There's your roster and your syllabus. Come on, and I'll show you some of the equipment you'll be working with. GalacTech's got two projects in the wind they're thinking of finally turning these Cay Project quaddies loose on."

"Quaddies?"

"The official nickname."

"It's not, um . . . pejorative?"

Van Atta stared, then snorted. "No. What you do not call them out loud, however, is 'mutants,' genetic paranoia being what it is after that Nuovo Brasilian military cloning fiasco. This whole project could have been carried out

much more conveniently in Earth orbit, but for the
assorted legal hysterias about human gene manipulation.
Anyway, the projects. One to assemble jumpships in orbit
around Orient IV, and another building a deep space transfer facility at some nexus away the hell-and-gone beyond
Tau Ceti called Kline Station—cold work, no habitable
planets in the system and its sun is a cinder, but the local
space harbors no less than six wormhole exits. Potentially
very profitable. Lots of welding under the most difficult
free-fall conditions—"

Leo's brief angst was swallowed in interest. It had always
been the work itself, not the pay and perks, that held him in
thrall. Screw executive privilege—didn't it mostly mean
being stuck downside? He followed Van Atta out of the
office back into the corridor where Tony still waited
patiently with his luggage.

"I suppose it was the development of the uterine replicators that made it all possible," Van Atta opined while Leo
stowed his gear in his new quarters. More than a mere sleep
cubicle, the chamber included private sanitary facilities
and a comconsole as well as comfortable-looking sleep
restraints—no morning backache on this job, Leo thought
with minor satisfaction. Headache was another problem.

"I'd heard something about those things," said Leo.
"Another invention from Beta Colony, wasn't it?"

Van Atta nodded. "The outer worlds are getting too
damn clever these days. Earth's going to lose its edge if it
doesn't shape up."

Too true, Leo thought. Yet the history of innovation suggested this was an inevitable pattern. Management who
had made huge capital investments in one system were naturally loath to scrap it, and so the latecomers forged

ahead—to the frustration of loyal engineers. . . . "I'd thought the use of uterine replicators was limited to obstetrical emergencies."

"Actually, the only limitation on their use is the fact that they're hideously expensive," said Van Atta. "It's probably only a matter of time before rich women everywhere start ducking their biological duties and cooking up their kids in 'em. But for GalacTech, it meant that human bioengineering experiments could at last be carried out without involving a lot of flaky foster-mothers to carry the implanted embryos. A neat, clean, controlled engineering approach. Better still, these quaddies are total constructs—that is, their genes are taken from so many sources, it's impossible to identify their genetic parents either. Saves quantities of legal grief."

"I'll bet," said Leo faintly.

"This whole thing was Dr. Cay's obsession, I gather. I never met him, but he must have been one of those, you know, charismatic types, to push through a project with this enormous lead time before any possible pay-off. The first batch is just turning twenty. The extra arms are the wildest part—"

"I've often wished I had four hands, in free fall," Leo murmured, trying not to sound too dubious out loud.

"—but most of the changes were this bunch of metabolic stuff. They never get motion-sick—something about re-wiring the vestibular system—and their muscles maintain tone with an exercise regimen of barely fifteen minutes a day, max—nothing like the hours you and I would have to put in during a long stint in null-gee. Their bones don't deteriorate at all. They're even more radiation-resistant than us. Bone marrow and gonads can take four and five times the rems we can absorb before GalacTech grounds us—although the medical types are pushing for them to do their reproducing early in life, while all those expensive genes are still pristine. After that, it's all gravy for us: workers who never require downside leave; so healthy they'll go on and on, cutting high-cost turnover; they're even," Van Atta snickered, "self-replicating."

Leo secured the last of his scanty personal possessions. "Where . . . will they go when they, uh, retire?" he asked slowly.

Van Atta shrugged. "I suppose the company will have to work something out, when the time comes. Not my problem, fortunately. *I'll* be retired before then."

"What happens if they—quit, go elsewhere? Suppose somebody offers them higher pay? GalacTech will be out-of-pocket for all the R&D."

"Ah. I don't think you've quite grasped the beauty of this set-up. They don't quit. They aren't employees. They're capital equipment. They aren't paid in money—though I wish *my* salary was equal to what GalacTech is spending yearly to maintain 'em. But that will get better as the last replicator cohort gets older and more self-sufficient. They stopped producing new ones about five years ago, see, in anticipation of turning that job over to the quaddies themselves." Van Atta licked his lips and raised his eyebrows, as if in enjoyment of a salacious joke. Leo could not regret missing its point.

Leo turned, curling in air and crossing his arms. "Spacer's Union is going to call it slave labor, you know," he said at last.

"The Union's going to call it worse names than that. Their productivity is going to look sick," growled Van Atta. "Loaded language bullshit. These little chimps have cradle to grave security. GalacTech couldn't be treating them better if they were made of solid platinum. You and I should have so good a deal, Leo."

"Ah," said Leo, and no more.

Chapter 2

The observation bubble on the side of the Cay Habitat had a televiewer, Leo discovered to his delight, and furthermore it was unoccupied at the moment. His own quarters lacked a viewport. He slipped within. His schedule allowed this one free day to recover from trip fatigue and jump lag before his course was to begin. A good night's sleep in free fall had already improved his tone of mind vastly over yesterday, after Van Atta's—Leo could only dub it "disorientation tour."

The curve of Rodeo's horizon bisected the view from the bubble, and beyond it the vast sweep of stars. Just now one of Rodeo's little mice moons crept across the panorama. A glint above the horizon caught Leo's eye.

He adjusted the televiewer for a close-up. A GalacTech shuttle was bringing up one of the giant cargo pods, refined petrochemicals or bulk plastics bound for petroleum-depleted Earth perhaps. A collection of similar pods floated in orbit. Leo counted. One, two, three . . . six, and the one arriving made seven. Two or three little manned pushers were already starting to bundle the pods, to be locked together and attached to one of the big orbit-breaking thruster units.

Once grouped and attached to their thruster, the pods would be aimed toward the distant wormhole exit point that gave access to Rodeo local space. Velocity and direction imparted, the thruster would detach and return to Rodeo orbit for the next load. The unmanned pod bundle would continue on its slow, cheap way to its target, one of a long train stretching from Rodeo to the anomaly in space that was the jump point.

Once there, the cargo pods would be captured and decelerated by a similar thruster, and positioned for the jump. Then the superjumpers would take over, cargo carriers as specially designed as the thrusters for their task. The monster cargo jumpers were hardly more than a pair of Necklin field generator rods in their protective housings so positioned as to be fitted around a constellation of pod bundles, a bracketing pair of normal space thruster arms, and a small control chamber for the jump pilot and his neurological headset. Without their balancing pod bundles attached, the superjumpers reminded Leo of some exceptionally weird and attenuated long-legged insects.

Each jump pilot, neurologically wired to his ship to navigate the wavering realities of wormhole space, made two hops a day, inbound to Rodeo with empty pod bundles and back out again with cargo, followed by a day off; two months on duty followed by a month's unpaid but compulsory gravity leave, usually financially augmented with shuttle duties. Jumps were more wearing on pilots than null-gee was. The pilots of the fast passenger ships like the one Leo had ridden in on yesterday called the superjumper pilots puddle-jumpers and merry-go-round riders. The cargo pilots just called the passenger pilots snobs.

Leo grinned, and considered that train of wealth gliding through space. No doubt about it, the Cay Habitat, fascinating as it was, was just the tail of the dog to the whole of GalacTech's Rodeo operation. That single thruster-load of pods being bundled now could maintain a whole town full of stockholding widows and orphans in style for a year, and it was just one of an apparently endless string. Base production was like an inverted pyramid, those at the bottom apex supporting a broadening mountain of ten-percenters, a fact which usually gave Leo more secret pride than irritation.

"Mr. Graf?" an alto voice interrupted his thoughts. "I'm Dr. Sondra Yei. I head up the psychology and training department for the Cay Habitat."

The woman hovering in the door wore pale green company coveralls. Pleasantly ugly, pushing middle-aged, she had the bright Mongolian eyes, broad nose and lips and coffee-and-cream skin of her mixed racial heritage. She pushed herself through the aperture with the concise relaxed movements of one accustomed to free fall.

"Ah, yes, they told me you'd be wanting to talk to me." Leo courteously waited for her to anchor herself before attempting to shake hands.

Leo gestured at the televiewer. "Got a nice view of the orbital cargo marshaling here. Seems to me that might be another job for your quaddies."

"Indeed. They've been doing it for almost a year now." Yei smiled satisfaction. "So, you don't find adjusting to the quaddies too difficult? So your psyche profile suggested. Good."

"Oh, the quaddies are all right." Leo stopped short of expanding on his unease. He was not sure he could put it into words anyway. "I was just surprised, at first."

"Understandable. You don't think you'll have trouble teaching them, then?"

Leo smiled. "They can't possibly be worse than the crew of roustabouts I trained at Jupiter Orbital #4."

"I didn't mean trouble *from* them." Yei smiled again. "You will find they are very intelligent and attentive students. Quick. Quite literally, good children. And that's what I want to talk about." She paused, as if marshaling her thoughts like the distant cargo pushers.

"The GalacTech teachers and trainers occupy a parental role here for the Habitat family. Although parentless, the quaddies themselves must someday—indeed, are already becoming parents. From the beginning we've been at pains to assure they were provided with role models of stable adult responsibility. But they *are* still children. They will be watching you closely. I want you to be aware, and take care. They'll be learning more than welding from you. They'll also be picking up your other patterns of behavior. In short, if you have any bad habits—and we all have some—they must be parked downside for the duration of your stay. In other words," Yei went on, "watch yourself. Watch your language." An involuntary grin crinkled her eyes. "For example, one of our crèche personnel once used the clichè 'spit in your eye' in some context or other . . . not only did the quaddies think it was hilarious, but it started an epidemic of spitting among the five-year-olds that took weeks to suppress. Now, you'll be working with much older children, but the principle remains. For instance—ah—did you bring any personal reading or viewing matter with you? Vid dramas, newsdiscs, whatever."

"I'm not much of a reader," said Leo. "I brought my course material."

"Technical information doesn't concern me. What we've been having a problem with lately is, um, fiction."

Leo raised an eyebrow and grinned. "Pornography? I'm not sure I'd worry about that. When I was a kid we passed around—"

"No, no, not pornography. I'm not sure the quaddies would understand about pornography anyway. Sexuality is an open topic here, part of their social training. Biology. I'm far more concerned about fiction that clothes false or dangerous values in attractive colors, or biased histories."

Leo wrinkled his forehead, increasingly dismayed. "Haven't you taught these kids any history? Or let them have stories . . . ?"

"Of course we have. The quaddies are well-supplied with both. It's simply a matter of correct emphasis. For example—a typical downsider history of, say, the settlement of Orient IV usually gives about fifteen pages to the year of the Brothers' War, a temporary if bizarre social aberration—and about two to the actual hundred or so years of settlement and building-up of the planet. Our text gives one paragraph to the war. But the building of the Witgow trans-trench monorail tunnel, with its subsequent beneficial economic effects to both sides, gets five pages. In short, we emphasize the common instead of the rare, building rather than destruction, the normal at the expense of the abnormal. So that the quaddies may never get the idea that the abnormal is somehow expected of them. If you'd like to read the texts, I think you'll get the idea very quickly."

"I—yeah, I think I'd better," Leo murmured. The degree of censorship imposed upon the quaddies implied by Yei's brief description made his skin crawl—and yet, the idea of a text that devoted whole sections to great engineering works made him want to stand up and cheer. He contained his confusion in a bland smile. "I really didn't bring anything on board," he offered in placation.

She led him off for a tour of the dormitories, and the supervised crèches of the younger quaddies.

The little ones amazed Leo. There seemed to be so many—maybe it was just because they moved so fast. Thirty or so five-year-olds bounced around the free fall gym like a barrage of demented ping pong balls when their crèche mother, a plump pleasant downsider woman they called Mama Nilla, assisted by a couple of quaddie teenage girls, first let them out of their reading class. But then she clapped her hands and put on some music, and they fell to and demonstrated a game, or a dance, Leo was not sure which, with many sidelong looks at him and much giggling. It involved creating a sort of duo-decahedron in mid-air, like a human pyramid only more complex, hand to hand to hand changing its formation in time to music. Cries of dismay went up when an individual slipped up and spoiled the group's formation. When perfection was achieved, everybody won. Leo couldn't help liking that game. Dr. Yei, watching Leo laugh when the young quaddies swarmed around him afterwards, seemed to purr with contentment.

But at the end of the tour she studied him with a little smile quirking her mouth. "Mr. Graf, you're still disturbed. You sure you're not harboring just a little of the old Frankenstein complex about all this? It's all right to admit it to me—in fact, I want you to talk about it."

"It's not that," said Leo slowly. "It's just . . . well, I can't really object to your trying to make them as group-centered as possible, given that they'll be living all their lives on crowded space stations. They're disciplined to a high degree for their ages, also good—"

"Vital to their survival, rather, in a space environment!"

"Yes . . . but what about—about their self-defense?"

"You'll have to define that term for me, Mr. Graf. Defense from what?"

"Well, it seems to me you've succeeded in raising about a thousand technical-whiz—doormats. Nice kids, but aren't they a little—feminized?" He was getting in deeper and deeper; her smile had quirked to a frown. "I mean—they just seem ripe for exploitation by—by somebody. Was this whole social experiment your idea? It seems like a woman's dream of a perfect society. Everybody's so *well behaved*." He was uncomfortably conscious of having expressed his thought badly, but surely she must see the validity . . .

She took a deep breath, and lowered her voice. Her smile had become fixed. "Let me set you straight, Mr. Graf. I did not invent the quaddies. I was assigned here six years ago. It's the GalacTech specs that call for *maximum socialization*. But I did inherit them. And I care about them. It's not your job—or your business—to understand about their legal status, but it concerns me greatly. Their safety lies in their socialization.

"You seem to be free of the common prejudices against the products of genetic engineering, but there are many who are not. There are planetary jurisdictions where this degree of genetic manipulation of humans would even be illegal. Let those people—just once—perceive the quaddies as a threat, and—" she clamped her lips on further confidences, and retreated onto her authority. "Let me put it this way, Mr. Graf. The power to approve—or disapprove— training personnel for the Cay Project is mine. Mr. Van

Atta may have called you in, but I can have you removed. And I will do so without hesitation if you fail in speech or behavior to abide by psych department guidelines. I don't think I can put it any more clearly than that."

"No, you're—quite clear," Leo said.

"I'm sorry," she said sincerely. "But until you've been on the Habitat a while, you really must refrain from making snap judgments."

I'm a testing engineer, lady, thought Leo. *It's my job to make judgments all day long.* But he did not speak the thought aloud. They managed to part on a note of only slightly strained cordiality.

The entertainment vid was titled "Animals, Animals, Animals." Silver set the re-run for the "Cats" sequence for the third time.

"Again?" Claire, sharing the vid viewing chamber with her, said faintly.

"Just one more time," Silver pleaded. Her lips parted in fascination as the black Persian appeared over the vid plate, but out of deference to Claire she turned down the music and narration. The creature was crouched lapping milk from a bowl, stuck to its floor by downside gravity. The little white droplets flying off its pink tongue arced back into the dish as though magnetized.

"I wish I could have a cat. They look so soft . . ." Silver's left lower hand reached out to pantomime-pat the life-sized image. No tactile reward, only the colored light of the holovid licking without sensation over her skin. She let her hand fall through the cat and sighed. "Look, you can pick it up just like a baby." The vid shrank to show the cat's downsider owner carting it off in her arms. Both looked smug.

"Well, maybe they'll let you have a baby soon," offered Claire.

"It's not the same thing," said Silver. She could not help glancing a little enviously at Andy, though, curled up asleep in midair near his mother. "I wonder if I'll ever get a chance to go downside?"

"Ugh," said Claire. "Who'd want to? It looks so uncomfortable. Dangerous, too."

"Downsiders manage. Besides, everything interesting seems to—to come from planets." Everyone interesting, too, her thought added. She considered Mr. Van Atta's former teacher, Mr. Graf, met on her last working shift yesterday in Hydroponics. Yet another legged Somebody who got to go places and make things happen. He'd actually been born on old Earth, Mr. Van Atta said.

There came a muffled tap on the door of the soundproof bubble, and Silver keyed her remote control to open the door. Siggy, in the yellow shirt and shorts of Airsystems Maintenance, stuck his head through. "All clear, Silver."

"All right, come on."

Siggy slipped inside. She keyed the door shut again, and Siggy turned over, reached into the tool pouch on his belt, jimmied open a wall plate, and jammed the door's mechanism. He left the wall plate open in case of urgent need for re-access, such as Dr. Yei knocking on the door to inquire brightly, What were they doing? Silver by this time had the back cover off the holovid. Siggy reached delicately past her to clip his home-made electronic scrambler across the power lead cable. Anyone monitoring their viewing through it would get static.

"This is a great idea," said Siggy enthusiastically.

Claire looked more doubtful. "Are you sure we won't get into a whole lot of trouble if we're caught?"

"I don't see why," said Silver. "Mr. Van Atta disconnects the smoke alarm in his quarters whenever he has a jubajoint."

"I thought downsiders weren't allowed to smoke on board," said Siggy, startled.

"Mr. Van Atta says it's a privilege of rank," said Silver. *I wish I had rank. . . .*

"Has he ever given you one of his jubas?" asked Claire in a tone of gruesome fascination.

"Once," said Silver.

"Wow," said Siggy, grinning in admiration. "What was it like?"

Silver made a face. "Not much. It tasted kind of nasty. Made my eyes red. I really couldn't see the point to it. Maybe downsiders have some biochemical reaction we don't get. I asked Mr. Van Atta, but he just laughed at me."

"Oh," said Siggy, and switched his interest to the holovid display. All three quaddies settled around it. An anticipatory silence fell in the chamber as the music swelled and the bold red title letters rotated before their eyes—"The Prisoner of Zenda."

The scene opened on an authentically-detailed street scene from the dawn of civilization, before space travel or even electricity. A quartet of glossy horses, harness jingling, drew an elaborate box on wheels across the ground.

"Can't you get any more of the 'Ninja of the Twin Stars' series?" complained Siggy. "This is more of your darned dirtball stuff. I want something realistic, like that chase scene through the asteroid belt . . ." His hands pursued each other as he made nasal sound effects indicating machinery undergoing high acceleration.

"Shut up and look at all the animals," said Silver. "So many—and it's not even a zoo. The place is littered with them."

"Littered is right," giggled Claire. "They're not wearing diapers, you know. Think about that."

Siggy sniffed. "Earth must have been a really disgusting place to live, back in the old days. No wonder people grew legs. Anything, to prop them up in the air away from—"

Silver switched the vid off with a snap. "If you can't think of anything else to talk about," she said dangerously, "I'll go back to my dorm. *With* my vid. And you all can go back to watching 'Cleaning and Maintenance Techniques for Food Service Areas.'"

"Sorry." Siggy curled his four arms around himself in a submissive ball and tried to look contrite. Claire refrained from further comment.

"Huh." Silver switched the vid back on, and continued watching in rapt and uninterrupted silence. When the railway scenes began, even Siggy stopped squirming.

Leo was well launched into his first class lecture.

"Now, here is a typical length of electron beam weld . . ." He fiddled with the controls of his holovid display. A ghost image in bright blue light, the computer-generated x-ray inspection record of the original object, sprang into being in the center of the room. "Spread out, kids, so you can all get a good look at it."

The quaddies arranged themselves around the display in a spherical shell of attentiveness, automatically extending helping hands to neighbors to absorb and trade momentum so that all achieved a tolerable hover. Dr. Yei, sitting in—if you could call it that—floated unobtrusively in the background. Monitoring him for his political purity, Leo supposed, not that it mattered. He did not propose to alter his lecture one jot for her presence.

Leo rotated the image so that each student could see it from every angle. "Now let's magnify this part. You see the deep-V cross section from the high-energy-density beam, familiar from your basic welding courses, right? Note the small round porosities here . . ." The magnification jumped again. "Would you say this weld is defective or not?" He almost added, *Raise your hand*, before realizing what a particularly unintelligible directive that was here. Several of the red-clad students solved the dilemma for him by crossing their upper arms formally across their chests instead, looking properly hesitant. Leo nodded toward Tony.

"Those are gas bubbles, aren't they sir? It must be defective."

Leo smiled thanks for the desired straight line. "They are indeed gas porosities. Oddly enough, though, when we crunch the numbers through, they do not appear to be defects. Let us run the computer scan down this length, with an eye to the digital read-out. As you see," the numbers flickered at a corner of the display as the cross-section moved dizzyingly, "at no point do more than two porosities appear in a cross-section, and at all points the voids occupy less than five percent of the section. Also, spherical cavities like these are the least damaging of all potential shapes of discontinuities, the least likely to propagate cracks in service. A non-critical defect is called a *discontinuity*." Leo paused politely while two dozen heads bent in unison to highlight this pleasingly unambiguous fact on the autotranscription of their light boards, braced between lower hands for a portable recording surface. "When I add that this weld was in a fairly low-pressure liquid storage tank, and not, for example, in a thruster propulsion chamber with its massively greater stresses, the slipperiness of this definition becomes clearer. For in a thruster the particular degree of defect that shows up here *would* have been critical.

"Now." He switched the holovid display to one in red light. "This is a holovid of the same weld from data bits mapped by an ultrasonic pulse reflective scan. Looks quite different, doesn't it? Can anyone identify *this* discontinuity?" He zoomed in on a bright area.

Several sets of arms crossed again. Leo nodded toward another student, a striking boy with aquiline nose, brilliant black eyes, wiry muscles, and dark mahogany skin contrasting elegantly with his red T-shirt and shorts. "Yes, Pramod?"

"It's an unbonded lamination."

"Right!" Leo tapped his holovid controls. "But check down this scan—where have all our little bubbles gone? Anybody think they magically closed between tests? Thank you," he said to their knowing grins, "I'm glad you don't think that. Now let's put both maps together." Red and blue melded to purple at overlapping points as the computer integrated the two displays.

"And *now* we see the little bugger," said Leo, zooming in again. "These two porosities, plus this lamination, all in the same plane. You can see the fatal crack starting to propagate already, on this rotation—" The holovid turned, and Leo emphasized the crack with a bright pink light. "That, children, is a defect."

They oohed in gratifying fascination. Leo grinned and plunged on. "Now, here's the point. Both these test scans were valid pictures—as far as they went. But neither one was complete, neither alone sufficient. The maps were not the territories. You have to know that x-radiography is excellent for revealing voids and inclusions, but poor at finding cracks except at certain chance alignments, and ultrasound is optimum for just those laminar discontinuities x-rays are most likely to miss. Both maps, intelligently integrated, yielded a judgment."

"Now." Leo smiled a bit grimly, and replaced the gaudy image with another, monochrome green this time. "Look at this. What do you see?" He nodded at Tony again.

"A laser weld, sir."

"So it would appear. Your identification is quite understandable—and quite wrong. I want you all to memorize this piece of work. Look well. Because it may be the most evil object you ever encounter."

They looked wildly impressed, but totally bewildered. He commanded their absolute silence and utmost attention.

"*That,*" he pointed for emphasis, his voice growing heavy with scorn, "is a falsified inspection record. Worse, it's one of a series. A certain subcontractor of GalacTech supplying thruster propulsion chambers for jumpships found its profit margin endangered by a high volume of its work being rejected—after it had been placed in the systems. So instead of tearing the work apart and doing it over right, they chose to lean on the quality control inspectors. We will never know for certain if the chief inspector refused a bribe or not, because he wasn't around to tell us. He was found accidentally very dead due to an apparent power suit malfunction, attributed to his own errors made when attempting to don it while drunk. The autopsy found a high percentage of alcohol in his bloodstream. It was only much later that it was pointed out that the percentage was so high, he oughtn't to have been able to walk, let alone suit up.

"The assistant inspector *did* accept the bribe. The welds passed the computer certification all right—because it was the same damn good weld, replicated over and over and inserted into the data bank in place of real inspections, which for the most part were never even made. Twenty propulsion chambers were put online. Twenty time-bombs.

"It wasn't until the second one blew up eighteen months later that the whole story was finally uncovered. This isn't hearsay; I was on the probable-cause investigating team. It was I who found it, by the oldest test in the world, eye-and-brain inspection. When I sat there in that station chair, running those hundreds of holovid records through one by one, and first recognized the piece when I saw it again—and again—and again—for the computer only recognized that the series was free of defects—and I *realized* what those bastards had done . . ." His hands were shaking, as they always did at this point of the lecture, as the old memories flickered back. Leo clenched them by his sides.

"The judgment of the map was falsified in these electronic dream images. But the universal laws of physics yielded a judgment of blood that was absolutely real. Eighty-six people died altogether. *That*," Leo pointed again, "was not merely fraud, it was coldest, crudest murder."

He gathered his breath. "This is the most important thing I will ever say to you. The human mind is the ultimate testing device. You can take all the notes you want on the technical data, anything you forget you can look up again, but this must be engraved on your hearts in letters of fire.

"There is *nothing, nothing, nothing* more important to me in the men and women I train than their absolute personal integrity. Whether you function as welders or inspectors, the laws of physics are implacable lie-detectors. You may fool men. You will never fool the metal. That's all."

He let his breath out, and regained his good humor, looking around. The quaddie students were taking it with proper seriousness, good, no class cut-ups making sick jokes in the back row. In fact, they were looking rather shocked, staring at him with terrified awe.

"So," he clapped his hands together and rubbed them cheerfully, to break the spell, "now let's go over to the shop and take a beam welder apart, and see if we can find everything that can possibly go wrong with it. . . ."

They filed out obediently ahead of him, chattering among themselves again. Yei was waiting by the door aperture as Leo followed his class. She gave him a brief smile.

"An impressive presentation, Mr. Graf. You become quite articulate when you talk about your work. Yesterday I thought you must be the strong silent type."

Leo flushed faintly and shrugged. "It's not so hard, when you have something interesting to talk about."

"I would not have guessed welding engineering to be so entertaining a subject. You are a gifted enthusiast."

"I hope your quaddies were equally impressed. It's a great thing, when I can get somebody fired up. It's the greatest work in the world."

"I begin to think so. Your story . . ." she hesitated. "Your fraud story had great impact. They've never heard anything like it. Indeed, I never heard about that one."

"It was years ago."

"Really quite disturbing, all the same." Her face bore a look of introspection. "I hope not overly so."

"Well, I hope it's very disturbing. It's a true story. I was there." He eyed her. "Someday, they may be there. Criminally negligent, if I fail to prepare them."

"Ah." She smiled shortly.

The last of his students had vanished up the corridor. "Well, I better catch up with them. Will you be sitting in on my whole course? Come on along, I'll make a welder of you yet."

She shook her head ruefully. "You actually make it sound attractive. But I'm afraid I have a full-time job. I have to turn you loose." She gave him a short nod. "You'll do all right, Mr. Graf."

Chapter 3

Andy stuck out his tongue, extruding the blob of creamed rice Claire had just spooned into his mouth. "Beh," he remarked. The blob, spurned as food, apparently exerted new fascination as a plaything, for he caught it between his upper right and lower left hands as it slowly rotated off. "Eh!" he protested as his new satellite was reduced to a mere smear.

"Oh, Andy," Claire muttered in frustration, and removed the smear from his hands with a vigorous swipe from a rather soiled high-capillarity towel. "Come on, baby, you've got to try this. Dr. Yei says it's *good* for you!"

"Maybe he's full," Tony offered helpfully.

The nutritional experiment was taking place in Claire's private quarters, awarded her upon the birth of Andy and shared with the baby. She often missed her old dormitory mates, but reflected ruefully that the company had been right; her popularity and Andy's fascination would probably not have survived too many night feedings, diaper changes, gas attacks, mysterious diarrheas and fevers, or other infant nocturnal miseries.

Of late she'd missed Tony, too. In the last six weeks she'd hardly seen him, his new welding instructor was keeping him so busy. The pace of life seemed to be picking up all over the Habitat. There were days when there scarcely seemed to be time to draw breath.

"Maybe he doesn't like it," suggested Tony. "Have you tried mixing it with that other goo?"

"Everybody's an expert," sighed Claire. "Except me . . . He ate some yesterday, anyway."

"How does it taste?"

"I don't know, I never tried it."

"Hm." Tony plucked the spoon from her hand and twirled it in the opened seal-a-cup, picked up a blob, and popped it in his mouth.

"Hey—!" began Claire indignantly.

"Beh!" Tony choked. "Give me that towel." He rid himself of his sample. "No wonder he spits it out. It's Gag Station."

Claire grabbed the spoon back, muttered "Huh!", and floated over to her kitchenette to push it through the handholes to the water dispenser and give it a steaming rinse. "Germs!" she snapped accusingly at Tony.

"You try it!"

She sniffed the food cup in renewed doubt. "I'll take your word for it."

Andy in the meantime had captured his lower right hand with his uppers and was gnawing on it.

"You're not supposed to have meat yet," Claire sighed, straightening him back out. Andy inhaled, preparing for complaint, but let it go in a mere "Aah," as the door slid open revealing a new object of interest.

"How's it going, Claire?" asked Dr. Yei. Her thick useless downsider legs trailed relaxed from her hips as she pulled herself into the cabin.

Claire brightened. She liked Dr. Yei; things always seemed to calm down a bit when she was around. "Andy won't eat the creamed rice. He liked the strained banana well enough."

"Well, next feeding try introducing the oatmeal instead," said Dr. Yei. She floated over to Andy, held out her hand; he captured it with his uppers. She peeled off his hands, held her hand down farther; he grasped at it with his lowers, and giggled. "His lower body coordination is coming along nicely. Bet it will nearly match the upper by his first birthday."

"And that fourth tooth broke through day before yesterday," said Claire, pointing it out.

"Nature's way of telling you it's time to eat creamed rice," Dr. Yei lectured the baby with mock seriousness. He clamped to her arm, beady eyes intent upon her gold loop earrings, nutrition quite forgotten. "Don't fret too much, Claire. There's always this tendency to push things with the first child, just to reassure yourself it can all be done. It will be more relaxed with the second. I guarantee all babies master creamed rice before they're twenty no matter *what* you do."

Claire laughed, secretly relieved. "It's just that Mr. Van Atta was asking about his progress."

"Ah." Dr. Yei's lips twitched in a rather compressed smile. "I see." She defended her earring from a determined assault by placing Andy in air just beyond reach. A frustrated paroxysm of swimming-motions gave him only an unwanted spin. He opened his mouth to howl protest; Dr.

Yei surrendered instantly, but bought time by holding out just her fingertips.

Andy again headed earring-ward, hand over hand over hand. "Yeah, go for it, baby," Tony cheered him on.

"Well." Dr. Yei turned her attention to Claire. "I actually stopped by to pass on some good news. The company is so pleased with the way things have turned out with Andy, they've decided to move up the date for you to start your second pregnancy."

Tony's face split in a delighted grin, beyond Dr. Yei's shoulder. His upper hands clasped in a gesture of victory. Claire made embarrassed-suppression motions at him, but couldn't help grinning back.

"Wow," said Claire, warm with pleasure. So, the company thought she was doing *that* well. There had been down days when she'd thought no one noticed how hard she'd been trying. "How much up?"

"Your monthly cycles are still being suppressed by the breast feeding, right? You have an appointment at the infirmary tomorrow morning. Dr. Minchenko will give you some medicine to start them up again. You can start trying on the second cycle."

"Oh my goodness. That soon." Claire paused, watching the wriggling Andy and remembering how the first pregnancy had drained her energy. "I guess I can handle it. But whatever happened to that two-and-a-quarter-year ideal spacing you were talking about?"

Dr. Yei bit her words off carefully. "There is a Project-wide push to increase productivity. In all areas." Dr. Yei, always straightforward in Claire's experience, smiled falsely. She glanced at Tony, hovering happily, and pursed her lips.

"I'm glad you're here, Tony, because I have some good news for you too. Your welding instructor Mr. Graf has rated you tops in his class. So you've been picked as gang foreman to go out on the first Cay Project contract GalacTech has landed. You and your co-workers will be shipping out in about a month to a place called Kline Station. It's on the far end of the wormhole nexus, beyond Earth, and it's a long ride, so Mr. Graf will be going along to complete your training en route, and double as engineering supervisor."

Tony surged across the room in excitement. "At last! Real work! But—" He paused, stricken. Claire, one thought ahead of him, felt her face becoming mask-like. "But how's Claire supposed to start a baby next month if I'm on my way to where?"

"Dr. Minchenko will freeze a couple of sperm samples before you go," suggested Claire. "Won't he . . . ?"

"Ah—hm," said Dr. Yei. "Well, actually, that wasn't in the plans. Your next baby is scheduled to be fathered by Rudy, in Microsystems Installation."

"Oh, no!" gasped Claire.

Dr. Yei studied both their faces, and arranged her mouth in a severe frown. "Rudy is a very nice boy. He would be very hurt by that reaction, I'm sure. This can't be a surprise, Claire, after all our talks."

"Yes, but—I was hoping, since Tony and I did so well, they'd let us—I was going to ask Dr. Cay!"

"Who is no longer with us," Dr. Yei sighed. "And so you've gone and let yourselves become pair-bonded. I warned you not to do that, didn't I?"

Claire hung her head. Tony's face was mask-like, now.

"Claire, Tony, I know this seems hard. But you in the first generations have a special burden. You are the first step in a very detailed long-range plan for GalacTech, spanning literally generations. Your actions have a multiplier effect all out of proportion—Look, this isn't by any means the end of the world for you two. Claire has a long reproductive career scheduled. It's quite probable you'll be getting back together again someday. And you, Tony—you're tops. GalacTech's not going to waste you, either. There will be other girls—"

"I don't want other girls," said Tony stonily. "Only Claire."

Dr. Yei paused, went on. "I shouldn't be telling you this yet, but Sinda in Nutrition is next for you. I've always thought she was an extraordinarily pretty girl."

"She has a laugh like a hacksaw."

Dr. Yei blew out her breath impatiently. "We'll discuss it later. At length. Right now I *have* to talk with Claire." She thrust him firmly out the door and keyed it shut on his frown and muffled objections.

Dr. Yei turned back to Claire and fixed her with a stern gaze. "Claire—did you and Tony continue to have sexual relations after you became pregnant?"

"Dr. Minchenko said it wouldn't hurt the baby."

"Dr. Minchenko knew?"

"I don't know . . . I just asked him, like, in a general way." Claire studied her hands guiltily. "Did you expect us to stop?"

"Well, yes!"

"You didn't tell us to."

"You didn't ask. In fact, you were quite careful not to bring up the subject, now that I think back—oh, how could I have been so blind-sided?"

"But downsiders do it all the time," Claire defended herself.

"How do you know what downsiders do?"

"Silver says Mr. Van Atta—" Claire stopped abruptly.

Dr. Yei's attention sharpened, knife-like and uncomfortable. "What do you know about Silver and Mr. Van Atta?"

"Well—everything, I guess. I mean, we all wanted to know how downsiders did it." Claire paused. "Downsiders are *strange*," she added.

After a paralyzed moment, Dr. Yei buried her suffused face in her hands and sniggered helplessly. "And so Silver's been supplying you with detailed information?"

"Well, yes." Claire regarded the psychologist with wary fascination.

Dr. Yei stifled her chortles, a strange light growing in her eyes, part humor, part irritation. "I suppose—I suppose you'd better pass the word to Tony not to let on. I'm afraid Mr. Van Atta would become a little upset if he realized his personal activities had a second-hand audience."

"All right," Claire agreed doubtfully. "But—you always wanted to know all about me and Tony."

"That's different. We were trying to help you."

"Well, we and Silver are trying to help each other."

"You're not supposed to help yourselves." The sting of Dr. Yei's criticism was blunted by her suppressed smile. "You're supposed to wait until you're served." Yei paused. "Just how many of you are privy to this, ah, Silver-mine of information, anyway? Just you and Tony, I trust?"

"Well, and my dormitory mates. I take Andy over there in my off hours and we all play with him. I used to have my sleep restraints opposite Silver's until I moved out. She's my best friend. Silver's so—so brave, I guess—she'll try things I'd never dare." Claire sighed envy.

"Eight girls," Yei muttered. "Oh, lord Krishna . . . I trust none of them have been inspired to emulation yet?"

Claire, not wishing to lie, said nothing. She didn't need to; the psychologist, watching her face, winced.

Yei turned indecisively in air. "I've got to have a talk with Silver. I should have done it when I first suspected—but I thought the man had the wit not to contaminate the experiment—asleep on my feet. Look, Claire, I want to talk with you more about your new assignment. I'm here to try and make it as easy and pleasant as possible—you know I'll help, right? I'll get back to you as soon as I can."

Yei peeled Andy off her neck where he was now attempting to taste her earring and handed him back to Claire, and exited the airseal door muttering something about "containing the damage . . ."

Claire, alone, held her baby close. Her troubled uncertainty turned like a lump of metal under her heart. She had tried so hard to be good. . . .

Leo squinted approvingly against the harsh light and dense shadows of the vacuum as a pair of his space-suited students horsed the locking ring accurately into place on the end of its flex tube. Between the two of them their eight gloved hands made short work of the task.

"Now Pramod, Bobbi, bring up the beam welder and the recorder and put them in their starting position. Julian, you run the optical laser alignment program and lock them on."

A dozen of the four-armed figures, their names and numbers printed in large clear figures on the front of each helmet and across the backs of their silvery work suits, bobbed about. Their suit jets puffed as they jockeyed for a better view.

"Now, in these high-energy-density partial penetration welds," Leo lectured into his space suit's audio pick-up, "the electron beam must not be allowed to achieve a penetrating steady-state. This beam can punch through half a meter of steel. Even one spiking event and your, say, nuclear pressure vessel or your propulsion chamber can lose its structural integrity. Now, the pulser that Pramod is checking right now"—Leo made his voice heavy with hint; Pramod jerked, and hastily began punching up the system readout on his machine—"utilizes the natural oscillation of the point of beam impingement within the weld cavity to set up a pulsing schedule that maintains its frequency, eliminating the spiking problem. *Always* double-check its function before you start."

The locking ring was firmly welded to its flex tube and duly examined for flaws by eye, hologram scan, eddy current, the examination and comparison of the simultaneous x-ray emission recording, and the classic kick-and-jerk test. Leo prepared to move his students on to the next task.

"Tony, you bring the beam welder over—TURN IT OFF FIRST!" Feedback squeal lanced through everyone's earphones, and Leo modulated his voice from his first urgent panicked bellow. The beam had in fact been off, but the controls live; one accidental bump, as Tony swung the machine around, and—Leo's eye traced the hypothetical slice through the nearby wing of the Habitat, and he shuddered.

"Get your head out of your ass, Tony! I saw a man cut in half by one of his friends once by just that careless trick."

"Sorry . . . thought it would save time . . . sorry . . ." Tony mumbled.

"You know better." Leo calmed, as his heart stopped palpitating. "In this hard vacuum that beam won't stop till it hits the third moon, or whatever it might encounter in between." He almost continued, stopped himself; no, not over the public com channel. Later.

Later, as his students unsuited in the equipment locker, laughing and joking as they cleaned and stored their work suits, Leo drifted over to the silent and pale Tony. *Surely I didn't bark at him* that *hard*, Leo thought to himself. *Figured he was more resilient* . . . "Stop and see me when you're finished here," said Leo quietly.

Tony flinched guiltily. "Yes, sir."

After his fellows had all swooped out, eager for their end-of-shift meal, Tony hung in the air, both sets of arms crossed protectively across his torso. Leo floated near, and spoke in a grave tone.

"Where were you, out there today?"

"Sorry, sir. It won't happen again."

"It's been happening all week. You got something on your mind, boy?"

Tony shook his head. "Nothing—nothing to do with you, sir."

Meaning, nothing to do with work, Leo interpreted that. All right, so. "If it's taking your mind off your work, it does have something to do with me. Want to talk about it? You got girl trouble? Little Andy all right? You have a fight with somebody?"

Tony's blue eyes searched Leo's face in sudden uncertainty, then he grew closed and inward once again. "No, sir."

"You worried about going out on that contract? I guess it will be the first time away from home for you kids, at that."

"It's not that," denied Tony. He paused, watching Leo again. "Sir—are there a great many other companies out there besides ours?"

"Not a great many, for deep interstellar work," Leo replied, a little baffled by this new turn in the conversation. "We're the biggest, of course, though there's maybe a half dozen others that can give us some real competition. In the heavily populated systems, like Tau Ceti or Escobar or Orient or of course Earth, there's always a lot of little companies operating on a smaller scale. Super-specialists, or entrepreneurial mavericks, this and that. The outer worlds are coming on strong lately."

"So—so if you ever quit GalacTech, you could get another job in space."

"Oh, sure. I've even had offers—but our company does the most of the sort of work I want to do, so there's no reason to go elsewhere. And I've got a lot of seniority accumulated by now, and all that goes with it. I'll probably be with GalacTech till I retire, if I don't die in harness." *Probably from a heart attack brought on by watching one of my students try to accidentally kill himself.* Leo did not speak the thought aloud; Tony seemed chastised enough. But still abstracted.

"Sir . . . tell me about *money*."

"Money?" Leo raised his brows. "What's to tell? The stuff of life."

"I've never seen any—I'd understood it was sort of coded value-markers to, to facilitate trade, and keep count."

"That's right."

"How do you get it?"

"Well—most people work for it. They, ah, trade their labor for it. Or if they own or manufacture or grow something, they can sell it. I work."

"And GalacTech gives you *money*?"

"Uh, yes."

"If I asked, would the company give me money?"

"Ah . . ." Leo became conscious of skating on very thin ice. His private opinion of the Cay Project had perhaps better remain just that, while he ate the company's bread. His job was to teach safe quality welding procedures, not—foment union demands, or whatever this conversation was sliding toward. "Whatever would you spend it on, up here? GalacTech gives you everything you need. Now, when I'm downside, or not on a company installation, I have to buy my own food, clothing, travel and what-not. Besides"—Leo reached for a less queasily specious argument—"up till now, you haven't actually done any work for GalacTech, although it's done plenty for you. Wait till you've actually been out on a contract and done some real producing. Then maybe it might be time to talk about money." Leo smiled, feeling hypocritical, but at least loyal.

"Oh." Tony seemed to fold inward on some secret disappointment. His blue eyes flicked up, probing Leo again. "When one of the company jumpships leaves Rodeo—where does it go first?"

"Depends on where it's wanted, I guess. Some run straight all the way to Earth. If there's cargo or people to divide up for other destinations, the first stop is usually Orient Station."

"GalacTech doesn't own Orient Station, does it?"

"No, it's owned by the government of Orient IV. Although GalacTech leases a good quarter of it."

"How long does it take to get to Orient Station from Rodeo?"

"Oh, usually about a week. You'll probably be stopping there yourself quite soon, if only to pick up extra equipment and supplies, when you're sent out on your first construction contract."

The boy was looking more outer-directed now, perhaps thinking about his first interstellar trip. That was better. Leo relaxed slightly.

"I'll be looking forward to that, sir."

"Right. If you don't cut your foot, er, hand off meanwhile, eh?"

Tony ducked his head and grinned. "I'll try not to, sir."

And what was that all about? Leo wondered, watching Tony sail out the door. Surely the boy could not be thinking of trying to strike out on his own? Tony had not the least conception of what a freak he would seem, beyond his familiar Habitat. If he would only open up a little more . . .

Leo shrank from the thought of confronting him. Every downsider staff member in the Habitat seemed to feel they had a right to the quaddies' personal thoughts. There wasn't a lockable door anywhere in the quaddies' living quarters. They had all the privacy of ants under glass.

He shook off the critical thought, but could not shake off his queasiness. All his life he had placed his faith in his own technical integrity—if he followed that star, his feet would not stumble. It was ingrained habit by now; he had brought that technical integrity to the teaching of Tony's work gang almost automatically. And yet . . . this time, it did not seem to be quite enough. As if he had memorized the answer, only to discover the question had been changed.

Yet what more could be demanded of him? What more could he be expected to give? What, after all, could one man do?

A spasm of vague fear made him blink, the hard-edged stars in the viewport smearing, as the looming shadow of the dilemma clouded on the horizon of his conscience. *More* . . .

He shivered, and turned his back to the vastness. It could swallow a man, surely.

✧   ✧   ✧

Ti, the freight shuttle co-pilot, had his eyes closed. Perhaps that was natural at times like this, Silver thought, studying his face from a distance of ten centimeters. At this range her eyes could no longer superimpose their stereoscopic images, so his twinned face overlapped itself. If she squinted just right, she could make him appear to have three eyes. Men really were rather alien. Yet the metal contact implanted in his forehead, echoed at both temples, did not have that effect, seeming more a decoration or a mark of rank. She blinked one eye closed, then the other, causing his face to shift back and forth in her vision.

Ti opened his eyes a moment, and Silver quickly flinched into action. She smiled, half-closed her own eyes, picked up the rhythm of her flexing hips. "Oooh," she murmured, as Van Atta had taught her. *Let's hear some feedback, honey,* Van Atta had demanded, so she'd hit on a collection of noises that seemed to please him. They worked on the pilot, too, when she remembered to make them.

Ti's eyes squeezed shut, his lips parting as his breath came faster, and Silver's face relaxed into pensive stillness once again, grateful for the privacy. Anyway, Ti's gaze didn't make her as uncomfortable as Mr. Van Atta's, which always seemed to suggest that she ought to be doing something else, or more, or differently.

The pilot's forehead was damp with sweat, plastering down one curl of brown hair around the shiny plug. Mechanical mutant, biological mutant, equally touched by differing technologies; perhaps that was why Ti had first seen her as approachable, being an odd man out himself. Both freaks together. On the other hand, maybe the jump pilot just wasn't very fussy.

He shivered, gasped convulsively, clutched her tightly to his body. Actually, he looked—rather vulnerable. Mr. Van

Atta never looked vulnerable at this moment. Silver was not sure just what it was he did look like.

What's he getting out of this that I'm not? What's wrong with me? Maybe she really was, as Van Atta had once accused, frigid—an unpleasant word, it reminded her of machinery, and the trash dumps locked outside the Habitat—so she had learned to make noises for him, and twitch pleasingly, and he had commended her for loosening up.

Silver reminded herself that she had another reason for keeping her eyes open. She glanced again past the pilot's head. The observation window of the darkened control booth where they trysted overlooked the freight loading bay. The staging area between the bay's control booth and the entrance to the freight shuttle's hatch remained dimly lit and empty of movement. *Hurry up Tony, Claire,* Silver worried. *I can't keep this guy occupied all shift.*

"Wow," breathed Ti, coming out of his trance and opening his eyes and grinning. "When they designed you folks for free fall they thought of *everything*." He released his own clutch on the wings of Silver's shoulder blades to slide his hands down her back, around her hips, and along her lower arms, ending with an approving pat on her hands locked around his muscular downsider flanks. "*Truly* functional."

"How *do* downsiders keep from, um, bouncing apart?" Silver inquired curiously, taking practical advantage of having cornered an apparent expert on the subject.

His grin widened. "Gravity keeps us together."

"How strange. I always thought of gravity as something you had to fight all the time."

"No, only half the time. The other half, it works for you," he assured her.

He undocked from her body rather gracefully—perhaps it was all that piloting experience showing through—and planted a kiss in the hollow of her throat. "Pretty lady."

Silver blushed a little, grateful for the dim lighting. Ti turned his attention momentarily to a necessary clean-up chore. A quick whistle of air, and the spermicide-permeated condom was gone down the waste chute. Silver suppressed a faint twinge of regret. It was just too bad Ti wasn't one of them. Too bad she was such a long way down the roster of those scheduled for motherhood. Too bad . . .

"Did you find out from your doctor fellow if we really need those?" Ti asked her.

"I couldn't exactly ask Dr. Minchenko directly," Silver replied. "But I gather he thinks any conceptus between a downsider and one of us would abort spontaneously, pretty early on—but nobody knows for sure. Could be a baby might make it to birth with lower limbs that were neither arms nor legs, but just some mess in between." *And they probably wouldn't let me keep it. . . .* "Anyway, it saves chasing body fluids around the room with a hand vac."

"Too true. Well, I'm certainly not ready to be a daddy."

How incomprehensible, thought Silver, for a man that old. Ti must be at least twenty-five, much older than Tony, who was nearly the eldest of them all. She was careful to float facing the window, so that the pilot had his back to it. *Come on, Tony, do it if you're going to. . . .*

A cool draft from the ventilators raised goose bumps on all her arms, and Silver shivered.

"Chilly?" Ti asked solicitously, and rubbed his hands up and down her arms rapidly to warm them by friction, then retrieved her blue shirt and shorts from the side of the room where they had drifted. Silver shrugged into them gratefully. The pilot dressed too, and Silver watched with covert fascination as he fastened his shoes. Such inflexible, heavy coverings, but then feet were inflexible, heavy things in their own right. She hoped he'd be careful how he swung them around. Shod, his feet reminded her of mallets.

Ti, smiling, unhooked his flight bag from a wall rack where he had stowed it when they'd retreated to the control booth half an hour earlier. "Gotcha something."

Silver perked up, and her four hands clasped each other hopefully. "Oh! Were you able to find any more book-discs by the same lady?"

"Yes, here you go—" Ti produced some thin squares of plastic from the inner reaches of his flight bag. "Three titles, all new."

Silver pounced on them and read their labels eagerly. Rainbow Illustrated Romances: *Sir Randan's Folly, Love in the Gazebo, Sir Randan and the Bartered Bride*, all by Valeria Virga. "Oh, wonderful!" She wrapped her upper right arm around Ti's neck and gave him a quite spontaneous and vigorous kiss.

He shook his head in mock despair. "I don't know how you can read that dreck. I think the author is a committee, anyway."

"It's *great*!" Silver defended her beloved literature indignantly. "It's so, so full of color, and strange places and times—a lot of them are set on old Earth, way back when *everybody* was still downside—they're amazing. People kept animals all around them—these enormous creatures called horses actually used to carry them around on their backs. I suppose the gravity tired people out. And these rich people, like—like company executives, I guess—called 'lords' and 'nobles' lived in the most fantastic habitats, stuck to the surface of the planet—and there was *nothing* about all this in the history *we* were taught!" Her indignation peaked.

"That stuff's not history, though," he objected. "It's fiction."

"It's nothing like the fiction they give us, either. Oh, it's all right for the little kids—I used to love *The Little Compressor That Could*—we made our crèche mother read it over and over. And the Bobby BX-99 series was all right . . . *Bobby BX-99 Solves the Excess Humidity Mystery* . . . *Bobby BX-99 and the Plant Virus* . . . it was then I asked to specialize in Hydroponics. But downsiders are ever so much more interesting to read about. It's so—so—when I'm reading this"—she clutched the little plastic squares tightly—"it's like they're real, and I'm not." Silver sighed hugely.

Although perhaps Mr. Van Atta *was* a bit like Sir Randan . . . high of status, commanding, short-tempered. . . . Silver wondered briefly why short temper in Sir Randan always seemed so exciting and attractive, full of fascinating consequences. When Mr. Van Atta became angry, it merely made her sick to her stomach. Perhaps downsider women had more courage.

Ti shrugged baffled amusement. "Whatever turns you on, I guess. Can't see the harm in it. But I brought something better for you, this trip—" he rummaged in his flight bag again and shook out a froth of ivory fabric, intricate lace and ribbony satin. "I figured you could wear a regular woman's blouse all right. It's got flowers in the pattern, thought you'd like that, being in hydroponics and all."

"Oh . . ." One of Valeria Virga's heroines might have been at home in such a garment. Silver reached for it, drew her hand back. "But—but I can't take it."

"Why not? You take the book-discs. It wasn't *that* expensive."

Silver, who felt she was beginning to have a fairly clear idea of how money worked from her reading, shook her head. "It's not that. It's, well—you know, I don't think Dr. Yei would approve of our meeting like this. Neither would—would a lot of other people." Actually, Silver was fairly sure that "disapprove" would barely begin to cover the consequences should her secret transactions with Ti be found out.

"Prudes," scoffed Ti. "You're not going to let them start telling you what to do *now*, are you?" But his scorn was tinged with anxiety.

"I'm not going to start telling them what I *am* doing either," said Silver pointedly. "Are you?"

"God, no." He waved his hands in horrified negation.

"So, we are in agreement. Unfortunately, that"—she pointed regretfully at the blouse—"is something I can't hide. I couldn't wear it without someone demanding that I explain where I got it."

"Oh," he said, in the blunted tone of one struck by incontrovertible fact. "Yeah, I—guess I should have thought of that. Do you suppose you could put it away for a time? I've only been taking my gravity leaves on the Rodeo side because all the shuttle bonus berths at Orient IV get nailed by the senior guys. Well, and you can log a lot more hours here faster, with all the freight hauling. But I'll have my shuttle commander's rating and be back to permanent jump status in just a few more cycles."

"It can't be shared, either," said Silver. "You see, the thing about the books and the vid dramas and things, besides being small and easy to hide, is that they can be passed all around the group without being used up. Nobody gets left out. So I can get, um, a lot of cooperation when I want to, say—get away for a little time by myself?" A toss of her head indicated the privacy they were presently enjoying.

"Ah," gulped Ti. He paused. "I—hadn't realized you were passing the stuff around."

"Not share?" said Silver. "That would be *really* wrong." She stared at him in mild offense, and pushed the blouse back toward him on the surge of the emotion, quickly, before she weakened. She almost explained further, then thought better of it.

Best Ti didn't know about the uproar when one of the book-discs, accidentally left in a viewer, had been found by one of the Habitat's downsider staff and turned over to Dr. Yei. The search—barely alerted, they had scrambled successfully to hide the rest of the contraband library, but the fierce intensity of the search had been warning enough to Silver of how serious was her offense in the eyes of her authorities. There had been two more surprise inspections since, even though no more discs had been found. She could take a hint.

Mr. Van Atta himself had taken her aside—her!—and urged her to spy out the leak for him among her comrades. She had started to confess, stopped just in time, as his rising rage tightened her throat with fear. "I'm going to crucify the little sneak when I get my hands on him," Van Atta had snarled. Maybe Ti would not find Mr. Van Atta and Dr. Yei and all their staffs ranked together so intimidating—but she dared not risk losing her one sure source of downsider delights. Ti at least was willing to barter for what was in effect a bit of Silver's labor, the one invisible commodity not accounted for in any inventory; who knew, another pilot might want *things* of some kind, far more difficult to smuggle out of the Habitat unnoticed.

A long-awaited movement in the loading area caught her eye. *And you thought you were risking trouble for a few books*, Silver thought to herself. *Wait'll this shit gets on the loose. . . .*

"Thank you anyway," said Silver hastily, and grabbed Ti around the neck for a prolonged thank-you kiss. He closed his eyes—wonderful reflex, that—and Silver rolled hers toward the view out the control booth window. Tony, Claire, and Andy were just disappearing into the shuttle hatch flex tube.

There, that's it. I've done what I can—the rest is up to you. Good luck, double-luck. And more sharply, *I wish I was going with you.*

"Oof! Look at the time!" Ti broke off their embrace. "I've got to get this checklist completed before Captain Durrance gets back. Guess you're right about the shirt." He stuffed it unceremoniously back into his flight bag. "What *do* you want me to bring you next time?"

"Siggy in Airsystems Maintenance asked me if there were any more holovids in the *Ninja of the Twin Stars* series," Silver said promptly. "He's up to Number 7, but he's missing 4 and 5."

"Ah," said Ti. "Now, that was decent entertainment. Did you watch them yourself?"

"Yes." Silver wrinkled her nose "But I'm not sure—the people in them did such horrible things to one another—they are fiction, you say?"

"Well, yes."

"That's a relief."

"Yes, but what would you like for yourself?" he persisted. "I'm not risking reprimand to gratify Siggy, whoever he is. Siggy doesn't have your," he sighed in remembered pleasure, "dear double-jointed hips."

Silver fanned out the three new book cards in her lower right hand. "More, please, sir."

"If it's dreck you want"—he captured each of her hands in turn and kissed their palms—"it's dreck you shall have. Uh, oh, here comes my fearless captain." Ti hastily straightened his shuttle pilot's uniform, turned up the light level, and picked up his report panel as an airseal door at the far end of the loading bay swished open. "He hates being saddled with junior jumpers. Tadpoles, he calls us. I think he's uncomfortable because on my jumpship, I'd outrank him. Still, better not give the old guy something to pick on."

Silver made the book cards disappear into her work bag and took up the pose of an idle bystander as Captain Durrance, the shuttle commander, floated into the control booth.

"Snap it up, Ti, we've had a change of itinerary," said Captain Durrance.

"Yes, sir. What's up?"

"We're wanted downside."

"Hell," Ti swore mildly. "What a pain. I had a hot date lined—er"—his eye fell on Silver—"was supposed to meet a friend for dinner tonight at the transfer station."

"Fine," said Captain Durrance, ironically unsympathetic. "File a complaint with Employee Relations—your work schedule is interfering with your love life. Maybe they can arrange that you not have a work schedule."

Ti took the hint and moved hastily out to continue his duties, as a Habitat technician arrived to take over the loading bay control booth.

Silver made herself small in a corner, frozen in horror and confusion. At the transfer station, Tony and Claire had planned to stow away on a jumpship for Orient IV, get beyond the reach of GalacTech, find work when they got there; a horribly risky plan, in Silver's estimation, a measure of their desperation. Claire had been terrified, but at last persuaded by Tony's plan of carefully thought out stages. At least, the first stages had been carefully thought out; they had seemed to get vaguer, farther away from Rodeo and home. They had not planned on a downside detour in any version.

Tony and Claire had surely hidden themselves by now in the shuttle's cargo bay. There was no way for Silver to warn them—should she betray them to save them? The ensuing uproar was guaranteed to be ghastly—her dismay wrapped like a steel band around her chest, constricting breathing, constricting speech.

She watched on the control booth's vid display in miserable paralysis as the shuttle kicked away from the Habitat and began to drop toward Rodeo's swirling atmosphere.

Chapter 4

Chapter 4

The dim cargo bay seemed to groan all around Claire as deceleration strained its structure. Buffeting, accompanied by a hissing whistle, vibrated through the shuttle's metal skin.

"What's wrong?" gasped Claire. She released an anchoring hand upon the plastic crate behind which they had hidden to double her grasp of Andy and hold him closer. "Are we sideswiping something? What's that funny noise?"

Tony hurriedly licked a finger and held it out. "No draft to speak of." He swallowed, testing his Eustachian tubes. "We're not depressurizing." Yet the whistle was rising.

Two mechanical ka-chunks, one after the other, that were nothing at all like the familiar thump and click of a hatch seal seating itself properly, shot terror through Claire. The deceleration went on and on, much too long, confused by a strange new vector of thrust that seemed to emanate from the shuttle's ventral side. The side of the cargo bay to which the crates were anchored seemed to push against her. She nervously put her back to it, and cushioned Andy upon her belly.

The baby's eyes were round, his mouth an echoing "o" of bewilderment. *No, please, don't start crying!* She dared not release the cry locked in her own throat; it would set him off like a siren. "Patty cake, patty cake, baker's man," Claire choked. "Microwave a cake as fast as you can . . ." She tickled his cheek, flicking her eyes at Tony in mute appeal.

Tony's face was white. "Claire—I think this shuttle's going downside! I bet those bangs were the airfoils deploying."

"Oh, no! Can't be. Silver checked the schedule—"

"It looks like Silver made a big mistake."

"I checked it too. This shuttle was supposed to be picking up a load of stuff at the transfer station, *then* going downside."

"Then you *both* made a big mistake." Tony's voice was harsh and shaking, anger masking fear.

Oh, help, don't yell at me—if I don't stay calm, neither will Andy—this wasn't my idea. . . .

Tony rolled over on his stomach and levered his body away from the thrusting surface of the—the *floor,* downsiders called the direction from which the vector of gravitational force came—and crept to the nearest window, pulling himself alongside it. The light that poured through it was taking on a strange diffuse quality, diminishing. "It's all white—Claire, I think we must be entering a cloud!"

Claire had watched clouds from orbit above for hours, as they slowly billowed in the convection of Rodeo's atmosphere. They had always seemed massive as moons. She longed to go look.

Andy was clutching her blue T-shirt. She rolled over, as Tony had, palms to the surface, and pushed up. Andy, turning his head toward his father, reached out with his upper hands and tried to shove off from Claire with his lowers. The floor leaped up and smacked him.

For a moment he was too stunned to howl. Then his little mouth went from round to square and poured out the vibrating scream of true pain. The sound knifed through every nerve in Claire's body.

Tony too jerked at the noise, and scrambled down from the window and back toward them. "Why did you drop him? What do you think you're doing? Oh, make him be quiet, quick!"

Claire rolled onto her back again, pulling Andy onto the elastic softness of her abdomen, and patted and kissed him frantically. The timbre of his screams began to change from the frightening high-pitched cry of pain to the less piercing bellows of indignation, but the volume was just as loud.

"They'll hear him all the way up in the pilot's compartment!" Tony hissed in anguish. "*Do* something!"

"I'm *trying*," Claire hissed back. Her hands shook. She tried to push Andy's head toward her breast, standard comfort, but he turned his head away and screamed louder. Fortunately, the sound of the atmosphere rushing over the shuttle's skin had risen to a deafening thunder. By the time the noise peaked and faded, Andy's cries had become whimpering hiccups. He rubbed his face, slimy with tears and mucous, mournfully against Claire's T-shirt. His weight on Claire's stomach and diaphragm half stopped her breath, but she dared not lay him down.

Another set of clunks reverberated through the shuttle. The engines' vibrations changed their pitch, and Claire was plucked this way and that by changing acceleration vectors, none as strong as the one emanating from the floor. She spared two hands from comforting Andy to brace herself against the plastic crates.

Tony lay beside them, biting his lips in helpless anxiety. "We must be coming down to land on the surface."

Claire nodded. "At one of the shuttleports. There'll be people there—downsiders—maybe we can tell them we got trapped aboard this shuttle by accident. Maybe," she added hopefully, "they'll send us right back up home."

Tony's right upper hand clenched. "No! We can't give up now! We'd never get another chance!"

"But what else can we do?"

"We'll sneak off this ship and hide, until we can get on another one, one that's going to the transfer station." His voice turned earnest with urgent pleading as a puff of dismay escaped Claire's parted lips. "We did it once, we can do it again."

She shook her head doubtfully. Further argument was interrupted by a startling series of thumps that shook the whole ship and then blended into a low continuous rumble. The light falling through the window shifted its beam around the cargo bay as the shuttle landed, taxied, and turned. Then it winked out, the cargo bay dimmed, and the engines whined to an equally startling silence.

Claire cautiously unbraced herself. Of all the acceleration vectors, only one remained. Isolated, it became overwhelming.

Gravity. Silent, implacable, it pressed against her back— she struggled with a nasty illusion that it might suddenly cease, and the thrust it imparted slam her into the ceiling above, smashing Andy between. In an accompanying optical illusion, the whole cargo bay seemed to be chugging in a slow circle around her. She closed her eyes in self-defense.

Tony's hand tightened in warning on her left lower wrist. She looked up and froze as the outside cargo bay door at the forward end of the compartment slid open.

A pair of downsiders wearing company maintenance coveralls entered. The access door in the center of the shuttle's fuselage dilated, and Ti the shuttle co-pilot stuck his head through.

"Hi, guys. What's the big rush-rush?"

"We're supposed to have this bird turned around and reloaded in an hour, that's what," replied the maintenance man. "*You* have just time to pee and eat lunch."

"What's the cargo? I haven't seen this much hopping around since the last medical emergency."

"Equipment and supplies for some sort of show they're supposed to be putting on up at your Habitat for the Vice President of Operations."

"That's not till next week."

The maintenance man snickered. "That's what everybody thought. The VP just flew in a week early on her private courier, with a whole commando squad of accountants. Seems she likes surprise inspections. Management, naturally, is overjoyed."

"Don't laugh too soon," Ti warned. "Management has ways of sharing their joy with the rest of us."

"Don't I know it," the maintenance man groaned. "C'mon, c'mon, you're blocking the door . . ." The three of them clattered forward.

"*Now*," whispered Tony, with a nod at the open cargo bay door.

Claire rolled to her side and laid Andy gently on the deck. His face crumpled, working up to a cry. Claire quickly rolled onto her palms, tested her balance. Her right lower arm seemed to be the one she could most easily spare. She scooped Andy back up one-handed and held him under her torso.

Plastered against the planet-ward side of the cargo bay by the dreadful gravity, she began a three-handed crawl toward the door. Andy's weight pulled at her arm as though a strong spring were drawing him to the floor, and his head bobbed backwards at an alarming angle. Claire inched her palm up under his head to support it, painfully awkward for her arm.

Beside her, Tony too achieved a three-handed stance. With his free hand he jerked the cord to their pack of supplies. The pack, stuck to the downside surface as if by suction, didn't budge.

"Shit," Tony swore under his breath. He swarmed over the pack, gripped and lifted it, but it was too bulky to carry under his belly. "*Double-shit.*"

"Can we give up yet?" Claire asked in a tiny voice, knowing the answer.

"*No!*" He grabbed the pack backwards over both shoulders with his upper hands and rocked forward violently. It came up and balanced precariously on his back. He kept his left upper hand on it to steady it and hopped forward on his right, his lower palms shuffling along under his hips. "I got it, go, go!"

The shuttle was parked in a cavernous hangar, a vast dim gulf of space roofed by girders. The girders behind the overhead lights would have been an excellent hiding place, if only one could swoop up there. But everything not rigidly fastened was doomed to fly to the one side of the room only, and stick there until forcibly removed. There was a lopsided fascination to it. . . .

"Oh . . ." Claire hesitated. Leading from the hatch to the hangar floor was a kind of corrugated ramp. Clearly, it was designed to break down the dangerous fight with the omnipresent gravity into little manageable increments. "*Stairs.*"

Claire paused, head down. Her blood seemed to pool diz-zyingly in her face. She gulped.

"Don't *stop*," Tony gasped pleadingly behind her, then gulped himself.

"Uh . . . uh . . ." In a moment of inspiration, Claire turned around and began to back down, her free lower palm slap-ping the metal treads with each hop. It was still uncomfortable, but at least possible. Tony followed.

"Where now?" Claire panted when they reached the bottom.

Tony pointed with his chin. "Hide in that jumble of equipment over there, for now. We daren't get too far from the shuttles."

They scuttled along over the downside surface of the hangar. Claire's hands quickly became smudged with oil and dirt, a psychological irritation as fierce as an unscratchable itch; she felt she might gladly risk death for a chance to wash them. Claire remembered watching beads of condensed humidity creeping by capillarity across sur-faces in the Habitat, until she'd smeared them to oblivion with her dry-rag, just as she and Tony crept now.

As they reached the area where some pieces of heavy equipment were parked, a loader rolled into the hangar and a dozen coveralled men and women jumped off it and began swarming over the shuttle, organized confusion. Claire was glad for their noise, for Andy was still emitting an occasional whimper. Fearfully, she watched the mainte-nance crew through the metal arms of the machinery. How late was too late to surrender?

Leo, half suited-up in the equipment locker, glanced up anxiously as Pramod swooped across the room to fetch up gracefully beside him.

"Did you find Tony?" Leo asked. "As gang foreman, he's supposed to be leading this parade. I'm only supposed to be watching."

Pramod shook his head. "He's not in any of the usual places, sir."

Leo hissed under his breath, not quite swearing. "He should've answered his page by now." He drifted to the plexiport.

Outside in the vacuum, a small pusher was just depositing the last of the sections for the shell of the new hydroponics bay in their carefully arranged constellation. It was to be built before the Operations Vice President's eyes by the quaddies. So much for Leo's faint hope that screwups and delays in other departments might cover those in his own. It was time for his welding crew to make its debut.

"All right, Pramod, get suited up. You'll take over Tony's position, and Bobbi from Gang B will take yours." Leo hurried on before the startled look in Pramod's eyes could turn to stage fright. "It's nothing you haven't practiced a dozen times. And if you have the least doubts about the quality or safety of any procedure, I'll be right there. Reality first— you people are going to be living in the structure you build today long after Vice President Apmad and her traveling circus are gone. I guarantee she'll have more respect for a job done right, however slowly, than for a piece of slapdash fakery."

For God's sake make it look smooth, Van Atta had instructed Leo urgently, earlier. *Keep to the schedule, no matter what—we'll fix the problems later, after she's gone. We're supposed to be making these chimps seem cost-effective.*

"You don't have to try to seem to be anything but what you are," Leo told Pramod. "You *are* efficient—and you are good. Instructing you all has been one of the great unexpected pleasures of my career. Be off, now, I'll catch up with you shortly."

Pramod sped away to find Bobbi. Leo frowned briefly to himself, then floated up the length of the locker room to the comconsole terminal at the end.

He keyed in his ID. "Page," he instructed it. "Dr. Sondra Yei." At the same moment a message square in the corner of the vid began to blink with his own name, and a number. "Cancel that instruction."

He punched up the number and raised his brows in surprise as Dr. Yei's face appeared on his vid. "Sondra! I was just about to call you. Do you know where Claire is?"

"How odd. I was calling to ask you if you knew where I could reach Tony."

"Oh?" said Leo, in a voice suddenly drained to neutrality. "Why?"

"Because I can't find her anywhere, and I thought Tony might know where she is. She's supposed to be giving a demonstration of child care techniques in free fall to Vice President Apmad after lunch."

"Is, um"—Leo swallowed—"Andy at the crèche, or with Claire, do you know?"

"With Claire, of course."

"Ah."

"Leo . . ." Dr. Yei's attention sharpened, her lips pursed. "Do you know something I don't?"

"Ah . . ." He eyed her. "I know Tony has been unusually inattentive at work for the last week. I might even say—depressed, except that's supposed to be your department, eh? Not his usual cheerful self, anyway." A knot of unease, tightening in Leo's stomach, gave his tongue an unaccustomed edge. "You, ah, got any concerns that you may have forgotten to share with me, lady?"

Her lips thinned, but she ignored the bait. "Schedules have been moved up in all departments, you know. Claire received her new reproduction assignment. It didn't include Tony."

"Reproduction assignment? You mean, having a baby?" Leo could feel his face flushing. Somewhere within him, a long-controlled steam pressure began to build. "Do you hide what you're really doing from yourselves with those weasel-words, too? And here I thought the propaganda was just for us peons." Yei started to speak, but Leo overrode her, bursting out, "Good God! Were you born inhuman, or did you grow so by degrees—M.S., M.D., Ph.D. . . ."

Yei's face darkened; her accent grew clipped. "An engineer with romance in his soul? Now I've seen everything. Don't get carried away with your scenario, Mr. Graf. Tony and Claire were assigned to each other in the first place by the exact same system, and if *certain people* had been willing to abide by my original timetable, this problem could have been avoided. I fail to see the point of paying for an expert and then blithely ignoring her advice, really I do. Engineers . . . !"

Ah, hell, she's suffering from as bad a case of Van Atta as I am, Leo realized. The insight blunted his momentum, without bleeding off his internal pressure.

"—I didn't invent the Cay Project, and if I were running it I'd do it differently, but I have to play the hand I'm dealt, Mr. Graf. Blast—" She controlled herself, almost visibly wrenching the conversation back on its original track. "I've got to find her soon, or I'll have no choice but to let Van Atta start the show ass-backwards. Leo, it's absolutely essential that Vice President Apmad get the crèche tour first, before she has time to start forming any—do you have any idea at all where those kids may be?"

Leo shook his head; an inspiration turned the truthful gesture to a lie even before he'd finished it. "But will you give me a call if you find them before I do?" he pleaded, his humble tone offering truce.

Yei's stiffness wilted a bit. "Yes, certainly." She shrugged wryly, a silent apology, and broke off.

Leo swung back to his locker, peeled out of his work suit, donned coveralls, and hastened off to track down his inspiration before Dr. Yei duplicated it independently. He was certain she would, and shortly, too.

Silver checked the work schedule on her vid display. Bell peppers. She floated across the hydroponics bay to the seed locker, found the correctly labeled drawer, and withdrew a pre-counted paper packet. She gave the packet an absent shake, and the dried seeds made a pleasing rattle.

She collected a plastic germination box, tore open the packet, and coaxed the little pale seeds into the container, where they bounced about cheerfully. To the hydration spigot next. She thrust the water tube through the rubber doughnut seal on the side of the germination box and administered a measured squirt, and gave the box an extra shake to break up the shimmering globule of liquid that formed. Shoving the germination box into its slot in the incubation rack, she set it for the optimum temperature for peppers, bell, hybrid phototropic non-gravitational axial differentiating clone 297-X-P, and sighed.

The light from the filtered windows plucked insistently at her attention, and she paused for the fourth or fifth time this shift to weave among the grow tubes and stare out at the portion of Rodeo this bay's angle of view allowed her to see. Somewhere down there, at the bottom of that well of air, Claire and Tony were crawling now—if they had not already surrendered—or managed to make it to another shuttle—or met some horrible catastrophe. . . . Silver's imagination, unbidden, supplied her with a string of sample catastrophes.

She tried to crowd them out with a firm mental picture of Tony and Claire and Andy successfully sneaking onto a shuttle bound for the transfer station, but the picture wavered into a scenario of Claire, attempting to jump some gap to the shuttle's hatchway (what gap? from where, for pity's sake?) forgetting that all such tangents were bent to parabolas by the gravitational force, and missing the target. Silver thought of the peculiar ways things moved in dense gravitational fields. The scream, chopped off by the splat on the concrete below—no, surely Claire would be holding Andy—the *double* splat on the concrete below. . . . Silver kneaded her forehead with the heels of her upper hands, as if she might physically press the grisly vision back out of her brain. Claire had seen the same vids of life downside, surely she'd remember.

The hiss of the airseal doors twitched Silver back to present reality. Better look busy—what was she supposed to be doing next? Oh, yes, cleaning used grow tubes, in preparation for their placement day after tomorrow in the new bay they were building to show off everybody's skills to the Ops VP. Damn the Ops VP. But for her, there'd be a chance Tony and Claire might go un-missed for two shifts, even three. Now . . .

Her heart shrank, as she saw who had entered the hydroponics bay. Now, indeed.

Ordinarily, Silver would have been glad to see Leo. He seemed a big, clean man—no, not large, but solid somehow, full of a prosaic calmness that spilled over in the very scent of him, reminiscent of downsider things Silver had chanced to handle, wood and leather and certain dried herbs. In the light of his slow smile, ghastly scenarios thinned to mist. She might yet be glad to talk to Leo. . . .

He was not smiling now. "Silver . . . ? You in here?"

For a wild moment Silver considered trying to hide among the grow tubes, but the foliage rustled as she turned, giving away her position. She peeked over the leaves. "Uh . . . hi, Leo."

"Have you seen Tony or Claire lately?" Trust Leo to be direct. *Call me Leo*, he'd told her the first time she'd "Mr. Graf'd" him. *It's shorter.* He drifted over to the grow tubes; they regarded each other across a barrier of bush beans.

"I haven't seen anybody but my supervisor all shift," said Silver, momentarily relieved to be able to give a perfectly honest answer.

"When did you last see either one of them?"

"Oh—last shift, I guess." Silver tossed her head airily.

"Where?"

"Uh . . . around." She giggled vacuously. Mr. Van Atta might have flung up his hands in disgust at this point, and abandoned any attempt to wring sense from so empty a head as hers.

Leo frowned at her thoughtfully. "You know, one of the charms of you kids is the literal precision with which you answer any question."

The comment hung in air expectantly, as Leo did. The picture of Tony, Claire, and Andy scooting across the shuttle loading bay flashed in Silver's mind with hallucinatory clarity. She groped in memory for their prior meeting, where the final plans had been laid, to offer up as a half-truth. "We had the mid-shift meal together last shift at Nutrition Station Seven."

Leo's lips quirked. "I see." He tilted his head, studying her as if she were some puzzle, such as two metallurgically incompatible surfaces he had to figure out how to join.

"You know, I just heard about Claire's new, ah, reproduction assignment. I'd wondered what was bothering Tony the last few weeks. He was pretty broken up about it, eh? Pretty . . . distraught."

"They'd had plans," Silver began, caught herself, shrugged casually. "I don't know. *I'd* be glad to get any reproduction assignment. There's no pleasing some people."

Leo's face grew stern. "Silver—just how distraught were they? Kids often mistake a temporary problem for the end of the world. They have no sense of the fullness of time. Makes 'em excitable. Think they might have been upset enough to do something . . . desperate?"

"Desperate?" Silver smiled rather desperately herself.

"Like a suicide pact or something?"

"Oh, no!" said Silver, shocked. "Oh, they'd never do anything like that."

Did relief flash for a moment in Leo's brown eyes? No, his face puckered in intensified concern.

"That's just what I'm afraid they might have done. Tony didn't show up for his work shift, and that's unheard of; Andy's gone too. They can't be found. If they felt so desperate—trapped—what could be easier than slipping out an airlock? A flash of cold, a moment's pain, and then—escape forever." His single pair of hands clasped earnestly. "And it's all my fault. I should have been more perceptive—said something . . ." He paused, looking at her hopefully.

"Oh, no, it was nothing like that!" Silver, horrified, hastened to dissuade him. "How awful for you to think that. Look . . ." She glanced around the hydroponics bay, lowered her voice. "Look, I shouldn't tell you this, but I can't let you go around thinking—thinking those fearful things." She had his entire attention, grave and intent. How much dare she tell him? Some suitably edited reassurance . . . "Tony and Claire—"

"Silver!" Dr. Yei's voice rang out as the airseal doors slid open. Echoed by Van Atta's bellow, "Silver, what do you know about all this?"

"Aw, shit," Leo snarled under his breath. His piously clasped hands clenched to fists of frustration.

Silver drew back in understanding and indignation. "You—!" And yet she almost laughed—Leo, so subtle and tricksy? She'd underestimated him. Did they both wear masks before the world, then? If so, what unknown territories did his bland face conceal?

"Please, Silver, before they get here—I can't help you if . . ."

It was too late. Van Atta and Yei tumbled into the room.

"Silver, do you know where Tony and Claire have gone?" Dr. Yei demanded breathlessly. Leo drew back into reserved silence, appearing to take an interest in the fine structure of the white bean blossoms.

"Of course she knows," Van Atta snapped, before Silver could reply. "Those girls are in each others' pockets, I tell you—"

"Oh, I *know*," Yei muttered.

Van Atta turned sternly to Silver. "Cough it up, Silver, if you know what's good for you."

Silver's lips closed, firmed into a line; her chin lifted.

Dr. Yei rolled her eyes at her superior's back. "Now, Silver," she began placatingly, "this isn't a good time for games.

If, as we suspect, Tony and Claire have tried to leave the Habitat, they could be in very serious trouble by now, even physical danger. I'm pleased that you feel you should be loyal to your friends, but I beg you, make it a responsible loyalty—friends don't let friends get hurt."

Silver's eyes puddled in doubt; her lips parted, inhaling for speech.

"Damn it," cried Van Atta, "I don't have time to stand around sweet-talking this little cunt. That snake-eyed bitch that runs Ops is waiting up there *right now* for the show to go on. She's starting to ask questions, and if she doesn't get the answers pronto she'll come looking for 'em herself. That one plays hardball. Of all the times to pick for this outbreak of idiocy, this has gotta be the worst possible. It's got to be deliberate. Nothing this fouled up could be by chance."

His red-faced rage was having its usual effect on Silver; her belly trembled, her vision blurred with unshed tears. She had once felt she would give him anything, do anything at all, if only he would calm down and smile and joke again.

But not this time. Her initial awed infatuation with him had been emptied out of her, bit by bit, and it startled her to realize how little was left. A hollowed shell could be rigid and strong. . . . "You," she whispered, "can't *make* me say anything."

"Just as I thought," snarled Van Atta. "Where's your *total socialization* now, Dr. Yei?"

"If you would," said Dr. Yei through her teeth, "kindly refrain from teaching my subjects anti-social behavior, you wouldn't have to deal with its consequences."

"I don't know what you're whining about. I'm an executive. It's my job to be hard-assed. That's why GalacTech put me in charge of this orbiting money-sink. Behavior control is your department's responsibility, Yei, or so you claimed. So do your job."

"Behavior *shaping*," Dr. Yei corrected frostily.

"What the hell's the use of that if it breaks down the minute the going gets tough? I want something that works all the time. If you were an engineer you'd never get past the reliability specs. Isn't that right, Leo?"

Leo snapped off a bean leaf stem, smiled blandly. His eyes glittered. He must have been chewing on his reply; at any rate, he swallowed *something*.

Silver grasped at a simple plan. So simple, surely she could carry it out. All she had to do was nothing. Do nothing, say nothing; eventually, the crisis must pass. They could not physically damage her, after all—she was valuable GalacTech property. The rest was only noise. She shrank into the safety of thing-ness, and stony silence.

The silence grew thick as cold oil. She nearly choked on it.

"So," hissed Van Atta to her, "that's the way you want to play it. Very well. Your choice." He turned to Yei. "You got something in the infirmary like fast-penta, Doctor?"

Yei's lips rippled. "Fast-penta is only legal for police departments, Mr. Van Atta."

"Don't they need a court order to use it, too?" inquired Leo, not looking up from the bean leaf he twirled between his fingers.

"On citizens, Leo. That," Van Atta pointed at Silver, "is not a citizen. What about it, Doctor?"

"To answer your question, *Mr.* Van Atta, no, our infirmary does *not* stock illegal drugs!"

"I didn't say fast-penta, I said something *like* it," said Van Atta irritably. "Some sort of anesthetic or something, to do in a pinch."

"Are we in a pinch?" asked Leo in a mild tone, still twirling his leaf; it was getting frayed. "Pramod is substituting for Tony, surely one of the other girls with babies can take over for Claire. Why should the Ops VP know the difference?"

"If we end up having to scrape two of our workers off the pavement downside—"

Silver winced at this echo of her own ghastly scenario.

"—or find them floating freeze-dried outside somewhere up here, it'll be damned hard to conceal from her. You haven't met the woman, Leo. She has a nose for trouble like a weasel's."

"Mm," said Leo.

Van Atta turned back to Yei. "What about it, Doctor? Or would you rather wait until someone calls us up asking what to do with the bodies?"

"IV Thalizine-5 is a bit like fast-penta," muttered Dr. Yei reluctantly, "in certain doses. It will make her sick for a day, though."

"That's her choice." He wheeled on Silver. "Your last chance, Silver. I've had it. I despise disloyalty. Where did they go? Tell me, or it's the needle for you, right now."

She was driven from thing-ness at last to a more painful, active human courage. "If you do that to me," Silver whispered in desperate dignity, "we're through."

Van Atta recoiled in sputtering outrage. "Through? You and your little friends conspire to sabotage my career in front of the company brass and you tell *me* we're through? You're damn right we're through!"

"Company Security, Shuttleport Three, Captain Bannerji speaking," George Bannerji recited into his comconsole. "May I help you?"

"You in charge here?" the well-dressed man in his vid began abruptly. He was clearly laboring under strong emotion, breathing rapidly. A muscle jumped in his clamped jaw.

Bannerji took his feet off his desk and leaned forward. "Yes, sir?"

"I'm Bruce Van Atta, Head of Project at the Habitat. Check my voiceprint, or whatever it is you do."

Bannerji sat up straight, tapped out the check-code; the word "cleared" flashed for a moment across Van Atta's face. Bannerji sat up straighter still. "Yes, sir, go ahead."

Van Atta paused as if groping for words, speaking slowly despite the jostling urgency of thought apparent in his tense face. "We have a little problem here, Captain."

Red lights and sirens went off in Bannerji's head. He could recognize an ass-covering understatement when he heard one. "Oh?"

"Three of our—experimental subjects have escaped the Habitat. We interrogated their co-conspirator, and we believe they stowed away on shuttle flight B119, and are now loose somewhere in Shuttleport Three. It is of the utmost urgency that they be captured and returned to us as quickly as possible."

Bannerji's eyes widened. Information about the Habitat was under a tight company security lid, but no one could work on Rodeo for long without learning that some kind of genetic experiments on humans were taking place up there, in careful isolation. It usually took a little longer for new employees to figure out that the more exotic monster stories told by the old hands were a form of hazing, practiced upon their credulity. Bannerji had transferred in to Rodeo about a month ago.

The project chief's words rang through Bannerji's head. *Escaped. Captured.* Criminals escaped. Dangerous zoo animals escaped, when their keepers screwed up, then some poor shmuck of a cop got the job of capturing them. Occasionally, horrifying biological weapons escaped. What the hell was he dealing with?

"How will we recognize them, sir? Do they," Bannerji swallowed, "look like human beings?"

"No." Van Atta evidently read the dismay in Bannerji's face, for he snorted ironically, "You'll have no trouble recognizing them, I assure you, Captain. And when you do find them, call me at once on my private code. I don't want this going out over broadcast channels. For God's sake keep it quiet, understand?"

Bannerji envisioned public panic. "Yes, sir. I understand completely."

His own panic was a private matter. He wouldn't be collecting the fat salary he did if security was expected to be all extended coffee breaks and pleasant evening strolls around perfectly deserted property. He'd always known the day would come when he'd have to earn his pay.

Van Atta broke off with a grim nod. Bannerji put in a call on the comconsole for his subordinate and placed pages for both his off-duty men as well. Something that had the executive hierarchy pouring sweat was nothing for a newly-promoted security grunt to take chances with.

He unlocked the weapons cabinet and signed out stunners and holsters for himself and his team. He weighed a stunner thoughtfully in his palm. It was such a light little diddly thing, almost a toy; GalacTech risked no lawsuits over stray shots from weapons like these.

Bannerji stood a moment, then turned to his own desk and keyed open the drawer with his personal palm-lock.

The unregistered pistol nestled in its own locked box, its shoulder holster coiled around it like a sleeping snake. By the time Bannerji had buckled it on and shrugged his uniform jacket back over it, he was feeling much better. He turned decisively to greet his patrolmen reporting for duty.

Chapter 5

Leo paused outside the airseal doors to the Habitat's infirmary to gather his nerve. He had been secretly relieved when a frantic call from Pramod had pulled him, shaking inside, away from the excruciating interrogation of Silver; as secretly ashamed of his relief. Pramod's problem—fluctuating power levels in his beam welder, traced at last to poisoning of the electron-emitting cathode by gas contamination—had occupied Leo for a time, but with the welding show over, shame had driven him back here.

So what are you going to do for her at this late hour? his conscience mocked him. *Assure her of your continued moral support, as long as it doesn't involve you in anything inconvenient or unpleasant? What a comfort.* He shook his head, tapped the door control.

Leo drifted silently past the medtech's station without signing in. Silver was in a private cubicle, a quarter-wedge of the infirmary's circumference at the very end of the module. The distance had helped muffle the yelling and crying.

Leo peered through the observation window. Silver was alone, floating limply in the locked sleep restraints against the wall. In the light from the fluoros her face was greenish, pale and damp. Her eyes seemed drained of their sparkling blue color, blurred leaden smudges. A yet-unused space-sick sack was clutched, hot and wrinkled, in an upper hand.

Sickened himself, Leo glanced up the corridor to be sure he was still unobserved, swallowed the clot of impotent rage growing in his throat, and slipped inside.

"Uh . . . hi, Silver," Leo began with a weak smile. "How you doing?" He cursed himself silently for the inanity of his own words.

Her smeary eyes found and focused on him uncomprehendingly. Then, "Oh. Leo. I think I was asleep for . . . for a while. Funny dreams . . . I still feel sick."

The drug must be wearing off. Her voice had lost the slurred, dreamy quality it had had during the interrogation earlier; now it was small and tight and self-aware. She added with a quaver of indignation, "That stuff made me throw up. And I've never thrown up before, not ever. It *made* me."

There were, Leo had learned, the most intense social inhibitions against vomiting in free fall, in Silver's little world. She would probably have been far less embarrassed at being stripped naked in public.

"It wasn't your fault," he hastened to reassure her.

She shook her head, her hair waving in lank strands unlike its usual bright aureole, her mouth pinched. "I should have—I thought I could . . . the Red Ninja never told *his* enemies his secrets, and they drugged and tortured him both!"

"Who?" asked Leo, startled.

"Oh . . . !" Silver's voice flattened to a wail. "They found out about our books, too! This time they'll find them all. . . ." Her lashes clotted with tears that could not fall, but only accumulate until blotted away. When her eyes widened to stare at Leo in a horrified realization, two or three droplets flew off in shimmering tangents. "And now Mr. Van Atta thinks Ti must have known Tony and Claire were on his shuttle—collusion—he says he's going to get Ti fired! And he'll find Tony and Claire down there—I don't know what he'll do to them. I've never seen Mr. Van Atta so angry."

Leo's set jaw had ground his smile to a grimace. Still he tried to speak reasonably. "But you told them—under drugs—that Ti didn't know, surely."

"He didn't believe it. Said I was lying."

"But that would be logically inconsistent—" Leo began, cut himself short. "No, you're right, that wouldn't faze him. God, what an asshole."

Silver's mouth opened in shock. "You mean—Mr. Van Atta?"

"I mean Brucie-baby. You can't tell me you've been around the man for what, eleven months, and not figured that out."

"I thought it was me—something wrong with me . . ." Silver's voice was still small and teary, but her eyes began to brighten with a sort of pre-dawn light. She overcame her inner miseries enough to regard Leo with increased attention. ". . . Brucie-baby?"

"Huh." The memory of one of Dr. Yei's lectures about *maintaining unified and consistent authority* gave Leo pause. It had seemed to make great sense at the time. . . . "Never mind. But there's nothing wrong with you, Silver."

Her regard was sharpening to something almost scientific. "You're not afraid of him." Her tone of wonder suggested she found this an unexpected and remarkable discovery.

"Me? Afraid? Of Bruce Van Atta?" Leo snorted. "Not likely."

"When he first came, and took over Dr. Cay's position, I thought—thought he would be like Dr. Cay."

"Look, ah . . . there is a very ancient rule of thumb that states, people tend to get promoted to the level of their incompetence. So far I think I've managed to avoid that unenviable plateau. So, I gather, did your Dr. Cay." *Screw Yei's scruples*, Leo thought, and added bluntly, "Van Atta hasn't."

"Tony and Claire would never have tried to run away if Dr. Cay were still here." A straggling species of hope began in her eyes. "Are you saying you think this mess could be Mr. Van Atta's fault?"

Leo stirred uneasily, pronged by secret convictions he had not yet voiced even to himself. "Your s—, s—," *slavery* "situation seems intrinsically, intrinsically," *wrong* his mind supplied, while his mouth fishtailed, "susceptible to abuse, mishandling of all sorts. Because Dr. Cay was so passionately dedicated to your welfare—"

"Like a father to us," Silver confirmed sadly.

"—this, er, susceptibility remained latent. But sooner or later it's inevitable that someone begin to exploit it, and you. If not Van Atta, someone else down the line. Someone . . ." *worse?* Leo had read enough history. Yes. "Much worse."

Silver looked as if she was struggling to imagine something worse than Van Atta, and failing. She shook her head dolefully. She raised her face to Leo; eyes like morning glories, targeting the sun. The target, struck, jerked out an involuntary smile.

"What's going to happen now, to Tony and Claire? I tried not to give them away, but that stuff made me so woozy—it was dangerous for them before, and now it's worse. . . ."

Leo attempted a tone of bluff and hearty reassurance. "Nothing's going to happen to them, Silver. Don't let Bruce's snit spook you. There's not really much he can do to them. They're much too valuable to GalacTech. He'll yell at them, no doubt, and you can't blame him for that; I'm ready to yell at them myself. Security will pick them up downside—they can't have gone far—they'll get the lecture of their young lives, and in a few weeks it'll all blow over. Lessons learned," Leo faltered. Just what lessons would they learn from this fiasco? "—all around."

"You act like—like getting yelled at—was nothing."

"It comes with age," he offered. "Someday you'll feel that way too." Or was it power that this particular immunity came with? Leo was suddenly unsure. But he had no power to speak of, except the ability to build things. Knowledge as power. Yet who had power over him? The line of logic trailed off in confusion; he turned his thoughts impatiently from it. Mental wheel-spinning, as unproductive as philosophy class in college.

"I don't feel that way now," said Silver practically.

"Look, uh . . . tell you what. If it'll make you feel better, I'll go along downside when they locate those kids. Maybe I can kind of keep things under control."

"Oh, would you? Could you?" Silver asked with relief. "Like you were trying to help me?"

Leo felt like biting off his tongue. "Uh, yeah. Something like that."

"You're not afraid of Mr. Van Atta. You can stand up to him." Her eyebrows quirked self-deprecatingly, and she waved her lower arms. "As you can see, I'm not equipped to stand up to anybody. Thank you, Leo." There was even a little color in her face now.

"Uh, right. I better hustle along now, if I'm to catch the shuttle going down to 'Port Three. We'll have 'em back safe and sound by breakfast. Think of it this way; at least GalacTech can't dock their pay for the extra shuttle trip." This even won a brief smile from her.

"Leo . . ." Her voice sobered, and he paused on his way out the door. "What are we going to do if . . . if there's ever anyone worse than Mr. Van Atta?"

Cross that bridge when you come to it, he wanted to say, evading the question. But one more platitude and he'd gag. He smiled and shook his head, and fled.

The warehouse made Claire think of a crystal lattice. It was all right angles, stretching away at ninety degrees in each dimension, huge slotted shelves reaching to the ceilings, endless rows, cross corridors. Blocking vision, blocking flight.

But there was no flight here. She felt like a stray molecule caught in the interstices of a doped crystal wafer, out of place but trapped. In retrospect the cozy curves of the Habitat seemed like enclosing arms.

They huddled now in one empty cell of a shelf stack, one of the few they had not found occupied by supplies, measuring some two meters on a side. Tony had insisted on climbing to the third tier, to be above the eye level of any chance downsider walking along the corridor upright on his long legs. The ladders set at intervals along the shelves had actually proved easier to manage than creeping along the floor, but getting the pack up had been a dreadful struggle, as its cord was too short to climb up and draw it up after themselves.

Claire was secretly unnerved. Andy was already finding an ability to push and grunt and wriggle against the gravity, still only a few centimeters at a time, but she had a nasty vision of him falling over the edge. Claire was developing a distaste for edges.

A robotic forklift whirred past. Claire froze, cowering in the back of their recess, clutching Andy to her, grabbing one of Tony's hands. The whirring trailed off into the distance. She breathed again.

"Relax," Tony squeaked. "Relax . . ." He breathed deeply in an apparent effort to follow his own advice.

Claire peered doubtfully out of the cubicle at the forklift, which had stopped farther down the corridor and was engaged in retrieving a plastic carton from its coded cell.

"Can we eat now?" She had been nursing Andy on and off for the last three hours in an effort to keep him quiet, and was drained in every sense. Her stomach growled, and her throat was dry.

"I guess," said Tony, and dug a couple of ration bars out of their hoard in the pack. "And then we'd better try to work our way back to the hangar."

"Can't we rest here a little longer?"

Tony shook his head. "The longer we wait, the more chance they'll be looking for us. If we don't get on a shuttle for the transfer station soon, they may start searching the outbound jumpships, and there goes our chance of stowing away undiscovered until after they boost past the point of no return."

Andy squeaked and gurgled; a familiar aroma wafted from his vicinity.

"Oh, dear. Would you please get out a diaper?" Claire asked Tony.

"Again? That's the fourth time since we left the Habitat."

"I don't think I brought near enough diapers," Claire worried, smoothing out the laminated paper and plastic form Tony handed her.

"Half our pack is filled with diapers. Can't you—make it last a little longer?"

"I'm afraid he may be getting diarrhea. If you leave that stuff on his bottom too long, it eats right through his skin—gets all red—even bleeds—gets infected—and then he screams and cries every time you touch it to try to clean it. Real loud," she emphasized.

The fingers of Tony's lower right hand drummed on the shelf floor, and he sighed, biting back frustration. Claire wrapped the used diaper tightly in itself and prepared to stash it back in their pack.

"Do we have to cart those along?" Tony asked suddenly. "Everything in the pack is going to reek after a while. Besides, it's heavy enough already."

"I haven't seen a disposal unit anywhere," said Claire. "What else can we do with them?"

Tony's face screwed up with inner struggle. "Just leave it," he blurted. "On the floor. It's not like it's going to float off down the corridor and get into the air recirculation, here. Leave them all."

Claire gasped at this horrific, revolutionary idea. Tony, following up his own suggestion before his nerve failed, collected the four little wads and stuffed them into the far corner of the storage cubicle. He smiled shakily, in mixed guilt and elation. Claire eyed him in worry. Yes, the situation was extraordinary, but what if Tony was developing a habit of criminal behavior? Would he return to normal when they got—wherever they were going?

If they got wherever they were going. Claire pictured their pursuers following the dirty diapers, like a trail of flower petals dropped by that heroine in one of Silver's books, across half the galaxy. . . .

"If you've got him back together," said Tony with a nod at his son, "maybe we better start back toward the hangar. That mob of downsiders may be cleared out by now."

"How are we going to pick a shuttle this time?" asked Claire. "How will we know that it's not just going right back up to the Habitat—or taking up a cargo to be unloaded in the vacuum? If they vent the cargo bay into space while we're in it . . ."

Tony shook his head, lips tight. "I don't know. But Leo says—to solve a big problem, or complete a big project, the secret is to break it down into little parts and tackle them one at a time, in order. Let's—just get back to the hangar, first. And see if there's any shuttles there at all."

Claire nodded, paused. Andy was not the only one of them plagued by biology, she reflected grimly. "Tony, do you think we can find a toilet on the way back? I need to go."

"Yeah, me too," Tony admitted. "Did you see any on the way here?"

"No." Locating the facilities had not been uppermost on her mind then, on that nightmare journey, creeping over the floors, dodging hurrying downsiders, squeezing Andy tightly to her for fear that he might cry out. Claire wasn't even sure she could reconstruct the route they'd taken, when they'd been driven out of their first hiding place by the busy work crew descending upon their machines and powering them up—

"There's got to be something," Tony reasoned optimistically. "People work here."

"Not in this section," Claire noted, gazing out at the wall of storage cells across the aisle. "It's all robots."

"Back toward the hangar, then. Say . . ." his voice faltered. "Uh . . . do you happen to know what a gravity-field toilet chamber looks like? How do they manage? Air suction couldn't possibly fight the gee forces."

One of Silver's smuggled historical vid dramas had involved a scene with an outhouse, but Claire was certain that was obsolete technology. "I think they use water, somehow."

Tony wrinkled his nose, shrugged away his bafflement. "We'll figure it out." His eye fell rather wistfully on the little wad of diapers in the corner. "It's too bad . . ."

"No!" said Claire, revolted. "Or at least—at least let's *try* to find a toilet first."

"All right . . ."

A distant rhythmic tapping was growing louder. Tony, about to swing out on the ladder, muttered "Oops," and recoiled back into the cubicle. He held a finger to his lips, panic in his face, and they all scuttled to the back of the cell.

"Aaah?" said Andy. Claire snatched him up and stuffed the tip of one breast into his mouth. Full and bored, he declined to nurse, turning his head away. Claire let her T-shirt fall back down and tried to distract him by silently counting all his busy fingers. He too had become smudged with dirt, as she had; no big surprise, planets were *made* of dirt. Dirt looked better from a distance. Say, a couple of hundred kilometers. . . .

The tapping grew louder, passed under their cell, faded.

"Company security man," Tony whispered in Claire's ear.

She nodded, hardly daring to breathe. The tapping was from those hard downsider foot-coverings striking the cement floor. A few minutes passed, and the tapping did not return. Andy made only small cooing noises.

Tony stuck his head cautiously out the chamber, looked right and left, up and down. "All right. Get ready to help me lower the pack as soon as this next forklift goes by. It'll have to fall the last meter, but maybe the sound of the forklift will cover that some."

Together they shoved the pack toward the edge of the cell, and waited. The whirring robolift was approaching down the corridor, an enormous plastic storage crate almost as large as a cubicle positioned on its lift.

The forklift stopped below them, beeped to itself, and turned ninety degrees. With a whine, its lift began to rise.

At this point, Claire recalled that theirs was the only empty cell in this stack.

"It's coming *here*! We're going to get squashed!"

"Get out! Get out on the ladder!" Tony yelped.

Instead she scuttled back to grab Andy, where she'd laid him at the rear of the chamber as far as possible from the frightening edge while she'd helped Tony shove the pack forward. The chamber darkened as the rising crate eclipsed the opening. Tony barely squeezed past it onto the ladder as it began to grind inward.

"Claire!" Tony screamed. He pounded uselessly on the side of the huge plastic crate. "Claire! No, no! Stupid robot! Stop, stop!"

But the forklift, clearly, was not voice-activated. It kept coming, bulldozing their pack before it. There were only a few centimeters' clearance on the sides and top of the crate. Claire retreated, so terrified her screams clotted in her throat like cotton, and she emitted only a smeary squeak.

Back, back; the cold metal wall behind froze her. She flattened against it as best she could, standing on her lower hands, holding Andy with her uppers. He was howling now, infected by her terror, earsplitting shrieks.

"Claire!" Tony cried from the ladder, a horrified bellow laced with tears. "*Andy!*"

The pack, beside them, compressed. Little crunching noises came from it. At the last moment, Claire transferred Andy to her lower arms, below her torso, bracing against the crate, against gravity, with her uppers. Perhaps her crushed body would hold the crate off just far enough to save him—the robolift's servos squealed with overload. . . .

And began to withdraw. Claire sent a silent apology to their oversized pack for all the curses she and Tony had heaped upon it in the past hours. Nothing in it would ever be the same, but it had saved them.

The robolift hiccuped, gears grinding bewilderedly. The crate shifted on its pallet, out of sync now. As the lift withdrew, the crate skidded with it, dragged by friction and gravity, skewing farther and farther from true.

Claire watched open-mouthed as it tilted and fell from the opening. She rushed forward. The crash shook the warehouse as the crate hit the concrete, followed by a booming shattered echo, the loudest sound Claire had ever heard. The crate took the forklift with it, its wheels whirring helplessly in air as it banged onto its side.

The power of gravity was stunning. The crate split, its contents spilling. Hundreds of round metal wheelcovers of some kind burst forth, ringing like a stampede of cymbals. A dozen or so rolled down the aisle in either direction as if bent on escape, wobbling into the corridor walls and falling onto their sides, still spinning, in ever-diminishing whanging pulses of sound. The echoes rang on in Claire's ears for a moment in the stupendous silence that followed.

"Oh, Claire!" Tony swarmed back into the cell and wrapped all his arms around her, Andy between them, as if he might never let go again. "Oh, Claire . . ." His voice cracked as he rubbed his face against her soft short hair.

Claire looked over his shoulder at the carnage they had created below. The overturned robolift was beeping again, like an animal in pain. "Tony, I think we better get out of here," she suggested in a small voice.

"I thought you were coming behind me, onto the ladder. Right behind me."

"I had to get Andy."

"Of course. You saved him, while I—saved myself. Oh, Claire! I didn't mean to leave you in there . . ."

"I didn't think you did."

"But I jumped—"

"It would have been plain stupid not to. Look, can we talk about it *later*? I *really* think we ought to get out of here."

"Yes, oh yes. Uh, the pack . . . ?" Tony peered into the dimness of the recess.

Claire didn't think they were going to have time for the pack, either—yet how far could they get without it? She helped Tony drag it back to the edge with frantic haste.

"If you brace yourself back there, while I hang onto the ladder, we can lower it—" Tony began.

Claire pushed it ruthlessly over the edge. It landed on the mess below, tumbled to the concrete. "I don't think there's any more point in worrying about the breakables now. Let's *go*," she urged.

Tony gulped, nodded, moved quickly onto the ladder, sparing one upper arm to help support Andy, whom Claire held in her lowers, her upper hands slapping down the rungs. Then they were back to the floor and their slow, frustrating, crabwise locomotion along it. Claire was beginning to hate the cold, dusty smell of concrete.

They were only a few meters down the corridor when Claire heard the pounding of downsider foot-coverings again, moving fast, with uncertain pauses as if for direction. A row or two over; the steps must shortly thread the lattice to them. Then an echo of the steps—no, another set.

What happened next seemed all in a moment, suspended between one breath and the next. Ahead of them, a gray-uniformed downsider leaped from a cross-corridor into their own with an unintelligible shout. His legs were braced apart to support his half-crouch, and he clutched a strange piece of equipment in both hands, held up half a meter in front of his face. His face was as white with terror as Claire's own.

Ahead of her, Tony dropped the pack and reared up on his lower arms, his upper hands flung wide, crying, "No!"

The downsider recoiled spasmodically, his eyes wide, mouth gaping in shock. Two or three bright flashes burst from his piece of equipment, accompanied by sharp cracking bangs that echoed, splintered, all through the great warehouse. Then the downsider's hands jerked up, the object flung away. Had it malfunctioned or short-circuited, burning or shocking him? His face drained further, from white to green.

Then Tony was screaming, flopping on the floor, all his arms curling in on himself in a tight ball of agony.

"Tony? Tony!" Claire scrambled toward him, Andy clamped tightly to her torso and crying and screaming in fear, his racket mingling with Tony's in a terrifying cacophony. "Tony, what's wrong?" She didn't see the blood on his red T-shirt until some drops spattered on the concrete. The bicep of his left lower arm, as he rolled toward her, was a scrambled, pulsing, scarlet and purple mess. "Tony!"

The company security guard had rushed forward. His face was harrowed with horror, his hands empty now and fumbling with a portable com link hooked to his belt. It took him three tries to detach it. "Nelson! Nelson!" he called into it. "Nelson, for God's sake call the medical squad, quick! It's just *kids*! I just shot a *kid*!" His voice shook. "It's just some crippled *kids*!"

Leo's stomach sank at the sight of the yellow pulses of light reflecting off the warehouse wall. Company medical squad; yes, there was their electric truck, blinkers flashing, parked in the wide central aisle. The breathless words of the clerk who'd met their shuttle tumbled through his brain— . . . *found in the warehouse . . . there's been an accident . . . injury . . .* Leo's steps quickened.

"Slow down, Leo, I'm getting dizzy," Van Atta, behind him, complained irritably. "Not everybody can bounce back and forth between null-gee and one-gee like you do with no effects, you know."

"They said one of the kids was hurt."

"So what are you going to do that the medics can't? I, personally, am going to crucify that idiot security team for this. . . ."

"I'll meet you there," Leo snarled over his shoulder, and ran.

Aisle 29 looked like a war zone. Smashed equipment, stuff scattered everywhere—Leo half tripped over a couple of round metal cover plates, kicked them impatiently out of his way. A pair of medics and a security guard were huddled over a stretcher on the floor, an IV bag hoisted on a pole like a flag above them.

Red shirt: Tony, it was Tony who'd been hurt. Claire was crouched on the floor a little farther down the aisle, clutching Andy, tears streaming silently down her ragged white mask of a face. On the stretcher, Tony writhed and cried out with a hoarse sob.

"Can't you at least give him something for pain?" the security guard urged the medtech.

"I don't *know.*" The medtech was clearly flustered. "I don't know what all they've done to their metabolisms. Shock is shock, I'm safe with the IV and the warmers and the synergine, but as for the rest of it—"

"Patch in an emergency com link to Dr. Warren Minchenko," Leo advised, kneeling beside them. "He's chief medical officer for the Cay Habitat, and he's on his month's downside leave right now. Ask him to meet you at your infirmary; he'll take over the case there."

The security guard eagerly unhooked his com link and began punching in codes.

"Oh, thank God," said the medtech, turning to Leo. "At last, somebody who knows what the hell they're doing. Do you know what I can give him for pain, sir?"

"Uh . . ." Leo did a quick mental review of his first aid. "Syntha-morph should be all right, until you get in touch with Dr. Minchenko. But adjust the dose—these kids weigh less than they look like they ought to—I think Tony masses about, um, 42 kilos."

The peculiar nature of Tony's injuries dawned on Leo at last. He had been picturing a fall, broken bones, maybe spinal cord or cranial damage. . . . "What *happened* here?"

"Gunshot wound," reported the medtech shortly. "Left lower abdomen and . . . and, um, not femur—left lower limb. That's just a flesh wound, but the abdominal one is serious."

"Gunshot!" Leo stared aghast at the guard, who reddened. "Did you—I thought you guys carried stunners—why in the name of God—"

"When that damned hysteric called down from the Habitat, yammering about his escaped monsters, I thought—I thought—I don't know what I thought." The guard glowered at his boots.

"Didn't you look before you fired?"

"I *damn* near shot the girl with the baby." The guard shuddered. "I hit this kid by accident, jerking my aim away."

Van Atta panted up. "Holy shit, what a mess!" His eye fell on the security guard. "I thought I told you to keep this quiet, Bannerji. What did you do, set off a bomb?"

"He shot Tony," said Leo through his teeth.

"You idiot, I told you to capture them, not murder them! How the hell am I supposed to sweep *this*—" he waved his arm down Aisle 29, "under the rug? And what the hell were you doing with a pistol anyway?"

"You said—I thought—" the guard began.

"I swear I'll have you canned for this. Of all the ass-backwards—did you think this was some kind of feelie-dream drama? I don't know whose judgment is worse, yours or the jerk's who hired you—"

The guard's face had gone from red to white. "Why you stupid son-of-a-bitch, you set me up for this—"

Somebody had better keep a level head, Leo thought wretchedly. Bannerji had retrieved and holstered his unauthorized weapon, a fact of which Van Atta seemed to be unconscious—the temptation to shoot the project chief shouldn't be allowed to get too overwhelming—Leo intervened. "Gentlemen, may I suggest that charges and defenses would be better saved for a formal investigation, where everyone will be cooler and, er, more reasoned. Meantime we have some hurt and frightened kids to take care of."

Bannerji fell silent, simmering with injustice. Van Atta growled assent, contenting himself with a black look toward Bannerji that boded ill for the guard's future career. The two medtechs snapped down the wheels of Tony's stretcher and began rolling him down the aisle toward their waiting truck. One of Claire's hands reached out after him, fell back hopelessly.

The gesture caught Van Atta's attention. Full of suppressed rage, he discovered he had an object on which to vent it after all. "You—!" he turned on Claire.

She flinched into a tighter huddle.

"Do you have any idea what this escapade of yours is going to cost the Cay Project, first to last? Of all the irresponsible—did you con Tony into this?"

She shook her head, eyes widening.

"Of course you did, isn't it always the way. The male sticks his neck out, the female gets it chopped off for him. . . ."

"Oh, no. . . ."

"And the timing—were you deliberately trying to smear me? How did you find out about the Ops VP—did you figure I'd cover up for you just because she was here? Clever, clever—but not clever enough!"

Leo's head, eyes, ears throbbed with the beating of his blood. "Lay off, Bruce. She's had enough for one day."

"The little bitch nearly gets your best student killed, and you want to stand up for her? Get serious, Leo."

"She's already scared out of her wits. Lay off."

"She damn well better be. When I get her back to the Habitat . . ." Van Atta strode past Leo, grabbed Claire by an upper arm, yanked her cruelly and painfully up. She cried out, nearly dropping Andy; Van Atta overrode her. "You wanted to come downside, you can bloody well just *try* walking—back to the shuttle, then."

Leo could not, afterwards, recall running forward or swinging Van Atta around to face him, but only Van Atta's surprised, open-mouthed expression. "Bruce," he sang through a red haze, "you smarmy creep—lay *off.*"

The uppercut to Van Atta's jaw that punctuated this command was surprisingly effective, considering it was the first time Leo had struck a man in anger in his life. Van Atta sprawled backwards on the concrete.

Leo surged forward in a kind of dizzy joy. He would rearrange Van Atta's anatomy in ways that even Dr. Cay had never dreamed of—

"Uh, Mr. Graf," the security guard began, touching him hesitantly on the shoulder.

"It's all right, I've been waiting to do this for weeks," Leo assured him, going for a grip on Van Atta's collar.

"It's not that, sir . . ."

A cold new voice cut in. "Fascinating executive technique. I must take notes."

Vice President Apmad, flanked by her flying wedge of accountants and assistants, stood behind Leo in Aisle 29.

Chapter 6

"Well, it wasn't *my* fault," snapped Shuttleport Administrator Chalopin. "I wasn't even told this was going on." She glowered pointedly at Van Atta. "How am I supposed to control my jurisdiction when *other* administrators hopscotch my properly established channels of command, blithely hand out orders to my people without even informing me, violate protocol . . ."

"The situation was extraordinary. Time was of the essence," muttered Van Atta truculently.

Leo secretly sympathized with Chalopin's testiness. Her smooth routine disrupted, her office abruptly appropriated for the Ops VP's inquest—Apmad did not believe in wasting time. The official company investigation of the incident had commenced, by her fiat, a bare hour ago in Aisle 29; he'd be surprised if it took her more than another hour to finish sifting the case.

The windows of Shuttleport Three's administrative offices, sealed against the internal pressure of the building, framed a panorama of the complex—the runways, loading zones, warehouses, offices, hangars, workers' dormitories, the monorail running off to the refinery glittering on the horizon and the eerily rugged mountains beyond. And the vital power plant; Rodeo's atmosphere had oxygen, nitrogen, and carbon dioxide, but in the wrong proportions and at too low a pressure to suit human metabolism. The air conditioning labored constantly to adjust the gas mix and filter out the contaminants. A human might live for fifteen minutes outside without a breath mask; Leo was uncertain whether to think of it as a safety margin or just a slow death. Definitely not a garden spot.

Bannerji had sidled around behind the shuttleport administrator. Hiding behind her, Leo thought. It might be the best strategy for the security guard at that. From her smart shoes through her trim GalacTech uniform to her swept-back coiffure, not a hair out of place, and her set, clean jawline, Chalopin radiated both the will and the ability to defend her turf.

Apmad, refereeing the scrimmage, was another type altogether. Dumpy, on the high end of middle age, frizzy gray hair cut short, she might have been somebody's grandmother, but for her eyes. She made no attempt to dress for success. As if she already possessed so much power, she was beyond that game. So far from regulating tempers, her laconic comments had served to stir the pot, as if she was curious what might float to the top. Definitely not a grandmother's eyes.

Leo was still close to a boil himself. "The project is twenty-five years old. Time can't be that much of the essence."

"God almighty," cried Van Atta, "am I the only man here conscious of what the bottom line means?"

"Bottom line?" said Leo. "GalacTech is closer to its pay-off from the Cay Project than ever before. To screw things up now with an impatient, premature attempt to wring profits is practically criminal. You're on the verge of the first real results."

"Not really," observed Apmad coolly. "Your first group of fifty workers is merely a token. It will take another ten years to bring the whole thousand online." Cool, yes; but Leo read a fierce concealed tension in her the source of which he could not yet identify.

"So, call it a tax loss. You can't tell me this," Leo waved a hand toward the window, indicating Rodeo, "can't use a tax loss or two."

Apmad rolled her eyes at the man who stood silently at her shoulder. "Tell this young man the facts of life, Gavin."

Gavin was a big rumpled goon with a broken nose whom Leo had taken at first for some kind of bodyguard. He was in fact the Ops VP's chief accountant, and when he spoke it was with startlingly precise and elegant elocution, in impressive rounded paragraphs.

"GalacTech has been offsetting the Cay Project's very considerable losses with Rodeo's paper profits since its inception. I'd better recapitulate a little history for you, Mr. Graf." Gavin scratched his nose thoughtfully.

"GalacTech holds Rodeo on a ninety-nine-year lease with the government of Orient IV. The original terms of the lease were extremely favorable to us, since Rodeo's unique mineral and petrochemical resources were at that time still undiscovered. And so they remained for the first thirty years of the lease.

"The next thirty years saw an enormous investment of materials and labor on the part of GalacTech to develop Rodeo's resources. Of course," he prodded the air with a didactic finger, "as soon as Orient IV began to see our profit passing through their wormhole nexus, they began to regret the terms of the lease, and to seek a larger cut of the action. Rodeo was chosen as the site for the Cay Project in the first place in part, besides certain unique legal advantages, precisely so that its projected expenses could be charged against Rodeo's profits generally, and reduce the, er, unhealthy excitement said profits were generating on Orient IV.

"GalacTech's lease of Rodeo now has some fourteen years left to run, and the government of Orient IV is getting, ah, how shall I put this, infected with anticipatory greed. They've just changed their tax laws, and from the end of this fiscal year they propose to tax the company's Rodeo operation upon gross not net profit. We lobbied against it, but we failed. Damn provincials," he added reflectively.

"So. After the end of this fiscal year, the Cay Project losses can no longer be offset against Orient IV tax savings; they will be real, and passed through to us. The terms of the new lease at the end of the next fourteen years are not expected to be favorable. In fact, we project Orient IV is preparing to drive GalacTech out and take over its Rodeo operations at a fraction of their real worth. Expropriation by any other name doth smell the same. The economic blockade is already beginning. The time to start limiting further investment and maximizing profit is now."

"In other words," said Apmad, a hard, angry glitter in her eyes, "let them take over a hollow shell."

Could be hard on the last guys out, Leo thought, chilled. Didn't those jerks on Orient IV realize that cooperation and compromise would increase everybody's profit, in the end? The GalacTech negotiators were probably not without fault, either, he reflected grimly. He'd seen other versions of the hostile takeover scenario before. He glanced out the window at the large, lively, *working* facilities laid out below, hard-won results of two generations of sincere labor, and groaned inwardly at the thought of the waste to come. From the horrified look on Chalopin's face, she had a similar vision, and Leo's heart went out to her. How much of her blood had gone into the building-up of this place? How many people's sweat and dedication, cancelled at the stroke of a pen?

"That was always your problem, Leo," said Van Atta rather venomously. "You always get your head balled up in the little details, and miss the big picture."

Leo shook his head to clear it, grasped for the lost thread of his original argument. "Nevertheless, the Cay Project's viability—" he paused abruptly, seized by a breathtaking inspiration as delicate as a soap bubble. The stroke of a pen. Could freedom be won with the stroke of a pen? As simply as that? He gazed at Apmad with a new intensity, two orders of magnitude more at least. "Tell me, ma'am," he said carefully, "what happens if the Cay Project's viability is disproved?"

"We shut it down," she said simply.

Oh, the tales out of school he might tell—and sink Brucie-baby forever as an added bonus—Leo's nerves thrilled. He opened his mouth to pour out destruction—

And closed it, sucked on his tongue, regarded his fingernails, and asked instead casually, "And what happens to the quaddies then?"

The Ops VP frowned as if she'd bitten into something nasty: that hidden tension again, the most expression Leo had yet seen upon her face. "That presents the most difficult problem of all."

"Difficult? Why difficult? Just let them go. In fact," Leo strove to conceal his rising excitement behind a bland face, "if GalacTech would let them go immediately, before the end of this fiscal year, it could still take whatever it chooses to calculate as its investment in them as a tax loss against Rodeo's profits. One last fling, as it were, one last bite out of Orient IV." Leo smiled attractively.

"Let them go where? You seem to forget, Mr. Graf, that the bulk of them are still mere children."

Leo faltered. "The older ones could help take care of the younger ones, they already do, some. . . . Perhaps they could be moved for a few years to some other sector that could absorb the loss from their upkeep—it couldn't cost GalacTech *that* much more than a like number of workers on pensions, and only for a few years. . . ."

"The company retirement pension fund is self-supporting," Gavin the accountant observed elliptically. "Roll-over."

"A moral obligation," Leo offered desperately. "Surely GalacTech must admit some moral obligation to them—we created them, after all." The ground was shifting under his feet, he could see it in her unsympathetic face, but he could not yet discern in what direction the tilt was going.

"Moral obligation indeed," agreed Apmad, her hands clenching. "And have you overlooked the fact that Dr. Cay created these creatures fertile? They are a new species, you know; he dubbed them *Homo quadrimanus*, not *Homo sapiens* race *quadrimanus*. He was the geneticist, we may presume he knew what he was talking about. What about GalacTech's moral obligation to society at large? How do you imagine it will react to having these creatures and all their problems just dumped into its systems? If you think they overreact to chemical pollution, just imagine the flap over genetic pollution!"

"Genetic pollution?" Leo muttered, trying to attach some rational meaning to the term. It *sounded* impressive.

"No. If the Cay Project is proved to be GalacTech's most expensive mistake, we will containerize it properly. The Cay workers will be sterilized and placed in some suitable institution, there to live out their lives otherwise unmolested. Not an ideal solution, but the best available compromise."

"St—st . . ." Leo stuttered. "What crime have they committed, to be sentenced to life in prison? And where, if Rodeo is to be closed down, will you find or build another suitable orbital habitat? If you're worried about expense, lady, *that'll* be expensive."

"They will be placed planetside, of course, at a fraction of the cost."

A vision of Silver creeping uncomfortably across the floor like a bird with both wings broken burst in Leo's brain. "That's *obscene*! They'll be no better than cripples."

"The obscenity," snapped Apmad, "was in creating them in the first place. Until Dr. Cay's death brought his department under mine, I had no idea that his 'R&D—Biologicals' was concealing such enormously invasive manipulations of human genes. My home world embraced the most painfully draconian measures to ensure our gene pool not be overrun with accidental mutations—to go out and deliberately introduce mutations seems the most vile . . ." She caught her breath, contained her emotions again, except what escaped her nervously drumming fingers. "The *right* thing to do is euthanasia. Terrible as it seems at first glance, it might actually be less cruel in the long run."

Gavin the accountant, squirming, twitched an uncertain smile at his boss. His eyebrows had gone up in surprise, down in dismay, and at last settled on up again—not taking her seriously, perhaps. Leo didn't think she'd been joking, but Gavin added in a facetiously detached professional tone, "It *would* be more cost effective. If it were done before the end of this fiscal year, we could indeed take them as a loss—total—against Orient taxes."

Leo felt suspended in glass. "You can't do that!" he whispered. "They're people—children—it would be murder—"

"No, it would not," denied Apmad. "Repugnant, certainly, but not murder. That was the other half of the reason for locating the Cay Project in orbit around Rodeo. Besides physical isolation, Rodeo exists in legal isolation. It's in the ninety-nine-year lease. The only legal writ in Rodeo local space is GalacTech regulation. I fear this has less to do with foresight than with Dr. Cay's successful blocking of any interference with his schemes. But if GalacTech chooses not to define the Cay workers as human beings, company regulations regarding crimes do not apply."

"Oh, really?" Bannerji brightened slightly.

"How *does* GalacTech define them?" asked Leo, glassily curious. "Legally."

"Post-fetal experimental tissue cultures," said Apmad.

"And what do you call murdering them? Retroactive abortion?"

Apmad's nostrils grew pinched. "Simple disposal."

"Or," Gavin glanced sardonically at Bannerji, "vandalism, perhaps. Our one legal requirement is that experimental tissue be cremated upon disposal. IGS Standard Biolab rules."

"Launch them into the sun," Leo suggested tightly. "That'd be cheap."

Van Atta stroked his chin gently and regarded Leo uneasily. "Calm down, Leo. We're just talking contingency scenarios here. Military staffs do it all the time."

"Quite," agreed the Ops VP. She paused to frown at Gavin, whose flippancy apparently did not please her. "There are some hard decisions to be made here, which I am not anxious to face, but it seems they have been dealt to me. Better me than someone blind to the long-term consequences to society at large like Dr. Cay. But perhaps, Mr. Graf, you will wish to join Mr. Van Atta in showing how Dr. Cay's original vision might still be carried out at a profit, so we can *all* avoid having to make the hardest choices."

Van Atta smiled at Leo, smarmily triumphant. Vindicated, vindictive, calculating . . . "To return to the matter at hand," Van Atta said, "I've already requested that Captain Bannerji be summarily terminated for his poor judgment and"—he glanced at Gavin—"and vandalism. I might also suggest that the cost of TY-776-424-XG's hospitalization be charged to his department." Bannerji wilted; Administrator Chalopin stiffened.

"But it's increasingly apparent to me," Van Atta went on, fixing his most unpleasant smile on Leo, "that there's another matter to be pursued here. . . ."

Ah shit, thought Leo, *he's going to get me on an assault charge—an eighteen-year career up in smoke—and I did it to myself—and I didn't even get to* finish *the job. . . .*

"Subversion."

"Huh?" said Leo.

"The quaddies have been growing increasingly restive in the past few months. Coincidentally with *your* arrival, Leo." Van Atta's gaze narrowed. "After today's events I wonder if it was a coincidence. I rather think not. Isn't it so that," he wheeled and pointed dramatically at Leo, "*you* put Tony and Claire up to this escapade?"

"Me!" Leo sputtered in outrage, paused. "True, Tony did come to me once with some very odd questions, but I thought he was just curious about his upcoming work assignment. I wish now I'd . . ."

"You admit it!" Van Atta crowed. "You have encouraged defiant attitudes toward company authority among the hydroponics workers, and among your own students entrusted to you—ignored the psych department's carefully developed guidelines for speech and behavior while aboard the Habitat—infected the workers with your own bad attitudes—"

Leo realized suddenly that Van Atta was not going to let him get a word of defense in edgewise if he could possibly help it. Van Atta was onto something infinitely more valuable than mere vengeance for a punch in the jaw—a scapegoat. A perfect scapegoat, upon whom he could pin every glitch in the Project for the past two months—or longer, depending on his ingenuity—and sacrifice without qualm to the company gods, himself emerging squeaky-clean and sinless.

"No, by God!" Leo roared. "If I were running a revolution, I'd do a damn sight better job of it than *that*—" He waved in the general direction of the warehouse. His muscles bunched to launch himself at Van Atta again. If he was to be fired anyway, he'd at least get some satisfaction out of it—

"Gentlemen." Apmad's voice sluiced down like a bucket of ice water. "Mr. Van Atta, may I remind you that terminations from outlying facilities like Rodeo are discouraged. Not only is GalacTech contractually obligated to provide transportation home to the terminees, but there is also the expense and large time delay of importing their replacements. No, we shall finish it this way. Captain Bannerji shall be suspended for two weeks without pay, and an official reprimand added to his permanent record for carrying an unauthorized weapon on official company duty. The weapon shall be confiscated. Mr. Graf shall be officially reprimanded also, but returned immediately to his duties, as there is no one to replace him in them."

"But I was screwed," complained Bannerji.

"But I'm totally innocent!" cried Leo. "It's a fabrication—a paranoid fantasy—"

"You can't send Graf back to the Habitat *now*," yelped Van Atta. "Next thing you know he'll be trying to *unionize* 'em—"

"Considering the consequences of the Cay Project's failure," said the Ops VP coldly, "I think not. Eh, Mr. Graf?"

Leo shivered. "Eh."

She sighed without satisfaction. "Thank you. This investigation is now complete. Further complaints or appeals by any party may be addressed to GalacTech headquarters on Earth." *If you dare*, her quirked eyebrow added. Even Van Atta had the sense to keep his mouth shut.

The mood in the shuttle for the return trip to the Habitat was, to say the least, constrained. Claire, accompanied by one of the Habitat's infirmary nurses pulled off her downside leave three days early for the duty, huddled in the back clutching Andy. Leo and Van Atta sat as far from each other as the limited space allowed.

Van Atta spoke once to Leo. "I told you so."

"You were right," Leo replied woodenly. Van Atta nearly purred at the stroke, smug. Leo would rather have stroked him with a pipe wrench.

Could Van Atta be all right, as well? Was his disruptive pressure for instant results a sign of concern for the quaddies' welfare, even survival? No, Leo decided with a sigh. The only welfare that truly concerned Bruce was his own.

Leo let his head rest on the padded support and stared out his window as the acceleration of takeoff thrust him back in his seat. A shuttle ride was still a bit of a thrill to something deep in him, even after the countless trips he'd made. There were people—billions, the vast majority—who never set foot off their home planets in their lives. He was one of the lucky few.

Lucky to have his job. Lucky in the results he'd achieved, over the years. The vast Morita Deep Space Transfer Station had probably been the crown of his career, the largest project he was ever likely to work on. He'd first viewed the site when it was empty, icy vacuum, as nothing as nothing could possibly be. He'd passed through it again just last year, making a changeover from a ship from Ylla to a ship for Earth. Morita had looked good, really good; alive, even undergoing expansion of its facilities, several years sooner than anyone had expected. Smooth expansion; plans for it had been incorporated into the original designs. Over-ambitious they'd called it then. Far-sighted, they called it now.

And there had been other projects too. Every day, from one end of the wormhole nexus to the other, countless accidents of structural failure did *not* occur because he, and people he'd trained, had done their jobs well. The work of a harried week, the early detection of the propagating micro-cracks in the reactor coolant lines at the great Beni Ra orbital factory alone had saved, perhaps, three thousand lives. How many surgeons could claim to save three thousand lives in ten years of their careers? On that memorable inspection tour, he'd done it once a month for a year. Invisibly, unsung; disasters that never happen don't normally make headlines. But he knew, and the men and women who worked alongside him knew, and that was enough.

He regretted slugging Bruce. The moment's red joy had certainly not been worth risking his job for. The eighteen years of accumulating pension benefits, the stock options, the seniority, yes, maybe; with no family to support, they were all Leo's, to piss into the wind if he chose. But who would take care of the next Beni Ra?

When they returned to the Habitat, he would cooperate. Apologize handsomely to Bruce. Redouble his training efforts, increase his care. Bite his tongue, speak only when spoken to. Be polite to Dr. Yei. Hell, even do what she told him.

Anything else was impossibly risky. There were a thousand kids up there. So many, so varied—so *young*. A hundred five-year-olds, a hundred and twenty six-year-olds alone, cramming the crèche modules, playing games in their free-fall gym. No one individual could possibly take responsibility for risking all those lives on something chancy. It would be endless, all-consuming. Impossible. Criminal. Insane. Revolt—where could it lead? No one could possibly foresee all the consequences. Leo couldn't even see around the next corner. No one could. No one.

They docked at the Habitat. Van Atta shooed Claire and Andy and the nurse ahead of him through the hatchway, as Leo slowly unfastened his seat harness.

"Oh, no," Leo heard Van Atta say. "The nurse will take Andy to the crèche. You will return to your old dormitory. Taking that baby downside was criminally irresponsible. It's clear you are totally unfit to have charge of him. I can guarantee, you'll be struck from the reproduction roster, too."

Claire's weeping was so muffled as to be nearly inaudible.

Leo closed his eyes in pain. "God," he asked, "why me?" Releasing his last restraint, he fell blindly into his future.

Chapter 7

"Leo!" Silver anchored one hand and pounded softly and frantically with the other three on the door to the engineer's sleeping quarters. "Leo, quick! Wake up, help!" She laid her cheek against the cold plastic, muffling her bursting howl to a small, sliding "Leo?" She dared not cry louder, lest she attract more than Leo's ear.

His door slid open at last. He wore red T-shirt and shorts, barefoot. His sleep sack against the far wall hung open like an empty cocoon, and his thinning sandy hair stuck out in odd directions. "What the hell . . . Silver?" His face was rumpled with sleep, eyes dark-ringed but focusing fast.

"Come quick, come quick!" Silver hissed, grabbing his hand. "It's Claire. She tried to go out an airlock. I jammed the controls. She can't get the outer door open, but I can't get the inner door open either, and she's trapped in there. Our supervisor will be back soon, and then I don't know *what* they'll do to us. . . ."

"Son-of-a . . ." He allowed her to draw him into the corridor, then lurched back into his cabin to grab a tool belt. "All right, go, go, lead on."

They sped through the maze of the Habitat, offering strained bland smiles to those quaddies and downsiders they flew past in the corridors. At last, the familiar door to "Hydroponics D" closed behind them.

"What happened? How did this happen?" Leo asked her as they brushed through the grow-tubes to the far end of the module.

"They wouldn't let me go see Claire day before yesterday, when you brought her back on the shuttle, even though we were both in the infirmary. Yesterday we were on different work teams. I think it was on purpose. Today I made Teddie trade with me." Silver's voice smeared with her distress. "Claire said they won't even let her into the crèche to see Andy on her off-shift. I went to get fertilizer from Stores to charge the grow-tubes we were working on, and when I came back, the lock was just starting to cycle. . . ." If only she hadn't left Claire alone—if only she had not let the shuttle take them downside in the first place—if only she had not betrayed them to Dr. Yei's drugs—if only they'd been born downsiders—or not been born at all. . . .

The airlock at the end of the hydroponics module was almost never used, merely waiting to become the airseal door to the next module that future growth might demand. Silver pressed her face to the observation window. To her immense relief, Claire was still within.

But she was ramming herself back and forth between door and door, her face smeared with tears and blood, fingers reddened. Whether she gulped for air or only screamed Silver could not tell, for all sound was silenced by the barrier door, like a turned-down holovid. Silver's own chest seemed so tight she could scarcely breathe.

Leo glanced in. His lips drew back in a fierce scowl in his whitened face, and he turned to hiss at the lock mechanism, scrabbling at his tool belt. "You fixed it but good, Silver . . ."

"I had to do something quick. Shorting it that way blocked the alarm from going off in Central Systems."

"Oh." Leo's hands hesitated briefly. "Not so random a stab as it looks, then."

"Random? In an airlock control box?" She stared at him in surprise, and some indignation. "I'm not a five-year-old!"

"Indeed not." A crooked grin lightened his tense face for a moment. "Any quaddie of six would know better. My apologies, Silver. So the problem, then, is not how to open the door, but how to do so without tripping the alarm."

"Yes, right." She hovered anxiously.

He looked the mechanism over, glanced up rather more hesitantly at the airlock door, which vibrated to the thumping from within. "You sure Claire doesn't need—more help anyway?"

"She may need help," snapped Silver, "but what she'll get is Dr. Yei."

"Ah . . . right." His grin thinned out altogether. He clipped a couple of tiny wires and rerouted them. With one last doubtful look at the lock door, he tapped a pressure plate within the mechanism.

The inner door slid open and Claire tumbled out, gasping rawly, ". . . let me go, let me go, oh, why didn't you let me go—I can't stand this . . ." She curled up in a huddled ball in midair, face hidden.

Silver darted to her, wrapped her arms around her. "Oh, Claire! Don't *do* things like that. Think—think how Tony would feel, stuck in that hospital downside, when they told him . . ."

"What does it matter?" demanded Claire, muffled against Silver's blue T-shirt. "They'll never let me see him again. I might as well be dead. They'll never let me see Andy . . ."

"Yes," Leo chimed in, "think of Andy. Who will protect him, if you're not around? Not just today, but next week, next year."

Claire unwound, and fairly screamed at him. "They won't even let me see him! They threw me out of the crèche . . ."

Leo seized her upper hands. "Who? Who threw you out?"

"Mr. Van Atta . . ."

"Right, I might have known. Claire, listen to me. The proper response to Bruce isn't suicide, it's murder."

"Really?" said Silver, her interest sparking. Even Claire was drawn out of her tight wad of misery enough to meet Leo's eyes directly for the first time.

"Well . . . perhaps not literally. But you can't let the bastard grind you down. Look, we're all smart here, right? You kids are smart—I've been known to knock down a problem or two, in my time—we've got to be able to think our way out of this mess, if we try. You're not alone, Claire. We'll help. I'll help."

"But you're a company man—a downsider—why should you . . . ?"

"GalacTech's not God, Claire. You shouldn't have to sacrifice your firstborn to it. GalacTech—any company—is just a way, one way, for people to organize themselves to do a job that's too big for one person to do alone. It's not God, it's not even a being, for pity's sake. It doesn't have a free will to answer for. It's just a collection of people, working. Bruce is only Bruce. There's got to be some way to get around him."

"You mean go over his head?" asked Silver thoughtfully. "Maybe to that vice president who was here last week?"

Leo paused. "Well . . . maybe not to Apmad. But I've been thinking—for three days, I've been thinking of nothing else but how to blow up this whole rotten set-up. But you've got to hang on, for me to have time to work—Claire, can you hang on? Can you?" His hands tightened urgently on hers.

She shook her head in doubt. "It hurts so much . . ."

"You have to. Look, listen. There's nothing I can do here at Rodeo—it's in this peculiar legal bubble. If it were a regular planetary government, I swear I'd go into debt to my eyebrows and buy each and every one of you a ticket out of here, but then, if it were a regular planet, I wouldn't need to. Anyway GalacTech has a monopoly on jumpship seats here; you travel on a company ship or not at all. So we have to wait, and bide our time.

"But in a little time—just a few months—the first quaddies will leave Rodeo on the first real work assignments. Working in and passing through real planetary jurisdictions. Governments too big and powerful even for GalacTech to mess with. I'm sure—pretty sure, if I pick the right venue—not Apmad's planet, of course, but say, Earth—Earth's by far the best bet, I'm a citizen there—I can bring a class-action suit declaring you legal persons. I'll probably lose my job, and the costs will eat me, but it can be done. Not exactly the life's work I had in mind . . . but eventually, you can be cracked loose from GalacTech."

"So long a time," sighed Claire.

"No, no, delay is our friend. The little ones grow older every day. By the time the legal case goes through, you'll all be ready. Go as a group—hire out—find work—even GalacTech wouldn't be so bad as an employer if you were

citizens and regular employees, with all the legal protec-
tions. Maybe even the Spacer's Union would take you in,
though that might constrain—well, I'm not sure. If they
don't perceive you as a threat . . . anyway, something can be
worked out. But you've got to hang on! Promise me?"

Silver breathed again when Claire nodded slowly. She
drew Claire away to the first aid kit on the wall, to apply
antiseptics and plastic bandages to her torn fingernails,
and wipe the blood from her bruised face. "There. There.
Better . . ."

Leo meanwhile restored the airlock control to its original working order, then drifted over to them. "All right
now?" He turned his face to Silver. "Is she going to be all
right?"

Silver could not help glowering. "As all right as any of us
. . . it's not fair!" she burst out. "This is my home, but it's
beginning to feel like an over-pressurized oxy bottle.
Everybody's upset, all the quaddies, about Tony and Claire.
There hasn't been anything like this since Jamie was killed
in that awful pusher accident. But this—this was *on purpose*. If they'd do that to Tony, who was so good, what
about—about me? Any of us? What's going to happen
next?"

"I don't know." Leo shook his head grimly. "But I'm
pretty sure the idyll is over. This is only the beginning."

"But what will we do? What can we do?"

"Well—don't panic. And don't despair. Especially don't
despair—"

The airseal doors at the end of the module slid open,
and the downsider hydroponics supervisor's voice lilted in.
"Girls? We got the seed delivery on the shuttle after all—is
that grow-tube ready yet?"

Leo twitched, but turned back one last time before hastening away, to grasp a hand of each quaddie with determined pressure. "It's just an old saying, but I know it's true from personal experience. Chance favors the prepared mind. So stay strong—I'll get back to you." He escaped past the hydroponics supervisor with an elaborately casual yawn, as if he'd merely stopped in to kibitz a moment upon the work in progress.

Silver's stomach churned as she fearfully watched Claire. Claire sniffled and turned hurriedly away to busy herself with the grow tube, hiding her face from their supervisor. Silver shivered with relief. All right for now.

The churning in Silver's stomach was slowly replaced by something hot and unfamiliar, filling it, crowding out the fear. *How dare they do this to her—to me—to us? They have no right, no right, no right. . . .*

Rage made her head pound, but it was better than the knotting fear. There was almost an exultation in it. The expression Silver bent her head to conceal from the supervisor was a small, fierce frown.

The nutrition assistant, a quaddie girl of perhaps thirteen, handed Leo's lunch tray to him through the serving window without her usual bright smile. When Leo smiled and said, "Thank you," the responding upward twitch of her mouth was mechanical, and fell away instantly. Leo wondered in what scrambled form the story of Claire's and Tony's downside disaster of the previous week had reached her ears. Not that the correct facts weren't distressing enough. The whole Habitat seemed plunged into an atmosphere of wary dismay.

Leo felt a flash of horrible weariness of the quaddies and their everlasting troubles. He shied away from a collection of his students eating their lunches near the serving window, though they waved to him with assorted hands, and instead floated down the module until he saw a vacant space to velcro his tray next to somebody with legs. By the time Leo realized the legged person was the supply shuttle captain, Durrance, it was too late to retreat.

But Durrance's greeting grunt was without animosity. Evidently he did not, unlike some others Leo could name, hold the engineer obscurely responsible for his student Tony's spectacular fiasco. Leo hooked his feet into the straps to free his hands to attack his meal, returned the grunt, and sucked hot coffee from his squeeze bulb. There wasn't enough coffee in the universe to dissolve his dilemmas.

Durrance, it appeared, was even in the mood for polite conversation. "You going to be taking your downside leave soon?"

"Soon . . ." In about a week, Leo realized with a start. Time was getting away from him, like everything else around here. "What's Rodeo like?"

"Dull." Durrance spooned some sort of vegetable pudding into his mouth.

"Ah." Leo glanced around. "Is Ti with you?"

Durrance snorted. "Not likely. He's downside, on ice. He's appealing." A twisted grimace and raised eyebrows pointed up the double meaning. "Not, you understand, from my point of view. I got a reprimand on my record because of that damn tadpole. If it had been his first screwup, he might have been able to duck getting fired, but now I don't think he has a chance. Your Van Atta wants his pelt riveted to the airlock doors."

"He's not *my* Van Atta," Leo denied strenuously. "If he was, I'd trade him for a dog—"

"—and shoot the dog," finished Durrance. His mouth twitched, not quite a grin. "Van Atta. That's all right. If the rumor I heard is true, he may not have so long to strut either."

"Ah?" Leo's ears pricked hopefully.

"I was talking yesterday to the jump pilot from the weekly personnel ship from Orient IV—he'd just finished his month's gravity leave there—listen up to *this* one. He swears the Betan embassy there is demonstrating an artificial gravity device."

"What! How—?"

"Piping it in from wormhole space for all I know. You bet Beta Colony is sitting on the math of it, till they make their initial killing in the marketplace and recoup their R&D costs. It's apparently been kept under wraps by their military for a couple of years already, till they got their head start, damn 'em. GalacTech and everybody else will be on the scramble to catch up. Every other R&D project in the company is going to have to kiss their budget goodbye for a couple of years, you watch."

"My God." Leo glanced up the length of the cafeteria module, crowded with quaddies. *My God . . .*

Durrance scratched his chin reflectively. "If it's true, do you have any idea what it's going to do to the space transport industry? The jump pilot claims the Betans got the damned thing there in two months—from Beta Colony!— boosting at fifteen gees and insulating the crew from the acceleration using it. There'll be no limit to acceleration now but fuel costs. It probably won't affect bulk cargoes much for that very reason, but the passenger trade'll be revolutionized. The speed news travels, which'll affect the rate of exchange between planetary currencies—military transport, where they don't care what they spend on fuel—and you can bet *that'll* affect interplanetary politics—it's a whole new game all around."

Durrance finished scraping the last globs of food out of the pockets of his lunch tray. "Damn the colonials. Good old conservative Earth-based GalacTech left in the lurch again. You know, I'm really tempted to emigrate out to the farther end of the wormhole nexus sometimes. The wife's got family on Earth, though, so I don't suppose we ever will . . ."

Leo hung stunned in his straps as Durrance droned on. After a moment he swallowed the bite of squash still in his mouth, there being no more practical way to dispose of it. "Do you realize," he choked, "what this will do to the quaddies?"

Durrance blinked. "Not much, surely. There's still going to be plenty of jobs to do in free fall."

"It will destroy their edge in profitability versus ordinary workers, that's what. It was the downside medical leaves that were boosting the personnel costs. Eliminate them, and there's nothing to choose between—can this thing provide artificial gravity on a space station?"

"If they could mount it on a ship, they can put it on a station," opined Durrance. "It's not some kind of perpetual motion, though," he cautioned. "It sucks power like crazy, the jump pilot said. That'll cost something."

"Not as much—and surely they'll find more design efficiencies as they go along—oh, God."

This chance wasn't going to favor the quaddies. This chance favored no one. Damn, damn, damn the timing! Ten years from now, even one year from now, it could have been their salvation. Here, now, might it be—a death sentence? Leo flipped his feet out of the straps and coiled to launch himself toward the module doors.

"You just leaving this tray here?" asked Durrance. "Can I have your dessert . . . ?"

Leo waved a hand in impatient assent as he sprang away.

One look at Bruce Van Atta's glum and hostile face, as Leo swung into his Habitat office, confirmed Durrance's story. "Have you heard this artificial gravity rumor?" Leo demanded anyway, one last lurch of hope—let Van Atta deny it, name it fraud. . . .

Van Atta glared at him in profound irritation. "How the hell did you find out about it?"

"It's none of your business where I found out about it. Is it true?"

"Oh, yes it is my business. I want to keep this under wraps for as long as possible."

It was true, then. Leo's heart shrank. "Why? How long have you known about it?"

Van Atta's hand flipped the edges of a pile of plastic flimsies, computer printouts and communiqués, magnetized to his desk. "Three days."

"It's official, then."

"Oh, quite official." Van Atta's mouth twisted in disgust. "I got the word from GalacTech district headquarters on Orient IV. Apmad apparently met the news on her way home, and made one of her famous field decisions."

He rattled the flimsies again, and frowned. "There's no way around it. Do you know what came in yesterday on the heels of this thing? Kline Station has cancelled its construction contract with GalacTech, the first one we were going to send the quaddies out on. Paid the penalty without a murmur. Kline Station's out toward Beta Colony—they must have found out about this weeks ago—months. They've switched to a Betan contractor who, we may presume, is undercutting us. The Cay Project is cooked. Nothing left to do but wrap it up and get the hell out of here, the sooner the better. Damn! So now I'm associated with a loser project. I'll come out reeking with odor of loss."

"Wrap, wrap how? What do you mean, wrap?"

"That bitch Apmad's most favored scenario. I'll bet she was purring when she cut these orders—the quaddies gave her nervous palpitations, y'know. They're to be sterilized and stashed downside. Any pregnancies in progress to be aborted—shit, and we just started fifteen of 'em! What a fiasco. A year of my career down the tubes."

"My God, Bruce, you're not going to carry out those orders, are you?"

"Oh no? Just watch me." Van Atta stared at him, chewing his lip. Leo could feel himself tensing, pale with his suppressed fury. Van Atta sniffed. "What d'you want, Leo? Apmad could have ordered them exterminated. They're getting off lightly. It could have been worse."

"And if it had been—if she had ordered the quaddies killed—would you have carried it out?" inquired Leo, deceptively calm.

"She didn't. C'mon, Leo. I'm not inhuman. Sure, I'm sorry for the little suckers. I was doing my damndest to make 'em profitable. But there's no way I can fight this. All I can do is make the wrap as quick and clean and painless as possible, and cut the losses as much as I can. Maybe *somebody* in the company hierarchy will appreciate it."

"Painless to whom?"

"To everybody." Van Atta grew more intent, and leaned toward Leo with a scowl. "That means I don't need a lot of panic and wild rumors floating around, you hear? I want business as usual right up to the last minute. You and all the other instructors will go on teaching your classes just as if

the quaddies really were going out on a work project, until
the downside facility is ready and we can start shuttling
'em. Maybe take the little ones first—the salvageable parts
of the Habitat are supposed to be moved around the orbit
to the transfer station, we might cut some costs by using
quaddies for that last job."

"To imprison them downside—"

"Oh, come off the dramatics. They're being placed in a
perfectly ordinary drilling workers' dormitory, only abandoned six months ago when the field ran dry." Van Atta
brightened slightly in self-congratulation. "I found it
myself, looking over the possible sites to place 'em. It'll cost
next to nothing to refurbish it, compared to building new."

Leo could just picture it. He shuddered. "And what happens in fourteen years, when and if Orient IV expropriates
Rodeo?"

Van Atta ruffled his hair with both hands in exasperation. "How the hell should I know? At that point, it
becomes Orient IV's problem. There's only so much one
human being can do, Leo."

Leo smiled slowly, in grim numbness. "I'm not sure . . .
what one human being can do. I've never pushed myself to
the limit. I thought I had, but I realize now I hadn't. My
self-tests were always carefully non-destructive."

This test was a higher order of magnitude altogether.
This Tester, perhaps, scorned the merely humanly possible.
Leo tried to remember how long it had been since he'd
prayed, or even believed. Never, he decided, like this. He'd
never *needed* like this before. . . .

Van Atta frowned suspiciously at him. "You're weird,
Leo." He straightened his spine, as if seeking a posture of
command. "Just in case you missed my message, let me
repeat it loud and clear. You are to mention this artificial

gravity business to no one, that means especially no quaddies. Likewise, keep their downside destination secret. I'll let Yei figure out how to make them swallow it without kicking, it's time she earned her over-inflated salary. No rumors, no panics, no goddamn workers' riots—and if there are, I'll know just whose hide to nail to the wall. Got it?"

Leo's smile was canine, concealing—everything. "Got it." He withdrew without turning his back, or speaking another word.

Dr. Yei was not usually easy to track down, it being her habit to circulate often among the quaddies, observing behavior, taking notes, making suggestions. But this time Leo found her at once, in her office, with plastic flimsies stuck to every available surface and her desk console lit like a Christmas tree. Did they have Christmas at the Cay Habitat? Leo wondered. Somehow, he thought not.

"Did you hear—"

Her glum slouch answered his question, even as his white face and rapid breathing finished asking it.

"Yes, I've heard," she said wearily, glancing up at him. "Bruce just dumped the whole Habitat's personnel evacuation logistics on my desk to organize. He, he tells me, being an engineer, will be doing facility dismantling and equipment salvage flow charts. Just as soon as I get the bodies out of his way. Excuse me, the damned bodies."

Leo shook his head helplessly. "Are you going to do it?"

She shrugged, her lips compressed. "How can I not do it? Quit in high dudgeon? It wouldn't change a thing. This affair would not be rendered one iota less brutal for my walking out, and it could get a lot worse."

"I don't see how," Leo ground out.

"You don't?" She frowned. "No, I don't suppose you do. You never appreciated what a dangerous legal edge the quaddies are balanced on here. But I did. One wrong move and—oh, damn it all. I knew Apmad needed careful handling. Everything got away from me. Although I suppose this artificial gravity thing would have killed the project whoever was in charge, we are very, very lucky that she didn't order the quaddies exterminated. You have to understand, she had something like four or five pregnancies terminated for genetic defects, back on her home world when she was a young woman. It was the law. She eventually gave up, got divorced, took an off-planet job with GalacTech—came up through the ranks. She has a deep emotional vested interest in her prejudices against genetic tampering, and I knew it. And blew it . . . She still could order the quaddies killed—do you understand that? Any report of trouble, unrest, magnified by her genetic paranoias, and . . ." She squeezed her eyes shut, massaged her forehead with her fingertips.

"She could order it—who says you've got to carry it out? You said you cared about the quaddies. We've got to *do* something!" said Leo.

"What?" Yei's hands clenched, spread wide. "What, what, what? One or two—even if I could adopt one or two, take them away with me—smuggle them out somehow, who knows?—what then? To live on a planet with me, socially isolated as cripples, freaks, mutants—and sooner or later they would grow to adulthood, and then what? And what about the others? A *thousand*, Leo!"

"And if Apmad did order them exterminated, what excuse would you find then for doing nothing?"

"Oh, go *away*," she groaned. "You have no appreciation for the complexities of the situation, none. What do you think one person can do? I used to have a life of my own, once, before this job swallowed it. I've given six years— which is five and three-quarters more than *you* have—I've given all I can. I'm burned out. When I get away from this hole, I never want to hear of quaddies again. They're not my children. I haven't had *time* to have children."

She rubbed her eyes angrily, and sniffed, inhaling— tears?—or just bile. Leo didn't know. Leo didn't care.

"They're not anybody's children," Leo growled. "That's the trouble. They're some kind of . . . genetic orphans or something."

"If you're not going to say anything useful, please go *away*," she repeated. A wave of her hand encompassed the mass of flimsies. "I have work to do."

Leo had not struck a female since he was five years old. He removed himself, shaking.

He drifted slowly through the corridors, back toward his own quarters, cooling. And whatever had he hoped to get from Yei anyway? Relief from responsibility? Was he to dump his conscience on her desk, a la Bruce, and say, "Take care of it . . ."

And yet, and yet, and yet . . . there was a solution in here somewhere. He could feel it, a palpable dim shape, like a tightness in the gut, a mounting, screaming frustration. The problem that refused to fall into the right pieces, the elusive solution—he'd solved engineering problems that presented themselves at first as such solid, unscalable walls. He did not know where the leaps beyond logic that ultimately topped them came from, except that it was not a conscious process, however elegantly he might diagram it post facto. He could not solve it and he could not leave it alone, but picked uselessly at it, counterproductive like picking a scab, in a rising compulsive frenzy. The wheels spun, imparting no motion.

"It's in here," he whispered, touching his head. "I can feel it. I just . . . can't . . . *see* it . . ."

They had to get out of Rodeo local space somehow, that much was certain. All the quaddies. There was no future here. It was the damn peculiar legal set-up. What was he to do—hijack a jumpship? But the personnel jumpships carried no more than three hundred passengers. He could, just barely, picture himself holding a—a what? what weapon? he had no gun, his pocket knife featured mainly screwdrivers —right, hold a screwdriver to the pilot's head and cry, "Jump us to Orient IV!"—where he would promptly be arrested and jailed for the next twenty years for piracy, leaving the quaddies to do . . . what? In any case, he could not possibly hijack three ships at the same time, and that was the minimum number needed.

Leo shook his head. "Chance favors," he muttered, "chance favors, chance favors . . ."

Orient IV would not want the quaddies. Nobody was going to want the quaddies. What, indeed, could their future be even if freed from GalacTech? Gypsy orphans, alternately ignored, exploited, or abused, in their dependency on the narrow environment of humanity's chain of space facilities. Talk about technology traps. He pictured Silver—he had little doubt just what sort of exploitation would be her lot, with that elegant face and body of hers. No place for her out there . . .

No! Leo denied silently. The universe was so damned *big.* There had to be a place. A place of their own, far, far from the trappings and traps of human so-called civilization. The histories of previous utopian social experiments in isolation were not encouraging, but the quaddies were exceptional in every way.

Between one breath and the next, the vision took him. It came not as a chain of reason, more words words words, but as a blinding image, all complete in its first moment, inherent, holistic, gestalt, inspired. Every hour of his life from now on would be but the linear exploration of its fullness.

A stellar system with an M or G or K star, gentle, steady, pouring out power for the catching. Circling it, a Jovian gas giant with a methane and water-ice ring, for water, oxygen, nitrogen, hydrogen. Most important of all, an asteroid belt.

And some equally important absences: no Earth-like planet orbiting there also to attract competition; not on a wormhole jump route of strategic importance to any potential conquistadors. Humanity had passed over hundreds of such systems, in its obsessive quest for new Earths. The charts were glutted with them.

A quaddie culture spreading out along the belt from their initial base, a society of the quaddies, by the quaddies, for the quaddies. Burrowing into the rocks for protection against radiation, and to seal in their precious air, expanding, leapfrogging from rock to rock, to drill and build new homes. Minerals all around, more than they could ever use. Whole hydroponics farms for Silver. A new world to build. A space world to make Morita Station look like a toy.

"Why"—Leo's eyes widened with delight—"it's an *engineering* problem after all!"

He hung limply in air, entranced; fortunately, the corridor was empty of passers-by at the moment, or they would surely have thought him mad or drugged.

The solution had been lying around him in pieces all this time, invisible until *he'd* changed. He grinned dementedly, possessed. He yielded himself up to it without reservation. All. All. There was no limit to what one man might do, if he gave all, and held back nothing.

Didn't hold back, didn't look back—for there would be no going back. Literally, medically, that was the heart of it. Men adapted to free fall, it was the going *back* that crippled them.

"*I* am a quaddie," Leo whispered in wonder. He regarded his hands, clenched and spread his fingers. "Just a quaddie with legs." He wasn't going back.

As for that initial base—he was floating in it right now. It merely required relocating. His cascading thought clicked over the connections too rapidly to analyze. He didn't need to hijack a spaceship; he was in one. All it needed was a bit of power.

And the power lay ready-to-hand in Rodeo orbit, being gratuitously wasted even at this moment to shove mere bulk petrochemicals out of orbit. What might a petrochemical pod-bundle mass, compared to a chunk of the Cay Habitat? Leo didn't know, but he knew he could find out. The numbers would be on his side, anyway, whatever their precise magnitudes.

The cargo thrusters could handle the Habitat, if it were properly reconfigured, and anything the thrusters could handle, one of the monster cargo superjumpers could manage too. It was all there, all—for the taking.

For the taking . . .

Chapter 8

It took an hour of stalking before Leo was able to catch Silver alone, in a monitor blind spot in a corridor leading from the free fall gym.

"Is there someplace we can talk in private?" he asked her. "I mean really private."

Her wary glance around confirmed that she understood him perfectly. Still she hesitated. "Is it important?"

"Vital. Life or death for every quaddie. That important."

"Well . . . wait a minute or two, then follow me."

He trailed her slowly and casually through the Habitat, a flash of shimmering hair and blue jersey at this or that cross-branching. Then, down one corridor, he suddenly lost her. "Silver . . . ?"

"Sh!" she hissed at his ear. A wall panel hinged silently inward, and one of her strong lower hands reached out to yank him in like a fish on a line.

It was dark and narrow behind the wall for only a moment, then airseal doors parted with a whisper to reveal an odd-shaped chamber perhaps three meters across. They slipped within.

"What's this?" asked Leo, stunned.

"The Clubhouse. Anyway, we call it that. We built it in this little blind pocket. You wouldn't notice it from Outside unless you were looking for it at just the right angle. Tony and Pramod did the outside walls. Siggy ran the ductwork in, others did the wiring . . . the airseals we built from spare parts."

"Weren't they missed?"

Her smile was not in the least innocent. "Quaddies do the computer records entry, too. The parts just sort of ceased to exist in inventory. A bunch of us worked together on it—we just finished it about two months ago. I was sure Dr. Yei and Mr. Van Atta would find out about it, when they were questioning me"—her smile faded to a frown in memory—"but they never asked just the right question. Now the only vids we have left are the ones that happened to be stored in here, and Darla doesn't have the vid system up yet."

Leo followed her glance to a dead holovid set, obviously in process of repair, fixed to the wall. There were other comforts: lighting, handy straps, a wall cabinet that proved to be stuffed with little bags of dried snacks abstracted from Nutrition, raisins, peanuts and the like. Leo orbited the room slowly, nervously examining the workmanship. It was tight. "Was this place your idea?"

"Sort of. I couldn't have done it alone, though. You understand, it's strictly against our rules for me to bring you in here," Silver added somewhat truculently. "So this better be good, Leo."

"Silver," said Leo, "it's your uniquely pragmatic approach to rules that makes you the most valuable quaddie in the Habitat right now. I need you—your daring, and all the other qualities that Dr. Yei would doubtless call anti-social.

I've got a job to do that I can't do alone either." He took a deep breath. "How would you quaddies like to have your own asteroid belt?"

"What?" Her eyes widened.

"Brucie-baby is trying to keep it under wraps, but the Cay Project has just been scheduled for termination—and I mean that in the most sinister sense of the word."

He detailed the anti-gravity rumor to her, all that he had yet heard, and Van Atta's secret plans for the quaddies' disposal. With rising passion, he described his vision of escape. He didn't have to explain anything twice.

"How much time do we have left?" she asked whitely, when he had finished.

"Not much. A few weeks at most. I have only six days until I'm forced downside by my gravity leave. I've got to figure out some way to duck that; I'm afraid I might not be able to get back here. We—you quaddies—have to choose *now*. And I can't do it for you. I can only help with some of the parts. If you cannot rescue yourselves, you will be lost, guaranteed."

She blew out her breath in a silent whistle, looking troubled indeed. "I thought—watching Tony and Claire—they were doing it the wrong way. Tony talked about finding work, but do you know, he didn't think to take a work suit with him? I didn't want to make the same mistakes. We aren't made to travel alone, Leo. Maybe it's something that was built into us."

"But can you bring in the others?" Leo asked anxiously. "In secret? Let me tell you, the quickest end-scenario for this little revolution I can imagine would be for some quaddie to panic and tell, trying to be good. This is a real conspiracy, all rules off. I sacrifice my job, risk legal prosecution, but you risk much more."

"There are some who, um, should be told last," said Silver thoughtfully. "But I can bring the important ones in. We've got some ways of keeping things private from the downsiders."

Leo glanced around the chamber, subtly reassured.

"Leo . . ." Her blue eyes targeted him, searching. "*How* are we going to get rid of the downsiders?"

"Well, we won't be able to shuttle them down to Rodeo, that's for certain. From the moment this thing comes out in the open, you can count on the Habitat being cut off from re-supply." *Besieged*, was the word Leo's mind suggested, and carefully edited. "The way I thought of was to collect them all in one module, throw in some emergency oxygen, cut it off the Habitat, and use one of the cargo pushers to move it around orbit to the transfer station. At that point they become GalacTech's problem, not ours. Hopefully it'd ball things up a bit at the transfer station, too, and give us a little more time."

"How do you plan to—to make them all get into the module?"

Leo stirred uncomfortably. "Well, that's the point of no return, Silver. There are weapons all around us here. We just don't recognize them because we call them 'tools'. A laser-solderer with the safety removed is as good as a gun. There's a couple of dozen of them in the workshops. Point it at the downsiders and say 'Move!'—and they'll move."

"What if they don't?"

"Then you must fire it. Or choose not to, and be taken downside to a slow and sterile death. And you choose for everybody, when you make that choice, not just for yourself."

Silver was shaking her head. "I don't think that's such a good idea, Leo. What if somebody panicked and actually fired one? The downsider would be horribly burned!"

"Well . . . yes, that's the idea."

Her face crumpled with dismay. "If I have to shoot Mama Nilla, I'd rather go downside and die!"

Mama Nilla was one of the quaddies' most popular crèche mothers, Leo recalled vaguely, a big elderly woman—he'd barely met her, as his classes didn't involve the younger quaddies. "I was thinking more in terms of shooting Bruce," Leo confessed.

"I'm not sure I could even do that to Mr. Van Atta," said Silver slowly. "Have you ever seen a bad burn, Leo?"

"Yes."

"So have I."

A brief silence fell.

"We can't bluff our teachers," said Silver finally. "All Mama Nilla would have to do is say 'Give that over now, Siggy!' in that *voice* of hers, and he would. It's not—it's not a *smart* scenario, Leo."

Leo's hands clenched in exasperation. "But we must get the downsiders off the Habitat, or nothing else can be done! If we can't, they'll just re-take it, and you'll be worse off than when you started."

"All right, all right! We've got to get rid of them. But that's not the way." She paused, looking at him more doubtfully. "Could you shoot Mama Nilla? Do you really think—say—Pramod, could shoot you?"

Leo sighed. "Probably not. Not in cold blood. Even soldiers in battle have to be brought to a special state of mental excitement to shoot total strangers."

Silver looked relieved. "All right, so what else would have to be done? Saying we could take over the Habitat."

"Re-configuring the Habitat can be done with tools and supplies already aboard, though everything will have to be carefully rationed. The Habitat will have to be defended from any attempt by GalacTech to recapture it while this is going on. The high-energy-density beam welders could be quite effective discouragement to shuttles attempting to board us—if anybody could be induced to fire one," he added with a dry edge. "Company inventory doesn't include armored attack ships, fortunately. A real military force would make short work of this little revolution, you realize." His imagination supplied the details, and his stomach bunched queasily. "Our only real defense is to get gone before GalacTech can produce one. That will require a jump pilot."

He studied her anew. "That's where you come in, Silver. I know a pilot who's going to be passing through the transfer station very soon who might be, um, easier to kidnap than most. Especially if *you* came along to lend your personal persuasion."

"Ti."

"Ti," he confirmed.

She looked dubious. "Maybe."

Leo fought down another and stronger wave of queasiness. Ti and Silver had a relationship pre-dating his arrival. He wasn't really playing pimp. Logic dictated this. He realized suddenly that what he really wanted was to remove her as far from the jump pilot as possible. *And do what? Keep her for yourself? Get serious. You're too old for her.* Ti was what—twenty-five, maybe? Perhaps violently jealous, for all Leo knew. She must prefer him. Leo tried virtuously to feel old. It wasn't hard; most of the quaddies made him feel about eighty anyway. He wrenched his mind back to business.

"The third thing that has to be done first"—Leo thought over the wording of that, and concluded unhappily that it was all too accurate—"is nail down a cargo jumper. If we wait until we boost the Habitat all the way out to the wormhole, GalacTech will have time to figure out how to defend them. Such as jumping them all to the Orient IV side and thumbing their noses at us until we are forced to surrender." He contemplated the next logical step with some dismay. "That means we've got to send a force out to the wormhole to hijack one. And I can't go with it and be here to defend and reconfigure the Habitat both . . . it'll have to be a force of quaddies. I don't know . . ." Leo ran down. "Maybe this isn't such a great idea after all."

"Send Ti with them," suggested Silver reasonably. "He knows more about the cargo jumpers than any of us."

"Mm," said Leo, drawn back to optimism. If he was going to pay attention to the odds against this escapade succeeding, he might as well give up now and avoid the rush. Screw the odds. He would believe in Ti. If necessary, he would believe in elves, angels, and the tooth fairy.

"That makes, um, suborning Ti step one in the flow chart," Leo reasoned aloud. "From the moment he's missed we're out in the open, racing the clock. That means all the advance planning for moving the Habitat had better be done—in advance. And—oh. Oh, my." Leo's eyes lit.

"What?"

"I just had a *brilliant* idea to buy us a head start . . ."

Leo timed his entrance carefully, waiting until Van Atta had been holed up in his Habitat office nearly the first two hours of the shift. The project chief would be starting to think about his coffee break by now, and reaching the degree of frustration that always attended the first attack on a new problem, in this case dismantling the Habitat. Leo could picture the entangled stage of his planning precisely; he'd gone through it himself about eight hours previously, locked in his own quarters, brainstorming on his computer console after a brief pause to render his programs inaccessible to snoops. The leftover military security clearance from the Argus cruiser project worked wonders. Leo was quite sure no one in the Habitat, not Van Atta and certainly not Yei, possessed a higher key.

Van Atta frowned at him from the clutter of printouts, his computer vid scintillating multi-screened and colorful with assorted Habitat schematics. "Now what, Leo? I'm busy. Those who can, do; those who can't, teach."

And those who can't teach, Leo finished silently, *go into administration*. He maintained his usual bland smile, not letting the edged thought show by any careless gleam or reflection. "I've been thinking, Bruce," Leo purred. "I'd like to volunteer for the job of dismantling the Habitat."

"You would?" Van Atta's brows rose in astonishment, lowered in suspicion. "Why?"

Van Atta would hardly believe it was out of the goodness of his heart. Leo was prepared. "Because as much as I hate to admit it, you were right again. I've been thinking about what I'm going to bring away from this assignment. Counting travel time, I've shot four months of my life—more, before this is done—and I've got nothing to show for it but some black marks on my record."

"You did it to yourself." Van Atta, reminded, rubbed his chin upon which the bruise was fading to a green shadow, and glowered.

"I lost my perspective for a little while, it's true," Leo admitted. "I've got it back."

"A bit late," sneered Van Atta.

"But I could do a good job," argued Leo, wondering how one could achieve the effect of a hangdog shuffle in free fall. Better not overdo it. "I really need a commendation, something to counterweight those reprimands. I've had some ideas that could result in an unusually high salvage ratio, cut the losses. It would take all the scut work off your hands and leave you free to administer."

"Hm," said Van Atta, clearly enticed by a vision of his office returning to its former pristine serenity. He studied Leo, his eyes slitting. "Very well—take it. There're my notes, they're all yours. Ah, just send the plans and reports through my office, I'll send 'em on. That's my real job, after all, administration."

"Certainly." Leo swept up the clutter. *Yes, send 'em through you—so you can replace my name with your own.* Leo could almost see the wheels turn, in the smug light of Van Atta's eyes. Let Leo do the work, and Van Atta siphon off the credit. *Oh, you'll get the credit for how this project ends all right, Brucie-baby—all of it.*

"I'll need a few other things," Leo requested humbly. "I want all the quaddie pusher crews that can be spared from their regular duties, in addition to my own classes. These useless children are going to learn to work like they never worked before. Supplies, equipment, authorization to sign out pushers and fuel—gotta start some on-site surveying— and I need to be able to commandeer other quaddie spot labor as needed. All right?"

"Oh, are you volunteering for the hands-on part too?" A fleeting vindictive greediness crossed Van Atta's face, followed by doubt. "What about keeping this under wraps till the last minute?"

"I can present the pre-planning as a theoretical class exercise, at first. Buy a week or two. They'll have to be told eventually, you know."

"Not too soon. I'll hold you responsible for keeping the chimps under control, you copy?"

"I copy. Do I have my authorization? Oh—and I'll need to get an extension against my downside gravity leave."

"HQ doesn't like that. Liability."

"It's either me or you, Bruce."

"True . . ." Van Atta waved a hand, already sinking back gratefully from harried to languid mode. "All right. You got it."

A blank check. Leo tamped a wolfish grin into a fawning smile. "You'll remember this, won't you Bruce—later?"

Van Atta's lips too drew back. "I guarantee, Leo, I'll remember *everything*."

Leo bowed himself out, mumbling gratitude.

Silver poked her head through the door to the crèche mother's private sleep cubicle. "Mama Nilla?"

"Sh!" Mama Nilla held her finger to her lips and nodded toward Andy, asleep in a sack on the wall with his face peeping out. She whispered, "For heaven's sake don't wake the baby. He's been so fussy—I think the formula disagrees with him. I wish Dr. Minchenko were back. Here, I'll come out in the corridor."

The airseal doors swished shut behind her. In preparation for sleep Mama Nilla had exchanged her pink working coveralls for a set of flowered pajamas cinched in around her ample waist. Silver suppressed an urge to clamp herself to that soft torso as she had in desperate moments when she was little—she was much too grown-up to be cuddled anymore, she told herself sternly. "How's Andy doing?" she asked instead, with a nod toward the closed doors.

"Hm. All right," said Mama Nilla. "Though I hope I can get this formula problem straightened out soon. And . . . well . . . I'm not sure you could call it depression, exactly, but his attention span seems shorter, and he fusses—don't tell Claire that, though, poor dear, she has enough troubles. Tell her he's all right."

Silver nodded. "I understand."

Mama Nilla frowned introspectively. "I wrote up a protest, but my supervisor blocked it. Ill-timed, she said. Ha. More like Mr. Van Atta has her spooked. I could just . . . ahem. Anyway, I've been turning in overtime chits like crazy, and I requested an extra assistant be assigned to my crèche unit. Maybe when they realize that this foolishness is costing them money, they'll give in. You can tell Claire that, I think."

"Yes," said Silver, "she could use a little hope."

Mama Nilla sighed. "I feel so badly about this. Whatever possessed those children to try to run off, anyway? I could just shake Tony. And as for that stupid security guard, I could just . . . well." She shook her head.

"Have you heard any more about Tony, that I could pass on to Claire?"

"Ah. Yes." Mama Nilla glanced up and down the corridor, to assure herself of their privacy. "Dr. Minchenko called me last night on the personal channel. He assures me Tony's out of danger now. They got that infection under control. But he's still very weak. Dr. Minchenko means to bring him back up to the Habitat when he finishes his own gravity leave. He thinks Tony will complete his recovery faster up here. So that's a bit of good news you can pass on to Claire."

Silver calculated, her lower fingers tapping out the days unobtrusively below Mama Nilla's line of sight, and breathed relief. That was one massive problem she could report to Leo as solved. Tony would be back before their revolt broke into the open. His safe return might even become the signal for it. A smile lit her face. "Thanks, Mama Nilla. That is good news."

Revolution 101 for the Bewildered, Leo decided grimly, should be his course title. Or worse—*050: Remedial Revolution . . .*

The shell of floating quaddies hovering expectantly around him in the lecture module had been officially augmented by both the off-duty pusher crews, and loaded with all the off-shift older quaddies Silver had been able to contact covertly. Sixty or seventy altogether. The lecture module was jammed, causing Leo to jump ahead mentally and think about oxygen consumption and regeneration plans for the reconfigured Habitat. There was tension, as well as carbon dioxide, in the air. Rumors were afloat already, Leo realized, God knew in what mutant forms. It was time to replace rumors with facts.

Silver waved all clear from the airseal doors, turning all four thumbs up and grinning at Leo, as one last T-shirted quaddie scurried within. The airseal doors slid shut, eclipsing her as she turned to take up guard duty in the corridor.

Leo took up his lecture station in the center. The center, the hub of the wheel, where stresses are most concentrated. After some initial whispering, poking, and prodding, they hushed for him to an almost frightening attentiveness. He could hear them breathing. *We would need you even if you weren't an engineer, Leo*, Silver had remarked. *We're all too used to taking orders from people with legs.*

Are you saying you need a front man? he'd asked, amused.

Is that what it's called? Her gaze upon him had been coolly pragmatic.

He was getting too old; his brain was short-circuiting to some distant rock beat, slipping back to the noisier rhythms of his adolescence. *Let me be your front man, baby. Call me Leo. Call me anytime, day or night. Let me help.* He eyed the closed airseal doors. Was the man waving the baton at the front of the parade pulling it after him—or being pushed along ahead of it? He had a queasy premonition he was going to learn the answer. He woofed a breath, and returned his attention to the lecture chamber.

"As some of you have already heard," Leo began, his words like pebbles in the pool of silence, "a new gravity technology has arrived from the outlying planets. It's apparently based on a variation of the Necklin field tensor equations, the same mathematics that underlie the technology we use to punch through those wrinkles in space-time we call wormholes. I haven't been able to get hold of the tech specs yet myself, but it seems it's already been developed to the marketable stage. The theoretical possibility was not, strictly speaking, new, but I for one never expected to see its practical capture in my lifetime. Evidently, neither did the people who created you quaddies.

"There is a kind of strange symmetry to it. The spurt forward in genetic bioengineering that made you possible was based on the perfection of a new technology, the uterine replicator, from Beta Colony. Now, barely a generation later, the new technology that renders you obsolete has arrived from the same source. Because that's what you have become, before you even got online—technologically

obsolete. At least from GalacTech's point of view." Leo drew
breath, watching for their reactions.

"Now, when a machine becomes obsolete, we scrap it.
When a man's training becomes obsolete, we send him
back to school. But your obsolescence was bred in your
bones. It's either a cruel mistake, or, or, *or*," he paused for
emphasis, "the greatest opportunity you will ever have to
become a free people.

"Don't . . . don't take notes," Leo choked, as heads bent
automatically over their scribble boards, illuminating his
key words with their light pens as the auto-transcription
marched across their displays. "This isn't a class. This is real
life." He had to stop a moment to regain his equilibrium. He
was positive some child at the back was still highlighting
"no notes—real life", in reflexive virtue.

Pramod, floating near, looked up, his dark eyes agitated.
"Leo? There was a rumor going around that the company
was going to take us all downside and shoot us. Like Tony."

Leo smiled sourly. "That's actually the least likely scenario. You are to be taken downside, yes, to a sort of prison
camp. But this is how guilt-free genocide is handled. One
administrator passes you on to the next, and him to the
next, and him to the next. You become a routine expense
on the inventory. Expenses rise, as they always do. In
response, your downsider support employees are gradually
withdrawn, as the company names you 'self-sufficient.' Life
support equipment deteriorates with age. Breakdowns happen more and more often, maintenance and re-supply
become more and more erratic.

"Then one night—without anybody ever giving an
order or pulling a trigger—some critical breakdown
occurs. You send a call for help. Nobody knows who you
are. Nobody knows what to do. Those who placed you

there are all long gone. No hero takes initiative, initiative having been drained by administrative bitching and black hints. The investigating inspector, after counting the bodies, discovers with relief that you were merely inventory. The books are quietly closed on the Cay Project. Finis. Wrap. It might take twenty years, maybe only five or ten. You are simply forgotten to death."

Pramod's hand touched his throat, as if he already felt the rasp of Rodeo's toxic atmosphere. "I think I'd rather be shot," he muttered.

"*Or*," Leo raised his voice, "you can take your lives into your own hands. Come with me and put all your risks up front. The big gamble for the big payoff. Let me tell you"— he gulped for courage, mustered megalomania—for surely only a maniac could drive this through to success—"let me tell you about the Promised Land. . . ."

Chapter 9

Leo stretched for a look out the viewport of the cargo pusher at the rapidly-enlarging transfer station. Damn. The weekly passenger ship from Orient IV was already docked at the hub of the wheel. Newly arrived, it was doubtless still in the off-loading phase, but nothing seemed more likely to Leo than for a pilot—or ex-pilot—like Ti to invite himself aboard early, to kibitz.

The jumpship was blocked from view as they spiraled around the station to their own assigned shuttle hatch. The quaddie piloting the pusher, a dark-haired, copper-skinned girl named Zara in the purple T-shirt and shorts of the pusher crews, brought her ship smartly into alignment and clicked it delicately into the clamps on the landing spoke. Leo was encouraged toward belief in her top rating among the pusher pilots after all, despite his qualms about her age, barely fifteen.

The mild acceleration vector of the Station's spin at this radius tugged at Leo, and his padded chair swung in its gimbals to the newly-defined "upright" position. Zara grinned over her shoulder at Leo, clearly exhilarated by the sensation. Silver, in the quaddie-formfit acceleration couch beside Zara, looked more dubious.

Zara completed the formal litany of cross-checks with transfer station traffic control and shut down her systems. Leo sighed illogical relief that traffic control hadn't questioned the vaguely-worded purpose of their filed flight plan—"Pick up material for the Cay Habitat." There was no reason they should have. Leo wasn't even close to exceeding his powers of authorization. Yet.

"Watch, Silver," said Zara, and let a light-pen fall from her fingers. It fell slowly to the padded strip on the wall-now-floor and bounced in a graceful arc. Zara's lower hand scooped it back out of the air.

Leo waited resignedly while Silver tried it once too, then said, "Come on. We've got to catch Ti."

"Right." Silver pulled herself up by her upper hands on her headrest, swung her lowers free, and hesitated. Leo shook out his pair of gray sweat pants he'd brought for the purpose, and gingerly helped her pull them over her lower arms and up to her waist. She waved her hands and the ends of the pant legs flopped and flapped over them. She grimaced at the unaccustomed constraint of the bundled cloth upon her dexterity.

"All right, Silver," said Leo, "now the shoes you borrowed from that girl running Hydroponics."

"I gave them to Zara to stow."

"Oh," said Zara. One of her upper hands flew to her lips.

"What?"

"I left them in the docking bay."

"Zara!"

"Sorry . . ."

Silver blew out her breath against Leo's neck. "Maybe your shoes, Leo," she suggested.

"I don't know . . ." Leo kicked out of his shoes, and Zara helped Silver slip her lower hands into them.

"How do they look?" said Silver anxiously.

Zara wrinkled her nose. "They look kinda big."

Leo sidled around to catch their reflection in the darkened port. They looked absurd. Leo regarded his feet as though he'd never seen them before. Did they look that absurd on him? His socks seemed suddenly like enormous white worms. Feet were insane appendages. "Forget the shoes. Give 'em back. Just let the pant legs cover your hands."

"What if someone asks what happened to my feet?" Silver worried aloud.

"Amputated," suggested Leo, "due to a terrible case of frostbite suffered on your vacation to the Antarctic Continent."

"Isn't that on Earth? What if they start asking questions about Earth?"

"Then I'll—I'll quash them for rudeness. But most people are pretty inhibited about asking questions like that. We can still use the original story about your wheelchair being lost luggage, and we're on our way to try to get it back. They'll believe that. Come on." Leo backed up to her. "All aboard." Her upper arms twined around his neck, and her lowers clamped around his waist with slightly paranoid pressure, as she cautiously entrusted her newfound weight to him. Her breath was warm, and tickled his ear.

They ducked through the flex tube and into the transfer station proper. Leo headed for the elevator stack that ran up—or down—the length of the spoke to the rim where the transient rest cubicles were to be found.

Leo waited for an empty elevator. But it stopped again, and others boarded. Leo had a brief spasm of terror that Silver might try to strike up a friendly conversation—he should have told her explicitly not to talk to strangers—but she maintained a shy reserve. Transfer station personnel gave them a few uncomfortable covert stares, but Leo gazed coldly at the wall and no one attempted to broach the silence.

Leo staggered, exiting the elevator at the outer rim where the gee forces were maximized. Little though he wished to admit it, three months of null-gee deconditioning had had its inevitable effect. But at half-gee, Silver's weight didn't even bring their combined total up to his Earthside norm, Leo told himself sternly. He shuffled off as rapidly as possible away from the populated foyer.

Leo knocked on the numbered cubicle door. It slid open. A male voice: "Yeah, what?" They had cornered the jump pilot. Leo plastered an inviting smile on his face, and they entered.

Ti was propped up on the bed, dressed in dark trousers, T-shirt, and socks, idly scanning a hand-viewer. He glanced up in mild irritation at Leo, unfamiliar to him, then his eyes widened as he saw Silver. Leo dumped Silver as unceremoniously as a cat on the foot of the bed, and plopped into the cubicle's sole chair to catch his breath. "Ti Gulik. Gotta talk to you."

Ti had recoiled to the head of the bed, knees drawn up, hand viewer rolled aside and forgotten. "Silver! What the hell are you doing here? Who's this guy?" He jerked a thumb at Leo.

"Tony's welding teacher. Leo Graf," answered Silver smearily. Experimentally, she rolled over and pushed her torso upright with her upper hands. "This feels weird." She raised her upper hands, balancing, Leo thought, for all the world like a seal on a tripod formed by her lower arms. "Huh." She returned her upper hands to the bed, to lend support, achieving a dog-like posture, fine hair flattened, all her grace stolen by gravity. No doubt about it, quaddies belonged in null-gee.

"We need your help, Lieutenant Gulik," Leo began as soon as he could. "Desperately."

"Who's *we*?" asked Ti suspiciously.

"The quaddies."

"Hah," said Ti darkly. "Well, the first thing I would like to point out is that I am not Lieutenant Gulik any more. I'm plain Ti Gulik, unemployed, and quite possibly unemployable. Thanks to the quaddies. Or at any rate, one quaddie." He frowned at Silver.

"I told them it wasn't your fault," said Silver. "They wouldn't listen to me."

"You might at least have covered for me," said Ti petulantly. "You owed me that much."

He might as well have hit her, from the look on her face. "Back off, Gulik," Leo growled. "Silver was drugged and tortured to extract that confession. Seems to me any owing in here goes in the other direction."

Ti flushed. Leo bit back his annoyance. They couldn't afford to piss off the jump pilot; they needed him too much. Besides, this wasn't the conversation Leo had rehearsed. Ti should be leaping through hoops for those morning-glory eyes of Silver's, the psychology of reward and all that—surely he must respond to a plea for her good. If the young lout didn't appreciate her, he didn't deserve to have her—Leo forced his thoughts back to the matter at hand.

"Have you heard about this new artificial gravity field technology yet?" Leo began again.

"Something," admitted Ti warily.

"Well, it's killed the Cay Project. GalacTech's dropping out of the quaddie business."

"Huh. Yeah, well, that makes sense."

Leo waited a beat for the next logical question, which didn't come. Ti wasn't an idiot; he was therefore being deliberately dense. Leo pushed on relentlessly. "They plan to ship the quaddies downside to Rodeo, to an abandoned workers' barracks—" He repeated the forgotten-to-death scenario he had described to Pramod a week earlier, and looked up to gauge its effect.

The pilot's face was closed and neutral. "Well, I'm very sorry for them"—Ti did not look at Silver—"but I totally fail to see what I'm supposed to do about it. I'm leaving Rodeo in six hours, never to return—which is just fine with me, by the way. This place is a pit."

"And Silver and the quaddies are being dropped into that pit and the lid clamped over them. And the only crime they've committed is to become technologically obsolete. Doesn't that mean anything to you?" cried Leo heatedly.

Ti bolted upright indignantly. "You want to talk about technological obsolescence? I'll show you technological obsolescence. This!" His hand touched the implant plugs at mid-forehead and temples, the cannula at the nape of his neck. "This! I trained for two years and waited in line for a year for the surgery to implant my jump set. It's a tensor bit-code version, because that's the jump system GalacTech uses, and they underwrote part of the cost of it. Trans-Stellar Transport and a few independents also use it. Everybody else in the universe is gearing up to Necklin color-drive. You know what my chances of being hired by TST are, after being fired by GalacTech? Zilch. Zero. Nada. If I want a jump pilot's job, I need this surgically removed and a new implant. Without a job, I can't afford an implant. Without an implant, I can't get a job. Screw you, Ti Gulik!" He sat, panting.

Leo leaned forward. "I'll give you a pilot's berth, Gulik," he said clearly. "On the biggest jumpship ever to fly." Rapidly, before the pilot could interrupt, he detailed his vision of the Habitat converted to colony ship. "It's all here. All we need is a pilot. A pilot who can plug into the GalacTech drive system. All we need—is you."

Ti looked perfectly appalled. "You're not just talking grand lunacy—you're talking grand larceny! Do you realize what the cash value of the total configuration would *be*? They wouldn't let you out of jail till the next millennium!"

"I'm not going to jail. I'm going to the stars with the quaddies."

"*Your* cell will be padded."

"This isn't crime. This is—war, or something. Crime is turning your back and walking away."

"Not by any legal code I know of."

"All right then; sin."

"Oh, brother." Ti rolled his eyes. "Now it comes out. You're on a mission from God, right? Let me off at the next stop, please."

God's not here. Somebody's got to fill in. Leo backed off hastily from that line of thought. Padded cells, indeed. "I thought you were in love with Silver. How can you abandon her to a slow death?"

"Ti's not in love with me," interrupted Silver in surprise. "Whatever gave you that idea, Leo?"

Ti gave her an unsettled look. "No, of course not," he agreed faintly. "You, ah—you always knew, right? We just had a mutually beneficial little arrangement, is all."

"That's right," confirmed Silver. "I got books and vids, Ti got relief from physiological stress. Downsider males need sex to stay healthy, you know, they can't cope with stress. It makes them disruptive. Wild genes, I suppose."

"Where did *that* line of bullshit come from—?" Leo began, and broke off "Never mind." He could guess. He closed his eyes, pressed them with his fingertips, and groped for his lost argument. "Right. So to you, Silver is just . . . disposable. Like a tissue. Sneeze in her and toss her away."

Ti looked stung. "Give it up, Graf. I'm no worse than anyone else."

"But I'm giving you the chance to be better, don't you see—"

"Leo," Silver interrupted again. She was now sprawled on her stomach on the bed, her chin propped awkwardly on one upper hand. "After we get to our asteroid belt— wherever it turns out to be—what are we going to do with the superjumper?"

"The superjumper?"

"We'll be detaching the Habitat and opening it out again, surely—building on to it—the jumper unit would just be sitting there in parking orbit. Can't we give it to Ti?"

"What?" said Leo and Ti together.

"As payment. He jumps us to our destination, he gets to keep the jumpship. Then he can go off and be a pilot-owner, set up his own transport business, whatever he likes."

"In a stolen ship?" yipped Ti.

"If we're far enough away that GalacTech can't catch up with us, we're far enough away that GalacTech can't catch up with you," said Silver logically. "Then you'll have a ship that fits your neural implant, and nobody will be able to fire you again, because you'll be working for yourself."

Leo bit his tongue. He'd brought Silver along expressly to help persuade Ti—so what if it wasn't the blandishment he'd envisioned? From the blitzed look on the pilot's face, they'd gotten through to his launch-button at last. Leo lidded his eyes and smiled encouragement at her.

"Besides," she went on, her eyelashes fluttering in return, "if we do succeed in jumping out of here, Habitat and all, Mr. Van Atta's going to be left looking an awful fool." She let her head flop back on the bed and smiled sideways at Ti.

"Oh," said Ti in a tone of enlightenment. "Ah . . ."

"Are your bags all packed?" asked Leo helpfully.

"Over there." Ti nodded to a pile of luggage in the corner. "But . . . but . . . dammit, if this thing crashes, they'll crucify me!"

"Ah," said Leo. "Here, see . . ." He opened his red coveralls at the neck and drew out the laser-solderer concealed in an inner pocket. "I jimmied the safety on this thing; it'll fire an extremely intense beam for quite a distance now, until the atmosphere dissipates it—farther than the distance across this room, certainly." He waved it negligently; Ti ducked, eyes widening. "If we end up under arrest, you can truthfully testify that you were kidnapped at gunpoint by a crazed engineer and his mad mutant assistant and made to cooperate under duress. You may be a hero one way—or another."

The mad mutant assistant smiled blindingly at Ti, her eyes like stars.

"You, ah—wouldn't really fire that thing, would you?" choked Ti.

"Of course not," Leo said jovially, baring his teeth. He put the solderer away.

"Ah." Ti's mouth twitched briefly in response. But his eye returned often thereafter to the lump in Leo's coveralls.

When they made it back to the shuttle hatch where the pusher was docked, Zara was gone.

"Oh, God," moaned Leo. Had she wandered off? Gotten lost? Been forcibly removed? A frantic inventory found no message left on the com, no note pinned anywhere.

"Pilot, she's a pilot," Leo reasoned aloud. "Is there anything she could have needed to do? We've plenty of fuel—communicating with traffic control is done right from here . . ." He realized, with a cold chill, that he hadn't actually forbidden her to leave the pusher. It had been so self-evident that she was to stay out of sight, and on guard. Self-evident to himself, Leo realized. Who could say what was self-evident to a quaddie?

"I could fly this thing, if necessary," said Ti in a most unpressing tone, looking over the control deck. "It's all manual."

"That's not the point," said Leo. "We can't leave without her. The quaddies aren't supposed to be over here at all. If she gets picked up by the Station authorities and they start asking questions—always assuming she hasn't been picked up by something worse . . ."

"What worse?"

"I don't *know* what worse, that's the trouble."

Silver meanwhile had rolled off the acceleration couch to the deck strip. After a moment of thoughtful experimentation, she achieved a four-handed forward shuffle, and marched off past Leo's knees, pant legs trailing.

"Where are you going?"

"After Zara."

"Silver, stay with the ship. We don't need two of you lost, for God's sake," Leo ordered sternly. "Ti and I can move much faster, we'll find her."

"I don't think so," murmured Silver distantly. She reached the flex tube and stared up and down the corridor which curved away to right and left, ringing the spoke. "You see, I don't think she's gone far."

"If she got on the elevator, she could be practically anywhere on the Station by now," said Ti.

Silver reared up on her tripoded lower arms, raised her uppers over her head, and narrowed her eyes for a look around the elevator foyer to her left. "The controls would be hard for a quaddie to reach. Besides, she'd know she was more likely to run into downsiders there. I think she went this way." She raised her chin and shuffled determinedly off to her right on all fours. After a moment she picked up speed by changing her gait to a series of gazelle-like bounds in the low-gee of the spoke. Leo and Ti, of necessity, bounded after her. Leo felt absurdly like a man chasing a runaway pet. It was an optical illusion of the quadrimanual locomotion—quaddies even *looked* more human in free fall.

A strange rumbling noise approached around the curve of the corridor. Silver hooted, and skidded to one side against the outer wall.

"Oh, sorry!" cried Zara, whizzing past torso-down and chin up on a low roller-pallet, all four hands going like paddle wheels to propel her along the deck. Braking proved more difficult than acceleration, and Zara fetched up beside Silver with a crash.

Leo, horrified, bounded over to them, but Zara was already disentangling herself and sitting up cheerfully. Even the roller pallet was undamaged.

"Look Silver," Zara said, flipping the pallet over, "wheels! I wonder how they're beating the friction, inside those casings? Feel, they're not hot at all."

"Zara," cried Leo, "why did you leave the ship?"

"I wanted to see what a downsider toilet chamber looked like," said Zara, "but there wasn't one on this level. All I found was a closet full of cleaning supplies, and this." She patted the roller pallet. "Can I take the wheels apart and see what's inside?"

"No!" roared Leo.

She looked quite put-out. "But I want to know!"

"Bring it along," Silver suggested, "and take it apart later." Her eyes flicked up and down the corridor; Leo was slightly consoled that at least one quaddie shared his sense of urgency.

"Yes, later," Leo agreed, for the sake of expediency. "Let's go now." He tucked the roller pallet firmly under his arm, to thwart further experimentation. The quaddies, he reflected, didn't seem to have a very clear idea of private property. Probably came from a lifetime spent in a communal space habitat, with its tight ecology. Planets were communal in the same way, really, except that their enormous size put so much slack in their systems, it was disguised.

Habits of thought, indeed. Here he was worried over the theft of a roller pallet, while planning the greatest space heist in human history. Ti almost bolted when he found out what the rest of the assignment they had planned for him was to be. Leo, prudently, didn't fill in these details until the pusher was safely launched from the transfer station and halfway back to the Habitat.

"You want *me* to hijack the superjumper!" yelped Ti.

"No, no," Leo soothed him. "You're only going along as an advisor. The quaddies will take the ship."

"But *my* ass will depend on whether or not *they* can—"

"Then I suggest you advise well."

"Ye gods."

"The trouble with you, Ti," lectured Leo kindly, "is that you lack teaching experience. If you had it, you'd have faith that the most unlikely people can learn the most amazing things. After all, you weren't born knowing how to pilot a jump—yet lives depended on your doing it right the first time, and every time thereafter. Now you'll know how your instructors felt, that's all."

"How do instructors feel?"

Leo lowered his voice and grinned. "Terrified. Absolutely terrified."

A second pusher, packed with fuel and supplies for its long-range excursion, was waiting in the slot next to theirs as they docked at the Habitat. Leo resisted a strong urge to take Ti aside and fill his ear with advice and suggestions for his mission. Alas, their experience in criminal theft was all too comparable—zero equaled zero no matter how unequal the years each was multiplied by.

They floated through the hatch into the docking module to find several anxious quaddies waiting for them.

"I've modified more solderers, Leo," Pramod began unnecessarily—three of his four hands clutched the improvised arsenal to his torso. "One each for five people."

Claire, hovering at his shoulder, eyed the weapons with dread fascination.

"Good. Give them to Silver. She'll have charge of them until the pusher gets to the wormhole," said Leo.

They made their way down the hand grips to the next hatch. Zara swung within to begin her pre-flight checks.

Ti craned his neck after her nervously. "Are we leaving right now?"

"Time is critical," said Leo. "We don't have more than four hours till you're missed at the transfer station."

"Shouldn't there be a—a briefing, or something?"

Ti too, Leo appreciated, was having trouble committing himself to falling free. Well, *jumped* or *was pushed*, after the initial impulse it would make no practical difference.

"You'll have almost twenty-four hours, boosting at one gee to midpoint and then flipping and braking the rest of the way, to work out your plan of attack. Silver will be depending on your knowledge of the superjumpers. We've already discussed various methods of achieving surprise. She'll fill you in."

"Oh, is Silver going?"

"Silver," Leo enlightened him gently, "is in command."

Ti's face flickered through an array of expressions, settling on dismay. "Screw this. There's still time for me to go back and catch my ship—"

"And *that*," Leo overrode him, "is precisely why Silver is in charge. Your capture of a cargo jumper is the signal for a quaddie uprising here on the Habitat. And that uprising is their death warrant. When GalacTech discovers it cannot control the quaddies, it will almost certainly be frightened into an attempt to violently exterminate them. Escape must be assured before we tip our hand. The ship you must catch is out that way." Leo pointed. "I can depend on Silver to remember that. You"—Leo smiled thinly—"are no worse than anyone else."

Ti subsided at that, although not happily.

Silver, Zara, Siggy, a particularly husky quaddie from the pusher crews named Jon, and Ti. Five, crammed into a ship meant for a crew of two and not designed for overnight use in any case. Leo sighed. The superjumpers carried a pilot and an engineer. Five-to-two wasn't altogether bad odds, but Leo wished he could have loaded them even more overwhelmingly in the quaddies' favor.

They filed through the flex tube into the pusher. Silver, at the end, paused to embrace Pramod and Claire, who had lingered to see them off.

"We're going to get Andy back," Silver murmured to Claire. "You'll see."

Claire nodded, and hugged her hard.

Silver turned last to Leo, who was gazing doubtfully at the flex tube through which the crew he'd drafted had gone.

"I thought the quaddies were going to be the weak link in this hijacking operation," jittered Leo, "now I'm not so sure. Don't let Ti cave on you, eh, Silver? Don't let him bring you down. You have to succeed."

"I know. I'll try. Leo . . . why did you think Ti was in love with me?"

"I don't know. . . . You were intimate—the power of suggestion, maybe. All those romances."

"Ti doesn't read romances, he reads *Ninja of the Twin Stars*."

"Weren't you in love with him? At first, anyway?"

She frowned. "It was exciting, to be beating the rules with him. But Ti is . . . well, is Ti. Love like in the books—I always knew it wasn't really real. When I got to looking around, at our own downsiders, nobody was like that. I guess I was stupid, to like those stories so much."

"I suppose they're not realistic—I haven't read them either, to tell you the truth. But it's not stupid to want something more, Silver."

"More than what?"

More than to be worked over by a lot of self-centered legged louts, that's what. We're not all like that . . . are we? Why, after all, was he being moved *now* to lay a load of his own on her, when she needed all her concentration for the task ahead? Leo shook his head. "Anyway, don't let Ti get confused between his Ninja-whatsit and what you're trying to do, either."

"I don't think even Ti could mistake a company jump-ship crew for the Black League of Eridani," said Silver.

Leo could have wished for more certainty in her tone. "Well . . ." He cleared his throat, inexplicably blocked. "Take care. Don't get hurt."

"You be careful too." She did not hug him, as she had Pramod and Claire.

"Right."

And don't ever believe, his mind cried after her as she vanished into the flex tube, *that nobody could love you, Silver . . .* But it was too late to call the words aloud. The airseal doors shut with a sigh like regret.

Chapter 10

The freight shuttle docking bay was chilly, and Claire rubbed all her hands together to warm them. Only her hands seemed cold; her heart beat hot with anticipation and dread. She looked sideways at Leo, floating as seeming-stolid as ever by the airseal doors with her.

"Thanks, for pulling me off my work shift for this," Claire said. "Are you sure you won't get into trouble, when Mr. Van Atta finds out?"

"Who's to tell him?" said Leo. "Besides, I think Bruce is losing interest in tormenting you. Everything's so obviously futile. All the better for us. Anyway, I want to talk to Tony too, and I figure I'll have a better chance of getting his undivided attention after you've got the reunion-bit over with." He smiled reassuringly.

"I wonder what condition he'll be in?"

"You may be sure he's much better, or Dr. Minchenko wouldn't be subjecting him to the stresses of travel, even to keep him close under his eye."

A thump, and the whir and grind of machinery, told Claire that the shuttle had arrived in its clamps. Her hands reached out, drew in self-consciously. The quaddie manning the control booth waved to two others in the bay, and they locked the flex tubes into position and sealed them. The personnel tube opened first. The shuttle's engineer stuck his head through to double check everything, then whipped back out of sight. Claire's heart lurched in her chest, and her throat constricted dryly.

Dr. Minchenko emerged at last and hovered a moment, one hand anchored to a grip by the hatch. A leathery-faced, vigorous man, his hair was as white as the GalacTech medical service coveralls he wore. He had been a big man, now shrunken to his frame like a withered apricot, but, like a withered apricot, still sound. Claire had the impression he only needed to be re-hydrated and he'd pop back to like-new condition.

Dr. Minchenko shoved off from the hatchway and crossed the bay toward them, landing accurately by the grips around the airseal doors. "Why, hullo, Claire," he said in a surprised voice. "And, ah—Graf," he added less cordially. "You're the one. Let me tell you, I don't appreciate being leaned on to authorize violation of sound medical protocol. You are to spend double time in the gym for the duration of your extension, you hear?"

"Yes, Dr. Minchenko, thank you," said Leo promptly, who was not, as far as Claire knew, spending any time in the gym at all these days. "Where's Tony? Can we help you get him to the infirmary?"

"Ah." He looked more closely at Claire. "I see. Tony's not with me, dear, he's still in hospital downside."

Claire stifled a gasp. "Oh, no—is he worse?"

"Not at all. I had fully intended to bring him with me. In my opinion, he needs free fall to complete his recovery. The problem is, um, administrative, not medical. And I'm on my way right now to resolve it."

"Did Bruce order him kept downside?" asked Leo.

"That's right." He frowned at Leo. "And I'm not pleased to have my medical responsibilities interfered with, either. He'd better have a mighty convincing explanation. Daryl Cay wouldn't have permitted a screw-up like this."

"You, um . . . haven't heard the new orders yet, then?" said Leo carefully, with a warning glance at Claire—*hush*. . . .

"What new orders? I'm on my way to see the little schmuck—that is, the man right now. Get to the bottom of this . . ." He turned to Claire, switching firmly to a kinder tone. "It's all right, we'll get it straightened out. All Tony's internal bleeding is stopped, and there's no further sign of infection. You quaddies are tough. You hold your health much better in gravity than we downsiders do in free fall. Well, we explicitly designed you not to undergo de-conditioning. I could only wish the confirming experiment hadn't happened under such distressing conditions. Of course," he sighed, "youth has something to do with it. . . . Speaking of youth, how's little Andy? Sleeping better for you now?"

Claire almost burst into tears. "I don't know," she squeaked, and swallowed hard.

"What?"

"They won't let me see him."

"What?"

Leo, studying his fingernails distantly, put in, "Andy was removed from Claire's care. On charges of child-endangering, or some such thing. Didn't Bruce tell you that either?"

Dr. Minchenko's face was darkening to a brick-red hue. "Removed? From a breast-feeding mother—obscene!" His eyes swept back over Claire.

"They gave me some medicine to dry me up," explained Claire.

"Well, that's something . . ." His mollification seemed slight. "Who did?"

"Dr. Curry."

"He didn't report it to me."

"You were on leave."

"'On leave' doesn't mean 'incommunicado.' You, Graf! Spit it out. What the hell's going on around here? Has that pocket-martinet lost his mind?"

"You really haven't heard. Well, you'd better ask Bruce. I'm under direct orders not to discuss it."

Minchenko gave Leo a stabbing glare. "I shall." He pushed off and entered the corridor through the airseal doors, muttering under his breath.

Claire and Leo were left looking at each other in dismay.

"How are we going to get Tony back now?" cried Claire. "It's less than twenty-four hours till Silver's signal!"

"I don't know—but don't cave now! Remember Andy. He's going to need you."

"I'm not going to cave," Claire denied. She took a steadying gulp of air. "Not ever again. What can we do?"

"Well, I'll see what strings I can pull, to try and have Tony brought up—bullshit Bruce, tell him I have to have Tony to supervise his welding gang or something—I'm not sure. Maybe Minchenko and I together can work something, though I don't want to risk rousing Minchenko's suspicions. If I can't"—Leo inhaled carefully—"we'll have to work out something else."

"Don't lie to me, Leo," said Claire dangerously.

"Don't leap to conclusions. Yes, I know—you know—the possibility exists that we won't be able to retrieve him, all right, I said it, right out loud. But please note any, er, alternative scenarios depend on Ti to pilot a shuttle for us, and must wait until we re-connect with the hijack crew. At which point we will have captured a jumpship, and I will begin to believe that anything is possible." His brows bent, stressed. "And if it's possible, we'll try it. Promise."

There was a growing coldness in her. She firmed her lips against their tremble. "You can't risk everybody for the sake of just one. That's not right."

"Well . . . there are a thousand things that can go wrong between now and some—point of no return for Tony. It may turn out to be quite academic. I do know, dividing our energies among a thousand what-ifs instead of concentrating them for the one sure next-step is a kind of self-sabotage. It's not what we do next week, it's what we do next that counts most. What must you do next?"

Claire swallowed and tried to pull her wits back together. "Go back to work . . . pretend like nothing's going on. Continue the secret inventory of all possible seed stocks. Uh, finish the plan of how we're going to hook up the grow-lights to keep the plants going while the Habitat is moved away from the sun. And as soon as the Habitat is ours, start the new cuttings and bring the reserve tubes online, to start building up extra food stocks against emergencies. And, uh, arrange cryo-storage of samples of every genetic variety we have on board, to re-stock in case of disaster—"

"That's enough!" Leo smiled encouragement. "The next step only! And you *know* you can do that."

She nodded.

"We need you, Claire," he added. "All of us, not just Andy. Food production is one of the fundamentals of our survival. We'll need every pair, er, every set of expert hands. And you'll have to start training youngsters, passing on that how-to knowledge that the library, no matter how technically complete, can't duplicate."

"I am not going to cave," Claire reiterated through her teeth, answering the undercurrent, not the surface, of his speech.

"You scared me, that time in the airlock," he apologized, embarrassed.

"I scared myself," she admitted.

"You had a right to be angry. Just remember, your true target isn't in here—" he touched her collarbone, above her heart, fleetingly. "It's out there."

So, he had recognized it was rage, rage blocked and turned inward, and not despair that had brought her to the airlock that day. In a way, it was a relief to put the right name to her emotion. In a way it was not.

"Leo . . . that scares me too."

He smiled quizzically. "Welcome to the human club."

"The next step," she muttered. "Right. The next *reach*." She gave Leo a wave and swung into the corridor.

Leo turned back to the freight bay with a sigh. The next-step speech was all very well, except when people and changing conditions kept switching your route around in front of you while your foot was in the air. His gaze lingered a moment on the quaddie docking crew, who had connected the flex tube to the shuttle's large freight hatch and were unloading the cargo into the bay with their power handlers. The cargo consisted of man-high gray cylinders that Leo did not at first recognize.

But the cargo wasn't supposed to be unrecognizable.

The cargo was supposed to be a massive stock of spare cargo-pusher fuel rods. "For dismantling the Habitat," Leo had sung dulcetly to Van Atta, when jamming the requisition through. "So I won't have to stop and reorder. So what if we have leftovers, they can go to the transfer station with the pushers when they're relocated. Credit them to the salvage."

Disturbed, Leo drifted over to the cargo workers. "What's this, kids?"

"Oh, Mr. Graf, hello. Well, I'm not quite sure," said the quaddie boy in the canary-yellow T-shirt and shorts of Air-systems Maintenance, of which Docks & Locks was a subdivision. "I don't think I've ever seen it before. It's massive, anyway." He paused to unhook a report panel from his power-handler and gave it to Leo. "There's the freight manifest."

"It was supposed to be cargo-pusher fuel rods. . . ." The cylinders *were* about the right size. They surely couldn't have redesigned them. Leo tapped the manifest keypad—item, a string of code numbers, quantity, astronomical.

"They gurgle," the yellow-shirted quaddie added helpfully.

"Gurgle?" Leo looked at the code number on the report panel more closely, glanced at the gray cylinders—they matched. Yet he recognized the code for the pusher rods—or did he? He entered 'Fuel Rods, Orbital Cargo Pusher Type II, cross ref, inventory code.' The report panel blinked and a number popped up. Yes, it was the same—no, by God! G77618PD, versus the G77681PD emblazoned on the cylinders. Quickly he tapped in 'G77681PD.' There was a long pause, not for the report panel but for Leo's brain to register.

"Gasoline?" Leo croaked in disbelief. "*Gasoline?* Those idiots actually shipped a hundred tons of gasoline to a space station . . . ?"

"What is it?" asked the quaddie.

"Gasoline. It's a hydrocarbon fuel used downside, to power their land rovers. A freebie by-product from the petrochemical cracking. Atmospheric oxygen provides the oxidant. It's a bulky, toxic, volatile, flammable—explosive!—liquid at room temperature. For God's sake don't let any of those barrels get open."

"Yes, *sir*," promised the quaddie, clearly impressed with Leo's list of hazards.

The legged supervisor of the orbital pusher crews arrived at that moment in the bay, trailed by a gang of quaddies from his department.

"Oh, hello, Graf. Look, I think it was a mistake letting you talk me into ordering this load—we're going to have a storage problem—"

"Did you order this?" Leo demanded.

"What?" the supervisor blinked, then took in the scene before him. "What the—where are my fuel rods? They told me they were here."

"I mean did you, personally, place the order. With your own little fingers."

"Yes. You asked me to, remember?"

"Well"—Leo took a breath, and handed him the report panel—"you made a typo."

The super glanced at the report panel and paled. "Oh, God."

"And they did it," Leo gibbered, running his hands through what was left of his hair. "They filled it—I can't believe they filled it. Loaded all this stuff onto the shuttle without once questioning it, sent a hundred tons of gasoline to a space station without *once* noticing that it was utterly absurd. . . ."

"I can believe it," sighed the super. "Oh, God. Oh, well. We'll just have to send it back, and reorder. It'll probably take about a week. It's not like our fuel rod stocks are really low, in spite of the rate you've been using them up for that 'special project' you're so hushy-hush about."

I don't have a week, thought Leo frantically. *I have twenty-four hours, maybe.*

"I don't have a week," Leo found himself raging. "I want them *now*. Put it on a rush order." He lowered his voice, realizing he was becoming conspicuous.

The super was offended enough to overcome his guilt. "There's no need to throw a fit, Graf. It was my mistake and I'll probably have to pay for it, but it's plain stupid to charge my department for a rush shuttle trip on top of this one when we can perfectly well wait. This is going to be bad enough as it is." He waved at the gasoline. "Hey, kids," he added, "stop unloading! This load's a mistake, it's all gotta go back downside."

The shuttle pilot was just exiting the personnel hatch in time to hear this. "What?" He floated over to them, and Leo gave him a brief explanation in very short words of the error.

"Well, you can't send it back this trip," said the shuttle pilot firmly. "I'm not fueled up to take a full load. It'll have to wait." He shoved off, to take his mandatory safety break in the cafeteria.

The quaddie cargo handlers looked quite reproachful, as the direction of their work was reversed for the second time. But they limited their implied criticism to a plaintive, "Are you sure now, sir?"

"Yes," sighed Leo. "But find some place to store this stuff in a detached module. You can't leave it in here."

"Yes, sir."

Leo turned again to the pusher crew supervisor. "I've still got to have those fuel rods."

"Well, you'll just have to wait. I won't do it. Van Atta's going to have enough of my blood for this already."

"You can charge it to my special project. I'll sign for it."

The super raised his eyebrows, slightly consoled. "Well . . . I'll try, all right, I'll try. But what about your blood?"

Already sold, thought Leo. "That's my look-out, isn't it?"

The super shrugged. "I guess." He exited, muttering. One of the pusher crew quaddies, trailing him, gave Leo a significant look; Leo returned a severe shake of his head, emphasized by a throat-cutting gesture with his index finger, indicating, Silence!

He turned and nearly rammed Pramod, waiting patiently at his shoulder. "Don't sneak up on me like that!" he yelped, then got better control of his fraying nerves. "Sorry, you startled me. What is it?"

"We've run into a problem, Leo."

"But of course. Who ever tracks me down to impart good news? Never mind. What is it?"

"Clamps."

"Clamps?"

"There're a lot of clamped connections Outside. We were going over the flow chart for the Habitat disassembly, for, um, tomorrow, you know—"

"I know, don't say it."

"We thought a little practice might speed things up."

"Yes, good . . ."

"Hardly any of the clamps will unclamp. Even with power tools."

"Uh . . ." Leo paused, taken aback, then realized what the problem was. "Metal clamps?"

"Mostly."

"Worse on the sun side?"

"Much worse. We couldn't get any of those to come at all. Some of them are visibly fused. Some idiot must have welded them."

"Welded, yes. But not by some idiot. By the sun."

"Leo, it doesn't get *that* hot—"

"Not directly. What you're seeing is spontaneous vacuum diffusion welding. Metal molecules are evaporating off the surfaces of the pieces in the vacuum. Slowly, to be sure, but it's a measurable phenomenon. On the clamped areas they migrate into their neighboring surfaces and eventually achieve quite a nice bond. A little faster for the hot pieces on the sun side, a little slower for the cold pieces in the shade—but I'll bet some of those clamps have been in place for twenty years."

"Oh. But what do we do about them?"

"They'll have to be cut."

Pramod's lips pursed in worry. "That will slow things down."

"Yeah. And we'll have to have a way set up to re-clamp each connection in the new configuration, too . . . gonna need more clamps, or something that can be made to work as clamps. . . . Go round up all your off-shift work gang. We're going to have to have a little emergency scrounging session."

Leo stopped wondering if he was going to survive the Great Takeover, and started wondering if he was going to survive *until* the Great Takeover. He prayed devoutly that Silver was having an easier time of it than himself.

Silver hoped earnestly that Leo was having an easier time of it than herself.

She hitched herself around in the acceleration couch, increasingly uncomfortable after their first eight hours of flight, and rested her chin on the padding to regard her crew, crammed in the pusher's cabin. The other quaddies were drooped and draped as she was; only Ti seemed comfortable, feet propped up and leaning back in his seat in the steady gee-forces.

"I saw this great holovid"—Siggy waved some hands enthusiastically—"that had a boarding battle. The marines used magnetic mines to blow holes like bubble cheese in the side of the mothership and just poured through." He added a weird ululating cry for sound effects. "The aliens were running every which way, stuff flying everywhere as the air blew out—"

"I saw that one," said Ti. "*Nest of Doom*, right?"

"You got it for us," reminded Silver.

"Did you know it had a sequel?" said Ti aside to Siggy. "*The Nest's Revenge.*"

"No, really? Do you suppose—"

"First of all," said Silver, "nobody has found any intelligent aliens yet, hostile or not, secondly, we don't have any magnetic mines," *thanks be*, "and thirdly, I don't think Ti wants a lot of unsightly holes blown in the side of his ship."

"Well, no," conceded Ti.

"We will go in through the airlock," said Silver firmly, "which was designed for just that purpose. I think the jumpship crew will be surprised enough when we put them in their escape pod and launch it, without, um, frightening them into doing who-knows-what with a lot of premature whooping. Even if Colonel Wayne in *Nest of Doom* led his troops into battle with his rebel yell over their com links, I don't think real marines would do that. It would be bound to interfere with their communications." She frowned Siggy into submission.

"We'll just do it Leo's way," Silver went on, "and point the laser-solderers at them. They don't know us—they wouldn't know whether we'd fire or not." How, after all, could strangers know what she didn't know herself? "Speaking of which, how do we know which superjumper to," she groped for terminology, "cut out of the herd? It ought to be easier to get permission to come aboard if the crew's someone Ti knows well. On the other hand, it might be harder to . . ." She trailed off, disliking the thought. "Especially if they tried to fight back."

"Jon could wrestle them into submission," offered Ti. "That's what he's here for, after all."

Husky Jon gave him a woeful look. "I thought I was here as the pusher backup pilot. You wrestle them if you want—they're your friends. I'll hold a solderer."

Ti cleared his throat. "Anyway, I'd like to get D771, if it's there. We aren't going to have much choice, though. There's only likely to be a couple of superjumpers working this side of the wormhole at any one time anyway. Basically, we go for whatever ship that's just jumped over from Orient IV and dumped its empty pod bundles, and hasn't started to load on new ones yet. That'll give us the quickest getaway. There's not that much to plan, we just go *do* it."

"The real trouble will start," said Silver, "when they've figured out what we're really up to and start trying to take the ship back."

A glum silence fell. For the moment, even Siggy had no suggestions.

Leo found Van Atta in the downsiders' gym, tramping determinedly on the treadmill. The treadmill was a medical torture device like a rack in reverse. Spring-loaded straps pulled the walker toward the tread surface, against which his or her feet pushed, for an hour or more a day by prescription, an exercise designed to slow, if not stop, the lower body deconditioning and long bone demineralization of free fall dwellers.

By the expression on Van Atta's face he was stamping out the measured treads today with considerable personal animosity. Cultivated irritation was indeed one way to muster the energy to tackle the boring but necessary task. After a moment's thoughtful study Leo decided upon a casual and oblique approach. He slipped out of his coveralls and velcroed them to the wall-strip, retaining his red T-shirt and shorts, and floated over and hooked himself into the belt and straps of the unoccupied machine next to Van Atta's.

"Have they been lubricating these things with glue?" he puffed, grasping the hand holds and straining to start the treads moving against his feet.

Van Atta turned his head and grinned sardonically. "What's the matter, Leo? Did Minchenko the medical minidictator order a little physiological revenge on you?"

"Yeah, something like that . . ." He got it started at last, his legs flexing in an even rhythm. He *had* skipped too many sessions lately. "Have you talked to him since he came up?"

"Yeah." Van Atta's legs drove against his machine, and angry whirring spurted from its gears.

"Have you told him what's going to be happening to the Project yet?"

"Unfortunately, I had to. I'd hoped to put him off to the last, with the rest. Minchenko is probably the most arrogant of Cay's Old Guard—he's never made it a secret that he thought he should have succeeded Cay as Head of Project, instead of bringing in an outsider, namely me. If he hadn't been slated for retirement in a year, I'd damn well have taken steps to get rid of him before this."

"Did he, ah—voice objections?"

"You mean, did he yowl like a stuck pig? You bet he did. Carried on like *I* was personally responsible for inventing the damned artificial gravity. I don't need this shit." Van Atta's treadmill moaned in counterpoint to his words.

"If he's been with the Project from the beginning, I guess the quaddies are practically his life's work," allowed Leo reasonably.

"Mm." Van Atta marched. "It doesn't give him the right to go on strike in a snit, though. Even you had more sense, in the end. If he doesn't show signs of a more cooperative attitude when he's had a chance to calm down and think through how useless it is, it may be easier to extend Curry's rotation and just send Minchenko back downside."

"Ah." Leo cleared his throat. This didn't exactly smell like the good opening he'd been hoping for. But there was so little time. "Did he talk to you about Tony?"

"Tony!" Van Atta's treadmill buzzed like a hornet for a moment. "If I never see that little geek again in my life it will be too soon. He's been nothing but trouble, trouble and expense."

"I was rather hoping to get some more use out of him, myself," said Leo carefully. "Even if he's not medically ready to go back on regular Outside work shifts, I've got a lot of computer console work and supervisory tasks I could delegate to him, if he was here. If we could bring him up."

"Nonsense," snapped Van Atta. "You could much more easily tap one of your other quaddie work gang leaders— Pramod, say—or pull any quaddie in the place. I don't care who, that's what I gave you the authorization for. We're going to start moving the little freaks *down* in just two weeks. It makes no sense to bring up one Minchenko wouldn't let out of the infirmary till then. And so I told him." He glared at Leo. "I don't want to hear one more word about Tony."

"Ah," said Leo. Damn. Clearly, he should have taken Minchenko aside before he'd muddied the waters with Van Atta. Too late now. It wasn't just the exercise that was making Van Atta red in the face. Leo wondered what all Minchenko had really said—doubtless pretty choice, it would have been a pleasure to hear. Too expensive a pleasure for the quaddies, though. Leo schooled his features to what he hoped would be read through his puffing and blowing as sympathy for Van Atta.

"How's the salvage planning going?" asked Van Atta after a while.

"Almost complete."

"Oh, really?" Van Atta brightened. "Well, that's something, at least."

"You'll be amazed at how totally the Habitat can be recycled," Leo promised with perfect truth. "So will the company brass."

"And fast?"

"Just as soon as we get the go-ahead. I've got it laid out like a war game." He closed his teeth on further double entendres. "You still planning the grand announcement to the rest of the staff at thirteen-hundred tomorrow?" Leo inquired casually. "In the main lecture module? I really want to be in on that. I have a few visual aids to present when you're done."

"Naw," said Van Atta.

"What?" Leo gulped. He missed a step, and the springs slammed him painfully down on one knee on the treadmill, padded against just such clumsiness. He struggled back to his feet.

"Did you hurt yourself?" said Van Atta. "You look funny...."

"I'll be all right in a minute." He stood, leg muscles straining against the elastic pull, regaining his breath and equilibrium in the face of pain and panic. "I thought—that was how you were going to drop the shoe. Get everybody together, just go over the facts once."

"After Minchenko, I'm tired of arguing about it," said Van Atta. "I've told Yei to do it. She can call them into her office in small groups, and hand out the individual and department evacuation schedules at the same time. Much more efficient."

And so Leo and Silver's beautiful scheme for peacefully detaching the downsiders, hammered out through four secret planning sessions, was blown away on a breath. Wasted was the flattery, the oblique suggestion, that had gone into convincing Van Atta that it was his idea to gather, unusually, the entire Habitat downsider staff at once and make his announcement in a speech persuading them all they were being commended, not condemned....

The shaped charges to cut the lecture module away from the Habitat at the touch of a button were all in place. The emergency breath masks to supply the nearly three hundred bodies with oxygen for the few hours necessary to push the module around the planet to the transfer station were carefully hidden within. The two pusher crews were drilled, their pushers fueled and ready.

Fool he had been, to lay plans that depended on Van Atta following through on anything.... Leo felt suddenly sick.

It was going to have to be the second-choice plan, then, the emergency one they'd discussed and discarded as too risky, too potentially uncontrolled in its results. Numbly, he detached his springs and harness and hooked them back in their slots on the treadmill frame.

"That wasn't an hour," said Van Atta.

"I think I did something to my knee," lied Leo.

"I'm not surprised. Think I didn't know you've been skipping exercise sessions? Just don't try to sue GalacTech, 'cause we can prove personal neglect." Van Atta grinned and marched on virtuously.

Leo paused. "By the way, did you know that Rodeo Warehousing just mis-shipped the Habitat a hundred tons of gasoline? And they're charging it to us."

"What?"

As Leo turned away he had the small vindictive satisfaction of hearing Van Atta's treadmill stop and the snap of a too-hastily-detached harness rebounding to slap its wearer. "Ow!" Van Atta cried.

Leo did not look back.

Dr. Curry met Claire as she arrived for her appointment at the infirmary. "Oh, good, you're just on time."

Claire glanced up and down the corridor, and her eyes searched the treatment room into which Dr. Curry shoo'd her. "Where's Dr. Minchenko? I thought he'd be here."

Dr. Curry flushed faintly. "Dr. Minchenko is in his quarters. He won't be coming on duty."

"But I wanted to talk to him."

Dr. Curry cleared his throat. "Did they tell you what your appointment was for?"

"No . . . I supposed it was for more medication for my breasts."

"Ah, I see."

Claire waited a moment, but he did not expand further. He busied himself, laying out a tray of instruments by their velcro collars and placing them in the sterilizer, not meeting Claire's eyes. "Well, it's quite painless."

Once, she might have asked no questions, docilely submitting—she had undergone thousands of obscure medical tests starting even before she had been freed as an infant from the uterine replicator, the artificial womb that had gestated her in a now-closed section of this very infirmary. Once, she had been another person, before the downside disaster with Tony. For a little time thereafter she had hovered close to being no one at all. Now she felt strangely thrilled, as if she trembled on the edge of a new birth. Her first had been mechanical and painless; perhaps that was why it had failed to take root. . . .

"What—" she began to squeak. Too tiny a voice. She raised it, loud in her own ears. "What is this appointment for?"

"Just a small local abdominal procedure," said Dr. Curry airily. "It won't take long. You don't even have to get undressed, just roll up your shirt and push down your shorts a bit. I'll prep you. You have to be immobilized under the sterile-air-flow shield, in case a drop or two of blood gets on the loose."

You're not immobilizing me . . . "What is the procedure?"

"It won't hurt, and will do you no harm at all. Come on over, now." He smiled, and tapped the shield unit, which folded out from the wall.

"What?" repeated Claire, not moving.

"I can't discuss it. It's—classified. Sorry. You'll have to ask—Mr. Van Atta, or Dr. Yei, or somebody. Tell you what, I'll send you over to Dr. Yei right after, and you can talk to her, all right?" He licked his lips; his smile grew steadily more nervous.

"I wouldn't ask . . ." Claire groped after a phrase she had heard a downsider use once, "I wouldn't ask Bruce Van Atta for the time of day."

Dr. Curry looked quite startled. "Oh." And muttered, not quite under his breath, "I wondered why you were second on the list."

"Who was first on the list?" asked Claire.

"Silver, but that engineering instructor has her on some kind of assignment. Friend of yours, right? You'll be able to tell her it doesn't hurt."

"I don't care—I don't give a *damn* if it hurts, I want to know what it *is*." Her eyes narrowed, as the connections clicked at last, then widened in outrage. "The sterilizations," she breathed. "You're starting the sterilizations!"

"How did you—you weren't supposed—I mean, whatever makes you think that?" gulped Curry.

She dodged for the doorway. He was closer and quicker, and sealed it in front of her nose. She caromed off the closing panel.

"Now, Claire, calm down!" panted Curry, zigzagging after her. "You'll only hurt yourself, totally unnecessarily. I can put you under a general anesthetic, but it's better for you to use a local, and just lie still. You do have to lie still. I have to do this, one way or another—"

"Why do you *have* to do this?" cried Claire. "Did Dr. Minchenko *have* to do this—or is that why he isn't here? Who's making you, and how, that you *have* to?"

"If Minchenko was here, I *wouldn't* have to," snapped Curry, infuriated. "He ducked out and left me holding the bag. Now come over here and position yourself under the steri-shield, and let me set up the scanners, or I'll have to get—get quite *firm* with you." He inhaled deeply, psyching himself up.

"Have to," Claire taunted, "have to, have to! It's amazing, some of the things downsiders think they have to do. But they're almost never the same things they think quaddies have to do. Why is that, do you suppose?"

His breath woofed out, and his lips tightened angrily. He plucked a hypodermic off his tray of instruments.

He laid it out in advance, Claire thought. *He's rehearsed this, in his mind—he made his mind up before I ever got here. . . .*

He launched himself over to where she hovered, and grabbed her left upper arm, stabbing the needle towards it in a swift silver arc. She grabbed his right wrist, slowing it to a straining standstill; so they were locked for a moment, muscles trembling, tumbling slowly in the air.

Then she brought up her lower arms to join her uppers. Curry gasped in surprise, and for breath, as she parted his arms wide, overpowering even his young male torso. He kicked, his knees thumping her, but with nothing to push against he couldn't drive them with enough force to really hurt.

She grinned in wild exhilaration, brought his arms in, out again at will. *I'm stronger! I'm stronger! I'm stronger than him and I never even knew it. . . .*

Carefully, she locked her power-gripping lower hands around his wrists, and freed her uppers. Both hands working together easily peeled his clutching fingers from the hypodermic. She held it up and crooned, "This won't hurt a bit."

"No, no—"

He was wriggling too much for her inexperience to try for a swift venous injection, so she went for a deltoid muscle instead, and went on holding him until he grew woozy and weak, which took several minutes. After that, it was easy to immobilize him under the steri-shield.

She looked over his tray of instruments, and touched them wonderingly. "How far should I carry this turnabout, do you think?" she asked aloud.

He whimpered in his wooziness and twitched feebly against the soft restraints, panic in his eyes. Claire's eyes lit; she threw back her head and laughed, really laughed, for the first time in—how long? She couldn't remember.

She put her lips near his ear, and spoke clearly. "*I don't have to.*"

She was still laughing softly when she sealed the doors to the treatment room behind her and flew down the corridor toward refuge.

Chapter 11

It had been a mistake to let Ti insist on docking to the superjumper, Silver realized, as the crunch and shudder of their impact with the docking clamps reverberated through the pusher. Zara, hovering anxiously, emitted a tiny moan. Ti snarled wordlessly over his shoulder at her, returned his fraying attention to the controls.

No—*her* mistake, to let his downsider, male, legged authority override her own reason—she knew he wasn't rated for these pushers, he'd told her so himself. He was only the authority after they got inside the superjumper.

No, she told herself firmly, *not even then*.

"Zara," she called, "take the controls."

"Dammit," Ti began, "if you'd just—"

"We need Ti too much on the com channels to spare him for piloting," Silver inserted, hoping desperately Ti would not spurn this offered sop for his pride.

"Mm." Grudgingly, Ti let Zara shoulder him aside.

The flex tube docking ring wouldn't seal properly. A second docking, and all the hopeful jiggling the auto-waldos could supply, couldn't make the locking ring seal properly. Silver either feared she would die, or wished she could, she wasn't sure. All her palms sweated, and transferring the laser-solderer from one to another only made the grip clammier.

"See," said Ti to Zara, "you can't do any better."

Zara glared at him. "You bent one of the rings, you dipstick. You better hope it's theirs and not ours."

"That's 'dipshit,'" Jon, laboring back by the hatch trying to make it seal, corrected helpfully. "If you're going to use downsider terminology, get it right."

"Pusher R-26 calling GalacTech Superjumper D-620," Ti quavered into the com. "Von, we're going to have to disengage and come around to the other side. This isn't working."

"Go ahead, Ti," came the jump pilot's voice in return. "Are you sick? You don't sound so good. That was a miserable docking. Just what *is* this emergency, anyway?"

"I'll explain when we're aboard." Ti glanced up, got a confirming nod from Zara. "Disengaging now."

Their luck was better on the starboard hatch. *No*, Silver reminded herself again. *We make our own luck. And it's my responsibility to see it's good and not bad.*

Ti pushed through the flex tube first. The jumpship's engineer was waiting for him on the other side. Silver could hear his angry voice, "Gulik, you bent our portside docking ring. You wireheads all think you're Mr. Twinkletoes when you're plugged into your sets, but on manual you are, without exception, the most ham-handed—" He broke off, his voice thinning out in a little hiss, as Silver flitted through the hatch and hovered, her laser-solderer pointed sturdily at his stomach. It actually took him a moment to notice the weapon. His eyes widened and his mouth opened as Siggy and Jon backed her up from behind.

"Take us to where the pilot is, Ti," said Silver. She hoped the fear that edged her voice made her sound angry and fierce, not pale and weak. All her strength seemed washed out of her, leaving her limp-stomached. She swallowed and took a tighter grip on the solderer.

"What the hell is this?" began the engineer, his voice a taut octave higher than before. He cleared his throat and brought it back down. "Who are you . . . people, anyway? Gulik, are they with you?"

Ti shrugged and produced a sickly smile that was either very well acted, or real. "Not exactly. I'm kind of with them."

Siggy, reminded, pointed his solderer at Ti. Silver, when approving this ploy, had kept her inner thoughts about it most secret. Going in with Ti unarmed, apparently under the quaddies' guns, covered him in case of later capture and legal prosecution. Equally, it disguised the possibility of making his ersatz kidnapping real, should he decide to bolt back to the side of his legged companions at the last moment. Wheels within wheels; did all leaders have to think on multiple levels? It made her head hurt.

They filed quickly through the compact crew's section to Nav and Com. The jump pilot sat enthroned in his padded chair, plugged into the massive crown of his control headset, a temporary, regal cyborg. His purple company coveralls were stitched with gaudy patches proudly proclaiming his rank and specialization. His eyes were closed, and he hummed tunelessly in time to the throbbing biofeedback from his ship.

He yelped in surprise as his headset detached and rose, cutting his communion with his machine, when Ti thumbed the disconnect control. "God, Ti, don't *do* things like that—you know better—" A second yelp at the sight of the quaddies was swallowed with a gulp. He smiled at Silver in complete bewilderment, his eyes, after one shocked pass over her anatomy, locked politely on her face. She wriggled the laser-solderer, to bring it to his attention.

"Get out of your chair," she ordered.

He shrank back into it. "Look, lady . . . uh . . . what is that?"

"Laser gun. Get out of your chair."

His eyes measured her, measured Ti, flicked to his engineer. His hand stole to his seat harness buckle, hesitated. His muscles tensed.

"Get out slowly," Silver added.

"Why?" he asked.

Stalling, Silver thought.

"These people want to borrow your ship," Ti explained.

"Hijackers!" breathed the engineer. He coiled, floating in his position near the airseal door. Jon's and Siggy's solderers swivelled toward him. "Mutants . . ."

"Get *out*," Silver repeated, her voice rising uncontrollably.

The pilot's face was drawn and thoughtful. His hands floated from his belt to rest in a parody of relaxation over his knees. "What if I don't?" he challenged softly.

She fancied she could feel control of the situation slipping from her to him, sucked up by his superior imitation of coolness. She glanced at Ti, but he was staying safely and firmly in his part of helpless—and unhelpful—victim, *lying low* as the downsiders phrased it.

A heartbeat passed, another, another. The pilot began to relax, visibly in his long exhalation, a smug light of triumph in his eyes. He had her number; he knew she could not fire.

His hand went to his belt buckle, and his legs curled under him, seeking launch leverage.

She had rehearsed it in her mind so many times, the actual event was almost an anticlimax. It had a glassy clarity, as if she observed herself from a distance, or from another time, future or past. The moment shaped the choice of target, something she had turned over and over without decision before; she sighted the solderer at a point just below his knees because no valuable control surfaces lay behind them.

Pressing the button was surprisingly easy, the work of one small muscle in her upper right thumb. The beam was dull blue, not enough to even make her blink, though a brief bright yellow flame flared at the edge of the melted fabric of his supposedly nonflammable coveralls, then winked out. Her nostrils twitched with the stink of the burnt fabric, more pungent than the smell of burnt flesh. Then the pilot was bent over himself, screaming.

Ti was babbling, voice strained, "What d'ja do that for? He was still strapped to his *chair*, Silver!" His eyes were wells of astonishment. The engineer, after a first convulsive movement, froze in a submissive ball, eyes flickering from quaddie to quaddie. Siggy's mouth hung open; Jon's was a tight line.

The pilot's screams frightened her, swelled up her nerves to lance through her head. She pointed the solderer at him again. "Stop that noise!" she demanded.

Amazingly, he stopped. His breath whistled past his clenched teeth as he twisted his head to stare at her through pain-slitted eyes. The centers of the burns across his legs seemed to be cauterized, shadowed black and ambiguous— she was torn between revulsion, and the curious desire to go take a closer look at what she had done. The edges of the burns were swelling red, yellow plasma already seeping through but clinging to his skin, no need for a hand-vac. The injury did not seem to be immediately life-threatening.

"Siggy, unstrap him and get him out of that control chair," Silver ordered. For once, Siggy zipped to obey with no argument, not even a suggestion of how to do it better gleaned from his holodrama viewing.

In fact, the effect of her action on everyone present, not just their captives, was most gratifying. Everyone moved faster. *This could get addictive*, Silver thought. No arguments, no complaints—

Some complaints. "Was that necessary?" Ti asked, as the prisoners were bundled ahead of them through the corridor. "He was getting out of his seat for you . . ."

"He was going to try to jump me."

"You can't be sure of that."

"I didn't think I could hit him once he was moving."

"It's not like you had no choice—"

She turned toward him with a snap; he flinched away. "If we do not succeed in taking this ship, a thousand of my friends are going to die. I had a choice. I chose. I'd choose again. You got that?" *And you choose for everybody, Silver,* Leo's voice echoed in her memory.

Ti subsided instantly. "Yes, ma'am."

Yes, *ma'am?* Silver blinked, and pushed ahead of him to hide her confusion. Her hands were shaking in reaction now. She entered the life-pod first, ostensibly to yank all the communications equipment but for the emergency directional finder beeper, and to check for the first-aid kit—it was there, and complete—also to be alone for a moment, away from the wide eyes of her companions.

Was this the pleasure in power Van Atta felt, when everyone gave way before him? It was obvious what firing the weapon had done to the defiant pilot; what had it done to her? For every action, an equal and opposite reaction. This was a somatic truth, visceral knowledge ingrained in every quaddie from birth, clear and demonstrable in every motion.

She exited the pod. A hoarse moan broke from the pilot's lips as his legs accidentally bumped against the hatch, as they stuffed him and the engineer through into the life-pod, sealed it, and fired it away from the jumpship.

Silver's agitation gave way to a cool pool of resolve within her, even though her hands still trembled with distress for the pilot's pain. So. Quaddies were no different than downsiders after all. Any evil they could do, quaddies could do too. If they chose.

There. By placing the grow-tubes at this angle, with a six-hour rotation, they could get by with four fewer spectrum lights in the hydroponics module and still have enough lumens falling on the leaves to trigger flowering in fourteen days. Claire entered the command on her lap board computer and made the analog model cycle all the way through once on fast-forward, just to be sure. The new growth configuration would cut the power drain of the module by some twelve percent from her first estimate. Good: for until the Habitat reached its destination and they unfurled the delicate solar collectors again, power would be at a premium.

She shut off the lap board and sighed. That was the last of the planning tasks she could do while still locked up here in the Clubhouse. It was a good hiding place, but too quiet. Concentration had been horribly difficult, but having nothing to do, she discovered as the seconds crept on, was worse. She floated over to the cupboard and took a pack of raisins and ate them one at a time. When she finished the gluey silence closed back in.

She imagined holding Andy again, his warm little fingers clutching hers in mutual security, and wished for Silver to hurry up and send her signal. She pictured Tony, medically imprisoned downside, and hoped in anguish Silver might delay, that by some miracle they might yet regain him at the last minute. She didn't know whether to push or pull at the passing minutes, only that each one seemed to physically pelt her.

The airseal doors hissed, jolting her with anxiety. Was she discovered—? No, it was three quaddie girls, Emma, Patty, and Kara the infirmary aide.

"Is it time?" Claire asked hoarsely.

Kara shook her head.

"Why doesn't it start, what's keeping Silver . . ." Claire broke off. She could imagine all too many disastrous reasons for Silver's delay.

"She'd better signal soon," said Kara. "The hunt is up all over the Habitat for you. Mr. Wyzak, the Airsystems Maintenance supervisor, finally thought of looking behind the walls. They're over in the docking bay section now. Everybody on his crew is having the most terrific outbreak of clumsiness"—a curved moon of a grin winked in her face—"but they'll be working this way eventually."

Emma gripped one of Kara's lower arms. "In that case, is this really the best place for *us* to hide?"

"It'll have to do, for now. I hope things break before Dr. Curry works all the way down his list, or it's going to get awfully crowded in here," said Kara.

"Is Dr. Curry recovered, then?" asked Claire, not certain if she wanted to hear a yes or a no. "Enough to do surgery? I'd hoped he'd be out longer."

Kara giggled. "Not exactly. He's kind of hanging there all squinty-eyed and puffy, just supervising while the nurse gives the injections. Or he would be, if they could find any of the girls to give injections to."

"Injections?"

"Abortifacient." Kara grimaced.

"Oh. A different list from mine, then." So, that was why Emma and Patty looked pale, as from a narrow escape.

Kara sighed. "Yeah. Well, we're all on one list or another, in the end, I guess." She slipped back out.

Claire was cheered by the company of the other two quaddies, even though it represented a growing danger of discovery not only of themselves but of their plans. How much more could go wrong before the Habitat's downsider staff started asking the right questions? Suppose the entire plot was discovered prematurely, following up the loose end she'd left? Should she have submitted docilely to Curry's procedure, just to keep the secret a little longer? Suppose "a little longer" was all it took to make the difference between success and disaster?

"Now what, I wonder?" said Emma in a thin voice.

"Just wait. Unless you brought something to do," said Claire.

Emma shook her head. "Kara just grabbed me off my work shift in Small Repairs about ten minutes ago. I didn't think to bring anything."

"She got me out of my sleep sack," Patty confirmed. A yawn escaped her despite the tension. "I'm so tired, these days . . ."

Emma rubbed her abdomen absently with her lower palms in a circular motion familiar to Claire; so, the girls had already started childbirth training.

"I wonder how all this is going to go," sighed Emma. "How it will turn out. Where we'll all be in seven months . . ."

Hardly a figure chosen at random, Claire realized. "Away from Rodeo, anyway. Or dead."

"If we're dead, we won't have a problem," Patty said. "If not . . . Claire, how is labor? What's it *really* like?" Her eyes were urgent, seeking reassurance from Claire's expertise, as the sole initiate present in the maternal mysteries of the body.

Claire, understanding, responded, "It wasn't exactly comfortable, but it's nothing you can't handle. Dr. Minchenko says we have it a lot better than downsider women. We have a more flexible pelvis with a wider arch, and our pelvic floor is more elastic, on account of not having to fight the gravitational forces. He says that was his own design idea, like eliminating the hymen—whatever that was. Something painful, I gather."

"Ugh, poor things," said Emma. "I wonder if their babies ever get sucked from their bodies by the gravity?"

"I never heard of such a thing," said Claire doubtfully. "He did say they had trouble close to term with the weight of the baby cutting off circulation and squeezing their nerves and organs and things."

"I'm glad I wasn't born a downsider," said Emma. "At least not a female one. Think of the poor downsider mothers who have to worry about their helpers dropping their newborns." She shuddered.

"It's horrible, down there," Claire confirmed fervently, remembering. "It's worth risking anything, not to have to go there. Truly."

"But we'll be by ourselves, in seven months, that is," said Patty. "You had help. You had Dr. Minchenko. Emma and me—we'll be all alone."

"No, you won't," said Claire. "What a nasty thought. Kara will be there—I'll come—we'll all help."

"Leo will be coming with us," Emma offered, trying to sound optimistic. "He's a downsider."

"I'm not sure that's exactly his field of expertise," said Claire honestly, trying to picture Leo as a medtech. He didn't care for hydraulic systems, he'd said. She went on more firmly, "Anyway, all the complicated stuff in Andy's birth mostly had to do with data collecting, because I was one of the first, and they were working out the procedures, Dr. Minchenko said. Just having the baby wasn't all that much. Dr. Minchenko didn't do it—really, I didn't do it, my body did. About all he did was hold the hand-vac. Messy, but straightforward." *If nothing goes wrong biologically,* she thought, and had the last-minute wit not to say aloud.

Patty still looked unhappy. "Yes, but birth is only the beginning. Working for GalacTech kept us busy, but we've been working three times as hard since this escape-thing came up. And you'd have to be a dim bulb not to see it's going to get harder later. There's no end in sight. How are we going to handle it all and babies too? I'm not sure I think much of this freedom-stuff. Leo talks it up, but freedom for who? Not me. I had more free time working for the company."

"You want to go report to Dr. Curry?" suggested Emma.

Patty shrugged uncomfortably. "No . . ."

"I don't think by freedom he means free time," said Claire thoughtfully. "More like survival. Like—like not having to work for people who have a right to shoot us if they want." A twinge of harsh memory edged her voice, and she softened it self-consciously. "We'll still have to work, but it will be for ourselves. And our children."

"Mostly our children," said Patty glumly.

"That's not all bad," remarked Emma.

Claire thought she caught a glimpse of the source of Patty's pessimism. "And next time—if you want a next time—*you* can choose who will father your baby. There won't be anybody around to tell you."

Patty brightened visibly. "That's true."

Claire's reassurances seemed effective; the talk drifted to less threatening channels for a while. Much later, the airseal doors parted, and Pramod stuck his head in.

"We got Silver's signal," he said simply.

Claire sang out in joy; Patty and Emma hugged each other, whirling in air.

Pramod held out a cautionary hand. "Things haven't started yet. You've got to stay in here a while longer."

"No, why?" Emma cried.

"We're waiting for a special supply shuttle from downside. When it docks is the new signal for things to start happening."

Claire's heart thumped. "Tony—did they get Tony aboard?"

Pramod shook his head, his dark eyes sharing her pain. "No, fuel rods. Leo's really anxious about them. He's afraid that without them we might not have enough power to boost the Habitat all the way out to the wormhole."

"Oh—yes, of course." Claire folded back into herself.

"Stay in here, hang on, and ignore any emergency klaxons you may hear," said Pramod. His lower hands clenched together in a gesture of encouragement, and he withdrew.

Claire settled back to wait. She could have wept with the tension of it, but Patty and Emma didn't need the bad example.

Bruce Van Atta pressed a finger to one side of his nose, squeezing the nostril shut, and sniffed mightily, then switched sides and repeated the procedure. Damn free fall and its lack of proper sinus drainage, among its other discomforts. He could hardly wait to get back to Earth. Even dismal Rodeo would be an improvement. He wondered idly if he could whip up some excuse—go inspect the quaddie barracks being readied, perhaps. That could be stretched out to about five days, if he worked it right.

He drifted over and shored himself across one corner of Dr. Yei's pie-wedge-shaped office, sighting over her desk, his back to a flat inner wall and his feet braced where her magnet-board curved, thick with stuck-on papers and flimsies. Yei's lips tightened with annoyance as she swiveled to face him. He hitched his feet to a comfortably crossed position, deliberately letting them muss her papers, outpsyching the psycher. She glanced back to her holovid display, declining to rise to the bait, and he mussed a few more. *Female wimp*, he thought. A relief, that they had only a few weeks left to work together, and he didn't have to jolly her up any more.

"So," he prodded, "how far along are we?"

"Well, I don't know how you're doing—in fact," she added rather venomously, "I don't even know what you're doing—"

Van Atta grinned in appreciation. So the worm could wriggle after all. Some administrators might have taken offense at the implied insubordination; he congratulated himself upon his sense of humor.

"—but so far I've finished orienting about half the staff to their new assignments."

"Anybody give you a hard time? I'll play bad guy, if necessary," he offered nobly, "and go lean on the non-cooperative."

"Everybody is naturally rather shocked," she replied, "however, I don't think your . . . direct intervention will be required."

"Good," he said jovially.

"I do think it would have been better to tell them all at once. This business of releasing the information in bits and dribbles invites just the sort of rumor-mongering that is least desirable."

"Yeah, well, it's too late now—"

His words were cut short by the startling hoot of an alarm klaxon, shrilling out over the intercom. Yei's holovid was abruptly overridden by the Central Systems emergency channel.

A hoarse male voice, a strained face—good God, it was Leo Graf—sprang from the display.

"Emergency, emergency," Graf called—where was he calling from?—"we are having a depressurization emergency. This is not a drill. All Habitat downsider staff should proceed at once to the designated safe area and remain there until the all-clear sounds—"

On the holovid, a computer-generated map sketched itself showing the shortest route from this terminal to the designated safe modules—module, Van Atta saw. Holy shit, the pressurization drop must be Habitat-wide. What the hell was going on?

"Emergency, emergency, this is not a drill," Graf repeated.

Yei too was staring bug-eyed at the map, looking more like a frog than ever. "How can that be? The sealing system is supposed to isolate the problem area from the rest—"

"I bet I know," spat Van Atta. "Graf's been messing with the Habitat's structure, preparatory to salvage—I'll bet he, or his quaddies, just screwed something up royally. Unless it was that idiot Wyzak did something—come on!"

"Emergency, emergency," Graf's voice droned on, "this is not a drill. All Habitat downsider staff should proceed at once—son-of-a-*bitch*!" His head snapped around, winked out, leaving only the urgently pulsing map on the display.

Van Atta beat Yei, whose eye was still caught by the map, out the door to her office and through the airseal doors at the end of the module that should have been sealed and weren't. The doors seemed to sag half-opened, controls dead, useless, as Van Atta and Yei joined a babbling stream of staffers speeding toward safety. Van Atta swallowed, cursing his sinuses, as one ear popped and the other, throbbing, failed to. Adrenaline-spurred anxiety shivered in his stomach.

Lecture Module C was already mobbed when they arrived, with downsiders in every state of dress and undress. One of the Nutrition staff had a case of frozen food clutched under her arm—Van Atta rejected the notion that she had inside information about the duration of the emergency and decided she must have simply had it in her hands when the alarm sounded and not thought to drop it before she fled.

"Close the door!" howled a chorus of voices as his and Yei's group entered. A distinct breeze sighed past them, rising to a whistle cut to silence as the doors sealed.

Chaos and babble ruled in the crowded lecture module.

"What's going on?"

"Ask Wyzak."

"He's out there, surely, dealing with it."

"If not, he'd better *get* the hell out there—"

"Is everybody here?"

"Where are the quaddies? What about the quaddies?"

"They have their own safe area, this isn't big enough."

"Their gym, probably."

"I didn't catch any directions for them on the holovid, to the gym or anywhere else—"

"Try the com."

"Half the channels are dead."

"Can't you even raise Central Systems?"

"Lady, I *am* Central Systems—"

"Shouldn't we have a head-count? Does anybody know exactly how many there are up on rotation right now?"

"Two hundred seventy-two, but how can you know which are missing because they're trapped and which are missing because they're out there dealing with it—"

"Let me at that damned com unit—"

"CLOSE THE DOOR!" Van Atta himself joined the chorus this time, semi-involuntarily. The pressure differential was becoming more marked. He was glad he wasn't a latecomer. If this went on it would shortly become his duty to see the doors stayed closed at any cost, no matter who was pounding for admittance from the other side. He had a little list . . . Well, anybody who lacked the wit to respond quickly to emergency instructions shouldn't be on a space station. Survival of the fittest.

If they hadn't amassed the whole two hundred seventy-two by now, they were surely getting close. Van Atta pushed his way through the bobbing crowd toward the center of the module, stealing momentum from this or that person at the price of their own displacement. A few turned to object, saw who had nudged them, and bit short their complaints. Somebody had the cover off the com unit and was peering into its guts in frustration, lacking delicate diagnostic tools doubtless dropped somewhere back in the Habitat.

"Can't you at least raise the quaddies' gym?" demanded a young woman. "I've got to know if my class made it there."

"Well, why didn't you go with 'em, then?" the would-be repairman snapped logically.

"One of the older quaddies took them. He told me to come here. I didn't think to argue with him, with that alarm howling in our ears—"

"No go." Grimacing, the man clicked the cover shut.

"Well, I'm going back and find out," said the young woman decisively.

"No, you're not," interrupted Van Atta. "There's too many people breathing in here to open the door and lose air unnecessarily. Not till we find out what's going on, how extensive this is, and how long it's likely to last."

The man tapped the holovid cover. "If this thing doesn't cut in, the only way we're going to find out anything is to send out somebody with a breath mask to go check."

"We'll give it a few more minutes." Damn that overweening fool Graf. What had he done? And where was he? In a breath mask somewhere, Van Atta trusted, or better yet a pressure suit—although if Graf had indeed caused this unholy mess, Van Atta wasn't sure he wished him a pressure suit. Let him have a breath mask, and a nasty case of the bends for just punishment. Idiot Graf.

So much for Graf's famous safety record. Blessings in disguise, at least the engineer wouldn't be able to jam that down his throat any more. A little humility would be good for him.

And yet—the situation was so damned anomalous. It shouldn't be possible to depressurize the whole Habitat at once. There were backups on the backups, interlocks, separated bays—any accident so system-wide would take foresight and planning.

A little hiss escaped his teeth, and Van Atta locked into himself in a sudden bubble of furious concentration, eyes widening. A planned accident—could it be, could it possibly be . . . ?

Genius Graf. An accident, an accident, a *perfect* accident, the very accident he'd most desired but had never dared wish for aloud. Was that it? That had to be it! Fatal disaster for the quaddies, now, at the last moment when they were all together and it could be accomplished at one stroke?

A dozen clues fell into place. Graf's insistence upon handling all the details of the salvage planning himself, his secretiveness, his anxiety for constant updates on the evacuation schedule—his withdrawal from social contacts that Yei had observed with disfavor, obsessive work schedule, general air of a man with a secret agenda driven to exhaustion—it was all culminating in this.

Of course it was secret. Now that he had penetrated the plot himself, Van Atta could only concur. The gratitude of the GalacTech hierarchy to Graf for relieving them of the quaddie problem must appear indirectly, in better assignments, quicker promotions—he would have to think up some suitably oblique way of transmitting it.

On the other hand—why share? Van Atta's lips drew back in a vulpine grin. This was hardly a situation where Graf could demand credit where it was due, after all. Graf had been subtle—but not subtle enough. There would have to be a sacrifice, for the sake of form, after the accident. All he had to do was keep his mouth shut, and . . . Van Atta had to wrench his attention back to his present surroundings.

"I've *got* to check on my quaddies!" The young woman was growing wild-eyed. She gave up on the com unit and began to shove her way back toward the airseal doors.

"Yes," another man joined her, "and I've got to find Wyzak. He's still not here. He's bound to need help. I'll go with you—"

"No!" cried Van Atta urgently, almost adding *You'll spoil everything!* "You're to wait for the all-clear. I won't have a panic. We'll all just sit tight and wait for instructions."

The woman subsided, but the man said skeptically, "Instructions from whom?"

"Graf," said Van Atta. Yes, it was not too early to start making it clear to witnesses where the hands-on responsibility lay. He controlled his excitement-spurred rapid breathing, trying for an aura of steady calm. Though not too calm—he must appear as surprised as any—no, more surprised than any—when the full extent of the disaster became apparent.

He settled down to wait. Minutes dragged past. One last panting group of refugees made it through the airseal doors; the Habitat-wide rate of depressurization must be slowing. One of the administrators from inventory control—old habits die hard—presented him with an unsolicited head-count of those present.

He silently cursed the census-taker's initiative, even as he accepted the results with thanks. The proof that all were not present might compel him to action he did not desire to take.

Only eleven downsider staff members had not made it. *A necessary price to pay*, Van Atta assured himself nervously. Some were doubtless holed up in other pressurized pockets, or so he could maintain he had believed, later. Their fatal mistakes could be pinned on Graf.

A group by the airseal doors was making ready to bolt. Van Atta inhaled, then paused, momentarily uncertain how to stop them without giving away everything. But a cry of dismay went up from one woman—"All the air is out of the corridor now! We can't get through without pressure suits!" Van Atta exhaled in relief.

He made his way to one of the module's viewports; it framed a dull vista of unwinking stars. The port on the other side gave an oblique view back toward the Habitat. Movement caught his eye, and he mashed his nose to the cold glass in an attempt to make out the details.

The silvery flash of work suits, bobbing over the outside surface of the Habitat. Refugees? Or a repair party? Could his first hypothesis of a real accident be correct after all? Not good, but in any case it was still Graf's baby.

But there were quaddies out there, dammit, quaddie survivors. He could see the arms. Graf had not made his stroke complete. Just two quaddie survivors, if one was male and the other female, would be as bad as a thousand, from Apmad's point of view. Perhaps the work party was all-male.

There was Graf himself, among the flitting figures! They carried an assortment of equipment. The wavering distortion of his transverse view through the port prevented him from making out just what. He twisted his neck, craning painfully. Then the work party was eclipsed by a curve of the Habitat. A pusher slid into, and out of, his view, arcing smoothly over the lecture module. More escapees? Quaddie or downsider?

"Hey." An excited voice from within the lecture module disrupted his frantic observations. "We're in luck, gang. This whole cupboard is filled with breath masks. There must be three hundred of 'em."

Van Atta swiveled his head to spot the cupboard in question. The last time he'd been in this module that storage had been filled with audiovisual equipment. Who the hell had made that switch, and why . . . ?

A bang reverberated through the module with a peculiar sharp resonance, like having one's head in a metal bucket when someone whacked it with a hammer. Hard. Shrieks and screams. The lights dimmed, then came up to about a quarter of their former brilliance. They were on the module's own emergency power. Power from the Habitat had been cut off.

Power wasn't all that had been cut off. Stunned, Van Atta saw the Habitat begin to turn slowly past his viewport. No, it wasn't the Habitat—it was the module that was moving. A generalized "Aaah!" went up from the mob within, as they began to drift toward one wall and pile up there against the gentle acceleration being imparted from without. Van Atta clung convulsively to the handholds by the viewport.

Realization washed over him almost physically, radiating hotly from his chest down his arms, his legs, pounding up through the top of his head as if to burst through his skull.

Betrayed! He was betrayed, betrayed completely and on every level. A space-suited figure with legs was waving a cheery farewell at the module from beside a gaping hole burned in the side of the Habitat. Van Atta shook with chagrin. *I'll get you, Graf! I'll get you, you double-crossing son-of-a-bitch! You and every one of those four-armed little creeps with you—*

"Calm down, man!" Dr. Yei was saying, having somehow snagged up by his viewport. "What is it?"

He realized he'd been mumbling aloud. He wiped saliva from the corners of his mouth and glared at Yei. "You— you—you *missed* it. You were supposed to be keeping track of everything that's going on with those little monsters, and you totally *missed* it—" He advanced on her, intending he knew not what, slipped from a handhold, swung and skidded down the wall. His blood beat so hard in his ears he was afraid he was having a coronary. He lay a moment with his eyes closed, gasping, temporarily overwhelmed by his emotions. *Control,* he told himself in a mortal fear of his imminent self-destruction. *Control, stay in control—and get Graf later. Get him, get them all. . . .*

Chapter 12

Leo unsuited to the wails of disturbed quaddies.

"What do you mean, we didn't get them all?" he asked, his elation draining away. He had so hoped that his troubles—or at least the downsider parts of them—would be over with the ignition of the jet cord cutting off Lecture Module C.

"Four of the area supervisors are locked in the vegetable cooler with breath masks and won't come out," reported Sinda from Nutrition.

"And the three crewmen from the shuttle that just docked tried to make it back to their ship," said a yellow-shirted quaddie from Docks & Locks. "We trapped them between two airseal doors, but they've been working on the mechanism and we don't think we can hold them much longer."

"Mr. Wyzak and two of the life-support systems supervisors are, um, tied up in Central Systems. To the wall hand grips," reported another quaddie in yellow, adding nervously, "Mr. Wyzak sure is mad."

"Three of the crèche mothers refused to leave their kids," said an older quaddie girl in pink. "They're all still in the gym with the rest of the little ones. They're pretty upset. Nobody's told them what's going on yet, at least not when I'd left."

"And, um, there's one other person," added red-clad Bobbi from Leo's own welding and joining work gang in a faint tone. "We're not quite sure what to do about him . . ."

"Immobilize him, to start," began Leo wearily. "We'll just have to arrange a life pod to take the stragglers."

"That may not be so easy," said Bobbi.

"You outnumber him, take ten—take twenty—you can be as careful as you like—is he armed?"

"Not exactly," admitted Bobbi, seeming to find her lower fingernails objects of new fascination. The quaddie equivalent of foot-shuffling, Leo realized.

"Graf!" boomed an authoritative voice, as the airseals at the end of the work-suit locker room slid open. Dr. Minchenko launched himself across the module to thump to a halt beside Leo, and gave the locker an extra bang with his fist for emphasis. One could not, after all, stomp in free fall. The unused breath mask trailing from his hand bounced and quivered. "What the hell is going on here? There's no bleeding pressurization emergency—" He inhaled vigorously, as if to prove his point.

The quaddie girl Kara in the white T-shirt and shorts of Medical trailed him, looking mortified. "Sorry, Leo," she apologized. "I couldn't get him to go."

"Am I to run off to some closet while all my quaddies asphyxiate?" Minchenko demanded indignantly of her. "What do you take me for, girl?"

"Most everybody else did," she offered hesitantly.

"Cowards—scoundrels—*idiots*," he sputtered.

"They followed their computerized emergency instructions," said Leo. "Why didn't you?"

Minchenko glared at him. "Because the whole thing stank. A Habitat-wide pressurization loss should be almost impossible. A whole chain of interlocking accidents would have to occur."

"Such chains do occur, though," said Leo, speaking from wide experience. "They're practically my specialty."

"Just so," purred Minchenko, lidding his eyes. "And that vermin Van Atta billed you as his pet engineer when he brought you in. Frankly, I thought—ahem!" he looked only mildly embarrassed, "that you might be his triggerman. The accident seemed so suspiciously convenient just now, from his point of view. Knowing Van Atta, that was practically the first thing I thought of."

"Thanks," snarled Leo.

"I knew Van Atta—I didn't know you." Minchenko paused, and added more mildly, "I still don't. What do you think you're doing?"

"Isn't it obvious?"

"Not entirely, no. Oh, certainly, you can hold out in the Habitat for a few months, cut off from Rodeo—perhaps years, barring counterattacks, if you were conservative and clever enough—but what then? There is no public opinion to come to your rescue here, no audience to grandstand for. It's half-baked, Graf. You've made no provisions for reaching help—"

"We're not asking for help. The quaddies are going to rescue themselves."

"How?" Minchenko's tone scoffed, though his eyes were alight.

"Jump the Habitat. Then keep going."

Even Minchenko was silenced momentarily. "Oh . . ."

Leo finished struggling into his red coveralls, and found the tool he wanted. He pointed the laser-solderer firmly at Minchenko's midsection. It did not appear to be a task he could safely delegate to the quaddies. "And you," he said stiffly, "can go to the transfer station in the life pod with the rest of the downsiders. Let's go."

Minchenko barely glanced at the solderer. His lips curled with contempt for the weapon and, Leo felt, its wielder. "Don't be more of an idiot than you can help, Graf. I know they foxed that cretin Curry, so there are still at least fifteen pregnant quaddie girls out there. Not counting the results of unauthorized experiments, which judging from the way the level is dropping in that box of condoms in the unlocked drawer in my office, are becoming significant."

Kara started in guilty dismay, and Minchenko added aside to her, "Why do you think I pointed them out to you, dear? Be that as it may, Graf," he fixed Leo with a stern eye, "if you throw me off what do you plan to do if one of them presents at labor with placenta praevia? Or a post-partum prolapsed uterus? Or any other medical emergency that requires more than a band-aid?"

"Well . . . but . . ." Leo was taken aback. He wasn't quite sure what placenta praevia was, but somehow he didn't think it was medical gobbledy-gook for a hangnail. Nor that a precise explanation of the term would do anything to ease the ominous anxiety it engendered in him. Was it something likely to occur, given the alterations of quaddie anatomy? "There is no choice. To stay here is death for every quaddie. To go is a chance—not a guarantee—of life."

"But you need me," argued Minchenko.

"You have to—what?" Leo's tongue stumbled.

"You need me. You can't throw me off." Minchenko's eyes flicked infinitesimally to the solderer.

"Well, huh," Leo choked, "I can't kidnap you, either."

"Who's asking you to?"

"You are, evidently . . ." He cleared his throat. "Look, I don't think you understand. I'm taking this Habitat out, and we're not coming back, not ever. We're going out as far as we can go, beyond every inhabited world. It's a one-way ticket."

"I'm relieved. At first I thought you were going to try something stupid."

Leo found his emotions churning, a mixture of suspicion, jealousy?—and a sharp rising anticipation—what a *relief* it would be, not to have to carry it all alone. . . . "You sure?"

"They're *my* quaddies . . ." Minchenko's hands clenched, opened. "Daryl's and mine. I don't think you half understand what a job we did. What a *good* job, developing these people. They're finely adapted to their environment. Superior in every way. Thirty-five years' work—am I to let some total stranger drag them off across the galaxy to who-knows-what fate? Besides, GalacTech was going to retire me next year."

"You'll lose your pension," Leo pointed out. "Maybe your freedom—possibly your life."

Minchenko snorted. "Not much of that left."

Not true, Leo thought. The bio-scientist possessed enormous life, over three-quarters of a century of accumulation. When this man died, a universe of specialized knowledge would be extinguished. Angels would weep for the loss. Unless—"Could you train quaddie doctors?"

"It's a forgone conclusion *you* couldn't." Minchenko ran his hands through his clipped white hair in a gesture part exasperation, part pleading.

Leo glanced around at the anxiously hovering quaddies, listening in—listening in while men with legs decided their fate, again. Not right . . . the words popped out of his mouth before reasoned caution could stop them. "What do you kids think?"

A ragged but immediate chorus of assent for Minchenko—relief in their eyes, too. Minchenko's familiar authority would clearly be an immense comfort to them, as they traveled farther into the unknown. Leo was suddenly put in mind of the way the universe had changed to a stranger place the day his father had died. *Just because we're adults doesn't automatically mean we can save you . . .* But this was a discovery each quaddie would have to make in their own time. He took a deep breath. "All right . . ." How could one suddenly feel a hundred kilos lighter when already weightless? Placenta praevia, God.

Minchenko did not react with immediate pleasure. "There's just one thing," he began, arranging his features in a humble smile quite horribly out of place on his face.

What's he sweating for now? Leo wondered, suspicions renewed. "What?"

"Madame Minchenko."

"Who?"

"My wife. I have to get her."

"I didn't—realize you were married. Where is she?"

"Downside. On Rodeo."

"Hell . . ." Leo suppressed an urge to start tearing out the remains of his hair.

Pramod, listening, reminded, "Tony's down there too."

"I know, I know—and I promised Claire—I don't know how we're going to work this . . ."

Minchenko was waiting, his expression intense—not a man used to begging. Only his eyes pleaded. Leo was moved. "We'll try. We'll try. That's all I can promise."

Minchenko nodded, dignified.

"How's Madame Minchenko going to feel about all this, anyway?"

"She's loathed Rodeo for twenty-five years," Minchenko promised—somewhat airily, Leo thought. "She'll be delighted to get away." Minchenko didn't add *I hope* aloud, but Leo heard it anyway.

"All right. Well, we've still got to round up these stragglers and get rid of them. . . ." Leo wondered wistfully if it was possible to drop dead painlessly from an anxiety attack. He led his little troop from the locker room.

Claire flew from hand-grip to hand-grip along the branching corridors, done with patience at last. Her heart sang with anticipation. The airseal doors to the raucous gym were crowded with quaddies, and she had to restrain herself from forcibly elbowing them out of her way. One of her old dormitory mates, in the pink T-shirt and shorts of crèche duty, recognized her with a grin and reached out with a lower hand to pull her through the mob.

"The littlest ones are by Door C," said her dorm mate. "I've been expecting you." After a quick visual check to be sure her flight plan didn't violently intersect anyone else's taking a similar shortcut, her dorm mate helped her launch herself in that direction by the most direct route, across the diameter of the big chamber.

The buxom figure in pink coveralls Claire sought was practically buried in a swarm of excited, frightened, chattering, crying five-year-olds. Claire felt a twinge of real guilt, that it had been judged too dangerous to their secrecy to warn the younger quaddies in advance of the great changes about to sweep over them. *The little ones didn't get a vote, either,* she thought.

Andy was tethered to Mama Nilla, weeping miserably. Mama Nilla was desperately trying to pacify him with a squeeze bottle of formula with one hand while holding a reddening gauze pad to the forehead of a crying five-year-old with the other. Two or three more clung for comfort to her legs as she tried to verbally direct the efforts of a sixth to help a seventh who had torn open a package of protein chips too wide and accidentally allowed the contents to spill into the air. Through it all her calm familiar drawl was only slightly more compressed than usual, until she saw Claire approaching. "Oh, dear," she said in a weak voice.

"Andy!" Claire cried.

His head swiveled toward her, and he launched himself away from Mama Nilla with frantic swimming motions, only to fetch up at the end of his tether and rebound back to the crèche mother's side. At this point he began screaming in true earnest. As if by resonance, the bleeding boy started crying harder too.

Claire braked by the wall and closed in on them.

"Claire, honey, I'm sorry," said Mama Nilla, twitching her hips around to eclipse Andy, "but I can't let you have him. Mr. Van Atta said he'd fire me on the spot, twenty years or no twenty years—and God knows who they'd get then—there's so few I can really trust to have their heads screwed on right—" Andy interrupted her by launching himself again; he batted the proffered bottle violently out of her hand and it spun away, a few drops of formula adding tangentially to the general environmental degradation. Claire's hands reached for him.

"—I can't, I really can't—oh, hell, *take* him!" It was the first time Claire had ever heard Mama Nilla swear. She unhooked the tether and her freed left side was instantly set upon by the waiting five-year-olds.

Andy's screams faded at once to a muffled weeping, as his little hands clamped her fiercely. Claire folded him to her with all four arms no less fiercely. He rooted in her shirt—uselessly, she realized. Just holding him might be enough for her, but the reverse was not necessarily true. She nuzzled in his scant hair, delighting in the clean baby smell of him, tender sculptured ears, translucent skin, fine eyelashes, every part of his wriggling body. She wiped his nose happily with the edge of her blue shirt.

"It's Claire," she overheard one of the five-year-olds explaining knowledgeably to another. "She's a real mommy." She glanced up to catch them gravely inspecting her; they giggled. She grinned back. A seven-year-old from an adjoining group had retrieved the bottle, and hung about watching Andy with interest.

The cut on the little quaddie's forehead having clotted enough, Mama Nilla was at last able to carry on a conversation. "You don't happen to know where Mr. Van Atta is, do you?" she asked Claire in worry.

"Gone," said Claire joyously, "gone forever! *We're* taking over."

Mama Nilla blinked. "Claire, they won't let you . . ."

"We have help." She nodded across the gym, where Leo in his red coveralls caught her eye—he must have just arrived. With him was another legged figure in white coveralls. What was Dr. Minchenko still doing here? A sudden fear twinged through her. Had they failed to clear the Habitat of downsiders after all? For the first time it occurred to her to question Mama Nilla's presence. "Why didn't you go to your safe zone?" Claire asked her.

"Don't be silly, dear. Oh, Dr. Minchenko!" Mama Nilla waved to him. "Over here!"

The two downsider men, lacking the free-flying confidence of the quaddies, crossed the chamber via a rope net hung across a farther arc, and made their way toward Mama Nilla's group.

"I've got one here who needs some biotic glue," Mama Nilla, hugging the cut quaddie, said to Dr. Minchenko as soon as he drew near enough to hear. "What's going on? Is it safe to take them back to the crèche modules yet?"

"It's safe," replied Leo, "but you're going to have to come with me, Ms. Villanova."

"I don't leave my kids till my relief arrives," said Mama Nilla tartly, "and nine-tenths of the department seems to have evaporated, including my department head."

Leo frowned. "Have you had your briefing from Dr. Yei yet?"

"No . . ."

"They were saving the best for last," said Dr. Minchenko grimly, "for obvious reasons." He turned to the crèche mother. "GalacTech has just terminated the Cay Project, Liz. Without even consulting me!" Bluntly, he outlined the termination scenario for her. "I was writing up protests, but Graf here beat me to it. Rather more effectively, I suspect. The inmates are taking over the asylum. He thinks he can convert the Habitat into a colony ship. I think . . . I choose to believe he can."

"You mean you're responsible for this mess?" Mama Nilla glared at Leo, and looked around, clearly stunned. "I thought Claire was babbling . . ." The other two downsider crèche mothers had come over during the explanation and hung in the air looking equally nonplused. "GalacTech's not *giving* you the Habitat . . . are they?" Mama Nilla asked Leo faintly.

"No, Ms. Villanova," said Leo patiently. "We are stealing it. Now, I wouldn't ask you to get involved in anything illegal, so if you'll just follow me to the life pod—"

Mama Nilla stared around the gym. A few groups of youngsters were already being herded out by some older quaddies. "But these kids can't handle all these kids!"

"They're going to have to," said Leo.

"No, no—I don't think you have the foggiest idea how labor-intensive this department is!"

"He doesn't," confirmed Dr. Minchenko, rubbing his lips thoughtfully with a forefinger.

"There's *no choice*," said Leo through his teeth. "Now kids, let go of Ms. Villanova," he addressed the quaddies clutching her. "She has to leave."

"No!" said the one wrapped around her left knee. "She's gotta read our stories after lunch, she *promised*." The one with the cut began crying again. Another one tugged her left sleeve and whispered loudly, "Mama Nilla! I gotta go to the toilet!"

Leo ran his hands through his hair, unclenched them with a visible effort. "I need to be suited up and Outside *right now*, lady, I don't have *time* to argue. All of you," his glare took in the other two crèche mothers, "move it!"

Mama Nilla's eyes glinted. She held out her left arm with the quaddie attached, blue eyes peering in fright at Leo around Mama Nilla's sturdy bicep. "Are you going to take this little girl to the bathroom, then?"

The quaddie girl and Leo stared at each other in equal horror. "Certainly not," the engineer choked. He looked around "Another quaddie will. Claire . . . ?"

After a barracuda-like investigation, Andy chose this moment to begin wailing protests at the lack of expected milk from his mother's breasts. Claire tried to soothe him, patting his back; she felt like crying herself for his disappointment.

"I don't suppose," Dr. Minchenko interjected mildly, "that you would care to come along with us, Liz? There would be no going back, of course."

"Us?" Mama Nilla regarded him sharply. "Are you going along with this nonsense?"

"I rather think so."

"That's all right, then." She nodded.

"But you can't—" Leo began.

"Graf," Dr. Minchenko said, "did your little depressurization drama just now give these ladies any reason to think they were still going to have air to breathe if they stayed with their quaddies?"

"It shouldn't have," said Leo.

"I didn't even think about it," said one of the crèche mothers, looking suddenly dismayed.

"I did," said the other, frowning at Leo.

"I knew there were emergency air supplies in the gym module," said Mama Nilla, "it's in the regular drill, after all. The whole department ought to have come here."

"I diverted 'em," said Leo shortly.

"The whole department should have told you to go screw yourself," Mama Nilla added evenly. "Allow me to speak for the absent." She smiled icily at the engineer.

One of the crèche mothers addressed Mama Nilla in distress. "But I can't come with you. My husband works downside!"

"Nobody's asking you to!" roared Leo.

The other crèche mother, ignoring him, added to Mama Nilla, "I'm sorry. I'm sorry, Liz, I just can't. It's just too much."

"Yes, exactly." Leo's hand hesitated over a lump in his coveralls, abandoned it, and switched to trying to herd them all along with broad arm-waving gestures.

"It's all right girls, I understand," Mama Nilla soothed their evident anxiety. "I'll stay and hold the fort, I guess. Got nobody waiting for this old body, after all," she laughed. It was a little forced.

"Will you take over the department, then?" Dr. Minchenko confirmed with Mama Nilla. "Keep it going any way you can—come to me when you can't."

She nodded, looking withdrawn, as if the bottomless complexity of the task before her was just beginning to dawn.

Dr. Minchenko took charge of the quaddie boy with the still-oozing cut on his forehead; Leo at last successfully pried loose the other two downsider women, saying, "Come *on*. I have to go empty the vegetable cooler next."

"With all this going on, what is he doing spending time cleaning out a refrigerator?" Mama Nilla muttered under her breath. "Madness . . ."

"Mama Nilla, I gotta go *now*." The little quaddie wrapped all her arms tightly around her torso by way of emphasis, and Mama Nilla perforce broke away.

Andy was still wailing his indignant disappointment in intermittent bursts.

"Hey, little fellow," Dr. Minchenko paused to address him, "that's no way to talk to your mama. . . ."

"No milk," explained Claire. Glumly, feeling dreadfully inadequate, she offered him the bottle, which he batted away. When she attempted to detach him momentarily in

order to dive after it, he wrapped himself around her arm
and screamed frantically. One of the five-year-olds twisted
up and put all four of his hands over his ears, pointedly.

"Come with us to the infirmary," said Dr. Minchenko
with an understanding smile. "I think I have something
that will fix that problem. Unless you want to wean him
now, which I don't recommend."

"Oh, please," said Claire hopefully.

"It will take a couple of days to get your systems inter-
locked again," he warned, "the biofeedback lag time being
what it is. But I haven't had a chance to examine you two
since I came up anyway . . ."

Claire floated after him with gratitude. Even Andy
stopped crying.

Pramod hadn't been joking about the clamps, Leo
thought with a sigh, as he studied the fused lump of metal
before him. He punched up the specs on the computer
board floating beside him, a bit slowly and clumsily with
his pressure-gloved hands. This particular insulated pipe
conducted sewage. Unglamorous, but a mistake here could
be just as much a disaster as any other.

And a lot messier, Leo thought with a grim grin. He
glanced up at Bobbi and Pramod hovering at the ready
beside him in their silvery work suits; five other quaddie
work teams were visible along the Habitat's surface, and a
pusher jockeyed into position nearby. Rodeo's sunlit cres-
cent wheeled in the background. Well, they must certainly
be the galaxy's most expensive plumbers.

The mess of variously-coded pipes and tubing before
him formed the umbilical connections between one module and the next, shielded by an outer casing from
microdust pitting and other hazards. The task at hand was

to re-align the modules in uniform longitudinal bundles to withstand acceleration. Each bundle, strapped together like the cargo pods, would form a sturdy, self-supporting, balanced mass, at least in terms of the relatively low thrusts Leo was contemplating. Just like driving a team of yoked hippopotamuses. But re-aligning the modules entailed re-aligning all their connections, and there were lots and lots and *lots* of connections.

A movement caught the corner of Leo's eye. Pramod's helmet followed the tilt of Leo's.

"There they go," Pramod remarked. Both triumph and regret mingled in his voice.

The life pod with the last remnant of downsiders aboard fled silently into the void, a flash of light winking off a port even as it shrank from sight around Rodeo's curvature. That was it, then, for the legged ones, bar himself, Dr. Minchenko, Mama Nilla, and a slightly demented young supervisor waving a spanner they'd pried out of a duct who declared his violent love for a quaddie girl in Airsystems Maintenance and refused to be budged. If he came to his senses by the time they reached Orient IV, Leo decided, they could drop him off. Meantime it was a choice between shooting him or putting him to work. Leo had eyed the spanner, and put him to work.

Time. The seconds seemed to wriggle over Leo's skin like bugs, beneath his suit. The remnant group of evicted downsiders must soon catch up with the bewildered first batch and start comparing notes. It wouldn't be long after that, Leo judged, that GalacTech must start making its counter-moves. It didn't take an engineer to see a thousand ways in which the Habitat was vulnerable. The only option left to the quaddies now was speedy flight.

Phlegmatic calm, Leo reminded himself, was the key to getting out of this alive. *Remember that.* He turned his attention back to the job at hand. "All right, Bobbi, Pramod, let's do it. Get ready with the emergency shut-offs on both ends, and we'll get this monster horsed around . . ."

Chapter 13

His fellow refugees gave way before him as Bruce Van Atta stormed out of the boarding tube and into the passenger arrival lounge of Rodeo Shuttleport Three. He had to pause a moment, hands braced on his knees, to overcome a wave of dizziness induced by his abrupt return to planetside gravity. Dizziness and rage.

For several hours during the ride around Rodeo orbit in the cut-off lecture module Van Atta had been horribly certain that Graf was intending to murder them all, despite the contrary evidence of the breath masks. If this was war, Graf would never make a good soldier. *Even I know better than to humiliate a man like this, and then leave him alive. You'll be sorry you double-crossed me, Graf; sorrier still you didn't kill me when you had the chance.* He restrained his rage with an effort.

Van Atta had ordered himself aboard the first available shuttle down from a transfer station overburdened by the surprise arrival of almost three hundred unexpected bodies. He had not slept in the twenty hours since the detached lecture module's airlock had, with agonizing glitches and delays, finally been married to that of a Station personnel carrier. He and the other Cay Habitat employees had disembarked in disorganized batches from their cramped prison-mobile and been ferried to the transfer station, where yet more time had been wasted.

Information. It had been almost a full day since they had been evicted from the Cay Habitat. He must have information. He boarded a slide tube and headed for Shuttleport Three's administration building, with its communications center. Dr. Yei pattered after him, wimping about something; he paid little attention.

He caught sight of his own wavering reflection in the plexiplastic walls of the tube as he was carried along above the shuttleport tarmac. Haggard. He straightened and sucked in his gut. It would not do to appear before other administrators looking beaten or weak. The weak went under.

He gazed through his pale image and across the shuttleport laid out below. On the far side of the tarmac at the monorail terminal cargo pods were already starting to pile up. Ah, yes: the damned quaddies were a link in that chain, too. A weak link, a broken link, soon to be replaced.

He arrived at the communications center at the same moment as Shuttleport Three's chief administrator, Chalopin. She was trailed by her security captain, what's-his-name, oh, yes, that idiot Bannerji.

"What the hell is going on here?" Chalopin snapped without preamble. "An accident? Why haven't you requested assistance? They told us to hold all flights—we've got a major production run backed up halfway to the refinery."

"Keep holding it, then. Or call the transfer station. Moving your cargo is not my department."

"Oh, yes it is! Orbital cargo marshaling has been under Cay Project aegis for a year."

"*Ex*-perimentally." He frowned, stung. "It may be my department, but it's not my biggest worry right now. Look, lady, I got a full-scale crisis here." He turned to one of the com controllers. "Can you punch me through to the Cay Habitat at all?"

"They're not answering our calls," said the com controller doubtfully. "Almost all of the regular telemetry has been cut off."

"Anything. Telescopic sighting, anything."

"I might be able to get a visual off one of the comsats," said the controller. He turned to his panel, muttering. In a few minutes his screen coughed up a distant flat view of the Cay Habitat as seen from synchronous orbit. He stepped up the magnification.

"What are they *doing*?" asked Chalopin, staring.

Van Atta stared too. What insane vandalism was this? The Habitat resembled a complex three-dimensional puzzle pulled apart by an idle child. Detached modules seemed spilled carelessly, floating at all angles in space. Tiny silver figures jetted among them. The solar power panels had mysteriously shrunk to a quarter of their normal area. Was Graf embarked on some nutty scheme for fortifying the Habitat against counterattack, perhaps? Well, it would do him no good, Van Atta swore silently.

"Are they . . . preparing for a siege or something?" Dr. Yei asked aloud, evidently following a similar line of thought. "Surely they must realize how futile it would be."

"Who knows what that damn fool Graf thinks?" Van Atta growled. "The man's run mad. There are a dozen ways we can stand off at a distance and knock that installation to bits even without military supplies. Or just wait and starve them out. They've trapped themselves. He's not just crazy, he's stupid."

"Maybe," said Yei doubtfully, "they mean to just go on quietly living up there, in orbit. Why not?"

"The hell you say. I'm going to hook them out of there, and double-quick, too. Somehow . . . No bunch of miserable mutants are going to get away with sabotage on *this* scale. Sabotage—theft—terrorism . . ."

"They are not mutants," began Yei, "they are genetically-engineered childr—"

"Mr. Van Atta, sir?" piped up another com controller. "I have an urgent memo for you listed on my all-points. Can you take it here?" Yei, cut off, spread her hands in frustration.

"Now what?" Van Atta muttered, seating himself before the com unit.

"It's a recorded message from the manager of the cargo marshaling station out at jump point. I'll put it online," said the tech.

The vaguely familiar face of the jump point station manager wavered into focus before Van Atta. Van Atta had met him perhaps once, early in his stint here. The small jump point station was manned from the Orient IV side, and was under Orient IV's operations division, not Rodeo's. Its employees were regular Union downsiders and did not normally have contact with Rodeo, nor with the quaddies once destined to replace them.

The station manager looked harried. He gabbled through the preliminary IDs, then came abruptly to the meat of his matter: "What the hell is going on with you people, anyway? A crew of mutant freaks just came out of nowhere, kidnapped a jump pilot, shot another, and hijacked a GalacTech cargo superjumper. But instead of jumping *out*, they've headed back with it toward Rodeo. When we notified Rodeo Security, they indicated the mutants probably belonged to you. Are there more out there? Are they running wild or something? I want answers, dammit. I've got a pilot in the infirmary, a terrorized engineer, and a crew on the verge of panic." From the look on his face the station manager was on the verge of panic himself. "Jump point station out!"

"How old is this memo?" said Van Atta rather blankly.

"About," the com tech checked his monitor, "twelve hours, sir."

"Does he think the hijackers are quaddies? Why wasn't I informed"—Van Atta's eye fell on Bannerji, standing blandly at attention by Chalopin's elbow—"why wasn't I informed of this at once by Security?"

"At the time the incident was first reported, you were unavailable," said the security captain, devoid of expression. "Since then we've been tracking the D-620, and it's continued to boost straight toward Rodeo. It doesn't answer our calls."

"What are you doing about it?"

"We're monitoring the situation. I have not yet received orders to do anything about it."

"Why not? Where's Norris?" Norris was Operations manager for the entire Rodeo local space area; he ought to be on this thing. True, the Cay Project was not in his chain of command proper, as Van Atta reported directly to company Ops.

"Dr. Norris," said Chalopin, "is attending a materials development conference on Earth. In his absence, I am acting Operations manager. Captain Bannerji and I have discussed the possibility of his taking his men and the Shuttleport Three Security and Rescue shuttle and attempting to board the hijacked ship. We're still not sure who these people are or what they want, but they appear to have taken a hostage, compelling caution on our part. So we've let them continue to decrease their range while we *attempt* to gain more information about them. This"—she eyed him beadily—"brings us to you, Mr. Van Atta. Is this incident somehow connected to your crisis at the Cay Habitat?"

"I don't see how—" Van Atta began, and broke off, because suddenly he did see how. "Son-of-a-bitch . . ." he whispered.

"Lord Krishna," Dr. Yei said, and wheeled to stare again at the live vid of the Habitat half-dismantled in orbit far above them. "It can't be . . ."

"Graf's crazy. He's crazy. The man's a flaming megalomaniac. He can't *do* this—" The engineering parameters paraded inexorably through Van Atta's mind. Mass— power—distance—yes, a pared-down Habitat, a percentage of its less-essential components dropped, might just barely be torqued by a superjumper into wormhole space, if it could be wrestled into position at the distant jump point. The whole damn thing . . . "They're hijacking the whole damn thing!" Van Atta cried aloud.

Yei wrung her hands, half-circling the vid. "They'll never manage. They're barely more than children! He'll lead them to their deaths! It's criminal!"

Captain Bannerji and the shuttleport administrator glanced at each other. Bannerji pursed his lips and opened his hand to her, as if to say, *Ladies first*.

"Do you think the two incidents are connected, then?" Chalopin pressed.

Van Atta too paced back and forth, as if he could so coax an angle from flat view of the Habitat. ". . . the whole damn thing!"

Yei answered for him. "Yes, we think so."

Van Atta paced on. "Hell, and they've got it apart already! We aren't going to have time to starve 'em out. Got to stop 'em some other way."

"The Cay Project workers were very upset at the abrupt termination of the Project," Yei explained. "They found out about it prematurely. They were afraid of being remanded downside, being unaccustomed to gravity. I never had a chance to introduce the idea gradually. I think they may actually be trying to—run away, somehow."

Captain Bannerji's eyes widened. He leaned across the console on one hand and stared into the vid. "Consider the lowly snail," he muttered, "who carries its house on its back. On cold rainy days when it goes for a walk, it never has to backtrack. . . ."

Van Atta put an extra half meter of distance between himself and the suddenly poetic security captain.

"Weapons," Van Atta said. "What kind of weapons does Security have on tap?"

"Stunners," answered Bannerji, straightening up and studying his right thumbnail. Was there a flash of mockery in his eyes? No, he wouldn't dare.

"I mean on your shuttle," said Van Atta irritably. "Ship-mounted weapons. Teeth. You can't make a threat without teeth."

"There are two medium-power ship-mounted laser units. Last time we used them was—let me see—to burn through a log snag that had backed up flood waters threatening an exploration camp."

"Yes, well, it's more than *they* have, anyway," said Van Atta excitedly. "We can attack the Habitat—or the superjumper—either, really. The main thing is to keep them from connecting with each other. Yes, get the jump-ship first. Without it the Habitat is a sitting target we can polish off at our leisure. Is your security shuttle fueled up and ready to go, Bannerji?"

Dr. Yei had paled. "Hold on! Who's talking about attack-ing anything? We haven't even made verbal contact yet. If the hijackers are indeed quaddies, I'm sure I could per-suade them to listen to reason—"

"It's too late for reason. This situation calls for *action*." Van Atta's humiliation burned hot in his stomach, fueled by fear. When the company brass found out how totally he had lost control—well, he'd better be firmly back in control by then.

"Yes, but . . ." Yei licked her lips, "it's all very well to threaten, but the actual use of force is dangerous—maybe destructive—hadn't you better get some kind of authoriza-tion first? If something went horribly wrong, you wouldn't want to be left holding the bag, surely."

Van Atta paused. "It would take too much time," he objected at last. "Maybe a day, to reach District HQ on Ori-ent IV and return. And if they decided it was too hot and bounced it all the way to Apmad on Earth, it could be sev-eral days before we got a reply."

"But it's going to be several days, isn't it?" said Yei, watching him intently. "Even if they succeed in fitting the Habitat to the superjumper, they aren't going to be able to swing it around and boost it like a fast courier. It would never stand the strain, it would use too much fuel—there's lots of time yet. Wouldn't it be better to get authorization, to be safe? Then, if anything went wrong—it wouldn't be *your* fault."

"Well . . ." Van Atta slowed still further. How typical of Yei's wishy-washy, wimpy indecision. He could almost hear her, in his head; *Now, let's all sit down and discuss this like reasonable people. . . .* He loathed letting her push his buttons; still, she had a valid point: cover-your-ass was a fundamental rule for survival even of the fittest.

"Well . . . no, dammit! One thing I can damn well guarantee is that GalacTech is going to want this whole fiasco kept quiet. The last thing they'll want is a lot of rumors flying around about their pet mutants running wild. Better for all of us if this is handled strictly inside Rodeo local space." He turned to Bannerji. "That's the first priority, then—you and your men have got to get that jumpship back, or at least disable it."

"That," remarked Bannerji to the air, "would be vandalism. Besides, as has been pointed out before—Shuttleport Three Security is not in your chain of command, Mr. Van Atta." He glanced significantly at his boss, who stood listening and pulling worriedly on a strand of hair escaped from her sleek coiffure.

"True," she agreed. "The Habitat may be your problem, Mr. Van Atta, but this jumpship hijacking is clearly under my jurisdiction, regardless of their connections. And there's still a cargo shuttle docked up there that's mine, too, though the transfer station reported they picked up its crew from a life pod."

Van Atta stood fuming, blocked. Blocked by the damned women. It had been Chalopin's buttons Yei had been aiming for, he realized suddenly, and she'd scored a hit, too. "That's it, then," he said through his teeth at last.

"We'll bounce it to HQ. And then we'll see who's in charge here."

Dr. Yei closed her eyes briefly, as if in relief. At a word from Chalopin a com tech began readying his system for the relay of a scrambled emergency message to District, to be radioed at the speed of light to the wormhole station, recorded and jumped through on the next available transport, and radio-relayed again to its destination.

"In the meantime," said Van Atta to Chalopin, "what are you going to do about *your*"—he drew the word out sarcastically—"hijacking?"

"Proceed with caution," she replied levelly. "We believe there is a hostage involved, after all."

"We're not sure if all the GalacTech staff is off the Habitat yet, either," put in Dr. Yei.

Van Atta growled, unable to contradict her. But if there were still downsiders being held aboard, senior management must surely realize the need for a swift and vigorous response. He must call the transfer station next and get the final head count. If all these dithering idiots were going to force him to sit on his hands for the next several days, he could at least lay his plans for action when he was unleashed.

And he was certain he would be unleashed, sooner or later. He had not failed to read Apmad's underlying horror of the mutant quaddies. When word of this mess finally arrived on her desk it would goose her three meters straight up in the air, hostages or no hostages—Van Atta's eyes narrowed. "Hey," he said suddenly, "we're not as helpless as you think. Two can play that game—*I* have a hostage too!"

"You do?" said Dr. Yei, puzzled. Then her hand went to her throat.

"Damn straight. And to think I almost forgot. That four-armed geek Tony is down here!"

Tony was Graf's teacher's pet—and that little cunt Claire's favorite prick, and *she* was surely a ringleader—if he couldn't swing this to his advantage, he was dead in the head. He spun on his heel. "Come on, Yei! Those little suckers are going to answer our calls now!"

Jump pilots might swear their ships were beautiful, but really, Leo thought as the D-620 heaved silently into view, the superjumper looked like nothing so much as a mutant mechanical squid. A pod-like section at the front end contained the control room and crew quarters, protected from the material hazards encountered during acceleration by an oblate laminated shield and from the hazards of radiation by an invisible magnetic cone. Arcing out behind trailed four enormously long, mutually braced arms. Two housed normal space thrusters; two housed the heart of the ship's purpose, the Necklin field generator rods that spun the ship through wormhole space during a jump. Between the four arms was a huge empty space normally occupied by cargo pods. The bizarre ship would look more sensible when that space was filled with Habitat modules, Leo decided. At that point he would even break down and call it beautiful himself.

With a jerk of his chin Leo called up a vid of his work suit's power and supply levels, displayed on the inside of his faceplate. He would have just time to see the first module bundle pushed into place and attached before being forced to take a break and restock his suit. Not that he hadn't been ready for a break hours ago. He blinked sand and water from his itching, no-doubt-bloodshot eyes, wishing he could rub them, and sucked another mouthful of hot coffee from his drink tube. He wanted fresh coffee, too. The stuff he was drinking now had been out here as long as he had, and was growing just as chemically vile, opaque and greenish.

The D-620 sidled near the Habitat, matching velocities precisely, and shut down its engines. The flight lights blinked out and the parking lights, signaling that it was safe to approach, flicked on. Banks of floods suddenly illuminated the vast cargo space, as if to say, *Welcome aboard.*

Leo's gaze strayed to the crew's section, dwarfed by the arcing arms. From the corner of his eye he saw a personnel pod peel away from the superjumper's starboard side and ferry off toward the Habitat modules. Somebody heading home—Silver? Ti? He had to talk to Ti as soon as possible. A previously unrealized knot unwound in his stomach. *Silver's back safe.* He caught himself up; *everybody* was back. But not safe yet. He activated his suit jets and caught up with his quaddie crew.

Thirty minutes later Leo's heart eased as the first module bundle slid smoothly into place in the D-620's embrace. In a minor nightmare, undispelled by checking and re-checking his figures, he'd envisioned something Not Fitting, followed by endless delays for correction. The fact that they'd heard nothing from downside yet apart from repeated pleas for communication did not reassure him much. GalacTech management on Rodeo had to respond eventually, and there wasn't a thing he could do to counter that response until it shaped itself. Rodeo's apparent paralysis couldn't last much longer.

Meanwhile, it was half past breaktime. Maybe Dr. Minchenko could be persuaded to disgorge something for his throbbing head, to replace the eight hours sleep he wasn't going to get. Leo punched up his work gang leaders' channel on his suit com.

"Bobbi, take over as foreman. I'm going Inside. Pramod, bring in your team as soon as that last strap is bolted down. Bobbi, be sure that second module bundle is tied in solid before you adjust and seal all the end airlocks, right?"

"Yes, Leo. I'm on it." Bobbi waved acknowledgment from the far end of the module bundle with a lower arm.

As Leo turned away, one of the one-man mini-pushers that had helped tug the module bundle into place detached itself and rotated, preparing to thrust away and help the next bundle already being aligned beyond the super-jumper. One of its attitude jets puffed, then, even as Leo watched, emitted a sudden intense blue stream. Its rotation picked up speed.

That's uncontrolled! Leo thought, his eyes widening. In the bare moment it took him to call up the right channel on his suit com, the rotation became a spin. The pusher jetted off wildly, missing colliding with a work-suited quaddie by a scant meter. As Leo watched in horror it caromed off a nacelle on one of the superjumper's Necklin rod arms and tumbled into space beyond.

The com channel from the pusher emitted a wordless scream. Leo bounced channels. "Vatel!" he called the quaddie manning the nearest other little pusher. "Go after her!"

The second pusher rotated and sped past him; he saw the flash of one of Vatel's gloved hands visually acknowledging the order through the pusher's wide-angle front viewport. Leo restrained a heart-wrenching urge to jet after them himself. Damn little he could do in a power-depleted work suit. It was up to Vatel.

Had it been human—or quaddie—error, or a mechanical defect that had caused the accident? Well, he would be able to tell quickly enough once the pusher was retrieved. *If the pusher was retrieved . . .* He squelched that thought. Instead he jetted over to the Necklin rod nacelle.

The nacelle housing was deeply dented where the pusher had collided with it. Leo tried to reassure himself. *It's only a housing. It's put there just to protect the guts from accidents like this, right?* Hissing in dismay, he pulled himself around to shine his work suit light into the man-high dark aperture at one end of the housing.

Oh, God.

The vortex mirror was cracked. Over three meters wide at its elliptical lip, mathematically shaped and polished to angstrom-unit precision, it was an integral control surface of the jump system, reflecting, bleeding or amplifying the Necklin field generated by the main rods at the will of the pilot. Not just cracked—shattered in a starry burst, cold titanium deformed past its limits. Leo moaned.

A second light shone in past him. Leo glanced around to find Pramod at his shoulder.

"Is that as bad as it looks?" Pramod's voice choked over the suit com.

"Yes," sighed Leo.

"You can't—do a welded repair on those, can you?" Pramod's voice was rising. "What are we going to do?"

Fatigue and fear, the worst possible combination—Leo kept his own tired voice flat. "My suit supply-level readout says we're going to go Inside and take a break right now. After that we'll see."

To Leo's immense relief, by the time he had unsuited, Vatel had retrieved the errant pusher and brought it back to dock at its Habitat module. They unloaded a frightened, bruised quaddie pilot.

"It locked on, I couldn't get it off," she wept. "What did I hit? Did I hit somebody? I didn't *want* to dump the fuel—it was the only way I could think of to kill the jet. I'm sorry I wasted it. I couldn't shut it off . . ."

She was, Leo guessed, all of fourteen years old. "How long have you been on work shift?" he demanded.

"Since we started," she sniffed. She was shaking, all four of her hands trembling, as she hung in air sideways to him. He resisted an urge to straighten her "up".

"Good God, child, that's over twenty-six hours straight. Go take a break. Eat something and go sleep."

She looked at him in bewilderment. "But the dorm units are all cut off and bundled with the crèches. I can't get there from here."

"Is that why . . . ? Look, three-fourths of the Habitat is inaccessible right now. Stake out a corner of the suit locker room or anywhere you can find." He gazed at her tears in bafflement a moment, then added, "It's *allowed*." She clearly wanted her own familiar sleep sack, which Leo was in no position to supply.

"All by myself?" she said in a very small voice.

She'd probably never slept with less than seven other kids in the room in her life, Leo reflected. He took a deep, controlling breath—he would *not* start screaming at her, no matter how wonderfully it would relieve his own feelings— how had he gotten sucked into this children's crusade, any- way? He could not at the moment recall.

"Come along." He took her by the hand off to the locker room, found a laundry bag to hook to the wall, and helped stuff her into it along with a packaged sandwich. Her face peered from the opening, making him feel for a weird moment like a man in process of drowning a sack of kittens.

"There." He forced a smile. "All better, huh?"

"Thank you, Leo," she sniffed. "I'm sorry about the pusher. And the fuel."

"We'll take care of it." He winked heroically. "Get some sleep, huh? There'll still be plenty of work to do when you wake up. You're not going to miss anything. Uh . . . nighty-night."

"'Night . . ."

In the corridor he rubbed his hands over his face. "*Nng . . .*"

Three-fourths of the Habitat inaccessible? It was more like nine-tenths by now. And all the module bundles were running on emergency power, waiting to be reattached to the main power supply as they were loaded into the super-jumper. It was vital to the safety and comfort of those trapped aboard various sub-units that the Habitat be fully reconfigured and made operational as swiftly as possible.

Not to mention everyone's having to start to learn their way around a new maze. Multiple compromises had driven the design—crèche units, for example, could go in an interior bundle; docks and locks had to be positioned facing out into space; some garbage vents were unavoidably cut off, power mods had to be positioned just so, the nutrition units, now serving some three thousand meals a day, required certain kinds of access to storage. . . . Getting everyone's routines readjusted was going to be an unholy mess for a while, even assuming all the module bundles were loaded in right-side-up and attached head-end-round when Leo wasn't personally supervising—or even when he *was* watching, Leo admitted to himself. His face was numb.

And now the kicker-question—should they continue loading at all onto a superjumper that was, just possibly, fatally disabled? The vortex mirror, God. Why couldn't she have rammed one of the normal space thruster arms? Why couldn't she have run over Leo himself?

"Leo!" called a familiar male voice.

Floating down the corridor, his arms crossed angrily, came the jump pilot, Ti Gulik. Silver starfished from hand-grip to hand-grip behind him, trailed by Pramod. Gulik grabbed a grip and swung to a halt beside Leo. Leo's gaze crossed Silver's in a frustratingly brief and silent *Hello!* before the jump pilot pinned him to the wall.

"What have your damned quaddies done to my Necklin rods?" sputtered Ti. "We go to all this trouble to catch this ship, bring it here, and practically the first thing you do is start smashing it up—I barely got it parked!" His voice faded "Please—tell me that little mutant," he waved at Pramod, "got it wrong . . . ?"

Leo cleared his throat. "One of the pusher attitude jets apparently got stuck in an 'on' position, throwing the pusher into an uncontrollable spin. The term 'unpreventable accident' is not in my vocabulary, but it certainly wasn't the quaddie's fault."

"Huh," said Ti. "Well, at least you're not trying to pin it on the pilot . . . but what was the damage, really?"

"The rod itself wasn't hit—"

Ti let out a relieved breath.

"—but the portside titanium vortex mirror was smashed."

Ti's breath became a howl in a minor key. "That's just as bad!"

"Calm down! Maybe not quite as bad. I have one or two ideas yet. I wanted to talk to you anyway. When we took over the Habitat, there was a freight shuttle in dock."

Ti eyed him suspiciously. "Lucky you. So?"

"Planning, not luck. Something Silver doesn't know yet"—Leo caught her eye; she braced herself visibly, soberly intent upon his words—"we weren't able to get Tony back before we took over the Habitat. He's still in hospital downside on Rodeo."

"Oh, no," Silver whispered. "Is there any way—?"

Leo rubbed his aching forehead. "Maybe. I'm not sure it's good military thinking—the precedent had to do with sheep, I believe—but I don't think I could live with myself if we didn't at least try to get him back. Dr. Minchenko has also promised to go with us if we can somehow pick up Madame Minchenko. She's downside too."

"Dr. Minchenko stayed?" Silver clapped her hands, clearly thrilled. "Oh, good."

"Only if we retrieve the Madame," Leo cautioned. "So that's two reasons to chance a downside foray. We have a shuttle, we have a pilot—"

"Oh, no," began Ti, "now, wait a minute—"

"—and we desperately need a spare part. If we can locate a vortex mirror in a Rodeo warehouse—"

"You won't," Ti cut in firmly. "Jumpship repairs are handled solely by the District orbital yards at Orient IV. Everything's warehoused on that end. I know 'cause we had a problem once and had to wait four days for a repair crew to arrive from there. Rodeo's got nothing to do with superjumpers, nothing." He crossed his arms.

"I was afraid of that," said Leo lowly. "Well, there's one other possibility. We could try to fabricate a new one, here on the spot."

Ti looked like a man sucking on a lemon. "Graf, you don't weld those things together out of scrap iron. I know damn well they make 'em all in one piece—something about joins impeding the field flow—and that sucker's three meters wide at the top end! The thing they stamp them out with weighs multi tons. And the precision required—it would take you six months to put a project like that together!"

Leo gulped, and held up both hands, fingers spread. Had he been a quaddie he might have been tempted to double the estimate, but, "Ten hours," he said. "Sure, I'd like to have six months. Downside. In a foundry. With a monster alloy-steel press die machined to the millimicron, just like the big boys. And mass water-cooling, and a team of assistants, and unlimited funding—I'd be all set up to make ten thousand units. But we don't need ten thousand units. There *is* another way. A quick-and-dirty one-shot, but one shot's all we're going to have time for. But I can't be up *here*, refabricating a vortex mirror, and down *there*, rescuing Tony, both at the same time. The quaddies can't go. I need you, Ti. I'd have needed you to pilot the shuttle in any case. Now I'll just need you to do a little more."

"Look, you," Ti began. "Theory was, I was going to get out of this with a whole skin 'cause GalacTech would think I was kidnapped, and had jumped you out with a gun to my head. A nice, simple, believable scenario. This is getting too damned complicated. Even if I could pull off a stunt like that, they're not going to believe I did it under duress. What would keep me from flying downside—and just turning myself in? That's the sort of questions they'll be asking, you can bet your ass. No, dammit. Not for love nor money."

"I know," Leo growled. "We've offered both." Ti glared at him, but ducked his head to evade Silver's eyes.

A thin young voice was echoing down the corridor. "Leo? Leo . . . !"

"Here!" Leo answered. What now . . . ?

One of the younger quaddies swung into sight and darted toward them. "Leo! We've been looking all over for you. Come quick!"

"What is it?"

"An urgent message. On the com. From downside."

"We're not answering their messages. Total blackout, remember? The less information we give them, the longer it's going to take them to figure out what to do about us."

"But it's Tony!"

Leo's guts knotted, and he lurched after the messenger. Silver, pale, and the others followed hot behind.

The holovid solidified, showing a hospital bed. Tony was braced against the raised backrest, looking directly into the vid. He wore T-shirt and shorts, a white bandage around his left lower bicep, a thick stiffness to his torso hinting at wrappings beneath. His face was furrowed, flushed over a pale underlay. His blue eyes shifted nervously, white-rimmed like a frightened pony's, to the right of his bed where Bruce Van Atta stood.

"Took you long enough to answer your call, Graf," Van Atta said, smirking unpleasantly.

Leo swallowed hard. "Hullo, Tony. We haven't forgotten you, up here. Claire and Andy are all right, and back together—"

"You're here to listen, Graf, not talk," Van Atta interrupted. He fiddled with a control. "There, I've just cut your audio, so you can save your breath. All right, Tony"—Van Atta prodded the quaddie with a silver-colored rod—what was it? Leo wondered fearfully—"say your piece."

Tony's gaze shifted back, to the silent vid image Leo guessed, and his eyes widened urgently. He took a deep breath and began gabbling, "Whatever you're doing, Leo, keep doing it. Never mind about me. Get Claire away—get Andy away—"

The holovid blacked out abruptly, although the audio channel remained open a moment longer. It emitted a strange spatting noise, a scream, and Van Atta swearing, "Hold still, you little shit!" before the sound cut off too.

Leo found himself gripping one of Silver's hands.

"Claire was on her way over," Silver said lowly, "to be in on this call."

Leo's eyes met hers. "I think you'd better go divert her."

Silver nodded grim understanding. "Right." She swung away.

The vid came back up. Tony was huddled silently in the far corner of the bed, head down, hands over his face. Van Atta stood glaring, rocking furiously on his heels.

"The kid's a slow learner, evidently," Van Atta snarled to Leo. "I'll make it short and clear, Graf. You may hold hostages, but if you so much as touch 'em, you can be swung in any court in the galaxy. *I've* got a hostage I can do anything I want to, legally. And if you don't think I will, just try me. Now, we're going to be sending a security shuttle up there in a little while to restore order. And you *will* cooperate with it." He held up the silvery rod, pressed something; Leo saw an electric spark spit from its tip. "This is a simple device, but I can get real creative with it, if you force me to. Don't force me to, Leo."

"Nobody's forcing you to—" Leo began.

"Ah," Van Atta interrupted, "just a minute . . ."—he touched his holovid control—"now talk so's I can hear you. And it had better be something I want to hear."

"Nobody here can force you to do anything," Leo grated. "Whatever you do, you do of your own free will. We don't have any hostages. What we have is three volunteers, who chose to stay for—for their consciences' sake, I guess."

"If Minchenko's one of them, you'd better watch your back, Leo. Conscience hell, he wants to hang onto his own little empire. You're a fool, Graf. Here . . ."—he made a motion off-vid—"come talk to him in his own language, Yei."

Dr. Yei stepped stiffly into view, met Leo's eyes and moistened her lips. "Mr. Graf, please, stop this madness. What you are trying to do is incredibly dangerous, for all concerned—" Van Atta illustrated this by waving the electric prod over her head with a sour grin; she glanced at him in irritation, but said nothing and plowed on grimly. "Surrender now, and the damage can at least be minimized. Please. For everyone's sake. You have the power to stop this."

Leo was silent for a moment, then leaned forward. "Dr. Yei, I'm forty-five thousand kilometers up. You're there in the same room . . . *you* stop him." He flicked the holovid off, and floated in numb silence.

"Is that wise?" choked Ti uncertainly.

Leo shook his head. "Don't know. But without an audience, there's no reason to carry on a show, surely."

"Was that acting? How far will that guy really go?"

"In the past I've known him to have a pretty uncontrolled temper, when he got wound up. An appeal to his self-interest usually unwound him. But as you've realized yourself, the, um career rewards in this mess are minimal. I don't know how far he'll go. I don't think even he knows."

After a long pause Ti said, "Do you, ah—still need a shuttle pilot, Leo?"

Chapter 14

Silver clutched the arms of the shuttle co-pilot's seat tightly in mixed exhilaration and fear. Her lower hands curled over the seat's front edge, seeking purchase. Deceleration and gravity yanked at her. She spared a hand to double-check the latch of the shoulder-harness snugging her in as the shuttle altered its attitude to nose-down and the ground heaved into view. Red desert mountains, rocky and forbidding, wrinkled and buckled below them, passing faster and faster as they dropped closer.

Ti sat beside her in the commander's chair, his hands and feet barely moving the controls in tiny, constant corrections, eyes flicking from readout to readout and then to the real horizon, totally absorbed. The atmosphere roared over the shuttle's skin and the craft rocked violently in some passing wind shear. Silver began to see why Leo, despite his expressed anguish at the risk to them all of losing Ti downside, had not substituted Zara or one of the other pusher pilots in Ti's stead. Even barring the foot pedals, landing on a planet was definitely a discipline apart from jetting about in free fall, especially in a vehicle nearly the size of a Habitat module.

"There's the dry lake bed," Ti nodded forward, addressing her without taking his eyes from his work. "Right on the horizon."

"Will it be—very much harder than landing on a shuttleport runway?" Silver asked in worry.

"No problem." Ti smiled. "If anything, it's easier. It's a big puddle—it's one of our emergency alternate landing sites anyway. Just avoid the gullies at the north end, and we're home free."

"Oh," said Silver, reassured. "I hadn't realized you'd landed out here before."

"Well, I haven't, actually," Ti murmured, "not having had an emergency yet. . . ." He sat up more intently, taking a tighter grip on the controls, and Silver decided perhaps she would not distract him with further conversation just now.

She peeked around the edge of her seat at Dr. Minchenko, holding down the engineer's station behind them, to see how he was taking all this. His return smile was sardonic, as if to tease her for her anxiety, but she noticed his hand checking his seat straps, too.

The ground rushed up from below. Silver was almost sorry they had not, after all, waited for the cover of night to make this landing. At least she wouldn't have been able to see her death coming. She could, of course, close her eyes. She closed her eyes, but opened them again almost immediately. Why miss the last experience of one's life? She was sorry Leo had never made a pass at her. He must suffer from stress accumulation too, surely. Faster and faster . . .

The shuttle bumped, bounced, banged, rocked, and roared out over the flat cracked surface. She was sorry *she* had never made a pass at Leo. Clearly, you could die while waiting for other people to start your life for you. Her seat harness cut across her breasts as deceleration sucked her forward and the rumbling vibration rattled her teeth.

"Not quite as smooth as a runway," Ti shouted, grinning and sparing her a bright glance at last. "But good enough for company work . . ."

All right, so nobody else was gibbering in terror, maybe this was the way a landing was supposed to be. They rolled to a quite demure stop in the middle of nowhere. Toothed carmine mountains ringed an empty horizon. Silence fell.

"Well," said Ti, "here we are. . . ." He released his harness with a snap and turned to Dr. Minchenko, struggling up out of the engineer's seat. "Now what? Where is she?"

"If you would be good enough," said Dr. Minchenko, "to provide us with an exterior scan . . ."

A view of the horizon scrolled slowly several times through a monitor, as the minutes ticked by in Silver's brain. The gravity, Silver discovered, was not nearly so awful as Claire had described it. It was much like the time spent under acceleration on the way to the wormhole, only very still and without vibration, or like at the transfer station only stronger. It would have helped if the design of the seat had matched the design of her body.

"What if Rodeo Traffic Control saw us land?" she said. "What if GalacTech gets here first?"

"It's more frightening to think traffic control might have missed us," said Ti. "As for who gets here first—well, Dr. Minchenko?"

"Mm," he said glumly. Then he brightened, leaned forward and froze the scan, and put his finger on a small smudge in the screen, perhaps 15 kilometers distant.

"Dust devil?" said Ti, plainly trying to control his hopes.

The smudge focused. "Land rover," said Dr. Minchenko, smiling in satisfaction. "Oh, *good* girl."

The smudge grew into a boiling vortex of orange dust spun up behind a speeding land rover. Five minutes later the vehicle braked to a halt beside the shuttle's forward hatchway. The figure under the dusty bubble canopy paused to adjust a breath mask, then the bubble swung up and the side ramp swung down.

Dr. Minchenko adjusted his own breath mask firmly over his nose and, followed by Ti, rushed down the shuttle stairs to assist the frail, silver-haired woman who was struggling with an assortment of odd-shaped packages. She gave them all up to the men with evident gladness but for a thick black case shaped rather like a spoon which she clutched to her bosom in much the same way, Silver thought, as Claire clutched Andy. Dr. Minchenko shepherded his lady anxiously upward toward the airlock—her knees moved stiffly, on the stairs—and through, where they could at last pull down their masks and speak clearly.

"Are you all right, Warren?" Madame Minchenko asked.

"Perfectly," he assured her.

"I could bring almost nothing—I scarcely knew what to choose."

"Think of the vast amounts of money we shall save on shipping charges, then."

Silver was fascinated by the way gravity gave form to Madame Minchenko's dress. It was a warm, dark fabric with a silver belt at the waist, and hung in soft folds about her booted ankles. The skirt swirled as Madame Minchenko stepped, echoing her agitation.

"It's utter madness. We're too old to become refugees. I had to leave my harpsichord!"

Dr. Minchenko patted her sympathetically on the shoulder. "It wouldn't work in free fall anyway. The little pluckers fall back into place by gravity." His voice cracked with urgency, "But they're trying to kill my quaddies, Ivy!"

"Yes, yes, I understand . . ." Madame Minchenko twitched a somewhat strained and absent smile at Silver, who hung one-handed from a strap listening. "You must be Silver?"

"Yes, Madame Minchenko," said Silver breathlessly in her most-politest voice. This woman was quite the most aged downsider Silver had ever seen, bar Dr. Minchenko and Dr. Cay himself.

"We must go now, to get Tony," Dr. Minchenko said. "We'll be back as quick as we can drive. Silver will help you; she's very good. Hold the ship!"

The two men hustled back out, and within moments the land rover was boiling off across the barren landscape.

Silver and Madame Minchenko were left regarding each other.

"Well," said Madame Minchenko.

"I'm sorry you had to leave all your things," said Silver diffidently.

"H'm. Well, I can't say I'm sorry to be leaving here." Madame Minchenko's glance around the shuttle's cargo bay took in Rodeo by implication.

They shuffled forward to the pilot's compartment and sat; the monitor scanned the monotonous horizon. Madame Minchenko still clutched her giant spoon suitcase in her lap. Silver hitched herself around in her wrong-shaped seat and tried to imagine what it would be like to be married to someone for more than twice the length of her own life. Had Madame Minchenko been young once? Surely Dr. Minchenko had been old forever.

"However did you come to be married to Dr. Minchenko?" Silver asked.

"Sometimes I wonder," Madame Minchenko murmured dryly, half to herself.

"Were you a nurse, or a lab tech?"

She looked up with a little smile. "No, dear, I was never a bioscientist. Thank God." Her hand caressed the black case. "I'm a musician. Of sorts."

Silver perked with interest. "Synthavids? Do you program? We've had some synthavids in our library, the company library that is."

The corner of Madame Minchenko's mouth twisted up in a half-smile. "There's nothing synthetic in what I do. I'm a registered historian-performer. I keep old skills alive— think of me as a live museum exhibit, somewhat in need of dusting—only a few spider webs clinging to my elbow. . . ." She unlatched her case and opened it to Silver's inspection. Burnished reddish wood, satin-smooth, caught and played back the colored lights of the pilot's compartment. Madame Minchenko lifted the instrument and tucked it under her chin. "It's a violin."

"I've seen pictures of them," Silver offered. "Is it real?"

Madame Minchenko smiled, and drew her bow across the strings in a quick succession of notes. The music ran up and down like—like quaddie children in the gym, was the only simile Silver could think of. The volume was astounding.

"Where do those wires on top attach to the speakers?" Silver inquired, pushing up on her lower hands and craning her neck.

"There are no speakers. The sound all comes from the wood."

"But it filled the compartment!"

Madame Minchenko's smile became almost fierce. "*This* instrument could fill an entire concert hall."

"Do you . . . play concerts?"

"Once, when I was very young—your age, maybe . . . I went to a school that taught such skills. The only school for music on my planet. A colonial world, you see, not much time for the arts. There was a competition—the winner was to travel to Earth, and have a recording career. Which he subsequently did. But the recording company underwriting the affair was only interested in the very best. *I* came in second. There is room for so very few . . ." Her voice faded in a sigh. "I was left with a pleasing personal accomplishment that no one wanted to listen to. Not when they had only to plug in a disc to hear not just the best from my world, but the best in the galaxy. Fortunately, I met Warren about then. My permanent patron and audience of one. Probably as well I wasn't trying to make a career of it, we moved so often in those days, when he was finishing school and starting work with GalacTech. I've done some teaching here and there, to interested antiquarians . . ." She tilted her head at Silver. "And did they teach you any music, with all the things they've been teaching you up on that satellite?"

"We learned some songs when we were little," said Silver shyly. "And then there were the flute-toots. But they didn't last long."

"Flute-toots?"

"Little plastic things you blew in. *They* were real. One of the crèche mothers brought them up when I was about, oh, eight. But then they sort of got all over the place, and people were complaining about the, um, tooting. So she had to take them all back."

"I see. Warren never mentioned the flute-toots." Madame Minchenko's eyebrows quirked. "Ah . . . what sort of songs?"

"Oh . . ." Silver drew breath, and sang, "Roy G. Biv, Roy G. Biv, he's the color quaddie that the spectrum gives; Red-orange-yellow, green and blue, indigo, violet, all for you—" she broke off, flushing. Her voice sounded so wavery and weak, compared to that astonishing violin.

"I see," said Madame Minchenko in a strangely choked voice. Her eyes danced, though, so Silver didn't think she was offended. "Oh, Warren," she sighed, "the things you have to answer for . . ."

"May I," Silver began, and stopped. Surely she would not be permitted to touch that lavish antique. What if she forgot to hold onto it for a moment and the gravity pulled it from her hands?

"Try it?" Madame Minchenko finished her thought. "Why not? We appear to have a little time to kill, here."

"I'm afraid—"

"Tut. Oh, I used to protect this one. It sat unplayed for years, locked up in climate-controlled vaults . . . dead. Then of late I began to wonder what I was saving it for. Here, now. Raise your chin, so; tuck, so," Madame Minchenko curled Silver's fingers around the violin's neck. "What nice long fingers you have, dear. And, er . . . what a *lot* of them. I wonder . . ."

"What?" asked Silver as Madame Minchenko trailed off.

"Hm? Oh. I was just having a mental picture of a quaddie in free fall with a twelve-string guitar. If you weren't squashed into a chair as you are now you could bring that lower hand up . . ."

It was a trick of the light, perhaps, of Rodeo's westering sun sinking toward the sawtoothed horizon and sending its

red beams through the cabin windows, but Madame
Minchenko's eyes seemed to gleam. "Now arch your fingers, so . . ."

Fire.

The first problem had been to find enough pure scrap
titanium around the Habitat to add to the mass of the
ruined vortex mirror to allow for the inevitable losses during re-fabrication. A forty-percent extra mass margin
would have been enough for Leo to feel comfortable with.

There ought to have been titanium storage tanks for
nasty corrosive liquids—a single, say, hundred-liter tank
would have done the trick—conduits, valves, something.
For the first desperate hour of scrounging Leo was convinced his plan would come to grief right there in Step
One. Then he found it in, of all places, Nutrition; a cooler
full of titanium storage canisters massing a good half-kilo
apiece. Their varied contents were hastily dumped into
every substitute container Leo and his quaddie raiders
could find. "Clean-up," Leo had called guiltily over his
shoulder to the appalled quaddie girl now running Nutrition, "is left as an exercise for the student."

The second problem had been to find a place to work.
Pramod had pointed out one of the abandoned Habitat
modules, a cylinder some four meters in diameter. It was
the work of another two hours to tear holes in the side for
entry and pack one end of it with all the conductive scrap
metal mass they could find. The mass was then surfaced
with more abandoned Habitat module skin, pounded out
and rendered as nearly glass-smooth as they could make it
in a shallow concave bowl of carefully calculated arc that
spanned the diameter of the module.

Now their mass of scrap titanium hung weightless in the center of the module. The broken-up pieces of the vortex mirror and the flattened-out food canisters were all bound together by a spool of pure titanium wire some brilliant quaddie child had produced for them out of Stores. The dense gray metal glittered and glowed in their work-lights and the reflection from a shaft of hard-edged sunlight falling through one of their entry holes.

Leo glanced around the chamber one last time. Four work-suited quaddies each manned a laser unit braced around the walls, bracketing the titanium mass. Leo's measuring instruments floated tethered to his belt, ready to his pressure-gloved hands. It was time. Leo touched his helmet control, darkening his faceplate.

"Commence firing," said Leo into his suit com.

Four beams of laser light lanced out in unison, pouring into the scrap. For the first few minutes, nothing appeared to be happening. Then it began to glow, dark red, bright red, yellow, white—then, visibly, one of the ex-food canisters began to sag, flowing into the jumble. The quaddies continued to pour in the energy.

The mass was beginning to drift slightly, one of Leo's readouts told him, although the effect was not yet visible to the naked eye. "Unit Four, power-up about ten percent," Leo instructed. One of the quaddies flashed a lower palm in acknowledgment and touched his control box. The drift stopped. Good, his bracketing was working. Leo had had a horrid vision of the molten mass of metal drifting off into the side wall, or worse, fatally brushing into somebody, but the very beams that melted it seemed enough to control its motion, at least in the absence of stronger sources of momentum.

Now the melt was obvious, the metal becoming a white glowing blob of liquid floating in the vacuum, struggling toward the shape of a perfect sphere. *Boy, is that stuff ever going to be pure when we're done*, Leo reflected with satisfaction.

He checked his monitoring devices. Now they were coming up on a moment of critical judgment: when to stop? They must pour in enough energy to achieve an absolutely uniform melt, no funny lumps left in the middle of the gravy. But not too much; even though it was not visible to the eye Leo knew there was metal vapor pouring off that bubble now, part of his calculated loss.

More importantly, looking ahead to the next step—every kilocalorie they dumped into that titanium mass was going to have to be brought back out. Planetside, the shape he was trying to get would have been formed against a copper mold, with lots and lots of water to carry away the heat at the desired rate, in this case rapidly; single-crystal splat-cooling, it was called. Well, at least he'd figured out how to achieve the splat part of it. . . .

"Cease firing," Leo ordered.

And there it hung, their sphere of molten metal, blue-white with the violent heat energy contained within it, perfect. Leo checked and re-checked its centered position, and had laser number two give it one more half-second blast not for melt but for momentum's sake.

"All right," said Leo into his suit com. "Now let's get everything out of this module that's going out, and double-check everything that's staying. Last thing we need now is for somebody to drop his wrench in the soup pot, right?"

Leo joined the quaddies in shoving their equipment unceremoniously out the holes torn in the side of the module. Two of his laser operators went with it, two stayed with

Leo. Leo checked centering again, and then they all strapped themselves to the walls.

Leo switched channels in his suit com. "Ready, Zara?" he called.

"Ready, Leo," the quaddie pilot responded from her pusher, now attached to the gutted module's stern.

"Now remember, slow and gentle does it. But firm. Pretend your pusher is a scalpel, and you're just about to operate on one of your friends or something."

"Right, Leo." There was a grin in her voice. *Don't swagger, girl*, Leo prayed inwardly.

"Go when you're ready."

"Going. Hang on up there!"

There was at first no perceivable change. Then Leo's harness straps began to tug gently at him. It was the Habitat module, not the molten ball of titanium, that was moving, Leo reminded himself. The metal did not drift; it was the back wall that moved forward and engulfed it.

It was working, by God it was working! The metal bubble touched the back wall, spread out, and settled into its shallow bowl mold.

"Increase acceleration by the first increment," Leo called into his com. The pusher powered up, and the molten titanium circle spread, its edges growing toward the desired diameter some three meters wide, already losing its bright glow. Creating a titanium blank of controlled thickness, ready (after cooling) for explosive molding into its final subtle form.

"Steady on. That does it!"

Splat-cooling? Well, not exactly. Leo was uncomfortably aware that they were probably not going to achieve a perfect internal single-crystal freeze. But it would be good, good enough—as long as it was good enough that they didn't have to melt it down and start all over again, that was the most Leo dared pray for. They might, barely, have time to make one of these suckers. Not two. And when *was* the threatened response from Rodeo arriving? Soon, surely.

He wondered briefly what the new gravity technology was going to do to fabrication problems in space like this. Revolutionize seemed too mild a term, certainly. *Too bad we didn't have some now*, he thought. Still—he grinned, concealed within his helmet—they were doing all right.

He pointed his temperature gauge at the back wall. The piece was cooling almost as rapidly as he had hoped. They were still due for a couple of hours of driving around until it had dumped enough heat to remove from the wall and handle without danger of deformation.

"All right, Bobbi, I'm leaving you and Zara in charge here," Leo said. "It's looking good. When the temperature drops to about five hundred degrees centigrade, bring it on back. We'll try to be ready for the final cooling and the second phase of the shaping."

Carefully, trying not to add excess vibration to the walls, Leo loosed his harness and climbed to the exit hole. From this distance he had a fine view of the D-620, now more than half loaded, and Rodeo beyond. Better go now, before the view became more distant than his suit jets could close.

He activated his jets and zipped quickly away from the side of the still-gently-accelerating module-and-pusher unit. It chugged off, looking a drunken, jury-rigged wreck indeed, concealing hope in its heart.

Leo aimed toward the Habitat, and Phase II of his Jumpships-Repaired-While-U-Wait scheme.

It was sunset on the dry lake bed. Silver gazed anxiously into the monitor in the shuttle control cabin as it swept the

horizon, brightening and darkening each time the red ball
of the sun rolled past.

"They can't possibly be back for at least another hour,"
Madame Minchenko, watching her, pointed out, "in the
best case."

"That's not who I'm looking for," answered Silver.

·"Hm." Madame Minchenko drummed her long, age-
sculptured fingers on the console, unlatched and tilted
back the co-pilot's seat, and stared thoughtfully at the cabin
roof. "No, I suppose not. Still—if GalacTech traffic control
saw you land and sent out a jetcopter to investigate, they
should have been here before now. Perhaps they missed
your landing after all."

"Perhaps they're just not very organized," suggested Silver, "and they'll be along any minute."

Madame Minchenko sighed. "All too likely." She
regarded Silver, pursing her lips. "And what are you supposed to do in that case?"

"I have a weapon." Silver touched the laser-solderer,
lying seductively on the console before the pilot-
commander's seat in which she sprawled. "But I'd rather
not shoot anybody else. Not if I can help it."

"Anybody *else*?" There was a shade more respect in
Madame Minchenko's voice.

Shooting people was such a *stupid* activity, why should
everybody—anybody!—be so impressed? Silver wondered
irritably. You would think she had done something truly
great, like discover a new treatment for black stem-rot. Her
mouth tightened.

Then her lips parted, and she leaned forward to stare
into the monitor. "Oh, oh. Here comes a groundcar."

"Not our boys already, surely," said Madame Minchenko
in some unease. "Has something gone wrong, I wonder?"

"It's not your land rover." Silver fiddled with the resolution. The slanting sunlight poured through the dust, turning it into a glowing red smokescreen. "I think . . . it's a GalacTech Security groundcar."

"Oh, dear." Madame Minchenko sat up straight. "Now what?"

"We don't open the hatches, anyway. No matter what."

In a few minutes the groundcar pulled up about fifty meters from the shuttle. An antenna rose from its roof and quivered demandingly. Silver switched on the com—it was so irritating, not to have the full use of her lower arms—and called up a menu of the com channels from the computer. The shuttle seemed to have access to an inordinate number of them. Security audio was 9999. She tuned them in.

"—by God! Hey, you in there—answer!"

"Yes, what do you want?" said Silver.

There was a spluttery pause. "Why didn't you answer?"

"I didn't know you were calling me," Silver answered logically.

"Yeah, well—this freight shuttle is the property of GalacTech."

"So am I. So what?"

"Eh . . . ? Look, lady, this is Sergeant Fors of GalacTech Security. You have to disembark and turn this shuttle over to us."

A voice in the background, not quite sufficiently muffled, inquired, "Hey, Bern—d'you think we'll get the ten percent bonus for recovering stolen property on *this* one?"

"Dream on," growled another voice. "Nobody's gonna give *us* a quarter million."

Madame Minchenko held up a hand, and leaned forward to cut in, quavering, "Young man, this is Ivy

Minchenko. My husband, Dr. Minchenko, has comman-
deered this craft in order to respond to an urgent medical
emergency. Not only is this his right, it's his legally compelled duty—and *you* are required by GalacTech regulation
to assist, not hinder him."

A somewhat baffled growl greeted this. "I'm required to
take this shuttle back. Those are my orders. Nobody told
me anything about any medical emergency."

"Well, I'm telling you!"

The background voice again, ". . . it's just a couple of
women. Come on!"

The sergeant: "Are you going to open the hatch, lady?"

Silver did not respond. Madame Minchenko raised an
inquiring eyebrow, and Silver shook her head silently.
Madame Minchenko sighed and nodded.

The sergeant repeated his demands, his voice fraying—
he stopped just short, Silver felt, of degenerating into
obscenities. After a minute or two he broke off.

After a few more minutes the doors of the groundcar
winged up and the three men, now wearing breath masks,
clambered out to stamp over and stare up at the hatches of
the shuttle high over their heads. They returned to the
groundcar, got in—it circled. Going away? Silver hoped
against hope. No, it came up and parked again under the
forward shuttle hatch. Two of the men rummaged in the
back for tools, then climbed to the car's roof.

"They've got some kind of cutting things," said Silver in
alarm. "They must be going to try to cut their way in."

Banging reverberated through the shuttle.

Madame Minchenko nodded toward the laser-solderer.
"Is it time for that?" she asked fearfully.

Silver shook her head unhappily. "No. Not again. Besides, I can't let them damage the ship either—it's got to stay spaceworthy or we can't get home."

She had watched Ti. . . . She inhaled deeply and reached for the shuttle controls. The foot pedals were hopelessly awkward to grope for; she would have to get along without them. Right engine, activate; left engine, activate—a purr ran through the ship. Brakes—there, surely. She pulled the lever gently to the "release" position. Nothing happened.

Then the shuttle lurched forward. Frightened at the abrupt motion, Silver hit the brake lever again and the ship rocked to a halt. She searched the outside monitors wildly. Where—?

The shuttle's starboard airfoil had swept over the roof of the security groundcar, missing it by half a meter. Silver realized with a guilty shudder that she should have checked its height before she began to move. She might have torn the wing right off, with ghastly chaining consequences to them all.

The security guards were nowhere to be seen—no, there they were, scattered out onto the dry lake bed. One picked himself up out of the dirt and started back toward the groundcar. Now what? If she parked, or even rolled some distance and parked, they would only try again. It couldn't take too many more attempts till they got smart and shot out the shuttle's tires or otherwise immobilized it. A dangerously unstable stand-off.

Silver sucked on her lower lip. Then, leaning forward awkwardly in a seat never designed for quaddies, she released the brakes partway and powered up the port engine. The shuttle shuddered a few meters farther forward, skidding and yawing. Behind them, the monitor showed the groundcar half obscured by orange dust kicked up by the exhaust, its image wavering in the heat of it.

She set the brakes as hard as they would go and powered up the port engine yet more. Its purr became a whine—she dared not bring it to the howling pitch Ti had used during landing, who knew what would happen then?

The groundcar's plastic canopy cracked in a crazed starburst and began to sag. If Leo had been right in his description of that hydrocarbon fuel they used downside here for their vehicles, in just a second more she ought to get . . .

A yellow fireball engulfed the groundcar, momentarily brighter than the setting sun. Pieces flew off in all directions, arcing and bouncing fantastically in the gravity field. A glance at her monitors showed Silver the security men now all running in the other direction.

Silver powered down the port engine, released the brakes, and let the shuttle roll forward across the hard-baked mud. Fortunately, the old lake bed was quite uniform, so she didn't have to worry about the fine points of shuttle operation such as steering.

One of the security men ran after them for a minute or two, waving his arms, but he fell behind quickly. She let the shuttle roll on for a couple of kilometers, braked again, and shut the engines off.

"Well," she sighed, "that takes care of *them*."

"It certainly does," said Madame Minchenko faintly, adjusting the monitor magnification for a last glance behind. A column of black smoke and a dying orange glow in the distant gathering dusk marked their former parking place.

"I hope all their breath masks were well filled," Silver added.

"Oh, dear," said Madame Minchenko. "Perhaps we ought to go back and . . . do something. Surely they'll have the sense to stay with their car and wait for help, though, and not try to walk off into the desert. The company safety vids always emphasize that. 'Stay with your vehicle and wait for Search and Rescue.'"

"Aren't they supposed to *be* Search and Rescue?" Silver studied the tiny images in the monitor. "Not much vehicle left. But they all three seem to be staying there. Well . . ." She shook her head. "It's too dangerous for us to try and pick them up. But when Ti and the doctor get back with Tony, maybe the security guards could have your land rover to go home in. If, um, nobody else gets here first."

"Oh," said Madame Minchenko, "that's true. Good idea. I feel much better." She peered reflectively into the monitor. "Poor fellows."

Ice.

Leo watched from the sealed control booth overlooking the Habitat freight bay as four work-suited quaddies eased the intact vortex mirror taken from the D-620's second Necklin rod through the hatch from Outside. The mirror was an awkward object to handle, in effect an enormous shallow titanium funnel, three meters in diameter and a centimeter thick at its broad lip, mathematically curved and thickening to about two centimeters at the central, closed dip. A lovely curve, but definitely non-standard, a fact Leo's re-fabrication ploy must needs cope with.

The undamaged mirror was jockeyed into place, nested into a squiggle of freezer coils. The space-suited quaddies exited. From the control booth, Leo sealed the Outside hatch and set the air to pump back into the loading bay. In his anxiety Leo literally popped out of the control booth, with a *whoosh* of air from the remaining pressure differential, and had to work his jaw to clear his ears.

The only freezer coils big enough to be adequate to the task had been found by Bobbi in a moment of inspiration, once more in Nutrition. The quaddie girl running the department had moaned when she saw Leo and his work gang approach again. They had ruthlessly ripped the guts out of her biggest freezer compartment and carried them off to their work space, in the largest available docking module now installed as part of the D-620. Less than a quarter of the final Habitat re-assembly was left to go, Leo estimated, despite the fact that he'd pulled a dozen of the best workers onto this project.

In a few minutes three of his quaddies joined Leo in the freight bay. Leo checked them over. They were bundled up in extra T-shirts and shorts and long-sleeved coveralls left by the evicted downsiders, with the legs wrapped tight to their lower arms and secured by elastic bands. They had scrounged enough gloves to go around; good, Leo had been worried about frostbite with all those exposed fingers. His breath smoked in the chilled air.

"All right, Pramod, we're ready to roll. Bring up the water hoses."

Pramod unrolled several lengths of tubing and gave them to the waiting quaddies; another quaddie ran a final check of their connections to the nearest water spigot. Leo switched on the freezer coils and took a hose.

"All right, kids, watch me and I'll show you the trick of it. You must bleed the water slowly onto the cold surfaces, avoiding splash into the air; at the same time you must keep it going constantly enough so that your hoses don't freeze up. If you feel your fingers going numb, take a short break in the next chamber. We don't need any injuries out of this."

Leo turned to the back side of the vortex mirror, nestled among but not touching the freezer coils. The mirror had been in the shade for the last several hours Outside, and was good and cold now. He thumbed his valve and let a silvery blob of water flow onto the mirror's surface. It spread out in swift feathers of ice. He tried some drops on the coils; they froze even faster.

"All right, just like that. Start building up the ice mold around the mirror. Make it as solid as you can, no air pockets. Don't forget to place the little tube to let the air evacuate from the die chamber, later."

"How thick should it be?" asked Pramod, following suit with his hose and watching in fascination as the ice formed.

"At least one meter. At a minimum the mass of the ice must be equal to the mass of the metal. Since we've only got one shot at this, we'll go for at least twice the mass of the metal. We aren't going to be able to recover any of this water, unfortunately. I want to double-check our water reserves, because two meters thick would certainly be better, if we can spare it."

"However did you think of this?" asked Pramod in an awed tone.

Leo snorted, as he realized Pramod had the impression that he was making up this entire engineering procedure out of his head in the heat of the moment. "I didn't invent it. I read about it. It's an old method they used to use for preliminary test designs, before fractal theory was perfected and computer simulations improved to today's standards."

"Oh." Pramod sounded rather disappointed.

Leo grinned. "If you ever have to make a choice between learning and inspiration, boy, choose learning. It works more of the time."

I hope. Critically, Leo drew back and watched his quaddies work. Pramod had two hoses, one in each set of hands, and was rapidly alternating between them, blob after blob of water flowing onto the coils and the mirror, the ice already starting to thicken visibly. So far he hadn't lost a drop. Leo heaved a weary sigh of relief; it seemed he could safely delegate this part of the task. He gave Pramod a high sign, and left the bay to pursue a part of the job he dared not delegate to anyone else.

Leo got lost twice, threading his way through the Habitat to Toxic Stores, and he'd designed the reconfiguration himself. It was no wonder he passed so many bewildered-looking quaddies on the way. Everyone seemed frantically busy; on the principle of misery-loves-company, Leo could only approve.

Toxic Stores was a chill module sharing no connections whatsoever with the rest of the Habitat but a triple-chambered and always-closed airlock of thick steel. Leo entered to meet one of his own welding and joining gang quaddies still assigned to Habitat reconfiguration on his way out.

"How's it going, Agba?" Leo asked him.

"Pretty good." Agba looked tired. His tan face and skin were marked with red lines, telltales of recent and pro-longed time in his work suit. "Those stupid frozen clamps were really slowing us up, but we're just about to the end of them. How's your thing going?"

"All right so far. I came in to prepare the explosive. We're that far along. Do you remember where the devil in all this"—the module's curved walls were packed with sup-plies—"we keep the slurry explosive?"

"It *was* over there," Agba pointed.

"Good—" Leo's stomach shrank suddenly. "What do you mean, *was*?" *He only means it's been moved*, Leo suggested hopefully to himself.

"Well, we've been using it up at a pretty good clip, blowing open clamps."

"Blowing them open? I thought you were cutting them off."

"We were, but then Tabbi figured out how to pack a small charge that cracked them apart on the line of the vacuum fuse. About half the time they're reusable. The other half they're no more ruined than if we'd cut 'em." Agba looked quite proud of himself.

"You haven't used it *all* for that, surely!"

"Well, there was a little spillage. Outside, of course," Agba, misapprehending, added in response to Leo's horrified look. He held out a sealed half-liter flask to Leo's inspection. "This is the last of it. I figure it will just about finish the job."

"Nng!" Leo's snatching hands closed around the bottle and clutched it to his stomach like a man smothering a grenade. "I need that! I have to have it!" *I have to have ten times that much!* his thought howled silently.

"Oh," said Agba. "Sorry." He gave Leo a look of limpid innocence. "Does this mean we have to go back to cutting clamps?"

"Yes," squeaked Leo. "Go," he added. Yes, before he exploded himself.

Agba, with an uncertain smile, ducked back out the airlock. It sealed, leaving Leo alone a moment to hyperventilate in peace.

Think, man, think, Leo told himself. *Don't panic.* There was something, some elusive fact or factor in the back of his mind, trying to tell him this wasn't the end, but he could not at present recall . . . Unfortunately, a careful mental review of his calculations, keeping track on his fingers (oh, to be a quaddie!) only confirmed his initial fear.

The explosive fabrication of the titanium blank into the complex shape of the vortex mirror required, besides an assortment of spacers, rings, and clamps, three main parts; the ice die, the metal blank, and the explosive to marry the two. Shotgun wedding indeed. And what is the most important leg of a three-legged stool? The one that is missing, of course. And he'd thought the slurry explosive was going to be the *easy* part . . .

Forlorn, Leo began systematically going around the Toxic Stores module, checking its contents. An extra flask of slurry explosive *might* have been misplaced somewhere. Alas, the quaddies were all too conscientious in their inventory control. Each bin contained only what its label proclaimed, no more, no less. Agba had even updated the label on the bin just now; *Contents, Slurry Explosive Type B-2, one-half liter flasks. Quantity, 0.*

About this time Leo stumbled, literally, over a barrel of gasoline. No, some six barrels of the damn stuff, which had somehow washed up here, now strapped firmly to the walls. God knew where the rest of the hundred tons had gone. Leo wished it all in Hell, where it might at least be of some conceivable use. He would gladly trade the whole hundred tons of it for four aspirins. A hundred tons of gasoline, of which—

Leo blinked, and let out an "aaah" of exultation.

Of which a liter or so, mixed with tetranitromethane, would make an even *more* powerful explosive.

He would have to look it up, to be sure—he would have to look up the exact proportions in any case—but he was certain he had remembered aright. Learning *and* inspiration, that was the best combination of all. Tetranitromethane was used as an emergency oxygen source in several Habitat and pusher systems. It yielded more O_2 per cc than liquid oxygen, without the temperature and pressure problems of storage, in a highly refined version of the early tetranitromethane candles which, when burned, gave *off* oxygen. Now—oh, God—if only the TNM hadn't all been used by somebody, to—to blow up balloons for quaddie children or some damn thing—they *had* been losing air during the Habitat reconfiguration . . . Pausing only to put the flask back in its bin and arrange a sign on the barrels reading, in large red print, THIS IS LEO GRAF'S GASOLINE. IF ANYONE ELSE TOUCHES IT HE WILL BREAK ALL THEIR ARMS, he raced out of the Toxic Stores module and away to find the nearest working library computer terminal.

Chapter 15

Twilight lingered on the dry lake bed, the luminous bowl of the sky darkening gradually through a deep turquoise to a star-flecked indigo. Silver found her attention constantly distracted from horizon-scan by the entrancing color changes of the planetary atmosphere seen through the ports. What subtle variety downsiders enjoyed: bands of purple, orange, lemon, green, blue, with cobalt feathers of water vapor melting in the western sky. It was with some regret that Silver switched the scan to infra-red. Its computer-enhanced colors gave clarity to her vision, but seemed crude and garish after the real thing.

At last came the sight her heart desired: a land rover, bouncing over the distant hilly pass and skidding down the last rocky slopes, then peeling out over the lake bed at maximum acceleration. Madame Minchenko hurried out of the pilot's compartment to let down the hatch stairs as the land rover roared to a halt beside the shuttle.

Silver clapped all her hands with delight as she saw Ti thump up the ramp, burdened with Tony clinging piggy-back just as Leo had carted her at the transfer station. *They got him! They got him!* Dr. Minchenko followed close behind.

There was a short argument back at the airlock, Doctor and Madame Minchenko's muffled voices, then Dr. Minchenko galloped back down the stairs to crack a cold flare and stick it to the land rover's roof. It gave off a brilliant green glare. Good, the stranded security guards should have no trouble seeing that beacon, Silver decided with some relief.

Silver scrambled back across to the co-pilot's seat as Ti staggered into the pilot's compartment, dumped Tony into the engineer's seat, and vaulted into the command chair. He yanked his breath mask down around his neck with one hand while switching on controls with the other. "Hey, who's been messing with my ship . . . ?"

Silver turned and pulled herself up to look over the top of her seat at Tony, who had rid himself of his own breath mask and was trying to get his seat straps in order. "You made it!" She grinned.

He grinned back. "'ust bar-ry. 'Er right behin' us." His blue eyes, Silver realized, were huge with pain as well as excitement, his lips swollen.

"What happened to you—?" Silver turned to Ti. "What happened to Tony?"

"That shit Van Atta burned him in the mouth with his damn cattle prod, or whatever the hell that thing was he had," said Ti grimly, his hands dancing over the controls. The engines came alive, lights flickered, and the shuttle began to roll. Ti hit his intercom. "Dr. Minchenko? You folks strapped down back there yet?"

"Just a moment—" came Dr. Minchenko's reply. "There. Yes, go!"

"Did you have any trouble?" asked Silver, sliding back into her seat and groping for her own straps as the shuttle taxied.

"Not at first. We got to the hospital all right, walked right in with no problem. I thought sure the nurses were going to question our taking Tony, but evidently they all think Minchenko is God, there. We just blasted right through and were on our way out, with me playing donkey—that's all I am, just transportation, y'know?— when who should we meet, going out the door, but that son-of-a-bitch Van Atta coming in."

Silver gasped.

"We tripped him up—Dr. Minchenko wanted to stop and beat the shit out of him, on account of Tony's mouth, but he would have had to delegate the most of it to me—he is an old man, little though he wants to admit it—I dragged him out to the land rover. I last heard Van Atta running off screaming for a security jetcopter. He's surely found one by now . . ." Ti scanned the monitors nervously. "Yes. Damn. There." He pointed. A colorized flare swooped over the mountains, marking the following 'copter's position in the monitor. "Well, they can't catch us now."

The shuttle rocked in a wide circle, then halted; the engines' pitch rose from purr to whine to scream. Its white landing lights tunneled the darkness in front of them. Ti released the brakes and the ship sprang forward, gobbling up the light, with a terrifying noisy rumble that ceased abruptly as they rotated into the air. The acceleration shoved them all back in their seats.

"What the *hell* does that idiot think he's doing?" Ti muttered through his teeth as the jetcopter grew rapidly in the tracking monitor. "Try to play chicken with *me*, will you . . . ?"

It was swiftly apparent that was exactly the jetcopter's intent. It arced toward them, diving as they rose, evidently with some idea of forcing them down.

Ti's mouth thinned to a white line, his eyes blazing, and he powered his ship up further. Silver gritted her teeth, but kept her eyes open.

They passed close enough to see the 'copter out the ports, whipping in a strobe-like flash through their lights. In the blink Silver could see faces through the bubble canopy, frozen white blurs with dark round holes of eyes and mouths, but for one individual, possibly the pilot, who had his hands pressed over his eyes.

Then there was nothing between them and the silver stars.

Fire and ice.

Leo rechecked the tightness of every C-clamp personally, then jetted back a few meters in his work suit to give his efforts one last visual inspection. They floated in space a safe kilometer's distance from the D-620–Habitat configuration, which hung huge and complete now above Rodeo's arc. Anyway, it looked complete on the outside, as long as you didn't know too much about the hysterical last-minute tie-downs still going on within.

The ice die, when finished, had turned out over three meters wide and nearly two meters thick. Its outer surface was irregular; it might have been a tumbling bit of space debris from some gas giant's ice ring. Its secret inner side precisely duplicated the smooth curve of the vortex mirror that had molded it.

The evacuated inner chamber was capped by layers. First, the titanium blank; next, a layer of pure gasoline for a spacer—a handy second use Leo had found for it: unlike other possible liquids it would not freeze at the ice's present temperature—then the thin plastic divider circle, then his precious TNM-gasoline explosive, then a cap of scrap Habitat skin, then the bars and clamps—all in all, quite a birthday cake. Time to light the candle and make his wish come true, before the ice die began to sublimate in the sunlight.

Leo turned to motion his quaddie helpers to get behind the protective barrier of one of the abandoned Habitat modules floating nearby. Another quaddie, he saw, was just jetting over from the D-620–Habitat configuration. Leo waited a moment, to give him or her time to come up and get behind their shelter. Not a messenger, surely, he had his suit com for that. . . .

"Hai, Leo," said Tony's voice thickly through the suit comm. "Sorry I'm la'e for work—d'you leave any for me?"

"Tony!"

It wasn't easy, trying to embrace someone through a work suit, but Leo did his best. "Hey, hey, you're just in time for the best part, boy!" said Leo excitedly. "I saw the shuttle dock a bit ago." Yes, and a horrid turn it had given him for a moment, thinking it was Van Atta's threatened security force at last, until he'd correctly identified it as theirs. "Didn't think Dr. Minchenko'd let you go anywhere but the infirmary. Is Silver all right? Shouldn't you be resting?"

"She's fine. Dr. Minchenko had a lot t' do, 'n Claire 'n Andy's asleep—I looked in—didn't want to wake the baby."

"You sure you're feeling all right, son? Your voice sounds funny."

"Hurt mah mout'. S'all right."

"Ah." Briefly, Leo explained the task in progress. "You've arrived for the grand finale."

Leo jockeyed his suit around until he could just see over the abandoned module. "What we've got out there, in that box on top—the cherry-bomb on the icing, as it were—is a charge capacitor with a couple thousand volts stored in it. Leads down into a filament placed in the liquid explosive— I used an incandescent light bulb filament with the poly-glass envelope knocked off—that thing sticking up is an electric eye swiped from a door control. When we hit it with a burst from this optical laser, it closes the switch—"

"And the 'lectricity sets the ex'losive off?"

"Not exactly. The high voltage pouring through the fila-ment literally explodes the wire, and it's the shock wave from the exploding wire that sets off the TNM and gaso-line. Which blows the titanium blank out until it hits the ice die and transfers its momentum, whereupon the titanium stops and the ice, ah, carries the momentum away. Quite spectacularly, which is why we're behind this module . . ." he turned to check his quaddie crew. "Everybody ready?"

"If you can stick your head up and watch, why can't we?" complained Pramod.

"I have to have line-of-sight for the laser," said Leo primly.

Leo aimed the optical laser carefully, and paused a moment for the anxiety rush. So many things could go wrong—he'd checked and re-checked—but there comes a time when one must let all the doubts go and commit to action. He gave himself up to God and pressed the button.

A brilliant, soundless flash, a cloud of boiling vapor, and the ice die exploded, shards flying off in all directions. The effect was utterly enchanting. With an effort Leo tore his gaze away and ducked hastily back behind the module. The afterimage danced across his retinas, teal green and magenta. His pressure-gloved hand, resting against the module's skin, transmitted sharp vibrations as a few high-speed ice cubes pelted against the other side and ricocheted off into space.

Leo remained hunkered a moment, staring rather blankly at Rodeo. "*Now* I'm afraid to look."

Pramod jetted around the module. "It's all in one piece, anyway. It's tumbling—hard to see the exact shape."

Leo inhaled. "Let's go catch it, kids. And see what we've got."

It was the work of a few minutes to capture the workpiece. Leo refused to let himself call it "the vortex mirror" just yet—it might still turn out to be scrap metal. The quaddies ran their various scanners over the curving gray surface.

"I can't find any cracks, Leo," said Pramod breathlessly. "It's a few millimeters over-thick in spots, but nowhere too thin."

"Thick we can take care of during the final laser-polish. Thin we can't remedy. I'll take thick," said Leo.

Bobbi waved her optical laser, crossing and re-crossing the curved surface, numbers blurring in her digital readout. "It's in spec! Leo, it's within spec! We did it!"

Leo's innards were melting wax. He breathed a long and very tired sigh of happiness. "All right, kids, let's take it Indoors. Back to the—the—darn it, we can't keep calling it the 'D-620-and-Habitat-Reconfiguration.'"

"Ah sure can't," agreed Tony.

"So what are we going to name it?" An assortment of possibilities flitted through Leo's mind—*the Ark—the Freedom Star—Graf's Folly*. . . .

"Home," said Tony simply after a moment. "Let's go home, Leo."

"Home." Leo rolled the name in his mouth. It tasted good. It tasted very good. Pramod nodded, and one of Bobbi's upper hands touched her helmet in salute of the choice.

Leo blinked. Some irritating vapor in his suit's air was making his eyes water, no doubt, and tightening his chest. "Yeah. Let's take our vortex mirror home, gang."

Bruce Van Atta paused in the corridor outside Chalopin's office at Shuttleport Three, to catch his breath and control his trembling. He had a stitch in his side, too. He wouldn't be the least surprised if he was developing an ulcer out of all this. The fiasco out on the dry lake bed had been infuriating. To pave the way, and then have fumbling subordinates totally fail him—utterly infuriating.

Sheer chance, that having returned to his own downside quarters for a much-needed shower and some sleep, he'd awakened to take a piss and called Shuttleport Three to check progress. They might not even have told him about the shuttle landing otherwise! Anticipating Graf's next move, he had flung on his clothes and rushed to the hospital—if he'd been moments sooner, he might have trapped Minchenko within.

He had already chewed out the jetcopter pilot, reamed his ass for his cowardice in failing to force down the launching shuttle, for his dilatory failure to arrive at the lake bed faster. The red-faced pilot had clamped his jaw and his fists and said nothing, doubtless properly ashamed of himself. But the real failure lay higher up—on the other side of these very office doors. He jabbed the control, and they slid aside.

Chalopin, her security captain Bannerji, and Dr. Yei had their heads together around Chalopin's computer vid display. Captain Bannerji had his finger on it, and was saying to Yei, ". . . can get in here. But how *much* resistance, d'you think?"

"You'll surely frighten them very much," said Yei.

"Hm. I'm not crazy about asking my men to go up with stunners against desperate folk with much more lethal weapons. What *is* the real status of those so-called hostages?"

"Thanks to you," snarled Van Atta, "the hostage ratio is now five to zero. They got away with Tony, damn them. Why didn't you put a twenty-seven-hour guard on that quaddie like I told you? We should have put a guard on Madame Minchenko, too."

Chalopin's head came up, and she gave him an expressionless stare. "Mr. Van Atta, you seem to be laboring under some misconceptions about the size of my security forces here. I have only ten men, to cover three shifts, seven days a week."

"Plus ten each from each of the other two shuttleports. That's thirty. Properly armed, they'd be a substantial strike force."

"I've already borrowed six men from the other two 'ports to cover our own routine, while my entire force is devoted to this emergency."

"Why haven't you stripped them all?"

"Mr. Van Atta, Rodeo Ops is a big company—but a very small town. There are not ten thousand employees here altogether, plus an equal number of dependents not also employed by GalacTech. My security is a police force, not a military one. They have to cover their own duties, double for emergency squad and search and rescue, and be ready to assist Fire Control."

"Dammit—I drove a wedge for you with Tony. Why didn't you follow up immediately and board the Habitat?"

"I had a force of eight ready to go up to orbit," said Chalopin tartly, "upon your assurance of cooperation from your quaddies. We were not, however, able to get any confirmation of that cooperation from the Habitat itself. They went right back to maintaining com silence. Then we spotted our freight shuttle returning, so we diverted the forces to capture it—first a groundcar, and then, as you yourself came howling in here demanding not two hours ago, a jetcopter."

"Well, get them back together and get them into orbit, dammit!"

"For one thing, *you* left three of them out on the lake bed," remarked Captain Bannerji. "Sergeant Fors just reported in—says their groundcar was disabled. They're returning in Dr. Minchenko's abandoned land rover. It'll be at least another hour before they're back. For another, as Dr. Yei has several times pointed out, we have not yet received authorization to use any kind of deadly force."

"Surely you've got some kind of hot pursuit clause," argued Van Atta. "*That*," he pointed upward, indicating the events now going on in Rodeo orbit, "is grand theft in progress at the very least. And don't forget, a GalacTech employee has already been shot by them!"

"I haven't overlooked that fact," murmured Bannerji.

"But," Dr. Yei put in, "having asked HQ for authorization to use force, we are now obliged to wait for their reply. What, after all, if they deny the request?"

Van Atta frowned at her, his eyes narrowing. "I knew we should never have asked. You maneuvered us into that, damn you. They'd have swallowed any fait accompli we presented, and been glad of it. Now . . ." he shook his head in frustration. "Anyway, you're overlooking other sources of personnel. The Habitat staff itself can be used to follow up the opening Security drives into the Habitat."

"They're scattered all over Rodeo by now," Dr. Yei remarked, "back to their downside leave quarters, most of them."

Bannerji cringed visibly. "And do you have any idea the kind of legal liability that situation would present to Security?"

"So deputize 'em—"

A beeping from Chalopin's desk console interrupted Van Atta; a com tech's face appeared in the vid.

"Administrator Chalopin? Com Center here. You asked us to advise you of any change in the status of the Habitat or the D-620. They, um—appear to be preparing to leave orbit."

"Put it on up here," Chalopin ordered.

The com tech produced the flat view from the satellite again. He upped the magnification, and the Habitat–D-620 configuration half-filled the vid. The D-620's two normal-space thruster arms had been augmented by four of the big thruster units the quaddies used to break cargo bundles out of orbit. Even as Van Atta watched in horror, the array of engines flared into life. Stirring a glittering wake of space trash, the monstrous vehicle began to move.

Dr. Yei stood staring open-mouthed, her hands clapped to her chest, her eyes glistening strangely. Van Atta felt like weeping with rage himself.

"You see"—he pointed, his voice cracking—"you see what all this interminable dithering has resulted in? They're getting *away*!"

"Oh, not yet," purred Dr. Yei. "It will be at least a couple of days before they can possibly arrive at the wormhole.

There is no just cause for panic." She blinked at Van Atta, went on in an almost hypnotically cloying voice, "You are extremely fatigued, of course, as are we all. Fatigue invites mistakes in judgment. You should rest—get some sleep. . . ."

His hands twitched; he burned to strangle her on the spot. The shuttleport administrator and that idiot Bannerji were nodding, reasonable agreement. A choked growl steamed from Van Atta's throat. "Every minute you wait is going to complicate our logistics—increase the range—increase the risk—"

They all had the same bland stare on their faces. Van Atta didn't need his nose rubbed in it—he could recognize concerted non-cooperation when he smelled it. Damn, damn, damn! He glowered suspiciously at Yei. But his hands were tied, his authority undercut by her sweet reason. If Yei and all her ilk had their way, nobody would ever shoot anybody, and chaos would rule the universe.

He snarled inarticulately, wheeled on his heel, and stalked out.

Claire woke without yet opening her eyes, snugged in her sleep sack. The exhaustion that had drenched her at the end of last shift was slow to ebb from her limbs. She could not hear Andy stirring yet; good, a brief respite before diaper change. In ten minutes she would wake him, and they would exchange services; he relieving her tingling breasts of milk, the milk relieving his hungry tummy—moms need babes, she thought sleepily, as much as babes need moms, an interlocking design, two individuals sharing one biological system . . . so the quaddies shared the technological system of the Habitat, each dependent on all the others. . . .

Dependent on her work, too. What was next? Germination boxes, grow tubes—no, she could not yank grow tubes around today, today was Acceleration Day—her eyes sprang open. And widened in joy.

"Tony!" she breathed. "How long have you been here?"

"Been watching you abou' fifteen minutes. You sleep pretty. Can I come in?" He hung in air, dressed again in his familiar, comfortable red T-shirt and shorts, watching her in the half-light of her chamber. "Gotta tie down anyway, acceleration's about to start."

"Already . . . ?" She wriggled aside and made room for him, entwining all their arms, touching his face and the alarming bandage still wrapping his torso. "Are you all right?"

"All right now," he sighed happily. "Lying there, in that hospital—well, I didn't expect anyone to come after me. Horrible risk to you—not worth it!" He nuzzled her hair.

"We talked about it, the risk. But we couldn't leave you. Us quaddies—we've got to stick together." She was fully awake now, reveling in his physical reality, muscled hands, bright eyes, fuzzy blond brows. "Losing you would have diminished us, Leo said, and not just genetically. We have to be a people now, not just Claire and Tony and Silver and Siggy—and Andy—I guess it's what Leo calls 'synergistic.' We're something synergistic now."

A strange vibration purred through the walls of her chamber. She hitched around to scoop Andy out of his sleep restraints beside her, and fold him to her with her upper hands while still holding Tony's lowers with her lowers, under the sleep sack's cover. Andy squeaked, lips smacking, and fell back to sleep. Slowly, gently, her shoulderblades began to press against the wall.

"We're on our way," she whispered. "It's starting. . . ."

"It's holding together," Tony observed in wonder. They clung to each other. "Wanted to be with you, at this moment. . . ."

She let the acceleration have her, laying her head against the wall, cushioning Andy on her chest. Something went *clunk* in her cupboard; she'd check it later.

"This is the way to travel," sighed Tony. "Beats stowing away. . . ."

"It's going to be strange, without GalacTech," said Claire after a while. "Just us quaddies . . . what will Andy's world be like, I wonder?"

"That'll be up to us, I guess," said Tony soberly. "That's almost scarier than downsiders with guns, y'know? Freedom. Huh." He shook his head. "Not like I'd pictured it."

Yei's suggested sleep was out of the question. Morosely, Van Atta returned not to his living quarters, but to his own downside office. He had not checked in there for a couple of weeks. It was about midnight now, Shuttleport Three time; his downside secretary was off-shift. It suited his foul humor to sulk alone.

After about twenty minutes spent muttering to himself in the dim light, he decided to scan his accumulated electronic mail. His usual office routine had gone to pot these last few weeks anyway, and of course the events of the last two days had blown it entirely to hell. Perhaps a dose of boring routine would calm him enough to consider sleep after all.

Obsolete memos, out-of-date requests for instructions, irrelevant progress reports—the quaddie downside barracks, he noted with a grim snort, were advertised as ready for occupancy at fifteen percent over budget. If he could catch any quaddies to put in them. Instructions from HQ

viz wrapping up the Cay Project, unsolicited advice upon
salvage and disposal of its various parts . . .

Van Atta stopped abruptly, and backed up two screens
on his vid. What had that said again?

Item: Post-fetal experimental tissue cultures. Quantity:
1000. Disposition: cremation by IGS Standard Biolab
Rules.

He checked the source of the order. No, it hadn't come
through Apmad's office, as he'd first guessed. It came from
General Accounting & Inventory Control, part of a long
computer-generated list including a variety of lab stores.
The order was signed by a human, though, some unknown
middle manager in the GA&IC back on Earth.

"By damn," Van Atta swore softly, "I don't think this twit
even knows what quaddies *are*." The order had been signed
some weeks before.

He read the opening paragraph again. *The Project Chief
will oversee the termination of this project with all due speed.
The quick release of personnel for other assignments is particularly desirable. You are authorized to make whatever
temporary requisitions of material or personnel from adja-
cent divisions you require to complete this termination by 6/1.*

After another minute his lips drew back in a furious
grin. Carefully, he pulled the precious message disc from
the machine, pocketed it, and left to go find Chalopin. He
hoped he might rout her out of bed.

Chapter 16

"Aren't you about done out there yet?" Ti's taut voice crackled through Leo's work suit com.

"One last weld, Ti," Leo answered. "Check that alignment one more time, Tony."

Tony waved a gloved hand in acknowledgment and ran the optical laser check up the line that the electron beam welder would shortly follow. "You're clear, Pramod," he called, and moved aside.

The welder advanced in its tracks across the workpiece, stitching a flange for the last clamp to hold the new vortex mirror in place in its housing. A light on the beam welder's top flashed from red to green, the welder shut itself off, and Pramod moved in to detach it. Bobbi floated up immediately behind to check the weld with a sonic scan. "It's good, Leo. It'll hold."

"All right. Clear the stuff out and bring the mirror in."

His quaddies moved fast. Within minutes the vortex mirror was fitted into its insulated clamps, its alignment checked. "All right, gang. Let's move back and let Ti run the smoke test."

"Smoke test?" Ti's voice came over the com. "What's that? I thought you wanted a ten-percent power-up."

"It's an ancient and honorable term for the final step in any engineering project," Leo explained. "Turn it on, see if it smokes."

"I should have guessed," Ti choked. "How very scientific."

"Use is always the ultimate test. But power-up slowly, eh? Gently does it. We've got a delicate lady here."

"You've said that about eight or ten times, Leo. Is that sucker in spec or out?"

"In. On the surface, anyway. But the internal crystalline structure of the titanium—well, it just isn't as controlled as it would have been in a normal fabrication."

"Is it *in* spec or out? I'm not going to jump a thousand people to their deaths, dammit. Especially if I'm included."

"In, in," Leo spoke through his teeth. "But just—don't horse it around, huh? For the sake of my blood pressure, if nothing else."

Ti muttered something; it might have been, *Screw your blood pressure*, but Leo wasn't sure. He didn't ask for a repeat.

Leo and his quaddie work gang gathered their equipment and jetted a safe distance from the Necklin rod arm. They hung a hundred meters or so above Home. The light of Rodeo's sun was pale and sharp here within an hour of the wormhole jump point; more than a bright star, but far less than the nuclear furnace that had warmed the Habitat in Rodeo orbit.

Leo seized the moment to gaze upon their cobbled-together colony ship from this rare exterior vantage. Over a hundred modules had finally been bundled together along the ship's axis, all carrying on—more or less—their previous functions. Damned if the design didn't look almost intended, in a lunatic-functional sort of way. It reminded Leo a bit of the thrilling ugliness of the early space probes of the Twentieth and Twenty-first Centuries.

Miraculously, it had held together under two days' steady acceleration and deceleration. Inevitably items here and there Inside had been found to have been overlooked. The younger quaddies had crawled about bravely, cleaning up; Nutrition had managed to get everyone fed something, though the menu was a trifle random; thanks to yeoman efforts on the part of the young airsystems maintenance supervisor who had stayed on and his quaddie work gang, they no longer had to cease accelerating periodically for the plumbing to work. For a while Leo had been convinced the potty stops were going to be the death of them all, not that he hadn't grabbed the opportunities himself for the final touching-up on their vortex mirror.

"See any smoke?" Ti's voice inquired in his ear.

"Nope."

"That's it, then. You people better get your asses Inside. And as soon as you've got everything nailed down, Leo, I'd appreciate it if you'd come up to Nav and Com."

Something in the timbre of Ti's voice chilled Leo. "Oh? What's up?"

"There's a security shuttle closing on us from Rodeo. Your old buddy Van Atta's aboard, and ordering us to halt and desist. I don't think there's much time left."

"You're still maintaining com silence, I trust?"

"Oh, yeah, sure. But that doesn't prevent me from listening, eh? There's a lot of chatter from the jump station—but that doesn't worry me as much as what's coming up from behind. I, um . . . don't think Van Atta handles frustration too well."

"On edge, is he?"

"Over the edge, I think. Those security shuttles are armed, y'know. And a lot faster than this monster in normal space. Just 'cause their lasers are classed as 'light weaponry' doesn't mean it's exactly healthy to stand around in front of 'em. I'd just as soon jump *before* they got in range."

"I read you." Leo waved his work gang toward the entry hatch to the work-suit locker module.

So it was coming at last. Leo had devised a dozen defenses in his mind—upended beam welders, explosive mines—for the long-anticipated physical confrontation with GalacTech employees trying to retake the Habitat. But all his time had been gobbled up by the vortex mirror, and as a result only the most instant of weapons, such as the beam welders, were now available, and even they would have no use Indoors in a boarding battle. He could just picture one missing its target and slicing through a wall into an adjoining crèche module. Hand-to-hand in free fall the quaddies might have some advantage; weapons cancelled that, being more dangerous to the defenders than the attackers. It all depended on what kind of attack Van Atta launched. And Leo hated depending on Van Atta.

Van Atta swore into the com one last time, then dealt the OFF key an angry blow. He had run out of fresh invective hours before, and was conscious of repeating himself. He turned from the comconsole and glowered around the security shuttle's control compartment.

The pilot and co-pilot, up front, were busy about their work. Bannerji, commanding the force, and Dr. Yei—and how had she inserted herself into this expedition, anyway?—were strapped to their acceleration couches, Yei in the engineer's seat, Bannerji holding down the weapons console across the aisle from Van Atta.

"That's it, then," snapped Van Atta. "Are we in range for the lasers yet?"

Bannerji checked a readout. "Not quite."

"Please," said Dr. Yei, "let me try to talk to them just once more—"

"If they're half as sick of the sound of your voice as I am, they're not going to answer," growled Van Atta. "You've spent hours talking to them. Face it—they're not *listening* any more, Yei. So much for psychology."

The security sergeant, Fors, stuck his head through from the rear compartment where he rode with his twenty-six fellow GalacTech guards. "What's the word, Captain Bannerji? Should we suit up for boarding yet?"

Bannerji quirked an eyebrow at Van Atta. "Well, Mr. Van Atta? Which plan is it to be? It appears we're going to have to cross off all the scenarios that started with their surrendering."

"You got that shit straight." Van Atta brooded at the com, which emitted only a gray empty hiss on its vid. "As soon as we're in range, start firing on 'em, then. Disable the Necklin rod arms first, then the normal space thrusters if you can. Then we blast a hole in the side, march in, and mop up."

Sergeant Fors cleared his throat. "You did say there were a *thousand* of those mutants aboard, didn't you, Mr. Van Atta? What about the plan of skipping the boarding part and just taking the whole vessel in tow, back to wherever you want it? Aren't the odds a little, um, lopsided for boarding?"

"Complain to Chalopin, she's the one who balked at drafting help from outside Security proper. But the odds aren't what they appear. The quaddies are creampuffs. Half of them are children under twelve, for God's sake. Just go in, and stun anything that moves. How many five-year-old girls do you figure you're equal to, Fors?"

"I don't know, sir," Fors blinked. "I never pictured myself fighting five-year-old girls."

Bannerji drummed his fingers on his weapons console and glanced at Yei. "Is that girl with the baby aboard, the ones I almost shot that day in the warehouse, Dr. Yei?"

"Claire? Yes," she replied levelly.

"Ah." Bannerji glanced away from her intent gaze, and shifted in his seat.

"Let's hope your aim is better this time, Bannerji," said Van Atta.

Bannerji rotated a computer schematic of a super-jumper in his vid, running calculations. "You realize," he said slowly, "that the real event is going to have some uncontrolled factors—the probability is good that we're going to end up punching some extra holes in the inhabited modules while we're going for the Necklin rods."

"That's all right," said Van Atta. Bannerji's lips screwed up doubtfully. "Look, Bannerji," added Van Atta impatiently, "the quaddies are—ah, have made themselves expendable by turning criminal. It's no different than shooting a thief fleeing from any other kind of robbery or break-in. Besides, you can't make an omelet without breaking eggs."

Dr. Yei ran her hands hard over her face. "Lord Krishna," she groaned. She favored Van Atta with a tight, peculiar smile. "I've been wondering when you were going to say that. I should have put a side bet on it—run a pool—"

Van Atta bristled defensively. "If you had done your job right," he returned no less tightly, "we wouldn't be here now breaking eggs. We could have boiled them in their shells back on Rodeo at the very least. A fact I intend to point out to management later, believe me. But I don't have to argue with you any more. For everything I intend to do, I have a proper authorization."

"Which you have not shown to me."

"Chalopin and Captain Bannerji saw it. If I have my way you'll get a termination out of this, Yei."

She said nothing, but acknowledged the threat with a brief ironic tilt of her head. She leaned back in her chair and crossed her arms, apparently silenced at last. *Thank God*, Van Atta added to himself.

"Get suited up, Fors," he told the security sergeant.

Nav and Com in the D-620 was a crowded chamber. Ti ruled from his control chair, enthroned beneath his head-set; Silver manned the com; and Leo—held down the post of chief engineer, he supposed. The chain of command became rather blurred at this point. Perhaps his title ought to be Official Ship's Worrier. His guts churned and his throat tightened as all lines of action approached their intersection at the point of no return.

"The security shuttle has stopped broadcasting," Silver reported.

"That's a relief," said Ti. "You can turn the sound back up, now."

"Not a relief," denied Leo. "If they've stopped talking, they may be getting ready to open fire." And it was too late, too close to jump point to put a beam welder and crew Outside to fire back.

Ti's mouth twisted in dismay. He closed his eyes; the D-620 seemed to tilt, lumbering under acceleration. "We're almost in position to jump," he said.

Leo eyed a monitor. "They're almost in range to fire." He paused a moment, then added, "They *are* in range to fire."

Ti made a squeaking noise, and pulled his headset down. "Powering-up the Necklin field—"

"*Gently,*" yelped Leo. "My vortex mirror—"

Silver's hand sought Leo's. He was overwhelmed by a desire to apologize, to Silver, to the quaddies, to God, he didn't know who. *I got you into this . . . I'm sorry . . .*

"If you open a channel, Silver," said Leo desperately, his head swimming in panic—all those children—"we could still surrender."

"Never," said Silver. Her grip tightened on his hand, and her blue eyes met his. "And I choose for all, not just for myself. We go."

Leo ground his teeth, and nodded shortly. The seconds thudded in his brain, syncopated with the hammering of his heart. The security shuttle grew in the monitor.

"Why don't they fire now?" asked Silver.

"Fire," ordered Van Atta.

Bannerji's bright computer schematics drew toward alignment, numbers flickering, lights converging. Dr. Yei, Van Atta noticed, was no longer in her seat. Probably hiding out in the toilet chamber. This dose of real life and real consequences was doubtless too much for her. *Just like one of those wimp politicians*, Van Atta thought scathingly, *who talks people into disaster and disappears when the shooting starts. . . .*

"Fire *now,*" he repeated to Bannerji, as the computer blinked readiness, locked onto its target.

Bannerji's hand moved toward the firing switch, hesitated. "Do you have a work order for this?" he asked suddenly.

"Do I have a *what*?" said Van Atta.

"A work order. It occurs to me that, technically, this could be considered an act of hazardous waste disposal. It takes a work order signed by the originator of the request—that's you—my supervisor—that's Administrator Chalopin—and the company Hazardous Waste Management Officer."

"Chalopin has turned you over to me. That makes it official, mister!"

"But not complete. The Hazardous Waste Management Officer is Laurie Gompf, and she's back on Rodeo. You don't have *her* authorization. The work order is incomplete. Sorry, sir." Bannerji vacated the weapons console and plunked himself down in the empty engineer's seat, crossing his arms. "It's as much as my job is worth to complete an act of hazardous waste disposal without a proper order. The Environmental Impact Assessment has to be attached, too."

"This is mutiny!" yelled Van Atta.

"No, it isn't," Bannerji disagreed cordially. "This isn't the military."

Van Atta glared red-faced at Bannerji, who studied his fingernails. With an oath, Van Atta flung himself into the weapons console seat and reset the aim. He might have known—anything you wanted done right you had to do yourself—he hesitated, the engineering parameters of the D-class superjumpers racing through his mind. Where on that complex structure might a hit not merely disable the rods, but cause the main thrusters to blow entirely?

Cremation, indeed. And the deaths of the four or five downsiders aboard could, at need, be blamed on Bannerji—*I did my best, ma'am—if he'd done his job as I'd first requested . . .*

The schematic spun in the vid display. There must be a point in the structure—*yes*. There and there. If he could knock out both *that* control nexus and *those* coolant lines, he could start an uncontrolled reaction that would result in—promotion, probably, after the dust had settled. Apmad would kiss him. Just like a heroic doctor, single-handedly stopping a plague of genetic abomination from spreading across the galaxy . . .

The target schematic pulled toward alignment again. Van Atta's sweating palm closed around the firing switch. In a moment—just a moment—

"What are you doing with *that*, Dr. Yei?" asked Bannerji's voice, startled.

"Applying psychology."

The back of Van Atta's head seemed to explode with a sickening crack. He pitched forward, cutting his chin on the console, bumping the keypads, turning his firing program to confetti-colored hash in the vid. He saw stars *inside* the shuttle, blurring purple and green spots—gasping, he straightened back up.

"Dr. Yei," Bannerji objected, "if you're trying to knock a man out you've got to hit him a *lot* harder than that."

Yei recoiled fearfully as Van Atta surged up out of his seat. "I didn't want to risk killing him. . . ."

"Why not?" muttered Bannerji under his breath.

Furiously, Van Atta's hands closed around Yei's wrist. He yanked the metal wrench from her grasp. "You can't do anything right, can you?" he snarled.

She was gasping and weeping. Fors, space-suited but still minus his helmet, stuck his head through again from the rear compartment. "What the hell is going on up here?"

Van Atta shoved Yei toward him. Bannerji, squirming uncomfortably in his seat, was clearly not to be trusted.

"Hold onto this crazy bitch. She just tried to kill me with a wrench."

"Oh? She told *me* she needed it to adjust a seat attitude," remarked Fors. "Or—*did* she say 'seat'?" But he held Yei's arms. Her struggle, as ever, was weak and futile.

With a hiss, Van Atta heaved himself back into the weapons console seat and called up the targeting program again. He reset it, and switched on the view from the exterior scanners. The D-620–Habitat configuration stood out vividly in the vid, the cold and distant sunlight silver-gilding its structure. The schematics converged, caging it.

The D-620 wavered, rotated, and vanished.

The lasers fired, lances of light striking into empty space.

Van Atta howled, beating his fists on the console, blood droplets flicking from his chin. "They got *out*. They got *out*. They got *out*—"

Yei giggled.

Leo hung limply in his seat restraints, laughter bubbling in his throat. "We made it!"

Ti swung his headset up and sat no less limply, his face white and lined—jumps drained pilots. Leo felt as if he'd just been twisted inside out himself, squeaking, but the nausea passed quickly.

"Your mirror was in spec, Leo," Ti said faintly.

"Yes. I'd been afraid it might explode, during the stresses of the jump."

Ti eyed him indignantly. "That's not what you *said*. I thought you were the hot-shot testing engineer."

"Look, I'd never made one of those things before," Leo protested. "You never *know*. You only make the best possible guesses." He sat up, trying to gather his scattered wits.

"We're here. We made it. But what's going on Outside, was there any damage to the Habitat—Silver, see what you can get on the com."

She too was pale. "My goodness," she blinked. "So that was a jump. Sort of like six hours of Dr. Yei's truth serum all squeezed into a second. Ugh. Are we going to be doing this a lot?"

"I certainly hope so," said Leo. He unstrapped himself and floated over to assist her.

Space around the wormhole was empty and serene—Leo's secret paranoid vision of jumping into waiting military fire was not to be, he noted gladly. But wait, a ship was approaching them—not a commercial vessel, something dangerous and official-looking. . . .

"It's some sort of police ship from Orient IV," Silver guessed. "Are we in trouble?"

"Undoubtedly," Dr. Minchenko's voice cut in as he floated into Nav and Com. "GalacTech will certainly not take this lying down. You will do us all a favor, Graf, if you let me do the talking just now." He elbowed both Silver and Leo aside, taking over the com. "The Minister of Health of Orient IV happens to be a professional colleague of mine. While his is not a position of great political power, it is a channel of communication to the highest levels of government. If I can get through to him we will be in a much better position than if we try to deal with some low level police sergeant, or worse, military officer." Minchenko's eyes glinted. "There is no love lost between GalacTech and Orient IV at the moment. Whatever GalacTech's charges, we can counter—tax fraud—oh, the possibilities. . . ."

"What do we do while you're talking?" asked Ti.

"Keep boosting," advised Minchenko.

"It's not over, is it?" Silver said quietly to Leo, as they floated out of Minchenko's way. "Somehow, I thought our troubles would be over if only we could get away from Mr. Van Atta."

Leo shook his head. A jubilant grin still kept crooking up the corner of his mouth. He took one of her upper hands. "Our troubles would have been over if Brucie-baby had scored a hit. Or if the vortex mirror had blown up in the middle of the jump, or if—don't be afraid of troubles, Silver. They're a sign of life. We'll deal with them together—tomorrow."

She breathed a long sigh, the tension draining from her face, her body, her arms. An answering smile at last lighted her eyes, making them bright like stars. She turned her face expectantly toward his.

He found himself grinning quite foolishly, for a man pushing forty. He tried to twitch his face into more dignified lines. There was a pause.

"Leo," said Silver in a tone of sudden insight, "are you *shy*?"

"Who, me?" said Leo.

The blue stars squeezed for a moment into quite predatory glitters. She kissed him. Leo, indignant at her accusation, kissed her back more thoroughly. Now it was her turn to grin foolishly. A lifetime with the quaddies, Leo reflected, could be all right. . . .

They turned their faces to the new sun.

Labyrinth

Labyrinth

Miles contemplated the image of the globe glowing above the vid plate, crossed his arms, and stifled queasiness. The planet of Jackson's Whole, glittering, wealthy, corrupt . . . Jacksonians claimed their corruption was entirely imported—if the galaxy were willing to pay for virtue what it paid for vice, the place would be a pilgrimage shrine. In Miles's view this seemed rather like debating which was superior, maggots or the rotten meat they fed off. Still, if Jackson's Whole didn't exist, the galaxy would probably have had to invent it. Its neighbors might feign horror, but they wouldn't permit the place to exist if they didn't find it a secretly useful interface with the sub-economy.

The planet possessed a certain liveliness, anyway. Not as lively as a century or two back, to be sure, in its hijacker-base days. But its cutthroat criminal gangs had senesced into Syndicate monopolies, almost as structured and staid as little governments. An aristocracy, of sorts. Naturally. Miles wondered how much longer the major Houses would be able to fight off the creeping tide of integrity.

House Dyne, detergent banking—launder your money on Jackson's Whole. House Fell, weapons deals with no questions asked. House Bharaputra, illegal genetics. Worse, House Ryoval, whose motto was "Dreams Made Flesh," surely the damndest—Miles used the adjective precisely— procurer in history. House Hargraves, the galactic fence, prim-faced middlemen for ransom deals—you had to give them credit, hostages exchanged through their good offices came back alive, mostly. And a dozen smaller syndicates, variously and shiftingly allied.

Even we find you useful. Miles touched the control and the vid image vanished. His lip curled in suppressed loathing, and he called up his ordnance inventory for one final check of his shopping list. A subtle shift in the vibrations of the ship around him told him they were matching orbits— the fast cruiser *Ariel* would be docking at Fell Station within the hour.

His console was just extruding the completed data disk of weapons orders when his cabin door chimed, followed by an alto voice over its com, "Admiral Naismith?"

"Enter." He plucked off the disk and leaned back in his station chair.

Captain Thorne sauntered in with a friendly salute. "We'll be docking in about thirty minutes, sir."

"Thank you, Bel."

Bel Thorne, the *Ariel*'s commander, was a Betan hermaphrodite, man/woman descendant of a centuries-past genetic-social experiment every bit as bizarre, in Miles's private opinion, as anything rumored to be done for money by House Ryoval's ethics-free surgeons. A fringe effort of Betan egalitarianism run amok, hermaphroditism had not caught on, and the original idealists' hapless descendants remained a minority on hyper-tolerant Beta Colony.

Except for a few stray wanderers like Bel. As a mercenary officer Thorne was conscientious, loyal, and aggressive, and Miles liked him/her/it—Betan custom used the neuter pronoun—a lot. *However . . .*

Miles could smell Bel's floral perfume from here. Bel was emphasizing the female side today. And had been, increasingly, for the five days of this voyage. Normally Bel chose to come on ambiguous-to-male, soft short brown hair and chiselled, beardless facial features counteracted by the gray-and-white Dendarii military uniform, assertive gestures, and wicked humor. It worried Miles exceedingly to sense Bel soften in his presence.

Turning to his computer console's holovid plate, Miles again called up the image of the planet they were approaching. Jackson's Whole looked demure enough from a distance, mountainous, rather cold—the populated equator was only temperate—ringed in the vid by a lacy schematic net of colored satellite tracks, orbital transfer stations, and authorized approach vectors. "Have you ever been here before, Bel?"

"Once, when I was a lieutenant in Admiral Oser's fleet," said the mercenary. "House Fell has a new baron since then. Their weaponry still has a good reputation, as long as you know what you're buying. Stay away from the sale on neutron hand grenades."

"Heh. For those with strong throwing arms. Fear not, neutron hand grenades aren't on the list." He handed the data disk to Bel.

Bel sidled up and leaned over the back of Miles's station chair to take it. "Shall I grant leaves to the crew while we're waiting for the baron's minions to load cargo? How about yourself? There used to be a hostel near the docks with all the amenities, pool, sauna, great food . . ." Bel's voice lowered. "I could book a room for two."

"I'd only figured to grant day passes." Necessarily, Miles cleared his throat.

"I *am* a woman, too," Bel pointed out in a murmur.

"Among other things."

"You're so hopelessly monosexual, Miles."

"Sorry." Awkwardly, he patted the hand that had somehow come to rest on his shoulder.

Bel sighed and straightened. "So many are."

Miles sighed too. Perhaps he ought to make his rejection more emphatic—this was only about the seventh time he'd been round with Bel on this subject. It was almost ritualized by now, almost, but not quite, a joke. You had to give the Betan credit for either optimism or obtuseness . . . or, Miles's honesty added, genuine feeling. If he turned round now, he knew, he might surprise an essential loneliness in the hermaphrodite's eyes, never permitted on the lips. He did not turn round.

And who was he to judge another, Miles reflected ruefully, whose own body brought him so little joy? What did Bel, straight and healthy and of normal height, if unusual genital arrangements, find so attractive in a little half-crippled part-time crazy man? He glanced down at the gray Dendarii officer's uniform he wore. The uniform he had won. *If you can't be seven feet tall, be seven feet smart.* His reason had so far failed to present him with a solution to the problem of Thorne, though.

"Have you ever thought of going back to Beta Colony, and seeking one of your own?" Miles asked seriously.

Thorne shrugged. "Too boring. That's why I left. It's so very safe, so very narrow. . . ."

"Mind you, a great place to raise kids." One corner of Miles's mouth twisted up.

Thorne grinned. "You got it. You're an almost perfect Betan, y'know? Almost. You have the accent, the in-jokes..."

Miles went a little still. "Where do I fail?"

Thorne touched Miles's cheek; Miles flinched.

"Reflexes," said Thorne.

"Ah."

"I won't give you away."

"I know."

Bel was leaning in again. "I could polish that last edge..."

"Never mind," said Miles, slightly flushed. "We have a mission."

"Inventory," said Thorne scornfully.

"That's not a mission," said Miles, "that's a cover."

"Ah ha." Thorne straightened up. "At last."

"At last?"

"It doesn't take a genius. We came to purchase ordnance, but instead of taking the ship with the biggest cargo capacity, you chose the *Ariel*—the fleet's fastest. There's no deader dull routine than inventory, but instead of sending a perfectly competent quartermaster, you're overseeing it personally."

"I do want to make contact with the new Baron Fell," said Miles mildly. "House Fell is the biggest arms supplier this side of Beta Colony, and a lot less picky about who its customers are. If I like the quality of the initial purchase, they could become a regular supplier."

"A quarter of Fell's arms are Betan manufacture, marked up," said Thorne. "Again, ha."

"And while we're here," Miles went on, "a certain middle-aged man is going to present himself and sign on to the Dendarii Mercenaries as a medtech. At that point all Station passes are cancelled, we finish loading cargo as quickly as possible, and we leave."

Thorne grinned in satisfaction. "A pick-up. Very good. I assume we're being well-paid?"

"Very. If he arrives at his destination alive. The man happens to be the top research geneticist of House Bharaputra's Laboratories. He's been offered asylum by a planetary government capable of protecting him from the long arms of Baron Luigi Bharaputra's enforcers. His soon-to-be-former employer is expected to be highly irate at the lack of a month's notice. We are being paid to deliver him to his new masters alive and not, ah, forcibly debriefed of all his trade secrets.

"Since House Bharaputra could probably buy and sell the whole Dendarii Free Mercenary Fleet twice over out of petty cash, I would prefer we not have to deal with Baron Luigi's enforcers either. So we shall be innocent suckers. All we did was hire a bloody medtech, sir. And we shall be irate ourselves when he deserts after we arrive at fleet rendezvous off Escobar."

"Sounds good to me," conceded Thorne. "Simple."

"So I trust," Miles sighed hopefully. Why, after all, shouldn't things run to plan, just this once?

The purchasing offices and display areas for House Fell's lethal wares were situated not far from the docks, and most of House Fell's smaller customers never penetrated further into Fell Station. But shortly after Miles and Thorne placed their order—about as long as needed to verify a credit chit—an obsequious person in the green silk of House Fell's uniform appeared, and pressed an invitation into Admiral

Naismith's hand to a reception in the Baron's personal quarters.

Four hours later, giving up the pass cube to Baron Fell's majordomo at the sealed entrance to the station's private sector, Miles checked Thorne and himself over for their general effect. Dendarii dress uniform was a gray velvet tunic with silver buttons on the shoulders and white edging, matching gray trousers with white side piping, and gray synthasuede boots—perhaps just a trifle effete? Well, he hadn't designed it, he'd just inherited it. Live with it.

The interface to the private sector was highly interesting. Miles's eye took in the details while the majordomo scanned them for weapons. Life-support—in fact, all systems—appeared to be run separately from the rest of the station. The area was not only sealable, it was detachable. In effect, not Station but Ship—engines and armament around here somewhere, Miles bet, though it could be lethal to go looking for them unescorted. The majordomo ushered them through, pausing to announce them on his wrist com: "Admiral Miles Naismith, commanding, Dendarii Free Mercenary Fleet. Captain Bel Thorne, commanding the fast cruiser *Ariel*, Dendarii Free Mercenary Fleet." Miles wondered who was on the other end of the com.

The reception chamber was large and gracefully appointed, with iridescent floating staircases and levels creating private spaces without destroying the illusions of openness. Every exit (Miles counted six) had a large green-garbed guard by it trying to look like a servant and not succeeding very well. One whole wall was a vertigo-inducing transparent viewport overlooking Fell Station's busy docks and the bright curve of Jackson's Whole bisecting the star-spattered horizon beyond. A crew of elegant women in green silk saris rustled among the guests offering food and drink.

Gray velvet, Miles decided after one glance at the other guests, was a positively demure choice of garb. He and Bel would blend right into the walls. The thin scattering of fellow privileged customers wore a wide array of planetary fashions. But they were a wary bunch, little groups sticking together, no mingling. Guerrillas, it appeared, did not speak to mercenaries, nor smugglers to revolutionaries; the Gnostic Saints, of course, spoke only to the One True God, and perhaps to Baron Fell.

"Some party," commented Bel. "I went to a pet show with an atmosphere like this once. The high point was when somebody's Tau Cetan beaded lizard got loose and ate the Best-In-Show from the canine division."

"Hush." Miles grinned with one corner of his mouth. "This is business."

A green-sari'd woman bowed silently before them, offering a tray. Thorne raised a brow at Miles—*do we . . . ?*

"Why not?" Miles murmured. "We're paying for it, in the long run. I doubt the baron poisons his customers, it's bad for business. Business is emperor, here. Laissez-faire capitalism gone completely over the edge." He selected a pink tid-bit in the shape of a lotus and a mysterious cloudy drink. Thorne followed suit. The pink lotus, alas, turned out to be some sort of raw fish. It squeaked against his teeth. Miles, committed, swallowed it anyway. The drink was potently alcoholic, and after a sip to wash down the lotus he regretfully abandoned it on the first level surface he could find. His dwarfish body refused to handle alcohol, and he had no desire to meet Baron Fell while either semi-comatose or giggling uncontrollably. The more metabolically fortunate Thorne kept beverage in hand.

A most extraordinary music began from somewhere, a racing rich complexity of harmonics. Miles could not identify the instrument—instruments, surely. He and Thorne exchanged a glance, and by mutual accord drifted toward the sound. Around a spiraling staircase, backed by the panoply of station, planet, and stars, they found the musician. Miles's eyes widened. *House Ryoval's surgeons have surely gone too far this time. . . .*

Little decorative colored sparkles defined the spherical field of a large null-gee bubble. Floating within it was a woman. Her ivory arms flashed against her green silk clothes as she played. All *four* of her ivory arms. . . . She wore a flowing, kimono-like belted jacket and matching shorts, from which the second set of arms emerged where her legs should have been. Her hair was short and soft and ebony black. Her eyes were closed, and her rose-tinted face bore the repose of an angel, high and distant and terrifying.

Her strange instrument was fixed in air before her, a flat polished wooden frame strung across both top and bottom with a bewildering array of tight gleaming wires, soundboard between. She struck the wires with four felted hammers at blinding speed, both sides at once, her upper hands moving at counterpoint to her lowers. Music poured forth in a cascade.

"Good God," said Thorne, "it's a quaddie."

"It's a what?"

"A quaddie. She's a long way from home."

"She's—not a local product?"

"By no means."

"I'm relieved. I think. Where the devil does she come from, then?"

"About two hundred years ago—about the time hermaphrodites were being invented," a peculiar wryness flashed across Thorne's face, "there was this rush of genetic experimentation on humans, in the wake of the development of the practical uterine replicator. Followed shortly by a rush of laws restricting such, but meanwhile, somebody thought they'd make a race of free-fall dwellers. Then artificial gravity came in and blew them out of business. The quaddies fled—their descendants ended up on the far side of nowhere, way beyond Earth from us in the Nexus. They're rumored to keep to themselves, mostly. Very unusual, to see one this side of Earth. H'sh." Lips parted, Thorne tracked the music.

As unusual as finding a Betan hermaphrodite in a free mercenary fleet, Miles thought. But the music deserved undivided attention, though few in this paranoid crowd seemed to even be noticing it. A shame. Miles was no musician, but even he could sense an intensity of passion in the playing that went beyond talent, reaching for genius. An evanescent genius, sounds woven with time and, like time, forever receding beyond one's futile grasp into memory alone.

The outpouring of music dropped to a haunting echo, then silence. The four-armed musician's blue eyes opened, and her face came back from the ethereal to the merely human, tense and sad.

"Ah," breathed Thorne, stuck its empty glass under its arm, raised hands to clap, then paused, hesitant to become conspicuous in this indifferent chamber.

Miles was all for being inconspicuous. "Perhaps you can speak to her," he suggested by way of an alternative.

"You think?" Brightening, Thorne tripped forward, swinging down to abandon the glass on the nearest handy floor and raising splayed hands against the sparkling bubble. The hermaphrodite mustered an entranced, ingra-tiating smile. "Uh . . ." Thorne's chest rose and fell.

Good God, Bel, tongue-tied? Never thought I'd see it. "Ask her what she calls that thing she plays," Miles supplied helpfully.

The four-armed woman tilted her head curiously, and starfished gracefully over her boxy instrument to hover politely before Thorne on the other side of the glittering barrier. "Yes?"

"What do you call that extraordinary instrument?" Thorne asked.

"It's a double-sided hammer dulcimer, ma'am—sir . . ." her servant-to-guest dull tone faltered a moment, fearing to give insult, "Officer."

"Captain Bel Thorne," Bel supplied instantly, beginning to recover accustomed smooth equilibrium. "Command-ing the Dendarii fast cruiser *Ariel*. At your service. How ever did you come to be here?"

"I had worked my way to Earth. I was seeking employ-ment, and Baron Fell hired me." She tossed her head, as if to deflect some implied criticism, though Bel had offered none.

"You are a true quaddie?"

"You've heard of my people?" Her dark brows rose in surprise. "Most people I encounter here think I am a *man-ufactured* freak." A little sardonic bitterness edged her voice.

Thorne cleared its throat. "I'm Betan, myself. I've fol-lowed the history of the early genetics explosion with a rather more personal interest." Thorne cleared its throat again, "Betan hermaphrodite, you see," and waited anx-iously for the reaction.

Damn. Bel never waited for reactions, Bel sailed on and let the chips fall anyhow. *I wouldn't interfere with this for all the world.* Miles faded back slightly, rubbing his lips to wipe off a twitching grin as all Thorne's most masculine mannerisms reasserted themselves from spine to fingertips and outward into the aether.

Her head tilted in interest. One upper hand rose to rest on the sparkling barrier not far from Bel's. "*Are* you? You're a genetic too, then."

"Oh, yes. And tell me, what's your name?"

"Nicol."

"Nicol. Is that all? I mean, it's lovely."

"My people don't use surnames."

"Ah. And, uh, what are you doing after the party?"

At this point, alas, interference found them. "Heads up, *Captain*," Miles murmured. Thorne drew up instantly, cool and correct, and followed Miles's gaze. The quaddie floated back from the force barrier and bowed her head over her hands held palm-to-palm and palm-to-palm as a man approached. Miles too came to a polite species of attention.

Georish Stauber, Baron Fell, was a surprisingly old man to have succeeded so recently to his position, Miles thought. In the flesh he looked older than the holovid Miles had viewed of him at his own mission briefing. The baron was balding, with a white fringe of hair around his shiny pate, jovial and fat. He looked like somebody's grandfather. Not Miles's; Miles's grandfather had been lean and predatory even in his great age. And the old Count's title had been as real as such things got, not the courtesy-nobility of a Syndicate survivor. Jolly red cheeks or no, Miles reminded himself, Baron Fell had climbed a pile of bodies to attain this high place.

"Admiral Naismith. Captain Thorne. Welcome to Fell Station," rumbled the baron, smiling.

Miles swept him an aristocratic bow. Thorne somewhat awkwardly followed suit. Ah. He must copy that awkwardness next time. Of such little details were cover identities made. And blown.

"Have my people been taking care of your needs?"

"Thank you, yes." So far the proper businessmen.

"So glad to meet you at last," the baron rumbled on. "We've heard a great deal about you here."

"Have you," said Miles encouragingly. The baron's eyes were strangely avid. *Quite a glad-hand for a little tin-pot mercenary, eh?* This was a little more stroke than was reasonable even for a high-ticket customer. Miles banished all hint of wariness from his return smile. *Patience. Let the challenge emerge, don't rush to meet what you cannot yet see.* "Good things, I hope."

"Remarkable things. Your rise has been as rapid as your origins are mysterious."

Hell, hell, what kind of bait was this? Was the baron hinting that he actually knew "Admiral Naismith's" real identity? This could be sudden and serious trouble. No— fear outran its cause. Wait. Forget that such a person as Lieutenant Lord Vorkosigan, Barrayaran Imperial Security, ever existed in this body. *It's not big enough for the two of us anyway, boy.* Yet why was this fat shark smiling so ingratiatingly? Miles cocked his head, neutrally.

"The story of your fleet's success at Vervain reached us even here. So unfortunate about its former commander."

Miles stiffened. "I regret Admiral Oser's death."

The baron shrugged philosophically. "Such things happen in the business. Only one can command."

"He could have been an outstanding subordinate."

"Pride is so dangerous," smiled the baron.

Indeed. Miles bit his tongue. *So he thinks I "arranged" Oser's death. So let him.* That there was one less mercenary than there appeared in this room, that the Dendarii were now through Miles an arm of the Barrayaran Imperial Service so covert most of them didn't even know it themselves . . . it would be a dull Syndicate baron who couldn't find profit in those secrets somewhere. Miles matched the baron's smile and added nothing.

"You interest me exceedingly," continued the baron. "For example, there's the puzzle of your apparent age. And your prior military career."

If Miles had kept his drink, he'd have knocked it back in one gulp right then. He clasped his hands convulsively behind his back instead. Dammit, the pain lines just didn't age his face enough. If the baron was indeed seeing right through the pseudo-mercenary to the twenty-three-year-old Security lieutenant—and yet, he usually carried it off—

The baron lowered his voice. "Do the rumors run equally true about your Betan rejuvenation treatment?"

So *that's* what he was on about. Miles felt faint with relief. "What interest could you have in such treatments, my lord?" he gibbered lightly. "I thought Jackson's Whole was the home of practical immortality. It's said there are some here on their third cloned body."

"I am not one of them," said the baron rather regretfully.

Miles's brows rose in genuine surprise. Surely this man didn't spurn the process as murder. "Some unfortunate medical impediment?" he said, injecting polite sympathy into his voice. "My regrets, sir."

"In a manner of speaking." The baron's smile revealed a sharp edge. "The brain transplant operation itself kills a certain irreducible percentage of patients—"

Yeah, thought Miles, *starting with 100% of the clones, whose brains are flushed to make room. . . .*

"—another percentage suffer varying sorts of permanent damage. Those are the risks anyone must take for the reward."

"But the reward is so great."

"But then there are a certain number of patients, indistinguishable from the first group, who do not die on the operating table by accident. If their enemies have the subtlety and clout to arrange it. I have a number of enemies, Admiral Naismith."

Miles made a little who-would-think-it gesture, flipping up one hand, and continued to cultivate an air of deep interest.

"I calculate my present chances of surviving a brain transplant to be rather worse than the average," the baron went on. "So I've an interest in alternatives." He paused expectantly.

"Oh," said Miles. Oh, indeed. He regarded his fingernails and thought fast. "It's true, I once participated in an . . . unauthorized experiment. A premature one, as it happens, pushed too eagerly from animal to human subjects. It was not successful."

"No?" said the baron. "You appear in good health."

Miles shrugged. "Yes, there was some benefit to muscles, skin tone, hair. But my bones are the bones of an old man, fragile." *True.* "Subject to acute osteoinflammatory attacks—there are days when I can't walk without medication." *Also true, dammit.* A recent and unsettling medical development. "My life expectancy is not considered good." *For example, if certain parties here ever figure out who "Admiral Naismith" really is, it could go down to as little as fifteen minutes.* "So unless you're extremely fond of pain and think you would enjoy being crippled, I fear I must dis-recommend the procedure."

The baron looked him up and down. Disappointment pulled down his mouth. "I see."

Bel Thorne, who knew quite well there was no such thing as the fabled "Betan rejuvenation treatment," was listening with well-concealed enjoyment and doing an excellent job of keeping the smirk off its face. Bless its little black heart.

"Still," said the baron, "your . . . scientific acquaintance may have made some progress in the intervening years."

"I fear not," said Miles. "He died." He spread his hands helplessly. "Old age."

"Oh." The baron's shoulders sagged slightly.

"Ah, there you are, Fell," a new voice cut across them. The baron straightened and turned.

The man who had hailed him was as conservatively dressed as Fell, and flanked by a silent servant with "bodyguard" written all over him. The bodyguard wore a uniform, a high-necked red silk tunic and loose black trousers, and was unarmed. Everyone on Fell Station went unarmed except Fell's men; the place had the most strictly-enforced weapons regs Miles had ever encountered. But the pattern of calluses on the lean bodyguard's hands suggested he might not need weapons. His eyes flickered and his hands shook just slightly, a hyper-alertness induced by artificial aids—if ordered, he could strike with blinding speed and adrenalin-insane strength. He would also retire young, metabolically crippled for the rest of his short life.

The man he guarded was also young—some great lord's son? Miles wondered. He had long shining black hair dressed in an elaborate braid, smooth dark olive skin, and a high-bridged nose. He couldn't be older than Miles's real age, yet he moved with a mature assurance.

"Ryoval," Baron Fell nodded in return, as a man to an equal, not a junior. Still playing the genial host, Fell added, "Officers, may I introduce Baron Ryoval of House Ryoval. Admiral Naismith, Captain Thorne. They belong to that Illyrican-built mercenary fast cruiser in dock, Ry, that you may have noticed."

"Haven't got your eye for hardware, I'm afraid, Georish." Baron Ryoval bestowed a nod upon them, of a man being polite to his social inferiors for the principle of it. Miles bowed clumsily in return.

Dropping Miles from his attention with an almost audible thump, Ryoval stood back with his hands on his hips and regarded the null-gee bubble's inhabitant. "My agent didn't exaggerate her charms."

Fell smiled sourly. Nicol had withdrawn—recoiled— when Ryoval first approached, and now floated behind her instrument, fussing with its tuning. Pretending to be fussing with its tuning. Her eyes glanced warily at Ryoval, then returned to her dulcimer as if it might put some magic wall between them.

"Can you have her play—" Ryoval began, and was interrupted by a chime from his wrist com. "Excuse me, Georish." Looking slightly annoyed, he turned half-away from them and spoke into it. "Ryoval. And this had better be important."

"Yes, m'lord," a thin voice responded. "This is Manager Deem in Sales and Demonstrations. We have a problem. That creature House Bharaputra sold us has savaged a customer."

Ryoval's greek-statue lips rippled in a silent snarl. "I told you to chain it with duralloy."

"We did, my lord. The chains held, but it tore the bolts right out of the wall."

"Stun it."

"We have."

"Then punish it suitably when it awakes. A sufficiently long period without food should dull its aggression—its metabolism is unbelievable."

"What about the customer?"

"Give him whatever comforts he asks for. On the House."

"I . . . don't think he'll be in shape to appreciate them for quite some time. He's in the clinic now. Still unconscious."

Ryoval hissed. "Put my personal physician on his case. I'll take care of the rest when I get back downside, in about six hours. Ryoval out." He snapped the link closed. "Morons," he growled. He took a controlled, meditative breath, and recalled his social manner as if booting it up out of some stored memory bank. "Pardon the interruption, please, Georish."

Fell waved an understanding hand, as if to say, *Business.*

"As I was saying, can you have her play something?" Ryoval nodded to the quaddie.

Fell clasped his hands behind his back, his eyes glinting in a falsely benign smile. "Play something, Nicol."

She gave him an acknowledging nod, positioned herself, and closed her eyes. The frozen worry tensing her face gradually gave way to an inner stillness, and she began to play, a slow, sweet theme that established itself, rolled over, and began to quicken.

"Enough!" Ryoval flung up a hand. "She's precisely as described."

Nicol stumbled to a halt in mid-phrase. She inhaled through pinched nostrils, clearly disturbed by her inability to drive the piece through to its destined finish, the frustration of artistic incompletion. She stuck her hammers into their holders on the side of the instrument with short, savage jerks, and crossed her upper and lower arms both. Thorne's mouth tightened, and it crossed its arms in unconscious echo. Miles bit his lip uneasily.

"My agent conveyed the truth," Ryoval went on.

"Then perhaps your agent also conveyed my regrets," said Fell dryly.

"He did. But he wasn't authorized to offer more than a certain standard ceiling. For something so unique, there's no substitute for direct contact."

"I happen to be enjoying her skills where they are," said Fell. "At my age, enjoyment is much harder to obtain than money."

"So true. Yet other enjoyments might be substituted. I could arrange something quite special. Not in the catalog."

"Her *musical* skills, Ryoval. Which are more than special. They are unique. Genuine. Not artificially augmented in any way. Not to be duplicated in your laboratories."

"My laboratories can duplicate anything, sir." Ryoval smiled at the implied challenge.

"Except originality. By definition."

Ryoval spread his hands in polite acknowledgment of the philosophical point. Fell, Miles gathered, was not just enjoying the quaddie's musical talent, he was vastly enjoying the possession of something his rival keenly wanted to buy, that he had absolutely no need to sell. One-upmanship was a powerful pleasure. It seemed even the famous Ryoval was having a tough time coming up with a better—and yet, if Ryoval could find Fell's price, what force on Jackson's Whole could save Nicol? Miles suddenly realized he knew what Fell's price could be. Would Ryoval figure it out too?

Ryoval pursed his lips. "Let's discuss a tissue sample, then. It would do her no damage, and you could continue to enjoy her unique services uninterrupted."

"It would damage her uniqueness. Circulating counterfeits always brings down the value of the real thing, you know that, Ry." Baron Fell grinned.

"Not for some time," Ryoval pointed out. "The lead time for a mature clone is at least ten years—ah, but you know that." He reddened and made a little apologetic bow, as if he realized he'd just committed some faux pas.

By the thinning of Fell's lips, he had. "Indeed," said Fell coldly.

At this point Bel Thorne, tracking the interplay, interrupted in hot horror, "You can't sell her tissues! You don't own them. She's not some Jackson's Whole construct, she's a freeborn galactic citizen!"

Both barons turned to Bel as if the mercenary were a piece of furniture that had suddenly spoken. Out of turn. Miles winced.

"He can sell her contract," said Ryoval, mustering a glassy tolerance. "Which is what we are discussing. A *private* discussion."

Bel ignored the hint. "On Jackson's Whole, what practical difference does it make if you call it a contract or call it flesh?"

Ryoval smiled a little cool smile. "None whatsoever. Possession is rather more than nine points of the law, here."

"It's totally illegal!"

"Legal, my dear—ah—you are Betan, aren't you? That explains it," said Ryoval. "And illegal, are whatever the planet you are on chooses to call so and is able to enforce. I don't see any Betan enforcers around here to impose their peculiar version of morality on us all, do you, Fell?"

Fell was listening with raised brows, caught between amusement and annoyance.

Bel twitched. "So if I were to pull out a weapon and blow your head off, it would be perfectly legal?"

The bodyguard tensed, balance and center-of-gravity flowing into launch position.

"Quash it, Bel," Miles muttered under his breath.

But Ryoval was beginning to enjoy baiting his Betan interruptor. "You have no weapon. But legality aside, my subordinates have instructions to avenge me. It is, as it were, a natural or virtual law. In effect you'd find such an ill-advised impulse to be illegal indeed."

Baron Fell caught Miles's eyes and tilted his head just slightly. Time to intervene. "Time to move on, Captain," Miles said. "We aren't the baron's only guests here."

"Try the hot buffet," suggested Fell affably.

Ryoval pointedly dropped Bel from his attention and turned to Miles. "Do stop by my establishment if you get downside, Admiral. Even a Betan could stand to expand the horizons of his experience. I'm sure my staff could find something of interest in your price range."

"Not any more," said Miles. "Baron Fell already has our credit chit."

"Ah, too bad. Your next trip, perhaps." Ryoval turned away in easy dismissal.

Bel didn't budge. "You can't sell a galactic citizen down there," gesturing jerkily to the curve of the planet beyond the viewport. The quaddie Nicol, watching from behind her dulcimer, had no expression at all on her face, but her intense blue eyes blazed.

Ryoval turned back, feigning sudden surprise. "Why, Captain, I just realized. Betan—you must be a genuine genetic hermaphrodite. You possess a marketable rarity yourself. I can offer you an eye-opening employment experience at easily twice your current rate of pay. And you wouldn't even have to get shot at. I guarantee you'd be extremely popular. Group rates."

Miles swore he could see Thorne's blood pressure skyrocketing as the meaning of what Ryoval had just said sunk in. The hermaphrodite's face darkened, and it drew breath. Miles reached up and grasped Bel by the shoulder, hard. The breath held.

"No?" said Ryoval, cocking his head. "Oh, well. But seriously, I would pay well for a tissue sample, for my files."

Bel's breath exploded. "My clone-siblings, to be—be—some sort of sex-slaves into the next century! Over my dead body—or yours—you—"

Bel was so mad it was stuttering, a phenomenon Miles had never seen in seven years' acquaintance including combat.

"So Betan," smirked Ryoval.

"Stop it, Ry," growled Fell.

Ryoval sighed. "Oh, very well. But it's so easy."

"We can't win, Bel," hissed Miles. "It's time to withdraw." The bodyguard was quivering.

Fell gave Miles an approving nod.

"Thank you for your hospitality, Baron Fell," Miles said formally. "Good day, Baron Ryoval."

"Good day, Admiral," said Ryoval, regretfully giving up what was obviously the best sport he'd had all day. "You seem a cosmopolitan sort, for a Betan. Perhaps you can visit us sometime without your moral friend, here."

A war of words should be won with words. "I don't think so," Miles murmured, racking his brain for some stunning insult to withdraw on.

"What a shame," said Ryoval. "We have a dog-and-dwarf act I'm sure you'd find *fascinating.*"

There was a moment's absolute silence.

"Fry 'em from orbit," Bel suggested tightly.

Miles grinned through clenched teeth, bowed, and backed off, Bel's sleeve clutched firmly in his hand. As he turned he could hear Ryoval laughing.

Fell's majordomo appeared at their elbows within moments. "This way to the exit, please, officers," he said, smiling. Miles had never before been thrown out of any place with such exquisite politeness.

Back aboard the *Ariel* in dock, Thorne paced the wardroom while Miles sat and sipped coffee as hot and black as his own thoughts.

"Sorry I lost my temper with that squirt Ryoval," Bel apologized gruffly.

"Squirt, hell," said Miles. "The brain in that body has got to be at least a hundred years old. He played you like a violin. No. We couldn't expect to count coup on him. I admit, it would have been nice if you'd had the sense to shut up." He sucked air to cool his scalded tongue.

Bel made a disturbed gesture of acknowledgement and paced on. "And that poor girl, trapped in that bubble—I had one chance to talk to her, and I blew it—I *blithered. . . .*"

She really had brought out the male in Thorne, Miles reflected wryly. "Happens to the best of us," he murmured. He smiled into his coffee, then frowned. No. Better not to encourage Thorne's interest in the quaddie after all. She was clearly much more than just one of Fell's house servants. They had one ship here, a crew of twenty; even if he had the whole Dendarii fleet to back him he'd want to think twice about offending Baron Fell in Fell's own territory.

They had a mission. Speaking of which, where was their blasted pick-up? Why hadn't he yet contacted them as arranged?

The intercom in the wall bleeped.

Thorne strode to it. "Thorne here."

"This is Corporal Nout at the portside docking hatch. There's a . . . woman here who's asking to see you."

Thorne and Miles exchanged a raised-brows glance. "What's her name?" asked Thorne.

An off-side mumble, then, "She says it's Nicol."

Thorne grunted in surprise. "Very well. Have her escorted to the wardroom."

"Yes, Captain." The corporal failed to kill his intercom before turning away, and his voice drifted back, " . . . stay in this outfit long enough, you see one of *everything*."

Nicol appeared in the doorway balanced in a float chair, a hovering tubular cup that seemed to be looking for its saucer, enameled in a blue that precisely matched her eyes. She slipped it through the doorway as easily as a woman twitching her hips, zipped to a halt near Miles's table, and adjusted the height to that of a person sitting. The controls, run by her lower hands, left her uppers entirely free. The lower body support must have been custom-designed just for her. Miles watched her maneuver with great interest. He hadn't been sure she could even live outside her null-gee bubble. He expected her to be weak. She didn't look weak. She looked determined. She looked at Thorne.

Thorne looked all cheered up. "Nicol. How nice to see you again."

She nodded shortly. "Captain Thorne. Admiral Naismith." She glanced back and forth between them, and fastened on Thorne. Miles thought he could see why. He sipped coffee and waited for developments.

"Captain Thorne. You are a mercenary, are you not?"

"Yes. . . ."

"And . . . pardon me if I misunderstood, but it seemed to me you had a certain . . . empathy, for my situation. An understanding of my position."

Thorne rendered her a slightly idiotic bow. "I understand you are dangling over a pit."

Her lips tightened, and she nodded mutely.

"She got herself into it," Miles pointed out.

Her chin lifted. "And I intend to get myself out of it."

Miles turned a hand palm-out, and sipped again.

She readjusted her float chair, a nervous gesture ending at about the same altitude it began.

"It seems to me," said Miles, "that Baron Fell is a formidable protector. I'm not sure you have anything to fear from Ryoval's, er, carnal interest in you as long as Fell's in charge."

"Baron Fell is dying." She tossed her head. "Or at any rate, he thinks he is."

"So I gathered. Why doesn't he have a clone made?"

"He did. It was all set up with House Bharaputra. The clone was fourteen years old, full-sized. Then a couple of months ago, somebody assassinated the clone. The baron still hasn't found out for sure who did it, though he has a little list. Headed by his half-brother."

"Thus trapping him in his aging body. What a . . . fascinating tactical maneuver," Miles mused. "What's this unknown enemy going to do next, I wonder? Just wait?"

"I don't know," said Nicol. "The Baron's had another clone started, but it's not even out of the replicator yet. Even with growth accelerators it'd be years before it would be mature enough to transplant. And . . . it has occurred to me that there are a number of ways the baron could die besides ill health between now and then."

"An unstable situation," Miles agreed.

"I want out. I want to buy passage out."

"Then why, he asked," said Miles dryly, "don't you just go plunk your money down at the offices of one of the three galactic commercial passenger lines that dock here, and buy a ticket?"

"It's my contract," said Nicol. "When I signed it back on Earth, I didn't realize what it would mean once I got to Jackson's Whole. I can't even buy my way out of it, unless the baron chooses to let me. And somehow, it seems to cost more and more just to live here. I ran a calculation . . . it gets much worse before my time is up."

"How much time?" asked Thorne.

"Five more years."

"Ouch," said Thorne sympathetically.

"So you, ah, want us to help you jump a Syndicate contract," said Miles, making little wet coffee rings on the table with the bottom of his mug. "Smuggle you out in secret, I suppose."

"I can pay. I can pay more right now than I'll be able to next year. This wasn't the gig I expected, when I came here. There was talk of recording a vid demo . . . it never happened. I don't think it's ever going to happen. I have to be able to reach a wider audience, if I'm ever to pay my way back home. Back to my people. I want . . . *out* of here, before I fall down that gravity well." She jerked an upper thumb in the general direction of the planet they orbited. "People go downside here, who never come up again." She paused. "Are you *afraid* of Baron Fell?"

"No!" said Thorne, as Miles said, "Yes." They exchanged a sardonic look.

"We are inclined to be careful of Baron Fell," Miles suggested. Thorne shrugged agreement.

She frowned, and maneuvered to the table. She drew a wad of assorted planetary currencies out of her green silk jacket and laid it in front of Miles. "Would this bolster your nerve?"

Thorne fingered the stack, flipped through it. At least a couple thousand Betan dollars worth, at conservative estimate, mostly in middle denominations, though a Betan single topped the pile, camouflaging its value to a casual glance. "Well," said Thorne, glancing at Miles, "and what do we mercenaries think of that?"

Miles leaned back thoughtfully in his chair. The kept secret of Miles's identity wasn't the only favor Thorne could call in if it chose. Miles remembered the day Thorne had helped capture an asteroid mining station and the pocket dreadnought *Triumph* for him with nothing but sixteen troops in combat armor and a hell of a lot of nerve. "I encourage creative financing on the part of my commanders," he said at last. "Negotiate away, Captain."

Thorne smiled, and pulled the Betan dollar off the stack. "You have the right idea," Thorne said to the musician, "but the amount is wrong."

Her hand went uncertainly to her jacket and paused, as Thorne pushed the rest of the stack of currency, minus the single, back at her. "What?"

Thorne picked up the single and snapped it a few times. "This is the right amount. Makes it an official contract, you see." Bel extended a hand to her; after a bewildered moment, she shook it. "Deal," said Thorne happily.

"Hero," said Miles, holding up a warning finger, "beware, I'll call in my veto if you can't come up with a way to bring this off in dead secret. That's my cut of the price."

"Yes, *sir*," said Thorne.

Several hours later, Miles snapped awake in his cabin aboard the *Ariel* to an urgent bleeping from his comconsole. Whatever he had been dreaming was gone in the instant, though he had the vague idea it had been something unpleasant. Biological and unpleasant. "Naismith here."

"This is the duty officer in Nav and Com, sir. You have a call originating from the downside commercial com net. He says to tell you it's Vaughn."

Vaughn was the agreed-upon code name of their pickup. His real name was Dr. Canaba. Miles grabbed his uniform jacket and shrugged it on over his black T-shirt, passed his hands futilely through his hair, and slid into his console station chair. "Put him through."

The face of a man on the high side of middle age materialized above Miles's vid plate. Tan-skinned, racially indeterminate features, short wavy hair graying at the temples; more arresting was the intelligence that suffused those features and quickened the brown eyes. *Yep, that's my man,* thought Miles with satisfaction. *Here we go.* But Canaba looked more than tense. He looked distraught.

"Admiral Naismith?"

"Yes. Vaughn?"

Canaba nodded.

"Where are you?" asked Miles.

"Downside."

"You were to meet us up here."

"I know. Something's come up. A problem."

"What sort of problem? Ah—is this channel secure?"

Canaba laughed bitterly. "On this planet, nothing is secure. But I don't think I'm being traced. But I can't come up yet. I need . . . help."

"Vaughn, we aren't equipped to break you out against superior forces—if you've become a prisoner—"

He shook his head. "No, it's not that. I've . . . lost something. I need help to get it back."

"I'd understood you were to leave everything. You would be compensated later."

"It's not a personal possession. It's something your employer wants very badly. Certain . . . samples, have been removed from my . . . power. They won't take me without them."

Dr. Canaba took Miles for a mercenary hireling, entrusted with minimum classified information by Barrayaran Security. So. "All I was asked to transport was you and your skills."

"They didn't tell you everything."

The hell they didn't. Barrayar would take you stark naked, and be grateful. What was this?

Canaba met Miles's frown with a mouth set like iron. "I *won't* leave without them. Or the deal's off. And you can whistle for your pay, mercenary."

He meant it. Damn. Miles's eyes narrowed. "This is all a bit mysterious."

Canaba shrugged acknowledgment. "I'm sorry. But I *must* . . . Meet with me, and I'll tell you the rest. Or go, I don't care which. But a certain thing must be accomplished, must be . . . expiated." He trailed off in agitation.

Miles took a deep breath. "Very well. But every complication you add increases your risk. And mine. This had better be worth it."

"Oh, Admiral," breathed Canaba sadly, "it is to me. It is to me."

Snow sifted through the little park where Canaba met them, giving Miles something new to swear at if only he hadn't run out of invective hours ago. He was shivering even in his Dendarii-issue parka by the time Canaba walked past the dingy kiosk where Miles and Bel roosted. They fell in behind him without a word.

Bharaputra Laboratories were headquartered in a downside town Miles frankly found worrisome: guarded shuttleport, guarded Syndicate buildings, guarded municipal buildings, guarded walled residential compounds; in between, a crazy disorder of neglected aging structures that didn't seem to be guarded by anyone, occupied by people who *slunk*. It made Miles wonder if the two Dendarii troopers he'd detailed to shadow them were quite enough. But the slithery people gave them a wide berth; they evidently understood what guards meant. At least during the daylight.

Canaba led them into one of the nearby buildings. Its lift tubes were out-of-order, its corridors unheated. A darkly-dressed maybe-female person scurried out of their way in the shadows, reminding Miles uncomfortably of a rat. They followed Canaba dubiously up the safety ladder set in the side of a dead lift tube, down another corridor, and through a door with a broken palm-lock into an empty dirty room, grayly lit by an unpolarized but intact window. At least they were out of the wind.

"I think we can talk safely here," said Canaba, turning and pulling off his gloves.

"Bel?" said Miles.

Thorne pulled an assortment of anti-surveillance detectors from its parka and ran a scan, as the two guards prowled the perimeters. One stationed himself in the corridor, the second near the window.

"It scans clean," said Bel at last, as if reluctant to believe its own instruments. "For now." Rather pointedly, Bel walked around Canaba and scanned him too. Canaba waited with bowed head, as if he felt he deserved no better. Bel set up the sonic baffler.

Miles shrugged back his hood and opened his parka, the better to reach his concealed weapons in the event of a trap. He was finding Canaba extraordinarily hard to read. What were the man's motivations anyway? There was no doubt House Bharaputra had assured his comfort—his coat, the rich cut of his clothing beneath it, spoke of that—and though his standard of living surely would not drop when he transferred his allegiance to the Barrayaran Imperial Science Institute, he would not have nearly the opportunities to amass wealth on the side that he had here. So, he wasn't in it for the money. Miles could understand that. But why work for a place like House Bharaputra in the first place unless greed overwhelmed integrity?

"You puzzle me, Dr. Canaba," said Miles lightly. "Why this mid-career switch? I'm pretty well acquainted with your new employers, and frankly, I don't see how they could out-bid House Bharaputra." There, that was a properly mercenary way to put it.

"They offered me protection from House Bharaputra. Although, if *you're* it . . ." He looked doubtfully down at Miles.

Ha. And, hell. The man really was ready to bolt. Leaving Miles to explain the failure of his mission to Chief of Imperial Security Illyan in person. "They bought our services," said Miles, "and therefore you command our services. They want you safe and happy. But we can't begin to protect you when you depart from a plan designed to maximize your safety, throw in random factors, and ask us to operate in the dark. I need full knowledge of what's going on if I'm to take full responsibility for the results."

"No one is asking you to take responsibility."

"I beg your pardon, doctor, but they surely have."

"Oh," said Canaba. "I . . . see." He paced to the window, back. "But will you do what I ask?"

"I will do what I can."

"Happy," Canaba snorted. "God . . ." He shook his head wearily, inhaled decisively. "I never came here for the money. I came here because I could do research I couldn't do anywhere else. Not hedged round with outdated legal restrictions. I dreamed of breakthroughs . . . but it became a nightmare. The freedom became slavery. The things they wanted me to do . . . ! Constantly interrupting the things I wanted to do. Oh, you can always find someone to do anything for money, but they're second-raters. These labs are full of second-raters. The very best can't be bought. I've done things, unique things, that Bharaputra won't develop because the profit would be too small, never mind how many people it would benefit—I get no credit, no standing for my work—every year, I see in the literature of my field galactic honors going to lesser men, because I cannot publish my results . . ." He stopped, lowered his head. "I doubtless sound like a megalomaniac to you."

"Ah . . ." said Miles, "you sound quite frustrated."

"The frustration," said Canaba, "woke me from a long sleep. Wounded ego—it was only wounded ego. But in my pride, I rediscovered shame. And the weight of it stunned me, stunned me where I stood. *Do* you understand? Does it matter if you understand? Ah!" He paced away to the wall, and stood facing it, his back rigid.

"Uh," Miles scratched the back of his head ruefully, "yeah. I'd be glad to spend many fascinating hours listening to you explain it to me—on my ship. Outbound."

Canaba turned with a crooked smile. "You are a practical man, I perceive. A soldier. Well, God knows I need a soldier now."

"Things are that screwed up, eh?"

"It . . . happened suddenly. I thought I had it under control."

"Go on," sighed Miles.

"There were seven synthesized gene-complexes. One of them is a cure for a certain obscure enzyme disorder. One of them will increase oxygen-generation in space station algae twenty-fold. One of them came from outside Bharaputra Labs, brought in by a man—we never found out who he really was, but death followed him. Several of my colleagues who had worked on his project were murdered all in one night, by the commandos who pursued him—their records destroyed—I never told anyone I'd borrowed an unauthorized tissue sample to study. I've not unravelled it fully yet, but I can tell you, it's absolutely unique."

Miles recognized that one, and almost choked, reflecting upon the bizarre chain of circumstances that had placed an identical tissue sample in the hands of Dendarii Intelligence a year ago. Terrence See's telepathy complex—and the main reason *why* His Imperial Majesty suddenly wanted a top geneticist. Dr. Canaba was in for a little surprise when he arrived at his new Barrayaran laboratory. But if the other six complexes came anywhere near matching the value of the known one, Security Chief Illyan would peel Miles with a dull knife for letting them slip through his fingers. Miles's attention to Canaba abruptly intensified. This side-trip might not be as trivial as he'd feared.

"Together, these seven complexes represent tens of thousands of hours of research time, mostly mine, some of others—my life's work. I'd planned from the beginning to take them with me. I bundled them up in a viral insert and placed them, bound and dormant, in a live . . ." Canaba faltered, "organism, for storage. An organism, I thought, that no one would think to look at for such a thing."

"Why didn't you just store them in your own tissue?" Miles asked irritably. "Then you couldn't lose 'em."

Canaba's mouth opened. "I . . . never thought of that. How elegant. Why didn't I think of that?" His hand touched his forehead wonderingly, as if probing for systems failure. His lips tightened again. "But it would have made no difference. I would still need to . . ." he fell silent. "It's about the organism," he said at last. "The . . . creature." Another long silence.

"Of all the things I did," Canaba continued lowly, "of all the interruptions this vile place imposed on me, there is one I regret the most. You understand, this was years ago. I was younger, I thought I still had a future to protect. And it wasn't all my doing—guilt by committee, eh? Spread it around, make it easy, say it was *his* fault, *her* doing . . . well, it's mine now."

You mean it's *mine* now, thought Miles grimly. "Doctor, the more time we spend here, the greater the chance of compromising this operation. Please get to the point."

"Yes . . . yes. Well, a number of years ago, House Bharaputra Laboratories took on a contract to manufacture a . . . new species. Made to order."

"I thought it was House Ryoval that was famous for making people, or whatever, to order," said Miles.

"They make slaves, one-off. They are very specialized. And small—their customer base is surprisingly small. There are many rich men, and there are, I suppose, many depraved men, but a House Ryoval customer has to be a member of both sets, and the overlap isn't as large as you'd think. Anyway, our contract was supposed to lead to a major production run, far beyond Ryoval's capabilities. A certain sub-planetary government, hard-pressed by its neighbors, wanted us to engineer a race of super-soldiers for them."

"What, again?" said Miles. "I thought that had been tried. More than once."

"This time, we thought we could do it. Or at least, the Bharaputran hierarchy was willing to take their money. But the project suffered from too much input. The client, our own higher-ups, the genetics project members, everybody had ideas they were pushing. I swear it was doomed before it ever got out of the design committee."

"A super-soldier. Designed by committee. Ye gods. The mind boggles." Miles's eyes were wide in fascination. "So then what happened?"

"It seemed to . . . several of us, that the physical limits of the merely human had already been reached. Once a, say, muscle system has been brought to perfect health, stimulated with maximum hormones, exercised to a certain limit, that's all you can do. So we turned to other species for special improvements. I, for instance, became fascinated by the aerobic and anaerobic metabolism in the muscles of the thoroughbred horse—"

"What?" said Thorne, shocked.

"There were other ideas. Too many. I swear, they weren't all mine."

"You mixed human and animal genes?" breathed Miles.

"Why not? Human genes have been spliced into animals from the crude beginnings—it was almost the first thing they tried. Human insulin from bacteria and the like. But till now, no one dared do it in reverse. I broke the barrier, cracked the codes . . . It looked good at first. It was only when the first ones reached puberty that all the errors became fully apparent. Well, it was only the initial trial. They were meant to be formidable. But they ended up monstrous."

"Tell me," Miles choked, "were there any actual combat-experienced soldiers on the committee?"

"I assume the client had them. They supplied the parameters," said Canaba.

Said Thorne in a suffused voice, "*I see.* They were trying to re-invent the *enlisted* man."

Miles shot Thorne a quelling glower, and tapped his chrono. "Don't let us interrupt, doctor."

There was a short silence. Canaba began again. "We ran off ten prototypes. Then the client . . . went out of business. They lost their war—"

"Why am I not surprised?" Miles muttered under his breath.

"—funding was cut off, the project was dropped before we could apply what we had learned from our mistakes. Of the ten prototypes, nine have since died. There was one left. We were keeping it at the labs due to . . . difficulties, in boarding it out. I placed my gene complexes in it. They are there still. The last thing I meant to do before I left was kill it. A mercy . . . a responsibility. My expiation, if you will."

"And then?" prodded Miles.

"A few days ago, it was suddenly sold to House Ryoval. As a novelty, apparently. Baron Ryoval collects oddities of all sorts, for his tissue banks—"

Miles and Bel exchanged a look.

"—I had no idea it was to be sold. I came in in the morning and it was gone. I don't think Ryoval has any idea of its real value. It's there now, as far as I know, at Ryoval's facilities."

Miles decided he was getting a sinus headache. From the cold, no doubt. "And what, pray, d'you want us soldiers to do about it?"

"Get in there, somehow. Kill it. Collect a tissue sample. Only then will I go with you."

And stomach twinges. "What, both ears and the tail?"

Canaba gave Miles a cold look. "The left gastrocnemius muscle. That's where I injected my complexes. These storage viruses aren't virulent, they won't have migrated far. The greatest concentration should still be there."

"I see." Miles rubbed his temples, and pressed his eyes. "All right. We'll take care of it. This personal contact between us is very dangerous, and I'd rather not repeat it. Plan to report to my ship in forty-eight hours. Will we have any trouble recognizing your critter?"

"I don't think so. This particular specimen topped out at just over eight feet. I . . . want you to know, the fangs were *not* my idea."

"I . . . see."

"It can move very fast, if it's still in good health. Is there any help I can give you? I have access to painless poisons . . ."

"You've done enough, thank you. Please leave it to us professionals, eh?"

"It would be best if its body can be destroyed entirely. No cells remaining. If you can."

"That's why plasma arcs were invented. You'd best be on your way."

"Yes." Canaba hesitated. "Admiral Naismith?"

"Yes. . . ."

"I . . . it might also be best if my future employer didn't learn about this. They have intense military interests. It might excite them unduly."

"Oh," said Miles/Admiral Naismith/Lieutenant Lord Vorkosigan of the Barrayaran Imperial Service, "I don't think you have to worry about that."

"Is forty-eight hours enough for your commando raid?" Canaba worried. "You understand, if you don't get the tissue, I'll go right back downside. I will not be trapped aboard your ship."

"You will be happy. It's in my contract," said Miles. "Now you'd better get gone."

"I must rely on you, sir." Canaba nodded in suppressed anguish, and withdrew.

They waited a few minutes in the cold room, to let Canaba put some distance between them. The building creaked in the wind; from an upper corridor echoed an odd shriek, and later, a laugh abruptly cut off. The guard shadowing Canaba returned. "He made it to his groundcar all right, sir."

"Well," said Thorne, "I suppose we'll need to get hold of a plan of Ryoval's facilities, first—"

"I think not," said Miles.

"If we're to raid—"

"Raid, hell. I'm not risking my men on anything so idiotic. I said I'd slay his sin for him. I didn't say how."

The commercial comconsole net at the downside shuttleport seemed as convenient as anything. Miles slid into the booth and fed the machine his credit card while Thorne lurked just outside the viewing angle and the guards, outside, guarded. He encoded the call.

In a moment, the vid plate produced the image of a sweet-faced receptionist with dimples and a white fur crest instead of hair. "House Ryoval, Customer Services. How may I help you, sir?"

"I'd like to speak to Manager Deem, in Sales and Demonstrations," said Miles smoothly, "about a possible purchase for my organization."

"Who may I say is calling?"

"Admiral Miles Naismith, Dendarii Free Mercenary Fleet."

"One moment, sir."

"You really think they'll just sell it?" Bel muttered from the side as the girl's face was replaced by a flowing pattern of colored lights and some syrupy music.

"Remember what we overheard yesterday?" said Miles. "I'm betting it's *on* sale. Cheap." He must try not to look too interested.

In a remarkably short time, the colored glop gave way to the face of an astonishingly beautiful young man, a blue-eyed albino in a red silk shirt. He had a huge livid bruise up one side of his white face. "This is Manager Deem. May I help you, Admiral?"

Miles cleared his throat carefully. "A rumor has been brought to my attention that House Ryoval may have recently acquired from House Bharaputra an article of some professional interest to me. Supposedly, it was a prototype of some sort of new improved fighting man. Do you know anything about it?"

Deem's hand stole to his bruise and palpated it gently, then twitched away. "Indeed, sir, we do have such an article."

"Is it for sale?"

"Oh, *ye*—I mean, I think some arrangement is pending. But it may still be possible to bid on it."

"Would it be possible for me to inspect it?"

"Of course," said Deem with suppressed eagerness. "How soon?"

There was a burst of static, and the vid image split, Deem's face abruptly shrinking to one side. The new face was only too familiar. Bel hissed under its breath.

"I'll take this call, Deem," said Baron Ryoval.

"Yes, my lord." Deem's eyes widened in surprise, and he cut out. Ryoval's image swelled to occupy the space available.

"So, Betan." Ryoval smiled. "It appears I have something you want after all."

Miles shrugged. "Maybe," he said neutrally. "If it's in my price range."

"I thought you gave all your money to Fell."

Miles spread his hands. "A good commander always has hidden reserves. However, the actual value of the item hasn't yet been established. In fact, its existence hasn't even been established."

"Oh, it exists, all right. And it is . . . impressive. Adding it to my collection was a unique pleasure. I'd hate to give it up. But for you," Ryoval smiled more broadly, "it may be possible to arrange a special cut rate." He chuckled, as at some secret pun that escaped Miles.

A special cut throat is more like it. "Oh?"

"I propose a simple trade," said Ryoval. "Flesh for flesh."

"You may overestimate my interest, Baron."

Ryoval's eyes glinted. "I don't think so."

He knows I wouldn't touch him with a stick if it weren't something pretty compelling. So. "Name your proposal, then."

"I'll trade you even, Bharaputra's pet monster—ah, you should see it, Admiral!—for three tissue samples. Three tissue samples that will, if you are clever about it, cost you nothing." Ryoval held up one finger. "One from your Betan hermaphrodite," a second finger, "one from yourself," a third finger, making a W, "and one from Baron Fell's quaddie musician."

Over in the corner, Bel Thorne appeared to be suppressing an apoplectic fit. Quietly, fortunately.

"That third could prove extremely difficult to obtain," said Miles, buying time to think.

"Less difficult for you than me," said Ryoval. "Fell knows my agents. My overtures have put him on guard. You represent a unique opportunity to get in under that guard. Given sufficient motivation, I'm certain it's not beyond you, mercenary."

"Given sufficient motivation, very little is beyond me, Baron," said Miles semi-randomly.

"Well, then. I shall expect to hear from you within— say—twenty-four hours. After that time my offer will be withdrawn." Ryoval nodded cheerfully. "Good day, Admiral." The vid blanked.

"Well, then," echoed Miles.

"Well, what?" said Thorne with suspicion. "You're not actually seriously considering that—vile proposal, are you?"

"What does he want my tissue sample for, for God's sake?" Miles wondered aloud.

"For his dog and dwarf act, no doubt," said Thorne nastily.

"Now, now. He'd be dreadfully disappointed when my clone turned out to be six feet tall, I'm afraid." Miles cleared his throat. "It wouldn't actually hurt anyone, I suppose. To take a small tissue sample. Whereas a commando raid risks lives."

Bel leaned back against the wall and crossed its arms. "Not true. You'd have to fight me for mine. And *hers*."

Miles grinned sourly. "So."

"So?"

"So let's go find a map of Ryoval's flesh pit. It seems we're going hunting."

House Ryoval's palatial main biologicals facility wasn't a proper fortress, just some guarded buildings. Some bloody big guarded buildings. Miles stood on the roof of the lift-van and studied the layout through his night-glasses. Fog droplets beaded in his hair. The cold damp wind searched for chinks in his jacket much as he searched for chinks in Ryoval's security.

The white complex loomed against the dark forested mountainside, its front gardens floodlit and fairy-like in the fog and frost. The utility entrances on the near side looked more promising. Miles nodded slowly to himself and climbed down off the rented lift-van, artistically broke-down on the little mountain side-trail overlooking Ryoval's. He swung into the back, out of the piercing wind.

"All right, people, listen up." His squad hunkered around as he set up the holovid map in the middle. The colored lights of the display sheened their faces, tall Ensign Murka, Thorne's second-in-command, and two big troopers. Sergeant Laureen Anderson was the van driver, assigned to outside backup along with Trooper Sandy Herald and Captain Thorne. Miles harbored a secret Barrayaran prejudice against taking female troops inside Ryoval's, that he trusted he concealed. It went double for Bel Thorne. Not that one's sex would necessarily make any difference to the adventures that might follow in the event of capture, if even a tenth of the bizarre rumors he'd heard were true. Nevertheless . . . Laureen claimed to be able to fly any vehicle made by man through the eye of a needle, not that Miles figured she'd ever done anything so domestic as thread a needle in her life. She would not question her assignment.

"Our main problem remains, that we still don't know where exactly in this facility Bharaputra's creature is being kept. So first we penetrate the fence, the outer courts, and the main building, here and here." A red thread of light traced their projected route at Miles's touch on the control board. "Then we quietly pick up an inside employee and fast-penta him. From that point on we're racing time, since we must assume he'll be promptly missed.

"The key word is quietly. We didn't come here to kill *people*, and we are not at war with Ryoval's employees. You carry your stunners, and keep those plasma arcs and the rest of the toys packed till we locate our quarry. We dispatch it fast and quietly, I get my sample," his hand touched his jacket, beneath which rested the collection case that would keep the tissue alive till they got back to the *Ariel*. "Then we fly. If anything goes wrong before I get that very expensive cut of meat, we don't bother to fight our way out. Not worth it. They have peculiar summary ways of dealing with murder charges here, and I don't see the need for any of us to end up as spare parts in Ryoval's tissue banks. We wait for Captain Thorne to arrange a ransom, and then try something else. We hold a lever or two on Ryoval in case of emergencies."

"Dire emergencies," Bel muttered.

"If anything goes wrong after the butcher-mission is accomplished, it's back to combat rules. That sample will then be irreplaceable, and must be got back to Captain Thorne at all costs. Laureen, you sure of our emergency pick-up spot?"

"Yes, sir." She pointed on the vid display.

"Everybody else got that? Any questions? Suggestions? Last minute observations? Communications check, then, Captain Thorne."

Their wrist coms all appeared to be in good working order. Ensign Murka shrugged on the weapons pack. Miles carefully pocketed the blueprint map cube, that had cost them a near-ransom from a certain pliable construction company just a few hours ago. The four members of the penetration team slipped from the van and merged with the frosty darkness.

They slunk off through the woods. The frozen crunchy layer of plant detritus tended to slide underfoot, exposing a layer of slick mud. Murka spotted a spy eye before it spotted them, and blinded it with a brief burst of microwave static while they scurried past. The useful big guys made short work of boosting Miles over the wall. Miles tried not to think about the ancient pub sport of dwarf tossing. The inner court was stark and utilitarian, loading docks with big locked doors, rubbish collection bays, and a few parked vehicles.

Footsteps echoed, and they ducked down in a rubbish bay. A red-clad guard passed, slowly waving an infra-red scanner. They crouched and hid their faces in their infra-red blank ponchos, looking like so many bags of garbage no doubt. Then it was tiptoe up to the loading docks.

Ducts. The key to Ryoval's facility had turned out to be ducts, for heating, for access to power-optics cables, for the com system. Narrow ducts. Quite impassable to a big guy.

Miles slipped out of his poncho and gave it to a trooper to fold and pack.

Miles balanced on Murka's shoulders and cut his way through the first ductlet, a ventilation grille high on the wall above the loading dock doors. Miles handed the grille down silently, and after a quick visual scan for unwanted company, slithered through. It was a tight fit even for him. He let himself down gently to the concrete floor, found the door control box, shorted the alarm, and raised the door about a meter. His team rolled through, and he let the door back down as quietly as he could. So far so good; they hadn't yet had to exchange a word.

They made it to cover on the far side of the receiving bay just before a red-coveralled employee wandered through, driving an electric cart loaded with cleaning robots. Murka touched Miles's sleeve, and looked his inquiry—*This one?* Miles shook his head, *Not yet.* A maintenance man seemed less likely than an employee from the inner sanctum to know where their quarry was kept, and they didn't have time to litter the place with the unconscious bodies of false trials. They found the tunnel to the main building, just as the map cube promised. The door at the end was locked as expected.

It was up on Murka's shoulders again. A quick zizz of Miles's cutters loosened a panel in the ceiling, and he crawled through—the frail supporting framework would surely not have held a man of greater weight—and found the power cables running to the door lock. He was just looking over the problem and pulling tools out of his pocketed uniform jacket when Murka's hand reached up to thrust the weapons pack beside him and quietly pull the panel back into place. Miles flung himself to his belly and pressed his eye to the crack as a voice from down the corridor bellowed, "Freeze!"

Swear words screamed through Miles's head. He clamped his jaw on them. He looked down on the tops of his troopers' heads. In a moment, they were surrounded by half-a-dozen red-clad black-trousered armed guards. "What are you doing here?" snarled the guard sergeant.

"Oh, shit!" cried Murka. "*Please,* mister, don't tell my CO you caught us in here. He'd bust me back to private!"

"Huh?" said the guard sergeant. He prodded Murka with his weapon, a lethal nerve disruptor. "Hands up! Who are you?"

"M'name's Murka. We came in on a mercenary ship to Fell Station, but the captain wouldn't grant us downside passes. Think of it—we come all the way to Jackson's Whole, and the sonofabitch wouldn't let us go downside! Bloody pure-dick wouldn't let us see Ryoval's!"

The red-tunic'd guards were doing a fast scan-and-search, none too gently, and finding only stunners and the portion of security-penetration devices that Murka had carried.

"I made a bet we could get in even if we couldn't afford the front door." Murka's mouth turned down in great discouragement. "Looks like I lost."

"Looks like you did," growled the guard sergeant, drawing back.

One of his men held up the thin collection of baubles they'd stripped off the Dendarii. "They're not equipped like an assassination team," he observed.

Murka drew himself up, looking wonderfully offended. "We aren't!"

The guard sergeant turned over a stunner. "AWOL, are you?"

"Not if we make it back before midnight." Murka's tone went wheedling. "Look, m'CO's a right bastard. Suppose there's any way you could see your way clear that he doesn't find out about this?" One of Murka's hands drifted suggestively past his wallet pocket.

The guard sergeant looked him up and down, smirking. "Maybe."

Miles listened with open-mouthed delight. *Murka, if this works I'm promoting you. . . .*

Murka paused. "Any chance of seeing inside first? Not the girls even, just the place? So I could say that I'd seen it."

"This isn't a whorehouse, soldier boy!" snapped the guard sergeant.

Murka looked stunned. "What?"

"This is the *biologicals* facility."

"Oh," said Murka.

"You *idiot*," one of the troopers put in on cue. Miles sprinkled silent blessings down upon his head. None of the three so much as flicked an eyeball upward.

"But the man in town told me—" began Murka.

"What man?" said the guard sergeant.

"The man who took m'money," said Murka.

A couple of the red tunic'd guards were beginning to grin. The guard sergeant prodded Murka with his nerve disruptor. "Get going, soldier boy. Back that way. This is your lucky day."

"You mean we get to see inside?" said Murka hopefully.

"No," said the guard sergeant, "I mean we aren't going to break both your legs before we throw you out on your ass." He paused and added more kindly, "There's a whorehouse back in town." He slipped Murka's wallet out of his pocket, checked the name on the credit card and put it back, and removed all the loose currency. The guards did the same to the outraged-looking troopers, dividing the assorted cash up among them. "They take credit cards, and you've still got till midnight. Now move!"

And so Miles's squad was chivied, ignominiously but intact, down the tunnel. Miles waited till the whole mob was well out of earshot before keying his wrist com. "Bel?"

"Yes," came back the instant reply.

"Trouble. Murka and the troops were just picked up by Ryoval's security. I believe the boy genius has just managed to bullshit them into throwing them out the back door, instead of rendering them down for parts. I'll follow as soon as I can, we'll rendezvous and regroup for another try." Miles paused. This was a total bust. They were now worse off than when they'd started. Ryoval's security would be stirred up for the rest of the long Jacksonian night. He added to the com, "I'm going to see if I can't at least find out the location of the critter before I withdraw. Should improve our chances of success next round."

Bel swore in a heartfelt tone. "Be careful."

"You bet. Watch for Murka and the boys. Naismith out."

Once he'd identified the right cables it was the work of a moment to make the door slide open. He then had an interesting dangle by his fingertips while coaxing the ceiling panel to fall back into place before he dropped from maximum downward extension, fearful for his bones. Nothing broke. He slipped across the portal to the main building and took to the ducts as soon as possible, the corridors having been proved dangerous. He lay on his back in the narrow tube and balanced the blueprint holocube on his belly, picking out a new and safer route not necessarily passable to a couple of husky troopers. And where did one look for a monster? A closet?

It was about the third turn, inching his way through the system dragging the weapon pack, that he became aware that the territory no longer matched the map. Hell and damnation. Were these changes in the system since its construction, or a subtly sabotaged map? Well, no matter, he wasn't really lost; he could still retrace his route.

He crawled along for about thirty minutes, discovering and disarming two alarm sensors before they discovered him. The time factor was getting seriously pressing. Soon he would have to—ah, there! He peered through a vent grille into a dim room filled with holovid and communications equipment. *Small Repairs,* the map cube named it. It didn't look like a repairs shop. Another change since Ryoval had moved in? But a man sat alone with his back to Miles's wall. Perfect, too good to pass up.

Breathing silently, moving slowly, Miles eased his dart-gun out of the pack and made sure he loaded it with the right cartridge, fast-penta spiked with a paralyzer, a lovely cocktail blended for the purpose by the *Ariel's* medtech. He sighted through the grille, aimed the needle-nose of the dart gun with tense precision, and fired. Bullseye. The man slapped the back of his neck once and sat still, hand falling nervelessly to his side. Miles grinned briefly, cut his way through the grille, and lowered himself to the floor.

The man was well-dressed in civilian-type clothes—one of the scientists, perhaps? He lolled in his chair, a little smile playing around his lips, and stared with unalarmed interest at Miles. He started to fall over.

Miles caught him and propped him back upright. "Sit up now, that's right, you can't talk with your face in the carpet now, can you?"

"Nooo . . ." The man bobbled his head and smiled agreeably.

"Do you know anything about a genetic construct, a monstrous creature, just recently bought from House Bharaputra and brought to this facility?"

The man blinked and smiled. "Yes."

Fast-penta subjects did tend to be literal, Miles reminded himself. "Where is it being kept?"

"Downstairs."

"Where exactly downstairs?"

"In the sub-basement. The crawl-space around the foundations. We were hoping it would catch some of the rats, you see." The man giggled. "Do cats eat rats? Do rats eat cats . . . ?"

Miles checked his map-cube. Yes. That looked good, in terms of the penetration team getting in and out, though it was still a large search area, broken up into a maze by structural elements running down into the bedrock, and specially-set low-vibration support columns running up into the laboratories. At the lower edge, where the mountainside sloped away, the space ran high-ceilinged and very near the surface, a possible break-out point. The space thinned to head-cracking narrowness and then to bedrock at the back where the building wedged into the slope. All right. Miles opened his dart case to find something that would lay his victim out cold and non-questionable for the rest of the night. The man pawed at him and his sleeve slipped back to reveal a wrist com almost as thick and complex as Miles's own. A light blinked on it. Miles looked at the device, suddenly uneasy. This room . . . "By the way, who are you?"

"Moglia, Chief of Security, Ryoval Biologicals," the man recited happily. "At your service, sir."

"Oh, indeed you are." Miles's suddenly-thick fingers scrabbled faster in his dart case. Damn, damn, *damn*.

The door burst open. "Freeze, mister!"

Miles hit the tight-beam alarm/self-destruct on his own wrist com and flung his hands up, and the wrist com off, in one swift motion. Not by chance, Moglia sat between Miles and the door, inhibiting the trigger reflexes of the entering guards. The com melted as it arced through the air—no chance of Ryoval security tracing the outside squad through it now, and Bel would at least know something had gone wrong.

The security chief chuckled to himself, temporarily fascinated by the task of counting his own fingers. The red-clad guard sergeant, backed by his squad, thundered into what was now screamingly obvious to Miles as the Security Operations Room, to jerk Miles around, slam him face-first into the wall, and begin frisking him with vicious efficiency. Within moments he had separated Miles from a clanking pile of incriminating equipment, his jacket, boots, and belt. Miles clutched the wall and shivered with the pain of several expertly-applied nerve jabs and the swift reversal of his fortune.

The security chief, when un-penta'd at last, was not at all pleased with the guard sergeant's confession about the three uniformed men he had let go with a fine earlier in the evening. He put the whole guard shift on full alert, and sent an armed squad out to try to trace the escaped Dendarii. Then, with an apprehensive expression on his face very like the guard-sergeant's during his mortified admission— compounded with sour satisfaction, contemplating Miles, and drug-induced nausea—he made a vid call.

"My lord?" said the security chief carefully.

"What is it, Moglia?" Baron Ryoval's face was sleepy and irritated.

"Sorry to disturb you sir, but I thought you might like to know about the intruder we just caught here. Not an ordinary thief, judging from his clothes and equipment. Strange-looking fellow, sort of a tall dwarf. He squeezed in through the ducts." Moglia held up tissue-collection kit, chip-driven alarm-disarming tools, and Miles's weapons, by way of evidence. The guard sergeant bundled Miles, stumbling, into range of the vid pick-up. "He was asking a lot of questions about Bharaputra's monster."

Ryoval's lips parted. Then his eyes lit, and he threw back his head and laughed. "I should have guessed. Stealing when you should be buying, Admiral?" he chortled. "Oh, very good, Moglia!"

The security chief looked fractionally less nervous. "Do you know this little mutant, my lord?"

"Yes, indeed. He calls himself Miles Naismith. A mercenary—bills himself as an admiral. Self-promoted, no doubt. Excellent work, Moglia. Hold him, and I'll be there in the morning and deal with him personally."

"Hold him how, sir?"

Ryoval shrugged. "Amuse yourselves. Freely."

When Ryoval's image faded, Miles found himself pinned between the speculative glowers of both the security chief and the guard sergeant.

Just to relieve feelings, a burly guard held Miles while the security chief delivered a blow to his belly. But the chief was still too ill to really enjoy this as he should. "Came to see Bharaputra's toy soldier, did you?" he gasped, rubbing his own stomach.

The guard sergeant caught his chief's eye. "You know, I think we should give him his wish."

The security chief smothered a belch, and smiled as at a beatific vision. "Yes . . ."

Miles, praying they wouldn't break his arms, found himself being frog-marched down a complex of corridors and lift tubes by the burly guard, followed by the sergeant and the chief. They took a last lift-tube to the very bottom, a dusty basement crowded with stored and discarded equipment and supplies. They made their way to a locked hatch set in the floor. It swung open on a metal ladder descending into obscurity.

"The last thing we threw down there was a rat," the guard sergeant informed Miles cordially. "Nine bit its head right off. Nine gets very hungry. Got a metabolism like an ore furnace."

The guard forced Miles onto the ladder and down it a meter or so by the simple expedient of striking at his clinging hands with a truncheon. Miles hung just out of range of the stick, eyeing the dimly-lit stone below. The rest was pillars and shadows and a cold dankness.

"Nine!" called the guard sergeant into the echoing darkness. "Nine! Dinner! Come and catch it!"

The security chief laughed mockingly, then clutched his head and groaned under his breath.

Ryoval had said he'd deal with Miles personally in the morning; surely the guards understood their boss wanted a live prisoner. Didn't they? Didn't he? "Is this the dungeon?" Miles spat blood and peered around.

"No, no, just a basement," the guard sergeant assured him cheerily. "The dungeon is for the *paying* customers. Heh, heh, heh." Still chortling at his own humor, he kicked the hatch closed. The chink of the locking mechanism rained down; then silence.

The bars of the ladder bit chill through Miles's socks. He hooked an arm around an upright and tucked one hand into the armpit of his black T-shirt to warm it briefly. His gray trousers had been emptied of everything but a ration bar, his handkerchief, and his legs.

He clung there for a long time. Going up was futile; going down, singularly uninviting. Eventually the startling ganglial pain began to dull, and the shaking physical shock to wear off. Still he clung. Cold.

It could have been worse, Miles reflected. The sergeant and his squad could have decided they wanted to play Lawrence of Arabia and the Six Turks. Commodore Tung, Miles's Dendarii chief of staff and a certified military history nut, had been plying Miles with a series of classic military memoirs lately. How had Colonel Lawrence escaped an analogous tight spot? Ah, yes, played dumb and persuaded his captors to throw him out in the mud. Tung must have pressed that book-fax on Murka, too.

The darkness, Miles discovered as his eyes adjusted, was only relative. Faint luminescent panels in the ceiling here and there shed a sickly yellow glow. He descended the last two meters to stand on solid rock.

He pictured the newsfax, back home on Barrayar—*Body of Imperial Officer Found in Flesh-Czar's Dream Palace. Death From Exhaustion?* Dammit, this wasn't the glorious sacrifice in the Emperor's service he'd once vowed to risk, this was just embarrassing. Maybe Bharaputra's creature would eat the evidence.

With this morose comfort in mind, he began to limp from pillar to pillar, pausing, listening, looking around. Maybe there was another ladder somewhere. Maybe there was a hatch someone had forgotten to lock. Maybe there was still hope.

Maybe there was something moving in the shadows just beyond that pillar. . . .

Miles's breath froze, then eased again, as the movement materialized into a fat albino rat the size of an armadillo. It shied as it saw him and waddled rapidly away, its claws clicking on the rock. Only an escaped lab rat. A bloody big rat, but still, only a rat.

The huge rippling shadow struck out of nowhere, at incredible speed. It grabbed the rat by its tail and swung it squealing against a pillar, dashing out its brains with a crunch. A flash of a thick claw-like fingernail, and the white furry body was ripped open from sternum to tail. Frantic fingers peeled the skin away from the rat's body as blood splattered. Miles first saw the fangs as they bit and tore and buried themselves in the rat's tissues.

They were functional fangs, not just decorative, set in a protruding jaw, with long lips and a wide mouth; yet the total effect was lupine rather than simian. A flat nose, ridged, powerful brows, high cheekbones. Hair a dark matted mess. And yes, fully eight feet tall, a rangy, tense-muscled body.

Climbing back up the ladder would do no good; the creature could pluck him right off and swing him just like the rat. Levitate up the side of a pillar? Oh, for suction-cup fingers and toes, something the bioengineering committee had missed somehow. Freeze and play invisible? Miles settled on this last defense by default—he was paralyzed with terror.

The big feet, bare on the cold rock, also had claw-like toenails. But the creature was dressed, in clothes made of green lab-cloth, a belted kimono-style coat and loose trousers. And one other thing.

They didn't tell me it was female.

She was almost finished with the rat when she looked up and saw Miles. Bloody-faced, bloody-handed, she froze as still as he.

In a spastic motion, Miles whipped the squashed ration bar from his trouser thigh-pocket and extended it toward her in his outstretched hand. "Dessert?" He smiled hysterically.

Dropping the rat's stripped carcass, she snatched the bar out of his hand, ripped off the cover, and devoured it in four bites. Then she stepped forward, grabbed him by an arm and his black T-shirt, and lifted him up to her face. The clawed fingers bit into his skin, and his feet dangled in the air. Her breath was about what he would have guessed. Her eyes were raw and burning. "Water!" she croaked.

They didn't tell me she talked.

"Um, um—water," squeaked Miles. "Quite. There ought to be water around here—look, up at the ceiling, all those pipes. If you'll, um, put me down, good girl, I'll try and spot a water pipe or something. . . ."

Slowly, she lowered him back to his feet and released him. He backed carefully away, his hands held out open at his sides. He cleared his throat, and tried to bring his voice back down to a low, soothing tone. "Let's try over here. The ceiling gets lower, or rather, the bedrock rises . . . over near that light panel, there, that thin composite plastic tube—white's the usual color for water. We don't want gray, that's sewage, or red, that's the power-optics . . ." No telling what she understood; tone was everything with creatures. "If you, uh, could hold me up on your shoulders like Ensign Murka, I could have a go at loosening that joint there . . ." He made pantomime gestures, uncertain if anything was getting through to whatever intelligence lay behind those terrible eyes.

The bloody hands, easily twice the size of his own, grabbed him abruptly by the hips and boosted him upward. He clutched the white pipe, inched along it to a screw-joint. Her thick shoulders beneath his feet moved along under him. Her muscles trembled; it wasn't all his own shaking. The joint was tight—he needed tools—he turned with all his strength, in danger of snapping his fragile finger bones. Suddenly the joint squeaked and slid. It gave, the plastic collar was moving, water began to spray between his fingers. One more turn and it sheared apart, and water arched in a bright stream down onto the rock beneath.

She almost dropped him in her haste. She put her mouth under the stream, wide open, let the water splash straight in and all over her face, coughing and guzzling even more frantically than she'd gone at the rat. She drank, and drank, and drank. She let it run over her hands, her face and head, washing away the blood, and then drank some more. Miles began to think she'd never quit, but at last she backed away and pushed her wet hair out of her eyes, staring down at him. She stared at him for what seemed like a full minute, then suddenly roared, "Cold!"

Miles jumped. "Ah . . . cold . . . right. Me too, my socks are wet. Heat, you want heat. Lessee. Uh, let's try back this way, where the ceiling's lower. No point here, the heat would all collect up there out of reach, no good . . ." She followed him with all the intensity of a cat tracking a . . . well . . . rat, as he skittered around pillars to where the crawl space's floor rose to genuine crawl-height, about four feet. There, that one, that was the lowest pipe he could find. "If we could get this open," he pointed to a plastic pipe about as big around as his waist, "it's full of hot air being pumped along under pressure. No handy joints though, this time." He stared at his puzzle, trying to think. This composite plastic was extremely strong.

She crouched and pulled, then lay on her back and kicked up at it, then looked at him quite woefully.

"Try this." Nervously, he took her hand and guided it to the pipe, and traced long scratches around the circumference with her hard nails. She scratched and scratched, then looked at him again as if to say, *This isn't working!*

"Try kicking and pulling again now," he suggested.

She must have weighed three hundred pounds, and she put it all behind the next effort, kicking then grabbing the pipe, planting her feet on the ceiling and arching with all her strength. The pipe split along the scratches. She fell with it to the floor, and hot air began to hiss out. She held her hands, her face to it, nearly wrapped herself around it, sat on her knees and let it blow across her. Miles crouched down and stripped off his socks and flopped them over the warm pipe to dry. Now would be a good opportunity to run, if only there was anywhere to run to. But he was reluctant to let his prey out of his sight. His prey? He considered the incalculable value of her left calf muscle, as she sat on the rock and buried her face in her knees.

They didn't tell me she wept.

He pulled out his regulation handkerchief, an archaic square of cloth. He'd never understood the rationale for the idiotic handkerchief, except, perhaps, that where soldiers went there would be weeping. He handed it to her. "Here. Mop your eyes with this."

She took it, and blew her big flat nose in it, and made to hand it back.

"Keep it," Miles said. "Uh . . . what do they call you, I wonder."

"Nine," she growled. Not hostile; it was just the way her strained voice came out of that big throat. ". . . What do they call you?"

Good God, a complete sentence. Miles blinked. "Admiral Miles Naismith." He arranged himself cross-legged.

She looked up, transfixed. "A soldier? A *real officer?*" And then more doubtfully, as if seeing him in detail for the first time, "You?"

Miles cleared his throat firmly. "Quite real. A bit down on my luck just at the moment," he admitted.

"Me, too," she said glumly, and sniffed. "I don't know how long I've been here in this basement, but that was my first drink."

"Three days, I think," said Miles. "Have they not, ah, given you any food, either?"

"No." She frowned; the effect, with the fangs, was quite overpowering. "This is worse than anything they did to me in the lab, and I thought that was bad."

It's not what you don't know that'll hurt you, the old saying went. *It's what you do know that isn't so.* Miles thought of his map cube; Miles looked at Nine. Miles pictured himself taking this entire mission's carefully-worked-out strategy plan delicately between thumb and forefinger and flushing it down a waste-disposal unit. The ductwork in the ceiling niggled at his imagination. Nine would never fit through it. . . .

She clawed her wild hair away from her face and stared at him with renewed fierceness. Her eyes were a strange light hazel, adding to the wolfish effect. "What are you *really* doing here? Is this another test?"

"No, this is real life." Miles's lips twitched. "I, ah, made a mistake."

"Guess I did too," she said, lowering her head.

Miles pulled at his lip and studied her through narrowed eyes. "What sort of life have you had, I wonder?" he mused, half to himself.

She answered literally. "I lived with hired fosterers till I was eight. Like the clones do. Then I started to get big and clumsy and break things—they brought me to live at the lab after that. It was all right, I was warm and had plenty to eat."

"They can't have simplified you too much if they seriously intended you to be a soldier. I wonder what your IQ is?"

"A hundred and thirty-five."

Miles fought off stunned paralysis. "I . . . see. Did you ever get . . . any training?"

She shrugged. "I took a lot of tests. They were . . . OK. Except for the aggression experiments. I don't like electric shocks." She brooded a moment. "I don't like experimental psychologists, either. They lie a lot." Her shoulders slumped. "Anyway, I failed. We all failed."

"How can they know if you failed if you never had any proper training?" Miles said scornfully. "Soldiering entails some of the most complex, cooperative learned behavior ever invented—I've been studying strategy and tactics for years, and I don't know half yet. It's all up *here*." He pressed his hands urgently to his head.

She looked across at him sharply. "If that's so," she turned her huge hands over, staring at them, "then why did they do *this* to me?"

Miles stopped short. His throat was strangely dry. *So, admirals lie too. Sometimes, even to themselves.* After an unsettled pause he asked, "Did you never think of breaking open a water pipe?"

"You're punished, for breaking things. Or I was. Maybe not you, you're human."

"Did you ever think of escaping, breaking out? It's a soldier's duty, when captured by the enemy, to escape. Survive, escape, sabotage, in that order."

"Enemy?" She looked upward at the whole weight of House Ryoval pressing overhead. "Who are my friends?"

"Ah. Yes. There is that . . . point." And where would an eight-foot-tall genetic cocktail with fangs run to? He took a deep breath. No question what his next move must be. Duty, expediency, survival, all compelled it. "Your friends are closer than you think. Why do you think I came here?" *Why, indeed?*

She shot him a silent, puzzled frown.

"I came for you. I'd heard of you. I'm . . . recruiting. Or I was. Things went wrong, and now I'm escaping. But if you came with me, you could join the Dendarii Mercenaries. A top outfit—always looking for a few good men, or whatever. I have this master-sergeant who . . . who *needs* a recruit like you." Too true. Sergeant Dyeb was infamous for his sour attitude about women soldiers, insisting that they were too soft. Any female recruit who survived his course came out with her aggression highly developed. Miles pictured Dyeb being dangled by his toes from a height of about eight feet. . . . He controlled his runaway imagination in favor of concentration on the present crisis. Nine was looking . . . unimpressed.

"Very funny," she said coldly, making Miles wonder for a wild moment if she'd been equipped with the telepathy complex—no, she pre-dated that—"but I'm not even human. Or hadn't you heard?"

Miles shrugged carefully. "Human is as human does." He forced himself to reach out and touch her damp cheek. "Animals don't weep, Nine."

She jerked, as from an electric shock. "Animals don't lie. Humans do. All the time."

"Not *all* the time." He hoped the light was too dim for her to see the flush in his face. She was watching his face intently.

"Prove it." She tilted her head as she sat cross-legged. Her pale gold eyes were suddenly burning, speculative.

"Uh . . . sure. How?"

"Take off your clothes."

" . . . what?"

"Take off your clothes, and lie down with me as *humans* do. Men and women." Her hand reached out to touch his throat.

The pressing claws made little wells in his flesh. "Blrp?" choked Miles. His eyes felt wide as saucers. A little more pressure, and those wells would spring forth red fountains. *I am about to die. . . .*

She stared into his face with a strange, frightening, bottomless hunger. Then abruptly, she released him. He sprang up and cracked his head on the low ceiling, and dropped back down, the stars in his eyes unrelated to love at first sight.

Her lips wrinkled back on a fanged groan of despair. "Ugly," she wailed. Her clawed nails raked across her cheeks leaving red furrows. "Too *ugly* . . . animal . . . you *don't* think I'm human—" She seemed to swell with some destructive resolve.

"No, no, no!" gibbered Miles, lurching to his knees and grabbing her hands and pulling them down. "It's not that. It's just, uh—how old are you, anyway?"

"Sixteen."

Sixteen. God. He remembered sixteen. Sex-obsessed and dying inside every minute. A horrible age to be trapped in a twisted, fragile, abnormal body. God only knew how he had survived his own self-hatred then. No— he remembered how. *He'd* been saved by one who loved him. "Aren't you a little young for this?" he tried hopefully.

"How old were you?"

"Fifteen," he admitted, before thinking to lie. "But . . . it was traumatic. Didn't work out at all in the long run."

Her claws turned toward her face again.

"Don't *do* that!" he cried, hanging on. It reminded him entirely too much of the episode of Sergeant Bothari and the knife. The Sergeant had taken Miles's knife away from him by superior force. Not an option open to Miles here. "Will you *calm down?*" he yelled at her.

She hesitated.

"It's just that, uh, an officer and gentleman doesn't just fling himself onto his lady on the bare ground. One . . . one sits down. Gets comfortable. Has a little conversation, drinks a little wine, plays a little music . . . slows down. You're hardly warm yet. Here, sit over here where it's warmest." He positioned her nearer the broken duct, got up on his knees behind her, tried rubbing her neck and shoulders. Her muscles were tense—they felt like rocks under his thumbs. Any attempt on his part to strangle her would clearly be futile.

I can't believe this. Trapped in Ryoval's basement with a sex-starved teenage werewolf. There was nothing about this in any of my Imperial Academy training manuals. . . . He remembered his mission, which was to get her left calf muscle back to the *Ariel* alive. *Dr. Canaba, if I survive, you and I are going to have a little talk about this. . . .*

Her voice was muffled with grief and the odd shape of her mouth. "You think I'm too tall."

"Not at all." He was getting hold of himself a bit; he could lie faster. "I adore tall women, ask anyone who knows me. Beside, I made the happy discovery some time back that height difference only matters when we're standing up. When we're lying down it's, ah, less of a problem. . . ." A rapid mental review of everything he'd ever learned by trial and error, mostly error, about women was streaming uninvited through his mind. It was harrowing. What did women *want*?

He shifted around and took her hand, earnestly. She stared back equally earnestly, waiting for . . . *instruction.* At this point the realization came over Miles that he was facing his first virgin. He smiled at her in total paralysis for several seconds. "Nine . . . you've never done this before, have you?"

"I've seen vids." She frowned introspectively. "They usually start with kisses, but . . ." a vague gesture toward her misshapen mouth, "maybe you don't want to."

Miles tried not to think about the late rat. She'd been systematically starved, after all. "Vids can be very misleading. For women—especially the first time—it takes practice to learn your own body responses, woman friends have told me. I'm afraid I might hurt you." *And then you'll disembowel me.*

She gazed into his eyes. "That's all right. I have a very high pain threshold."

But I don't.

This was mad. She was mad. *He* was mad. Yet he could feel a creeping fascination for the—proposition—rising from his belly to his brain like a fey fog. No doubt about it, she was the tallest female thing he was ever likely to meet.

More than one woman of his acquaintance had accused him of wanting to go mountain-climbing. He could get that out of his system once for all. . . .

Damn, I do believe she'd clean up good. She was not without a certain . . . charm was *not* the word—whatever beauty there was to be found in the strong, the swift, the leanly athletic, the functioning form. Once you got used to the *scale* of it. She radiated a smooth heat he could feel from here—*animal magnetism?* the suppressed observer in the back of his brain supplied. Power? Whatever else it was, it would certainly be *astonishing.*

One of his mother's favorite aphorisms drifted through his head. *Anything worth doing,* she always said, *is worth doing well.*

Dizzy as a drunkard, he abandoned the crutch of logic for the wings of inspiration. "Well then, doctor," he heard himself muttering insanely, "let us experiment."

Kissing a woman with fangs was indeed a novel sensation. Being kissed back—she was clearly a fast learner—was even more novel. Her arms circled him ecstatically, and from that point on he lost control of the situation, somehow. Though some time later, coming up for air, he did look up to ask, "Nine, have you ever heard of the black widow spider?"

"No . . . what is it?"

"Never mind," he said airily.

It was all very awkward and clumsy, but sincere, and when he was done the water in her eyes was from joy, not pain. She seemed enormously (how else?) pleased with him. He was so unstrung he actually fell asleep for a few minutes, pillowed on her body.

He woke up laughing.

"You really do have the most elegant cheekbones," he told her, tracing their line with one finger. She leaned into his touch, cuddled up equally to him and the water pipe. "There's a woman on my ship who wears her hair in a sort of woven braid in the back—it would look just great on you. Maybe she could teach you how."

She pulled a wad of her hair forward and looked cross-eyed at it, as if trying to see past the coarse tangles and filth. She touched his face in turn. "You are very handsome, Admiral."

"Huh? Me?" He ran a hand over the night's beard stubble, sharp features, the old pain lines . . . *she must be blinded by my putative rank, eh?*

"Your face is very . . . alive. And your eyes see what they're looking at."

"Nine . . ." He cleared his throat, paused. "Dammit, that's not a name, that's a number. What happened to Ten?"

"He died." *Maybe I will too,* her strange-colored eyes added silently, before her lids shuttered them.

"Is Nine all they ever called you?"

"There's a long biocomputer code-string that's my actual designation."

"Well, we all have serial numbers," Miles had two, now that he thought about it, "but this is absurd. I can't call you Nine, like some robot. You need a proper name, a name that fits you." He leaned back onto her warm bare shoulder—she was like a furnace; they had spoken truly about her metabolism—and his lips drew back on a slow grin. "Taura."

"Taura?" Her long mouth gave it a skewed and lilting accent. ". . . it's too beautiful for me!"

"Taura," he repeated firmly. "Beautiful but strong. Full of secret meaning. Perfect. Ah, speaking of secrets . . ." Was now the time to tell her about what Dr. Canaba had planted in her left calf? Or would she be hurt, as someone falsely courted for her money—or his title—Miles faltered. "I think, now that we know each other better, that it's time for us to blow out of this place."

She stared around, into the grim dimness. "How?"

"Well, that's what we have to figure out, eh? I confess, ducts rather spring to my mind." Not the heat pipe, obviously. He'd have to go anorexic for months to fit in, besides, he'd cook. He shook out and pulled on his black T-shirt— he'd put on his trousers immediately after he'd woken; that stone floor sucked heat remorselessly from any flesh that touched it—and creaked to his feet. God. He was getting too old for this sort of thing already. The sixteen-year-old, clearly, possessed the physical resilience of a minor goddess. What was it he'd gotten into at sixteen? Sand, that was it. He winced in memory of what it had done to certain sensitive body folds and crevices. Maybe cold stone wasn't so bad after all.

She pulled her pale green coat and trousers out from under herself, dressed, and followed him in a crouch until the space was sufficient for her to stand upright.

They quartered and re-quartered the underground chamber. There were four ladders with hatches, all locked. There was a locked vehicle exit to the outside on the downslope side. A direct breakout might be simplest, but if he couldn't make immediate contact with Thorne it was a twenty-seven-kilometer hike to the nearest town. In the snow, in his sock feet—her bare feet. And if they got there, he wouldn't be able to use the vidnet anyway because his credit card was still locked in the Security Ops office upstairs. Asking for charity in Ryoval's town was a dubious proposition. So, break straight out and be sorry later, or linger and try to equip themselves, risking recapture, and be sorry sooner? Tactical decisions were such fun.

Ducts won. Miles pointed upward to the most likely one. "Think you can break that open and boost me in?" he asked Taura.

She studied it, nodded slowly, the expression closing on her face. She stretched up and moved along to a soft metal clad joint, slipped her claw-hard fingernails under the strip, and yanked it off. She worked her fingers into the exposed slot and hung on it as if chinning herself. The duct bent open under her weight. "There you go," she said.

She lifted him up as easily as a child, and he squirmed into the duct. This one was a particularly close fit, though it was the largest he had spotted as accessible in this ceiling. He inched along it on his back. He had to stop twice to suppress a residual, hysteria-tinged laughing fit. The duct curved upward, and he slithered around the curve in the darkness only to find that it split here into a Y, each branch half-sized. He cursed and backed out.

Taura had her face turned up to him, an unusual angle of view.

"No good that way," he gasped, reversing direction gymnastically at the gap. He headed the other way. This too curved up, but within moments he found a grille. A tightly-fitted, unbudgable, unbreakable, and with his bare hands uncuttable grille. Taura might have the strength to rip it out of the wall, but Taura couldn't fit through the duct to reach it. He contemplated it for a few moments. "Right," he muttered, and backed out again.

"So much for ducts," he reported to Taura. "Uh . . . could you help me down?" She lowered him to the floor, and he dusted himself futilely. "Let's look around some more."

She followed him docilely enough, though something in her expression hinted she might be losing faith in his admiralness. A bit of detailing on a column caught his eye, and he went to take a closer look in the dim light.

It was one of the low-vibration support columns. Two meters in diameter, set deep in the bedrock in a well of fluid, it ran straight up to one of the labs, no doubt, to provide an ultra-stable base for certain kinds of crystal generation projects and the like. Miles rapped on the side of the column. It rang hollow. *Ah yes, makes sense, concrete doesn't float too well, eh?* A groove in the side outlined . . . an access port? He ran his fingers around it, probing. There was a concealed . . . something. He stretched his arms and found a twin spot on the opposite side. The spots yielded slowly to the hard pressure of his thumbs. There was a sudden pop and hiss, and the whole panel came away. He staggered, and barely kept from dropping it down the hole. He turned it sideways and drew it out.

"Well, well," Miles grinned. He stuck his head through the port, looked down and up. Black as pitch. Rather gingerly, he reached his arm in and felt around. There was a ladder running up the damp inside, for access for cleaning and repairs; the whole column could apparently be filled with fluid of whatever density at need. Filled, it would have been self-pressure-sealed and unopenable. Carefully, he examined the inner edge of the hatch. Openable from either side, by God. "Let's go see if there's any more of these, further up."

It was slow going, feeling for more grooves as they ascended in the blackness. Miles tried not to think about the fall, should he slip from the slimy ladder. Taura's deep breathing, below him, was actually rather comforting. They had gone up perhaps three stories when Miles's chilled and numbing fingers found another groove. He'd almost missed it; it was on the opposite side of the ladder from the first. He then discovered, the hard way, that he didn't have nearly the reach to keep one arm hooked around the ladder and press both release catches at the same time. After a terrifying slip, trying, he clung spasmodically to the ladder till his heart stopped pounding. "Taura?" he croaked. "I'll move up, and you try it." Not much up was left. The column ended a meter or so above his head.

Her extra arm length was all that was needed—the catches surrendered to her big hands with a squeak of protest.

"What do you see?" Miles whispered.

"Big dark room. Maybe a lab."

"Makes sense. Climb back down and put that lower panel back on. No sense advertising where we went."

Miles slipped through the hatch into the darkened laboratory while Taura accomplished her chore. He dared not switch on a light in the windowless room, but a few instrument readouts on the benches and walls gave enough ghostly glow for his dark-adapted eyes that at least he didn't trip over anything. One glass door led to a hallway. A heavily electronically-monitored hallway. With his nose pressed to the glass Miles saw a red shape flit past a cross-corridor; guards here. What did they guard?

Taura oozed out of the access hatch to the column—with difficulty—and sat down heavily on the floor, her face in her hands. Concerned, Miles nipped back to her. "You all right?"

She shook her head. "No. Hungry."

"What, already? That was supposed to be a twenty-four-hour rat—er, ration bar." Not to mention the two or three kilos of meat she'd had for an appetizer.

"For you, maybe," she wheezed. She was shaking.

Miles began to see why Canaba dubbed his project a failure. Imagine trying to feed a whole army of such appetites. Napoleon would quail. Maybe the raw-boned kid was still growing. Daunting thought.

There was a refrigerator at the back of the lab. If he knew lab techs . . . ah, ha. Indeed, in among the test tubes was a package with half a sandwich and a large, if bruised, pear. He handed them to Taura. She looked vastly impressed, as if he'd conjured them from his sleeve by magic, and devoured them at once, and grew less pale.

Miles foraged further for his troop. Alas, the only other organics in the fridge were little covered dishes of gelatinous stuff with unpleasant multi-colored fuzz growing in them. But there were three big shiny walk-in wall freezers lined up in a row. Miles peered through a glass square in one thick door, and risked pressing the wall pad that turned on the light inside. Within were row on row on row of labelled drawers, full of clear plastic trays. Frozen samples of some kind. Thousands—Miles looked again, and calculated more carefully—hundreds of thousands. He glanced at the lighted control panel by the freezer door. The temperature inside was that of liquid nitrogen. Three freezers . . . *Millions* of . . . Miles sat down abruptly on the floor himself. "Taura, do you know where we *are*?" he whispered intensely.

"Sorry, no," she whispered back, creeping over.

"That was a rhetorical question. *I* know where we are."

"Where?"

"Ryoval's treasure chamber."

"What?"

"That," Miles jerked his thumb at the freezer, "is the baron's hundred-year-old tissue collection. My God. Its value is almost incalculable. Every unique, irreplaceable, mutant bizarre bit he's begged, bought, borrowed or stolen for the last three-fourths of a century, all lined up in neat little rows, waiting to be thawed and cultured and cooked up into some poor new slave. This is the living heart of his whole human biologicals operation." Miles sprang to his feet and pored over the control panels. His heart raced, and he breathed open-mouthed, laughing silently, feeling almost as if he was about to pass out. "Oh, shit. Oh, God." He stopped, swallowed. Could it be done?

These freezers had to have an alarm system, monitors surely, piped up to Security Ops at the very least. Yes, there was a complex device for opening the door—that was fine, he didn't want to open the door. He left it untouched. It was systems readout he was after. If he could bugger up just one sensor . . . Was the thing broadcast-output to several outside monitor locations, or did they run an optic thread to just one? The lab benches supplied him with a small hand light, and drawers and drawers of assorted tools and supplies. Taura watched him in puzzlement as he darted here, there, taking inventory.

The freezer monitor *was* broadcast output, inaccessible; could he hit it on the input side? He levered off a smoke-dark plastic cover as silently as he could. There, *there,* the optic thread came out of the wall, pumping continuous information about the freezer's interior environment. It fit into a simple standard receiver plug on the more daunting black box that controlled the door alarm. There'd been a whole drawer full of assorted optic threads with various ends and Y-adaptors. . . . Out of the spaghetti-tangle he drew what he needed, discarding several with broken ends or other damage. There were three optical data recorders in the drawer. Two didn't work. The third did.

A quick festoon of optic thread, a swift unplugging and plugging, and he had one freezer talking to two control boxes. He set the freed thread to talking to the datacorder. He simply had to chance the blip during transfer. If anyone checked they'd find all seemed well again. He gave the datacorder several minutes to develop a nice continuous replay loop, crouching very still with even the tiny hand light extinguished. Taura waited with the patience of a predator, making no noise.

One, two, three, and he set the datacorder to talking to all three control boxes. The real thread plugs hung forlornly loose. Would it work? There were no alarms going off, no thundering herd of irate security troops. . . .

"Taura, come here."

She loomed beside him, baffled.

"Have you ever met Baron Ryoval?" asked Miles.

"Yes, once . . . when he came to buy me."

"Did you like him?"

She gave him an are-you-out-of-your-mind? look.

"Yeah, I didn't much care for him either." Restrained murder, in point of fact. He was now meltingly grateful for that restraint. "Would you like to rip his lungs out, if you could?"

Her clawed hands clenched. "Try me!"

"Good!" He smiled cheerily. "I want to give you your first lesson in tactics." He pointed. "See that control? The temperature in these freezers can be raised to almost 200 degrees centigrade, for heat sterilization during cleaning. Give me your finger. One finger. Gently. More gently than that." He guided her hand. "The least possible pressure you can apply to the dial, and still move . . . Now the next," he pulled her to the next panel, "and the last." He exhaled, still not quite able to believe it.

"And the lesson is," he breathed, "it's not how much force you use. It's where you apply it."

He resisted the urge to scrawl something like *The Dwarf Strikes Back* across the front of the freezer with a flow pen. The longer the baron in his mortal rage took to figure out who to pursue, the better. It would take several hours to bring all that mass in there from liquid nitrogen temperature up to *well-done,* but if no one came in till morning shift, the destruction would be absolute.

Miles glanced at the time on the wall digital. Dear God, he'd spent a lot of time in that basement. Well-spent, but still . . . "Now," he said to Taura, who was still meditating on the dial, and her hand, with her gold eyes glowing, "we have to get out of here. Now we *really* have to get out of here." Lest her next tactics lesson turn out to be, Don't blow up the bridge you're standing on, Miles allowed nervously.

Contemplating the door-locking mechanism more closely, plus what lay beyond—among other things, the sound-activated wall-mounted monitors in the halls featured automatic laser fire—Miles almost went to turn the freezer temperatures back down. His chip-driven Dendarii tools, now locked in the Security Ops office, might barely have handled the complex circuitry in the pried-open control box. But of course, he couldn't get at his tools without his tools . . . a nice paradox. It shouldn't surprise Miles, that Ryoval saved his most sophisticated alarm system for this lab's one and only door. But it made the room a much worse trap than even the sub-basement.

He made another tour of the lab with the filched hand light, checking drawers again. No computer-keys came to hand, but he did find a big, crude pair of cutters in a drawer full of rings and clamps, and bethought him of the duct grille that had lately defeated him in the basement. So. The passage up to this lab had merely been the illusion of progress toward escape.

"There's no shame in a strategic retreat to a better position," he whispered to Taura when she balked at re-entering the support column's dark tube. "This is a dead-end, here. Maybe literally." The doubt in her tawny eyes was strangely unsettling, a weight in his heart. *Still don't trust me, eh? Well, maybe those who have been greatly betrayed need great proof.* "Stick with me, kid," he muttered under his breath, swinging into the tube. "We're going places." Her doubt was merely masked under lowered eyelids, but she followed him, sealing the hatch behind them.

With the hand light, the descent was slightly less nasty than the ascent into the unknown had been. There were no other exits to be found, and shortly they stood on the stone they had started from. Miles checked the progress of their ceiling waterspout, while Taura drank again. The splattering water ran off in a flat greasy trickle downslope; given the vast size of the chamber, it would be some days before the pool collecting slowly against the lower wall offered any useful strategic possibilities, though there was always the hope it might do a bit to undermine the foundations.

Taura boosted him back into the duct. "Wish me luck," he murmured over his shoulder, muffled by the close confines.

"Goodbye," she said. He could not see the expression on her face; there was none in her voice.

"See you later," he corrected firmly.

A few minutes of vigorous wriggling brought him back to his grille. It opened onto a dark room stacked with stuff, part of the basement proper, quiet and unoccupied. The snip of his cutters, biting through the grille, seemed loud enough to bring down Ryoval's entire security force, but none appeared. Maybe the security chief was sleeping off his drug hangover. A scrabbling noise, not of Miles's own making, echoed thinly through the duct and Miles froze. He flashed his light down a side-branching tube. Twin red jewels flashed back, the eyes of a huge rat. He briefly considered trying to clout it and haul it back to Taura. No. When they got back to the *Ariel*, he'd give her a steak dinner. Two steak dinners. The rat saved itself by turning and scampering away.

The grille parted at last, and he squeezed into the storage room. What time was it, anyway? Late, very late. The room gave onto a corridor, and on the floor at the end, one of the access hatches gleamed dully. Miles's heart rose in serious hope. Once he'd got Taura, they must next try to reach a vehicle. . . .

This hatch, like the first, was manual, no sophisticated electronics to disarm. It re-locked automatically upon closing, however. Miles jammed it with his clippers before descending the ladder. He aimed his light around— "Taura!" he whispered. "Where are you?"

No immediate answer; no glowing gold eyes flashing in the forest of pillars. He was reluctant to shout. He slapped down the rungs and began a silent fast trot through the chamber, the cold stone draining the heat through his socks and making him long for his lost boots.

He came upon her sitting silently at the base of a pillar, her head turned sideways resting on her knees. Her face was pensive, sad. Really, it didn't take long at all to begin reading the subtleties of feeling in her wolfish features.

"Time to march, soldier girl," Miles said.

Her head lifted. "You came back!"

"What did you think I was going to do? Of course I came back. You're my recruit, aren't you?"

She scrubbed her face with the back of a big paw—hand, Miles corrected himself severely—and stood up, and up. "Guess I must be." Her outslung mouth smiled slightly. If you didn't have a clue what the expression was, it could look quite alarming.

"I've got a hatch open. We've got to try to get out of this main building, back to the utility bay. I saw several vehicles parked there earlier. What's a little theft, after—"

With a sudden whine, the outside vehicle entrance, downslope to their right, began to slide upward. A rush of cold dry air swept through the dankness, and a thin shaft of yellow dawn light made the shadows blue. They shielded their eyes in the unexpected glare. Out of the bright squinting haze coalesced half-a-dozen red-clad forms, double-timing it, weapons at the ready.

Taura's hand was tight on Miles's. *Run,* he started to cry, and bit back the shout; no way could they outrun a nerve disruptor beam, a weapon which at least two of the guards now carried. Miles's breath hissed out through his teeth. He was too infuriated even to swear. They'd been so *close.* . . .

Security Chief Moglia sauntered up. "What, still in one piece, Naismith?" He smirked unpleasantly. "Nine must have finally realized it's time to start cooperating, eh, Nine?"

Miles squeezed her hand hard, hoping the message would be properly understood as, *Wait.*

She lifted her chin. "Guess so," she said coldly.

"It's about time," said Moglia. "Be a good girl, and we'll take you upstairs and feed you breakfast after this."

Good, Miles's hand signalled. She was watching him closely for cues, now.

Moglia prodded Miles with his truncheon. "Time to go, dwarf. Your friends have actually made ransom. Surprised me."

Miles was surprised himself. He moved toward the exit, still towing Taura. He didn't look at her, did as little as possible to draw unwanted attention to their, er, togetherness, while still maintaining it. He let go of her hand as soon as their momentum was established.

What the hell . . . ? Miles thought as they emerged into the blinking dawn, up the ramp and onto a circle of tarmac slick with glittering rime. A most peculiar tableau was arranged there.

Bel Thorne and one Dendarii trooper, armed with stunners, shifted uneasily—not prisoners? Half a dozen armed men in the green uniform of House Fell stood at the ready. A float truck emblazoned with Fell's logo was parked at the tarmac's edge. And Nicol the quaddie, wrapped in white fur against the frost, hovered in her float chair at the stunner-point of a big green-clad guard. The light was gray and gold and chilly as the sun, lifting over the dark mountains in the distance, broke through the clouds.

"Is that the man you want?" the green-uniformed guard captain asked Bel Thorne.

"That's him." Thorne's face was white with an odd mixture of relief and distress. "Admiral, are you all right?" Thorne called urgently. Its eyes widened, taking in Miles's tall companion. "What the hell's *that?*"

"*She* is Recruit-trainee Taura," Miles said firmly, hoping 1) Bel would unravel the several meanings packed in that sentence and 2) Ryoval's guards wouldn't. Bel looked stunned, so evidently Miles had got at least partly through; Security Chief Moglia looked suspicious, but baffled. Miles was clearly a problem Moglia thought he was about to get rid of, however, and he thrust his bafflement aside to deal with the more important person of Fell's guard captain.

"What *is* this?" Miles hissed at Bel, sidling closer until a red-clad guard lifted his nerve disruptor and shook his head. Moglia and Fell's captain were exchanging electronic data on a report panel, heads bent together, evidently the official documentation.

"When we lost you last night, I was in a panic," Bel pitched its voice low toward Miles. "A frontal assault was out of the question. So I ran to Baron Fell to ask for help. But the help I got wasn't quite what I expected. Fell and Ryoval cooked up a deal between them to exchange Nicol for you. I swear, I only found out the details an hour ago!" Bel protested at Nicol's thin-lipped glower in its direction.

"I . . . see." Miles paused. "Are we planning to refund her dollar?"

"*Sir,*" Bel's voice was anguished, "we had *no idea* what was happening to you in there. We were expecting Ryoval to start beaming up a holocast of obscene and ingenious tortures, starring you, at any minute. Like Commodore Tung says, on hemmed-in ground, use subterfuge."

Miles recognized one of Tung's favorite Sun Tzu aphorisms. On bad days Tung had a habit of quoting the 4000-year-dead general in the original Chinese; when Tung was feeling benign they got a translation. Miles glanced around, adding up weapons, men, equipment. Most of the green guards carried stunners. Thirteen to . . . three? Four? He glanced at Nicol. Maybe five? *On desperate ground,* Sun Tzu advised, *fight.* Could it get much more desperate than this?

"Ah . . ." said Miles. "Just what the devil did we offer Baron Fell in exchange for this extraordinary charity? Or is he doing it out of the goodness of his heart?"

Bel shot him an exasperated look, then cleared its throat. "I promised you'd tell him the real truth about the Betan rejuvenation treatment."

"Bel . . ."

Thorne shrugged unhappily. "I thought, once we'd got you back, we'd figure something out. But I never thought he'd offer Nicol to Ryoval, I swear!"

Down in the long valley, Miles could see a bead moving on the thin gleam of monorail. The morning shift of bioengineers and technicians, janitors and office clerks and cafeteria cooks, was due to arrive soon. Miles glanced at the white building looming above, pictured the scene to come in that third floor lab as the guards deactivated the alarms and let them in to work, as the first one through the door sniffed and wrinkled his nose and said plaintively, "What's that awful *smell?*"

"Has 'Medtech Vaughn' signed aboard the *Ariel* yet?" Miles asked.

"Within the hour."

"Yeah, well . . . it turns out we didn't need to kill his fatted calf after all. It comes with the package." Miles nodded toward Taura.

Bel lowered its voice still further. "*That's* coming with us?"

"You'd better believe it. Vaughn didn't tell us everything. To put it mildly. I'll explain later," Miles added as the two guard captains broke up their tete-a-tete. Moglia swung his truncheon jauntily, heading toward Miles. "Meantime, you made a slight miscalculation. This isn't hemmed-in ground. This is *desperate* ground. Nicol, I want you to know, the Dendarii don't give refunds."

Nicol frowned in bewilderment. Bel's eyes widened, as it checked out the odds—calculating them thirteen to three, Miles could tell.

"Truly?" Bel choked. A subtle hand signal, down by its trouser seam, brought the trooper to full alert.

"Truly desperate," Miles reiterated. He inhaled deeply. "Now! Taura, attack!"

Miles launched himself toward Moglia, not so much actually expecting to wrestle his truncheon from him as hoping to maneuver Moglia's body between himself and the fellows with the nerve disruptors. The Dendarii trooper, who had been paying attention to details, dropped one of the nerve disruptor wielders with his first stunner shot, then rolled away from the second's return fire. Bel dropped the second nerve disruptor man and leapt aside. Two red guards, aiming their stunners at the running hermaphrodite, were lifted abruptly by their necks. Taura cracked their heads together, unscientifically but hard; they fell to hands and knees, groping blindly for their lost weapons.

Fell's green guards hesitated, not certain just whom to shoot, until Nicol, her angel's face alight, suddenly shot skyward in her float chair and dropped straight down again on the head of her guard, who was distracted by the fight. He fell like an ox. Nicol flipped her floater sideways as green-guard stunner fire found her, shielding herself from its flare, and shot upwards again. Taura picked up a red guard and threw him at a green one; they both went down in a tangle of arms and legs.

The Dendarii trooper closed on a green guard hand-to-hand, to shield himself from stunner blast. Fell's captain wouldn't buy the maneuver, and ruthlessly stunned them both, a sound tactic with the numbers on his side. Moglia got his truncheon up against Miles's windpipe and started to press, meanwhile yelling into his wrist com, calling for backup from Security Ops. A green guard screamed as Taura yanked his arm out of its shoulder socket and swung him into the air by the dislocated joint at another one aiming his stunner at her.

Colored lights danced before Miles's eyes. Fell's captain, focusing on Taura as the biggest threat, dropped to stunner fire from Bel Thorne as Nicol whammed her float chair into the back of the last green guard left standing.

"The float truck!" Miles croaked. "Go for the float truck!" Bel cast him a desperate look and sprinted toward it. Miles fought like an eel until Moglia got a hand down to his boot, drew a sharp, thin knife, and pressed it to Miles's neck.

"Hold still!" snarled Moglia. "That's better . . ." He straightened in the sudden silence, realizing he'd just pulled domination from disaster. "*Everybody* hold still." Bel froze with its hand on the float truck's door pad. A couple of the men splayed on the tarmac twitched and moaned.

"Now stand away from—glk," said Moglia.

Taura's voice whispered past Moglia's ear, a soft, soft growl. "Drop the knife. Or I'll rip your throat out with my bare hands."

Miles's eyes wrenched sideways, trying to see around his own clamped head, as the sharp edge sang against his skin.

"I can kill him, before you do," croaked Moglia.

"The little man is mine," Taura crooned. "You gave him to me yourself. He came *back* for me. Hurt him one little bit, and I'll tear your head off and then I'll drink your blood."

Miles felt Moglia being lifted off his feet. The knife clattered to the pavement. Miles sprang away, staggering. Taura held Moglia by his neck, her claws biting deep. "I still want to rip his head off," she growled petulantly, remembrance of abuse sparking in her eyes.

"Leave him," gasped Miles. "Believe me, in a few hours he's going to be suffering a more artistic vengeance than anything we can dream up."

Bel galloped back to stun the security chief at can't-miss range while Taura held him out like a wet cat. Miles had Taura throw the unconscious Dendarii over her shoulder while he ran around to the back of the float truck and released the doors for Nicol, who zipped her chair inside. They tumbled within, dropped the doors, and Bel at the controls shot them into the air. A siren was going off somewhere in Ryoval's.

"Wrist com, wrist com," Miles babbled, stripping his unconscious trooper of the device. "Bel, where is our drop shuttle parked?"

"We came in at a little commercial shuttleport just outside Ryoval's town, about forty kilometers from here."

"Anybody left manning it?"

"Anderson and Nout."

"What's their scrambled com channel?"

"Twenty-three."

Miles slid into the seat beside Bel and opened the channel. It took a small eternity for Sergeant Anderson to answer, fully thirty or forty seconds, while the float truck streaked above the treetops and over the nearest ridge.

"Laureen, I want you to get your shuttle into the air. We need an emergency pick-up, soonest. We're in a House Fell float truck, heading—" Miles thrust his wrist under Bel's nose.

"North from Ryoval Biologicals," Bel recited. "At about two hundred sixty kilometers per hour, which is all the faster this crate will go."

"Home in on our screamer," Miles set the wrist com emergency signal. "Don't wait for clearance from Ryoval's shuttleport traffic control, 'cause you won't get it. Have Nout patch my com through to the *Ariel*."

"You got it, sir," Anderson's thin voice came cheerily back over his com.

Static, and another few seconds excruciating delay. Then an excited voice, "Murka here. I thought you were coming out right behind us last night! You all right, sir?"

"Temporarily. Is 'Medtech Vaughn' aboard?"

"Yes, sir."

"All right. Don't let him off. Assure him I have his tissue sample with me."

"Really! How'd you—"

"Never mind how. Get all the troops back aboard and break from the station into free orbit. Plan to make a flying pick-up of the drop shuttle, and tell the pilot-officer to plot a course for the Escobar wormhole jump at max acceleration as soon as we're clamped on. Don't wait for clearance."

"We're still loading cargo. . . ."

"Abandon any that's still unloaded."

"Are we in serious shit, sir?"

"Mortal, Murka."

"Right, sir. Murka out."

"I thought we were all supposed to be as quiet as mice here on Jackson's Whole," Bel complained. "Isn't this all a bit splashy?"

"The situation's changed. There'd be no negotiating with Ryoval for Nicol, or for Taura either, after what we did last night. I struck a blow for truth and justice back there that I may live to regret, briefly. Tell you about it later. Anyway, do you really want to stick around while I explain to Baron Fell the real truth about the Betan rejuvenation treatment?"

"Oh," Thorne's eyes were alight, as it concentrated on its flying, "I'd pay money to watch that, sir."

"Ha. No. For one last moment back there, all the pieces were in our hands. Potentially, anyway." Miles began exploring the readouts on the float truck's simple control panel. "We'd never get everybody together again, never. One maneuvers to the limit, but the golden moment demands action. If you miss it, the gods damn you forever. And vice versa. . . . Speaking of action, did you see Taura take out *seven* of those guys?" Miles chortled in memory. "What's she going to be like after basic training?"

Bel glanced uneasily over its shoulder, to where Nicol had her float chair lodged and Taura hunkered in the back along with the body of the unconscious trooper. "I was too busy to keep count."

Miles swung out of his seat, and made his way into the back to check on their precious live cargo.

"Nicol, you were great," he told her. "You fought like a falcon. I may have to give you a discount on that dollar."

Nicol was still breathless, ivory cheeks flushed. An upper hand shoved a strand of black hair out of her sparkling eyes. "I was afraid they'd break my dulcimer." A lower hand stroked a big box-shaped case jammed into the float chair's cup beside her. "Then I was afraid they'd break Bel. . . ."

Taura sat leaning against the truck wall, a bit green.

Miles knelt beside her. "Taura dear, are you all right?" He gently lifted one clawed hand to check her pulse, which was bounding. Nicol gave him a rather strange look at his tender gesture. Her float chair was wedged as far from Taura as it could get.

"Hungry," Taura gasped.

"Again? But of course, all that energy expenditure. Anybody got a ration bar?" A quick check found an only-slightly-nibbled rat bar in the stunned trooper's thigh pocket, which Miles immediately liberated. Miles smiled benignly at Taura as she wolfed it down; she smiled back as best she could with her mouth full. *No more rats for you after this,* Miles promised silently. *Three steak dinners when we get back to the* Ariel, *and a couple of chocolate cakes for dessert. . . .*

The float truck jinked. Taura, reviving somewhat, extended her feet to hold Nicol's dented cup in place against the far wall and keep it from bouncing around. "Thank you," said Nicol warily. Taura nodded.

"Company," Bel Thorne called over its shoulder. Miles hastened forward.

Two aircars were coming up fast behind them. Ryoval's security. Doubtless beefed up tougher than the average civilian police car—yes. Bel jinked again as a plasma bolt boiled past, leaving bright green streaks across Miles's retinas. Quasi-military and seriously annoyed, their pursuers were.

"This is one of Fell's trucks, we ought to have *something* to fling back at them." There was nothing in front of Miles that looked like any kind of weapons-control.

A *whoomp,* a scream from Nicol, and the float truck staggered in air, righted itself under Bel's hands. A roar of air and vibration—Miles cranked his head around frantically—one top back corner of the truck's cargo area was blown away. The rear door was fused shut on one side, whanging loose along the opposite edge. Taura still braced the float chair;

Nicol now had her upper hands wrapped around Taura's ankles. "Ah," said Thorne. "No armor."

"What did they think this was going to be, a peaceful mission?" Miles checked his wrist com. "Laureen, are you in the air yet?"

"Coming, sir."

"Well, if you've ever itched to red-line it, now's your chance. Nobody's going to complain about your abusing the equipment this time."

"*Thank* you, sir," she responded happily.

They were losing speed and altitude. "Hang on!" Bel yelled over its shoulder, and suddenly reversed thrust. Their closing pursuers shot past them, but immediately began climbing turns. Bel accelerated again; another scream from the back as their live cargo was thus shifted toward the now-dubious rear doors.

The Dendarii hand stunners were of no use at all. Miles clambered into the back again, looking for some sort of luggage compartment, gun rack, anything—surely Fell's people did not rely only on the fearsome reputation of their House for protection. . . .

The padded benches along each side of the cargo compartment, upon which Fell's guard squad had presumably sat, swung up on storage space. The first was empty, the second contained personal luggage—Miles had a brief flash of strangling an enemy with someone's pajama pants, flinging underwear into thruster air-intakes—the third compartment was also empty. The fourth was locked.

The float truck rocked under another blast, part of the top peeled away in the wind, Miles grabbed for Taura, and the truck plummeted downward. Miles's stomach, and the rest of him, seemed to float upward. They were all flattened to the floor again as Bel pulled up. The float truck shivered and lurched, and all—Miles and Taura, the unconscious trooper, Nicol in her float chair—were flung forward in a tangle as the truck plowed to a tilted stop in a copse of frost-blackened scrub.

Bel, blood streaming down its face, clambered back to them crying "Out, out, out!" Miles stretched for the new opening in the roof, jerked his hand back at the burning touch of hot slagged metal and plastics. Taura, standing up, stuck her head out through the hole, then crouched back down to boost Miles through. He slithered to the ground, looked around. They were in an unpeopled valley of native vegetation, flanked by ropy, ridgy hills. Flying up the slot toward them came the two pursuing aircars, swelling, slowing—coming in for a capture, or just taking careful aim?

The *Ariel's* combat drop shuttle roared up over the ridge and descended like the black hand of God. The pursuing aircars looked suddenly *much* smaller. One veered off and fled; the second was smashed to the ground not by plasma fire but by a swift swat from a tractor beam. Not even a trickle of smoke marked where it went down. The drop shuttle settled demurely beside them in a deafening crackling crush of shrubbery. Its hatch extended and unfolded itself in a sort of suave, self-satisfied salute.

"Show-off," Miles muttered. He pulled the woozy Thorne's arm over his shoulder, Taura carried the stunned man, Nicol's battered cup stuttered through the air, and they all staggered gratefully to their rescue.

Subtle noises of protest emanated from the ship around him as Miles stepped into the *Ariel's* shuttle hatch corridor. His stomach twitched queasily from an artificial gravity not quite in synch with overloaded engines. They were on their way, breaking orbit already. Miles wanted to get to

Nav and Com as quickly as possible, though the evidence so far suggested that Murka was carrying on quite competently. Anderson and Nout hauled in the downed trooper, now moaning his way to consciousness, and turned him over to the medtech waiting with a float pallet. Thorne, who had acquired a temporary plas dressing for the forehead cut during the shuttle flight, sent Nicol in her damaged float chair after them and whisked off toward Nav and Com. Miles turned to encounter the man he least wanted to see. Dr. Canaba hovered anxiously in the corridor, his tanned face strained.

"You," said Miles to Canaba, in a voice dark with rage. Canaba stepped back involuntarily. Miles wanted, but was too short, to pin Canaba to the wall by his neck, and regretfully dismissed the idea of ordering Trooper Nout to do it for him. Miles pinned Canaba with a glare instead. "You cold-blooded double-dealing son-of-a-bitch. You set me up to murder a sixteen-year-old girl!"

Canaba raised his hands in protest. "You don't understand—"

Taura ducked through the shuttle hatch. Her tawny eyes widened in a surprise only exceeded by Canaba's. "Why, Dr. Canaba! What are you doing here?"

Miles pointed to Canaba. "You, stay there," he ordered thickly. He tampered his anger down and turned to the shuttle pilot. "Laureen?"

"Yes, sir?"

Miles took Taura by the hand and led her to Sergeant Anderson. "Laureen, I want you to take Recruit-trainee Taura here in tow and get her a square meal. All she can eat, and I do mean all. Then help her get a bath, a uniform, and orient her to the ship."

Anderson eyed the towering Taura warily. "Er . . . yes, sir."

"She's had a hell of a time," Miles felt compelled to explain, then paused and added, "Do us proud. It's important."

"Yes, sir," said Anderson sturdily, and led off, Taura following with an uncertain backward glance to Miles and Canaba.

Miles rubbed his stubbled chin, conscious of his stains and stink, fear-driven weariness stretching his nerves taut. He turned to the stunned geneticist. "All right, doctor," he snarled, "make me understand. Try real hard."

"I couldn't leave her in Ryoval's hands!" said Canaba in agitation. "To be made a victim, or worse, an agent of his, his merchandised depravities . . ."

"Didn't you ever think of asking us to rescue her?"

"But," said Canaba, confused, "why should you? It wasn't in your contract—a mercenary—"

"Doctor, you've been living on Jackson's Whole too damn long."

"I knew that back when I was throwing up every morning before going to work." Canaba drew himself up with a dry dignity. "But Admiral, you don't understand." He glanced down the corridor in the direction Taura had gone. "I couldn't leave her in Ryoval's hands. But I can't possibly take her to Barrayar. They kill mutants there!"

"Er . . ." said Miles, given pause. "They're attempting to reform those prejudices. Or so I understand. But you're quite right. Barrayar is not the place for her."

"I had hoped, when you came along, not to have to do it, to kill her myself. Not an easy task. I've known her . . . too long. But to leave her down there would have been the most vile condemnation . . ."

"That's no lie. Well, she's out of there now. Same as you."
If we can keep so. . . . Miles was frantic to get to Nav and
Com and find out what was happening. Had Ryoval
launched pursuit yet? Had Fell? Would the space station
guarding the distant wormhole exit be ordered to block
their escape?

"I didn't want to just abandon her," dithered Canaba,
"but I couldn't take her with me!"

"I should hope not. You're totally unfit to have charge of
her. I'm going to urge her to join the Dendarii Mercenaries.
It would seem to be her genetic destiny. Unless you know
some reason why not?"

"But she's going to die!"

Miles stopped short. "And you and I are not?" he said
softly after a moment, then more loudly, "Why? How
soon?"

"It's her metabolism. Another mistake, or concatenation
of mistakes. I don't know when, exactly. She could go
another year, or two, or five. Or ten."

"Or fifteen?"

"Or fifteen, yes, though not likely. But early, still."

"And yet you wanted to take from her what little she
had? Why?"

"To spare her. The final debilitation is rapid, but very
painful, to judge from what some of the other . . . prototypes, went through. The females were more complex than
the males, I'm not certain . . . But it's a ghastly death. Especially ghastly as Ryoval's slave."

"I don't recall encountering a lovely death yet. And I've
seen a variety. As for duration, I tell you we could all go in
the next fifteen minutes, and where is your tender mercy
then?" He *had* to get to Nav and Com. "I declare your

interest in her forfeit, doctor. Meanwhile, let her grab what life she can."

"But she was my project—I must answer for her—"

"No. She's a free woman now. She must answer for herself."

"How free can she ever be, in that body, driven by that metabolism, that face—a freak's life—better to die painlessly, than to have all that suffering inflicted on her—"

Miles spoke through his teeth. With emphasis. "No. It's. Not."

Canaba stared at him, shaken out of the rutted circle of his unhappy reasoning at last.

That's right, doctor, Miles's thought glittered. *Get your head out of your ass and look at me. Finally.*

"Why should . . . you care?" asked Canaba.

"I like her. Rather better than I like you, I might add." Miles paused, daunted by the thought of having to explain to Taura about the gene complexes in her calf. And sooner or later they'd have to retrieve them. Unless he could fake it, pretend the biopsy was some sort of medical standard operating procedure for Dendarii induction—no. She deserved more honesty than that.

Miles was highly annoyed at Canaba for putting this false note between himself and Taura and yet—without the gene complexes, would he have indeed gone in after her as his boast implied? Extended and endangered his assigned mission just out of the goodness of his heart, yeah? Devotion to duty, or pragmatic ruthlessness, which was which? He would never know, now. His anger receded, and exhaustion washed in, the familiar post-mission down—too soon, the mission was far from over, Miles reminded himself sternly. He inhaled. "You can't save her from being alive, Dr. Canaba. Too late. Let her go. Let *go.*"

Canaba's lips were unhappily tight, but, head bowing, he turned his hands palm-out.

"Page the Admiral," Miles heard Thorne say as he entered Nav and Com, then "Belay that," as heads swivelled toward the swish of the doors and they saw Miles. "Good timing, sir."

"What's up?" Miles swung into the com station chair Thorne indicated. Ensign Murka was monitoring ship's shielding and weapons systems, while their jump pilot sat at the ready beneath the strange crown of his headset with its chemical cannulae and wires.

Pilot Padget's expression was inward, controlled and meditative; his consciousness fully engaged, even merged, with the *Ariel*. Good man.

"Baron Ryoval is on the com for you," said Thorne. "Personally."

"I wonder if he's checked his freezers yet?" Miles settled in before the vid link. "How long have I kept him waiting?"

"Less than a minute," said the com officer.

"Hm. Let him wait a little longer, then. What's been launched in pursuit of us?"

"Nothing, so far," reported Murka.

Miles's brows rose at this unexpected news. He took a moment to compose himself, wishing he'd had time to clean up, shave, and put on a fresh uniform before this interview, just for the psychological edge. He scratched his itching chin and ran his hands through his hair, and wriggled his damp sock toes against the deck matting, which they barely reached. He lowered his station chair slightly, straightened his spine as much as he could, and brought his breathing under control. "All right, bring him up."

The rather blurred background to the face that formed over the vid plate seemed faintly familiar—ah yes, the Security Ops room at Ryoval Biologicals. Baron Ryoval had arrived personally on that scene as promised. It took only one glance at the dusky, contorted expression on Ryoval's youthful face to fill in the rest of the scenario. Miles folded his hands and smiled innocently. "Good morning, Baron. What can I do for you?"

"*Die,* you little mutant!" Ryoval spat. "You! There isn't going to be a bunker deep enough for you to burrow in. I'll put a price on your head that will have every bounty hunter in the galaxy all over you like a second skin—you'll not eat or sleep—I'll have you—"

Yes, the baron had seen his freezers all right. Recently. Gone entirely was the suave contemptuous dismissal of their first encounter. Yet Miles was puzzled by the drift of his threats. It seemed the baron expected them to escape Jacksonian local space. True, House Ryoval owned no space fleet, but why not rent a dreadnought from Baron Fell and attack now? That was the ploy Miles had most expected and feared, that Ryoval and Fell, and maybe Bharaputra too, would combine against him as he attempted to carry off their prizes.

"Can you afford to hire bounty hunters now?" asked Miles mildly. "I thought your assets were somewhat reduced. Though you still have your surgical specialists, I suppose."

Ryoval, breathing heavily, wiped spittle from his mouth. "Did my dear little brother put you up to this?"

"Who?" said Miles, genuinely startled. Yet another player in the game . . . ?

"Baron Fell."

"I was . . . not aware you were related," said Miles. "*Little* brother?"

"You lie badly," sneered Ryoval. "I knew he had to be behind this."

"You'll have to ask him," Miles shot at random, his head spinning as the new datum rearranged all his estimates. *Damn* his mission briefing, which had never mentioned this connection, concentrating in detail only on House Bharaputra. Half-brothers only, surely—yes, hadn't Nicol mentioned something about "Fell's half-brother"?

"I'll have your head for this," foamed Ryoval. "Shipped back frozen in a box. I'll have it encased in plastic and hang it over my—no, better. Double the money for the man who brings you in alive. You will die slowly, after infinite degradation—"

In all, Miles was glad the distance between them was widening at high acceleration.

Ryoval interrupted his own tirade, dark brows snapping down in sudden suspicion. "Or was it Bharaputra who hired you? Trying to block me from cutting in on their biologicals monopoly at the last, not merging as they promised?"

"Why, now," drawled Miles, "would Bharaputra really mount a plot against the head of another House? Do you have personal evidence that they do that sort of thing? Or—who did kill your, ah, brother's clone?" The connections were locking into place at last. Ye gods. It seemed Miles and his mission had blundered into the middle of an ongoing power struggle of byzantine complexity. Nicol had testified that Fell had never pinned down the killer of his young duplicate. . . . "Shall I guess?"

"You know bloody well," snapped Ryoval. "But which of them hired you? Fell, or Bharaputra? *Which?*"

Ryoval, Miles realized, knew absolutely nothing yet of the real Dendarii mission against House Bharaputra. And with the atmosphere among the Houses being what it apparently was, it could be quite a long time before they got around to comparing notes. The longer the better, from Miles's point of view. He began to suppress, then deliberately released, a small smile. "What, can't you believe it was just my personal blow against the genetic slave trade? A deed in honor of my lady?"

This reference to Taura went straight over Ryoval's head; he had his idée-fixe now, and its ramifications and his rage were an effective block against incoming data. Really, it should not be at all hard to convince a man who had been conspiring deeply against his rivals, that those rivals were conspiring against him in turn.

"Fell, or Bharaputra?" Ryoval reiterated furiously. "Did you think to conceal a theft for Bharaputra with that wanton destruction?"

Theft? Miles wondered intently. Not of Taura, surely—of some tissue sample Bharaputra had been dealing for, perhaps? Oh *ho.* . . .

"Isn't it obvious?" said Miles sweetly. "You gave your brother the motive, in your sabotage of his plans to extend his life. And you wanted too much from Bharaputra, so they supplied the method, placing their super-soldier inside your facility where I could rendezvous with her. They even made you pay for the privilege of having your security screwed! You played right into our hands. The master plan, of course," Miles buffed his fingernails on his T-shirt, "was mine."

Miles glanced up through his eyelashes. Ryoval seemed to be having trouble breathing. The baron cut the vid connection with an abrupt swat of his shaking hand. Blackout.

Humming thoughtfully, Miles went to get a shower.

He was back in Nav and Com in fresh gray-and-whites, full of salicylates for his aches and contusions and with a mug of hot black coffee in his hands as antidote to his squinting red eyes, when the next call came in.

So far from breaking into a tirade like his half-brother, Baron Fell sat silent a moment in the vid, just staring at Miles. Miles, burning under his gaze, felt extremely glad he'd had the chance to clean up. So, had Baron Fell missed his quaddie at last? Had Ryoval communicated to him yet any part of the smouldering paranoid misconceptions Miles had so lately fanned to flame? No pursuit had yet been launched from Fell Station—it must come soon, or not at all, or any craft light enough to match the *Ariel's* acceleration would be too light to match its firepower. Unless Fell planned to call in favors from the consortium of Houses that ran the Jumppoint Station. . . . One more minute of this heavy silence, Miles felt, and he would break into uncontrollable blither. Fortunately, Fell spoke at last.

"You seem, Admiral Naismith," Baron Fell rumbled, "whether accidentally or on purpose, to be carrying off something that does not belong to you."

Quite a few somethings, Miles reflected, but Fell referred only to Nicol if Miles read him right. "We were compelled to leave in rather a hurry," he said in an apologetic tone.

"So I'm told." Fell inclined his head ironically. He must have had a report from his hapless squad commander. "But you may yet save yourself some trouble. There was an agreed-upon price for my musician. It's of no great difference to me, if I give her up to you or to Ryoval, as long as I get that price."

Captain Thorne, working the *Ariel*'s monitors, flinched under Miles's glance.

"The price you refer to, I take it, is the secret of the Betan rejuvenation technique," said Miles.

"Quite."

"Ah . . . hum." Miles moistened his lips. "Baron, I cannot."

Fell turned his head. "Station commander, launch pursuit ships—"

"Wait!" Miles cried.

Fell raised his brows. "You reconsider? Good."

"It's not that I *will* not tell you," said Miles desperately, "it's just that the truth would be of no use to you. None whatsoever. Still, I agree you deserve some compensation. I have another piece of information I could trade you, more immediately valuable."

"Oh?" said Fell. His voice was neutral but his expression was black.

"You suspected your half-brother Ryoval in the murder of your clone, but could not chain any evidence to him, am I right?"

Fell looked fractionally more interested. "All my agents and Bharaputra's could not turn up a connection. We tried."

"I'm not surprised. Because it was Bharaputra's agents who did the deed." Well, it was possible, anyway.

Fell's eyes narrowed. "Killed their own product?" he said slowly.

"I believe Ryoval struck a deal with House Bharaputra to betray you," said Miles rapidly. "I believe it involved the trade of some unique biological samples in Ryoval's possession; I don't think cash alone would have been worth their risk. The deal was done on the highest levels, obviously. I don't know how they figured to divide the spoils of House

Fell after your eventual death—maybe they didn't mean to divide it at all. They seem to have had some ultimate plan of combining their operations for some larger monopoly of biologicals on Jackson's Whole. A corporate merger of sorts." Miles paused to let this sink in. "May I suggest you may wish to reserve your forces and favors against enemies more, er, intimate and immediate than myself? Besides, you have all our credit chit but we have only half our cargo. Will you call it even?"

Fell glowered at him for a full minute, the face of a man thinking in three different directions at once. Miles knew the feeling. He then turned his head, and grated out of the corner of his mouth, "Hold pursuit ships."

Miles breathed again.

"I thank you for this information, Admiral," said Fell coldly, "but not very much. I shall not impede your swift exit. But if you or any of your ships appear in Jacksonian space again—"

"Oh, Baron," said Miles sincerely, "staying far, far away from here is fast becoming one of my dearest ambitions."

"You're wise," Fell growled, and moved to cut the link.

"Baron Fell," Miles added impulsively. Fell paused. "For your future information—is this link secured?"

"Yes."

"The true secret of the Betan rejuvenation technique—is that there is none. Don't be taken in again. I look the age I do, because it is the age I am. Make of it what you will."

Fell said absolutely nothing. After a moment a faint, wintry smile moved his lips. He shook his head and cut the com.

Just in case, Miles lingered on in sort of a glassy puddle in one corner of Nav and Com until the Com Officer reported their final clearance from Jumppoint Station traffic control. But Miles calculated Houses Fell, Ryoval, and Bharaputra were going to be too busy with each other to concern themselves with him, at least for a while. His late transfer of information both true and false among the combatants—to each according to his measure—had the feel of throwing one bone to three starving, rabid dogs. He almost regretted not being able to stick around and see the results. Almost.

Hours after the jump he woke in his cabin, fully dressed but with his boots set neatly by his bed, with no memory of how he'd got there. He rather fancied Murka must have escorted him. If he'd fallen asleep while walking alone he'd surely have left the boots on.

Miles first checked with the duty officer as to the *Ariel*'s situation and status. It was refreshingly dull. They were crossing a blue star system between jump points on the route to Escobar, unpeopled and empty of everything but a smattering of routine commercial traffic. Nothing pursued them from the direction of Jackson's Whole. Miles had a light meal, not sure if it was breakfast, lunch, or dinner, his bio-rhythm being thoroughly askew from shiptime after his downside adventures. He then sought out Thorne and Nicol. He found them in Engineering. A tech was just polishing out the last dent in Nicol's float chair.

Nicol, now wearing a white tunic and shorts trimmed with pink piping, lay sprawled on her belly on a bench watching the repairs. It gave Miles an odd sensation to see her out of her cup. It was like looking at a hermit crab out of its shell, or a seal on the shore. She looked strangely vulnerable in one-gee, yet in null gee she'd looked so right, so clearly at ease, he'd stopped noticing the oddness of the extra arms very quickly. Thorne helped the tech fit the float cup's blue shell over its reconditioned antigrav mechanism, and turned to greet Miles as the tech proceeded to lock it in place.

Miles sat down-bench from Nicol. "From the looks of things," he told her, "you should be free of pursuit from Baron Fell. He and his half-brother are going to be fully occupied avenging themselves on each other for a while. Makes me glad I'm an only child."

"Hm," she said pensively.

"You should be safe," Thorne offered encouragingly.

"Oh—no, it's not that," Nicol said. "I was just thinking about my sisters. Time was I couldn't wait to get away from them. Now I can't wait to see them again."

"What are your plans now?" Miles asked.

"I'll stop at Escobar, first," she replied. "It's a good nexus crossing. From there I should be able to work my way back to Earth. From Earth I can get to Orient IV, and from there I'm sure I can get home."

"Is home your goal now?"

"There's a lot more galaxy to be seen out this way," Thorne pointed out. "I'm not sure if Dendarii rosters can be stretched to include a ship's musician, but—"

She was shaking her head. "Home," she said firmly. "I'm tired of fighting one-gee all the time. I'm tired of being alone. I'm starting to have nightmares about growing legs."

Thorne sighed faintly.

"We do have a little colony of downsiders living among us now," she added suggestively to Thorne. "They've fitted out their own asteroid with artificial gravity—quite like the real thing downside, only not as drafty."

Miles was faintly alarmed—to lose a ship commander of proven loyalty—

"Ah," said Thorne in a pensive tone to match Nicol's. "A long way from my home, your asteroid belt."

"Will you return to Beta Colony, then, someday?" she asked. "Or are the Dendarii Mercenaries your home and family?"

"Not quite that passionate, for me," said Thorne. "I mainly stick around due to an overwhelming curiosity to see what happens next." Thorne favored Miles with a peculiar smile.

Thorne helped load Nicol back into her blue cup. After a brief systems check she was hovering upright again, as mobile—more mobile—than her legged companions. She rocked and regarded Thorne brightly.

"It's only three more days to Escobar orbit," said Thorne to Nicol rather regretfully. "Still—seventy-two hours. 4,320 minutes. How much can you do in 4,320 minutes?"

Or how often, thought Miles dryly. *Especially if you don't sleep.* Sleep, per se, was not what Bel had in mind, if Miles recognized the signs. Good luck—to both of them.

"Meanwhile," Thorne maneuvered Nicol into the corridor, "let me show you around my ship. Illyrican-built— that's out your way a bit, I understand. It's quite a story, how the *Ariel* first fell into Dendarii hands—we were the Oseran Mercenaries, back then—"

Nicol made encouraging noises. Miles suppressed an envious grin, and turned the other way up the corridor, to search out Dr. Canaba and arrange the discharge of his last unpleasant duty.

Bemusedly, Miles set aside the hypospray he'd been turning over in his hands as the door to sickbay sighed open. He swivelled in the medtech's station chair and glanced up as Taura and Sergeant Anderson entered. "My *word*," he murmured.

Anderson sketched a salute. "Reporting as ordered, sir." Taura's hand twitched, uncertain whether to attempt to mimic this military greeting or not. Miles gazed up at Taura and his lips parted with involuntary delight. Taura's transformation was all he'd dreamed of and more.

He didn't know how Anderson had persuaded the stores computer to so exceed its normal parameters, but somehow she'd made it disgorge a complete Dendarii undress kit in Taura's size: crisp gray-and-white pocketed jacket, gray trousers, polished ankle-topping boots. Taura's face and hair were clean enough to outshine her boots. Her dark hair was now drawn back in a thick, neat, and rather mysterious braid coiling up the back of her head—Miles could not make out where the ends went—and glinting with unexpected mahogany highlights.

She looked, if not exactly well-fed, at least less rawly starving, her eyes bright and interested, not the haunted yellow flickers in bony caverns he'd first seen. Even from this distance he could tell that re-hydration and the chance to brush her teeth and fangs had cured the ketone-laced breath that several days in Ryoval's sub-basement on a diet of raw rats and nothing had produced. The dirt-encrusted scale was smoothed away from her huge hands, and— inspired touch—her clawed nails had been, not blunted, but neatened and sharpened, and then enamelled with an iridescent pearl-white polish that complemented her gray-and-whites like a flash of jewelry. The polish had to have been shared out of some personal stock of the sergeant's.

"Outstanding, Anderson," said Miles in admiration.

Anderson smirked proudly. "That about what you had in mind, sir?"

"Yes, it was." Taura's face reflected his delight straight back at him. "What did you think of your first wormhole jump?" he asked her.

Her long lips rippled—what happened when she tried to purse them, Miles guessed. "I was afraid I was getting sick, I was so dizzy all of a sudden, till Sergeant Anderson explained what it was."

"No little hallucinations, or odd time-stretching effects?"

"No, but it wasn't—well, it was quick, anyway."

"Hm. It doesn't sound like you're one of the fortunates— or unfortunates—to be screened for jump pilot aptitudes. From the talents you demonstrated on Ryoval's landing pad yesterday morning, Tactics should be loathe to lose you to Nav and Com." Miles paused. "Thank you, Laureen. What did my page interrupt?"

"Routine systems checks on the drop shuttles, putting them to bed. I was having Taura look over my shoulder while I worked."

"Right, carry on. I'll send Taura back to you when she's done here."

Anderson exited reluctantly, clearly curious. Miles waited till the doors swished closed to speak again. "Sit down, Taura. So your first twenty-four hours with the Dendarii have been satisfactory?"

She grinned, settling herself carefully in a station chair, which creaked. "Just fine."

"Ah." He hesitated. "You understand, when we reach Escobar, you do have the option to go your own way. You're not compelled to join us. I could see you got some kind of start, downside there."

"What?" Her eyes widened in dismay. "No! I mean . . . do I eat too much?"

"Not at all! You fight like four men, we can bloody well afford to feed you like three. But . . . I need to set a few things straight, before you make your trainee's oath." He cleared his throat. "I didn't come to Ryoval's to recruit you. A few weeks before Bharaputra sold you, do you remember Dr. Canaba injecting something into your leg? With a needle, not a hypospray."

"Oh, yes." She rubbed her calf half-consciously. "It made a knot."

"What, ah, did he tell you it was?"

"An immunization."

She'd been right, Miles reflected, when they'd first met. Humans did lie a lot. "Well, it wasn't an immunization. Canaba was using you as a live repository for some engineered biological material. Molecularly bound, dormant material," he added hastily as she twisted around and looked at her leg in disquiet. "It can't activate spontaneously, he assures me. My original mission was only to pick up Dr. Canaba. But he wouldn't leave without his gene complexes."

"He planned to take me with him?" she said in thrilled surprise. "So I should thank *him* for sending you to me!"

Miles wished he could see the look on Canaba's face if she did. "Yes and no. Specifically, no." He rushed roughly on before his nerve failed him. "You have nothing to thank him for, nor me either. He meant to take only your tissue sample, and sent me to get it."

"Would you rather have left me at—is that why Escobar—" she was still bewildered.

"It was your good luck," Miles plunged on, "that I'd lost my men and was disarmed when we finally met. Canaba lied to me, too. In his defense, he seems to have had some dim idea of saving you from a brutal life as Ryoval's slave.

He sent me to kill you, Taura. He sent me to slay a monster, when he should have been begging me to rescue a princess in disguise. I'm not too pleased with Dr. Canaba. Nor with myself. I lied through my teeth to you down in Ryoval's basement, because I thought I had to, to survive and win."

Her face was confused, congealing, the light in her eyes fading. "Then you didn't . . . really think I was human—"

"On the contrary. Your choice of test was an excellent one. It's much harder to lie with your body than with your mouth. When I, er, demonstrated my belief, it had to be real." Looking at her, he still felt a twinge of lurching, lunatic joy, somatic residual from that adventure-of-the-body. He supposed he always would feel something—male conditioning, no doubt. "Would you like me to demonstrate it again?" he asked half-hopefully, then bit his tongue. "No," he answered his own question. "If I am to be your commander—we have these non-fraternization rules. Mainly to protect those of lower rank from exploitation, though it can work both—ahem!" He was digressing dreadfully. He picked up the hypospray, fiddled with it nervously, and put it back down.

"Anyway, Dr. Canaba has asked me to lie to you again. He wanted me to sneak up on you with a general anesthetic, so he could biopsy back his sample. He's a coward, you may have noticed. He's outside now, shaking in his shoes for fear you'll find out what he intended for you. I think a local zap with a medical stunner would suffice. I'd sure want to be conscious and watching if he were working on *me,* anyway." He flicked the hypospray contemptuously with one finger.

She sat silent, her strange wolfish face—though Miles was getting used to it—unreadable. "You want me to let him . . . cut into my leg?" she said at last.

"Yes."

"Then what?"

"Then nothing. That will be the last of Dr. Canaba for you, and Jackson's Whole and all the rest of it. That, I promise. Though if you're doubtful of my promises, I can understand why."

"The last . . ." she breathed. Her face lowered, then rose, and her shoulders straightened. "Then let's get it over with." There was no smile to her long mouth now.

Canaba, as Miles expected, was not happy to be presented with a conscious subject. Miles truly didn't care how unhappy Canaba was about it, and after one look at his cold face, Canaba didn't argue. Canaba took his sample wordlessly, packaged it carefully in the biotainer, and fled with it back to the safety and privacy of his own cabin as soon as he decently could.

Miles sat with Taura in sickbay till the medical stun wore off enough for her to walk without stumbling. She sat without speaking for a long time. He watched her still features, wishing beyond measure he knew how to re-light those gold eyes.

"When I first saw you," she said softly, "it was like a miracle. Something magic. Everything I'd wished for, longed for. Food. Water. Heat. Revenge. Escape." She gazed down at her polished claws, "Friends . . ." and glanced up at him, " . . . touching."

"What else do you wish for, Taura?" Miles asked earnestly.

Slowly she replied. "I wish I were normal."

Miles was silent too. "I can't give you what I don't possess myself," he said at length. The words seemed to lie in inadequate lumps between them. He roused himself to a better effort. "No. Don't wish that. I have a better idea. Wish to be yourself. To the hilt. Find out what you're best at, and develop it. Hopscotch your weaknesses. There isn't time for them. Look at Nicol—"

"So beautiful," sighed Taura.

"Or look at Captain Thorne, and tell me what 'normal' is, and why I should give a damn for it. Look at me, if you will. Should I kill myself trying to overcome men twice my weight and reach in unarmed combat, or should I shift the ground to where their muscle is useless, 'cause it never gets close enough to apply its strength? I haven't got *time* to lose, and neither have you."

"Do you know how little time?" demanded Taura suddenly.

"Ah . . ." said Miles cautiously, "do you?"

"I am the last survivor of my creche mates. How could I not know?" Her chin lifted defiantly.

"Then don't wish to be normal," said Miles passionately, rising to pace. "You'll only waste your precious time in futile frustration. Wish to be great! That at least you have a fighting chance for. Great at whatever you are. A great trooper, a great sergeant. A great quartermaster, for God's sake, if that's what comes with ease. A great musician like Nicol—only think how horrible if she were wasting her talents trying to be merely normal." Miles paused self-consciously in his pep talk, thinking, *Easier to preach than practice. . . .*

Taura studied her polished claws, and sighed. "I suppose it's useless for me to wish to be beautiful, like Sergeant Anderson."

"It is useless for you to try to be beautiful *like* anyone but yourself," said Miles. "Be beautiful like Taura, ah, that you can do. Superbly well." He found himself gripping her hands, and ran one finger across an iridescent claw, "Though Laureen seems to have grasped the principle. You might be guided by her taste."

"Admiral," said Taura slowly, not releasing his hands, "are you actually my commander yet? Sergeant Anderson said something about orientation, and induction tests, and an oath. . . ."

"Yes, all that will come when we make fleet rendezvous. Till then, technically, you're our guest."

A certain sparkle was beginning to return to her gold eyes. "Then—till then—it wouldn't break any Dendarii rules, would it, if you showed me again how human I am? One more time?"

It must be, Miles thought, akin to the same drive that used to propel men to climb sheer rock faces without an antigrav belt, or jump out of ancient aircraft with nothing to stop them going splat but a wad of silk cloth. He felt the fascination rising in him, the death-defying laugh. "Slowly?" he said in a strangled voice. "Do it right this time? Have a little conversation, drink a little wine, play a little music? Without Ryoval's guard squad lurking overhead, or ice cold rock under my . . ."

Her eyes were huge and gold and molten. "You did say you liked to practice what you were great at."

Miles had never realized how susceptible he was to flattery from tall women. A weakness he must guard against. Sometime.

They retired to his cabin and practiced assiduously till halfway to Escobar.

Diplomatic Immunity

Chapter 1

In the image above the vid plate, the sperm writhed in elegant, sinuous curves. Its wriggling grew more energetic as the invisible grip of the medical micro-tractor grasped it and guided it to its target, the pearl-like egg: round, lustrous, rich with promise.

"Once more, dear boy, into the breach—for England, Harry, and Saint George!" Miles murmured encouragingly. "Or at least, for Barrayar, me, and maybe Grandfather Piotr. Ha!" With a last twitch, the sperm vanished within its destined paradise.

"Miles, are you looking at those baby pictures *again*?" came Ekaterin's voice, amused, as she emerged from their cabin's sybaritic bathroom. She finished winding up her dark hair on the back of her head, secured it, and leaned over his shoulder as he sat in the station chair. "Is that Aral Alexander, or Helen Natalia?"

"Well, Aral Alexander in the making."

"Ah, admiring your sperm again. I see."

"*And* your excellent egg, my lady." He glanced up at his wife, glorious in a heavy red silk tunic that he'd bought her on Earth, and grinned. The warm clean scent of her skin tickled his nostrils, and he inhaled happily. "Were they not a handsome set of gametes? While they lasted, anyway."

"Yes, and they made beautiful blastocysts. You know, it's a good thing we took this trip. I swear you'd be in there trying to lift the replicator lids to peek, or shaking the poor little things up like Winterfair presents to see how they rattled."

"Well, it's all new to *me*."

"Your mother told me last Winterfair that as soon as the embryos were safely implanted you'd be acting like you'd invented reproduction. And to think I imagined she was exaggerating!"

He captured her hand and breathed a kiss into its palm. "This, from the lady who sat in the nursery next to the replicator rack all spring to study? Whose assignments all suddenly seemed to take twice as long to complete?"

"Which, of course, had nothing to do with her lord popping in twice an hour to ask how she was going on?" The hand, released, traced his chin in a very flattering fashion. Miles considered proposing that they forgo the rather dull luncheon company in the ship's passenger lounge, order in room service, get undressed again, and go back to bed for the rest of the watch. Ekaterin didn't seem to regard anything about their journey as boring, though.

This galactic honeymoon was belated, but perhaps better so, Miles thought. Their marriage had had an awkward enough commencement; it was as well that their settling-in had included a quiet period of domestic routine. But in retrospect, the first anniversary of that memorable, difficult, mid-winter wedding had seemed to arrive in about fifteen subjective minutes.

They had long agreed they would celebrate the date by starting the children in their uterine replicators. The debate had never been about *when*, just *how many*. He still thought his suggestion of doing them all at once had an admirable efficiency. He'd never been serious about twelve; he'd just figured to start with that proposition, and fall back to six. His mother, his aunt, and what seemed every other female of his acquaintance had all mobilized to explain to him that he was insane, but Ekaterin had merely smiled. They'd settled on two, to begin with, Aral Alexander and Helen Natalia. A double portion of wonder, terror, and delight.

At the edge of the vid recording, Baby's First Cell Division was interrupted by a red blinking message light. Miles frowned faintly. They were three jumps out from Solar space, in the deep interstellar on a sub-light-speed run between wormholes expected to take four full days. En route to Tau Ceti, where they would make orbital transfer to a ship bound for Escobar, and there to yet another that would thread the jump route past Sergyar and Komarr to home. He wasn't exactly expecting any vid calls here. "Receive," he intoned.

Aral Alexander *in potentia* vanished, to be replaced by the head and shoulders of the Tau Cetan passenger liner's captain. Miles and Ekaterin had dined at his table some two or three times on this leg of their tour. The man favored Miles with a tense smile and nod. "Lord Vorkosigan."

"Yes, Captain? What can I do for you?"

"A ship identifying itself as a Barrayaran Imperial courier has hailed us and is requesting permission to match velocities and lock on. Apparently, they have an urgent message for you."

Miles's brows rose, and his stomach sank. This was not, in his experience, the way the Imperium delivered *good* news. On his shoulder, Ekaterin's hand tightened. "Certainly, Captain. Put them through."

The captain's dark Tau Cetan features vanished, to be replaced after a moment by a man in Barrayaran Imperial undress greens with lieutenant's tabs and Sector IV pins on his collar. Visions surged through Miles's mind of the Emperor assassinated, Vorkosigan House burned to the ground with the replicators inside, or, even more hideously likely, his father suffering a fatal stroke—he dreaded the day some stiff-faced messenger would begin by addressing him, *Count Vorkosigan, sir?*

The lieutenant saluted him. "Lord Auditor Vorkosigan? I'm Lieutenant Smolyani of the courier ship *Kestrel.* I have a message to hand-deliver to you, recorded under the Emperor's personal seal, after which I am ordered to take you aboard."

"We're not at war, are we? Nobody's died?"

Lieutenant Smolyani ducked his head. "Not so far as I've heard, sir." Miles's heart rate eased; behind him, Ekaterin let out her breath. The lieutenant went on, "But, apparently, a Komarran trade fleet has been impounded at some place called Graf Station, Union of Free Habitats. It's listed as an independent system, out near the edge of Sector V. My clear-code flight orders are to take you there with all safe speed, and to wait on your convenience thereafter." He smiled a bit grimly. "I hope it's not a war, sir, because they only seem to be sending us."

"Impounded? Not quarantined?"

"I gather it's some sort of legal entanglement, sir."

I smell diplomacy. Miles grimaced. "Well, no doubt the sealed message will make it more plain. Bring it to me, and I'll take a look while we get packed up."

"Yes, sir. The *Kestrel* will be locking on in just a few minutes."

"Very good, Lieutenant." Miles cut the com.

"We?" said Ekaterin in a quiet tone.

Miles hesitated. Not a quarantine, the lieutenant had said. Not, apparently, a shooting war either. *Or not yet, anyway.* On the other hand, he couldn't imagine Emperor Gregor interrupting his long-delayed honeymoon for something trivial. "I'd better see what Gregor has to say, first."

She dropped a kiss on the top of his head, and said simply, "Right."

Miles raised his personal wrist com to his lips and murmured, "Armsman Roic—on duty, to my cabin, now."

The data disk with the Imperial Seal upon it that the lieutenant handed to Miles a short time later was marked *Personal*, not *Secret*. Miles sent Roic, his bodyguard-cum-batman, and Smolyani off to sort and stow luggage, but motioned Ekaterin to stay. He slipped the disk into the secured player that the lieutenant had also brought, set it on the cabin's bedside table, and keyed it to life. He sat back on the edge of the bed beside her, conscious of the warmth and solidity of her body. For the sake of her worried eyes, he took her hand in a reassuring grip.

Emperor Gregor Vorbarra's familiar features appeared, lean, dark, reserved. Miles read profound irritation in the subtle tightening of his lips.

"I'm sorry to interrupt your honeymoon, Miles," Gregor began. "But if this has caught up with you, you haven't changed your itinerary. So you're on your way home now in any case."

Not *too* sorry, then.

"It's my good luck and your bad that you happen to be the man physically closest to this mess. Briefly, one of our Komarr-based trade fleets put in at a deep-space facility out near Sector V, for resupply and cargo transfer. One—or more, the reports are unclear—of the officers from its Barrayaran military escort either deserted, or was kidnapped. Or was murdered—the reports are unclear about *that*, too. The patrol the fleet commander sent to retrieve him ran into trouble with the locals. Shots—I phrase this advisedly—shots were fired, equipment and structures were damaged, people on both sides were apparently seriously injured. No other deaths reported yet, but that may have changed by the time you get this, God help us.

"The problem—or one of them, anyway—is that we're getting a significantly different version of the chain of events from the local ImpSec observer on the Graf Station side of the conflict than we're getting from our fleet commander. Yet more Barrayaran personnel are now reported either held hostage, or arrested, depending on which version one is to believe. Charges filed, fines and expenses mounting, and the local response has been to lock down all ships currently in dock until the muddle is resolved to their satisfaction. The Komarran cargomasters are now screaming back to us over the heads of their Barrayaran escort, with yet a third spin on events. For your, ah, delectation, all the original reports we've received so far from all the viewpoints are appended to this message. Enjoy." Gregor grimaced in a way that made Miles twitch.

"Just to add to the delicacy of the problem, the fleet in question is about fifty percent Toscane-owned." Gregor's new wife, Empress Laisa, was a Toscane heiress and a Komarran by birth, their political marriage of enormous importance to the peace of the fragile union of planets that was the Imperium. "The problem of how to satisfy my in-laws while simultaneously presenting the appearance of Imperial evenhandedness to all their Komarran commercial rivals—I leave to your ingenuity." Gregor's thin smile said it all.

"You know the drill. I request and require you, as my Voice, to get yourself to Graf Station with all safe speed and sort out the situation before it deteriorates further. Pry all my subjects out of the hands of the locals and get the fleet back on its way. Without starting a war, if you please, or breaking my Imperial budget.

"And, critically, find out who's lying. If it's the ImpSec observer, that's a problem to bounce to their chain of command. If it's the fleet commander—who is Admiral Eugin Vorpatril, by the way—it becomes . . . very much my problem."

Or rather, very much the problem of Gregor's proxy, his Emperor's Voice, his Imperial Auditor. Namely Miles. Miles considered the interesting pitfalls inherent in attempting, without backup, far from home, to arrest the ranking military officer out of the middle of his long-standing and possibly personally loyal command. A Vorpatril, too, scion of a Barrayaran aristocratic clan of far-flung and important political connections within the Council of Counts. Miles's own aunt and cousin were Vorpatrils. *Oh, thank you, Gregor.*

The Emperor continued, "In matters rather closer to Barrayar, something has stirred up the Cetagandans around Rho Ceta. No need to go into the peculiar details here, but I would appreciate it if you would settle this impoundment crisis as swiftly and efficiently as you can. If the Rho Cetan business becomes any more peculiar, I'll want you safely home. The communications lag between

Barrayar and Sector V is going to be too long for me to
breathe over your shoulder, but some occasional status or
progress reports from you would be a nice touch, if you
don't mind." Gregor's voice did not change to convey irony.
It didn't need to. Miles snorted. "Good luck," Gregor concluded. The image on the viewer returned to a mute display
of the Imperial Seal. Miles reached forward and keyed it
off. The detailed reports, he could study once he was en
route.

He? Or *we*?

He glanced up at Ekaterin's pale profile; she turned her
serious blue eyes toward him. He asked, "Do you want to
go with me, or continue on home?"

"*Can* I go with you?" she asked doubtfully.

"Of course you can! The only question is, would you like
to?"

Her dark brows rose. "Not the only question, surely. Do
you think I'd be of any use, or would I just be a distraction
from your work?"

"There's official use, and there's unofficial use. Don't bet
that the first is more important than the second. You know
the way people talk to you to try to get oblique messages to
me?"

"Oh, yes." Her lips twisted in distaste.

"Well, yes, I realize it's tedious, but you're very good at
sorting them out, you know. Not to mention the information to be obtained just from studying the kinds of lies
people tell. And, ah—not-lies. There may well be people
who will talk to you who won't talk to me, for one reason or
another."

She conceded the truth of this with a little wave of her
free hand.

"And . . . it would be a real relief for me to have someone along I can talk to freely."

Her smile tilted a little at this. "Talk, or vent?"

"I—hem!—suspect this one is going to entail quite a lot of venting, yes. D'you think you can stand it? It could get pretty thick. Not to mention boring."

"You know, you keep claiming your job is boring, Miles, but your eyes have gone all bright."

He cleared his throat and shrugged unrepentantly.

Her amusement faded, and her brows drew down. "How long do you think this sorting out will take?"

He considered the calculation she had doubtless just made. It would be six more weeks, give or take a few days, to the scheduled births. Their original travel plan would have put them back at Vorkosigan House a comfortable month early. Sector V was in the opposite direction from their present location to Barrayar, insofar as the network of jump points people navigated to get from *here* to *there* could be said to have a direction. Several days to get from here to Graf Station, plus an extra two weeks of travel at least to get home from there, even in the fastest of fast couriers. "If I can settle things in less than two weeks, we can both get home on time."

She breathed a short laugh. "For all that I try to be all modern and galactic, that feels so strange. All sorts of men don't make it home for the births of their children. But *My mother was out of town on the day I was born, so she missed it*, just seems . . . seems like a more profound complaint, somehow."

"If it runs over, I suppose I could send you home on your own, with a suitable escort. But I want to be there, too." He hesitated. *It's my first time, dammit, of course it's making me crazy,* was a statement of the obvious that he managed to stop on his lips. Her first marriage had left her riddled with sensitive scars, none of them physical, and this topic trod near several of them. *Rephrase, O Diplomat.* "Does it . . . make it any easier, that it's the second time, for you?"

Her expression grew introspective. "Nikki was a body birth; of course everything was harder. The replicators take away so many risks—our children could get all their genetic mistakes corrected, they won't be subject to damage from a bad birth—I know replicator gestation is better, more responsible, in every way. It's not as though they are being *shortchanged*. And yet . . ."

He raised her hand and touched her knuckles to his lips. "You're not shortchanging *me*, I promise you."

Miles's own mother was adamantly in favor of the use of replicators, with cause. He was reconciled now, at age thirty-odd, with the physical damage he had taken in her womb from the soltoxin attack. Only his emergency transfer to a replicator had saved his life. The teratogenic military poison had left him stunted and brittle-boned, but a childhood's agony of medical treatments had brought him to nearly full function, if not, alas, full height. Most of his bones had been replaced piecemeal with synthetics thereafter, emphasis on the *pieces*. The rest of the damage, he conceded, was all his own doing. That he was still alive seemed less a miracle than that he had won Ekaterin's heart. *Their* children would not suffer such traumas.

He added, "And if you think you're having it too luxuriously easy now to feel properly virtuous, why, just wait till they get *out* of those replicators."

She laughed. "Very good point!"

"Well." He sighed. "I'd intended this trip to show you the glories of the galaxy, in the most elegant and refined society. It appears I'm heading instead to what I suspect is the armpit of Sector V, and the company of a bunch of squabbling, frantic merchants, irate bureaucrats, and paranoid militarists. Life is full of surprises. Come with me, my love? For my sanity's sake?"

Her eyes narrowed in amusement. "How can I resist such an invitation? Of course I will." She sobered. "Would it violate security for me to send a message to Nikki telling him we'll be late?"

"Not at all. Send it from the *Kestrel*, though. It'll get through faster."

She nodded. "I've never been away from him so long before. I wonder if he's been lonely?"

Nikki had been left, on Ekaterin's side of the family, with four uncles and a great-uncle plus matching aunts, a herd of cousins, a small army of friends, and his Grandmother Vorsoisson. On Miles's side were Vorkosigan House's extensive staff and their extensive families, with Uncle Ivan and Uncle Mark and the whole Koudelka clan for backup. Impending were his doting Vorkosigan step-grandparents, who had planned to arrive after Miles and Ekaterin for the birthday bash, but who now might beat them home. Ekaterin might have to travel *ahead* to Barrayar, if he couldn't cut through this mess in a timely fashion, but by no rational definition of the word, *alone*.

"I don't see how," said Miles honestly. "I expect you miss him more than he misses us. Or he'd have managed more than that one monosyllabic note that didn't catch up with us till Earth. Eleven-year-old boys can be pretty self-centered. I'm sure *I* was."

Her brows rose. "Oh? And how many notes have you sent to *your* mother in the past two months?"

"It's a *honeymoon* trip. Nobody expects you to . . . Anyway, she's always gotten to see the reports from my security."

The brows stayed up. He added prudently, "I'll drop her a message from the *Kestrel* too."

He was rewarded with a League of Mothers smile. Come to think of it, perhaps he would include his father in the address as well, not that his parents didn't share his missives. And complain coequally about their rarity.

An hour of mild chaos completed their transfer to the Barrayaran Imperial courier ship. Fast couriers gained most of their speed by trading off carrying capacity. Miles was forced to divest all but their most essential luggage. The considerable remainder, along with a startling volume of souvenirs, would continue the journey back to Barrayar with most of their little entourage: Ekaterin's personal maid, Miss Pym, and, to Miles's greater regret, both of Roic's relief armsmen. It occurred to him belatedly, as he and Ekaterin fitted themselves into their new shared cabin, that he ought to have mentioned how cramped their quarters would be. He'd traveled on similar vessels so often during his own years in ImpSec, he took their limitations for granted—one of the few aspects of his former career where his undersized body had worked to his advantage.

So while he did spend the remainder of the day in bed with his wife after all, it was primarily due to the absence of other seating. They folded back the upper bunk for head space and sat up on opposite ends, Ekaterin to read quietly from a hand viewer, Miles to plunge into Gregor's promised Pandora's box of reports from the diplomatic front.

He wasn't five minutes into this study before he uttered a *Ha!*

Ekaterin indicated her willingness to be interrupted by looking up at him with a reciprocal *Hm?*

"I just figured out why Graf Station sounded familiar. We're headed for Quaddiespace, by God."

"Quaddiespace? Is that someplace you've been before?"

"Not personally, no." This was going to take more politic preparation than he'd anticipated. "Although I actually met a quaddie once. The quaddies are a race of bioengineered humans developed, oh, two or three hundred years ago. Before Barrayar was rediscovered. They were supposed to be permanent free fall dwellers. Whatever their creators' original plan for them was, it fell through when the new grav technologies came in, and they ended up as sort of economic refugees. After assorted travels and adventures, they finally settled as a group in what was at the time the far end of the wormhole Nexus. They were wary of other people by then, so they deliberately picked a system with no habitable planets, but with considerable asteroid and cometary resources. Planning to keep themselves to themselves, I guess. Of course, the explored Nexus has grown around them since then, so now they get some foreign exchange by servicing ships and providing transfer facilities. Which explains why our fleet came to be docked there, although not what happened afterwards. The, ah . . ." He hesitated. "The bioengineering included a lot of metabolic changes, but the most spectacular alteration was, they have a second set of arms where their legs should be. Which is really, um, handy in free fall. So to speak. I've often wished I'd had a couple of extra hands, when I was operating in vacuum."

He passed the viewer across and displayed the shot of a quaddie, dressed in bright yellow shorts and a singlet, handing himself along a gravity-less corridor with the speed and agility of a monkey navigating through treetops.

"*Oh*," gulped Ekaterin, then quickly regained control of her features. "How, uh . . . interesting." After a moment she added, "It does look quite practical, for their environment."

Miles relaxed a trifle. Whatever her buried Barrayaran reflexes were regarding visible mutations, they would be trumped by her iron grip on good manners.

The same, unfortunately, did not appear to be true of their fellow members of the Imperium now stranded in the quaddies' system. The difference between deleterious mutation and benign or advantageous modification was not readily grasped by Barrayarans from the backcountry. Given that one officer referred to them as *horrible spider mutants* right in his report, it was clear that Miles could add racial tensions to the mix of complications they were now racing toward.

"You get used to them pretty quickly," he reassured her.

"Where did you meet one, if they keep to themselves?"

"Um . . ." Some quick internal editing, here . . . "It was on an ImpSec mission. I can't talk about it. But she was a musician, of all things. Played the hammer dulcimer with all four arms." His attempt to mime this remarkable sight resulted in his banging his elbow painfully on the cabin wall. "Her name was Nicol. You would have liked her. We got her out of a tight spot. I wonder if she ever made it home?" He rubbed his elbow and added hopefully, "I'll bet the quaddies' free-fall gardening techniques would interest you."

Ekaterin brightened. "Yes, indeed."

Miles returned to his reports with the uncomfortable certainty that this was not going to be a good task to plunge into underprepared. He mentally added a review of quad-die history to his list of studies for the next few days.

Chapter 2

"Is my collar straight?"

Ekaterin's cool fingers made businesslike work upon the back of Miles's neck; he concealed the shiver down his spine. "Now it is," she said.

"Clothes make the Auditor," he muttered. The little cabin lacked such amenities as a full-length mirror; he had to use his wife's eyes instead. This did not seem a disadvantage. She stepped back as far as she could, a half-pace to the bulkhead, and looked him up and down to check the effect of his Vorkosigan House uniform: brown tunic with his family crest in silver thread upon the high collar, silver-embroidered cuffs, brown trousers with silver side piping, tall brown riding boots. The Vor class had been cavalry soldiers, in their heyday. No horse within God knew how many light-years now, that was certain.

He touched his wrist com, mate in function to the one she wore, though hers was made Vor-lady-like with a decorative silver bracelet. "I'll give you a heads-up when I'm ready to come back and change." He nodded toward the plain gray suit she'd already laid out on the bunk. A uniform for the military-minded, civvies for the civilians. And let the weight of Barrayaran history, eleven generations of Counts Vorkosigan at his back, make up for his lack of height, his faintly hunched stance. His less visible defects, he didn't need to mention.

"What should I wear?"

"Since you'll have to play the whole entourage, something effective." He smiled crookedly. "That red silk thing ought to be distractingly civilian enough for our Stationer hosts."

"Only the male half, love," she pointed out. "Suppose their security chief is a female quaddie? Are quaddies even attracted to downsiders?"

"One was, apparently," he sighed. "Hence this mess. . . . Parts of Graf Station are null-gee, so you'll likely want trousers or leggings instead of Barrayaran-style skirts. Something you can move in."

"Oh. Yes, I see."

A knock sounded at the cabin door, and Armsman Roic's diffident voice, "My lord?"

"On my way, Roic." Miles and Ekaterin exchanged places—finding himself at her chest height, he stole a pleasantly resilient hug in passing—and he exited to the courier ship's narrow corridor.

Roic wore a slightly plainer version of Miles's Vorkosigan House uniform, as befitted his liege-sworn armsman's status. "Do you want me to pack up your things now for transfer to the Barrayaran flagship, m'lord?" he asked.

"No. We're going to stay aboard the courier."

Roic almost managed to conceal his wince. He was a young man of imposing height and intimidating breadth of shoulder, and had described his bunk above the courier ship's engineer as *Sort of like sleeping in a coffin, m'lord, except for the snoring.*

Miles added, "I don't care to hand off control of my movements, not to mention my air supply, to either side in this squabble just yet. The flagship's bunks aren't much bigger anyway, I assure you, Armsman."

Roic smiled ruefully, and shrugged. "I'm afraid you should've brought Jankowski, sir."

"What, because he's shorter?"

"No, m'lord!" Roic looked faintly indignant. "Because he's a real veteran."

A Count of Barrayar was limited by law to a bodyguard of a score of sworn men; the Vorkosigans had by tradition recruited most of their armsmen from retiring twenty-year veterans of the Imperial Service. By political need, in the last decades they'd mostly been former ImpSec men. They were a keen but graying bunch. Roic was an interesting new exception.

"When did that become a concern?" Miles's father's cadre of armsmen treated Roic as a junior because he was, but if they were treating him as a second-class citizen . . .

"Eh . . ." Roic waved somewhat inarticulately around the courier ship, by which Miles construed that the problem lay in more recent encounters.

Miles, about to lead off down the short corridor, instead leaned against the wall and folded his arms. "Look, Roic—there's scarcely a man in the Imperial Service your age or younger who's faced as much live fire in the Emperor's employ as you have in the Hassadar Municipal Guard. Don't let the damned green uniforms spook you. It's empty swagger. Half of 'em would fall over in a faint if they were asked to take down someone like that murderous lunatic who shot up Hassadar Square."

"I was already halfway across the plaza, m'lord. It would've been like swimming halfway across a river, deciding you couldn't make it, and turning around to swim back. It was *safer* to jump him than to turn and run. He'd 'a had the same amount of time to take aim at me either way."

"But not the time to take out another dozen or so bystanders. Auto-needler's a filthy weapon." Miles brooded briefly.

"That it is, m'lord."

For all his height, Roic tended to shyness when he felt himself to be socially outclassed, which unfortunately seemed to be much of the time in the Vorkosigans' service. Since the shyness showed on his surface mainly as a sort of dull stolidity, it tended to get overlooked.

"You're a Vorkosigan armsman," said Miles firmly. "The ghost of General Piotr is woven into that brown and silver. They'll be spooked by *you*, I promise you."

Roic's brief smile conveyed more gratitude than conviction. "Wish I could've met your grandfather, m'lord. From all the tales they told of him back in the District, he was quite something. My great-grandfather served with him in the mountains during the Cetagandan Occupation, m'mother says."

"Ah! Did she have any good stories about him?"

Roic shrugged. "He died of t' radiation after Vorkosigan Vashnoi was destroyed. M'grandmother would never talk about him much, so I don't know."

"Pity."

Lieutenant Smolyani poked his head around the corner. "We're locked on to the *Prince Xav* now, Lord Auditor Vorkosigan. Transfer tube's sealed and they're ready for you to board."

"Very good, Lieutenant."

Miles followed Roic, who had to duck his head through the oval doorway, into the courier's cramped personnel hatch bay. Smolyani took up station by the hatch controls. The control pad twinkled and beeped; the door slid open onto the airlock and the flex tube, beyond it. Miles nodded to Roic, who took a visible breath and swung himself through. Smolyani braced to a salute; Miles returned him an acknowledging nod and a "Thank you, Lieutenant," and followed Roic.

A meter of stomach-lifting zero-gee in the flex tube ended at a similar hatchway. Miles grasped the handgrips and swung himself through and smoothly to his feet in the open airlock. He stepped from it into a very much more spacious hatch bay. On his left, Roic loomed formally, awaiting him. The flagship's door slid closed behind him.

Before him, three green-uniformed men and a civilian stood stiffly to attention. Not one of them changed expression at Miles's un-Barrayaran physique. Presumably Vorpatril, whom Miles barely recalled from a few passing encounters in Vorbarr Sultana's capital scene, remembered him more vividly, and had prudently briefed his staff on the mutoid appearance of Emperor Gregor's shortest, not to mention youngest and newest, Voice.

Admiral Eugin Vorpatril was of middle height, stocky, white-haired, and grim. He stepped forward and gave Miles a crisp and proper salute. "My Lord Auditor. Welcome aboard the *Prince Xav.*"

"Thank you, Admiral." He did not add *Happy to be here*; no one in this group could be happy to see him, under the circumstances.

Vorpatril continued, "May I introduce my Fleet Security commander, Captain Brun."

The lean, tense man, possibly even grimmer than his admiral, nodded curtly. Brun had been in operational charge of the ill-fated patrol whose hair-trigger exploits had blown the situation from minor legal brangle to major diplomatic incident. No, not happy at all.

"Senior Cargomaster Molino of the Komarran fleet consortium."

Molino too was middle-aged, and quite as dyspeptic-looking as the Barrayarans, though dressed in neat dark Komarran-style tunic and trousers. A senior cargomaster was the ranking executive and financial officer of the limited-term corporate entity that was a commercial convoy, and as such bore most of the responsibilities of a fleet admiral with a fraction of the powers. He also had the unenviable task of being the designated interface between a potentially very disparate bunch of commercial interests, and their Barrayaran military protectors, which was usually enough to account for dyspepsia even without a crisis. He murmured a polite, "My Lord Vorkosigan."

Vorpatril's tone took on a slightly gritty quality. "My fleet legal officer, Ensign Deslaurier."

Tall Deslaurier, pale and wan beneath a lingering touch of adolescent acne, managed a nod.

Miles blinked in surprise. When, under his old covert ops identity, he had run a supposedly independent mercenary fleet for ImpSec's galactic operations, Fleet Legal had been a major department; just negotiating the peaceful passage of armed ships through all the varied local space legal jurisdictions had been a full-time job of nightmarish complexity. "Ensign." Miles returned the nod, and chose his wording carefully. "You, ah . . . would seem to have a considerable responsibility, for your rank and age."

Deslaurier cleared his throat, and said in a nearly inaudible voice, "Our department chief was sent home earlier in the voyage, my Lord Auditor. Compassionate leave. His mother'd died."

I think I'm getting the drift of this already. "This your first galactic voyage, by chance?"

"Yes, my lord."

Vorpatril put in, possibly mercifully, "I and my staff are entirely at your disposal, my Lord Auditor, and are ready with our reports as you requested. Would you care to follow me to our briefing room?"

"Yes, thank you, Admiral."

Some shuffling and ducking through the corridors brought the party to a standard military briefing room: bolted-down holovid-equipped table and station chairs, friction matting underfoot harboring the faint musty odor of a sealed and gloomy chamber that never enjoyed sunlight or fresh air. The place *smelled* military. Miles suppressed the urge to take a long, nostalgic inhalation, for old times' sake. At his hand signal, Roic took up an impassive guard's stance just inside the door. The rest waited for him to seat himself, then disposed themselves around the table, Vorpatril on his left, Deslaurier as far away as possible.

Vorpatril, displaying a clear understanding of the etiquette of the situation, or at least some sense of self-preservation, began, "So. How may we serve you, my Lord Auditor?"

Miles tented his hands on the table. "I am an Auditor; my first task is to listen. If you please, Admiral Vorpatril, describe for me the course of events from your point of view. How did you arrive at this impasse?"

"From my point of view?" Vorpatril grimaced. "It started out seeming no more than the usual one damned thing after another. We were supposed to be in dock here at Graf Station for five days, for contracted cargo and passenger transfers. Since there was no reason at that time to think that the quaddies were hostile, I granted as many station leaves as possible, which is standard procedure."

Miles nodded. The purposes of Barrayaran military escorts for Komarran ships ranged from overt to subtle to never-spoken. Overtly, escorts rode along to repel hijackers from the cargo vessels and supply the military part of the fleet with maneuvering experience scarcely less valuable than war games. More subtly, the ventures provided opportunity for all sorts of intelligence gathering—economic, political, and social, as well as military. And it provided cadres of young provincial Barrayaran men, future officers and future civilians, with seasoning contact with the wider galactic culture. On the never-spoken side were the lingering tensions between Barrayarans and Komarrans, legacy of the, in Miles's view, fully justified conquest of the latter by the former a generation ago. It was the Emperor's express policy to move from a stance of occupation to one of full political and social assimilation between the two planets. That process was proving slow and rocky.

Vorpatril continued, "The Toscane Corporation's ship *Idris* put into dock for jump drive adjustments, and ran into unexpected complications when they pulled things apart. Repaired parts failed to pass calibration tests when reinstalled and were sent back to the Station shops for refabrication. Five days became ten, while that bickering was going back and forth. Then Lieutenant Solian turned up missing."

"Do I understand correctly that the lieutenant was the Barrayaran security liaison officer aboard the *Idris*?" Miles said. Fleet beat cop, charged with maintaining peace and order among crew and passengers, keeping an eye out for any illegal or threatening activities or suspicious persons—not a few historic hijackings were inside jobs—and being first line of defense in counterintelligence. More quietly, keeping an ear out for potential disaffection among the Emperor's Komarran subjects. Obliged to render all possible assistance to the ship in physical emergencies, coordinating evacuation or rescue with the military escort. Liaison officer was a job that could shift from yawningly boring to lethally demanding in an eyeblink.

Captain Brun spoke for the first time. "Yes, my lord."

Miles turned to him. "One of your people, was he? How would you describe Lieutenant Solian?"

"He was newly assigned," Brun answered, then hesitated. "I did not have a close personal acquaintance with him, but all his prior personnel evaluations gave him high marks."

Miles glanced at the cargomaster. "Did you know him, sir?"

"We met a few times," said Molino. "I mostly stayed aboard the *Rudra*, but my impression of him was that he was friendly and competent. He seemed to get along well with crew and passengers. Quite the walking advertisement for assimilation."

"Excuse me?"

Vorpatril cleared his throat. "Solian was Komarran, my lord."

"Ah." *Argh.* The reports hadn't mentioned this wrinkle. Komarrans were but lately permitted admittance into the Barrayaran Imperial Service; the first generation of such officers was handpicked, and on their marks to prove their loyalty and competence. *The Emperor's pets*, Miles had heard at least one Barrayaran fellow-officer describe them in covert disgruntlement. The success of this integration was a high personal priority of Gregor's. Admiral Vorpatril certainly knew it, too. Miles moved the mysterious fate of Solian up a few notches in his mental list of most-urgent priorities.

"What were the circumstances of his original disappearance?"

Brun answered, "Very quiet, my lord. He signed off-shift in the usual manner, and never showed up for his next watch. When his cabin was finally checked, it seemed that some of his personal effects and a valise were missing, although most of his uniforms were left. There was no record of his finally leaving the ship, but then . . . he'd know how to get out without being seen if anyone could. Which is why I posit desertion. The ship was very thoroughly searched after that. He has to have altered the records, or slipped out with the cargo, or *something*."

"Any sense that he was unhappy in his work or place?"

"Not—no, my lord. Nothing special."

"Anything not special?"

"Well, there was the usual chronic chaff about being a Komarran in this"—Brun gestured at himself—"uniform. I suppose, where he was placed, he was in position to get it from both sides."

We're trying to all be one side, now. Miles decided this was not the time or place to pursue the unconscious assumptions behind Brun's word-choice. "Cargomaster Molino—do you have any sidelights on this? Was Solian subject to, ah, reproof from his fellow Komarrans?"

Molino shook his head. "The man seemed to be well liked by the crew of the *Idris* as far as I could tell. Stuck to business, didn't get into arguments."

"Nevertheless, I gather that your first . . . impression, was that he had deserted?"

"It seemed possible," Brun admitted. "I'm not casting aspersions, but he *was* Komarran. Maybe he'd found it tougher than he thought it would be. Admiral Vorpatril disagreed," he added scrupulously.

Vorpatril waved a hand in a gesture of judicious balance. "The more reason not to think desertion. High command's been pretty careful of what Komarrans they admit to the Service. They don't want public failures."

"In any case," said Brun, "we put all our own security people on alert to search for him, and asked for help from the Graf Station authorities. Which they were not especially eager to offer. They just kept repeating they'd had no sign of him in either the gravity or null-gee sections, and no record of anyone of his description leaving the station on their local-space carriers."

"And then what happened?"

Admiral Vorpatril answered, "Time ran on. Repairs on the *Idris* were completed and signed off. Pressure," he eyed Molino without favor, "grew to leave Graf Station and continue on the planned route. Me—I don't leave my men behind if I can help it."

Molino said, rather through his teeth, "It made no economic sense to tie up the entire fleet over one man. You might have left one light vessel or even a small team of investigators to pursue the matter, to follow on when they were concluded, and let the rest continue."

"I also have standing orders not to split the fleet," said Vorpatril, his jaw tightening.

"But we haven't suffered a hijacking attempt in this sector for decades," argued Molino. Miles felt he was witnessing round n-plus-one of an ongoing debate.

"Not since Barrayar began providing you with free military escorts," said Vorpatril, with false cordiality. "Odd coincidence, that." His voice grew firmer. "I don't leave my men. I swore *that* at the Escobar debacle, back when *I* was a milk-faced ensign." He glanced at Miles. "Under your father's command, as it happened."

Uh-oh. This could be trouble. . . . Miles let his brows climb in curiosity. "What was your experience there, sir?"

Vorpatril snorted reminiscently. "I was a junior pilot on a combat drop shuttle, orphaned when our mothership was blown to hell by the Escos in high orbit. I suppose if we'd made it back during the retreat, we'd have been blown up with her, but still. Nowhere to dock, nowhere to run, even the few surviving ships that had an open docking cradle not pausing for us, a couple of hundred men on board including wounded—it was a right nightmare, let me tell you."

Miles felt the admiral had barely clipped off a "son," at the end of that last sentence.

Miles said cautiously, "I'm not sure Admiral Vorkosigan had much choice left, by the time he inherited command of the invasion after the death of Prince Serg."

"Oh, none at all," Vorpatril agreed, with another wave of his hand. "I'm not saying the man didn't do all he could with what he had. But he couldn't do it all, and I was among those sacrificed. Spent almost a year in an Escobaran prison camp, before the negotiators finally got me mustered home. The Escobarans didn't make it a holiday for us, I can tell you that."

It could have been worse. You might have been a female Escobaran prisoner of war in one of our *camps.* Miles decided not to suggest this exercise of the imagination to the admiral just now. "I would expect not."

"All I'm saying is, I know what it is to be abandoned, and I won't do it to men of mine for any trivial reason." His narrow glance at the cargomaster made it clear that evaporating Komarran corporate profits did not qualify as a weighty enough reason for this violation of principle. "Events proved—" He hesitated, and rephrased himself. "For a time, I thought events had proved me right."

"For a time," Miles echoed. "Not any more?"

"Now . . . well . . . what happened next was pretty . . . pretty disturbing. There was an unauthorized cycling of a personnel airlock in the Graf Station cargo bay next to where the *Idris* was locked on. No ship or personnel pod was sighted at it, however—the tube seals weren't activated. By the time the Station security guard got there, the bay was empty. But there was a quantity of blood on the floor, and signs of something dragged to the lock. The blood came up on testing as Solian's. It looked like he was trying to make it back to the *Idris,* and someone jumped him."

"Someone who didn't leave footprints," added Brun darkly.

At Miles's inquiring look, Vorpatril explained, "In the gravitational areas where the downsiders stay, the quaddies buzz around in these little personal floaters. They operate 'em with their lower hands, leaving their upper arms free. No footprints. No feet, for that matter."

"Ah, yes. I understand," said Miles. "Blood, but no body—has a body been found?"

"Not yet," said Brun.

"Searched for?"

"Oh, yes. In all the possible trajectories."

"I suppose it's occurred to you that a deserter might try to fake his own murder or suicide, to free himself from pursuit."

"I might have thought that," said Brun, "but I saw the loading bay floor. No one could lose that much blood and live. There must have been three or four liters at least."

Miles shrugged. "The first step in emergency cryonic prep is to exsanguinate the patient and replace his blood with cryo-fluid. That can easily leave several liters of blood on the floor, and the victim—well, potentially alive." He'd had close personal experience of the process, or so Elli Quinn and Bel Thorne had told him afterward, on that Dendarii Free Mercenary mission that had gone so disastrously wrong. Granted, he didn't remember that part, except through Bel's extremely vivid description.

Brun's brows flicked up. "I hadn't thought of that."

"It rather sprang to my mind," said Miles apologetically. *I could show you the scars.*

Brun frowned, then shook his head. "I don't think there would have been time before Station security arrived on the scene."

"Even if a portable cryochamber was standing ready?"

Brun opened his mouth, then closed it again. He finally said, "It's a complicated scenario, my lord."

"I don't insist on it," said Miles easily. He considered the other end of the cryo-revival process. "Except that I'd also point out that there are other sources of several liters of nice fresh one's-own-personal blood besides a victim's body. Such as a revival lab's or hospital's synthesizer. The product would certainly light up a cursory DNA scan. You couldn't even call it a false positive, exactly. A bio-forensics lab could tell the difference, though. Traces of cryo-fluid would be obvious, too, if only someone thought to look for them." He added wistfully, "I hate circumstantial evidence. Who ran the identification check on the blood?"

Brun shifted uncomfortably. "The quaddies. We'd downloaded Solian's DNA scan to them when he first went missing. But the security liaison officer from the *Rudra* had gone over by then—he was right there in the bay watching their tech. He reported the match to me as soon as the analyzer beeped. That's when I podded across to look at it all myself."

"Did he collect another sample to cross-check?"

"I . . . believe so. I can ask the fleet surgeon if he received one before, um, other events overtook us."

Admiral Vorpatril sat looking unpleasantly stunned. "I thought certainly poor Solian was murdered. By some—" He fell silent.

"It doesn't sound as though that hypothesis is ruled out either, yet," Miles consoled him. "In any case, you honestly believed it at the time. Have your fleet surgeon examine his samples more thoroughly, please, and report to me."

"And to Graf Station Security, too?"

"Ah . . . maybe not them yet." Even if the results were negative, the query would only serve to stir up more quaddie suspicions about Barrayarans. And if they were positive . . . Miles wanted to think about that first. "At any rate, what happened next?"

"That Solian was himself Fleet Security made his murder—apparent murder—seem especially sinister," Vorpatril admitted. "Had he been trying to get back with some warning? We couldn't tell. So I canceled all leaves, went to alert status, and ordered all ships to detach from dockside."

"With no explanation of *why*," put in Molino.

Vorpatril glowered at him. "During an alert, a commander does not stop to explain orders. He expects to be instantly obeyed. Besides, the way you people had been champing at the bit, complaining about the delays, I hardly thought I'd *need* to repeat myself." A muscle jumped in his jaw; he inhaled and returned to his narrative. "At this point, we suffered something of a communications breakdown."

Here comes the smokescreen, at last.

"*Our* understanding was that a two-man security patrol, sent to retrieve an officer who was late reporting in—"

"That would be Ensign Corbeau?"

"Yes. Corbeau. As we understood it at the time, the patrol and the ensign were attacked, disarmed, and detained by quaddies. The real story as it emerged later was more complex, but that was what I had to go on as I was trying to clear Graf Station of all our personnel and stand off for any contingency up to immediate evacuation from local space."

Miles leaned forward. "Did you believe it to be random quaddies who had seized your men, or did you understand it to have been Graf Station Security?"

Vorpatril didn't quite grind his teeth, but almost. He answered nonetheless, "Yes, we knew it was their security."

"Did you ask your legal officer to advise you?"

"No."

"Did Ensign Deslaurier volunteer advice?"

"No, my lord," Deslaurier managed to whisper.

"I see. Go on."

"I ordered Captain Brun to send a strike patrol in to retrieve, now, three men from a situation that I believed had just proved lethally dangerous to Barrayaran personnel."

"Armed with rather more than stunners, I understand?"

"I couldn't ask my men to go up against those numbers with only stunners, my lord," said Brun. "There are a *million* of those mutants out there!"

Miles let his brows climb. "On Graf Station? I thought its resident population was around fifty thousand. Civilians."

Brun made an impatient gesture. "A million to twelve, fifty thousand to twelve—regardless, they needed weapons with authority. My rescue party needed to get in and out as quickly as possible, having to deal with as little argument or resistance as possible. Stunners are useless as weapons of intimidation."

"I am familiar with the argument." Miles leaned back and rubbed his lips. "Go on."

"My patrol reached the place our men were being held—"

"Graf Station Security Post Number Three, was it not?" Miles put in.

"Yes."

"Tell me—in all the time since the fleet has been here, hadn't any of your men on leave had close encounters with Station Security? No drunk and disorderlies, no safety violations, nothing?"

Brun, looking as though the words were being pulled from his mouth with dental pliers, said, "Three men were arrested by Graf Station Security last week for racing float chairs in an unsafe manner while inebriated."

"And what happened to them? How did your fleet legal advisor handle it?"

Ensign Deslaurier muttered, "They spent a few hours in lock-up, then I went down and saw that their fines were paid, and pledged to the stationer adjudicator that they would be confined to quarters for the duration of our stay."

"So you were all by then familiar with standard procedures for retrieving men from contretemps with Station authorities?"

"These were not drunk and disorderlies this time. These were our own security forces carrying out their duties," said Vorpatril.

"Go on," sighed Miles. "What happened with your patrol?"

"I still don't have their own firsthand reports, my lord," said Brun stiffly. "The quaddies have only let one unarmed medical officer visit them in their current place of confinement. Shots were exchanged, both stunner and plasma fire, inside Security Post Three. Quaddies swarmed the place, and our men were overwhelmed and taken prisoner."

The "swarming" quaddies had included, not unnaturally in Miles's view, most of the Graf Station professional and volunteer fire brigades. *Plasma fire. In a civilian space station. Oh, my aching head.*

"So," said Miles gently, "after we shot up the police station and set the habitat on fire, what did we do for an encore?"

Admiral Vorpatril's teeth set, briefly. "I am afraid that, when the Komarran ships in dock failed to obey my urgent orders to cast off and instead allowed themselves to be locked down, I lost the initiative in the situation. Too many hostages had passed into quaddie control by then, the Komarran independent captain-owners were entirely laggard in obeying my position orders, and the quaddies' own militia, such as it is, was allowed to move into position around us. We froze in a standoff for almost two full days. Then we were ordered to stand down and wait your arrival."

Thank all the gods for that. Military intelligence was as nothing to military stupidity. But to slide halfway to stupid and *stop* was rare indeed. Vorpatril deserved some credit for that, at least.

Brun put in glumly, "Not much choice at that point. It's not as though we could threaten to blow up the station with our own ships in dock."

"You couldn't blow up the station in any case," Miles pointed out mildly. "It would be mass murder. Not to mention a criminal order. The Emperor would have you shot."

Brun flinched and subsided.

Vorpatril's lips thinned. "The Emperor, or you?"

"Gregor and I would flip a coin to see who got to go first."

A little silence fell.

"Fortunately," Miles continued, "it appears heads have cooled all round. For that, Admiral Vorpatril, I do thank you. I might add, the fates of your respective careers are a matter between you and your Ops command." *Unless you manage to make me late for the births of my very first children, in which case you'd better start looking for a deep, deep hole.* "*My* job is to talk out as many of the Emperor's subjects from quaddie hands, at the lowest prices, as I can. If I'm really lucky, when I'm done our trade fleets may be able to dock here again someday. You have not given me an especially strong hand of cards to play, here, unfortunately. Nonetheless, I'll see what I can do. I want copies of all raw transcripts pertaining to these late events provided for my review, please."

"Yes, my lord," growled Vorpatril. "But," his voice grew almost anguished, "that still doesn't tell me what happened to Lieutenant Solian!"

"I will undertake to give that question my keenest attention as well, Admiral." Miles met his eyes. "I promise you."

Vorpatril nodded shortly.

"But, Lord Auditor Vorkosigan!" Cargomaster Molino put in urgently. "Graf Station authorities are trying to fine our *Komarran* vessels for the damage done by *Barrayaran* troops. It must be made plain to them that the military stands alone in this . . . criminal activity."

Miles hesitated a long moment. "How fortunate for you, Cargomaster," he said at last, "that in the event of a genuine attack, the reverse would not be true." He tapped the table and rose to his feet.

Chapter 3

Miles stood on tiptoe to peer through the little port beside the *Kestrel's* personnel hatch as the ship maneuvered toward its assigned docking cradle. Graf Station was a vast jumbled aggregation, an apparent chaos of design not surprising in an installation in its third century of expansion. Somewhere buried in the core of the sprawling, bristling structure was a small metallic asteroid, honeycombed for both space and the material used in building this very oldest of the quaddies' many habitats. Also somewhere in its innermost sections could still be seen, according to the guidevids, actual elements from the broken-apart and reconfigured jumpship in which the initial band of hardy quaddie pioneers had made their historic voyage to this refuge.

Miles stepped back and gestured Ekaterin to the port for a look. He reflected on the political astrography of Quaddiespace, or rather, as it was formally designated, the Union of Free Habitats. From this initial point, quaddie groups had leapfrogged out to build daughter colonies in both

directions along the inner of the two rings of asteroids that
had made this system so attractive to their ancestors. Several generations and a million strong later, the quaddies
were in no danger whatsoever of running out of space,
energy, or materials. Their population could expand as fast
as it chose to build.

Only a handful of their many scattered habitats maintained areas supplied with artificial gravity for legged
humans, either visitor or resident, or even dealt with outsiders. Graf Station was one that did accept galactics and
their trade, as did the orbital arcologies dubbed Metropoli-
tan, Sanctuary, Minchenko, and Union Station. This last
was the seat of Quaddie government, such as it was; a vari-
ant of bottom-up representative democracy based, Miles
was given to understand, on the work gang as its primary
unit. He hoped to God he wasn't going to end up negotiating with a committee.

Ekaterin glanced around and, with an excited smile,
motioned Roic to take a turn. He ducked his head and
nearly pressed his nose to the port, staring in open curiosity. This was Ekaterin's first trip outside the Barrayaran
Empire, and Roic's first venture off Barrayar ever. Miles
paused to thank his habits of mild paranoia that before he'd
dragged them off world he'd troubled to send them both
through a short intensive course in space and free fall procedures and safety. He'd pulled rank and strings to get
access to the military academy facilities, albeit on a free
week between scheduled classes, for a tailored version of
the longer course that Roic's older armsmen colleagues had
received routinely in their former Imperial Service
training.

Ekaterin had been extremely startled when Miles had
invited—persuaded—well, hustled—her to join the

bodyguard in the orbital school: daunted at first, exhausted and close to mutiny partway through, proud and elated at the finish. For passenger liners in pressurization trouble, it was the usual method to stuff their paying customers into simple bubbles called bod pods to passively await rescue. Miles had been stuck in a bod pod a time or two himself. He'd sworn that no man, and most especially no wife, of his would ever be rendered so artificially helpless in an emergency. His whole party had traveled with their own personally tailored quick-donning suits at hand. Regretfully, Miles had left his old customized battle armor in storage. . . .

Roic unbent from the port, looking especially stoic, faint vertical lines of worry between his eyebrows.

Miles asked, "Has everyone had their antinausea pills?"

Roic nodded earnestly.

Ekaterin said, "Have you had *yours*?"

"Oh, yes." He glanced down his plain gray civilian tunic and trousers. "I used to have this nifty bio-chip on my vagus nerve that kept me from losing my lunch in free fall, but it got blown out with the rest of my guts in that unpleasant encounter with the needle-grenade. I should get it replaced one of these days. . . ." Miles stepped forward and took one more glance outside. The station had grown to occlude most of the view. "So, Roic. If some quaddies visiting Hassadar made themselves obnoxious enough to win a visit to the Municipal Guard's gaol, and then a bunch more quaddies popped up and tried to bust them out with military-grade weapons, and shot up the place and torched it and burned some of your comrades, just how would you feel about quaddies at that point?"

"Um . . . not too friendly, m'lord." Roic paused. "Pretty pissed, actually."

"That's what I figured." Miles sighed. "Ah. Here we go."

Clanks and thumps sounded as the *Kestrel* came gently to rest and the docking clamps felt their way to a firm grip. The flex tube whined, seeking its seal, guided by the *Kestrel*'s engineer at the hatch controls, and then seated itself with an audible chink. "All tight, sir," the engineer reported.

"All right, troops, we're on parade," Miles murmured, and waved Roic on.

The bodyguard nodded and slipped through the hatch; after a moment he called back, "Ready, m'lord."

All was, if not well, good enough. Miles followed through the flex tube, Ekaterin close behind him. He stole a glance over his shoulder as he floated forward. She was svelte and arresting in the red tunic and black leggings, her hair in a sophisticated braid around her head. Zero gee had a charming effect on well-developed female anatomy that he decided he had probably better not point out to her. As an opening move, setting this first meeting in the null-gee section of Graf Station was clearly calculated to put the visitors off balance, to emphasize just whose space this was. If they'd wanted to be polite, the quaddies would have received them in one of the grav sections.

The station-side airlock opened into a spacious cylindrical bay, its radial symmetry airily dispensing with the concepts of "up" and "down." Roic floated with one hand on the grip by the hatch, the other kept carefully away from his stunner holster. Miles craned his neck to take in the array of half a dozen quaddies, males and females, in paramilitary grade half-armor, floating in cross-fire positions around the bay. Their weapons were out but shouldered, formality masking threat. Lower arms, thicker and more muscular than their uppers, emerged from their hips. Both

sets of arms were protected by plasma-deflecting vam-
braces. Miles couldn't help reflecting that here were people
who actually could shoot and reload at the same time.
Interestingly, though two bore the insignia of Graf Station
Security, the rest were in the colors and badges of the
Union Militia.

Impressive window dressing, but these were not the
people he needed to be attending to. His gaze swept on to
the three quaddies and the legged downsider waiting
directly across from the hatch. Faintly startled expressions,
as they in turn took in his own nonstandard appearance,
were quickly suppressed on three out of four faces.

The senior Graf Station Security officer was instantly
recognizable by his uniform, weapons, and glower.
Another middle-aged quaddie male also wore some sort of
Stationer uniform, slate blue, in a conservative style
designed to reassure the public. A white-haired female
quaddie was more elaborately dressed in a maroon velvet
doublet with slashed upper sleeves, silky silver fabric puffing from the slits, with matching puffy shorts and tight
lower sleeves. The legged downsider also wore the slate-
blue uniform, except with trousers and friction boots.
Short, graying brown hair floated around the head that
turned toward Miles. Miles choked, trying not to swear
aloud in shock.

My God. It's Bel Thorne. What the devil was the
ex-mercenary Betan hermaphrodite doing *here*? The question answered itself as soon as it formed. *So. Now I know
who our ImpSec observer on Graf Station is.* Which,
abruptly, raised the reliability of *those* reports to a vastly
higher level . . . or did it? Miles's smile froze, concealing,
he hoped, his sudden mental disarray.

The white-haired woman was speaking, in a very chilly tone—some automatic part of Miles's mind pegged her as senior, as well as oldest, present. "Good afternoon, Lord Auditor Vorkosigan. Welcome to the Union of Free Habitats."

Miles, one hand still guiding a blinking Ekaterin into the bay, managed a polite return nod. He left the second handhold flanking the hatch to her for an anchor, and managed to set himself in air, without imparting an unwanted spin, right side up with relation to the senior quaddie woman. "Thank you," he returned neutrally. *Bel, what the hell . . . ? Give me a sign, dammit.* The hermaphrodite returned his brief wide-eyed stare with cool disinterest, and, as if casually, raised a hand to scratch the side of its nose, signaling, perhaps, *Wait for it. . . .*

"I am Senior Sealer Greenlaw," the quaddie woman continued, "and I have been assigned by my government to meet with you and provide arbitration between you and your victims on Graf Station. This is Crew Chief Venn of Graf Station Security, Boss Watts, who is supervisor of Graf Station Downsider Relations, and Assistant Portmaster Bel Thorne."

"How do you do, madam, gentlemen, honorable herm," Miles's mouth continued on autopilot. He was too shaken by the sight of Bel to take exception to that *your victims*, for now. "Permit me to introduce my wife, Lady Ekaterin Vorkosigan, and my personal assistant, Armsman Roic."

All the quaddies frowned disapprovingly at Roic. But now it was the turn for Bel's eyes to widen, staring with sudden attention at Ekaterin. A purely personal aspect of it all blazed across Miles's mind then, as he realized that he was shortly, very probably, going to be in the unsettling position of having to introduce his new wife to his old flame. Not that Bel's oft-expressed crush on him had ever been *consummated*, exactly, to his retrospective sometimes-regret. . . .

"Portmaster Thorne, ah . . ." Miles felt himself scrambling for firm footing in more ways than one. His voice went brightly inquiring. "Have we met?"

"I don't believe we've ever met, *Lord Auditor Vorkosigan*, no," returned Bel; Miles hoped his was the only ear that detected the slight emphasis on his Barrayaran name and title in that familiar alto drawl.

"Ah." Miles hesitated. *Throw out a lure, a line, something* . . . "My mother was Betan, you know."

"What a coincidence," Bel said blandly. "So was mine."

Bel, goddammit! "I have had the pleasure of visiting Beta Colony several times."

"I haven't been back but once in decades." The faint light of Bel's notably vile sense of humor faded in the brown eyes, and the herm relented as far as, "I'd like to hear about the old sandbox."

"It would be my pleasure to discuss it," Miles responded, praying this exchange sounded diplomatic and not cryptic. *Soon, soon, bloody soon.* Bel returned him a cordial, acknowledging nod.

The white-haired quaddie woman gestured toward the end of the bay with her upper right hand. "If you would please accompany us to the conference chamber, Lord and Lady Vorkosigan, Armsman Roic."

"Certainly, Sealer Greenlaw." Miles favored her with an *after you, ma'am* half-bow in air, then uncurled to get a foot to the wall to push off after her. Ekaterin and Roic followed. Ekaterin arrived and braked at the round airseal door with reasonable grace, though Roic landed crookedly with an audible thump. He'd used too much power pushing off, but

Miles couldn't stop to coach him on the fine points here. He'd come to the right of it soon enough, or break an arm. The next series of corridors featured a sufficiency of hand-grips. The downsiders kept up with the quaddies, who both preceded and followed; to Miles's secret satisfaction, none of the guards had to pause and collect any out-of-control spinning or helplessly becalmed Barrayarans.

They came at length to a chamber with a window-wall offering a panoramic view out across one arm of the station and into the deep, star-dusted void beyond. Any downsider suffering from a touch of agoraphobia or pressurization paranoia would doubtless prefer to cling to the wall on the opposite side. Miles floated gently up to the transparent barrier, stopping himself with two delicately extended fingers, and surveyed the spacescape; his mouth crooked up, unwilling. "This is very fine," he said honestly.

He glanced around. Roic had found a wall grip near the door, awkwardly shared with the lower hand of a quaddie guard, who glowered at him as they both shifted fingers trying not to touch the other. The majority of the honor guard had been shed in the adjoining corridor, and only two, one Graf Station and one Union, now hovered, albeit alertly. The chamber end-walls featured decorative plants growing out of illuminated spiraling tubes that held their roots in a hydroponic mist. Ekaterin paused by one, examining the multicolored leaves closely. She tore her attention away, and her brief smile faded, watching Miles, watching their quaddie hosts, watching for cues. Her eye fell curiously on Bel, who was surveying Miles in turn, the herm's expression—well, anyone else would see it as bland, probably. Miles suspected it was deeply ironic.

The quaddies took up position in a hemispherical arrangement around a central vid plate, Bel hovering near its comrade-in-slate-blue, Boss Watts. Arching posts of different heights featured the sort of com link control boards usually found on station-chair arms, looking a bit like flowers on stalks, which provided suitably spaced tethering points. Miles picked a post with his back to open space. Ekaterin floated over and took up a spot a little behind him. She'd gone into her silent, highly reserved mode, which Miles had to school himself not to read as unhappy; it might just mean that she was processing too hard to remember to be animated. Fortunately, the ivory-carved expression also simulated aristocratic poise.

A pair of younger quaddies, whose green shirt-and-shorts garb Miles's eye decoded as *servitor*, offered drink bulbs all around; Miles selected something billed to be tea, Ekaterin took fruit juice, and Roic, with a glance at his quaddie opposite numbers who were offered none, declined. A quaddie could grip a handhold and a drink bulb, and still have two hands left to draw and aim a weapon. It hardly seemed fair.

"Senior Sealer Greenlaw," Miles began. "My credentials, you should have received." She nodded, her short, fine hair floating in a wispy halo with the motion. He continued, "I am, unfortunately, not wholly familiar with the cultural context and meaning of your title. Who do you speak for, and do your words bind them in honor? That is to say, do you represent Graf Station, a department within the Union of Free Habitats, or some larger entity still? And who reviews your recommendations or sanctions your agreements?" *And how long does it usually take them?*

She hesitated, and he wondered if she was studying him with the same intensity that he studied her. Quaddies were even longer-lived than Betans, who routinely made it to one-hundred-and-twenty standard, and might expect to see a century and a half; how old was this woman?

"I am a Sealer for the Union's Department of Downsider Relations; I believe some downsider cultures would term this a minister plenipotentiary for their state department, or whatever body administers their embassies. I've served the department for the past forty years, including tours as junior and senior counsel for the Union in both our bordering systems."

The near neighbors to Quaddiespace, a few jumps away on heavily used routes; she was saying she'd spent time on planets. *And, incidentally, that she's been doing this job since before I was born.* If only she wasn't one of those people who figured that if you'd seen one planet, you'd seen 'em all, this sounded promising. Miles nodded.

"My recommendations and agreements will be reviewed by my work gang on Union Station—which is the Board of Directors of the Union of Free Habitats."

Well, so there was a committee, but happily, they weren't here. Miles pegged her as being roughly the equivalent of a senior Barrayaran minister in the Council of Ministers, well up to his own weight as an Imperial Auditor. Granted, the quaddies had nothing in their governmental structure equivalent to a Barrayaran Count, though they seemed none the worse for the deprivation—Miles suppressed a dry snort. One layer from the top, Greenlaw had a finite number of persons to please or persuade. He permitted himself his first faint hope for a reasonably supple negotiation.

Her white brows drew in. "They called you the Emperor's Voice. Do Barrayarans *really* believe their emperor's voice comes from your mouth, across all those light-years?"

Miles regretted his inability to lean back in a chair; he straightened his spine a trifle instead. "The name is a legal fiction, not a superstition, if that's what you're asking. Actually, Emperor's Voice is a nickname for my job. My real title is Imperial Auditor—a reminder that always my first task is to listen. I answer to—and for—Emperor Gregor alone." This seemed a good place to leave out such complications as potential impeachment by the Council of Counts, and other Barrayaran-style checks and balances. *Such as assassination.*

The security officer, Venn, spoke up. "So do you, or do you not, control the Barrayaran military forces here in Union space?" He'd evidently acquired enough experience of Barrayaran soldiers by now to have a little trouble picturing the slightly crooked runt floating before him dominating the bluff Vorpatril, or his no-doubt large and healthy troopers.

Yeah, but you should see my Da . . . Miles cleared his throat. "As the Emperor is commander-in-chief of the Barrayaran military, his Voice is automatically the ranking officer of any Barrayaran force in his vicinity, yes. If the emergency so demands it."

"So are you saying that if you ordered it, those thugs out there would shoot?" said Venn sourly.

Miles managed a slight bow in his direction, not easy in free fall. "Sir, if an Emperor's Voice so ordered it, they'd shoot *themselves.*"

This was pure swagger—well, part swagger—but Venn didn't need to know it. Bel remained straight-faced, somehow, thank whatever gods hovered here, though Miles could almost see the laugh getting choked back. *Don't pop your eardrums, Bel.* The Sealer's white eyebrows took a moment to climb back down to horizontal again.

Miles continued, "Nevertheless, while it's not hard to get any group of persons excited enough to shoot at things, one purpose of military discipline is to ensure they also *stop* shooting on command. This is not a time for shooting, but for talking—and listening. I am listening." He tented his fingers in front of what would be his lap, if he were sitting. "From your point of view, what was the sequence of events that led to this unfortunate incident?"

Greenlaw and Venn both started to speak at once; the quaddie woman opened an upper hand in a gesture of invitation to the security officer.

Venn nodded and continued, "It *started* when my department received an emergency call to apprehend a pair of your men who had assaulted a quaddie woman."

Here was a new player on stage. Miles kept his expression neutral. "Assaulted in what sense?"

"Broke into her living quarters, roughed her up, threw her around, broke one of her arms. They evidently had been sent in pursuit of a certain Barrayaran officer who had failed to report for duty—"

"Ah. Would that be Ensign Corbeau?"

"Yes."

"And was he in her living quarters?"

"Yes—"

"By her invitation?"

"Yes." Venn grimaced. "They had apparently, um, become friends. Garnet Five is a premier dancer in the Minchenko Memorial Troupe, which performs live zero-gee ballet for residents of the Station and for downsider visitors." Venn inhaled. "It is not entirely clear who went to whose defense when the Barrayaran patrol came to remove their tardy officer, but it degenerated into a noisy brawl. We arrested all the downsiders and took them to Security Post Three to sort out."

"By the way," Sealer Greenlaw broke in, "your Ensign Corbeau has lately requested political asylum in the Union."

This was new, too. "How lately?"

"This morning. When he learned you were coming."

Miles hesitated. He could imagine a dozen scenarios to account for this, ranging from the sinister to the foolish; he couldn't help it that his mind leapt to the sinister. "Are you likely to grant it?" he asked finally.

She glanced at Boss Watts, who made a little noncommittal gesture with a lower hand and said, "My department has taken it under advisement."

"If you want my advice, you'll bounce it off the far wall," growled Venn. "We don't need that sort here."

"I should like to interview Ensign Corbeau at the earliest convenience," said Miles.

"Well, he evidently doesn't want to talk to *you*," said Venn.

"Nevertheless. I consider firsthand observation and eyewitness testimony critical for my correct understanding of this complex chain of events. I'll also need to speak with the other Barrayaran—" he clipped the word *hostages*, and substituted, "detainees, for the same reason."

"It's not that complex," said Venn. "A bunch of armed thugs came charging onto my station, violated customs, stunned dozens of innocent bystanders and a number of Station Security officers attempting to carry out their duties, tried to effect what can only be called a jailbreak, and vandalized property. Charges against them for their crimes—documented on vid!—range from the discharge of illegal weapons to resisting arrest to arson in an inhabited area. It's a miracle that no one was killed."

"*That*, unfortunately, has yet to be demonstrated," Miles countered instantly. "The trouble is that from our point of view, the arrest of Ensign Corbeau was *not* the beginning of the sequence of events. Admiral Vorpatril had reported a man missing well before that—Lieutenant Solian. According to both your witnesses and ours, a quantity of his blood tantamount to a body part was found on the floor of a Graf Station loading bay. Military loyalty runs two ways—Barrayarans do not abandon our own. Dead or alive, *where* is the rest of him?"

Venn nearly ground his teeth. "We looked for the man. He is not on Graf Station. His body is not in space in any reasonable trajectory *from* Graf Station. We checked. We've told Vorpatril that, repeatedly."

"How hard—or easy—is it for a downsider to disappear in Quaddiespace?"

"If I may answer that," Bel Thorne broke in smoothly, "as that incident impinges on my department."

Greenlaw motioned assent with a lower hand, while simultaneously rubbing the bridge of her nose with an upper.

"Boarding to and from galactic ships here is fully controlled, not only from Graf Station, but from our other nexus trade depots as well. It is, if not impossible, at least difficult to pass through customs and immigration areas without leaving some sort of record, including general vid monitors of the areas. Your Lieutenant Solian does not show up anywhere in our computer or visual records for that day."

"Truly?" Miles gave Bel a look, *Is this the straight story?*

Bel returned a brief nod, *Yes*. "Truly. Now, in-system travel is much less strictly controlled. It is more . . . feasible, for someone to pass out of Graf Station to another Union habitat without notice. *If* that person is a quaddie. Any downsider, however, would stand out in the crowd. Standard missing-person procedures were followed in this case, including notifications of other habitat security departments. Solian has simply not been seen, on Graf Station or any other Union habitat."

"How do you account for his blood in the loading bay?"

"The loading bay is on the outboard side of the station access control points. It is my opinion that whoever created that scene came from and returned to one of the ships in that docks-and-locks sector."

Miles silently noted Bel's word choice, *whoever created that scene*, not *whoever murdered Solian*. Of course, Bel had been present at a certain spectacular emergency cryo-prep, too. . . .

Venn put in irritably, "All of which were ships from *your* fleet, at the time. In other words, you brought your own troubles with you. *We* are a peaceful people here!"

Miles frowned thoughtfully at Bel, and mentally reshuffled his plan of attack. "Is the loading bay in question very far from here?"

"It's on the other side of the station," said Watts.

"I think I would like to see it, and its associated areas, first, before I interview Ensign Corbeau and the other Barrayarans. Perhaps Portmaster Thorne would be so good as to conduct me on a tour of the facility?"

Bel glanced at Boss Watts and got an approving low sign.

"I should be very pleased to do so, Lord Vorkosigan," said Bel.

"Next, perhaps? We could take my ship around."

"That would be very efficient, yes," replied Bel, eyes brightening with appreciation. "I could accompany you."

"Thank you." *Good catch.* "That would be most satisfactory."

Wild as Miles now was to get away and shake Bel down in private, he had to smile his way through further formalities, including the official presentation of the list of charges, costs, fines, and punitive fines Vorpatril's strike force had garnered. He plucked the data disk Boss Watts spun to him delicately out of the air and intoned, "Note, please, I do not *accept* these charges. I will, however, undertake to review them fully at the earliest possible moment."

A lot of unsmiling faces greeted this pronouncement. Quaddie body language was a study in its own right. Talking with one's hands was fraught with so many more possibilities, here. Greenlaw's hands were very controlled, both uppers and lowers. Venn clenched his lower fists a lot, but then, Venn had helped carry out his burned comrades after the fire.

The conference drew to an end without achieving anything resembling closure, which Miles counted as a small victory for his side. He was getting away without committing himself or Gregor to anything much, so far. He didn't yet see how to twist this unpromising tangle his way. He needed more data, subliminals, people, some handle or lever he hadn't spotted yet. *I need to talk to Bel.*

That wish, at least, looked to be granted. At Greenlaw's word, the meeting broke up, and the honor guard escorted the Barrayarans back through the corridors to the bay where the *Kestrel* waited.

Chapter 4

At the *Kestrel's* lock, Boss Watts took Bel aside for a low-voiced conversation with some anxious hand waving. Bel shook its head, made *calm down* gestures, and finally turned to follow Miles, Ekaterin, and Roic through the flex tube and into the *Kestrel's* tiny and now crowded personnel hatch deck. Roic stumbled and looked a trifle dizzied, readjusting to the grav field, but then found his balance again. He frowned warily at the Betan hermaphrodite in the quaddie uniform. Ekaterin flashed a covertly curious glance.

"What was that all about?" Miles asked Bel as the airlock door slid shut.

"Watts wanted me to take a bodyguard or three. To protect me from the brutal Barrayarans. I told him there wouldn't be room aboard, and besides, you were a diplomat—not a soldier." Bel, head cocked, gave him an indecipherable look. "Is that so?"

"It is now. Uh . . ." Miles turned to Lieutenant Smolyani, manning the hatch controls. "Lieutenant, we're going to take the *Kestrel* around to the other side of Graf Station to another docking cradle. Their traffic control will direct you. Go as slowly as you can without looking odd. Take two or three tries to align with the docking clamps, or something."

"My lord!" said Smolyani indignantly. ImpSec fast courier pilots made a religion out of fast, tight maneuvering and swift, perfect dockings. "In front of *these* people?"

"Well, do it however you wish, but buy me some time. I need to talk with this herm. Go, go." He waved Smolyani out. He drew breath, and added to Roic and Ekaterin, "We'll take over the wardroom. Excuse us, please." Thus consigning her and Roic to their cramped cabins to wait. He gripped Ekaterin's hand in brief apology. He dared not say more until he'd decanted Bel in private. There were security angles, political angles, personal angles—how many angles could dance on the head of a pin?—and, as the first thrill of seeing that familiar face alive and well wore off, the nagging memory that the last time they'd met, the purpose had been to strip Bel of command and discharge it from the mercenary fleet for its unfortunate role in the bloody Jackson's Whole debacle. He *wanted* to trust Bel. Dare he?

Roic was too well trained to ask, *Are you sure you don't want me to come with you, m'lord?* out loud, but from the expression on his face he was doing his best to send it telepathically.

"I'll explain it all later," Miles promised Roic in an under-voice, and sent him on his way with what he hoped was a reassuring half-salute.

He led Bel the few steps to the tiny chamber that doubled as the *Kestrel*'s wardroom, dining room, and briefing room, shut both its doors, and activated the security cone.

A faint hum from the projector on the ceiling and a shimmer in the air surrounding the wardroom's circular dining/vid conference table assured him it was working. He turned to find Bel watching him, head a little to one side, eyes quizzical, lips quirked. He hesitated a moment. Then, simultaneously, they both burst into laughter. They fell on each other in a hug; Bel pounded him on the back, saying in a tight voice, "Damn, damn, damn, you sawed-off little half-breed maniac . . ."

Miles fell back, breathless. "Bel, by God. You look good."

"Older, surely?"

"That, too. But I don't think I'm the one to talk."

"*You* look terrific. Healthy. Solid. I take it that woman's been feeding you right? Or doing something right, anyway."

"Not *fat*, though?" Miles said anxiously.

"No, no. But the last time I saw you, right after they thawed you out of cryo-freeze, you looked like a skull on a stick. You had us all worried."

Bel remembered that last meeting with the same clarity as he did, evidently. More, perhaps.

"I worried about you, too. Have you . . . been all right? How the devil did you end up *here*?" Was that a delicate enough inquiry?

Bel's brows rose a trifle, reading who-knew-what expression on Miles's face. "I suppose I was a little disoriented at first, after I parted company with the Dendarii Mercenaries. Between Oser and you as commanders, I'd served there almost twenty-five years."

"I was sorry as hell about it."

"I'd say, not half as sorry as I was, but *you* were the one who did the dying." Bel looked away briefly. "Among other people. It wasn't as if either of us had a choice, at that point.

I couldn't have gone on. And—in the long run—it was a good thing. I'd got in a rut without knowing it, I think. I needed something to kick me out of it. I was ready for a change. Well, not *ready,* but . . ."

Miles, hanging on Bel's words, was reminded of their place. "Sit, sit." He gestured to the little table; they took seats next to each other. Miles rested his arm on the dark surface and leaned closer to listen.

Bel continued, "I even went home for a little while. But I found that a quarter of a century kicking around the Nexus as a free herm had put me out of step with Beta Colony. I took a few spacer jobs, some at the suggestion of our mutual employer. Then I drifted in here." Bel tucked its gray-brown bangs up off its forehead with spread fingers, a familiar gesture; they promptly fell back again, even more heart-catching.

"ImpSec's not my employer any more, exactly," Miles said.

"Oh? So what are they, exactly?"

Miles hesitated over this one. "My . . . intelligence utility," he chose at last. "By virtue of my new job."

Bel's eyebrows went up farther, this time. "This Imperial Auditor thing isn't a cover for the latest covert ops scam, then."

"No. It's the real thing. I'm done with scam."

Bel's lips twitched. "What, with that funny accent?"

"This is my real voice. The Betan accent I affected for Admiral Naismith was the put-on. Sort of. Not that I didn't learn it at my mother's knee."

"When Watts told me the name of the supposedly-hot-shot envoy the Barrayarans were sending out, I thought it had to be you. That's why I made sure to get myself onto the welcoming committee. But this Emperor's Voice thing sounded like something out of a fairy tale, to me. Until I got to the fine print. Then it sounded like something out of a really *gruesome* fairy tale."

"Oh, did you look up my job description?"

"Yeah, it's pretty amazing what's in the historical databases here. Quaddiespace is fully plugged in to the galactic information exchange, I've found. They're almost as good as Beta, despite having only a fraction of the population. Imperial Auditor's a pretty stunning promotion—whoever handed you that much unsupervised power on a platter has to be almost as much of a lunatic as you are. I want to hear your explanation of that."

"Yes, it can take some explaining, to non-Barrayarans." Miles took a breath. "You know, that cryo-revival of mine was a little dicey. Do you remember the seizures I was having, right after?"

"Yes . . ." said Bel cautiously.

"They turned out to be a permanent side effect, unfortunately. Too much for even ImpSec's version of the military to tolerate in a field officer. As I managed to demonstrate in a particularly spectacular manner, but that's another story. It was a medical discharge, officially. So that was the end of my galactic covert ops career." Miles's smile twisted. "I had to get an honest job. Fortunately, Emperor Gregor gave me one. Everyone assumes my appointment was high Vor nepotism at work, for my father's sake. Over time, I trust I'll prove them wrong."

Bel was silent for a moment, face set. "So. It seems I killed Admiral Naismith after all."

"Don't hog the blame. You had lots of help," Miles said dryly. "Including mine." He was reminded that this slice of privacy was precious and limited. "It's all blood over the dam now anyway, for you and me both. We have other crises on our plate today. Quickly, from the top—I've been assigned to straighten out this mess, to Barrayar's, if not benefit, least-cost. If you're our ImpSec informer here—are you?"

Bel nodded.

After Bel had handed in its resignation from the Dendarii Free Mercenaries, Miles had seen to it that the hermaphrodite had gone on ImpSec's payroll as a civilian informer. In part it was payback for all Bel had done for Barrayar before the ill-conceived disaster that had ended Bel's career directly and Miles's indirectly, but mostly it had been to keep ImpSec from getting lethally excited about Bel wandering the wormhole nexus with a head full of hot Barrayaran secrets. Aging, tepid secrets now, for the most part. Miles had figured the illusion that they held Bel's string would prove reassuring to ImpSec, and so it had apparently proved. "Portmaster, eh? What a superb job for an intelligence observer. Data on everyone and everything that passes in and out of Graf Station at your fingertips. Did ImpSec place you here?"

"No, I found this job on my own. Sector Five was happy, though. Which, at the time, seemed an added bonus."

"I'd think they damned well should be happy."

"The quaddies like me, too. It seems I'm good at handling all sorts of upset downsiders, without losing my equilibrium. I don't explain to them that after years of trailing around after *you*, my definition of an emergency is seriously divergent from theirs."

Miles grinned and made calculations in his head. "Then your most recent reports are probably still somewhere in transit between here and Sector Five headquarters."

"Yeah, that's what I figure."

"What are the most important things I need to know?"

"Well, for one, we *really* haven't seen your Lieutenant Solian. Or his body. Really. Union Security hasn't stinted on the search for him. Vorpatril—is he any relation to your cousin Ivan, by the way?"

"Yes, a distant one."

"I thought I sensed a family resemblance. In more ways than one. Anyway, he thinks we're lying. But we're not. Also, your people are idiots."

"Yes. I know. But they're *my* idiots. Tell me something new."

"All right, here's a good one. Graf Station Security has pulled all the passengers and crew off the Komarran ships impounded in dock and lodged 'em in station-side hostels, to prevent ill-considered actions and to put pressure on Vorpatril and Molino. Naturally, they're none too happy. The supercargo—non-Komarrans who just took passage for a few jumps—are wild to get away. Half a dozen have tried to bribe me to let them take their goods off the *Idris* or the *Rudra*, and transfer off Graf Station on somebody else's ships."

"Have any, ah, succeeded?"

"Not yet." Bel smirked. "Although if the price keeps going up at the current rate, even I could be tempted. Anyway, several of the most anxious ones struck me as . . . potentially interesting."

"Check. Have you reported this to your Graf Station employers?"

"I made a remark or two. But it's only suspicion. The individuals are all well behaved, so far—especially compared to Barrayarans—it's not like we have any pretext for fast-penta interrogations."

"Attempting to bribe an official," Miles suggested.

"I hadn't actually mentioned that last part to Watts yet." At Miles's raised eyebrows, Bel added, "Did you *want* more legal complications?"

"Ah—no."

Bel snorted. "Didn't think so." The herm paused a moment, as if marshaling its thoughts. "Anyway, back to the idiots. Your Ensign Corbeau, to wit."

"Yes. That political asylum request of his has got all my antennae quivering. Granted, he was in some trouble for being late reporting in, but why is he suddenly trying to desert? What connection does he have to Solian's disappearance?"

"Not any, as far as I've been able to make out. I actually met the fellow, before all this blew up."

"Oh? How and where?"

"Socially, as it happens. What is it about you people who run sexually segregated fleets that makes you all disembark insane? No, don't bother answering that, I think we all know. But the all-male military organizations who have that custom for religious or cultural reasons all come onto station leave like some horrible combination of kids let out of school and convicts let out of prison. The worst of both, actually—the judgment of children combined with the sexual deprivation of—never mind. The quaddies cringe when they see you coming. If you didn't spend money with such wild abandon, I think the commercial stations in the Union would all vote to quarantine you aboard your own ships and let you die of blue balls."

Miles rubbed his forehead. "Let's get back to Ensign Corbeau, shall we?"

Bel grinned. "We hadn't left. So, this backwoods Barrayaran boy on his first-ever trip into the glittering galaxy tumbles off his ship and, being under instructions, as I understand it, to enhance his cultural horizons—"

"That is actually correct."

"Goes off to see the Minchenko Ballet. Which is something to behold in any case. You should take it in while you're station-side."

"What, it isn't just, uh, exotic dancers?"

"Not in the advertising-for-the-sex-workers sense. Or even in the Betan Orb ultra-classy sexual smorgasbord and training academy sense."

Miles considered, then reconsidered, mentioning his and Ekaterin's honeymoon layover at the Orb of Unearthly Delights, possibly the most peculiarly *useful* stop on their itinerary . . . *Focus, my Lord Auditor.*

"It's exotic, and it's dancers, but it's real art, the real thing—it goes way beyond craft. A two-hundred-year-old tradition, a jewel of this culture. The fool boy *ought* to have fallen in love at first sight. It was his subsequent pursuit with all guns blazing—in the metaphorical sense, this time—that was a little out of line. Soldier on leave falls madly in lust with local girl is not precisely a new scenario, but what I *really* don't understand is what Garnet Five saw in him. I mean, he's a nice enough looking young male, but still . . . !" Bel smiled slyly. "Too tall for my taste. Not to mention too young."

"Garnet Five is this quaddie dancer, yes?"

"Yes."

Remarkable enough, for a Barrayaran to be attracted to a quaddie; the deeply ingrained cultural prejudice against anything that smacked of mutation would seem to work against it. Had Corbeau received less than the usual indulgent understanding from his fellows and superiors that a young officer in such a plight might ordinarily expect?

"And your connection with all this is—what?"

Did Bel take an apprehensive breath? "Nicol plays harp and hammer dulcimer in the Minchenko Ballet orchestra. You do remember Nicol, the quaddie musician we rescued during that personnel pickup that almost went down the disposer?"

"I remember Nicol vividly." And so, apparently, had Bel. "I gather she made it home safely after all."

"Yes." Bel's smile grew tenser. "Not surprisingly, she also remembers *you* vividly—Admiral Naismith."

Miles went still for a moment. At last he said cautiously, "Do, ah . . . you know her well? Can you command, or persuade, her discretion?"

"I live with her," said Bel briefly. "No one needs to command anything. She *is* discreet."

Oh. Much becomes clear . . .

"But she's a personal friend of Garnet Five's. Who is in a tearing panic over all of this. She's convinced, among other things, that the Barrayaran command wants to shoot her boyfriend out of hand. The pair of thugs that Vorpatril sent to pick up your stray evidently—well, it went beyond rude. They were insulting and brutal, for starters, and it slid downhill from there. I've heard the unabridged version."

Miles grimaced. "I know my countrymen. You can take the ugly details as read, thanks."

"Nicol has asked me to do what I can for her friend and her friend's friend. I promised I'd put in a word. This is it."

"I understand." Miles sighed. "I can't make any promises yet. Except to listen to everyone."

Bel nodded and looked away. It said after a moment, "This Imperial Auditor gig of yours—you're a big wheel in the Barrayaran machine now, huh?"

"Something like that," said Miles.

"The Emperor's Voice sounds like it would be pretty loud. People listen, do they?"

"Well, Barrayarans do. The rest of the galaxy"—one side of Miles's mouth turned up—"tend to think it's some kind of fairy tale."

Bel shrugged apologetically. "ImpSec is Barrayarans. So. The thing is, I've come to like this place—Graf Station, Quaddiespace. And these people. I like them a lot. I believe you'll see why, if I get much chance to show you around. I'm thinking of settling here permanently."

"That's . . . nice," said Miles. *Where are you taking me, Bel?*

"But if I *do* take an oath of citizenship here—and I've been thinking hard about it for a while—I want to take it honestly. I can't offer them a false oath, or divided loyalties."

"Your Betan citizenship never interfered with your career in the Dendarii Mercenaries," Miles pointed out.

"You never asked me to operate on Beta Colony," said Bel.

"And if I had?"

"I . . . would have faced a dilemma." Bel's hand stretched in urgent entreaty. "I want a clean start, with no secret strings attached. You claim ImpSec is your personal utility now. Miles—can you please fire me again?"

Miles sat back and chewed on his knuckle. "Cut you loose from ImpSec, you mean?"

"Yes. From all old obligations."

He blew out his breath. *But you're so valuable to us here!* "I . . . don't know."

"Don't know if you have the power? Or don't know if you want to use it?"

Miles temporized, "This power business has proved a lot stranger than I anticipated. You'd think more power would bring one more freedom, but I've found it's brought me less. Every word that comes out of my mouth has this *weight* that it never had before, when I was babbling Mad Miles, hustler of the Dendarii. I never had to watch my mass like this. It's . . . damned uncomfortable, sometimes."

"I'd have thought *you'd* love it."

"I'd have thought that too."

Bel leaned back, easing off. It would not make the request again, not soon, anyway.

Miles drummed his fingers on the cool, reflective surface of the table. "If there is anything more behind this mess than overexcitement and bad judgment—not that that isn't enough—it hinges on the evaporation of that Komarran fleet security fellow, Solian—"

Miles wrist com chimed, and he raised it to his lips. "Yes?"

"M'lord," came Roic's apologetic voice. "We're in dock again now."

"Right. Thanks. We'll be out directly." He rose from the table, saying, "You must meet Ekaterin properly, before we go back out there and have to play dumb again. She and Roic have full Barrayaran security clearances, by the way— they have to, to live this close to me. They both need to know who you are, and that they can trust you."

Bel hesitated. "Do they really need to know I'm ImpSec? Here?"

"They might, in an emergency."

"I would particularly like the quaddies not to know I've been selling intelligence to downsiders, you see. Maybe it would be safer if you and I were mere acquaintances."

Miles stared. "But Bel, she knows perfectly well who you are. Or were, anyway."

"What, have you been telling covert ops war stories to your wife?" Clearly disconcerted, Bel frowned. "Those rules always applied to someone else, didn't they?"

"Her clearance was earned, not just granted," Miles said a little stiffly. "But Bel, we sent you a wedding invitation! Or . . . did you get it? ImpSec notified me it was delivered—"

"Oh," said Bel, looking confused. "That. Yes. I did get it."

"Was it delivered too late? It should have included a travel voucher—if someone pocketed that, I'll have his hide—"

"No, the voucher came through all right. About a year and a half ago, yes? I could have made it, if I'd scrambled a bit. It just arrived at an awkward period for me. Kind of a low point. I'd just left Beta for the last time, and I was in the middle of a little job I was doing for ImpSec. Arranging a substitute would have been difficult. It was just effort, at a time when more effort . . . I wished you well, though, and hoped you'd finally got lucky." A wry grin flashed. "Again."

"Finding the right Lady Vorkosigan . . . was a bigger, rarer kind of luck than any I'd had before." Miles sighed. "Elli Quinn didn't come either. Though she sent a present and a letter." Neither especially demure.

"Hm," said Bel, smiling a little. And added rather slyly, "And Sergeant Taura?"

"*She* attended." Miles's lips curled up, unwilled. "Spectacularly. I had a burst of genius, and put my Aunt Alys in charge of getting her dressed civilian-style. It kept them both happily occupied. The old Dendarii contingent all missed you. Elena and Baz were there—with their new baby girl, if you can imagine it—and Arde Mayhew, too. So the very beginning of it all was fully represented. It was as well that the wedding was small. A hundred and twenty people is small, yes? It was Ekaterin's second, you see—she was a widow." And profoundly stressed thereby. Her tense, distraught state the night before the wedding had reminded Miles forcibly of a particular species of precombat nerves he'd seen in troops facing, not their first, but their second battle. The night after the wedding, now—that had gone much better, thank God.

Longing and regret had shadowed Bel's face during this recitation of old friends lifting a glass to new beginnings. Then the herm's expression sharpened. "Baz Jesek, back on Barrayar?" said Bel. "Someone must have worked out his little problems with the Barrayaran military authorities, eh?"

And if Someone could arrange Baz's relationship with ImpSec, maybe that same Someone might arrange Bel's? Bel didn't even need to make the point out loud. Miles said, "The old desertion charges made too good a cover when Baz was active in ops to allow them to be rescinded, but the need had become obsolete. Baz and Elena are both out of the Dendarii too, now. Hadn't you heard? We're all getting to be history." *All of us who made it out alive, anyway.*

"Yes," sighed Bel. "There is a deal of sanity to be saved in letting the past go, and moving on." The herm glanced up. "If the past will let you go too, that is. So let's keep this as simple as possible with your people, please?"

"All right," Miles agreed reluctantly. "For now, we'll mention the past, but not the present. Don't worry—they'll be, ah—discreet." He deactivated the security cone above the little conference table and unlocked the doors. Raising his wrist com to his lips, he murmured, "Ekaterin, Roic, could you step over to the wardroom, please."

When they had both arrived, Ekaterin smiling expectantly, Miles said, "We've had a piece of undeserved good fortune. Although Portmaster Thorne works for the quaddies now, the herm's an old friend of mine from an organization I worked with in my ImpSec days. You can rely on what Bel has to say."

Ekaterin held out her hand. "I'm so glad to meet you at last, Captain Thorne. My husband and his old friends have spoken highly of you. I believe you were much missed from their company."

Looking decidedly bemused, but rising to the challenge, Bel shook her hand. "Thank you, Lady Vorkosigan. But I don't go by that old rank here. Portmaster Thorne, or just call me Bel."

Ekaterin nodded. "And please call me Ekaterin. Oh—in private, I suppose." She looked a silent inquiry at Miles.

"Ah, right," said Miles. His gesture took in Roic, who looked attentive. "Bel knew me under another identity then. As far as Graf Station is concerned, we've just met. But we've hit it off splendidly, and Bel's talent for dealing with difficult downsiders is paying off for them."

Roic nodded. "Got it, m'lord."

Miles shepherded them into the hatch bay where the *Kestrel*'s engineer waited to pipe them back aboard Graf Station. He reflected that yet another reason Ekaterin's security clearance needed to be as high as his own was that, according to several persons' historical reports and her own witness, he talked in his sleep. Until Bel grew less nervy over the situation, he decided he'd probably better not mention this.

Two quaddie Station Security men waited for them in the freight loading bay. This being the section of Graf

Station supplied with artificially generated gravitational
fields for the comfort and health of its downsider visitors
and residents, the pair hovered in personal float chairs
with Station Security markings emblazoned on the sides.
The floaters were stubby cylinders, barely larger in diameter than a man's shoulders, and the general effect was of
people riding in levitating washtubs, or maybe the Baba
Yaga's magic flying mortar from Barrayaran folklore. Bel
gave the quaddie sergeant a nod and a murmured greeting as they emerged into the echoing cavern of the
loading bay. The sergeant returned the nod, evidently
reassured, and turned his close attention to the dangerous Barrayarans. Since the dangerous Barrayarans were
frankly gawking like tourists, Miles hoped the tough-
looking fellow would soon grow less twitchy.

"This personnel lock here," Bel pointed back to the one
by which they'd just entered, "was the one that was opened
by the unauthorized person. The blood trail ended in it, in
a smeary smudge. It started," Bel walked across the bay
toward the wall to the right, "a few meters away, not far
from the door to the next bay. This is where the large pool
of blood was found."

Miles walked after Bel, studying the deck. It had been
cleaned up in the several days since the incident. "Did you
see this yourself, Portmaster Thorne?"

"Yes, about an hour after it was first found. The mob had
arrived by then, but Security had been pretty good about
keeping the area uncontaminated."

Miles had Bel walk him around the bay, detailing all
exits. It was a standard sort of place, utilitarian, undeco-
rated, efficient; a few pieces of freight-handling equipment
stood silently in the opposite end, near a darkened,
airsealed control booth. Miles had Bel unlock it and give

him a look inside. Ekaterin too walked about, clearly glad to have room to stretch her legs after several days cooped up in the *Kestrel*. Her expression, gazing about the cool, echoing space, was thoughtfully reminiscent, and Miles smiled in appreciation.

They returned to the spot where the blood implied Lieutenant Solian's throat had been cut, and discussed the details of the spatter marks and smears. Roic observed with keen professional interest. Miles had one of the quaddie guards give up his float tub; scooped out of his shell, he sat up on the deck on his haunches and lower arms, looking a bit like a large, disgruntled frog. Quaddie locomotion in a gravity field without a floater was rather disturbing to watch. They either went on all fours, only slightly more mobile than a person on hands and knees, or managed a sort of forward-leaning, elbows-out, upright chicken-walk on their lower hands. Either mode looked very wrong and ungainly, compared to their grace and agility in zero gee.

With Bel, whom Miles judged to be about the right size for a Komarran, cooperatively playing the part of the corpse, they experimented with the problem of a person in a float chair shifting seventy or so kilos of inert meat the several meters to the airlock. Bel wasn't as slim and athletic as formerly, either; the added, ah, masses made it harder for Miles to fall back into his old subconscious default habit of thinking of Bel as male. Probably just as well. Miles found it extremely difficult, legs folded awkwardly in a seat not designed for them, trying to keep one hand on the float chair controls at roughly crotch level and also maintain a grip on Bel's clothing. Bel tried trailing either an arm or a leg artistically over the side; Miles stopped short of pouring water down Bel's sleeve to try to duplicate the smears. Ekaterin did little better than he did, and Roic, surprisingly, worse. His superior strength was counteracted by the awkwardness of squeezing his greater size into the cup-like space, his knees sticking up, and trying to work the hand controls in the constricted clearances. The quaddie sergeant managed it handily, but glowered at Miles afterwards.

Floaters, Bel explained, were not hard to come by, being considered shared public property, although quaddies who spent a lot of time on the grav side sometimes owned their own personalized models. The quaddies kept racks of floaters by the access ports between the grav and the free fall sections of the station, for any quaddie to grab and use, and drop off again upon returning. They were numbered for maintenance record purposes, but not tracked otherwise. Anyone could obtain one by simply walking up and getting in, apparently, even drunken Barrayaran soldiers on leave.

"When we came into that first docking cradle around on the other side, I noticed a lot of personal craft puttering around the outside of the station—pushers, personnel pods, in-system flitters," Miles said to Bel. "It occurs to me that someone could have picked up Solian's body within a short time of its being ejected from the airlock, and removed it damned near tracelessly. It could be anywhere by now, including still stored in a pod airlock or put through a disposer in one-kilo lumps or tucked away to mummify in some random asteroid crevice. Which offers an alternate explanation of why it hasn't been found floating out there. But that scenario requires either two persons, with prior planning, or one spontaneous murderer who moved very quickly. How much time would a single person have had between the throat-cutting and the pickup?"

Bel, straightening uniform and hair after the last drag across the loading bay, pursed its lips. "There were maybe five or ten minutes between the time the lock cycled, and the time the security guard arrived to check it. Maybe twenty minutes max after that before all sorts of people were looking around outside. In thirty minutes . . . yes, one person could just about have dumped the body, run to another bay and jumped in a small craft, zipped around, and collected it again."

"Good. Get me a list of everything that went out a lock in that period." For the sake of the listening quaddie guards he remembered to add a formal, "If you please, Portmaster Thorne."

"Certainly, Lord Auditor Vorkosigan."

"Seems damned odd to go to all that trouble to remove the body but leave the blood, though. Timing? Tried to get back to clean up, but it was too late? Something very, very strange to hide about the body?"

Maybe just blind panic, if the murder had not been planned in advance. Miles could imagine someone who was not a spacer shoving a body out an airlock, and only then realizing what poor concealment it really was. That didn't exactly jibe with a subsequent swift and handy outside pickup, though. And no quaddie qualified as not-a-spacer.

He sighed. "This is not getting us much forwarder. Let's go talk to my idiots."

Chapter 5

Graf Station Security Post Three lay on the border between the free fall and the grav sides of the station, with access to both. Construction quaddies in yellow shirts and shorts, and a few legged downsiders similarly dressed, were at work on repairs around the main grav-side entrance. Miles, Ekaterin, and Roic were escorted through by Bel and one of their quaddie outriders, the other having been left on dour guard at the *Kestrel's* docking hatch. The workers turned their heads to stare, frowning, as the Barrayarans passed.

They wound via a couple of corridors down one level, where they found the control booth at the portal to the grav-side detention block. A quaddie and a downsider were just collaborating on raising a new, possibly more plasma-fire-resistant, window into place in its frame; beyond, another yellow-clad quaddie could be seen putting the finishing touches on a monitor array while a uniformed quaddie in a Security floater, upper arms crossed, watched glumly.

In the tool-cluttered staging area in front of the booth they found Sealer Greenlaw and Chief Venn, now supplied with floaters, awaiting them. Venn immediately made sure to point out to Miles all the repairs completed and still in progress, in detail, with approximate costs, with a chronicle appended of all the quaddies who had been injured in the imbroglio, including names, ranks, prognoses, and the distress suffered by their family members. Miles made acknowledging yet neutral noises, and went into a short counter-riff on the missing Solian and the sinister testimony of the blood on the loading bay deck, with a brief dissertation on the logistics of his ejected body being spirited away by a possible outboard coconspirator. This last gave Venn pause, at least temporarily; his face twinged, like a man in stomach pain.

While Venn went to arrange Miles's entry to the cellblock with the guard in the control booth, Miles glanced at Ekaterin, and a little doubtfully around the less-than-inviting staging area. "Do you want to wait here, or sit in?"

"Do you want me to sit in?" she asked, with a lack of enthusiasm in her voice that even Miles could sense. "Not that you don't draft anyone in sight, as needed, but surely I'm not needed for this."

"Well, perhaps not. But it looks like it might be a trifle boring out here."

"I don't have quite your allergic response to boredom, love, but to tell the truth, I was rather hoping I could get more of a look around the station while you were tied up here this afternoon. The glimpses we saw on the way in seemed quite enticing."

"But I want Roic." He hesitated, the security triage problem turning in his head.

She glanced across in friendly speculation at Bel, listening. "I admit I would be glad for a guide, but do you really think I need a bodyguard here?"

Insult seemed possible, though only from quaddies who knew whose wife she was, but assault, Miles had to admit, seemed unlikely. "No, but . . ."

Bel smiled cordially back at her. "If you would accept my escort, Lady Vorkosigan, I would be pleased to show you around Graf Station while the Lord Auditor conducts his interviews."

Ekaterin brightened still further. "I would like that very much, yes, thank you, Portmaster Thorne. If things go well, as we must hope they do, we might not be here very long. I feel I should seize my opportunities."

Bel was more experienced than Roic in everything from hand-to-hand combat to fleet maneuvers, and vastly less likely to blunder into trouble here through ignorance. "Well . . . all right, why not? Enjoy." Miles touched his wrist com. "I'll call when I'm about finished. Maybe you can go shopping." He waved them off, smiling. "Just don't haul home any severed heads." He glanced up to find Venn and Greenlaw both staring at him in some dismay. "Ah—family joke," he explained weakly. The dismay did not abate.

Ekaterin smiled back, and sailed out on Bel's cheerfully proffered arm. It occurred to Miles belatedly that Bel was notably universal in its sexual tastes, and that maybe he ought to have warned Ekaterin that she needn't be especially delicate in redirecting Bel's attentions, should any be offered. But surely Bel wouldn't . . . on the other hand, maybe they'd just take turns trying things on.

Reluctantly, he turned back to business.

The Barrayaran prisoners were stacked three to a cell in chambers meant for two occupants, a circumstance about which Venn half complained, half apologized. Security Post Three, he gave Miles to understand, had been unprepared for such an abnormal influx of recalcitrant downsiders. Miles murmured comprehension, if not necessarily sympathy, and refrained from observing that the quaddies' cells were larger than the sleeping cabins housing four aboard the *Prince Xav.*

Miles began by interviewing Brun's squad commander. The man was shocked to find his exploits receiving the high-powered attention of an actual Imperial Auditor, and as a result defaulted to a thick MilSpeak in his account of events. The picture Miles unpacked behind such formal phrases as *penetrated the perimeter* and *enemy forces amassed* still made him wince. But allowing for the changed point of view, his testimony did not materially contradict the Stationer version of the events. Alas.

Miles spot-checked the squad commander's story with another cell full of fellows, who added details unfortunate but not surprising. As the squad had been attached to the *Prince Xav,* none of them were personally acquainted with Lieutenant Solian, posted on the *Idris.*

Miles emerged and tested an argument on the hovering Sealer Greenlaw. "It is quite improper for you to continue holding these men. The orders they were following, though perhaps ill thought out, were not in fact illegal in Barrayaran military definition. If their orders had been to plunder, rape, or massacre civilian quaddies, they would have been under a legal military obligation to resist them, but in fact they were specifically ordered not to kill. If they had disobeyed Brun, they could have faced court-martial. It's double jeopardy, and seriously unfair to them."

"I will consider this contention," said Greenlaw dryly, with the *For about ten seconds, after which I shall toss it out the nearest airlock* hanging unspoken.

"And, looking ahead," added Miles, "you can't wish to be stuck housing these men indefinitely. Surely it would be preferable for us to take them," he just managed to convert *off your hands* to, "with us when we leave."

Greenlaw looked even dryer; Venn grunted disconsolately. Miles gathered Venn would be just as glad for the Imperial Auditor to take them away *now*, except for the politics of the larger situation. Miles didn't push the point, but stored it up for near-future reference. He entertained a brief, wistful fantasy of trading Brun for his men, and leaving Brun here, to the net benefit of the Emperor's Service, but did not air it aloud.

His interview with the two service security men who'd initially been sent to pick up Corbeau was, in its way, even more wince-worthy. They were sufficiently intimidated by his Auditor's rank to give full and honest, if muttered, accounts of the contretemps. But such infelicitous phraseology as *I wasn't trying to break her arm, I was trying to bounce the mutie bitch off the wall*, and *All those clutching hands gave me the creeps—it was like having snakes wrapping around my boot*, convinced Miles that here were two men he wouldn't care to have testify in public, at least not in public in Quaddiespace. However, he was able to establish the significant point that at the time of the clash they, too, had been under the impression that Lieutenant Solian had just been murdered by an unknown quaddie.

He emerged from this interrogation to say to Venn, "I think I'd better speak privately to Ensign Corbeau. Can you find us a space?"

"Corbeau already has his own cell," Venn informed him coolly. "As a result of his being threatened by his comrades."

"Ah. Take me to him, then, if you please."

The cell door slid aside to reveal a tall young man sitting silently on a bunk, elbows on knees, his face propped in his hands. The metallic contact circles of a jump pilot's neural implant gleamed at his temples and mid-forehead, and Miles mentally tripled the young officer's recent training costs to the Imperium. He looked up and frowned in confusion at Miles.

He was a typical enough Barrayaran: dark haired, brown eyed, with an olive complexion made pale by his months in space. His regular features reminded Miles a bit of his cousin Ivan at the same feckless age. An extensive bruise around one eye was fading, turning yellowish green. His uniform shirt was open at the throat, sleeves rolled up. Some paling, irregular pink scars zigzagged over his exposed skin, marking him as a victim of the Sergyaran worm plague of some years back; he had evidently grown up, or at least been resident, on Barrayar's new colony planet during that difficult period before the oral vermicides had been perfected.

Venn said, "Ensign Corbeau, this is the Barrayaran Imperial Auditor, Lord Vorkosigan. Your emperor sent him out as the official diplomatic envoy to represent your side in negotiations with the Union. He wishes to interview you."

Corbeau's lips parted in alarm, and he scrambled to his feet and bobbed his head nervously at Miles. It made their height differential rather spring to the eye, and Corbeau's brow wrinkled in increased confusion.

Venn added, not so much kindly as punctiliously, "Due to the charges lodged against you, as well as your petition for asylum still pending for review, Sealer Greenlaw will *not* permit him to remove you from our custody at this time."

Corbeau exhaled a little, but still stared at Miles with the expression of a man introduced to a poisonous snake.

Venn added, a sardonic edge in his voice, "He has undertaken not to order you to shoot yourself, either."

"Thank you, Chief Venn," said Miles. "I'll take it from here, if you don't mind."

Venn took the hint, and his leave. Roic took up his silent guard stance by the cell door, which hissed closed.

Miles gestured at the bunk. "Sit down, Ensign." He seated himself on the bunk across from the young man and cocked his head in brief study as Corbeau refolded himself. "Stop hyperventilating," he added.

Corbeau gulped, and managed a wary, "My lord."

Miles laced his fingers together. "Sergyaran, are you?"

Corbeau glanced down at his arms and made an abortive move to roll down his sleeves. "Not born there, my lord. My parents emigrated when I was about five years old." He glanced at the silent Roic in his brown-and-silver uniform, and added, "Are you—" then swallowed whatever he'd been about to say.

Miles could fill in the blank. "I'm Viceroy and Vicereine Vorkosigan's son, yes. One of them."

Corbeau managed an unvoiced *Oh*. His look of suppressed terror did not diminish.

"I have just interviewed the two fleet patrollers sent to retrieve you from your station leave. In a moment, I'd like to hear your version of that event. But first—did you know

Lieutenant Solian, the Komarran fleet security officer aboard the *Idris*?"

The pilot's thoughts were so clearly focused on his own affairs that it took him a moment to parse this. "I met him once or twice at some of our prior stops, my lord. I can't say as I knew him. I never went aboard the *Idris*."

"Do you have any thoughts or theories about his disappearance?"

"Not . . . not really."

"Captain Brun thinks he might have deserted."

Corbeau grimaced. "Brun would."

"Why Brun especially?"

Corbeau's lips moved, halted; he looked still more miserable. "It would not be appropriate for me to criticize my superiors, my lord, or to comment on their personal opinions."

"Brun is prejudiced against Komarrans."

"I didn't say that!"

"That was *my* observation, Ensign."

"Oh."

"Well, let's leave that for the moment. Back to your troubles. Why didn't you answer your wrist com recall order?"

Corbeau touched his bare left wrist; the Barrayarans' com links had all been confiscated by their quaddie captors. "I'd taken it off and left it in another room. I must have slept through the beep. The first I knew of the recall order was when those two, two . . ." He struggled for a moment, then continued bitterly, "*thugs* came pounding at Garnet Five's door. They just pushed her aside—"

"Did they identify themselves properly, and relay your orders clearly?"

Corbeau paused, his glance at Miles sharpening. "I admit, my lord," he said slowly, "Sergeant Touchev announcing, 'All right, mutie-lover, this show's over,' did not exactly convey 'Admiral Vorpatril has ordered all Barrayaran personnel back to their ships' to *my* mind. Not right away, anyway. I'd just woken up, you see."

"Did they identify themselves?"

"Not—not verbally."

"Show any ID?"

"Well . . . they were in uniform, with their patrol armbands."

"Did you recognize them as fleet security, or did you think this was a private visit—a couple of comrades taking out their racial offense on their own time?"

"It . . . um . . . well—the two aren't exactly mutually exclusive, my lord. In my experience."

The kid has that one straight, unfortunately. Miles took a breath. "Ah."

"I was slow, still half asleep. When they shoved me around, Garnet Five thought they were attacking me. I wish she hadn't tried to . . . I didn't slug Touchev till he dumped her out of her float chair. At that point . . . everything sort of went down the disposer." Corbeau glowered at his feet, encased in prison-issue friction slippers.

Miles sat back. *Throw this boy a line. He's drowning.* He said mildly, "You know, your career is not necessarily cooked yet. You aren't, technically, AWOL as long as you are involuntarily confined by the Graf Station authorities, any more than Brun's strike patrol here is. For a little while yet, you're in a legal limbo. Your jump pilot's training and surgery would make you a costly loss, from command's viewpoint. If you make the right moves, you could still get out of this pretty cleanly."

Corbeau's face screwed up. "I don't . . ." He trailed off.

Miles made an encouraging noise.

Corbeau burst out, "I don't want my damned career any more. I don't want to be part of"—he waved around inarticulately—"*this*. This . . . idiocy."

Suppressing a certain sympathy, Miles asked, "What's your present status—how far along are you in your enlistment?"

"I signed up for one of the new five-year hitches, with the option to reenlist or go to reserve status for the next five. I've been in three years, two still to go."

At age twenty-three, Miles reminded himself, two years still seemed a long time. Corbeau could be barely more than an apprentice junior pilot at this stage of his career, although his assignment to the *Prince Xav* implied a superior rating.

Corbeau shook his head. "I see things differently these days, somehow. Attitudes I used to take for granted, jokes, remarks, just the way things are done—they bother me now. They grate. People like Sergeant Touchev, Captain Brun—God. Were we always this awful?"

"No," said Miles. "We used to be much worse. I can personally testify to that one."

Corbeau stared searchingly at him.

"But if all the progressive-minded men had opted out then, as you are proposing to do now, none of the changes I've seen in my lifetime could have happened. We've changed. We can change some more. Not instantly, no. But if all the decent folks quit and only the idiots are left to run the show, it won't be good for the future of Barrayar. About which I do care." It startled him to realize how passionately true that statement had become, of late. He thought of the two replicators in that guarded room in Vorkosigan House. *I always thought my parents could fix anything. Now it's my turn. Dear God, how did this happen?*

"I never imagined a place like this." Corbeau's jerky wave around, Miles construed, now meant Quaddiespace. "I never imagined a woman like Garnet Five. I want to stay here."

Miles had a bad sense of a desperate young man making permanent decisions for the sake of temporary stimuli. Graf Station was attractive at first glance, certainly, but Corbeau had grown up in open country with real gravity, real air—would he adapt, or would the techno-claustrophobia creep up on him? And the young woman for whom he proposed to throw his life over, was she worthy, or would Corbeau prove a passing amusement to her? Or, over time, a bad mistake? Hell, they'd known each other bare weeks—no one could know, least of all Corbeau and Garnet Five.

"I want out," said Corbeau. "I can't stand it any more."

Miles tried again. "If you withdraw your request for political asylum in the Union before the quaddies reject it, it might still be folded into your present legal ambiguity and made to disappear, without further prejudice to your career. If you don't withdraw it first, the desertion charge will certainly stick, and do you vast damage."

Corbeau looked up and said anxiously, "Doesn't this firefight that Brun's patrol had with the quaddie security here make it *in the heat?* The *Prince Xav's* surgeon said it probably did."

In the heat, desertion in the face of the enemy, was punishable by death in the Barrayaran military code. Desertion in peacetime was punishable by long stretches of time in some extremely unpleasant stockades. Either seemed excessively wasteful, all things considered. "I think it would require some pretty convoluted legal twisting to call this episode a battle. For one thing, defining it so runs directly counter to the Emperor's stated desire to maintain peaceful relations with this important trade depot. Still . . . given a sufficiently hostile court and ham-handed defense counsel . . . I shouldn't call court-martial a wise risk, if it can possibly be avoided." Miles rubbed his lips. "Were you drunk, by chance, when Sergeant Touchev came to pick you up?"

"No!"

"Hm. Pity. Drunk is a wonderfully safe defense. Not politically or socially radical, y'see. I don't suppose . . . ?"

Corbeau's mouth tightened in indignation. Suggesting Corbeau lie about his chemical state would not go over well, Miles sensed. Which gave him a higher opinion of the young officer, true. But it didn't make Miles's life any easier.

"I still want out," Corbeau repeated stubbornly.

"The quaddies don't much like Barrayarans this week, I'm afraid. Relying on them granting your asylum to pluck you out of your dilemma seems to me to be a grave mistake. There must be half a dozen better ways to solve your problems, if you'd open your mind to wider tactical possibilities. In fact, almost any other way would be better than this."

Corbeau shook his head, mute.

"Well, think about it, Ensign. I suspect the situation will remain murky until I find out what happened to Lieutenant Solian. At that point, I hope to unravel this tangle quickly, and the chance to change your mind about really bad ideas could run out abruptly."

He climbed wearily to his feet. Corbeau, after a moment of uncertainty, rose and saluted. Miles returned an acknowledging nod and motioned to Roic, who spoke into the cell's intercom and obtained their release.

He exited, frowning thoughtfully, to encounter the hovering Chief Venn. "I want *Solian*, dammit," Miles said grouchily to him. "This remarkable evaporation of his doesn't reflect any better on the competence of your security than it does on ours, y'know."

Venn glowered at him. But he didn't contradict this remark.

Miles sighed and raised his wrist com to his lips to call Ekaterin.

She insisted on having him rendezvous with her back at the *Kestrel*. Miles was just as glad for the excuse to escape the depressing atmosphere of Security Post Three. He couldn't call it moral ambiguity, alas. Worse, he couldn't call it legal ambiguity. It was quite clear which side was in the right; it just wasn't his side, dammit.

He found her in their little cabin, just hanging his brown-and-silver House uniform out on a hook. She turned and embraced him, and he tilted his head back for a long, luxurious kiss.

"So, how did your venture into Quaddiespace with Bel go?" he inquired, when he had breath to spare again.

"Very well, I thought. If Bel ever wants a change from being a portmaster, I believe it could go into Union public relations. I think I saw all the best parts of Graf Station that could be squeezed into the time we had. Splendid views, good food, history—Bel took me deep down into the free fall sector to see the preserved parts of the old jumpship that first brought the quaddies to this system. They have it set up as a museum—when we arrived it was full of quaddie schoolchildren, bouncing off the walls. Literally. They were incredibly cute. It almost reminded me of a Barrayaran ancestor-shrine." She released him and indicated a large box decorated with shiny, colorful pictures and schematics, occupying half the lower bunk. "I found this for

Nikki in the museum shop. It's a scale model of the D-620 Superjumper, modified with the orbital habitat configured on, that the quaddies' forebears escaped in."

"Oh, he'll like *that*." Nikki, at eleven, had not yet outgrown a passion for spaceships of every kind, but especially jumpships. It was still too early to guess whether the enthusiasm would turn into an adult avocation or fall by the wayside, but it certainly hadn't flagged yet. Miles peered more closely at the picture. The ancient D-620 had been an amazingly ungainly looking beast of a ship, appearing in this artist's rendition rather like an enormous metallic squid clutching a collection of cans. "Large-scale replica, I take it?"

She glanced rather doubtfully at it. "Not especially. It was a huge ship. I wonder if I should have chosen the smaller version? But it didn't come apart like this one. Now that I have it back here I'm not quite sure where to put it."

Ekaterin in maternal mode was quite capable of sharing her bunk with the thing all the way home, for Nikki's sake. "Lieutenant Smolyani will be happy to find a place to stow it."

"Really?"

"You have my personal guarantee." He favored her with a half-bow, hand over his heart. He wondered briefly if he ought to snag a couple more for little Aral Alexander and Helen Natalia while they were here, but the conversation with Ekaterin about *age-appropriate toys*, several times repeated during their sojourn on Earth, probably did not need another rehearsal. "What did you and Bel find to talk about?"

She smirked. "You, mostly."

Belated panic came out as nothing more self-incriminating than a brightly inquiring, "Oh?"

"Bel was wildly curious as to how we'd met, and obviously racking its brains to figure out how to ask without being rude. I took pity and told a little about meeting you on Komarr, and after. With all the classified parts left out, our courtship sounds awfully odd, do you know?"

He acknowledged this with a rueful shrug. "I've noticed. Can't be helped."

"Is it really true that the first time you met, you shot Bel with a stunner?"

The curiosity hadn't all run one way, evidently. "Well, yes. It's a long story. From a long time ago."

Her blue eyes crinkled with amusement. "So I understand. You were an absolute lunatic when you were younger, by all accounts. I'm not sure, if I'd met you back then, whether I'd have been impressed, or horrified."

Miles thought it over. "I'm not sure, either."

Her lips curled up again, and she stepped around him to lift a garment bag from the bunk. She drew from it a heavy fall of fabric in a blue-gray hue matching her eyes. It resolved itself into a jumpsuit of some swinging velvety stuff gathered to long, buttoned cuffs at the wrists and ankles, which gave the trouser legs a subtly sleeve-like look. She held it up to herself.

"*That's* new," he said approvingly.

"Yes, I can be both fashionable in gravity and demure in free fall." She laid the garment back down and stroked its silky nap.

"I take it Bel blocked any unpleasantness due to your being Barrayaran, when you two were out and about?"

She straightened. "Well, *I* didn't have any problems. Bel was accosted by one odd-looking fellow—he had the longest, narrowest hands and feet. Something funny about his chest, too, rather oversized. I wondered if he was genetically engineered for anything special, or if it was some sort of surgical modification. I suppose one meets all kinds, out here on the edge of the Nexus. He badgered Bel to tell how soon the passengers were to be let back aboard, and said there was a rumor someone had been allowed to take off their cargo, but Bel assured him—firmly!—that no one had been let on the ships since they were impounded. One of the passengers from the *Rudra*, worrying about his goods, I gather. He implied the seized cargoes were subject to rifling and theft by the quaddie dockhands, which didn't go over too well with Bel."

"I can imagine."

"Then he wanted to know what you were doing, and how the Barrayarans were going to respond. Naturally, Bel didn't say who I was. Bel said if he wanted to know what Barrayarans were doing, he'd do better to ask one directly, and to get in line to make an appointment with you through Sealer Greenlaw like everyone else. The fellow wasn't too happy, but Bel threatened to have him escorted back to his hostel by Station Security and confined there if he didn't give over pestering, so he shut up and went scurrying to find Greenlaw."

"Good for Bel." He sighed, and hitched his tight shoulders. "I suppose I'd better deal with Greenlaw again next."

"No, you shouldn't," Ekaterin said firmly. "You've done nothing but talk with committees of upset people since the first thing this morning. The answer, I expect, is no. The question is, did you ever stop to eat lunch, or take any sort of break?"

"Um . . . well, no. How did you guess?"

She merely smiled. "Then the next item on your schedule, my Lord Auditor, is a nice dinner with your wife and your old friends. Bel and Nicol are taking us out. And after that, we're going to the quaddie ballet."

"We are?"

"Yes."

"Why? I mean, I have to eat sometime, I suppose, but my wandering off in the middle of the case to, um, disport myself, won't thrill anyone who's waiting on me to solve this mess. Starting with Admiral Vorpatril and his staff, I daresay."

"It will thrill the quaddies. They're vastly proud of the Minchenko Ballet, and being seen to show an interest in their culture can do you nothing but good with them. The troupe only performs once or twice a week, depending on the passenger traffic in port and the season—do they have seasons here? time of year, anyway—so we might not get another chance." Her smile grew sly. "It was a sold-out show, but Bel had Garnet Five pull strings and get us a box. She'll be joining us there."

Miles blinked. "She wants to pitch her case to me about Corbeau, does she?"

"That's what I'd guess." At his dubiously wrinkled nose, she added, "I found out more about her today. She's a famous person on Graf Station, a local celebrity. The Barrayaran patrol's assault on her was news; because she's a performing artist, breaking her arm like that has put her out of work for a time, as well as being an awful thing in its own right—it was extra culturally offensive, in quaddie eyes."

"Oh, terrific." Miles rubbed the bridge of his nose. It wasn't just his imagination; he did have a headache.

"Yes. So the sight of Garnet Five at the ballet, chatting cordially with the Barrayaran envoy, all forgiven and amicable, is worth what to you, in propaganda points?"

"Ah ha!" He hesitated. "As long as she doesn't end up flouncing out of my presence in a public rage because I can't promise her anything yet about Corbeau. Tricky situation, that one, and the boy's not being as smart as he could be about it."

"She's apparently a person of strong emotions, but not stupid, or so I gather from Bel. I don't *think* Bel would have coaxed me to let it arrange this in order to engineer a public disaster . . . but perhaps you have reason to think otherwise?"

"No . . ."

"Anyway, I'm sure you'll be able to handle Garnet Five. Just be your usual charming self."

Ekaterin's vision of him, he reminded himself, was not exactly objective. Thank God. "I've been trying to charm quaddies all day, with no noticeable success."

"If you make it plain you like people, it's hard for them to resist liking you back. And Nicol will be playing in the orchestra tonight."

"Oh." He perked up. "*That* will be worth hearing." Ekaterin was shrewdly observant; he had no doubt she had spent the afternoon picking up cultural vibrations that went well beyond local fashions. The quaddie ballet it was. "Will you wear your fancy new outfit?"

"That's why I bought it. We honor the artists by dressing up for them. Now, skin back into your House uniform. Bel will be along to collect us soon."

"I'd better stick to my dull grays. I have a feeling that parading Barrayaran uniforms in front of the quaddies just now is a bad idea, diplomatically speaking."

"In Security Post Three, probably. But there's no point in being seen enjoying their art if we just look like any other anonymous downsiders. Tonight, I think we should both look as Barrayaran as possible."

His being seen with *Ekaterin* was good for a few points, too, he rather fancied, although not so much propaganda as pure swaggering one-upsmanship. He tapped his trouser seam, where no sword hung. "Right."

Chapter 6

Bel arrived promptly at the *Kestrel*'s hatch, having changed from its staid work uniform into a startling but cheerful orange doublet with glinting, star-decorated blue sleeves, slashed trousers bloused into cuffs at the knee, and color-coordinated midnight-blue hose and friction boots. Variations of the style seemed to be the local high fashion for both males and females, whether with or without legs, judging by Greenlaw's less blinding outfit.

The herm conducted them to a hushed and serene restaurant on the grav side of the station with the usual transparent window-wall overlooking station and starscape. An occasional tug or pod zipped silently past outside, adding interest to the scene. Despite the gravitation, which at least kept food on open plates, the place bowed to quaddie architectural ideals by having tables set on their own private pillars at varying heights, using all three dimensions of the room. Servers flitted back and forth and up and down in floaters. The design pleased everyone but Roic, who cranked his neck around in dismay, watching for trouble in 3-D. But Bel, ever thoughtful, as well as trained in security protocols, had provided Roic with his own perch above theirs, with an overview of the whole room; Roic mounted to his eyrie looking more reconciled.

Nicol was waiting for them at their table, which commanded a superior view out the window-wall. Her garments ran to form-fitting black knits and filmy rainbow scarves; otherwise, her appearance was not much changed from when Miles had first met her so many years and wormhole jumps ago. She was still slim, graceful of movement even in her floater, with pure ivory skin and short-clipped ebony hair, and her eyes still danced. She and Ekaterin regarded each other with great interest, and fell at once into conversation with very little prompting from Bel or Miles.

The talk ranged widely as exquisite food appeared in a smooth stream, presented by the place's well-trained and unobtrusive staff. Music, gardening, and station bio-recycling techniques led to discussion of quaddie population dynamics and the methods—technical, economic, and political—for seeding new habitats in the growing necklace along the asteroid belt. Only old war stories, by a silent, mutual agreement, failed to trickle into the conversational flow.

When Bel guided Ekaterin off to the lavatory between the last course and dessert, Nicol watched her out of earshot, then leaned over and murmured to Miles, "I am glad for you, Admiral Naismith."

He touched a finger briefly to his lips. "Be glad for Miles Vorkosigan. I certainly am." He hesitated, then asked, "Should I be equally glad for Bel?"

Her smile crimped a little. "Only Bel knows. I'm done with traveling the Nexus. I've found my place, home at last. Bel seems happy here too, most of the time, but—well, Bel is a downsider. They get *itchy feet*, I'm told. Bel talks about making a commitment to the Union, yet . . . somehow, never gets around to applying."

"I'm sure Bel's interested in doing so," Miles offered.

She shrugged, and drained the last of her lemon drink; anticipating her performance later, she had forgone the wine. "Maybe the secret of happiness is to live for today, to never look ahead. Or maybe that's just a habit of mind Bel got into in its former life. All that risk, all that danger—it takes a certain sort to thrive on it. I'm not sure Bel can change its nature, or how much it would hurt to try. Maybe too much."

"Mm," said Miles. *I can't offer them a false oath, or divided loyalties*, Bel had said. Even Nicol, apparently, was not aware of Bel's second source of income—and hazard. "I do note, Bel could have found a portmaster's berth in quite a few places. It traveled a very long way to get one here, instead."

Nicol's smile softened. "That's so." She added, "Do you know, when Bel arrived at Graf Station, it still had that Betan dollar I'd paid you on Jackson's Whole tucked in its wallet?"

Miles managed to stop the logical query, *Are you sure it was the same one?* on his lips before it fell out of his mouth leaving room for his downsider foot. One Betan dollar looked like any other. If Bel had claimed it for the same one, when making Nicol's reacquaintance, who was Miles to suggest otherwise? Not that much of a spoilsport, for damn sure.

After dinner they made their way under Bel and Nicol's guidance to the bubble-car system, its arteries of transit recently retrofitted into the three-dimensional maze Graf Station had grown to be. Nicol left her floater in a common rack on the passenger platform. It took their car about ten minutes to wend through the branching tubes to their destination; Miles's stomach lifted when they crossed into the free fall side, and he made haste to slip his antinausea meds from his pocket, swallow one, and offer them discreetly to Ekaterin and Roic.

The entrance to the Madame Minchenko Memorial Auditorium was neither large nor imposing, being just one of several accessible airseal doorways on different levels of the station here. Nicol kissed Bel and flitted off. No crowds yet clogged the cylindrical corridors, as they'd come early to give Nicol time to make her way backstage and change. Miles was therefore unprepared for the vast chamber into which they floated.

It was an enormous sphere. Nearly a third of its interior surface was a round, transparent window-wall, the universe itself turned into backdrop, thick with bright stars on this shaded side of the station. Ekaterin grabbed his hand rather abruptly, and Roic made a small choked noise. Miles had the sense of having swum inside a giant beehive, for the rest of the wall was lined with hexagonal cells like a silver-edged honeycomb filled with rainbow jewels. As they floated out toward the middle the cells resolved into velvet-lined boxes for the audience, varying in size from cozy niches for one patron to units spacious enough for parties of ten, if the ten were quaddies, not trailing long useless legs. Other sectors, interspersed, seemed to be dark, flat panels of various shapes, or to contain other exits. He tried at first to impose a sense of up and down upon the space, but then he blinked, and the chamber seemed to rotate around the window, and then he wasn't sure if he was looking up, down, or sideways through it. Down was a particularly disturbing mental construction, as it gave the dizzy impression of falling into a vast well of stars.

A quaddie usher wearing an air-jet belt took them in tow, after they had gawked their fill, and steered them gently wall-ward to their assigned hexagon. It was lined with some dark, soft, sound-baffling padding and convenient handgrips, and included its own lighting, the colored jewels seen from afar.

A dark shape and a gleam of motion in their generously sized box resolved itself, as they approached, as a quaddie woman. She was slim and long-limbed, with fine white-blond hair cut finger length and waving in an aureole around her head. It made Miles think of mermaids of legend. Cheekbones to inspire men to duel with each other, or perhaps scribble bad poetry, or drown in drink. Or worse, desert their brigade. She was clothed in close-fitting black velvet with a little white lace ruff at her throat. The cuff on the lower right elbow of her softly pleated black velvet pants . . . sleeve, Miles decided, not leg, had been left unfastened to make room for a medical air-filled arm immobilizer of a sort painfully familiar to Miles from his fragile-boned youth. It was the only stiff, ungraceful thing about her, a crude insult to the rest of the ensemble.

No mistaking her for anyone other than Garnet Five, but he waited for Bel to introduce them all properly, which Bel promptly did. They shook hands all around; Miles found her grip athlete-firm.

"Thank you for obtaining these—" *seats* did not apply, "this space for us on such short notice," Miles said, releasing her slim upper hand. "I understand we are to be privileged to view some very fine work." *Work* was a word with extra resonance in Quaddiespace, he had already gathered, like *honor* on Barrayar.

"My pleasure, Lord Vorkosigan." Her voice was melodious; her expression seemed cool, almost ironic, but an underlying anxiety glowed in her leaf-green eyes.

Miles opened his hand to indicate her broken lower right arm. "May I convey my personal apologies for the poor behavior of some of our men. They will be disciplined for it, when we get them back. Please do not judge all Barrayarans by our worst examples." *Well, she can't; we actually don't ship out our worst, Gregor be praised.*

She smiled briefly. "I do not, for I've also met your best." The urgency in her eyes tinged her voice. "Dmitri—what will happen to him?"

"Well, that depends to a great extent on Dmitri." Pitches, Miles suddenly realized, could run two ways, here. "It could range, when he is released and returns to duty, from a minor black mark on his record—he wasn't supposed to remove his wrist com while on station leave, you know, for just the sort of reason you unfortunately discovered—to a very serious charge of attempted desertion, if he fails to withdraw his request for political asylum before it is denied."

Her jaw set a trifle. "Perhaps it won't be denied."

"Even if granted, the long-term consequences could be more complex than you perhaps anticipate. He would at that point be plainly guilty of desertion. He would be permanently exiled from his home, never able to return or see his family. Barrayar might seem a world well lost now, in the first flush of . . . emotion, but I think—I'm sure—it's something he could come to deeply regret later." He thought of melancholy Baz Jesek, exiled for years over an even more badly managed conflict. "There are other, if less speedy, ways Ensign Corbeau might yet end up back here, if his desire to do so is true will and not temporary whim. It would take a little more time, but be infinitely less damaging—he's playing for the rest of his life with this, after all."

She frowned. "Won't the Barrayaran military have him shot, or horribly butchered, or—or assassinated?"

"We are not at war with the Union." *Yet, anyway.* It would take more heroic blundering than this to make that happen, but he ought not to underestimate his fellow Barrayarans, he supposed. And he didn't think Corbeau was politically important enough to assassinate. *So let's try to make sure he doesn't become so, eh?* "He wouldn't be executed. But twenty years in jail is hardly better, from your point of view. You don't serve him *or* yourself by encouraging him to this desertion. Let him return to duty, serve out his hitch, get passage back. If you're both still of the same mind then, continue your relationship without his unresolved legal status poisoning your future together."

Her expression had grown still more grimly stubborn. He felt horribly like some stodgy parent lecturing his angst-ridden teenager, but she was no child. He'd have to ask Bel her age. Her grace and authority of motion might be the results of her dancer's training. He remembered that they were supposed to be looking cordial, so tried to soften his words with a belated smile.

She said, "We wish to become partners. Permanently."

After only two weeks of acquaintance, are you so sure? He strangled this comment in his throat as Ekaterin's sideways glance at him put him in mind of just how many days—or was it hours?—it had taken him to fall in love with her. Granted, the *permanently* part had taken longer. "I can certainly see why Corbeau would wish that." The reverse was more puzzling, of course. In both cases. He himself did not find Corbeau lovable—his strongest emotion so far was a deep desire to whack the ensign on the side of the head—but this woman clearly didn't see him that way.

"Permanently?" said Ekaterin doubtfully. "But . . . don't you think you might wish to have children someday? Or might he?"

Garnet Five's expression grew hopeful. "We've talked about having children together. We're both interested."

"Um, er," said Miles. "Quaddies are not interfertile with downsiders, surely?"

"Well, one has to make choices, before they go into the replicators, just as a herm crossing with a monosexual has to choose whether to have the genetics adjusted to produce a boy or a girl or a herm. Some quaddie-downsider partnerships have quaddie children, some have downsiders, some have some of each—Bel, show Lord Vorkosigan your baby pictures!"

Miles's head swiveled around. "What?"

Bel blushed and dug in its trouser pocket. "Nicol and I . . . when we went to the geneticist for counseling, they ran a projection of all the possible combinations, to help us choose." The herm held up a holocube and turned it on. Six full-length still shots of children sprang into being above its hand. They were all frozen in their early teens, with the sense of adult features just starting to emerge from childhood's roundness. They had Bel's eyes, Nicol's jawline, hair a brownish black with that familiar swipe of a forelock. A boy, a girl, and a herm with legs; a boy, a girl, and a herm quaddie.

"Oh," said Ekaterin, reaching for it. "How *interesting*."

"The facial features are just an electronic blend of Nicol's and mine, not a genuine genetic projection," Bel explained, willingly giving the cube to her. "For that, they'd need an actual cell from a real conceptus, which, of course, they can't have till a real one is made for the genetic modifications."

Ekaterin turned the array back and forth, examining the portraits from all angles. Miles, looking over her shoulder, told himself firmly that it was probably just as well that his holovid of the blandly blastular Aral Alexander and Helen Natalia was still in his luggage back aboard the *Kestrel*. But maybe later he would have a chance to show Bel—

"Have you two finally decided what you want?" asked Garnet Five.

"A little quaddie girl, to start. Like Nicol." Bel's face softened, then, abruptly, recovered its habitual ironic smile. "Assuming I take the plunge and apply for my Union citizenship."

Miles imagined Garnet Five and Dmitri Corbeau with a string of handsome, athletic quaddie children. Or Bel and Nicol, with a clutch of smart, musical ones. It made his head spin. Roic, looking quietly boggled, shook his head at Ekaterin's profferment of a closer examination of the holo-array.

"Ah," said Bel. "The show's about to start." The herm retrieved the holocube and switched it off, and plunged it back safely deep in the pocket of its baggy blue knee breeches, carefully fastening the flap.

The auditorium had filled to capacity while they spoke, the honeycomb of cells now harboring an attentive crowd including a fair smattering of other downsiders, though whether Union citizen or galactic visitor Miles could not always tell. No green Barrayaran uniforms tonight, in any case. The lights dimmed; the hubbub quieted, and a few last quaddies sped across to their boxes and settled in. A couple of downsiders who had misjudged their momentum and were stranded in the middle were rescued by the ushers and towed to their box, earning a quiet snicker from the quaddies who noticed. An electric tension filled the air, the odd blend of hope and fear that any live performance bore, with its risk of imperfection, chance of greatness. The lights dimmed further, till only the blue-white starshine glinted off the chamber's array of now-crowded cells.

Lights flared, an exuberant fountain of red and orange and gold, and from all sides, the performers flowed in. *Thundered* in. Quaddie males, athletic and vastly enthusiastic, in skin-fitting ship knits made splendid with glitter. *Drumming.*

I wasn't expecting hand drums. Other free fall performances Miles had seen, whether dance or gymnastic, had been eerily silent except for the music and sound effects. Quaddies made their own noise, and still had hands left to play hands-across; the drummers met in the middle, clasped, gripped, exchanged momentum, turned, and doubled back in a shifting pattern. Two dozen men in free fall took up perfect station in the center of the spherical auditorium, their motion so controlled as to permit no sideways drift as the energy of their spins and duckings, twistings and turnings, flowed through their bodies one to another and on around again. The air pulsed with the rhythm of their drumming: drums of all sizes, round, oblong, two-headed; not only played by each holder, but some batted back and forth among them in an eye-and-ear-stunning cross between music and juggling, never missing a beat or a blow. The lights danced. Reflections spattered on the walls, picking out flashes from the boxes of upraised hands, arms, bright cloth, jewelry, entranced faces.

Then, from another entrance, a dozen female quaddies all in blues and greens geysered up into the growing, geodesic pattern and joined the dance. All Miles could think was, *Whoever first brought castanets to Quaddiespace has much to answer for.* They added a laughing descant note to the percussive braid of sound: hand drums and castanets, no other instruments. None needed. The round chamber reverberated, fairly rocked. He stole a glance sideways; Ekaterin's lips were parted, her eyes wide and shining, drinking in all this booming splendor without reserve.

Miles considered Barrayaran marching bands. It wasn't enough that humans did something so difficult as learning to play a musical instrument. Then they had to do it in *groups.* While *walking around.* In *complicated patterns.* And then they competed with one another to do it even *better.* Excellence, this kind of excellence, could never have any sane economic justification. It had to be done for the honor of one's country, or one's people, or the glory of God. For the joy of being human.

The piece ran for twenty minutes, until the players were gasping and sweat spun off them in tiny drops to speed in sparking streaks into the darkness, and still they whirled and thundered. Miles had to stop himself from hyperventilating in sympathy, heartbeat synchronized with their rhythms. Then, one last grand blast of joyous noise—and somehow the shifting net of four-armed men and women resolved itself into two chains, which flowed away into the exits from which they had emerged a revelation ago.

Darkness again. The silence was like a blow; behind him, Miles heard Roic exhale reverently, longingly, like a man home from war easing himself into his own bed for the first time.

The applause—hand-clapping, of course—rocked the room. No one in the Barrayaran party, Miles thought, had to *pretend* enthusiasm for quaddie culture now.

The chamber hushed again as the orchestra emerged from four points and filtered into positions all around the great window. The half-a-hundred quaddies bore a more standard array of instruments—all acoustic, Ekaterin observed to him in a fascinated whisper. They spotted Nicol, assisted by two more quaddies who helped manage and secure her harp, which was nearly the usual shape for a harp, and her double-sided hammer dulcimer, appearing to be a dull oblong box from this angle. But the piece that followed included a solo section for her with the dulcimer, her ivory face picked out in spotlights, and the music that poured forth between her four flashing hands was anything but dull. Radiantly ethereal; heartbreaking; electrifying.

Bel must have seen this dozens of times, Miles guessed, but the herm was surely as entranced as any newcomer. It wasn't just a lover's smile that illuminated Bel's eyes. *Yes. You would not be loving her properly if you did not also love her improvident, lavish, spendthrift excellence.* No jealous lover, greedy and selfish, could hoard it all; it had to be poured forth upon the world, or burst its wellspring. He glanced at Ekaterin and thought of her glorious gardens, much missed back on Barrayar. *I shall not keep you away from them much longer, love, I promise.*

There was a brief pause, while quaddie stagehands arranged a few mysterious poles and bars sticking in at odd angles around the interior of the sphere. Garnet Five, floating sideways with respect to Miles, murmured over her shoulder, "Coming up is the piece I usually dance. It's an excerpt from a larger work, Aljean's classic ballet *The Crossing*, which tells the story of our people's migration through the Nexus to Quaddiespace. It's the love duet between Leo and Silver. I dance Silver. I hope my understudy doesn't muck it up . . ." She trailed off as the overture swelled.

Two figures, a downsider male and a blond quaddie woman, floated in from opposite sides of the space, picked up momentum with hand-spins around a couple of the poles, and met in the middle. No drums this time, just sweet, liquid sound from the orchestra. The Leo character's legs trailed uselessly, and it took Miles a moment to realize that he was being played by a quaddie dancer with dummy legs. The woman's use of angular momentum, drawing in or extending various arms as she twirled or spun, was brilliantly controlled, her changes of trajectory around the various poles precise. Only a few indrawn breaths and critical mutters from Garnet Five suggested anything less than perfection to Miles's perceptions. The false-legged fellow was deliberately clumsy, earning a chuckle from the quaddie audience. Miles shifted uncomfortably, realizing he was watching a near-parody of how downsiders looked to quaddie eyes. But the woman's charming gestures of assistance made it seem more endearing than cruel. Bel, grinning, leaned over to murmur in Miles's ear, "It's all right. Leo Graf's supposed to dance like an engineer. He was."

The love angle of it all was clear enough. Affairs between quaddies and downsiders apparently had a long and honorable history. It occurred to Miles that certain aspects of his youth might have been rendered much easier if Barrayar had possessed a repertoire of romantic tales starring short, crippled heroes, instead of mutie villains. If this was a fair sample, it was clear that Garnet Five was culturally primed to play Juliet to her Barrayaran Romeo. *But let's not enact a tragedy this time, eh?*

The enchanting piece drew to a climax, and the two dancers saluted the enthusiastically clapping audience before making their way out. The lights came up; break time. Performance art was fundamentally constrained, Miles realized, by biology, in this case the capacity of the human bladder, whether downsider or quaddie.

When they all rendezvoused again in their box, he found Garnet Five explaining quaddie naming conventions to Ekaterin.

"No, it's not a surname," said Garnet Five. "When quaddies were first made by the GalacTech Corporation, there were only one thousand of us. Each had just one given name, plus a numerical designation, and with so few, each name was unique. When our ancestors fled to their freedom, they altered what the numbers coded, but kept the system of single, unique names, tracked in a register. With all of old Earth's languages to draw on, it was several generations before the system really began to be strained. The waiting lists for the really popular names were insanely long. So they voted to allow duplication, but only if the name had a numerical suffix, so we could always tell every Leo from every other Leo. When you die, your name-number goes back in the registry to be drawn again."

"I have a Leo Ninety-nine in my Docks and Locks crew," said Bel. "It's the highest number I've run across yet. Lower numbers, or none, seem to be preferred."

"I've never run across any of the other Garnets," said Garnet Five. "There were eight altogether somewhere in the Union, last time I looked it up."

"I'll bet there will be more," said Bel. "And it'll be your fault."

Garnet Five laughed. "I can wish!"

The second half of the show was as impressive as the first. During one of the musical interludes, Nicol had an exquisite harp part. There were two more large group dances, one abstract and mathematical, the other narrative, apparently based on a tragic pressurization disaster of a prior generation. The finale put everyone out in the middle, for a last vigorous, dizzying whirl, with drummers, castanet players, and orchestra combining in musical support that could only be described as massive.

It felt to Miles as though the performance ended all too soon, but his chrono told him four hours had passed in this dream. He bade a grateful but noncommittal farewell to Garnet Five. As Bel and Nicol escorted the three Barrayarans back to the *Kestrel* in the bubble car, he reflected on how cultures told their stories to themselves, and so defined themselves. Above all, the ballet celebrated the quaddie body. Surely no downsider could walk out of the quaddie ballet still imagining the four-armed people as mutated, crippled, or otherwise disadvantaged or inferior. One might even—as Corbeau had demonstrated—walk out having free-fallen in love.

Not that all crippling damage was visible to the eye. All this exuberant athleticism reminded him to check his brain chemical levels before bed, and see how soon his next seizure was likely to be.

Chapter 7

Miles woke from a sound sleep to tapping on his cabin door.

"M'lord?" came Roic's hushed voice. "Admiral Vorpatril wants to talk with you. He's on the secured comconsole in the wardroom."

Whatever inspiration his backbrain might have floated up to his consciousness in the drowsy interlude between sleep and waking flitted away beyond recall. Miles groaned and swung out of his bunk. Ekaterin's hand extended from the top bunk, and she peeked over blearily at him; he touched it and whispered, "Go back to sleep, love." She snuffled agreeably and rolled over.

Miles ran his hands through his hair, grabbed his gray jacket, shrugged it on over his underwear, and padded out barefoot into the corridor. As the airseal door hissed closed behind him, he checked his chrono. Since Quaddiespace didn't have to deal with inconvenient planetary rotations, they kept a single time zone throughout local space, to which Miles and Ekaterin had supposedly adjusted on the trip in. All right, so it wasn't the middle of the night, it was early morning.

Miles sat at the wardroom table, straightened his jacket and fastened it to the neck, and touched the control on his station chair. Admiral Vorpatril's face and torso appeared over the vid plate. He was awake, dressed, shaved, and had a coffee cup at his right hand, the rat-bastard.

Vorpatril shook his head, lips tight. "How the hell did you know?" he demanded.

Miles squinted. "I beg your pardon?"

"I just got back the report on Solian's blood sample from my chief surgeon. It *was* manufactured, probably within twenty-four hours of its being spilled on the deck."

"Oh." *Hell and damnation.* "That's . . . unfortunate."

"But what does it mean? Is the man still alive somewhere? I'd have sworn he wasn't a deserter, but maybe Brun was right."

Like the stopped clock, even idiots could be correct sometimes. "I'll have to think about this. It doesn't actually prove if Solian's alive or dead, either way. It doesn't even, necessarily, prove that he wasn't killed *there*, just not by getting his throat cut."

Armsman Roic, God bless and keep him forever, set a cup of steaming coffee down by Miles's elbow and withdrew to his station by the door. Miles cleared his mouth, if not his mind, with the first sluicing swallow, and took a second sip to buy a moment to think.

Vorpatril had a head start on both coffee and calculation. "Should we report this to Chief Venn? Or . . . not?"

Miles made a dubious noise in his throat. His one diplomatic edge, the only thing that had given him, so to speak, a leg to stand on here, had been the possibility that Solian had been murdered by an unknown quaddie. This was now rendered even more problematic, it seemed. "The blood had to have been manufactured somewhere. If you have the right equipment, it's easy, and if you don't, it's impossible. Find all such equipment on station—or aboard ships in dock—and the place it was done has to be one of 'em. The place plus the time should lead to the people. Process of elimination. It's the sort of footwork . . ." Miles hesitated, but went on, "that the local police are better equipped to carry out than we are. If they can be trusted."

"Trust the quaddies? Hardly!"

"What motivation do they have to lie or misdirect us?" *What, indeed?* "I have to work through Greenlaw and Venn. I have no authority on Graf Station in my own right." Well, there was Bel, but he had to use Bel sparingly or risk the herm's cover.

He wanted the truth. Ruefully, he recognized that he also would prefer to have a monopoly on it, at least until he had time to figure out how best to play for Barrayar's interests. *Yet if the truth doesn't serve us, what does that say about us, eh?* He rubbed his stubbled chin. "It does clearly prove that whatever happened in that freight bay, whether murder or cover-up, was carefully planned, and not spontaneous. I'll undertake to speak with Greenlaw and Venn about it. Talking to the quaddies is my job now, anyway." *For my sins, presumably. What god did I piss off this time?* "Thank you, Admiral, and thank your fleet surgeon from me for a good job."

Vorpatril gave a grudgingly pleased nod at this acknowledgment, and Miles cut the com.

"Dammit," he muttered querulously, frowning into the blank space. "Why didn't anyone pick up this information on the first pass? It's not *my* job to be a bloody forensic pathologist."

"I expect," began Armsman Roic, and stopped. "Uh . . . was that a question, m'lord?"

Miles swung around in his station chair. "A rhetorical one, but do you have an answer?"

"Well, m'lord," said Roic diffidently. "It's about the size of things here. Graf Station is a pretty big space habitat, but it's really a kind of a small city, by Barrayaran standards. And all these spacer types tend to be pretty law-abiding, in certain ways. All those safety rules. I don't imagine they *get* many murders here."

"How many did you used to get in Hassadar?" Graf Station boasted fifty thousand or so residents; the Vorkosigans' District capital's population was approaching half a million, these days.

"Maybe one or two a month, on average. They didn't come in smoothly. Seems there'd be a run of 'em, then a quiet period. More in the summer than the winter, except around Winterfair. Got a lot of multiples then. Most of 'em weren't *mysteries*, of course. But even in Hassadar there weren't enough really odd ones to keep our forensics folks in practice, y'see. Our medical people were part-timers from the District University, mostly, on call. If we ever got anything really strange, we'd call in one of Lord Vorbohn's homicide investigators from Vorbarr Sultana. They must get a murder every day or so up there—all sorts, lots of experience. I'll bet Chief Venn doesn't even have a forensics department, just some quaddie doctors he taps once in a while. So I wouldn't *expect* them to be, um, up to ImpSec standards like what you're used to. M'lord."

"That's . . . an interesting point, Armsman. Thank you." Miles took another swallow of his coffee. "Solian . . ." he said thoughtfully. "I don't know enough about Solian yet. Did he have enemies? Damn it, didn't the man have even one friend? Or a lover? If he *was* killed, was it for personal or for professional reasons? It makes a huge difference."

Miles had glanced through Solian's military record on the inbound leg, and found it unexceptionable. If the man had ever been to Quaddiespace before, it wasn't since he'd joined the Imperial service six years previously. He'd had two prior voyages, with different fleet consortiums and different military escorts; his experiences had apparently included nothing more exciting than handling an occasional inebriated crewman or belligerent passenger.

On average, more than half the military personnel on any tour of nexus escort duty would be new to each other. If Solian had made friends—or enemies—in the weeks since this fleet had departed Komarr, they almost had to have been on the *Idris*. If his disappearance had been closer to the time of the fleet's arrival in Quaddiespace, Miles would have pegged the professional possibilities to the *Idris* as well, but the ten days in dock was plenty of time for a nosy security man to find trouble stationside, too.

He drained his cup and punched up Chief Venn's number on the station-chair console. The quaddie security commander had also arrived early to work, apparently. His personal office was evidently on the free fall side of things. He appeared floating sideways to Miles in the vid view, a coffee bulb clutched in his upper right hand. He murmured a polite, "Good morning, Lord Auditor Vorkosigan," but undercut the verbal courtesy by not righting himself with respect to Miles, who had to exert a conscious effort to keep from tilting out of his chair. "What can I do for you?"

"Several things, but first, a question. When was the last murder on Graf Station?"

Venn's brows twitched. "There was one about seven years ago."

"And, ah, before that?"

"Three years before, I believe."

A veritable crime wave. "Did you have charge of those investigations?"

"Well, they were before my time—I became security chief for Graf Station about five years back. But there wasn't that much to investigate. Both suspects were downsider transients—one killed another downsider, the other murdered a quaddie he'd got into some stupid dispute over a payment with. Guilt confirmed by witnesses and fast-penta interrogation. It's almost always downsiders in these affairs, I notice."

"Have you *ever* investigated a mysterious killing before?"

Venn righted himself, apparently in order to frown more effectively at Miles. "I and my people are fully trained in the appropriate procedures, I assure you."

"I'm afraid I must reserve judgment on that point, Chief Venn. I have some rather curious news. I had the Barrayaran fleet surgeon reexamine Solian's blood sample. It appears that the blood in question was artificially produced, presumably using an initial specimen or template of Solian's real blood or tissue. You may wish to have your forensics people—whoever they are—retest your own archived evidence from the freight bay and confirm this."

Venn's frown deepened. "Then . . . he *was* a deserter—not murdered after all! No wonder we couldn't find a body!"

"You run—you hurry ahead, I believe. I grant you the scenario has grown extremely murky. My request, then, is that you locate all possible facilities on Graf Station where such a tissue synthesis could be carried out, and see if there is any record of such a batch being run off, and who for. Or if it could have been slipped through off the record, for that matter. I think we can safely assume that whoever had it done, Solian or some unknown, was keenly interested in concealment. The surgeon reports the blood likely was generated not much more than a day before it was spilled, but the inquiry had better be run back to the time the *Idris* first docked, to be sure."

"I . . . follow your logic, certainly." Venn held his coffee bulb to his mouth and squeezed, then transferred it absently to his lower left hand. "Yes, certainly," he echoed himself more faintly. "I'll see to it myself."

Miles felt satisfied that he'd rocked Venn off-balance to just the right degree to embarrass him into effective action, yet not freeze him into defensiveness. "Thank you."

Venn added, "I believe Sealer Greenlaw wished to speak with you this morning, also, Lord Vorkosigan."

"Very well. You may transfer my call to her, if you please."

Greenlaw was a morning person, it appeared, or else had drunk her coffee earlier. She appeared in the holovid dressed in a different elaborate doublet, stern, and fully awake. Perhaps more by diplomatic habit than any desire to please, she twitched herself around right-side-up to Miles.

"Good morning, Lord Auditor Vorkosigan. In response to their petitions, I have arranged you an appointment with the Komarran fleet's stranded passengers at ten-hundred. You may meet with them to answer their questions at the larger of the two hostels where they are presently housed. Portmaster Thorne will meet you at your ship and conduct you there."

Miles's head jerked back at this cavalier arrangement of his time and attention. Not to mention blatant pressure move. On the other hand . . . this delivered him a room *full* of suspects, just the people he wished to study. He split the difference between irritation and eagerness by remarking blandly, "Nice of you to let me know. Just what is it that you imagine I will be able to tell them?"

"That, I must leave to you. These people came in with you Barrayarans; they are your responsibility."

"Madam, if that were so, they would all be on their way already. There can be no responsibility without power. It is the Union authorities who have placed them under this house arrest, and therefore the Union authorities who must free them."

"When you finish settling the fines, costs, and charges your people have incurred here, we will be only too happy to do so."

Miles smiled thinly, and laced his hands together on the tabletop. He wished the only new card he had to play this morning were less ambiguous. Nevertheless, he repeated to her the news about Solian's manufactured blood sample, well-larded with complaint about quaddie Security not having determined this peculiar fact earlier. She bounced it back instantly, as Venn had, as evidence more supporting of desertion than murder.

"Fine," said Miles. "Then have Union Security produce the man. A foreign downsider wandering about in Quad-diespace can't be that hard for a *competent* police force to locate. Assuming they're actually trying."

"Quaddiespace," she sniffed back, "is not a *totalitarian* polity. As your Lieutenant Solian may perhaps have observed. Our guarantees of freedom of movement and personal privacy could well have been what attracted him to separate himself here from his former comrades."

"So why hasn't he asked for asylum like Ensign Cor-beau? No. I greatly fear what we have here is not a missing man, but a missing corpse. The dead cannot cry out for justice; it is a duty of the living to do so for them. And that *is* a responsibility of mine for mine, madam."

They closed the conversation on that note; Miles could only hope he'd made her morning as aggravating as she'd made his. He cut the com and rubbed the back of his neck. "Gah. That ties *me* down for the rest of the day, I'll bet." He glanced up at Roic, whose guard stance by the door had segued into at ease, his shoulders propped against the wall. "Roic."

Roic quickly drew himself upright. "My lord?"

"Have *you* ever conducted a criminal investigation?"

"Well . . . I was just a street guard, mostly. But I got to go along and help the senior officers on a few fraud and assault cases. And one kidnapping. We got her back alive. Several missing persons. Oh, and about a dozen murders, though like I said, they weren't hardly mysteries. And the series of arsons that time that—"

"Right." Miles waved a hand to stem this gentle tide of reminiscence. "I want you to do the detail work for me on Solian. First, the timetable. I want you to find out every documented thing the man did. His watch reports, where he was, what he ate, when he slept—and who with, if anyone—minute by minute, or as nearly as you can come to it, from the time of his disappearance right on back as far as you can take it. Especially any movements off the ship, and missing time. And then I want the personal slant—talk to the crew and captain of the *Idris*, try to find out anything you can about the fellow. I take it I don't need to give you the lecture on the difference between fact, conjecture, and hearsay?"

"No, m'lord. But . . ."

"Vorpatril and Brun will give you full cooperation and access, I promise you. Or if they don't, let me know." Miles smiled a bit grimly.

"It's not that, m'lord. Who'll run your personal security on Graf Station if I'm off poking around Admiral Vorpatril's fleet?"

Miles managed to swallow his airy, *I won't need a bodyguard*, upon the reflection that by his own pet theory, a desperate murderer might be floating around, possibly literally, on the station. "I'll have Captain Thorne with me."

Roic looked dubious. "I can't approve, m'lord. He's— it's—not even Barrayaran. What do you really know about, um, the portmaster?"

"Lots," Miles assured him. *Well, I used to, anyway.* He placed his hands on the table and pushed to his feet. "Solian, Roic. Find me Solian. Or his trail of breadcrumbs, or *something*."

"I'll try, m'lord."

Back in what he was starting to think of as their cabinet, Miles encountered Ekaterin returning from the shower, dressed again in her red tunic and leggings. They maneuvered for a kiss, and he said, "I've acquired an involuntary appointment. I have to go stationside almost immediately."

"You *will* remember to put on pants?"

He glanced down at his bare legs. "Planned to, yeah."

Her eyes danced. "You looked abstracted. I thought it would be safer to ask."

He grinned. "I wonder how strangely I *could* behave before the quaddies would say anything?"

"Judging by some of the stories my Uncle Vorthys tells me of the Imperial Auditors of past generations, a lot stranger than that."

"No, I'm afraid it would only be our loyal Barrayarans who'd have to bite their tongues." He captured her hand and rubbed it enticingly. "Want to come along with me?"

"Doing what?" she asked, with commendable suspicion.

"Telling the trade fleet's galactic passengers I can't do a damned thing for them, they're stuck till Greenlaw shifts, thank you very much, have a pleasant day."

"That sounds . . . really unrewarding."

"That would be my best guess."

"A Countess is by law and tradition something of an assistant Count. An Auditor's wife, however, is not an assistant Auditor," she said in a firm tone, reminiscent to Miles's ear of her aunt—Professora Vorthys was herself an Auditor's spouse of some experience. "Nicol and Garnet Five made arrangements to take me out this morning and show me quaddie horticulture. If you don't mind, I think I'll stick to my original plan." She softened this sensible refusal with another kiss.

A flash of guilt made him grimace. "Graf Station is not exactly what we had in mind for a honeymoon diversion, I'm afraid."

"Oh, I'm having a good time. *You're* the one who has to deal with all the difficult people." She made a face, and he was reminded again of her tendency to default to extreme reserve when painfully overwhelmed. He did fancy that it happened less often, these days. Her growing confidence and ease with the role of Lady Vorkosigan had been his secret delight to watch develop, this past year and a half. "Maybe, if you're free by lunch, we can rendezvous and you can vent at me," she added, rather in the tone of one offering a trade of hostages. "But not if I have to remind you to chew and swallow."

"Only the carpet." This won a snicker; a good-bye kiss, as he headed off to the shower, eased his heart in advance. He reflected that while he might feel lucky that she'd agreed to come with him to Quaddiespace, everyone on Graf Station from Vorpatril and Greenlaw on down was *much luckier*.

The crews of all four Komarran ships now locked into their docking cradles had been herded into one hostel, and held there under close arrest. The quaddie authorities had feigned not to charge the passengers, an odd lot of galactic businesspeople who, with their goods, had joined the convoy for various segments of its route as the most economical transport going their way. But of course, they could not be left aboard unmanned vessels, and so perforce had been removed to two other, more luxurious, hostels.

In theory, the erstwhile passengers were made free of the station with no more onerous requirement than to sign in and out with a couple of quaddie Security guards—armed with stunners only, Miles noted in passing—watching the hostel doors. It wasn't even that the passengers couldn't legally leave Quaddiespace—except that the cargoes most had been shepherding were still impounded aboard their respective ships. And so they were held on the principle of the monkey with its hand trapped in the jar of nuts, unwilling to let go of what they could not withdraw. The "luxury" of the hostel translated into another quaddie punishment, since the mandatory stay was being charged to the Komarran fleet corporation.

The hostel's lobby was faux-grandiose, to Miles's eye, with a high domed ceiling simulating a morning sky with drifting clouds that probably cycled through sunrise, sunset, and night with the day-cycle. Miles wondered which planet's constellations were displayed, or if they could be varied to flatter the transients du jour. The large open space was circled by a second-story balcony given over to a lounge, restaurant, and bar where patrons could meet, greet, and eat. In the center an array of drum-shaped fluted marble pillars, waist-high, supported a long double-curved sheet of thick glass that in turn held a large and complex live floral display. Where did they grow such flowers on Graf Station? Was Ekaterin viewing the source of them even now?

In addition to the usual lift tubes, a wide curving staircase led from the lobby down to the conference level. Bel guided Miles down it to a more utilitarian meeting room in the level below.

They found the chamber crammed with about eighty irate individuals of what seemed every race, dress, planetary origin, and gender in the Nexus. Galactic traders with a keenly honed sense of the value of their time, and no Barrayaran cultural inhibitions about Imperial Auditors, they unleashed several days of accumulated frustrations upon Miles the moment he stepped to the front and turned to face them. Fourteen languages were handled by nineteen different brands of auto-translators, several of which, Miles decided, must have been purchased at close-out prices from makers going deservedly belly-up. Not that his answers to their barrage of questions were any special tax on the translators—what seemed ninety percent of them came up either, "I don't know yet," or "Ask Sealer Greenlaw." The fourth iteration of this latter litany was finally met with a heartrending wail, in chorus, from the back of the room of, "But Greenlaw said to ask *you*!", except for the translation device that came up a beat later with, "Lawn rule sea-hunter inquiring altitude unit!"

Miles did get Bel to quietly point out to him the men who had attempted to bribe the portmaster into releasing their wares. Then he asked all passengers from the *Idris* who had ever met Lieutenant Solian to stay and debrief their experiences to him. This actually seemed to foster some illusion of Authority Doing Something, and the rest shuffled out merely grumbling.

An exception was an individual Miles's eye placed, after an uncertain pause, as a Betan hermaphrodite. Tall for a herm, the age suggested by its silver hair and eyebrows was belied by its firm posture and fluid movements. If a Barrayaran, Miles would have pegged the individual as a healthy and athletic sixty—which probably meant it had achieved its Betan century. A long sarong in a dark, conservative print, a high-necked shirt and long-sleeved jacket against what a Betan would doubtless interpret as the station chill, and fine leather sandals completed an expensive-looking ensemble in the Betan style. The handsome features were aquiline, the eyes dark, liquid, and sharply observant. Such extraordinary elegance seemed something Miles should remember, but he could not bring his dim sense of familiarity into focus. Damn cryo-freeze—he couldn't guess if it was a true memory, smudged as too many had been by the neural traumas of the revival process, or a false one, even more distorted.

"Portmaster Thorne?" said the herm in a soft alto.

"Yes?" Bel too, unsurprisingly, studied a fellow-Betan with special interest. Despite the herm's dignified age, its beauty drew admiration, and Miles was amused to note Bel's glance go to the customary Betan earring hanging in its left lobe. Disappointingly, it was of the style that coded, *Romantically attached, not looking.*

"I'm afraid I have a special problem with my cargo."

Bel's expression returned to bland, preparing no doubt to hear yet another woeful story, with or without bribes.

"I am a passenger on the *Idris*. I'm transporting several hundred genetically engineered animal fetuses in uterine replicators, which require periodic servicing. The servicing is due again. I really cannot put it off much longer. If they are not cared for, my creatures may be damaged or even die." One long-fingered hand pulled on the other, nervously. "Worse, they are nearing term. I really didn't expect such a long delay in my travels. If I am held here very much longer, they will have to be decanted or destroyed, and I will lose all the value of my cargo and of my time."

"What kind of animals?" Miles asked curiously.

The tall herm glanced down at him. "Sheep and goats, mostly. Some other specialty items."

"Mm. I suppose you could threaten to turn them loose on the station, and force the quaddies to deal with 'em. Several hundred custom-colored baby lambs running around the loading bays . . ." This earned an extremely dry look from Portmaster Thorne, and Miles continued smoothly, "But I trust it won't come to that."

"I'll submit your petition to Boss Watts," said Bel. "Your name, honorable herm?"

"Ker Dubauer."

Bel bowed slightly. "Wait here. I'll return shortly."

As Bel moved off to make a vid call in private, Dubauer, smiling faintly, murmured, "Thank you so much for assisting me, Lord Vorkosigan."

"No trouble." Brow wrinkling, Miles added, "Have we ever met?"

"No, my lord."

"Hm. Oh, well. When you were aboard the *Idris*, did you encounter Lieutenant Solian?"

"The poor young male everyone thought had deserted, but now it seems not? I saw him going about his duties. I never spoke with him at any length, to my regret."

Miles considered imparting his news about the synthetic blood, then decided to hold that close for a little while. There might yet prove some better, cleverer thing to do with it than unleash it with the rest of the rumors. Some half dozen other passengers from the *Idris* had shuffled forward during this conversation, waiting to volunteer their own experiences of the missing lieutenant.

The brief interviews were of dubious value. A bold murderer would surely lie, but a smart one might simply not come forward at all. Three of the passengers were wary and curt, but dutifully precise. The others were eager and full of theories to share, none consonant with the blood on the docking bay deck being a plant. Miles wistfully considered the charms of a wholesale fast-penta interview of every passenger and crew person aboard the *Idris*. Another task Venn, or Vorpatril, or both together should have done already, dammit. Alas, the quaddies had tedious rules about such invasive methods. These transients on Graf Station were off-limits to the more abrupt Barrayaran interrogation techniques; and the Barrayaran military personnel, with whose minds Miles might make free, were much farther down his current list of suspects. The Komarran civilian crew was a more ambiguous case, Barrayaran subjects now on quaddie—well, not soil—and under quaddie custody.

While this was going forth, Bel returned to Dubauer, waiting quietly by the side of the room with its hands folded, and murmured, "I can personally escort you aboard the *Idris* to service your cargo as soon as the Lord Auditor is finished here."

Miles cut short the last crime-theory enthusiast and sent him on his way. "I'm done," he announced. He glanced at the chrono in his wrist com. Could he catch up with Ekaterin for lunch? It seemed doubtful, by this hour, but on the other hand, she could spend unimaginable amounts of time looking at vegetation, so maybe there was still a chance.

The three exited the conference chamber together and mounted the broad stairs to the spacious lobby. Neither Miles nor, he supposed, Bel ever entered a room without running a visual sweep of every possible vantage for aim, a legacy of years of unpleasant shared learning experiences. Thus it was that they spotted, simultaneously, the figure on the balcony opposite hoisting a strange oblong box onto the railing. Dubauer followed his glance, eyes widening in astonishment.

Miles had a flashing impression of dark eyes in a milky face beneath a mop of brass-blond curls, staring down intently at him. He and Bel, on either side of Dubauer, reached spontaneously and together for the startled Betan's arms and flung themselves forward. Bright bursts from the box chattered with a loud, echoing, tapping noise. Blood spattered from Dubauer's cheek as the herm was yanked along; something like a swarm of angry bees seemed to pass directly over Miles's head. Then they were, all three, sliding on their stomachs to cover behind the wide marble drums holding the flowers. The bees seemed to follow them; pellets of safety glass exploded in all directions, and chips of marble fountained in a wide spray. A vast vibrato filled the room, shook the air, the thunderous thrumming noise sliced with screams and cries.

Miles, trying to raise his head for a quick glance, was crushed down again by Bel diving over the intervening

Betan and landing on him in a smothering clutch. He could only hear the aftermath: more yells, the sudden cessation of the hammering, a heavy *clunk*. A woman's voice sobbed and hiccoughed in the startling silence, then was choked down to a spasmodic gulping. His hand jerked at a soft, cool kiss, but it was only a few last shredded leaves and flower petals sifting gently down out of the air to settle all around them.

Chapter 8

Miles said in a muffled voice, "Bel, will you please get off my head?"

There was a brief pause. Then Bel rolled away and, cautiously, sat up, head hunched into collar. "Sorry," said Bel gruffly. "Thought for a moment there I was about to lose you. Again."

"Don't apologize." Miles, his heart still racing and his mouth very dry, pushed up and sat, his back pressed to a now-shorter marble drum. He spread his fingers to touch the cool synthetic stone of the floor. A little beyond the narrow, irregular arc of space shielded by the table pillars, dozens of deep gouges scored the pavement. Something small and bright and brassy rolled past, and Miles's hand reached for it, then sprang back at its branding heat.

The elderly herm, Dubauer, also sat up, hand going to pat its face where blood trickled. Miles's glance took quick inventory: no other hits, apparently. He shifted and drew his Vorkosigan-monogrammed handkerchief from his trouser pocket, folded it, and silently handed it across to the bleeding Betan. Dubauer swallowed, took it, and mopped at the minor wound. It held the pad out a moment to stare at its own blood as if in surprise, then pressed the cloth back to its hairless cheek.

In a way, Miles thought shakily, it was all rather flattering. At least *someone* figured he was competent and effective enough to be dangerous. *Or maybe I'm onto something. I wonder what the hell it is?*

Bel placed its hands upon the shattered drum top, peered cautiously over, then slowly pulled itself to its feet. A downsider in the uniform of the hostel staff scurried, a little bent over, around the ex-centerpiece and asked in a choked voice, "Are you people all right?"

"I think so," said Bel, glancing around. "What *was* that?"

"It came from the balcony, sir. The, the person up there dropped it over the side and fled. The door guard went after him."

Bel didn't bother to correct the gender of the honorific, a sure sign of distraction. Miles rose too, and nearly passed out. Still hyperventilating, he crunched around their bulwark through the broken glass pellets, marble chips, half-melted brass slugs, and flower salad. Bel followed in his path. On the far side of the lobby, the oblong box lay on its side, notably dented. They both knelt to stare.

"Automated hot riveter," said Bel after a moment. "He must have disconnected . . . quite a few safety devices, to make it do that."

A slight understatement, Miles felt. But it did explain their assailant's uncertain aim. The device had been designed to throw its slugs with vast precision a matter of millimeters, not meters. Still . . . if the would-be assassin had succeeded in framing Miles's head for even a short burst—he glanced again at the shattered marble—no cryorevival ever invented could have brought him back this time.

Ye gods—what if he hadn't missed? What would Ekaterin have done, this far from home and help, a messily decapitated husband on her hands before her honeymoon trip was even over, with no immediate support but the inexperienced Roic— *If they're shooting at me, how much danger is she in?*

In belated panic, he slapped his wristcom. "Roic! Roic, answer me!"

It was at least three agonizing seconds before Roic's drawl responded, "My lord?"

"Where are—never mind. Drop whatever you're doing and go at once to Lady Vorkosigan, and stay with her. Get her back aboard—" he clipped off *the Kestrel*. Would she be safer there? By now, any number of people knew that was where to look for Vorkosigans. Maybe aboard the *Prince Xav*, standing off a good safe distance from the station, surrounded by troops—*Barrayar's finest, God help us all—* "Just stay with her, till I call again."

"My lord, what's happening?"

"Someone just tried to rivet me to the wall. No, don't come here," he overrode Roic's beginning protest. "The fellow ran off, and anyway, quaddie security is beginning to arrive." Two uniformed quaddies in floaters were entering the lobby even as he spoke. At a hostel employee's gesticulations, one rose smoothly up over the balcony; the other approached Miles and his party. "I have to deal with these people now. I'm all right. Don't alarm Ekaterin. Don't let her out of your sight. Out."

He glanced up to see Dubauer unbend from examining a rivet-chewed marble drum, face very strained. The herm, hand still pressed to cheek, was visibly shaken as it walked over to glance at the riveter. Miles rose smoothly to his feet.

"My apologies, honorable herm. I should have warned you never to stand too close to me."

Dubauer stared at Miles. Its lips parted in momentary bewilderment, then made a small circle, *Oh*. "I believe you two gentlepersons saved my life. I . . . I'm afraid I didn't see anything. Until that thing—what was it?—hit me."

Miles bent and picked up a loose rivet, one of hundreds, now cooled. "One of these. Have you stopped bleeding?"

The herm pulled the pad away from its cheek. "Yes, I think so."

"Here, keep it for a souvenir." He held out the gleaming brass slug. "Trade you for my handkerchief back." Ekaterin had embroidered it by hand, for a present.

"Oh—" Dubauer folded the pad over the bloodstain. "Oh, dear. Is it of value? I'll have it cleaned, and return it to you."

"Not necessary, honorable herm. My batman takes care of such things."

The elderly Betan looked distressed. "Oh, no—"

Miles ended the argument by reaching over and plucking the fine cloth from the clutching fingers, and stuffing it back in his pocket. The herm's hand jerked after it, and fell back. Miles had met diffident people, but never before one who apologized for bleeding. Dubauer, unused to personal violence on low-crime Beta Colony, was on the edge of distraught.

A quaddie security patrolwoman hovered anxiously in her floater. "What the hell happened here?" she demanded, snapping open a recorder.

Miles gestured to Bel, who took over describing the incident into the recorder. Bel was as calm, logical, and detailed

as at any Dendarii debriefing, which possibly took the
woman more aback than the crowd of witnesses who clus-
tered eagerly around trying to tell the tale in more excited
terms. To Miles's intense relief, no one else had been hit
except for a few minor clips from ricocheting marble chips.
The fellow's aim might have been imperfect, but he apparently hadn't intended a general massacre.

Good for public safety on Graf Station, but not, upon
reflection, so good for Miles. . . . His children might have
been orphaned, just now, before they'd even had a chance
to be born. His will was spot up to date, the size of an academic dissertation complete with bibliography and
footnotes. It suddenly seemed entirely inadequate to the
task.

"Was the suspect a downsider or a quaddie?" the patrolwoman asked Bel urgently.

Bel shook its head. "I couldn't see the lower half of his
body below the balcony rail. I'm not even sure it was male,
really."

A downsider transient and the quaddie waitress who'd
been serving his drink on the lounge level chimed in with
the news that the assailant had been a quaddie, and had
fled down an adjoining corridor in his floater. The transient was sure he'd been male, although the waitress, now
that the question was raised, grew less certain. Dubauer
apologized for not having glimpsed the person at all.

Miles prodded the riveter with his toe, and asked Bel in
an under-voice, "How hard would it be to carry something
like that through Station Security checkpoints?"

"Easy," said Bel. "No one would even blink."

"Local manufacture?" It looked quite new.

"Yes, that's a Sanctuary Station brand. They make good
tools."

"First job for Venn, then. Find out where the thing was sold, and when. And who to."

"Oh, yeah."

Miles was nearly dizzy with a weird combination of delight and dismay. The delight was partly adrenaline high, a familiar and dangerous old addiction, partly the realization that having been potshotted by a quaddie gave him a stick to beat back Greenlaw's relentless attack on his Barrayaran brutality. Quaddies were killers too, hah. They just weren't as *good* at it. . . . He remembered Solian, and took back that thought. *Yeah, and if Greenlaw didn't set me up for this herself.* Now *there* was a nice, paranoid theory. He set it aside to reexamine when his head had cooled. After all, a couple of hundred people, both quaddies and transients—including all of the fleet's galactic passengers—must have known he'd be coming here this morning.

A quaddie medical squad arrived, and on their heels—immediately after them, Chief Venn. The security chief was instantly deluged with excited descriptions of the spectacular attack on the Imperial Auditor. Only the erstwhile victim Miles was calm, standing in wait with a certain grim amusement.

Amusement was an emotion notably lacking in Venn's face. "Were you hit, Lord Auditor Vorkosigan?"

"No." *Time to put in a good word—we may need it later.* "Thanks to the quick reactions of Portmaster Thorne, here. But for this remarkable herm, you—and the Union of Free Habitats—would have one hell of a mess on your hands just now."

A babble of confirmation solidified this view, with a couple of people breathlessly describing Bel's selfless defense of the visiting dignitary with the shield of its own body. Bel's eye glinted briefly at Miles, though whether with gratitude or its opposite Miles was not just sure. The portmaster's modest protests served only to firmly affix the picture of this heroism in the eyewitnesses' minds, and Miles suppressed a grin.

One of the quaddie security patrollers who had gone in pursuit of the assailant now returned, floating back over the balcony to jerk to a halt before Chief Venn and report breathlessly, "Lost him, sir. We've put all duty personnel on alert, but we don't have much of a physical description."

Three or four people attempted to supplement this lack, in vivid and contradictory terms. Bel, listening, frowned more deeply.

Miles nudged the herm. "Hm?"

Bel shook its head and murmured back, "Thought for a moment he looked like someone I'd seen recently, but that was a downsider, so—no."

Miles considered his own brief impression. Bright-haired, light-skinned, a trifle bulky, of indeterminate age, probably male—this could cover some several hundred quaddies on Graf Station. Laboring under intense emotion, but by that time, Miles had been too. Seen once, at that distance, under such circumstances, Miles didn't think even he could reliably pick the fellow out of a group of similar physical types. Unfortunately, none of the transients had happened just then to be doing a vid scan of the lobby décor or each other to show the folks back home. The waitress and her patron weren't even quite sure when the fellow had arrived, though they thought he'd been in position for a few minutes, upper hands resting casually upon the balcony railing, as if waiting for some last straggler from the passengers' meeting to mount the stairs. *And so he was.*

The still-shaken Dubauer fended off the medtechs, insisting it could treat the clotted rivet-graze itself and, reiterating a lack of anything to add to the testimonies, begged to be let go back to its room to lie down.

Bel said to its fellow Betan, "Sorry about all this. I may be tied up for a while. If I can't get away myself, I'll have Boss Watts send another supervisor to escort you aboard the *Idris* to take care of your critters."

"Thank you, Portmaster. That would be very welcome. You'll call my room, yes? It really is most urgent." Dubauer withdrew hastily.

Miles couldn't blame Dubauer for fleeing, for the quaddie news services were arriving, in the persons of two eager reporters in floaters emblazoned with the logo of their journalistic work gang. An array of little vidcam floaters bobbed after them. The vidcams darted about, collecting scans. Sealer Greenlaw followed hurriedly in their wake, and wove her floater determinedly through the growing mob to Miles's side. *She* was flanked by two quaddie bodyguards in Union Militia garb, with serious weapons and armor. However useless against assassins, they at least had the salutary effect of making the babbling bystanders back off.

"Lord Auditor Vorkosigan, were you hurt?" she demanded at once.

Miles repeated to her the assurances he'd made to Venn. He kept one eye on the robot vidcams floating up to him and recording his words, and not just to be sure his good side was turned to them. But none appeared to be mini-weapons-platforms in disguise. He made sure to loudly mention Bel's heroics again, which had the useful effect of turning them in pursuit of the Betan portmaster, now on the other side of the lobby being grilled in more detail by Venn's security people.

Greenlaw said stiffly, "Lord Auditor Vorkosigan, may I convey my profound personal apologies for this untoward incident. I assure you, all of the Union's resources will be turned to tracking down what I am certain must be an unbalanced individual and danger to us all."

Danger to us all indeed. "I don't know what's going on, here," said Miles. He let his voice sharpen. "And clearly, *neither do you.* This is no diplomatic chess game any more. Someone seems to be trying to start a damned war in here. They nearly succeeded."

She took a deep breath. "I am certain the person was acting alone."

Miles frowned thoughtfully. *The hotheads are always with us, true.* He lowered his voice. "For what? Retaliation? Did any of the quaddies injured by Vorpatril's strike force suddenly die last night?" He'd thought they all were on the recovering list. It was hard to imagine a quaddie relative or lover or friend taking bloody revenge for anything short of a fatality, but . . .

"No," said Greenlaw, her voice slowing as she considered this hypothesis. Regretfully, her voice firmed. "No. I would have been told."

So, Greenlaw was wishing for a simple explanation, too. But honest enough not to fool herself, at least.

His wrist com gave its high priority beep; he slapped it. "Yes?"

"My Lord Vorkosigan?" It was Admiral Vorpatril's voice, strained.

Not Ekaterin or Roic after all. Miles's heart climbed back down out of his throat. He tried not to let his voice go irritable. "Yes, Admiral?"

"Oh, thank God. We received a report that you were attacked."

"All over now. They missed. Station Security is here now."

There was a brief pause. Vorpatril's voice returned, fraught with implication: "My Lord Auditor, my fleet is on full alert, ready at your command."

Oh, crap. "Thank you, Admiral, but *stand down*, please," Miles said hastily. "Really. It's under control. I'll get back to you in a few minutes. Do nothing without my direct, personal orders!"

"Very well, my lord," said Vorpatril stiffly, still in a very suspicious tone. Miles cut the channel.

Greenlaw was staring at him. He explained to her, "I'm Gregor's Voice. To the Barrayarans, it's as if that quaddie had fired on the Emperor, almost. When I said someone had nearly started a war, it wasn't a figure of speech, Sealer Greenlaw. At home, this place would be crawling with ImpSec's best by now."

She cocked her head, her frown sharpening. "And how would an attack on an ordinary Barrayaran subject be treated? More casually, I daresay?"

"Not more casually, but on a lower organizational level. It would be a matter for their Count's District guard."

"So on Barrayar, what kind of justice you receive depends on who you are? Interesting. I do not regret to inform you, Lord Vorkosigan, that on Graf Station you will be treated like any other victim—no better, no worse. Oddly enough, this is no loss for you."

"How salutary for me," said Miles dryly. "And while you're proving how unimpressed you are with my Imperial authority, a dangerous killer remains at large. What will it be to lovely, egalitarian Graf Station if he goes for a less personal method of disposing of me next time, such as a large bomb? Trust me—even on Barrayar, we all die the same.

Shall we continue this discussion in private?" The vidcams, evidently finished with Bel, were zooming back toward him.

His head swiveled around at a breathless cry of, "Miles!" Also zooming toward him was Ekaterin, Roic lumbering at her shoulder. Nicol and Garnet Five followed in floaters. Pale of face and wide of eye, Ekaterin strode across the detritus in the lobby, gripped his hands, and, at his crooked smile, hugged him fiercely. Fully conscious of the vidcams avidly circling, he hugged her back, making sure that no journalists alive, no matter how many arms or legs they possessed, could resist putting *this* one up front and center. A human-interest shot, yeah.

Roic said apologetically, "I tried to stop her, m'lord, but she insisted on coming here."

"It's all right," said Miles in a muffled voice.

Ekaterin murmured unhappily in his ear, "I thought this was a safe place. It *felt* safe. The quaddies seemed like such peaceful people."

"The majority of them undoubtedly are," Miles said. Reluctantly, he released her, though he still kept a firm grip on one hand. They stood back and regarded each other anxiously.

Across the lobby, Nicol flew to Bel with much the same look on her face as had been on Ekaterin's, and the vidcams flocked after her.

Miles asked Roic quietly, "How far did you get on Solian?"

"Not far, m'lord. I decided to start with the *Idris*, and got all the access codes from Brun and Molino all right, but the quaddies wouldn't permit me to board her. I was about to call you."

Miles grinned briefly. "Bet I can fix that now, by damn."

Greenlaw returned to invite the Barrayarans to step into the hostel management's meeting room, hastily cleared as a refuge.

Miles tucked Ekaterin's hand into his arm, and they followed; he shook his head regretfully at a reporter who flitted purposefully toward them, and one of Greenlaw's Union Militia guards made a stern warding motion. Thwarted, the quaddie journalist pounced on Garnet Five instead. With a performer's reflex, she welcomed him with a blinding smile.

"Did you have a nice morning?" Miles asked Ekaterin brightly as they picked their way over the mess on the floor.

She eyed him in some bemusement. "Yes, lovely. Quaddie hydroponics are extraordinary." Her voice went dry as she glanced around the battle zone. "And you?"

"Delightful. Well, not if we hadn't ducked. But if I can't figure out how to use this to break our deadlock, I should turn in my Auditor's chain." He stifled a fox's smile, contemplating Greenlaw's back.

"The things one learns on a honeymoon. Now I know how to coax you out of your glum moods. Just hire someone to shoot at you."

"Peps me right up," he agreed. "I figured out years ago that I was addicted to adrenaline. I also figured out that it was going to be toxic, eventually, if I didn't taper off."

"Indeed." She inhaled. The slight trembling in the hand tucked in the crook of his elbow was lessening, and its clamp on his biceps was growing less circulation-stopping. Her face was back to being deceptively serene.

Greenlaw led them through the office corridor behind the reception area to a cluttered workroom. Its small central vid table had been swept clean of ringed cups, flaccid drink bulbs, and plastic flimsies, now piled haphazardly on a credenza shoved to one wall. Miles saw Ekaterin into a station chair and sat next to her. Greenlaw positioned her floater at chair-height opposite. Roic and one of the quaddie guards jockeyed for position at the door, frowning at each other.

Miles reminded himself to be indignant and not ecstatic. "Well." He let a distinct note of sarcasm creep into his voice. "That was a remarkable addition to my morning's speaking schedule."

Greenlaw began, "Lord Auditor, you have my apologies—"

"Your apologies are all very well, Madam Sealer, but I would happily trade them for your cooperation. Assuming *you* are not behind this incident," he overrode her indignant splutter, continuing smoothly, "and I don't see why you should be, despite the suggestive circumstances. Random violence does not seem to me to be in the usual quaddie style."

"It certainly is not!"

"Well, if it's not random, then it must be connected. The central mystery of this entire imbroglio remains the neglected disappearance of Lieutenant Solian."

"It was not neglected—"

"I disagree. The answer to it might—should!—have been put together days ago, except that Tab A seems to be on one side of an artificial divide from Slot B. If pursuing my quaddie assailant is the Union's task"—he paused and raised his eyebrows; she nodded grimly—"then pursuing Solian is surely mine. It's the one string I have in hand, and I intend to follow it up. And if the two investigations don't meet in the middle somewhere, I'll eat my Auditor's seal."

She blinked, seeming a little surprised by this turn of discourse. "Possibly . . ."

"Good. Then I want complete and unimpeded access for me, my assistant Armsman Roic, and anyone else I may designate to any and all areas and records pertinent to this search. Starting with the *Idris*, and starting immediately!"

"We cannot give downsiders license to roam at will over Station secure areas that—"

"Madam Sealer. You are here to promote and protect Union interests, as I am to promote and protect Barrayaran interests. But if there is anything at all about this mess that's good for either Quaddiespace *or* the Imperium, it's not apparent to me! Is it to you?"

"No, but—"

"Then you agree, the sooner we dig to the center of it, the better."

She tented her upper hands, regarding him through narrowed eyes. Before she could marshal further objections, Bel entered, having apparently escaped Venn and the media at last. Nicol bobbed along beside in her floater.

Greenlaw brightened, and seized on the one auspicious point for the quaddies in the chaos of the morning. "Portmaster Thorne. Welcome. I understand the Union owes you a debt of thanks for your courage and quick thinking."

Bel glanced at Miles—a trifle dryly, Miles thought—and favored her with a self-deprecating half salute. "All in a day's work, ma'am."

At one time, that would have been a statement of plain fact, Miles couldn't help reflecting.

Greenlaw shook her head. "I trust not on Graf Station, Portmaster!"

"Well, *I* certainly thank Portmaster Thorne!" said Ekaterin warmly.

Nicol's hand crept into Bel's, and she shot a look up from under her dark eyelashes for which a red-blooded soldier of any gender would gladly have traded medals, campaign ribbons, and combat bonuses all three, high command's boring speeches thrown in gratis. Bel began to look slightly more reconciled to being designated Heroic Person of the Hour.

"To be sure," Miles agreed. "To say that I'm pleased with the portmaster's liaison services is a profound understatement. I would take it as a personal favor if the herm might continue in this assignment for the duration of my stay."

Greenlaw caught Bel's eye, then nodded at Miles. "Certainly, Lord Auditor." Relieved, Miles gathered, to have something to hand to him that cost her no new concessions. A small smile moved her lips, a rare event. "Furthermore, I *shall* grant you and your designated assistants access to Graf Station records and secured areas— under the portmaster's direct supervision."

Miles pretended to consider this compromise, frowning artistically. "This places a substantial demand on Portmaster Thorne's time and attention."

Bel put in demurely, "I'll gladly accept the assignment, Madam Sealer, provided Boss Watts authorizes both all my overtime hours, and another supervisor to take over my routine duties."

"Not a problem, Portmaster. I'll direct Watts to add his increased departmental costs to the Komarran fleet's docking bill." Greenlaw delivered this promise with a glint of grim satisfaction.

Added to Bel's ImpSec stipend, this would put the herm on triple time, Miles estimated. Old Dendarii accounting tricks, hah. Well, Miles would see that the Imperium got its money's worth. "Very well," he conceded, endeavoring to appear stung. "Then I wish to proceed aboard the *Idris* immediately."

Ekaterin didn't crack a smile, but a faint light of appreciation glimmered in her eye.

And what if she had accepted his invitation to accompany him this morning? And had walked up those stairs next to him—his assailant's erratic aim would not have passed over *her* head. Picturing the probable results put an unpleasant knot in his stomach, and his lingering adrenaline high tasted suddenly very sour.

"Lady Vorkosigan,"—Miles swallowed—"I am going to arrange for Lady Vorkosigan to stay aboard the *Prince Xav* until Graf Station Security apprehends the would-be killer and this mystery is resolved." He added in an apologetic murmur aside to her, "Sorry . . ."

She returned him a brief nod of understanding. "It's all right." Not happy, to be sure, but she possessed too much good Vor sense to argue about security issues.

He continued, "I therefore request special clearance for a Barrayaran personnel shuttle to dock and take her out." Or the *Kestrel*? No, he dared not lose access to his independent transport, bolthole, and secure communications station.

Greenlaw twitched. "Excuse me, Lord Vorkosigan, but that's how the last Barrayaran assault arrived stationside. We do not care to host another such influx." She glanced at Ekaterin and took a breath. "However, I appreciate your concern. I would be glad to offer one of our pods and pilots to Lady Vorkosigan as a courtesy transport."

Miles replied, "Madam Sealer, an unknown quaddie just tried to kill me. I'll grant I don't really think it was your secret policy, but the key word here is *unknown*. We don't yet know that it wasn't some quaddie—or group of quaddies—still in a position of trust. There are several experiments I'd be willing to run to find out, but this isn't one of them."

Bel sighed audibly. "If you wish, Lord Auditor Vorkosigan, I will undertake to personally pilot Lady Vorkosigan out to your flagship."

But I need you here!

Bel evidently read his look, for the herm added, "Or some pilot of my choosing?"

With an unfeigned reluctance, this time, Miles agreed. The next step was to call Admiral Vorpatril and inform him of his ship's new guest. Vorpatril, when his face appeared above the vid plate on the conference table, passed no comment at the news other than, "Certainly, my Lord Auditor. The *Prince Xav* will be honored." But Miles could read in the admiral's shrewd glance his estimation of the increased seriousness of the situation. Miles ascertained that no hysterical preliminary dispatches about the incident had yet been squirted on their several-day trip to HQ; news and reassurances would therefore arrive, thankfully, simultaneously. Aware of their quaddie listeners, Vorpatril made no other remark than a bland request that the Lord Auditor bring him up to date on developments at his earliest convenience—in other words, as soon as he could reach a private secured comconsole.

The meeting broke up. More of Greenlaw's Union Militia guards had arrived, and they all exited back into the hostel's lobby, well screened, belatedly, by armed outriders. Miles made sure to walk as far from Ekaterin as possible. In the shattered lobby, quaddie forensics techs, under Venn's direction, were taking vid scans and measurements. Miles frowned up at the balcony, considering trajectories; Bel, walking beside him and watching his glance, raised its eyebrows. Miles lowered his voice and said suddenly, "Bel, you don't suppose that loon could have been firing at *you*, could he?"

"Why me?"

"Well, just so. How many people does a portmaster usually piss off, in the normal course of business?" He glanced around; Nicol was out of earshot, floating beside Ekaterin and engaged in some low-voiced, animated exchange with her. "Or not-business? You haven't been, oh, sleeping with anyone's wife, have you? Or husband," he added conscientiously. "Or daughter, or whatever."

"No," said Bel firmly. "Nor with their household pets, either. What a Barrayaran view of human motivations you do have, Miles."

Miles grinned. "Sorry. What about . . . *old* business?"

Bel sighed. "I thought I'd outrun or outlived all the old business." The herm eyed Miles sideways. "Almost." And added after a thoughtful moment, "You'd surely be way ahead of me in line for that one, too."

"Possibly." Miles frowned. And then there was Dubauer. *That* herm was certainly tall enough to be a target. Although how the devil could an elderly Betan dealer in designer animals, who'd spent most of its time on Graf Station locked in a hostel room anyway, have annoyed some quaddie enough to inspire him to try to blow its timid head off? *Too damned many possibles, here.* It was time to inject some hard data.

Chapter 9

The quaddie pilot of Bel's selecting arrived and whisked Ekaterin off, together with a couple of stern-looking Union Militia guards. Miles watched her go in mild anguish. As she turned to look over her shoulder, walking out the hostel door, he tapped his wrist com meaningfully; she silently raised her left arm, com bracelet glinting, in return.

Since they were all on their way to the *Idris* anyway, Bel used the delay to call Dubauer down to the lobby again. Dubauer, smooth cheek now neatly sealed with a discreet dab of surgical glue, arrived promptly, and stared in some alarm at their new quaddie military escort. But the shy, graceful herm appeared to have regained most of its self-possession, and murmured sincere gratitude to Bel for recollecting its creatures' needs despite all the tumult.

The little party walked or floated, variously, trailing Portmaster Thorne via a notably un-public back way through the customs and security zone to the array of loading bays devoted to galactic shipping. The bay serving the *Idris,* clamped into its outboard docking cradle, was quiet and dim, unpeopled except for the two Graf Station security patrollers guarding the hatches.

Bel presented its authorization, and the two patrollers floated aside to allow Bel access to the hatch controls. The door to the big freight lock slid upward, and, leaving their Union Militia escort to help guard the entry, Miles, Roic, and Dubauer followed Bel aboard the freighter.

The *Idris*, like its sister ship the *Rudra*, was of a utilitarian design that dispensed with elegance. It was essentially a bundle of seven huge parallel cylinders: the central-most devoted to personnel, four of the outer six given to freight. The other two nacelles, opposite each other in the outer ring, housed the ship's Necklin rods that generated the field to fold it through jump points. Normal-space engines behind, mass shield generators in front. The ship rotated around its central axis to bring each outer cylinder to alignment with the stationside freight lock for automated loading or unloading of containers, or hand loading of more delicate goods. The design was not without added safety value, for in the event of a pressurization loss in one or more cylinders, any of the others could serve as a refuge while repairs were made or evacuation effected.

As they walked now through one freight nacelle, Miles glanced up and down its central access corridor, which receded into darkness. They passed through another lock into a small foyer in the forward section of the ship. In one direction lay passenger staterooms; in the other, personnel cabins and offices. Lift tubes and a pair of stairs led up to the level devoted to ship's mess, infirmary, and recreation facilities, and downward to life support, engineering, and other utility areas.

Roic glanced at his notes and nodded down the corridor. "This way to Solian's security office, m'lord."

"I'll escort Citizen Dubauer here to its flock," said Bel, "and catch up with you." Dubauer made an abortive little bow, and the two herms passed onward into the lock leading to one of the outboard freight sections.

Roic counted doorways past a second connecting foyer and tapped a code into a lock pad near the stern. The door slid aside and the light came up revealing a tiny, spare chamber housing scarcely more than a computer interface and two chairs, and some lockable wall cabinets. Miles fired up the interface while Roic ran a quick inventory of the cabinets' contents. All security-issue weapons and their power cartridges were present and accounted for, all safety equipment neatly packed in its places. The office was void of personal effects, no vid displays of the girl back home, no sly—or political—jokes or encouraging slogans pasted inside the cabinet doors. But Brun's investigators had been through here once already, after Solian had disappeared but before the ship had been evacuated by the quaddies following the clash with the Barrayarans; Miles made a note to inquire if Brun—or Venn, for that matter—had removed anything.

Roic's override codes promptly brought up all of Solian's records and logs. Miles started from Solian's final shift. The lieutenant's daily reports were laconic, repetitive, and disappointingly free of comments on potential assassins. Miles wondered if he was listening to a dead man's voice. By rights, there ought to be some psychic frisson. The eerie silence of the ship encouraged the imagination.

While the ship was in port, its security system did keep continuous vid records of everyone and everything that boarded or departed through the stationside or other activated locks, as a routine antitheft, antisabotage precaution. Slogging through the whole ten days' worth of comings and goings before the ship had been impounded, even on fast forward, was going to be a time-consuming chore. The daunting possibility of records having been altered or deleted, as Brun suspected Solian had done to cover his desertion, would also have to be explored.

Miles made copies of everything that seemed even vaguely pertinent, for further examination, then he and Roic paid a visit to Solian's cabin, just a few meters down the same corridor. It too was small and spare and unrevealing. No telling what personal items Solian might have packed in the missing valise, but there certainly weren't many left. The ship had left Komarr, what, six weeks ago? With half a dozen ports of call between. When the ship was in-port was the busiest time for its security; perhaps Solian hadn't had much time to shop for souvenirs.

Miles tried to make sense of what was left. Half a dozen uniforms, a few civvies, a bulky jacket, some shoes and boots . . . Solian's personally fitted pressure suit. That seemed an expensive item one might want for a long sojourn in Quaddiespace. Not very anonymous, though, with its Barrayaran military markings.

Finding nothing in the cabin to relieve them of the chore of examining vid records, Miles and Roic returned to Solian's office and began. If nothing else, Miles encouraged himself, reviewing the security vids would give him a mental picture of the potential dramatis personae . . . buried somewhere in the mob of persons who had nothing to do with anything, to be sure. Looking at everything was a sure sign that he didn't know what the hell he was doing yet, but it was the only way he'd ever found to smoke out the non-obvious clue that everyone else had overlooked. . . .

He glanced up, after a time, at a movement in the office door. Bel had returned, and leaned against the jamb.

"Finding anything yet?" the herm asked.

"Not so far." Miles paused the vid display. "Did your Betan friend get its problems taken care of?"

"Still working. Feeding the critters and shoveling manure, or at least, adding nutrient concentrate to the replicator reservoirs and removing the waste bags from the filtration units. I can see why Dubauer was upset at the delay. There must be a thousand animal fetuses in that hold. Major financial loss, if it becomes a loss."

"Huh. Most animal husbandry people ship frozen embryos," said Miles. "That's the way my grandfather used to import his fancy horse bloodstock from Earth. Implanted 'em in a grade mare upon arrival, to finish cooking. Cheaper, lighter, less maintenance—shipping delays not an issue, if it comes to that. Although I suppose this way uses the travel time for gestation."

"Dubauer did say time was of the essence." Bel hitched its shoulders, frowning uncomfortably. "What do the *Idris*'s logs have to say about Dubauer and its cargo, anyway?"

Miles called up the records. "Boarded when the fleet first assembled in Komarr orbit. Bound for Xerxes—the next stop after Graf Station, which must make this mess especially frustrating. Reservation made about . . . six weeks before the fleet departed, via a Komarran shipping agent." A legitimate company; Miles recognized the name. This record did not indicate where Dubauer-and-cargo had originated, nor if the herm had intended to connect with another commercial—or private—carrier at Xerxes for some further ultimate destination. He eyed Bel shrewdly. "Something got your hackles up?"

"I . . . don't know. There's something funny about Dubauer."

"In what way? Would I get the joke?"

"If I could say, it wouldn't bother me so much."

"It seems a fussy old herm . . . maybe something on the academic side?" University, or former university, bioengineering research and development would fit the oddly precise and polite style. So would personal shyness.

"That might account for it," said Bel, in an unconvinced tone.

"Funny. Right." Miles made a note to especially observe the herm's movements on and off the *Idris*, in his records search.

Bel, watching him, remarked, "Greenlaw was secretly impressed with you, by the way."

"Oh, yeah? She's certainly managed to keep it a secret from me."

Bel's grin sparked. "She told me you appeared very *task oriented*. That's a compliment, in Quaddiespace. I didn't explain to her that you considered getting shot at to be a normal part of your daily routine."

"Well, not *daily*. By preference." Miles grimaced. "Nor normally, in the new job. I'm supposed to be rear echelon, now. I'm getting old, Bel."

The grin twisted half-up in sardonic amusement. "Speaking from the vantage of one not quite twice your age, and in your fine old Barrayaran phrase of yore, horseshit, Miles."

Miles shrugged. "Maybe it's the impending fatherhood."

"Got you spooked, does it?" Bel's brows rose.

"No, of course not. Or—well, yes, but not in that way. My father was . . . I have a lot to live up to. And perhaps even a few things to do differently."

Bel tilted its head, but before it could speak again, footsteps sounded down the corridor. Dubauer's light, cultured voice inquired, "Portmaster Thorne? Ah, there you are."

Bel moved within as the tall herm appeared in the doorway. Miles noted Roic's appraising eye flick, before the bodyguard pretended to return his attention to the vid display.

Dubauer pulled on its fingers anxiously and asked Bel, "Are you returning to the hostel soon?"

"No. That is, I'm not returning to the hostel at all."

"Oh. Ah." The herm hesitated. "You see, with strange quaddies flying around out there shooting at people, I didn't really want to go out on the station alone. Has anyone heard—he hasn't been apprehended yet, has he? No? I was hoping . . . can anyone go with me?"

Bel smiled sympathetically at this display of frazzled nerves. "I'll send one of the security guards with you. That all right?"

"I should be *extremely* grateful, yes."

"Are you all finished, now?"

Dubauer bit its lip. "Well, yes and no. That is, I have finished servicing my replicators, and done what little I can to slow the growth and metabolism of their contents. But if my cargo is to be held here very much longer, there'll not be time to get to my final destination before my creatures outgrow their containers. If I indeed have to destroy them, it will be a disastrous event."

"The Komarran fleet's insurance ought to make good on that, I'd think," said Bel.

"Or you could sue Graf Station," Miles suggested. "Better yet, do both, and collect twice." Bel spared him an exasperated glance.

Dubauer managed a pained smile. "That only addresses the immediate financial loss." After a longer pause, the herm continued, "To salvage the more important part, the proprietary bioengineering, I wish to take tissue samples and freeze them before disposal. I shall also require some equipment for complete biomatter breakdown. Or access to the ship's converters, if they won't become overloaded with the mass I must destroy. It's going to be a time-consuming and, I fear, extremely messy task. I was wondering, Portmaster Thorne—if you cannot obtain my cargo's release from quaddie impoundment, can you at least get me permission to stay aboard the *Idris* while I undertake its dispatch?"

Bel's brow wrinkled at the horrific picture the herm's soft words conjured. "Let's hope you're not forced to such extreme measures. How much time do you have, really?"

The herm hesitated. "Not very much more. And if I must dispose of my creatures—the sooner, the better. I'd prefer to get it over with."

"Understandable." Bel blew out its breath.

"There might be some alternate possibilities to stretch your time window," said Miles. "Hiring a smaller, faster ship to take you directly to your destination, for example."

The herm shook its head sadly. "And who would pay for this ship, my Lord Vorkosigan? The Barrayaran Imperium?"

Miles bit his tongue on either *Yeah, sure!* or alternate suggestions involving Greenlaw and the Union. He was supposed to be handling the big picture, not getting bogged down in all the human—or inhumane—details. He made a neutral gesture and let Bel shepherd the Betan out.

Miles spent a few more minutes failing to find anything exciting on the vid logs, then Bel returned.

Miles shut down the vid. "I think I'd like a look at that funny Betan's cargo."

"Can't help you there," said Bel. "I don't have the codes to the freight lockers. Only the passengers are supposed to have the access to the space they rent, by contract, and the quaddies haven't bothered to get a court order to make them disgorge 'em. Decreases Graf Station's liability for theft while the passengers aren't aboard, y'see. You'll have to get Dubauer to let you in."

"Dear Bel, I am an Imperial Auditor, and this is not only a Barrayaran-registered ship, it belongs to Empress Laisa's own family. I go where I will. Solian has to have a security override for every cranny of this ship. Roic?"

"Right here, m'lord." The armsman tapped his notation device.

"Very well, then, let's take a walk."

Bel and Roic followed him down the corridor and through the central lock to the adjoining freight section. The double-door to the second chamber down yielded to Roic's careful tapping on its lock pad. Miles poked his head through and brought up the lights.

It was an impressive sight. Gleaming replicator racks stood packed in tight rows, filling the space and leaving only narrow aisles between. Each rack sat bolted on its own float pallet, in four layers of five units—twenty to a rack, as high as Roic was tall. Beneath darkened display readouts on each, control panels twinkled with reassuringly green lights. For now.

Miles walked down the aisle formed by five pallets, around the end, and up the next, counting. More pallets lined the walls. Bel's estimate of a thousand seemed exactly right. "You'd think the placental chambers would be a larger size. These seem nearly identical to the ones at home." With which he'd grown intimately familiar, of late. These arrays were clearly meant for mass production. All twenty units stacked on a pallet economically shared reservoirs, pumps, filtration devices, and the control panel. He leaned closer. "I don't see a maker's mark." Or serial numbers or anything else that would reveal the planet of origin for what were clearly very finely made machines. He tapped a control to bring the monitor screen to life.

The glowing screen didn't contain manufacturing data or serial numbers either. Just a stylized scarlet screaming-bird pattern on a silver background. . . . His heart began to lump. What the hell was *this* doing *here* . . . ?

"Miles," said Bel's voice, seeming to come from a long way off, "if you're going to pass out, put your head down."

"Between my knees," choked Miles, "and kiss my ass good-bye. Bel, do you know what that sigil *is*?"

"No," said Bel, in a leery *now-what?* tone.

"Cetagandan Star Crèche. Not the military ghem-lords, not their cultivated—and I mean that in both senses—masters, the haut lords—not even the Imperial Celestial Garden. Higher still. The Star Crèche is the innermost core of the innermost ring of the whole damned giant genetic engineering project that is the Cetagandan Empire. The haut ladies' own gene bank. They design their emperors, there. Hell, they design the whole haut race, there. The haut ladies don't *work* in animal genes. They think it would be beneath them. They leave that to the ghem-ladies. Not, note, to the ghem-lords . . ."

Hand shaking slightly, he reached out to touch the monitor and bring up the next control level. General power and reservoir readouts, all in the green. The next level allowed individual monitoring of each fetus contained within one of the twenty separate placental chambers. Human blood temperature, baby mass, and if that weren't enough, tiny individual vid spy cameras built in, with lights, to view the replicators' inhabitants in real time, floating peacefully in their amniotic sacs. The one in the monitor twitched tiny fingers at the soft red glow, and seemed to scrunch up its big dark eyes. If not quite grown to term, it—no, she—was damned close to it, Miles guessed. He thought of Helen Natalia, and Aral Alexander.

Roic swung on his booted heel, lips parting in dismay, staring up the aisle of glittering devices. "D'you mean, m'lord, that all these things are full of *human* babies?"

"Well, now, that's a question. Actually, that's two questions. Are they full, and are they human? If they are haut infants, that latter is a most debatable point. For the first, we can at least look . . ." A dozen more pallet monitors, checked at random intervals around the room, revealed similar results. Miles was breathing rapidly by the time he gave it up for proven.

Roic said in a puzzled tone, "So what's a Betan herm doing with a bunch of Cetagandan replicators? And just because they're Cetagandan make, how d'you know it's Cetagandans inside 'em? Maybe the Betan bought the replicators used?"

Miles, lips drawn back on a grin, swung to Bel. "Betan? What do you think, Bel? How much did you two talk about the old sandbox while you were supervising this visit?"

"We didn't talk much at all." Bel shook its head. "But that doesn't prove anything. I'm not much for bringing up the subject of home myself, and even if I had, I'm too out of touch with Beta to spot inaccuracies in current events anyway. It wasn't Dubauer's *conversation* that was the trouble. There was just something . . . off, in its body language."

"Body language. Just so." Miles stepped to Bel, reached up, and turned the herm's face to the light. Bel did not flinch at his nearness, but merely smiled. Fine hairs gleamed on cheek and chin. Miles's eyes narrowed as he carefully revisualized the cut on Dubauer's cheek.

"You have facial down, like women. All herms do, right?"

"Sure. Unless they're using a really thorough depilatory, I suppose. Some even cultivate beards."

"Dubauer doesn't." Miles made to pace down the aisle, stopped himself, turned back, and held still with an effort. "Nary a sprout in sight, except for the pretty silver eyebrows and hair, which I'd wager Betan dollars to sand are recent implants. Body language, hah. Dubauer's not double-sexed at all—what *were* your ancestors thinking?"

Bel smirked cheerily.

"But altogether sexless. *Truly* 'it.'"

"*It*, in Betan parlance," Bel began in the weary tone of one who has had to explain this far too often, "does not carry the connotation of an inanimate object that it does in other planetary cultures. I say this despite a certain ex-boss of my very distant past, who did a pretty fair imitation of the sort of large and awkward piece of furniture that one can neither get rid of nor decorate around—"

Miles waved this aside. "Don't tell *me*—I got that lecture at my mother's knee. But Dubauer's not a herm. Dubauer's a ba."

"A who what?"

"To the casual outside eye, the ba appear to be the bred servitors of the Celestial Garden, where the Cetagandan emperor dwells in serenity in surroundings of aesthetic perfection, or so the haut lords would have you believe. The ba seem the ultimate loyal servant race, human dogs. Beautiful, of course, because everything inside the Celestial Garden must be. I first ran into the ba about ten years back, when I was sent to Cetaganda—not as Admiral Naismith, but as Lieutenant Lord Vorkosigan—on a diplomatic errand. To attend the funeral of Emperor Fletchir Giaja's mother, as it happened, the old Dowager Empress Lisbet. I got to see a lot of ba up close. Those of a certain age—relics of Lisbet's youth a century ago, mainly—had all been made hairless. It was a fashion, which has since passed.

"But the ba aren't servants, or anyway, aren't *just* servants, of the Imperial haut. Remember what I said about the haut ladies of the Star Crèche only working in human genes? The ba are where the haut ladies test out prospective new gene complexes, improvements to the haut race, before they decide if they're good enough to add to this year's new model haut cohort. In a sense, the ba are the haut's siblings. Elder siblings, almost. Children, even, from a certain angle of view. The haut and the ba are two sides of one coin.

"A ba is every bit as smart and dangerous as a haut lord. But not as autonomous. The ba are as loyal as they are sexless, because they're made so, and for some of the same reasons of control. At least it explains why I kept thinking I'd met Dubauer someplace before. If that ba doesn't share most of its genes with Fletchir Giaja himself, I'll eat my, my, my—"

"Fingernails?" Bel suggested.

Miles hastily removed his hand from his mouth. He continued, "If Dubauer's a ba, and I'll swear it is, these replicators have to be full of Cetagandan . . . somethings. But why *here*? Why transport them covertly, and on a ship of a once-and-future enemy empire, at that? Well, I hope not future—the last three rounds of open warfare we had with our Cetagandan neighbors were surely enough. If this was something open and aboveboard, why not travel on a Cetagandan ship, with all the trimmings? I guarantee it's not for economy's sake. Deathly secret, this, but who from, and why? What the hell is the Star Crèche up to, anyway?" He swung in a circle, unable to keep still. "And what is so *hellish* secret that this ba would bring these live growing fetuses all this way, but then plan to *kill* them all to keep the secret rather than ask for help?"

"Oh," said Bel. "Yeah, that. That's . . . a bit unnerving, when you think about it."

Roic said indignantly, "That's *horrible*, m'lord!"

"Maybe Dubauer doesn't really intend to flush them," said Bel in an uncertain tone. "Maybe it just said that to get us to put more pressure on the quaddies to give it a break, let it take its cargo off the *Idris*."

"Ah . . ." said Miles. *There* was an attractive idea—wash his hands of this whole unholy mess . . . "Crap. No. Not yet, anyway. In fact, I want you to lock the *Idris* back down. Don't let Dubauer—don't let *anyone* back on board. For once in my life, I actually *want* to check with HQ before I jump. And as quickly as possible."

What was it that Gregor had said—had talked around, rather? *Something has stirred up the Cetagandans around Rho Ceta.* Something *peculiar. Oh, Sire, do we ever have peculiar here now.* Connections?

"*Miles*," said Bel in aggravation, "I just jumped through hoops persuading Watts and Greenlaw to let Dubauer back *on* the *Idris*. How am I going to explain the sudden reversal?" Bel hesitated. "If this cargo and its owner are dangerous to Quaddiespace, I should report it. D'you think that quaddie in the hostel might have been shooting at Dubauer, instead of at you or me?"

"The thought has crossed my mind, yes."

"Then it's . . . wrong, to blindside the station on what may be a safety issue."

Miles took a breath. "You are Graf Station's representative here; you know, therefore the station knows. That's enough. For now."

Bel frowned. "That argument's too disingenuous even for *me*."

"I'm only asking you to wait. Depending on what information I get back from home, I could damn well end up *buying* Dubauer a fast ship to take its cargo away on. One not of Barrayaran registry, preferably. Just stall. I know you can."

"Well . . . all right. For a little while."

"I want the secured comconsole in the *Kestrel*. We'll seal this hold and continue later. Wait. I want to have a look at Dubauer's cabin, first."

"Miles, have you ever heard of the concept of a *search warrant*?"

"Dear Bel, how fussy you have grown in your old age. This is a Barrayaran ship, and I am Gregor's Voice. I don't ask for search warrants, I *issue* them."

Miles took one last turn completely around the cargo hold before having Roic lock it back up. He didn't spot anything different, just, dauntingly, more of the same. Fifty pallets added up to a lot of uterine replicators. There were no decomposing dead bodies tucked in behind any of the replicator racks, anyway, worse luck.

Dubauer's accommodation, back in the personnel module, proved unenlightening. It was a small economy cabin, and whatever personal effects the . . . individual of unknown gender had possessed, it had evidently packed and taken them all along when the quaddies had transferred the passengers to the hostels. No bodies under the bed or in the cabinets here, either. Brun's people had surely searched it at least cursorily once, the day after Solian vanished. Miles made a mental note to try to arrange a more microscopically thorough forensics examination of both the cabin, and the hold with the replicators. Although—by what organization? He didn't want to turn this over to Venn yet, but the Barrayaran fleet's medical people were mainly devoted to trauma. *I'll figure something out.* Never had he missed ImpSec more keenly.

"Do the Cetagandans have any agents here in Quaddiespace?" he asked Bel as they exited the cabin and locked up again. "Have you ever encountered your opposite numbers?"

Bel shook its head. "People from your region are pretty thinly spread out in this arm of the Nexus. Barrayar doesn't even keep a full-time consul's office on Union Station, and neither does Cetaganda. All they have is some quaddie lawyer on retainer over there who keeps the paperwork for about a dozen minor planetary polities, if anyone should want it. Visas and entry permissions and such. Actually, as I recall, she handles *both* Barrayar and Cetaganda. If there are any Cetagandan agents on Graf, I haven't spotted them. I can only hope the reverse is also true. Though if the Cetagandans do keep any spies or agents or informers in Quaddiespace, they're most likely to be on Union. I'm only here on Graf for, um, personal reasons."

Before they exited the *Idris*, Roic insisted Bel call Venn for an update on the search for the murderous quaddie from the hostel lobby. Venn, clearly discommoded, rattled off reports of vigorous activity on the part of his patrollers—and no results. Roic was jumpy on the short walk from the *Idris*'s docking bay to the one where the *Kestrel* was locked on, eyeing their armed quaddie escort with almost as much suspicion as he eyed shadows and cross corridors. But they arrived without further incident.

"How hard would it be to get Greenlaw's permission to fast-penta Dubauer?" Miles asked Bel, as they made their way through the *Kestrel*'s airlock.

"Well, you'd need a court order. And an explanation that would convince a quaddie judge."

"Hm. Ambushing Dubauer with a hypospray aboard the *Idris* suggests itself to my mind as a simpler alternate possibility."

"It would." Bel sighed. "And it would cost me my job if Watts found out I'd helped you. If Dubauer's innocent of wrongdoing, it would certainly complain to the quaddie authorities, afterward."

"Dubauer's not innocent. At the very least, it's lied about its cargo."

"Not necessarily. Its manifest just reads, *Mammals, genetically altered, assorted*. You can't say they aren't mammals."

"Transporting minors for immoral purposes, then. Slave trading. Hell, I'll think of something." Miles waved Roic and Bel off to wait, and took over the *Kestrel*'s wardroom again.

He seated himself, adjusted the security cone, and took a long breath, trying to round up his galloping thoughts. There was no faster way to get a tightbeam message, however coded, from Quaddiespace to Barrayar than via the commercial system of links. Message beams were squirted at the speed of light across local space systems between wormhole jump point stations. An hour's, or a day's, messages were collected at the stations and loaded on either scheduled dedicated communications ships, jumping back and forth on a regular schedule to squirt them across the next local space region, or, on less traveled routes, on whatever ship next jumped through. The round trip for a beamed message between Quaddiespace and the Imperium would take several days, at best.

He addressed the message triply, to Emperor Gregor, to ImpSec Chief Allegre, and to ImpSec galactic operations headquarters on Komarr. After a sketchy outline of the situation so far, including assurances of his assailant's bad aim, he described Dubauer, in as much detail as possible, and the startling cargo he'd found aboard the *Idris*. He requested full details on the new tensions with the Cetagandans that Gregor had alluded to so obliquely, and appended an urgent plea for information, if any, on known Cetagandan operatives and operations in Quaddiespace. He ran the results through the *Kestrel's* ImpSec encoder and squirted it on its way.

Now what? Wait for an answer that might be entirely inconclusive? Hardly . . .

He jumped in his chair when his wrist com buzzed. He gulped and slapped it. "Vorkosigan."

"Hello, Miles." It was Ekaterin's voice; his heart rate slowed. "Do you have a moment?"

"Not only that, I have the *Kestrel's* comconsole. A moment of privacy, if you can believe it."

"Oh! Just a second, then . . ." The wrist com channel closed. Shortly, Ekaterin's face and torso appeared over the vid plate. She was wearing that flattering slate-blue thing again. "Ah," she said happily. "There you are. That's better."

"Well, not quite." He touched his fingers to his lips and transferred the kiss in pantomime to the image of hers. Cool ghost, alas, not warm flesh. Belatedly, he asked, "Where are you?" Alone, he trusted.

"In my cabin on the *Prince Xav*. Admiral Vorpatril gave me a nice one. I think he evicted some poor senior officer. Are you all right? Have you had your dinner?"

"Dinner?"

"Oh, dear, I know that look. Make Lieutenant Smolyani at least open you a meal tray before you go off again."

"Yes, love." He grinned at her. "Practicing that maternal drill?"

"I was thinking of it more as a public service. Have you found something interesting and useful?"

"Interesting is an understatement. Useful—well—I'm not sure." He described his find on the *Idris*, in only slightly more colorful terms than the ones he'd just sent off to Gregor.

Ekaterin's eyes grew wide. "Goodness! And here I was all excited because I thought I'd found a fat clue for you! I'm afraid mine's just gossip, by comparison."

"Gossip away, do."

"Just something I picked up over dinner with Vorpatril's officers. They seemed a pleasant group, I must say."

I'll bet they made themselves pleasant. Their guest was beautiful, cultured, a breath of home, and the first female most of them had spoken to in weeks. And married to the Imperial Auditor, heh. *Eat your hearts out, boys.*

"I tried to get them to talk about Lieutenant Solian, but hardly anyone knew the man. Except that one fellow remembered that Solian had had to step out of a weekly fleet security officers' meeting because he'd sprung a nose-bleed. I gather that Solian was more embarrassed and annoyed than alarmed. But it occurred to me that it might be a chronic thing with him. Nikki had them for a while, and I had them occasionally for a couple of years when I was a girl, though mine went away on their own. But if Solian hadn't taken himself to his ship's medtech to get fixed yet, well, it might be another way someone could have obtained a tissue sample from him for that manufactured blood." She paused. "Actually, now I think on it, I'm not so sure that *is* a help to you. Anyone might have grabbed his used nose rag out of the trash, wherever he'd been. Although I supposed that if his nose was bleeding, at least he had to have been alive at the time. It seemed a little hopeful, anyway." Her thoughtful frown deepened. "Or maybe not."

"*Thank* you," said Miles sincerely. "I don't know if it's hopeful or not either, but it gives me another reason to see the medtechs next. Good!" He was rewarded with a smile. He added, "And if you come up with any thoughts on Dubauer's cargo, feel free to share. Although only with me, for the moment."

"I understand." Her brows drew down. "It is stunningly strange. Not strange that the cargo exists—I mean, if all the haut children are conceived and genetically engineered centrally, the way your friend the haut Pel described it to me when she came as an envoy to Gregor's wedding, the haut women geneticists have to be exporting thousands of embryos from the Star Crèche all the time."

"Not all the time," Miles corrected. "Once a year. The annual haut child ships to the outlying satrapies are all dispatched at the same time. It gives all the top haut-lady planetary consorts like Pel, who are charged with conducting them, a chance to meet and consult with each other. Among other things."

She nodded. "But to bring this cargo all the way here—and with only one handler to look after them . . . If your Dubauer, or whoever it is, really does have a thousand babies in tow, I don't care if they're normal human or ghem or haut or what, it had better have several hundred nursemaids waiting for them somewhere."

"Truly." Miles rubbed his forehead, which was aching again, and not just from the exploding possibilities. Ekaterin was right about that meal tray, as usual. If Solian could have tossed away a blood sample anywhere, any time . . .

"Oh, ha!" He rummaged in his trouser pocket and pulled out his handkerchief, forgotten there since this morning, and opened it on the heavy brown stain. Blood sample, indeed. He didn't have to wait for ImpSec HQ to get back to him on *this* identification. He would have undoubtedly remembered this accidental specimen eventually without the prompting. Whether before or after the efficient Roic had cleaned his clothes and returned them ready to don again, now, that was another question, wasn't it? "Ekaterin, I love you dearly. And I need to talk to the *Prince Xav*'s surgeon *right now.*" He made frantic kissing motions at her, which elicited that entrancing enigmatic smile of hers, and cut the com.

Chapter 10

Miles made an urgent heads-up call to the *Prince Xav*; a short delay followed while Bel negotiated clearance for the *Kestrel*'s message drone. Half a dozen armed Union Militia patrol vessels still floated protectively between Graf Station and Vorpatril's fleet lying in frustrated exile several kilometers off. It would not have done for Miles's precious sample to be shot out of space by some quaddie militia guard with a double quota of itchy trigger fingers. Miles didn't relax until the *Prince Xav* reported the capsule safely retrieved and taken inboard.

He finally settled down at the *Kestrel*'s wardroom table with Bel, Roic, and some military-issue ration trays. He ate mechanically, barely tasting the admittedly not-very-tasty hot food, one eye on the vid display still fast forwarding through the *Idris*'s lock records. Dubauer, it appeared, had never once left the vessel to so much as stroll about the station during the whole of the time the ship had been in dock, until forcibly removed with the other passengers to the stationside hostel by the quaddies.

Lieutenant Solian had left five times, four of them duty excursions for routine cargo checks, the fifth, most interestingly, after his work shift on his last day. The vid showed a good view of the back of his head, departing, and a clear shot of his face, returning about forty minutes later. Despite freezing the image, Miles could not certainly identify any of the spots or shadows on Solian's dark-green Barrayaran military tunic as nose-bloodstains, even in close-up. Solian's expression was set and frowning as he glanced up straight at the security vid pickup, part of his charge, after all—perhaps automatically checking its function. The young man didn't look relaxed, or happy, or as though he were looking forward to some interesting station leave, although he had been due some. He looked . . . intent on something.

It was the last documented time Solian had been seen alive. No sign of his body had been found when Brun's men had searched the *Idris* the next day, and they had searched thoroughly, requiring each passenger with cargo, including Dubauer, to unlock their cabins and holds for inspection. Hence Brun's strongly held theory that Solian must have smuggled himself out undetected. "So where did he go out to, during that forty minutes he was off the ship?" Miles asked in aggravation.

"He didn't cross my customs barriers, not unless someone rolled him in a damned carpet and carried him," said Bel positively. "And I don't have a record of anyone lugging in a carpet. We looked. He had pretty free access to the six loading bays in that sector, and any ships then in dock. Which were all your four, at the time."

"Well, Brun swears he doesn't have vids of him boarding any of the other vessels. I suppose I'd better check everyone else who entered or left any of the ships during that period.

Solian could have sat down for a quiet, unobserved chat—
or more sinister exchange—with someone in any number
of nooks in those loading bays. With or without a
nosebleed."

"The bays aren't that closely controlled or patrolled," Bel
admitted. "We let crew and passengers use the empty ones
for exercise spaces or games, sometimes."

"Hm." Someone had certainly used one to play games
with that synthesized blood, later.

After their utilitarian dinner, Miles had Bel conduct him
back through the customs checkpoints to the hostel where
the impounded ships' crews were housed. These digs were
notably less luxurious and more crowded than the ones
devoted to the paying galactic passengers, and the edgy
crews had been stuck in them for days with nothing but the
holovid and each other for entertainment. Miles was
instantly pounced upon by assorted senior officers, both
from the two Toscane Corporation ships and the two independents caught up in this fracas, demanding to know how
soon he was going to obtain their release. He cut through
the hubbub to request interviews with the medtechs
assigned to the four ships, and a quiet room to conduct
them in. Some shuffling produced, at length, a back office
and a quartet of nervous Komarrans.

Miles addressed the *Idris*'s medtech first. "How hard
would it be for an unauthorized person to gain access to
your infirmary?"

The man blinked. "Not hard at all, Lord Auditor. I mean,
it's not locked. In case of an emergency, people might need
to be able to get in right away, without hunting me up. I
might even *be* the emergency." He paused, then added, "A
few of my medications and some equipment are kept in
code-locked drawers, with tighter inventory controls, of

course. But for the rest, there's no need. In dock, who comes on and off the ship is controlled by ship's security, and in space, well, that takes care of itself."

"You haven't had trouble with theft, then? Equipment going for a walk, supplies disappearing?"

"Very little. I mean, the ship is public, but it's not that *kind* of public. If you see what I mean."

The medtechs from the two independent ships reported similar protocols when in space, but when in dock both were required to keep their little departments secured when they were not themselves on duty there. Miles reminded himself that one of these people might have been bribed to cooperate with whoever had undertaken the blood synthesis. Four suspects, eh. His next inquiry ascertained that all four ship's infirmaries did indeed keep portable synthesizers in inventory as standard equipment.

"If someone snuck in to one of your infirmaries to synthesize some blood, would you be able to tell that your equipment had been used?"

"If they cleaned up after themselves . . . maybe not," said the *Idris*'s tech. "Or—how much blood?"

"Three to four liters."

The man's anxious face cleared. "Oh, yes. That is, if they used my supplies of phyllopacks and fluids, and didn't bring in their own. I'd have noticed if *that* much were gone."

"How soon would you notice?"

"Next time I looked, I suppose. Or at the monthly inventory, if I didn't have occasion to look before then."

"*Have* you noticed?"

"No, but—that is, I haven't looked."

Except that a suitably bribed medtech ought to be perfectly capable of fudging the inventory of such bulky and noncontrolled items. Miles decided to turn up the heat. He said blandly, "The reason I ask is that the blood that was found on the loading bay floor that kicked off this unfortunate—and expensive—chain of events, while it was indeed initially DNA-typed as Lieutenant Solian's, was found to be synthesized. Quaddie customs claim to have no record of Solian ever crossing into Graf Station, which suggests, although it does not alas prove, that the blood might have been synthesized on the outboard side of the customs barrier too. I think we had better check each of your supply inventories, next."

The medtech from the *Idris*'s Toscane-owned sister ship, the *Rudra*, frowned suddenly. "There was—" She broke off.

"Yes?" Miles said encouragingly.

"There was that funny passenger, who came in to ask me about my blood synthesizer. I just figured he was one of the nervous sorts of travelers, although when he explained himself, I also thought he probably had good reason to be."

Miles smiled carefully. "Tell me more about your funny passenger."

"He'd just signed on to the *Rudra* here at Graf Station. He said he was worried, if he had any accidents en route, because he couldn't take standard blood substitutes on account of being so heavily gengineered. Which he was. I mean, I believed him about the blood compatibility problems. That's why we carry the synthesizers, after all. He had the longest fingers—with webs. He told me he was an amphibian, which I didn't *quite* believe, till he showed me his gill slits. His ribs opened out in the most astonishing fashion. He said he has to keep spraying his gills with moisturizer, when he travels, because the air on ships and stations is too dry for him." She stopped, and swallowed.

Definitely not "Dubauer," then. Hm. Another player? But in the same game, or a different one?

She continued in a scared voice, "I ended up showing him my synthesizer, because he seemed so worried and kept asking questions about it. I mainly worried about what sorts of tranquilizers were going to be safe to use on him, if he turned out to be one of those people who gets hysterical eight days out."

Leaping about and whooping, Miles told himself firmly, would likely just frighten the young woman more. He did sit up and favor her with a perky smile, which made her shrink back in her chair only slightly. "When was this? What day?"

"Um . . . two days before the quaddies made us all evacuate the ship and come here."

Three days after Solian's vanishing. *Better and better.* "What was the passenger's name? Could you identify him again?"

"Oh, sure—I mean, webs, after all. He told me his name was Firka."

As if casually, Miles asked, "Would you be willing to repeat this testimony under fast-penta?"

She made a face. "I suppose so. Do I have to?"

Neither panicked nor too eager; good. "We'll see. Physical inventory next, I think. We'll start with the *Rudra's* infirmary." And just in case he was being led up the path by his nose, the others to follow.

More delays ensued, while Bel negotiated over the com-console with Venn and Watts for the temporary release from house arrest of the medtechs as expert witnesses. Once those arrangements had been approved, the visit to the *Rudra's* infirmary was gratifyingly short, direct, and fruitful.

The medtech's supply of synthetic blood base was down by four liters. A phyllopack, with its hundreds of square meters of primed reaction surface stacked in microscopic layers in a convenient insert, was gone. And the blood synthesizing machine had been improperly cleaned. Miles smiled toothily as he personally scraped a tinge of organic residue from its tubing into a plastic bag for the delectation of the *Prince Xav*'s surgeon.

It all rang sufficiently true that he set Roic to collecting copies of the *Rudra*'s security records, with particular reference to Passenger Firka, and sent Bel off with the techs to cross-check the other three infirmaries without him. Miles returned to the *Kestrel* and handed off his new sample to Lieutenant Smolyani to convey promptly to the *Prince Xav*, then settled down to run a search for Firka's present location. He tracked him to the second of the two hostels taken up with the impounded ships' passengers, but the quaddie on security duty there reported that the man had signed out for the evening before dinner and had not yet returned. Firka's prior venture out that day had been around the time of the passengers' meeting; perhaps he'd been one of the men in the back of the room, although Miles certainly hadn't noticed a webbed hand raised for questions. Miles left orders with quaddie hostel security to call him or Armsman Roic when the passenger returned, regardless of the time.

Frowning, he called the first hostel to check on Dubauer. The Betan/Cetagandan herm/ba/whatever had indeed returned safely from the *Idris*, but had left again after dinner. Not in itself unusual: few of the trapped passengers stayed in their hostel when they could vary their evening boredom by seeking entertainment elsewhere on the station. But hadn't Dubauer just been the person who'd been too frightened to traverse Graf Station alone without an armed escort? Miles's frown deepened, and he left orders to this quaddie duty guard to notify him when Dubauer, too, came back.

He rescanned the *Idris*'s security vids on fast forward while waiting Roic's return. Paused close-up views of the hands of a number of otherwise unexceptional visitors to the ship revealed no webs. It was nearing station midnight when Roic and Bel checked in.

Bel was yawning. "Nothing exciting," the herm reported. "I think we got it in one. I sent the medtechs back to the hostel with a security escort to tuck 'em into bed. What's next?"

Miles chewed gently on the side of his finger. "Wait for the surgeon to report identifications on the two samples I sent over to the *Prince Xav*. Wait for Firka and Dubauer to return to their hostels, or else go running all over the station looking for them. Or better yet, make Venn's patrollers do it, except that I don't really want to divert them from hunting for my assassin till they nail the fellow."

Roic, who had begun to look alarmed, relaxed again. "Good thinking, m'lord," he murmured gratefully.

"Sounds like a golden opportunity to sleep, to me," opined Bel.

Miles, to his irritation, was finding Bel's yawns contagious. Miles had never quite mastered their old mercenary colleague Commodore Tung's formidable ability to sleep anywhere, any time a break in the action permitted. He was sure he was still too keyed up to doze. "A nap, maybe," he granted grudgingly.

Bel, intelligently, at once seized the chance to go home to Nicol for a time. Overriding the herm's argument that it *was* a bodyguard, Miles made Bel take a quaddie patroller along. Regretfully, Miles decided to wait until he had heard back from the surgeon to call and wake up Chief Venn; he could not afford mistakes in quaddie eyes. He cleaned up and lay down himself in his tiny cabin for whatever sleep he could snatch. If he had a choice between a good night's uninterrupted sleep and early news, he'd prefer news.

Venn would presumably let him know at once if Security effected an arrest of the quaddie with the rivet gun. Some space transfer stations were deliberately designed to be hard to hide in. Unfortunately, Graf wasn't one of them. Its architecture could only be described as an agglomeration. It had to be full of forgotten crannies. Best chance of catching the fellow would be if he attempted to leave; would he be cool enough to go to some den and lie low, instead? Or, having missed his target the first time— whoever his target had been—hot enough to circle back for another pass? Smolyani had disengaged the *Kestrel* from its lock and taken up position a few meters off the side of the station, just in case, while the Lord Auditor slept.

Replacing the question of who would want to shoot a harmless elderly Betan herm shepherding, well, sheep, with the question of who would want to shoot a Cetagandan ba smuggling a secret human—or superhuman—cargo of inestimable value, at least to the Star Crèche . . . opened up the range of possible complications in an extremely disturbing fashion. Miles had already quietly decided that Passenger Firka was due for an early rendezvous with fastpenta, with quaddie cooperation if Miles could get it, or without. But, upon reflection, it was doubtful that the truth drug would work on a ba. He entertained brief, wistful fantasies of older interrogation methods. Something from the ancestral era of Mad Emperor Yuri, perhaps, or great-great-grandfather Count Pierre "Le Sanguinaire" Vorrutyer.

He rolled over in his narrow bunk, conscious of how lonely the silence of his cabin was without the reassuring rhythmic breath of Ekaterin overhead. He had gradually become used to that nightly presence. This marriage thing was getting to be a habit, one of his better ones. He touched the chrono on his wrist, and sighed. She was probably asleep by now. Too late to call and wake her just to listen to his blither. He counted over the days to Aral Alexander and Helen Natalia's decanting. Their travel margin was narrowing each day he fooled around here. His brain was putting together a twisted jingle to an old nursery tune, something about fast-penta and puppy dog tails early in the morning, when he mercifully drifted off.

"M'lord?"

Miles snapped alert at Roic's voice on the cabin intercom. "Yes?"

"The *Prince Xav*'s surgeon is on the secured comconsole. I told him to hold, you'd wish to be wakened."

"Yes." Miles glanced at the glowing numerals of the wall chrono; he'd been asleep about four hours. Plenty enough for now. He reached for his jacket. "On my way."

Roic, again—no, still—in uniform, waited in the increasingly familiar little wardroom.

"I thought I told you to get some sleep," Miles said. "Tomorrow—today, it is now—could be a long one."

"I was checking through the *Rudra*'s security vids, m'lord. Think I might have something."

"All right. Show me them after this, then." He slid into the station chair, powered up the security cone, and activated the com vid image.

The senior fleet surgeon, who by the collar tabs on his green uniform held a captain's rank, looked to be one of the young and fit New Men of Emperor Gregor's progressive reign; by his bright, excited eyes, he wasn't regretting his lost night's sleep much. "My Lord Auditor. Captain Chris Clogston here. I have your blood work."

"Excellent. What have you found?"

The surgeon leaned forward. "The most interesting was the stain on that handkerchief of yours. I'd say it was Cetagandan haut blood, without question, except that the sex chromosomes are decidedly odd, and instead of the extra pair of chromosomes where they usually assemble their genetic modifications, there are two extra pairs."

Miles grinned. *Yes!* "Quite. An experimental model. Cetagandan haut indeed, but this one is a ba—genderless—and almost certainly from the Star Crèche itself. Freeze a portion of that sample and mark it top secret, and send it along home to ImpSec's biolabs by the first available courier, with my compliments. I'm sure they'll want it on file."

"Yes, my lord."

No wonder Dubauer had tried to retrieve that bloodied handkerchief. Quite aside from blowing its cover, high-level Star Crèche gene work was not the sort of thing the haut ladies cared to have circulating at large, not unless they'd released it themselves, filtered through a few select Cetagandan ghem clans via their haut trophy wives and mothers. Granted, the haut ladies saved their greatest vigilance for the genes they gated *in* to their well-guarded genome, generations-long work of art that it was. Miles wondered how tidy a profit one might make, offering pirate copies of those cells he'd inadvertently collected. Or maybe not—this ba wasn't, clearly, their *latest* work. A near-century out of date, in fact.

Their *latest* work lay in the hold of the *Idris. Urk.*

"The other sample," Clogston went on, "was Solian II—that is, Lieutenant Solian's synthesized blood. Identical to the earlier specimen—same batch, I'd say."

"Good! Now we're getting somewhere." *Where, for God's sake?* "Thank you, Captain. This is invaluable. Go get some sleep, you've earned it."

The surgeon, disappointment writ plainly on his face at this dismissal without further explication, signed off.

Miles turned back to Roic in time to catch him stifling a yawn. The armsman looked embarrassed, and sat up straighter.

"So what do we have?" Miles prompted.

Roic cleared his throat. "The passenger Firka actually joined the *Rudra* after it was first due to leave, during that delay for repairs."

"Huh. Suggests it wasn't part of a long-laid itinerary, then . . . maybe. Go on."

"I've filtered out quite a few records of the fellow passing on and off the ship, before it was impounded and the passengers evicted. Using his cabin as his hostel, it seems, which a lot of folks do to save money. Two of his trips bracket times Lieutenant Solian was away from the *Idris*—one overlaps his last routine cargo inspection, and t'other exactly brackets that last forty minutes we can't account for."

"Oh, very nice. So what does this self-declared amphibian look like?"

Roic fiddled a moment with the console and brought up a clear full-length shot from the *Rudra*'s lock vid records.

The man was tall, with pale unhealthy-looking skin and dark hair shaved close to his skull in a patchy, unflattering fuzz, like lichen on a boulder. Big nose, small ears, a lugubrious expression on his rubbery face—he looked strung out, actually, eyes dark and ringed. Long, skinny arms and legs; a loose tunic or poncho concealed the details of his big upper torso. His hands and feet were especially distinctive, and Miles zoomed in for close-ups. One hand was half-concealed in a cloth glove with the fingertips cut out, which hid the webs from a casual glance, but the other was ungloved and half-raised, and the webs showed distinctly, a dark rose color between the over-long fingers. The feet were concealed in soft boots or buskins, tied at the ankles, but they too were about double the length of a normal foot, though no wider. Could the fellow spread his webbed toes, when in the water, as he spread his webbed fingers, to make a broad flipper?

He recalled Ekaterin's description of the passenger who had accosted her and Bel on their outing, that first day—*he had the longest, narrowest hands and feet*. Bel should get a look at this shortly. Miles let the vid run. The fellow had a somewhat shambling gate when he walked, lifting and setting down those almost clownish feet.

"Where did he come from?" Miles asked Roic.

"His documentation *claims* he's an Aslunder." Roic's voice was heavy with disbelief.

Aslund was one of Barrayar's fairly near Nexus neighbors, an impoverished agricultural world in a local space cul-de-sac off the Hegen Hub. "Huh. Almost our neck of the woods."

"I dunno, m'lord. His Graf Station customs records show him disembarking from a ship he'd joined at Tau Ceti, which arrived here on the day before our fleet was originally due to leave. Don't know if he originated there or not."

"I'd bet not." Was there a water-world being settled somewhere on the fringes of the Nexus, whose colonists had chosen to alter their children instead of their environment? Miles hadn't heard of one, but it had to happen sometime. Or was Firka a one-off project, an experiment or prototype of some sort? He'd certainly run into a few of those, before. Neither exactly squared with an origin on Aslund. Though he might have immigrated there . . . Miles made a note to request an ImpSec background search on the fellow in his next report, even though any results were likely to trickle back too late to be of any immediate use. At least, he certainly hoped he'd have this mess wrapped up and shipped out before then.

"He originally tried to get a berth on the *Idris*, but there wasn't room," Roic added.

"Ah!" Or maybe that ought to be, *Huh?*

Miles sat back in his station chair, eyes narrowing. Reasoning in advance of his beloved and much-longed-for fast-penta—posit that this peculiar individual had had some personal contact with Solian before the lieutenant went missing. Posit that he had acquired, somehow, a sample of Solian's blood, perhaps in much the same accidental way that Miles had acquired Dubauer's. Why, then, in the name of reason, would he have subsequently gone to the trouble of running up a fake sample of Solian's blood and dribbling it all over a loading bay and out the airlock?

To cover up a murder elsewhere? Solian's disappearance had already been put down to desertion, by his own commanders. No cover needed: if a murder, it was already nearly the perfect crime at that point, with the investigation about to be abandoned.

A frame? Meant to pin Solian's murder on another? Attractive, but in that case, shouldn't some innocent have been tracked and accused by now? Unless Firka was the innocent, it was a frame with no portrait in it, at present.

To cover up a desertion? Might Firka and Solian be collaborating on Solian's defection? Or . . . when might a desertion not be a desertion? When it was an ImpSec covert ops scam, that's when. Except that Solian was Service Security, not ImpSec: a guard, not a spy or trained agent. Still . . . a *sufficiently* bright, loyal, highly motivated, and ambitious officer, finding himself in some complex imbroglio, might not wait for orders from on high to pursue a fast-moving long shot. As Miles had reason to know.

Of course, taking risky chances like that could get such an officer killed. As Miles also had reason to know.

Regardless of intent, what had the actual effect of the blood bait been? Or what would it have been if Corbeau and Garnet Five's star-crossed romance hadn't run afoul of Barrayaran prejudices and loutishness? The showy scarlet scenario on the loading bay deck would certainly have reaffixed official attention upon Solian's disappearance; it would almost certainly have delayed the fleet's departure, although not as spectacularly as the real events had. Assuming Garnet Five and Corbeau's problems had been accidental. She was an actress of sorts, after all. They had only Corbeau's word about his wrist com.

He said wistfully, "I don't suppose we have a clear shot of this frog-man lugging out half a dozen liter jugs at any point?"

"Afraid not, m'lord. He went back and forth with lots of packages and boxes at various times, though; they could well have been hid inside something."

Gah. The acquisition of facts was supposed to clarify thought. This was just getting murkier and murkier. He asked Roic, "Has quaddie security from either of the hostels called yet? Are Dubauer or Firka back yet?"

"No, m'lord. No calls, that is."

Miles called both to cross-check; neither of his two passengers of interest had yet returned. It was over four hours after midnight, now, 0420 on the twenty-four-hour, Earth-descended clock that Quaddiespace still kept, generations after their ancestors' unmodified ancestors had departed the home world.

After he'd cut the com, Miles asked querulously, "So where the hell have they gone, all night?"

Roic shrugged. "If it was t' obvious thing, I wouldn't look for them to be back till breakfast."

Miles considerately declined to take notice of Roic's distinct blush. "Our frog-man, maybe, but I guarantee the ba didn't go looking for feminine companionship. There's nothing obvious about any of this." Decisively, Miles reached for the call pad again.

Instead of Chief Venn, the image of a quaddie woman in a Security gray uniform appeared against the dizzying radial background of Venn's office. Miles wasn't sure what her rank markings decoded to, but she looked sensible, middle-aged, and harried enough to be fairly senior.

"Good morning," he began politely. "Where's Chief Venn?"

"Sleeping, I hope." The expression on her face suggested she was going to do her loyal best to keep it that way, too.

"At a time like this?"

"The poor man had a double shift and a half yester . . ." She squinted at him, and seemed to come to some recognition. "Oh. Lord Auditor Vorkosigan. I'm Chief Venn's third-shift supervisor, Teris Three. Is there anything I can do for you?"

"Night duty officer, eh? Very good. Yes, please. I wish to arrange for the detainment and interrogation, possibly with fast-penta, of a passenger from the *Rudra*. His name's Firka."

"Is there some criminal charge you wish to file?"

"Material witness, to start. I have found reason to suspect he may have something to do with the blood on the floor of the docking bay that started this mess. I want very much to find out for sure."

"Sir, we can't just go around arresting and drugging anyone we please, here. We need a formal charge. And if the transient doesn't volunteer to be interrogated, you'll have to get an adjudicator's order for the fast-penta."

That problem, Miles decided, he would bounce to Sealer Greenlaw. It sounded like her department. "All right, I charge him with suspected littering. Incorrect disposal of organics has to be some kind of illegal, here."

Despite herself, the corner of her mouth twitched. "It's a misdemeanor. Yes, that would do," she admitted.

"Any pretext that will fix it for you is all right by me. I *want* him, and I want him as quickly as you can lay hands on him. Unfortunately, he signed out of his hostel at about seventeen-hundred yesterday, and hasn't been seen since."

"Our security work gang is seriously overstretched, here, on account of yesterday's . . . unfortunate incident. Can this wait till morning, Lord Auditor Vorkosigan?"

"No."

For a moment, he thought she was going to go all bureaucratic on him, but after screwing up her lips in a thoughtfully aggravated way for a moment, she relented. "Very well. I'll put out a detention order on him, pending Chief Venn's review. But you'll have to see to the adjudicator as soon as we pick him up."

"Thank you. I promise you won't have any trouble recognizing him. I can download IDs and some vid shots to you from here, if you wish."

She allowed as how that would be useful, and the task was done.

Miles hesitated, mulling over the even more disturbing dilemma of Dubauer. There was not, to be sure, any obvious connection between the two problems. Yet. Perhaps the interrogation of Firka would reveal one?

Leaving Venn's myrmidon to get on with it, Miles cut the com. He leaned back in his station chair for a moment, then brought up the vids of Firka and reran them a couple of times.

"So," he said after a time. "How the devil did he keep those long, floppy feet out of the blood puddles?"

Roic stared over his shoulder. "Floater?" he finally said. "He'd have to be damned near double-jointed to fold those legs up in one, though."

"He *looks* damned near double-jointed." But if Firka's toes were as long and prehensile as his fingers suggested, might he have been able to manipulate the joystick controls, designed for quaddie lower hands, with his feet? In this new scenario, Miles needn't picture the person in the floater horsing a heavy body around, merely emptying his gurgling liter jugs overboard and supplying some artistic smears with a suitable rag.

After a few cross-eyed moments trying to imagine this, Miles dumped Firka's vid shots into an image manipulator and installed the fellow in a floater. The supposed amphibian didn't quite have to be double-jointed or break his legs to fit in. Assuming his lower body was rather more flexible than Miles's or Roic's, it folded pretty neatly. It looked a bit painful, but possible.

Miles stared harder at the image above the vid plate.

The first question one addressed in describing a person on Graf Station wasn't "man or woman?" It was "quaddie or downsider?" The very first cut, by which one discarded half or more of the possibilities from further consideration.

He pictured a blond quaddie in a dark jacket, speeding up a corridor in a floater. He pictured that quaddie's belated pursuers, whizzing past a shaven-headed downsider in light garb, walking the other way. That was all it would take, in a sufficiently harried moment. Step out of the floater, turn one's jacket inside out, stuff the wig in a pocket, leave the machine with a couple of others sitting waiting, stroll away . . . It would be much harder to work it the other way around, of course, for a quaddie to impersonate a downsider.

He stared at Firka's hollow, dark-ringed eyes. He pulled up a suitable mop of blond ringlets from the imager files and applied it to Firka's unhandsome head.

A fair approximation of the dark-eyed barrel-chested quaddie with the rivet gun? Glimpsed for a fraction of a second, at fifteen meters range, and truth to tell most of Miles's attention had been on the spark-spitting, chattering, hot-brass-chucking object in his hands . . . had those hands been webbed?

Fortunately, he could draw upon a second opinion. He called up Bel Thorne's home code from the comconsole.

Unsurprisingly, at this ungodly hour, the visual didn't come on when Nicol's sleepy voice answered. "Hello?"

"Nicol? Miles Vorkosigan here. Sorry to drag you out of your sleep sack. I need to talk to your housemate. Boot it out and make it come to the vid. Bel's had more sleep than I have, by now."

The visual came up. Nicol righted herself and drew a fluffy lace garment closer about her with a lower hand; this section of the apartment she shared with Bel was evidently on the free fall side. It was too dim to make out much beyond her floating form. She rubbed her eyes. "What? Isn't Bel with you?"

Miles's stomach went into free fall, for all that the *Kestrel*'s grav was in good working order. "No . . . Bel left over six hours ago."

Her frown sharpened. The sleep drained from her face, to be replaced by alarm. "But Bel didn't come home last night!"

Chapter 11

Graf Station Security Post One, housing most of the security police administrative offices including Chief Venn's, lay entirely on the free fall side of the station. Miles and Roic, trailed by a flustered quaddie guard from the *Kestrel*'s lock, floated into the post's radially arranged reception space, from which tubular corridors led off at odd angles. The place was still night-quiet, although shift change was surely due soon.

Nicol had beaten Miles and Roic there, but not by much. She was still awaiting the arrival of Chief Venn under the concerned eye of a uniformed quaddie whom Miles took to be the equivalent of a night desk sergeant. The quaddie officer's wariness increased when they entered, and one lower hand moved unobtrusively to touch a pad on his console; as if casually, and very promptly, another armed quaddie officer drifted down from one of the corridors to join his comrade.

Nicol wore a plain blue T-shirt and shorts, hastily donned with no artistic touches. Her face was pale with

worry. Her lower hands clenched each other. She returned
a short grateful nod to Miles's under-voiced greeting.

Chief Venn arrived at last and gave Miles a look unlov-
ing but resigned. He had apparently slept, if not enough,
and had pessimistically dressed for the day; no secret hope
of getting back into the sleep sack showed in his neat attire.
He waved off the armed guard and gruffly invited the Lord
Auditor and company to follow him to his office. The
third-shift supervisor Miles had spoken with a while ago—
might as well start calling it *last night*—brought coffee
bulbs along with her end-of-shift report. Meticulously, she
handed the bulbs out to the downsiders, instead of launching them through the air and expecting them to be caught
the way she served her crew chief and Nicol. Miles turned
the bulb's thermal control to the limit of the red zone and
sucked the hot bitter brew with gratitude, as did Roic.

"This panic may be premature," Venn began after his
own first swallow. "Portmaster Thorne's nonappearance
may have some very simple explanation."

And what were the top three complicated explanations
in Venn's mind right now? The quaddie wasn't sharing, but
then, neither was Miles. Bel had been missing for over six
hours, ever since it had dismissed its quaddie guard at a
bubble-car stop near its home. By now this panic might just
as easily be posthumous, but Miles didn't care to say so
aloud in front of Nicol. "I am extremely concerned."

"Thorne could be asleep somewhere else." Venn glanced
somewhat enigmatically at Nicol. "Have you checked with
likely friends?"

"The portmaster stated explicitly that it was heading
home to Nicol to rest, when it left the *Kestrel* about midnight," said Miles. "A well-earned rest by that time, I might

add. Your own guards should be able to confirm the exact time of Thorne's departure from my ship."

"We will, of course, provide you with another liaison officer to assist you in your inquiries, Lord Vorkosigan." Venn's voice was a little distant; buying time to think, was how Miles read him. He might be playing deliberately obtuse as well. Miles did not mistake him for actually obtuse, not when he'd cut his sleep shift short and come in for this within little more than minutes.

"I don't want another. I want Thorne. You mislay too damned many downsiders around here. It's beginning to seem bloody careless." Miles took a deep breath. "It has to have crossed your mind by now, as it has mine, that there were three persons in the line of fire in the hostel lobby yesterday afternoon. We all assumed that I was the obvious target. What if it was something less obvious? What if it was Thorne?"

Teris Three made a stemming motion at him with an upper hand, and interjected, "Speaking of that, the trace on that hot riveter came in a few hours ago."

"Oh, good," said Venn, turning to her with relief. "What have we got?"

"It was sold for cash three days back, from an engineering supply store near the free fall docks. Carried out, not delivered. The purchaser didn't fill out the warranty questionnaire. The clerk wasn't sure which customer took it, because it was a busy hour."

"Quaddie or downsider?"

"He couldn't say. Could have been either, it seems."

And if certain webbed hands had been covered with gloves as in the vid shot, they might well have been overlooked. Venn grimaced, his hopes for a break plainly frustrated.

The night supervisor glanced at Miles. "Lord Vorkosigan here also called, to request that we detain one of the passengers from the *Rudra*."

"Find him yet?" asked Miles.

She shook her head.

"Why do you want him?" asked Venn, frowning.

Miles repeated his own night's news about his interrogation of the medtechs and finding traces of Solian's synthesized blood in the *Rudra*'s infirmary.

"Well, that explains why *we* were having no luck at the station hospitals and clinics," grumbled Venn. Miles imagined him totting up his department's wasted quaddie-hours from the fruitless search, and let the grumble pass.

"I also flushed out one suspect, in the course of the conversation with the *Rudra*'s tech. All circumstantial speculation so far, but fast-penta is the drug to cure that." Miles described the unusual Passenger Firka, his own insufficient but nagging sense of recognition, and his suspicions about the creative use of a floater. Venn looked grimmer and grimmer. Just because Venn reflexively resisted being stampeded by a Barrayaran dirtsucker, Miles decided, didn't mean he wasn't listening. What he made of it all, through his provincial Quaddiespace cultural filters, was much harder to guess.

"But what about *Bel*?" Nicol's voice was tight with suppressed anguish.

Venn was obviously less immune to a plea from a beautiful fellow quaddie. He met his night supervisor's inquiring look and nodded agreement.

"Well, what's one more?" Teris Three shrugged. "I'll put out a call to all patrollers to start looking for Portmaster Thorne, too. As well as the fellow with the webs."

Miles nibbled on his lower lip in worry. Sooner or later, that live cargo secreted aboard the *Idris* must draw the ba back to it. "Bel—Portmaster Thorne *did* get back to you people last night about resealing the *Idris*, did it not?"

"Yes," said Venn and the night supervisor together. Venn gave her a short apologetic nod and continued, "Did that Betan passenger Thorne was trying to help get its animal fetuses taken care of all right?"

"Dubauer. Um, yes. They're fine for now. But, ah . . . I think I'd like to have you pick up Dubauer, as well as Firka."

"Why?"

"It left its hostel and vanished yesterday evening close to the same time that Firka went out, and also hasn't returned. And Dubauer was the third of our little triumvirate of targets yesterday. Let's just call it protective custody, for starters."

Venn screwed up his lips for a moment, considering this, and eyed Miles with shrewd disfavor. He'd have to be less bright than he appeared not to suspect Miles wasn't telling him everything. "Very well," he said at last. He waved a hand at Teris Three. "Let's go ahead and collect the whole set."

"Right." She glanced at the chrono on her left lower wrist. "It's oh-seven-hundred." Shift change, presumably. "Shall I stay?"

"No, no. I'll take over. Get the new missing-person traces started, then go get some rest." Venn sighed. "Tonight may be no better."

The night supervisor gave him an acknowledging thumbs-up with both lower hands and slipped out of the little office chamber.

"Would you prefer to wait at home?" Venn said suggestively to Nicol. "You'd be more comfortable there, I'm sure. We'll undertake to call you as soon as we find your partner."

Nicol took a breath. "I would rather be here," she said sturdily. "Just in case . . . just in case something happens soon."

"I'll keep you company," Miles volunteered. "For a little while, anyway." There, let Venn try to shift *his* diplomatic mass.

Venn at least managed to get them shifted out of his office by conducting them to a private waiting space, advertising it as more undisturbed. More undisturbed for Venn, anyway.

Miles and Nicol were left regarding each other in troubled silence. What Miles most wanted to know was if Bel had any other ImpSec business in train at present that might have impinged unexpectedly last night. But he was almost certain Nicol knew nothing of Bel's second source of income—and risk. Besides, that was wishful thinking. If any business had impinged, it was most probably the current mess. Which was now messy enough to raise every hackle Miles owned to quivering attention.

Bel had escaped its former career very nearly unscathed, despite Admiral Naismith's sometimes-lethal nimbus. For the Betan herm to have come all this way, to have come so close to regaining a private life and future, only to have its past reach out like some blind fate and swat it down *now* . . . Miles swallowed guilt and worry, and refrained from blurting some ill-timed and incoherent apology to Nicol. Something had certainly come upon Bel last night, but Bel was quick and clever and experienced; Bel could cope. Bel had always coped before.

But even the luck you made for yourself ran out some-times. . . .

Nicol broke the stretched silence by asking some random question of Roic about Barrayar, and the armsman returned clumsy but kind small talk to distract her from her nerves. Miles glanced at his wrist com. Was it too early to call Ekaterin?

What the bloody hell was next on his agenda, anyway? He'd planned to spend this morning conducting fast-penta interrogations. All the threads he'd thought he'd had in hand, winding in nicely, had come to these disturbingly similar cut ends; Firka vanished, Dubauer vanished, and now Bel vanished too. And Solian, don't forget him. Graf Station, for all its maze-like non-design, wasn't that big a place. Were they all sucked into the same oubliette? How many oubliettes could the damned labyrinth have?

To his surprise, his frustrated fretting was interrupted by the night supervisor sticking her head in through one of the round doors. Hadn't she been leaving?

"Lord Auditor Vorkosigan, may we see you for a moment?" she asked in a polite tone.

He excused himself to Nicol and floated after her, Roic trailing dutifully. She led the way back through a corridor to Venn's nearby office. Venn was finishing up a comconsole call, saying, "He's here, he's hot, and he's all over me. It's *your* job to handle him." He glanced over his shoulder and cut the com. Above the vid plate, Miles just glimpsed Sealer Greenlaw's form, wrapped in what might be a bathrobe, vanish with a sparkle.

When the door hissed closed again behind them, the supervisor turned in midair and stated, "The patroller that you detailed to escort Portmaster Thorne last night reports that Thorne dismissed him when they got to the Joint."

"The what?" said Miles. "When? *Why?*"

She glanced at Venn, who opened a hand in a go-ahead gesture. "The Joint is one of our main corridor hubs on the free fall side, with a bubble-car transfer station and a public garden—a lot of people meet there, to eat or whatever after their work shifts. Thorne evidently encountered Garnet Five at about oh-one-hundred, coming the other way, and went off to have some kind of conversation."

"Yes? They're friends, I believe."

Venn shifted in what Miles recognized after a belated moment as embarrassment, and said, "Do you happen to know how good of friends? I didn't wish to discuss this in front of that distressed young lady. But Garnet Five is known to, um, favor exotic downsiders, and the Betan herm is, after all, a Betan herm. Simple explanations, after all."

Half a dozen mildly outraged arguments coursed through Miles's mind, to be promptly rejected. He wasn't supposed to know Bel that well. Not that someone who did know Bel would be in the least shocked by Venn's delicate suggestion . . . no. Bel's sexual tastes might be eclectic, but the herm wasn't the sort to betray the trust of a friend. Had never been. *We all change.* "You might ask Boss Watts," he temporized. He caught Roic's rolling eye and head-jerk in the direction of Venn's comconsole, affixed to the curving office wall. Miles continued smoothly, "Better still, call Garnet Five. If Thorne's there, the mystery is solved. If not, she might at least know where Thorne was headed." He tried to decide which would be the worse cause for dismay. The memory of the hot rivets parting his hair inclined him to hope for the first result, despite Nicol.

Venn opened an upper hand in acknowledgment of the point, and half-turned to tap out a search-code on his comconsole with a lower. Miles's heart jumped as Garnet Five's serene face and crisp voice came on, but it was only an answering program. Venn's brows twitched; he left a brief request that she contact him at her earliest convenience, and cut the com.

"She could just be asleep," said the night-shift woman wistfully.

"Send a patroller to check," said Miles a little tightly. Remembering he was supposed to be a diplomat, he added, "If you please."

Teris Three, looking as though a vision of her sleep sack was receding before her eyes, departed again. Miles and Roic returned to Nicol, who turned anxious eyes upon them as they floated back into the waiting chamber. Miles barely hesitated before reporting the patroller's sighting to her.

"Can you think of any reason for them to have met?" he asked her.

"Lots," she answered without reserve, confirming Miles's secret judgment. "I'm sure she'd want news from Bel about Ensign Corbeau, or anything happening that might affect his chances. If she crossed trajectories with Bel coming home through the Joint, she'd be sure to grab the chance to try to get some news. Or she might have just wanted an ear to vent at. Most of her other friends are not too sympathetic about her romance, after the Barrayaran attack and the fire."

"All right, that might account for the first hour. But no more. Bel was tired. Then what?"

She turned all four hands out in helpless frustration. "I can't imagine."

Miles's own imagination was all too wildly active. *Need data dammit* was becoming his private mantra here. He left

Roic to make more distracting small talk with Nicol and, feeling a trifle selfish, took himself to the side of the chamber to call Ekaterin on his wrist com.

Her voice was sleepy but cheerful, and she stoutly maintained that she'd been awake already, and just about to get up. They exchanged a few verbal caresses that were no one's business but their own, and he described what he'd found as a result of the gossip she'd collected about Solian's nosebleeds, which seemed to please her greatly.

"So where are you now, and what have you had for breakfast?" she asked.

"Breakfast is delayed. I'm at the Station Security HQ." He hesitated. "Bel Thorne went missing last night, and they're putting together a search for it."

A little silence greeted this, and her return remark was as carefully neutral in tone as his own. "Oh. That's very worrisome."

"Yes."

"You *are* keeping Roic with you at all times, aren't you?"

"Oh, yes. The quaddies have armed guards trailing me around now, too."

"Good." Her breath drew in. "Good."

"The situation's getting pretty murky over here. I may have to send you home after all. We have four more days to decide, though."

"Well. In four more days we can talk about it, then."

Between his desire not to alarm her further, and hers not to distract him unduly, the conversation grew limping, and he mercifully tore himself from the calming sound of her voice to let her go bathe and dress and obtain her own breakfast.

He wondered if he and Roic ought, after all, to escort Nicol home, and perhaps after that try quartering the

station themselves in the hope of some random encounter.
Now, there was a tactically bankrupt plan if ever he'd
evolved one. Roic would have a fully justifiable, painfully
polite fit at the suggestion. It would feel just like old times.
But suppose there was some way to make it less random . . .

The night supervisor's voice floated in from the corridor. Dear God, was the poor woman never to get home to
sleep? "Yes, they're in here, but don't you think you ought
to see the medtech next to—"

"I have to see Lord Vorkosigan!"

Miles jerked to full alertness as he identified the sharp,
breathless female voice as Garnet Five's. The blond quaddie
practically tumbled through the round door from the corridor. She was trembling and haggard, almost greenish, an
unpleasant contrast to her rumpled carmine doublet. Her
eyes, huge and dark-ringed, flicked over the waiting trio.
"Nicol, oh, Nicol!" She flew to her friend in a fierce three-
armed hug, the immobilized fourth wavering slightly.

Nicol, looking bewildered, dutifully hugged her back,
but then pushed her away and asked urgently, "Garnet,
have you seen Bel?"

"Yes. No. I'm not sure. This is just insane. I thought we
were both knocked out together, but when I came to, Bel
wasn't there any more. I thought Bel might have waked up
first and gone for help, but the security crew"—she nodded
to her escort—"says not. Haven't you heard anything?"

"Came to? Wait—who knocked you out? Where? Are
you hurt?"

"I have the most horrible headache. It was some sort of
drug mist. Icy cold. It didn't smell like anything, but it
tasted bitter. He sprayed it in our faces. Bel yelled, 'Don't
breathe, Garnet!' but of course had to breathe to yell. I felt

Bel go all limp, and then everything sort of drained away. When I woke up, I was so sick I almost threw up, ugh!"

Nicol and Teris Three both grimaced in sympathy. Miles gathered this was the security woman's second time through this recitation, but her focus didn't flag.

"Garnet," Miles interjected, "please, take a deep breath, calm down, and begin at the beginning. A patroller reported he saw you and Bel somewhere in the Joint last night. Is that correct?"

Garnet Five scrubbed her pallid face with her upper hands, inhaled, and blinked; a little returning color relieved her gray-greenness. "Yes. I bumped into Bel coming out of the bubble-car stop. I wanted to know if Bel had asked—if you'd said anything—if anything had been decided about Dmitri."

Nicol nodded in bleak satisfaction.

"I bought us those peppermint teas that Bel likes at the Kabob Kiosk, hoping to get it to talk to me. But we hadn't been there five minutes when Bel went all distracted by this other pair who came in. One was a quaddie Bel knew from the Docks and Locks crew—Bel said he was someone it'd been keeping an eye on, because it suspected him of handling stolen stuff from the ships. The other was this really funny-looking downsider."

"Tall, lanky fellow with webbed hands and long feet, and a big barrel chest? Looks sort of like his mother might have married the Frog Prince, but the kiss didn't quite work out?" Miles asked.

Garnet Five stared. "Why, yes. Well, I'm not sure about the chest—he was wearing this loose, flippy cape-thing. How did you know?"

"This is about the third time he's turned up in this case. You might say he's riveted my attention. But go on, then what?"

"I couldn't get Bel to stay on the subject. Bel made me turn around and sit facing the pair, so Bel could keep its back to them, and made me report what they were doing. I felt silly, like we were playing spies."

No, not playing. . . .

"They had some sort of argument, then the quaddie from Docks and Locks spotted Bel and left in a hurry. The other fellow, the funny downsider, left too, and then Bel insisted on following him."

"And Bel left the bistro?"

"We both left together. I wasn't going to be dumped, and besides, Bel said, *Oh, all right, come along, you may be useful.* I think the downsider must have been some sort of spacer, because he wasn't as awkward as most tourists usually are on the free fall side. I didn't think he saw us, following, but he must have, because he wandered down Cross Corridor, weaving in and out of any shops that were open at that hour but not buying anything. Then he suddenly zigzagged over to the portal to the grav side. There weren't any floaters in the rack, so Bel boosted me onto its back and kept on after the fellow. He ducked into this utility section, where the shops on the next corridor—over on the grav side—move freight and supplies in and out of their back doors. He seemed to vanish around a corner, but then he just popped out in front of us and waved this little tube in our faces, that spit out that nasty spray. I was afraid it was a poison, and we were both dead, but evidently not." She hesitated in stricken doubt. "Anyway, *I* woke up."

"Where?" asked Miles.

"There. Well, not quite there—I was all in a heap stuck to the floor inside a recycle bin behind one of the shops, on top of a bundle of cartons. It wasn't locked, fortunately. That horrible downsider couldn't have stuffed me into it if it had been, I suppose. I had a bad time trying to climb out. The stupid lid kept pressing down. It almost smashed my fingers. I hate gravity. Bel wasn't anywhere around. I looked, and called. And then I had to walk on three hands back to the main corridor, till I could find help. I grabbed the first patroller I came to, and she brought me right here."

"You must have been out cold for six or seven hours, then," Miles calculated aloud. How different were quaddie metabolisms from those of Betan herms? Not to mention body mass, and the erratic dosage inhaled by two variously dodging persons. "You should be seen by a physician right away, and get a blood sample drawn while there are still traces of the drug in your system. We might be able to identify it, and maybe its place of origin, if it isn't just a local product."

The night supervisor endorsed this idea emphatically, and permitted the downsider visitors, as well as Nicol, to whom Garnet Five still clung, to trail along as she escorted the shaken blond quaddie to the post's infirmary. When Miles had assured himself that Garnet Five had been taken into competent medical hands, and plenty of them, he turned back to Teris Three.

"It isn't just my airy theories any more," he told her. "You have a valid assault charge on this Firka fellow. Can't you step up the search?"

"Oh, yes," she answered grimly. "This one's going out on all the com channels, now. He attacked a *quaddie*. *And* he released toxic volatiles into the *public air*."

Miles left the two quaddie women safely ensconced in the security post's infirmary. He then leaned on the night supervisor to supply him with the patroller who'd brought in Garnet Five to take him on an inspection of the scene of the crime, such as it was. The supervisor temporized, more delays ensued, and Miles harassed Crew Chief Venn in a nearly undiplomatic manner. But at length, he was issued a different quaddie patroller who did indeed escort him and Roic to the spot where Garnet Five had been so uncomfortably cached.

The dimly lit utility corridor had a flat floor and squared-off walls, and while not exactly cramped, shared its cross section with a great deal of duct work, which Roic had to bend to avoid. Around an obliquely angled turn, they found three quaddies, one in a Security uniform and two in shorts and shirts, working behind a stretched-out plastic ribbon printed with the Graf Station Security logo. Forensics techs at last, and about time. The young male rode in a floater broadly stenciled with a Graf Station technical school identification number. An intent-looking middle-aged female piloted a floater that bore the mark of one of the station clinics.

The shorts-and-shirt man in the tech school floater, hovering carefully, finished a laser scan for fingerprints along the edge and top of a large square bin sticking out into the corridor at a convenient height to bang the shins of the unwary passerby. He moved aside, and his colleague moved into place and began to run over the surfaces with what looked to be a standard sort of skin cell- and fiber-collecting hand-vac.

"Was that the bin where Garnet Five was hidden?" Miles asked the quaddie officer who was supervising.

"Yes."

Miles leaned forward, only to be waved back by the intently vacuuming tech. After extracting promises to be informed of any interesting cross-matches in the evidence, he strolled up and down the corridor instead, hands scrupulously tucked in his pockets, looking for . . . what? Cryptic messages written in blood on the walls? Or in ink, or spit, or snot, or *something*. He checked the floor, ceiling, and ducts, too, at Bel-height and lower, angling his head to catch odd reflections. Nothing.

"Were all these doors locked?" he asked the patroller who shadowed them. "Have they been checked yet? Could someone have bunged Bel—dragged Portmaster Thorne inside one?"

"You'll have to ask the officer in charge, sir," the quaddie guard replied, exasperation leaking into his service-issue neutral tone. "I only just got here with you."

Miles stared at the doors and their key pads in frustration. He couldn't very well go down the row trying them all, not unless the scanner man was finished. He returned to the bin.

"Finding anything?" he inquired.

"Not—" The medical quaddie glanced aside at the officer in charge. "Was this area swept before I got here?"

"Not as far as I know, ma'am," said the officer.

"Why do you ask?" Miles inquired instantly.

"Well, there isn't very much. I would have expected more."

"Try further away," suggested the scanner tech.

She cast him a somewhat bemused look. "That's not quite the point. In any case, after you." She gestured down the corridor, and Miles hurriedly confided his worries about the doors to the officer in charge.

The crew dutifully scanned everything, including, at Miles's insistence, the ductwork above, where the assailant might have braced himself in near-concealment to drop upon his victims. They tried each door. Fingers tapping impatiently on his trouser seam, Miles followed them up and down the corridor as they completed their survey. All doors proved locked . . . at least, they were now. One hissed open as they passed, and a blinking shopkeeper with legs poked his head through; the quaddie officer interrogated him briefly, and he in turn helped rouse his neighbors to cooperate in the search. The quaddie woman collected lots of little plastic bags of nothing much. No unconscious hermaphrodite was discovered in any bin, hallway, utility closet, or shop adjoining the passageway.

The utility corridor ran for about another ten meters before opening discreetly into a broader cross-corridor lined with shops, offices, and a small restaurant. The scene would have been quieter partway into third shift last night, but by no means reliably deserted, and just as well lit. Miles pictured the lanky Firka lugging or dragging Bel's compact but substantial form down the public way . . . wrapped in something for concealment? It would almost have to be. It would take a strong man to lug Bel far. Or . . . someone in a floater. Not necessarily a quaddie.

Roic, looming at his shoulder, sniffed. The spicy smells wafting into the corridor, into which the eatery cannily vented its bakery ovens, reminded Miles of his duty to feed his troops. Troop. The disgruntled quaddie guard could fend for himself, Miles decided.

The place was small, clean, and cozy, the sort of cheap café where the local working people ate. It was evidently past the breakfast rush and not yet time for lunch, because it was occupied only by a couple of legged young men who might be shop assistants, and a quaddie in a floater who, judging by her crowded tool belt, was an electrician on break. They stared covertly at the Barrayarans—more at tall Roic in his not-from-around-here brown-and-silver uniform than at short Miles in his unobtrusive gray civvies. Their quaddie security guard distanced himself slightly— with their party but not of it—and ordered coffee in a bulb.

A legged woman doubled as server and cook, assembling food on the plates with practiced speed. The spicy breads, apparently a specialty of the place, appeared hand-made, the slices of vat protein unexceptional, and the fresh fruit startlingly exquisite. Miles selected a large golden pear, its skin touched with a rose blush, unblemished; its flesh, when he cut into it, proved pale, perfect, and dripping with perfumed juice. If only they had more time, he'd love to sic Ekaterin onto the local agriculture— whatever plant-like matrix this had grown from had to have been genetically engineered to thrive in free fall. The Empire's space stations could use such stocks—if the Komarran traders hadn't snagged them already. Miles's plan to slip seeds into his pocket to smuggle home was thwarted by the fruit being seedless.

A holovid in the corner with the sound turned low had been mumbling to itself, ignored by everyone, but a sudden rainbow of blinking lights advertised an official safety bulletin. Heads turned briefly, and Miles followed the stares to find being displayed the shots of Passenger Firka from the *Rudra*'s locks that he had downloaded earlier to Station Security. He didn't need the sound to guess the content of the serious-looking quaddie woman's speech that followed: suspect wanted for questioning, may be armed and dangerous, if you see this dubious downsider call this code at once. A couple of shots of Bel followed, as the putative kidnapping victim, presumably; they were taken from yesterday's interviews after the assassination attempt in the hostel, which a newscaster came on to re-cap.

"Can you turn it up?" Miles asked belatedly.

The newscaster was just winding down; even as the café server aimed her remote, her image was replaced with an advertisement for an impressive selection of work gloves.

"Oh, sorry," said the server. "It was a repeat anyway. They've been showing it every fifteen minutes for the past hour." She provided Miles with a verbal summary of the alarm, which matched Miles's guess in most particulars.

So, on just how many holovids all over the station was this now appearing? It would be an order of magnitude harder for a wanted man to hide, with an order of magnitude more pairs of eyes looking for him . . . but was Firka himself seeing this? If so, would he panic, becoming more hazardous to anyone who crossed him? Or perhaps turn himself in, claiming it was all some sort of misunderstanding? Roic, studying the vid, frowned and drank more coffee. The sleep-deprived armsman was holding up all right for the moment, but Miles figured he would be dragging dangerously by mid-afternoon.

Miles had an unpleasant sensation of sinking in a quicksand of diversions and losing his grip on his initial mission. Which had been what? Oh, yes, free the fleet. He suppressed an internal snarl of *Screw the fleet, where the hell's Bel?* But if there was any way to use this disturbing development to pry his ships from quaddie hands, it was not apparent to him right now.

They returned to Security Post One to find Nicol waiting for them in the front reception space with the air of a hungry predator at a water hole. She pounced on Miles the moment he appeared.

"Did you find Bel? Did you see any sign?"

Miles shook his head in regret. "Neither hide nor hair. Well, there might be hairs—we'll know when the forensics tech gets her analysis done—but that won't tell us anything we don't already know from Garnet Five's testimony." The truth of which Miles didn't doubt. "I do have a better mental picture of the possible course of events, now." He wished it made more sense. The first part—Firka wishing to delay or shake his pursuers—was sensible enough. It was the blank afterward that puzzled.

"Do you think," Nicol's voice grew smaller, "he carried Bel away to murder someplace else?"

"In that case, why leave a witness alive?" He tossed this off instantly for her reassurance; upon reflection, he found it reassuring too. Maybe. But if not murder, what? What did Bel have or know that someone else might want? Unless, like Garnet Five, Bel had come to consciousness on its own, and gone off. But . . . if Bel had wandered away in some state of dazed or sick confusion, it should have been picked up by the patrollers or some solicitous fellow stationers by now. And if it had gone in hot pursuit of something, it should have reported in. *To me, at least, dammit . . .*

"If Bel was," Nicol began, and stopped. A startling crowd heaved through the main entry port, and paused for orientation.

A pair of husky male quaddies in the orange work shirts and shorts of Docks and Locks managed the two ends of a three-meter length of pipe. Firka occupied the middle.

The unhappy downsider's wrists and ankles were lashed to the pipe with swathes of electrical tape, bending him in a U, with another rectangle of tape plastered across his mouth, muffling his moans. His eyes were wide, and rolled in panic. Three more quaddies in orange, panting and rumpled, one with a red bruise starting around his eye, bobbed along beside as outriders.

The work crew took aim and floated with their squirming burden through free fall to fetch up with a thump at the reception desk. A quartet of uniformed security quaddies appeared from another portal to gather and stare at this unwilling prize; the desk sergeant hit his intercom, and lowered his voice to speak into it in a rapid undertone.

The spokes-quaddie for the posse bustled forward, a smile of grim satisfaction on his bruised face. "We caught him for you."

Chapter 12

"Where?" Miles asked.

"Number Two Freight Bay," the spokes-quaddie answered. "He was trying to get Pramod Sixteen, here"—his nod indicated one of the husky quaddies holding an end of the pipe, who nodded back in confirmation—"to take him out in a pod around the security zone to the galactic jumpship docks. So you can add attempted bribery of an airseal tech to violate regs to his list of charges, I'd say."

Ah, ha. Another way to get around Bel's customs barriers . . . Miles's mind jumped back to the missing Solian.

"Pramod told him he was making arrangements, and slipped out and called me. I rounded up the boys, and we made sure he'd come along and explain himself to you." The spokes-quaddie gestured to Chief Venn, who'd floated in hastily from the office corridor and was taking in the scene with unsurprised satisfaction.

The web-fingered downsider made a plaintive noise, beneath his electrical tape, but Miles took it more for protest than explanation.

Nicol put in urgently, "Did you see any sign of Bel?"

"Oh, hi, Nicol." The spokes-quaddie shook his head in regret. "We asked the fellow, but we didn't get an answer. If you all don't have better luck with him, we have a few more ideas we can try." His scowl suggested that these might run to the illicit utilization of airlocks, or perhaps innovative applications of freight-handling equipment definitely not covered in the manufacturer's warranties. "I bet we could make him stop screaming and start talking before his air ran out."

"I think we can take it from here, thanks," Chief Venn assured him. He glanced without favor at Firka, wriggling on his pole. "Although I'll keep your offer in mind."

"Do you know Portmaster Thorne?" Miles asked the Docks and Locks quaddie. "Do you work together?"

"Bel's one of our best supervisors," the quaddie replied. "About the most sensible downsider we've ever gotten. We don't care to lose it, eh?" He gave Nicol a nod.

She ducked her head in mute gratitude.

The citizens' arrest was duly recorded. The quaddie patrollers who'd assembled looked cautiously over the long, squirming captive, and elected to take him pole and all, for the moment. The Docks and Locks crew, with justifiable self-satisfaction, also presented the duffel bag Firka had been carrying.

So here was Miles's most wanted suspect, if not presented on a platter, at least *en brochette*. Miles itched to tear that tape off his rubbery face and start squeezing.

Sealer Greenlaw arrived while this was going forth, accompanied by a new quaddie man, dark-haired and fit-looking though not especially young. He wore neat, subdued garb much like that of Boss Watts and Bel, but black instead of slate blue. She introduced him as Adjudicator Leutwyn.

"So," said Leutwyn, staring curiously at the tape-secured suspect. "This is our one-man crime wave. Do I understand he, too, came in with the Barrayaran fleet?"

"No, Adjudicator," said Miles. "He joined the *Rudra* here on Graf Station, at the last minute. Actually, he didn't sign aboard until after the ship had originally been due to leave. I'd very much like to know why. I strongly suspect him of synthesizing and planting the blood in the loading bay, of attempting to assassinate . . . someone, in the hostel lobby yesterday, and of attacking Garnet Five and Bel Thorne last night. Garnet Five, at least, had a fairly close look at him, and should be able to confirm that identification shortly. But by far the most urgent question is, what has happened to Portmaster Thorne? Hot pursuit of a kidnap victim in danger is sufficient pretext for nonvoluntary penta interrogations in most jurisdictions, surely."

"Here as well," the adjudicator admitted. "But a fast-penta examination is a delicate undertaking. I've found, in the half dozen I've monitored, that it's not nearly the magic wand most people think it is."

Miles cleared his throat in fake diffidence. "I am tolerably familiar with the techniques, Adjudicator. I've conducted or sat in on over a hundred penta-assisted interrogations. And I've had it given to me twice." No need to go into his idiosyncratic drug reaction that had made those two events such dizzyingly surreal and notably uninformative occasions.

"Oh," said the quaddie adjudicator, sounding impressed despite himself, possibly especially with that last detail.

"I'm keenly aware of the need to keep the examination from being a mob scene, but you also need the right leading questions. I believe I have several."

Venn put in, "We haven't even processed the suspect yet. Me, I want to see what he's got in that bag."

The adjudicator nodded. "Yes, carry on, Chief Venn. I'd like further clarification, if I can get it."

Mob scene or no, they all followed the quaddie patrollers who maneuvered the unfortunate Firka, pole and all, into a back chamber. A pair of the patrollers, after first clapping proper restraints around the bony wrists and ankles, recorded retinal patterns and took laser scans of the fingers and palms. Miles had one curiosity satisfied when they also pulled off the prisoner's soft boots; the finger-length toes, prehensile or nearly so, flexed and stretched, revealing wide rose-colored webs between. The quaddies scanned them, too—of *course* the quaddies would routinely scan all four extremities—then cut through the bulky lashings of tape.

Meanwhile another patroller, assisted by Venn, emptied and inventoried the duffel. They removed an assortment of clothes, mostly in dirty wads, to find a large new chef's knife, a stunner with a dubiously corroded discharged power pack but no stunner permit, a long crowbar, and a leather folder full of small tools. The folder also contained a receipt for an automated hot riveter from a Graf Station engineering supply store, complete with incriminating serial numbers. It was at this point that the adjudicator stopped looking so carefully reserved and started to look grim instead. When the patroller held up something that looked at first glance to be a scalp, but when shaken out proved a brassy short blond wig of no particular quality, the evidence seemed almost redundant.

Of more interest to Miles was not one, but a dozen sets of identifying documentation. Half of them proclaimed their bearers to be natives of Jackson's Whole; the others were from local space systems all adjoining the Hegen Hub, a wormhole-rich, planet-poor system that was one of the Barrayaran Empire's nearest and most strategically important Nexus neighbors. Jump routes from Barrayar to both Jackson's Whole and the Cetagandan Empire passed, via Komarr and the independent buffer polity of Pol, through the Hub.

Venn ran the handful of IDs through a holovid station affixed to the chamber's curving wall, his frown deepening. Miles and Roic both maneuvered to watch over his shoulder.

"So," Venn growled after a bit, "which one really *is* the fellow?"

Two sets of documentation for "Firka" included physical vid shots of a man very different in appearance from their moaning captive: a big, bulky, but perfectly normal human male from either Jackson's Whole, no House affiliation, or Aslund, another Hegen Hub neighbor, depending on which—if either—ID was to be believed. Yet a third Firka ID, the one the present Firka seemed to have used to travel from Tau Ceti to Graf Station, portrayed the prisoner himself. Finally, his vid shots also matched up with the IDs of a person named Russo Gupta, also hailing from Jackson's Whole and lacking a proper House affiliation. That name, face, and associated retina scans came up again on a jump-ship engineer's license that Miles recognized as originating from a certain Jacksonian organization of the sub-economy he had dealt with in his covert ops days. Judging from the long file of dates and customs stamps appended, it had passed as genuine elsewhere. And recently. *A record of his travels, good!*

Miles pointed. "That is almost certainly a forgery."

The clustering quaddies looked genuinely shocked. Greenlaw said, "A false engineer's license? That would be *unsafe.*"

"If it's from the place I think, you could get a false neurosurgeon's license to go with it. Or any other job you cared to pretend to have, without going through all that tedious training and testing and certification." Or, in this case, really have—now, there was a disturbing thought. Although on-the-job apprenticeship and self-teaching might cover some of the gaps over time . . . *someone* had been clever enough to modify that hot riveter, after all.

Under no circumstances could this pale, lanky mutie pass for a stout, pleasantly ugly, red-haired woman named either Grace Nevatta of Jackson's Whole—no House affiliation—or Louise Latour of Pol, depending on which set of IDs she favored. Nor for a short, head-wired, mahogany-skinned jumpship pilot named Hewlet.

"Who *are* all these people?" Venn muttered in aggravation.

"Why don't we just ask?" suggested Miles.

Firka—or Gupta—had finally stopped struggling and just lay in midair, nostrils flexing with his panting above the blue rectangle of tape over his mouth. The quaddie patroller finished recording his last scans and reached for a corner of the tape, then paused uncertainly. "I'm afraid this is going to hurt a bit."

"He's probably sweated enough underneath the tape to loosen it," Miles offered. "Take it in one quick jerk. It'll hurt less in the long run. That's what I'd want, if I were him."

A muffled mew of disagreement from the prisoner turned into a shrill scream as the quaddie followed this plan. All right, so, the frog prince hadn't sweated as much around the mouth as Miles had guessed. It was still better to have the damned tape off than on.

But despite the noises he'd been making the prisoner did not follow up this liberation of his lips with outraged protests, swearing, complaints, or raving threats. He just kept panting. His eyes were peculiarly glassy—a look Miles recognized, of a man who'd been wound up far too tight for far too long. Bel's loyal stevedores might have roughed him up a bit, but he hadn't acquired *that* look in the brief time he'd been in quaddie hands.

Chief Venn held up a double handful, left and left, of IDs before the prisoner's eyes. "All right. Which one are you really? You may as well tell us the truth. We'll be cross-checking it all anyway."

With surly reluctance, the prisoner muttered, "I'm Guppy."

"Guppy? Russo Gupta?"

"Yeah."

"Who are these others?"

"Absent friends."

Miles wasn't quite sure if Venn had caught the intonation. He put in, "Dead friends?"

"Yeah, that too." Guppy/Gupta stared away into a distance Miles calculated as light-years.

Venn looked alarmed. Miles was torn between anxiety to proceed and an intense desire to sit down and study the place and date stamps on all those IDs, real and fake, before decanting Gupta. A world of revelation lay therein, he was fairly sure. But greater urgencies drove the sequencing now.

"Where is Portmaster Thorne?" Miles asked.

"I told those thugs before. I never heard of him."

"Thorne is the Betan herm you sprayed with knockout mist last night in a utility passage off Cross Corridor. Along with a blond quaddie woman named Garnet Five."

The surly look deepened. "Never seen either of 'em."

Venn turned his head and nodded to a patroller, who flitted off. A few moments later she returned through one of the chamber's other portals, ushering Garnet Five. Garnet's color looked vastly better now, Miles was relieved to note, and she had obviously managed to obtain whatever female grooming equipment she used to touch herself back up to her high-visibility norm.

"Ah!" she said cheerfully. "You caught him! Where's Bel?"

Venn inquired formally, "Is this the downsider who committed chemical assault on you and the portmaster, and released illicit volatiles into the public atmosphere last night?"

"Oh, yes," said Garnet Five. "I couldn't possibly mistake him. I mean, look at the webs."

Gupta clenched his lips, his fists, and his feet, but further pretense was clearly futile.

Venn lowered his voice to a quite nicely menacing official growl. "Gupta, where is Portmaster Thorne?"

"I don't know where the blighted nosy herm is! I left it in the bin right next to hers. It was all right then. I mean, it was breathing and all. They both were. I made sure. The herm's probably still sleeping it off in there."

"No," said Miles. "We checked all the bins in the passage. The portmaster was gone."

"Well, *I* don't know where it went after that."

"Would you be willing to repeat that assertion under fast-penta, and clear yourself of a kidnapping charge?" Venn inquired cannily, angling for a voluntary interrogation.

Gupta's rubbery face set, and his eyes shifted away. "Can't. I'm allergic to the stuff."

"Is that so?" said Miles. "Let's just check, shall we?" He dug in his trouser pocket and drew out the strip of test patches he'd borrowed earlier from the *Kestrel's* ImpSec supplies, in anticipation of just such an opportunity. Granted, he hadn't anticipated the added urgency of Bel's alarming vanishing act. He held up the strip and explained to Venn and the adjudicator, who was monitoring all this with a judicial frown, "Security-grade penta allergy skin test. If the subject has any of the six kinds of artificially induced anaphylaxes or even a mild natural allergy, the welt pops right up." By way of reassurance to the quaddie officials, he peeled off one of the burr-like patches and slapped it on the back of his own wrist, displaying it with a heartening wriggle of his fingers. The sleight of hand was sufficient that no one except the prisoner protested when he leaned over and pressed another to Gupta's arm. Gupta let out a yowl of horror that won him only stares; he reduced it to a pitiable whimper under the bemused eyes of the onlookers.

Miles peeled off his own patch to reveal a distinct reddish prickle. "As you see, I do have a slight endogenous sensitivity." He waited a few moments longer, to drive home the point, then reached over and peeled the patch off Gupta. The rather sickly natural—mushrooms were natural, right?—skin tone was unaffected.

Venn, getting into the rhythm of the thing like an old ImpSec hand, leaned toward Gupta and said, "That's two lies, so far, then. You can stop lying now. Or you can stop lying shortly. Either way will do." He raised narrowed eyes to his fellow quaddie official. "Adjudicator Leutwyn, do you rule that we have sufficient cause for an involuntary chemically assisted interrogation of this transient?"

The adjudicator looked less than wholly enthusiastic, but he replied, "In light of his admitted connection to the worrisome disappearance of a valued Station employee, yes, there can be no question. I do remind you that subjecting detainees in your charge to unnecessary physical discomfort is against regs."

Venn glanced at Gupta, hanging miserably in air. "How can he be uncomfortable? He's in free fall."

The adjudicator pursed his lips. "Transient Gupta, aside from your restraints, are you in any special discomfort at this time? Do you require food, drink, or downsider sanitary facilities?"

Gupta jerked his wrists against their soft bonds, and shrugged. "Naw. Well, yes. My gills are getting dry. If you're not gonna let me loose, I need somebody to spray them. The stuff's in my bag."

"This?" The female quaddie patroller held out what appeared to be a perfectly ordinary plastic sprayer, of the sort that Miles had seen Ekaterin use to mist some of her plants. She wriggled it, and it gurgled.

"What's in it?" asked Venn suspiciously.

"Water, mostly. And a bit of glycerin," said Gupta.

"Go ahead and check it," said Venn aside to his patroller. She nodded and floated out; Gupta watched her depart with some mistrust, but no particular alarm.

"Transient Gupta, it appears you're going to be our guest for a while," said Venn. "If we remove your restraints, are you going to give us any trouble, or are you going to behave yourself?"

Gupta was silent a moment, then vented an exhausted sigh. "I'll behave. Much good it'll do me either way."

A patroller floated forward and unshackled the prisoner's wrists and ankles. Only Roic seemed less than pleased with this unnecessary courtesy, tensing with a hand on a wall grip and one foot planted to a bit of bulkhead not occupied by equipment, ready to launch himself forward. But Gupta only chafed his wrists and bent to rub his ankles, and looked grudgingly grateful.

The patroller returned with the bottle, handing it to her chief. "The lab's chemical sniffer says it's inert. Should be safe," she reported.

"Very well." Venn pitched the bottle to Gupta, who despite his odd long hands caught it readily, with little downsider clumsiness, a fact Miles was sure the quaddie noted.

"Um." Gupta gave the crowd of onlookers a slightly embarrassed glance, and hitched up his loose poncho. He stretched and inhaled, and the ribs on his big barrel chest drew apart; flaps of skin parted to reveal red slashes. The substance beneath seemed spongy, rippling in the misting like densely laid feathers.

God almighty. He really does have gills under there. Presumably, the bellows-like movement of the chest helped pump water through, when the amphibian was immersed. Dual systems. So did he hold his breath, or did his lungs shut down involuntarily? By what mechanism was his blood circulation switched from one oxygenating interface to the other? Gupta pumped the bottle and sprayed mist into the red slits, handing it back and forth from right side to left, and seemed to draw some comfort thereby. He sighed, and the slits closed back down, his chest appearing merely ridged and scarred. He smoothed the drifting poncho back into place.

"Where *are* you from?" Miles couldn't help asking.

Gupta grew surly again. "Guess."

"Well, Jackson's Whole, by the weight of the evidence, but which House made you? Ryoval, Bharaputra, another? And were you a one-off, or part of a set? First-generation gengineered, or from a self-reproducing line of, of water people?"

Gupta's eyes widened in surprise. "You know Jackson's Whole?"

"Let's say, I've had several painfully educational visits there."

The surprise became edged with faint respect, and a certain lonely eagerness. "House Dyan made me. I *was* part of a set, once—we were an underwater ballet troupe."

Garnet Five blurted in unflattering astonishment, "*You* were a dancer?"

The prisoner hunched his shoulders. "No. They made me to be submersible stage crew. But House Dyan suffered a hostile takeover by House Ryoval—just a few years before Baron Ryoval was assassinated, pity *that* didn't happen sooner. Ryoval broke up the troupe for other, um, tasks, and decided he had no alternate use for me, so I was out of a job and out of protection. Could have been worse. He mighta kept me. I drifted around and took what tech jobs I could get. One thing led to another."

In other words, Gupta had been born into Jacksonian techno-serfdom, and dumped out on the street when his original owner-creators had been engulfed by their vicious commercial rival. Given what Miles knew of the late, unsavory Baron Ryoval, Gupta's fate was perhaps happier than that of his mer-cohort. By the known date of Ryoval's death, that last vague remark about things leading to things covered at least five years, maybe as many as ten.

Miles said thoughtfully, "You weren't shooting at *me* at all yesterday, then, were you. Nor at Portmaster Thorne." Which left . . .

Gupta blinked at him. "Oh! *That's* where I saw you before. Sorry, no." His brow corrugated. "So what were you doing there, then? You're not one of the passengers. Are you another Stationer squatter like that officious bloody Betan?"

"No. My name is"—he made an instant, almost subliminal decision to drop all the honorifics—"Miles. I was sent out to look after Barrayaran concerns when the quaddies impounded the Komarran fleet."

"Oh." Gupta grew uninterested.

What the devil was keeping that fast-penta? Miles softened his voice. "So what happened to your friends, Guppy?"

That fetched the amphibian's attention again. "Double-crossed. Subjected, injected, infected . . . rejected. We were all taken in. Damned Cetagandan bastard. That wasn't the Deal."

Something inside Miles went on overdrive. *Here's the connection, finally.* His smile grew charming, sympathetic, and his voice softened further. "Tell me about the Cetagandan bastard, Guppy."

The hovering mob of quaddie listeners had stopped rustling, even breathing more quietly. Roic had drawn back to a shadowed spot opposite Miles. Gupta glanced around at the Graf Stationers, and at Miles and himself, the only legged persons now in view in the center of the circle.

"What's the use?" The tone was not a wail of despair, but a bitter query.

"I *am* Barrayaran. I have a special stake in Cetagandan bastards. The Cetagandan ghem-lords left five million of my grandfather's generation dead behind them, when they finally gave up and pulled out of Barrayar. I still have his bag of ghem-scalps. For certain kinds of Cetagandans, I might know a use or two you'd find interesting."

The prisoner's wandering gaze snapped to his face and locked there. For the first time, he'd won Gupta's total attention. For the first time, he'd hinted he might have something that Guppy really wanted. Wanted? Burned for, lusted for, desired with mad obsessive hunger. His glassy eyes were ravenous for . . . maybe revenge, maybe justice—in any case, blood. But the frog prince clearly lacked personal expertise in retribution. The quaddies didn't deal in blood. Barrayarans . . . had a more sanguinary reputation. Which, for the first time this mission, might actually prove some *use*.

Gupta took a long breath. "I don't know *what* kind this one was. Is. He was like nothing I'd ever met before. Cetagandan bastard. He *melted* us."

"Tell me," Miles breathed, "everything. Why you?"

"He came to us . . . through our usual cargo agents. We thought it would be all right. We had a ship. Gras-Grace and Firka and Hewlet and me had this ship. Hewlet was our pilot, but Gras-Grace was the brains. Me, I had a knack for fixing things. Firka kept the books, and fixed regs, and passports, and nosy officials. Gras-Grace and her three husbands, we called us. We were a collection of rejects, but maybe we added up to one real spouse for her, I don't know. One for all and all for one, because it was damn sure that a crew of refugee Jacksonians, without a House or a Baron, wasn't going to get a break from anyone *else* in the Nexus."

Gupta was getting wound up in his story. Miles, listening with utmost care, prayed Venn would have the sense not to interrupt. Ten people hovered around them in this chamber, yet he and Gupta, mutually hypnotized by the increasing intensity of his confession, might almost be floating in a bubble of time and space altogether removed from this universe. "So where did you pick up this Cetagandan and his cargo, anyway?"

Gupta glanced up, startled. "You know about the cargo?"

"If it's the same one now aboard the *Idris*, yes, I've had a look. I found it rather disturbing."

"What's he got in there, really? I only saw the outsides."

"I'd rather not say, at this time. What did he," Miles elected not to go into the confusions of ba gender just now, "tell you it was?"

"Gengineered mammals. Not that we asked questions. We got paid extra for not asking questions. That was the Deal, we thought."

And if there was anything that the ethically elastic inhabitants of Jackson's Whole held nearly sacred, it was the Deal. "A good bargain, was it?"

"Looked like. Two or three more runs like that, we could have paid off the ship and owned it free and clear."

Miles took leave to doubt that, if the crew was in debt for their jumpship to a typical Jacksonian financial House. But perhaps Guppy and his friends had been terminal optimists. *Or terminally desperate.*

"The gig looked easy enough. Just take a little mixed-freight run through the fringes of the Cetagandan Empire. We jumped in through the Hegen Hub, via Vervain, and skirted round to Rho Ceta. All those arrogant, suspicious bastard inspectors who boarded us at the jump points turned up nothing to hold against us, though they'd have liked to, because there wasn't anything aboard but what our filed manifest said. Gave old Firka a good chuckle. Till we were heading out for the last jumps, for Rho Ceta through those empty buffer systems just before the route splits to Komarr. We made one little mid-space rendezvous there that didn't appear on our flight plan."

"What kind of ship did you rendezvous with? Jumpship, or just a local space crawler? Could you tell for sure, or was it disguised or camouflaged?"

"Jumpship. I don't know what else it might have really been. It looked like a Cetagandan government ship. It had lots of fancy markings, anyway. Not big, but fast—fresh and classy. The Cetagandan bastard moved his cargo all by himself, with float pallets and hand tractors, but he sure didn't waste any time. The moment the locks were closed, they went off."

"Where? Could you tell?"

"Well, Hewlet said they had an odd trajectory. It was that uninhabited binary system a few jumps out from Rho Ceta, I don't know if you know it—"

Miles nodded in encouragement.

"They went inbound, deeper into the grav well. Maybe they were planning to swing around the suns and approach one of the jump points from a disguised trajectory, I don't know. That would make sense, given all the rest of it."

"Just the one passenger?"

"Yeah."

"Tell me more about him."

"Not much to tell—then. He kept to himself, ate his own rations in his own cabin. He didn't talk to me at all. He had to talk to Firka, on account of Firka was fixing his manifest. By the time we reached the first Barrayaran jump point inspection, it had a whole new provenance. He was somebody else by then, too."

"Ker Dubauer?"

Venn twitched at this first mention of the familiar name in his hearing, and opened his mouth and inhaled, but closed it again without diverting Guppy's flow. The unhappy amphibian was in full spate now, pouring out his troubles.

"Not yet, he wasn't. He musta become Dubauer during his layover on the Komarran transfer station, I figure. I didn't track him by his identity, anyway. He was too good for that. Fooled you Barrayarans, didn't he?"

Indeed. An apparent Cetagandan agent of the highest caliber had passed through Barrayar's key Nexus trade crossroad like so much smoke. *ImpSec* would have a seizure when *this* report arrived. "How did you follow him here, then?"

The first smile-like expression Miles had seen on the rubbery face ghosted across Gupta's lips. "I was ship's engineer. I tracked him by his cargo's mass. It was kind of distinctive, when I went to look, later."

The ghastly smile faded into a black frown. "When we dumped him and his pallets off on the Komarran transfer station's loading bay, he seemed happy. Downright cordial. He went around to each of us for the first time, and gave us our no-problems bonuses personally. He shook Hewlet's and Firka's hands. He asked to see my webbing, so I spread my fingers for him, and he leaned over and gripped my arm and seemed real interested, and thanked me. He gave Gras-Grace a pat on her cheek, and smiled at her in this sappy way. He *smirked* as he touched her. *Knowing.* Since she was holding the bonus chit in her hand, she sort of smiled back and didn't deck him, though I could see it was a near thing. And then we bailed out. Hewlet and I wanted to take station leave and spend some of our bonus, but Gras-Grace said we could party later. And Firka said the Barrayaran Empire wasn't a healthy place for the likes of us to linger in." A distracted laugh that had nothing to do with humor puffed from his lips. So. That startling scream when Miles had touched the test patch to Guppy's skin hadn't been overreaction, exactly. It had been a flashback. Miles suppressed a shudder. *Sorry, sorry.*

"It was six days out from Komarr, past the jump to Pol, before the fevers began. Gras-Grace guessed it first, from the way it started. She always was the quickest of us. Four little pink wheals, like some kind of bug bites, on the backs of Hewlet and Firka's hands, on her cheek, on my arm where the Cetagandan bastard had touched me. They swelled up to the size of eggs, and throbbed, though not as much as our heads. It only took an hour. My head hurt so bad I could hardly see, and Gras-Grace, who wasn't doing any better, helped me to my cabin so's I could get into my tank."

"Tank?"

"I'd rigged up a big tank in my cabin, with a lid I could lock down from the inside, because the gravity on that old ship wasn't any too reliable. It was really comfortable to rest in, my own kind of water bed. I could stretch all the way out, and turn around. Good filtration system on the water, nice and clean, and extra oxygen sparkling up through it from a bubbler I'd rigged, all pretty with colored lights. And music. I miss my tank." He heaved a sigh.

"You . . . appear to have lungs, as well. Do you hold your breath underwater, or what?"

Gupta shrugged. "I have these extra sphincter muscles in my nose and ears and throat that shut down automatically, when my breathing switches over. That's always kind of an awkward moment, the switch; my lungs don't always seem to want to stop. Or start again, sometimes. But I can't stay in my tank forever, or I'd end up pissing in the water I breathe. That's what happened then. I floated in my tank for . . . hours, I'm not sure how many. I don't think I was quite in my right mind, I hurt so bad. But then I had to piss. Really bad. So I had to get out.

"I damn near passed out when I stood. I threw up on the floor. But I could walk. I made it to my cabin's head, finally. The ship was still running, I could feel the right vibrations through my feet, but it had gone all quiet. Nobody talking or arguing or snoring, no music. No laughing. I was cold and wet. I put on a robe—it was one of hers that Gras-Grace had given me, because she claimed being fat made her hot, and I was always too cold. She said it was because my designers gave me frog genes. For all I know, that might be true.

"I found her body . . ." He stopped. The light-years-gone look in his eyes intensified. "About five steps down the corridor. At least, I thought it was her. It was her braid, floating on the . . . At least, I thought it was a body. The size of the puddle seemed about right. It stank like . . . What kind of hell-disease liquefies *bones*?"

He inhaled, and continued unsteadily, "Firka had made it to the infirmary, for all the good it had done him. He was all flaccid, like he was deflating. And dripping. Over the side of the bunk. He stank worse than Gras-Grace. And he was *steaming*.

"Hewlet—what was left of him—was in his pilot's chair in Nav and Com. I don't know why he crawled up there, maybe it was a comfort to him. Pilots are strange that way. His pilot's headset kind of held his skull braced, but his face . . . his features . . . they were just sliding off. I thought he might have been trying to send an emergency message, maybe. *Help us. Biocontamination aboard.* But maybe not, because nobody ever came. Later I thought maybe he'd sent too much, and the rescuers stayed away on purpose. Why should the good citizens risk anything for *us*? Just Jacksonian smuggler scum. Better off dead. Saves the trouble and expense of prosecution, eh?" He looked at no one, now.

Miles feared he was falling silent, spent. But there was so much more, desperately important, to know . . . He dared to play out a lead—"So. No shit, there you were, trapped on a drifting ship with three dissolving corpses including a dead jump pilot. How did you get away?"

"The ship . . . the ship was no good to me now, not without Hewlet. And the others. Let the bastard financers have it, biocontamination and all. Murdered dreams. But I figured I was everybody's heir, by that time. Nobody had anybody else, not to speak to. I would've wanted them to have my stuff, if it had been the other way around. I went round and collected everybody's movables, spare cash, credit chits—Firka had a huge cache. He would. And he had all our doctored IDs. Gras-Grace, well, she probably gave hers away, or lost it gambling, or spent it on toys, or let it slip through her fingers somehow. Which made her smarter than Firka, in the long run. Hewlet, I guess he'd drunk most of his. But there was enough. Enough to travel to the ends of the Nexus, if I was clever about it. Enough to catch up with that Cetagandan bastard, stern chase or no. With that heavy cargo, I didn't figure he'd be traveling all that fast.

"I took it all and loaded it in an escape capsule. Decontaminated it all, and me, a dozen times first, trying to get that horrible death smell off. I wasn't . . . I wasn't at my best and brightest, I don't think, but I wasn't *that* far gone. Once I was in the capsule, it wasn't so hard. They're designed to get injured idiots to safety, automatically following the local space beacons . . . I got picked up three days later by a passing ship, and told a bullshit story about our ship coming apart—they believed *that* when they looked up the Jacksonian registry. I'd stopped crying by then." Tears were glistening at the corners of his eyes now. "Didn't mention the bio-shit, or they'd have jugged me good. They dropped me at the nearest Polian jump point station. From there I slipped away from the safety investigators and got me on the first ship I could bound for Komarr. I tracked the Cetagandan bastard's cargo by its mass to the Komarran trade fleet that had just pulled out. Ran a search to find a route that would catch me up to it at the first possible place. Which was here." He stared around, blinking at his quaddie audience as if surprised to find them all still in the room.

"How did Lieutenant Solian get sucked into it?" Miles had been waiting with nerves stretched to twanging to ask that one.

"I thought I could just lie in wait and ambush the Cetagandan bastard as soon as he came off the *Idris*. But he never came off. Stayed holed up in his cabin, I guess. Smart scum. I couldn't get through customs or the ship's security—I wasn't a registered passenger or a guest of one, though I tried to butter up a few. Scared the shit out of me when the fellow I tried to bribe to get me on board threatened to turn me in. Then I got smart and got me a berth on the *Rudra*, to at least get me legal entry past customs into those loading bays. And to be sure I'd be able to follow along if the fleet pulled out suddenly, which it was overdue to do by then. I wanted to kill him myself, for Gras-Grace and Firka and Hewlet, but if he was going to get away, I thought, if I turned him in to the Barrayarans as a Cetagandan spy, maybe . . . something interesting might happen, anyway. Something he wouldn't like. I didn't want to leave my trace on the vid call record, so I caught the *Idris*'s security officer in person when he was out in the loading bay. Tipped him off. I wasn't sure if he believed me or not, but I guess he went to check." Gupta hesitated. "He musta run into the Cetagandan bastard. I'm sorry. I'm afraid I got him melted. Like Gras-Grace and . . ." His litany ended in a shaken gulp.

"Is that when Solian had the nose bleed? When you were tipping him off?" Miles asked.

Gupta stared. "What are you, some kind of psychic?"

Check. "Why the faked blood on the docking bay floor?"

"Well . . . I'd heard the fleet was pulling out. They were saying that the poor bugger I'd got melted was supposed to have deserted, and they were writing him off, just like . . . like he didn't have a House or a Baron to put up any stake for him, and nobody cared. But I was afraid the Cetagandan bastard would pull another mid-space transfer, and I'd be stuck on the *Rudra*, and he'd get away . . . I thought it would focus attention back on the *Idris*, and what might be on it. I didn't dream those military morons would attack the quaddie station!"

"There were concatenating circumstances," Miles said primly, made conscious, for the first time in what seemed a small eternity of evoked horrors, of the hovering quaddie officialdom. "You certainly triggered events, but you could not possibly have anticipated them." He, too, blinked and looked around. "Er . . . did you have any questions, Chief Venn?"

Venn was giving him a most peculiar stare. He shook his head, slowly, from side to side.

"Uh . . ." A young quaddie patroller Miles had barely noticed enter during Guppy's urgent soliloquy held out a small, glittering object to his chief. "I have the fast-penta dose you ordered, sir . . . ?"

Venn took it and gazed over at Adjudicator Leutwyn.

Leutwyn cleared his throat. "Remarkable. I do believe, Lord Auditor Vorkosigan, that is the first time I've ever seen a fast-penta interrogation conducted without the fast-penta."

Miles glanced at Guppy, curled around himself in air, shivering a little. Smears of water still glistened at the corners of his eyes. "He . . . really wanted to tell somebody his story. He's been dying to for weeks. There was just no one in the entire Nexus he could trust."

"Still isn't," gulped the prisoner. "Don't get a swelled head, Barrayaran. I know nobody's on *my* side. But I missed my one shot, and he saw me. I was safe when he thought I was melted like the others. I'm a dead frog now, one way or another. But if I can't take him with me, maybe somebody else can."

Chapter 13

Chief Venn said, "So . . . this Cetagandan bastard Gupta here is raving about, that he says killed three of his friends and maybe your Lieutenant Solian—you really think this is the same as the Betan transient, Dubauer, that you wanted us to pick up last night? So is he a herm, or a man, or what?"

"Or what," answered Miles. "My medical people established from a blood sample I accidentally collected yesterday that Dubauer is a Cetagandan ba. The ba are neither male, female, nor hermaphrodite, but a genderless servant . . . caste, I guess is the best word, of the Cetagandan haut lords. More specifically, of the haut ladies who run the Star Crèche, at the core of the Celestial Garden, the Imperial residence on Eta Ceta." *Who almost never left the Celestial Garden, with or without their ba servitors. So what's this ba doing way out here, eh?* Miles hesitated, then went on, "This ba appears to be conducting a cargo of a thousand of what I suspect are the latest genetically modified haut fetuses in uterine replicators. I don't know where,

I don't know why, and I don't know who for, but if Guppy's telling us the straight story, the ba has killed four people, including our missing security officer, and tried to kill Guppy, to keep its secret and cover its tracks." *At least four people.*

Greenlaw's expression had grown stiff with dismay. Venn regarded Gupta, frowning. "I guess we'd better put out a public arrest call on Dubauer, then, too."

"No!" Miles cried in alarm.

Venn raised his brows at him.

Miles explained hastily, "We're talking about a possible trained Cetagandan agent who may be carrying sophisticated bioweapons. It's already extremely stressed by the delays into which this dispute with the trade fleet has plunged it. It's just discovered it's made one bad mistake at least, because Guppy here is still alive. I don't care how superhuman it is, it has to be rattled by now. The last thing you want to do is send a bunch of feckless civilians up against it. Nobody should even approach the ba who doesn't know exactly what they're doing and what they're facing."

"And *your* people brought this creature here, onto *my* station?"

"Believe me, if any of my people had known what the ba was before this, it would never have made it past Komarr. The trade fleet are dupes, innocent carriers, I'm sure." Well, he wasn't *that* sure—checking that airy assertion was going to be a high-priority problem for counterintelligence, back home.

"Carriers . . ." Greenlaw echoed, looking hard at Guppy. All the quaddies in the room followed her stare. "Could this transient still be carrying that . . . whatever it was, infection?"

Miles took a breath. "Possibly. But if he is, it's too damned late already. Guppy has been running all over Graf Station for days, now. Hell, if he's infectious, he's just spread a plague along a route through the Nexus touching half a dozen planets." *And me. And my fleet. And maybe Ekaterin too.* "I see two points of hope. One, by Guppy's testimony, the ba had to administer the thing by actual touch."

The patrollers who'd handled the prisoner looked apprehensively at each other.

"And secondly," Miles went on, "if the disease or poison is something bioengineered by the Star Crèche, it's likely to be highly controlled, possibly deliberately self-limiting and self-destructing. The haut ladies don't like to leave their trash lying around for anyone to pick up."

"But I got better!" cried the amphibian.

"Yes," said Miles. "Why? Obviously, something in your unique genetics or situation either defeated the thing, or held it at bay long enough to keep you alive past its period of activity. Putting you in quarantine is about useless by now, but the next highest priority after nailing the ba has got to be running you through the medical wringer, to see if what you have or did can save anyone else." Miles drew breath. "May I offer the facilities of the *Prince Xav*? Our medical people do have some specific training in Cetagandan bio-threats."

Guppy blurted to Venn in panic, "Don't give me to them! They'll dissect me!"

Venn, who had brightened at this offer, shot the prisoner an exasperated look, but Greenlaw said slowly, "I know something of the ghem and the haut, but I've never heard of these ba, or the Star Crèche."

Adjudicator Leutwyn added warily, "Cetagandans of any stripe haven't much come in my way."

Greenlaw continued, "What makes you think their work is so safe, so restricted?"

"Safe, no. Controlled, maybe." How far did he need to back up his explanation to make the dangers clear to them? It was vital that the quaddies be made to understand, and believe. "The Cetagandans . . . have this two-tiered aristocracy that is the bafflement of non-Cetagandan military observers. At the core are the haut lords, who are, in effect, one giant genetics experiment in producing the post-human race. This work is conducted and controlled by the haut women geneticists of the Star Crèche, the center where all haut embryos are created and modified before being sent back to their haut constellations—clans, parents—on the outlying planets of the empire. Unlike most prior historical versions of this sort of thing, the haut ladies didn't start by assuming they'd reached the perfected end already. They do not, at present, believe themselves to be done tinkering. When they are—well, who knows what will happen? What are the goals and desires going to be of the true post-human? Even the haut ladies don't try to second-guess their great-great-great-whatever grandchildren. I will say, it makes it uncomfortable to have them as neighbors."

"Didn't the haut try to conquer you Barrayarans, once?" asked Leutwyn.

"Not the haut. The ghem-lords. The buffer race, if you will, between the haut and the rest of humanity. I suppose you could think of the ghem as the haut's bastard children, except that they aren't bastards. In that sense, anyway. The haut leak selected genetic lines into the ghem via trophy haut wives—it's a complicated system. But the ghem-lords are the military arm of the empire, always anxious to prove their worth to their haut masters."

"The ghem, I've seen," said Venn. "We get them through here now and then. I thought the haut were, well, sort of degenerate. Aristocratic parasites. Afraid to get their hands dirty. They don't *work*." He gave a very quaddie sniff of disdain. "Or fight. You have to wonder how long the ghem-soldiers will put up with them."

"On the surface, the haut appear to dominate the ghem through pure moral suasion. Overawe by their beauty and intelligence and refinement, and by making themselves the source of all kinds of status rewards, culminating in the haut wives. All this is true. But beneath that . . . it is strongly suspected that the haut hold a biological and biochemical arsenal that even the ghem find terrifying."

"I haven't heard of anything like that being *used*," said Venn in a tone of skepticism.

"Oh, you bet you haven't."

"Why didn't they use it on you Barrayarans, back then, if they had it?" said Greenlaw slowly.

"That is a problem much studied, at certain levels of my government. First, it would have alarmed the neighborhood. Bioweapons aren't the only kind. The Cetagandan Empire apparently wasn't ready to face a posse of people scared enough to combine to burn off their planets and sterilize every living microbe. More importantly, we think it was a question of goals. The ghem-lords wanted the territory and the wealth, the personal aggrandizement that would have followed successful conquest. The haut ladies just weren't that interested. Not enough to waste their resources—not resources of weapons per se, but of reputation, secrecy, of a silent threat of unknown potency. Our intelligence services have amassed maybe half a dozen cases in the past thirty years of suspected use of haut-style bioweapons, and in every instance, it was a Cetagandan internal matter." He glanced at Greenlaw's intensely disturbed face and added in what he hoped didn't sound like hollow reassurance, "There was no spread or bio-backsplash from those incidents that we know of."

Venn looked at Greenlaw. "So do we take this prisoner to a clinic, or to a cell?"

Greenlaw was silent for a few moments, then said, "Graf Station University clinic. Straight to the infectious isolation unit. I think we want our best experts in on this, and as quickly as possible."

Gupta objected, "But I'll be an open target! I was hunting the Cetagandan bastard—now he—it, whatever—will be hunting me!"

"I agree with this evaluation," Miles said quickly. "Wherever you take Gupta, the location should be kept absolutely secret. The fact that he's even been taken into custody should be suppressed—dear God, this arrest hasn't gone out on your news services already, has it?" Piping the word of Gupta's location to every nook of the station . . .

"Not formally," said Venn uneasily.

It scarcely mattered, Miles supposed. Dozens of quaddies had seen the web-fingered man brought in, including everybody that Bel's crew of roustabouts had passed on the way. The Docks and Locks quaddies would certainly brag of their catch to everyone they knew. The gossip would be all over.

"I strongly urge—beg!—you to put out word of his daring escape, then. Complete with follow-up bulletins asking all the citizens to keep an eye out for him again." The ba had killed four to keep its secret—would it be willing to kill fifty thousand?

"A disinformation campaign?" Greenlaw's lips pursed in repugnance.

"The lives of everyone on the station might well depend on it. Secrecy is your best hope of safety. And Gupta's. After that, guards—"

"My people are already spread to their limit," Venn protested. He gave Greenlaw a beseeching look.

Miles opened a hand in acknowledgment. "Not patrollers. Guards who know what they're doing, trained in bio-defense procedures."

"We'll have to draw on Union Militia specialists," said Greenlaw in a decisive tone. "I'll put in the request. But it will take them . . . some time, to get here."

"In the meanwhile," said Miles, "I can loan you some trained personnel."

Venn grimaced. "I have a detention block full of your personnel. I'm not much impressed with their training."

Miles suppressed a wince. "Not *them*. Military medical corps."

"I will consider your offer," said Greenlaw neutrally.

"Some of Vorpatril's senior medical men must have some expertise in this area. If you won't let us take Gupta out to the safety of one of our vessels, please, let them come aboard the station to help you."

Greenlaw's eyes narrowed. "All right. We will accept up to four such volunteers. Unarmed. *Under* the direct supervision and command of our own medical experts."

"Agreed," said Miles instantly.

It was the best compromise he was likely to get, for the moment. The medical end of this problem, terrifying as it was, would have to be left to the specialists; it was out of Miles's range of expertise. Catching the ba before it could do any more damage, now . . .

"The haut are not immune to stunner fire. I . . . recommend"—he could not order, he could not demand, most of all, he could not scream—"you *quietly* inform all of your patrollers that the ba—Dubauer—be stunned on sight. Once it's down, we can sort things out at our leisure."

Venn and Greenlaw exchanged looks with the adjudicator. Leutwyn said in a constricted voice, "It would be against regs to so ambush the suspect if it is not in process of a crime, resisting arrest, or fleeing."

"Bioweapons?" muttered Venn.

The adjudicator swallowed. "Make damned sure your patrollers don't miss their first shot."

"Your ruling is noted, sir."

And if the ba stayed out of sight? Which it had certainly managed to do for most of the past twenty-four hours. . . .

What did the ba want? Its cargo freed, and Guppy dead before he could talk, presumably. What did the ba know, at this point? Or not know? It didn't know that Miles had identified its cargo . . . did it? *Where the hell is Bel?*

"Ambush," Miles echoed. "There are two places where you could set up an ambush for the ba. Wherever you take Guppy—or better still, wherever the ba *believes* you've taken Guppy. If you don't want to put it about that he's escaped, then take him to a concealed location, with a second, less secret one set up for bait. Then, another trap at the *Idris.* If Dubauer calls in requesting permission to go aboard again, which the last time we met, it fully intended to do, you should grant the petition. Then nail it as it enters the loading bay."

"That's what *I* was going to do," put in Gupta in a resentful voice. "If you people had just let well enough alone, this could have been all over by now."

Miles privately agreed, but it would hardly do to say so out loud; someone might point out just who had put on the pressure for Gupta's arrest.

Greenlaw was looking grimly thoughtful. "I wish to inspect this alleged cargo. It is possible that it violates enough regs to merit impoundment quite separately from the issue of its carrier ship."

The adjudicator cleared his throat. "That could grow legally complex, Sealer. More complex. Cargoes not off-loaded for transfer, even if questionable, are normally allowed to pass through without legal comment. They're considered to be the territorial responsibility of the polity of registration of the carrier, unless they are an imminent public danger. A thousand fetuses, if that's what they are, constitute . . . what menace?"

Impounding them could prove a horrific danger, Miles thought. It would certainly lock Cetagandan attention upon Quaddiespace. Speaking from both historical and personal experience, this was not necessarily a good thing.

"I want to confirm this for myself, too," said Venn. "And give my guards their orders in person, and figure out where to place my sharpshooters."

"And you need me along, to get into the cargo hold," Miles pointed out.

Greenlaw said, "No, just your security codes."

Miles smiled blandly at her.

Her jaw tightened. After a moment, she growled, "Very well. Let's go, Venn. You too, Adjudicator. And," she sighed briefly, "you, Lord Auditor Vorkosigan."

Gupta was wrapped in bio-barriers by the two quaddies who had handled him before—a logical choice, if not much to their liking. They donned wraps and gloves themselves and towed him out without allowing him to touch anything else. The amphibian suffered this without protest. He looked utterly exhausted.

Garnet Five left with Nicol for Nicol's apartment, where the two quaddie women planned to support each other while awaiting word of Bel. "*Call me,*" Nicol pleaded in an under-voice to Miles as they floated out. Miles nodded his promise, and prayed silently that it would not prove to be one of those hard calls.

His brief vid call out to the *Prince Xav* and Admiral Vorpatril was hard enough. Vorpatril was almost as white as his hair by the time Miles had finished bringing him up to date. He promised to expedite a selection of medical volunteers at emergency speed.

The procession to the *Idris* finally included Venn, Greenlaw, the adjudicator, two quaddie patrollers, Miles, and Roic. The loading bay was as dim and quiet as—had it only been yesterday? One of the two quaddie guards, watched bemusedly by the other, was out of his floater and crouched on the floor. He was evidently playing a game with gravity involving a scattering of tiny bright metal caltrops and a small rubber ball, which seemed to consist of bouncing the ball off the floor, catching it again, and snatching up the little caltrops between bounces. To make it more interesting for himself, he was switching hands with each iteration. At the sight of the visitors, the guard hastily pocketed the game and scrambled back into his floater.

Venn pretended not to see this, simply inquiring after any events of note during their shift. Not only had no unauthorized persons attempted to get past them, the investigation committee was the first live persons the bored men had seen since relieving the prior shift. Venn lingered with his patrollers to make his arrangements for the stunner ambush of the ba, should it appear, and Miles led Roic, Greenlaw, and the adjudicator aboard the ship.

The gleaming rows of replicator racks in Dubauer's leased cargo hold appeared unchanged from yesterday. Greenlaw grew tense about the lips, guiding her floater around the hold on an initial overview, then pausing to stare down the aisles. Miles thought he could almost see her doing the multiplication in her head. She and Leutwyn then hovered by Miles's side as he activated a few control panels to demonstrate the replicators' contents.

It was almost a repeat of yesterday, except . . . a number of the readout indicators showed amber instead of green. Closer examination revealed them as measures of an array of stressor-signals, including adrenaline levels. Was the ba right about the fetuses reaching some sort of biological limit in their containers? Was this the first sign of dangerous overgrowth? As Miles watched, a couple of the light bars dropped back on their own from amber to a more encouraging green. He went on to call up the vid monitor images of the individual fetuses for Greenlaw's and the adjudicator's views. The fourth one he activated showed amniotic fluid cloudy with scarlet blood when the lights came on. Miles caught his breath. *How . . . ?*

That surely wasn't normal. The only possible source of blood was the fetus itself. He rechecked the stressor levels—this one showed a lot of amber—then stood on tiptoe and peered more closely at the image. The blood appeared to be leaking from a small, jagged gash on the twitching haut infant's back. The low red lighting, Miles reassured himself uneasily, made it look worse than it was.

Greenlaw's voice by his ear made him jump. "Is there something wrong with that one?"

"He appears to have suffered some sort of mechanical injury. That . . . shouldn't be possible, in a sealed replicator." He thought of Aral Alexander, and Helen Natalia, and his stomach knotted. "If you have any quaddie experts in replicator reproduction, it might not be a bad idea to get them in here to look at these." He doubted this was a specialty where the military medicos from the *Prince Xav* were likely to be much help.

Venn appeared at the door of the hold, and Greenlaw repeated most of Miles's orienting patter for his benefit. Venn's expression was most disturbed as he regarded the replicators. "That frog fellow wasn't lying. This is *very* strange."

Venn's wrist com buzzed, and he excused himself to float to the side of the room and engage in some low-voiced conversation with whatever subordinate was reporting in. At least, it began as low-voiced, until Venn bellowed, "*What? When?*"

Miles abandoned his worried study of the injured haut infant and edged over to Venn.

"About 0200, sir," a distressed voice responded from the wrist com.

"This wasn't authorized!"

"Yes, it was, Crew Chief, duly. Portmaster Thorne authorized it. Since it was the same passenger it had brought on board yesterday, the one who had that live cargo to tend, we didn't think anything was odd."

"What time did they *leave*?" Venn asked. His face was a mask of dismay.

"Not on our shift, sir. I don't know what happened after that. I went straight home and went to bed. I didn't see the search bulletin for Portmaster Thorne on the news stream till I got up for breakfast just a few minutes ago."

"Why didn't you pass this on in your end-of-shift report?"

"Portmaster Thorne *said* not to." The voice hesitated. "At least . . . the passenger suggested we might want to leave this off the record, so that we wouldn't have to deal with all the other passengers demanding access too if they heard about it, and Portmaster Thorne nodded and said *Yes*."

Venn winced, and took a deep breath. "It can't be helped, Patroller. You reported as soon as you knew. I'm glad you at least picked up the news right away. We'll take it from here. Thank you." Venn cut the channel.

"What was that all about?" asked Miles. Roic had strolled up to loom over his shoulder.

Venn clutched his head with his upper hands, and groaned, "My night-shift guard on the *Idris* just woke up and saw the news bulletin about Thorne being missing. *He* says Thorne came here last night about oh-two-hundred and passed Dubauer through the guards."

"Where did Thorne go after that?"

"Escorted Dubauer aboard, apparently. Neither of them came off while my night-shift crew was watching. Excuse me. I need to go talk to my people." Venn grabbed his floater control and swung hastily out of the cargo hold.

Miles stood stunned. How could Bel have gone from an uncomfortable, but relatively safe, nap in a recycling bin to *this* action in little more than an hour? Garnet Five had taken six or seven hours to wake up. His high confidence in his judgment of Gupta's account was suddenly shaken.

Roic, eyes narrowing, asked, "Could your herm friend have gone renegade, m'lord? Or been bribed?"

Adjudicator Leutwyn looked to Greenlaw, who looked sick with uncertainty.

"I would sooner doubt . . . myself," said Miles. And that was slandering Bel. "Although the portmaster might have been bribed with a nerve disruptor muzzle pressed to its spine, or something equivalent." He wasn't sure he wanted to even try to imagine the ba's bioweapon equivalent. "Bel *would* play for time."

"How could this ba find the portmaster when we couldn't?" asked Leutwyn.

Miles hesitated. "The ba wasn't hunting Bel. The ba was hunting Guppy. If the ba had been closing in last night when Guppy counterattacked his shadowers . . . the ba might have come along immediately after, or even been a witness. And allowed itself to be diverted, or swapped its priorities, in the face of the unexpected opportunity to gain access to its cargo through Bel."

What priorities? What did the ba want? Well, Gupta dead, certainly, doubly so now that the amphibian was witness to both its initial clandestine operation, and to the murders by which the ba had attempted to completely erase its trail. But for the ba to have been so close to its target, and yet veer off, suggested that the other priority was overwhelmingly more important to it.

The ba had spoken of utterly destroying its purportedly animal cargo; the ba had also spoken of taking tissue samples for freezing. The ba had spoken lie upon lie, but suppose this was the truth? Miles wheeled to stare down the aisle of racks. The image formed itself in his mind: of the ba working all day, with relentless speed and concentration. Loosening the lid of each replicator, stabbing through membrane, fluid, and soft skin with a sampling needle, lining the needles up, row on row, in a freezer unit the size of a small valise. Miniaturizing the essence of its genetic payload to something it could carry away in one hand. At the cost of abandoning their originals? *Destroying the evidence?*

Maybe it has, and we just can't see the effects yet. If the ba could make adult-sized bodies steam away their own liquids within hours and turn to viscous puddles, what could it do with such tiny ones?

The Cetagandan wasn't stupid. Its smuggling scheme might have gone according to plan, but for the slipup with Gupta. Who had followed the ba here, and drawn in Solian—whose disappearance had led to the muddle with Corbeau and Garnet Five, which had led to the bungled raid on the quaddie security post, which had resulted in the impoundment of the fleet, including the ba's precious cargo. Miles knew exactly how it felt to watch a carefully planned mission slide down the toilet in a flush of random mischance. How would the ba respond to that sick, heart-pounding desperation? Miles had almost no sense of the person, despite meeting it twice. The ba was smooth and slick and self-controlled. It could kill with a touch, smiling.

But if the ba was paring down its payload to a minimum mass, it certainly wouldn't saddle its escape with a prisoner.

"I think," said Miles, and had to stop and clear a throat gone dry. Bel would play for time. But suppose time and ingenuity ran out, and no one came, and no one came, and no one came . . . "I think Bel might still be aboard the *Idris*. We must search the ship. At once."

Roic stared around, looking daunted. "All of it, m'lord?"

He started to cry *Yes!* but his laggard brain converted it to, "No. Bel had no access codes beyond quaddie control of the airlock. The ba had codes only for this hold and its own cabin. Anything that was locked before, should still be. For the first pass, check unsecured spaces only."

"Shouldn't we wait for Chief Venn's patrollers?" asked Leutwyn uneasily.

"If anyone even tries to come aboard who hasn't been exposed already, I swear I'll stun them myself before they can get through the airlock. I'm not fooling." Miles's voice was husky with conviction.

Leutwyn looked taken aback, but Greenlaw, after a frozen moment, nodded. "I quite see your point, Lord Auditor Vorkosigan. I must agree."

They spread out in pairs, the intent-looking Greenlaw followed by the somewhat bewildered adjudicator, Roic determinedly keeping to Miles's shoulder. Miles tried the ba's cabin first, to find it as empty as before. Four other cabins had been left unlocked, three presumably because they had been cleared of possessions, the last apparently through sheer carelessness. The infirmary was sealed, as it had been left after Bel's inspection with the medtechs last evening. Nav and Com was fully secured. On the deck above, the kitchen was open, as were some of the recreation areas, but no cheeky Betan herm or unnaturally decomposed remains were to be found. Greenlaw and Leutwyn passed through, to report that all of the other holds in the huge long cylinder shared by the ba's cargo were still properly sealed. Venn, they discovered, had taken over a comconsole in the passenger lounge; upon being apprised of Miles's new theory, he paled and attached himself to Greenlaw. Five more nacelles to check.

On the deck below the passengers' zone, most of the utility and engineering areas remained locked. But the door to the department of Small Repairs opened at Miles's touch on its control pad.

Three adjoining chambers were full of benches, tools, and diagnostic equipment. In the second chamber, Miles came upon a bench holding three deflated bod pods marked with the *Idris*'s logo and serial numbers. These tough-skinned human-sized balloons were furnished with enough air recycling equipment and power to keep a passenger alive in a pressurization emergency until rescue arrived. One had only to step inside, zip it up, and hit the power-on button. Bod pods required a minimum of instruction, mostly because there wasn't bloody much you could do once you were trapped inside one. Every cabin, hold, and corridor on the ship had them, stored in emergency lockers on the walls.

On the floor beside the bench, one bod pod stood fully inflated, as if it had been left there in the middle of testing by some tech when the ship had been evacuated by the quaddies.

Miles stepped up to one of the pod's round plastic ports and peered through.

Bel sat inside, cross-legged, stark naked. The herm's lips were parted, and its eyes glazed and distant. So still was that form, Miles feared he was looking at death already, but then Bel's chest rose and fell, breasts trembling with the shivers racking its body. On the blank face a fevered flush bloomed and faded.

No, God, no! Miles lunged for the pod's seal, but his hand stopped and fell back, clenching so hard his nails bit into his palm like knives. *No . . .*

Chapter 14

Step One. Seal the biocontaminated area.

Had the entry lock been closed behind them when their party entered the *Idris*? Yes. Had anyone opened it since?

Miles raised his wrist com to his lips and spoke Venn's contact code. Roic stepped closer to the bod pod, but stopped at Miles's upflung hand; he ducked his head and peered past Miles's shoulder, and his eyes widened.

The few seconds of delay while the wrist com's search program located Venn seemed to flow by like cold oil. Finally, the crew chief's edgy voice: "Venn here. What now, Lord Vorkosigan?"

"We've found Portmaster Thorne. Trapped in a bod pod in the engineering section. The herm appears dazed and very ill. I believe we have an urgent biocontamination emergency here, at least Class Three and possibly as bad as Class Five." The most extreme level, biowarfare plague. "Where are you all now?"

"In the Number Two freight nacelle. The sealer and the adjudicator are with me."

"No one has attempted to leave or enter the ship since we boarded? You didn't go out for any reason?"

"No."

"You understand the necessity for keeping it that way till we know what the devil we're dealing with?"

"What, do you think I'd be insane enough to carry some hell-plague back onto *my own station*?"

Check. "Very good, Crew Chief. I see we are of one mind in this." *Step Two. Alert the medical authority in your district.* To each their own. "I'm going to report this to Admiral Vorpatril and request medical assistance. I presume Graf Station has its own emergency protocols."

"Just as soon as you get off my com link."

"Right. At the earliest feasible moment, I also intend to break the tube seals and move the ship a little way out of its docking cradle, just to be sure. If you or the Sealer would warn station traffic control, plus clear whatever shuttle Vorpatril sends, that would be most helpful. Meanwhile—I strongly urge you seal the locks between your nacelle and this central section until . . . until we know more. Find the nacelle's atmosphere controls and put yourselves on internal circulation, if you can. I haven't . . . quite figured out what to do about this damned bod pod yet. Nai—Vorkosigan out."

He cut the com and stared in anguish at the thin wall between him and Bel. How good a biocontamination barrier was a sealed bod pod's skin? Probably quite good, for something not purpose-built for the task. A new and horrible idea of just where to look for Solian, or rather, whatever organic smear of the lieutenant might now remain, presented itself inescapably to Miles's imagination.

With that jump of deduction came new hope and new terror. Solian had been disposed of weeks ago, probably aboard this very vessel, at a time when passengers and crew had been moving freely between the station and the ship. No plague had broken out yet. If Solian had been dissolved by the same nightmare method Gupta testified had claimed his shipmates, inside a bod pod, which was then folded and set out of the way . . . leaving Bel in the pod with the seals unbroken might make everyone perfectly safe.

Everyone, of course, except Bel. . . .

It was unclear if the incubation or latency period of the infection was adjustable, although what Miles was seeing now suggested it was. Six days for Gupta and his friends. Six hours for Bel? But the disease or poison or bio-molecular device, whatever it was, had killed the Jacksonians quickly once it became active, in just a few hours. How long did Bel have until intervention became futile? Before the herm's brains began turning to some bubbling gray slime along with its body . . . ? Hours, minutes, too late already? And what intervention could help?

Gupta survived this. Therefore, survival is possible. His mind dug into that historical fact like pitons into a rock face. *Hang on and climb, boy.*

He held his wrist com to his lips and called up the emergency channel to Admiral Vorpatril.

Vorpatril responded almost immediately. "Lord Vorkosigan? The medical squad you requested reached the quaddie station a few minutes ago. They should be reporting in to you there momentarily to assist with the examination of your prisoner. Haven't they presented themselves yet?"

"They may have, but I'm now aboard the *Idris*, along with Armsman Roic. And, unfortunately, Sealer Greenlaw, Adjudicator Leutwyn, and Chief Venn. We've ordered the ship sealed. We appear to have a biocontamination incident aboard." He repeated the description of Bel he'd given Venn, with a few more details.

Vorpatril swore. "Shall I send a personnel pod to take you off, my lord?"

"Absolutely not. If there's anything contagious loose in here—which, while not certain, is not yet ruled out—it's um . . . already too late."

"I'll divert my medical squad to you at once."

"Not all of them, dammit. I want some of our people in with the quaddies, working on Gupta. It is of the highest urgency to find out why he survived. Since we may be stuck in here for a while, don't tie up more men than required. But do send me bright ones. In Level Five biotainer suits. You can send any equipment they want aboard with them, but nothing and no one goes back off this ship till this thing is locked down." Or until the plague took them all . . . Miles had a vision of the *Idris* towed away from the station and abandoned, the untouchable final tomb of all aboard. A damned *expensive* sepulchre, there was that consolation. He had faced death before and, once at least, lost, but the lonely ugliness of this one shook him badly. There would be no cheating with cryochambers this time, he suspected. Not for the last victims to go, certainly. "Volunteers only, you understand me, Admiral?"

"That I do," said Vorpatril grimly. "I'm on it, my Lord Auditor."

"Good. Vorkosigan out."

How much time did Bel have? Half an hour? Two hours? How much time would it take Vorpatril to muster his new set of medical volunteers and all their complex cargo? More than half an hour, Miles was fairly certain. And what could they do when they got here?

Besides his genetic engineering, what had been different from the others about Gupta?

His tank? Breathing through his gills . . . Bel didn't have gills, no help there. Cooling water, flowing over the froggish body, his fan-like webs, through the blood-filled, feathery gills, chilling his blood . . . could some of this biodissolvent's hellish development be heat-sensitive or temperature-triggered?

An ice-water bath? The vision sprang to his mind's eye, and his lips drew back on a fierce grin. A low-tech, but provably fast, way to lower body temperature, no question about it. He could personally guarantee the effects. *Thank you, Ivan.*

"My lord?" said Roic uncertainly to his apparent transfixed paralysis.

"We run like hell now. You go to the galley and check for ice. If there isn't any, start whatever machine they have full blast. Then meet me in the infirmary." He had to move fast; he didn't have to be stupid about it. "They may have biotainer gear there."

By the expression on Roic's face, he was notably not following any of this, but at least he followed Miles, who boiled out and down the corridor. They rose up the lift tube the two flights to the level that housed galley, infirmary, and recreation areas. More out of breath than he cared to reveal, Miles waved Roic on his way and galloped to the infirmary at the far end of the central nacelle. A frustrating pause while he tapped out the locking code, and he was through into the little sickbay.

The facilities were scant: two small wards, although both with at least Level Three bio-containment capabilities, plus an examining room equipped for minor surgery that also harbored the pharmacy. Major surgeries and severe injuries were expected to be transported to one of the military escort ship's more seriously equipped sickbays. Yes, one of the ward's bathrooms included a sterilizable treatment tub; Miles pictured unhappy passengers with skin infestations soaking therein. Lockers full of emergency equipment. He jerked them all open. There was the blood synthesizer, there a drawer of mysterious and unnerving objects perhaps designed for female patients, there was a narrow float pallet for patient transport, standing on end in a tall locker with two biotainer suits, yes! One too large for Miles, the other too small for Roic.

He could wear the too-large suit; it wouldn't be the first time. The other would be impossible. He couldn't justify endangering Roic so . . .

Roic jogged in. "Found the ice maker, m'lord. Nobody seems to have turned it off when the ship was evacuated. It's packed full."

Miles pulled out his stunner and dropped it on the examining table, then began to skin into the smaller biotainer suit.

"What t'hell do you think you're doing, m'lord?" asked Roic warily.

"We're going to bring Bel up here. Or at least, I am. It's where the medics will want to do treatments anyway." If there were any treatments. "I have an idea for some quick-and-dirty first aid. I think Guppy might have survived by the water in his tank keeping his body temperature down. Head for engineering. Try to find a pressure suit that will fit you. If—*when* you find the suit, let me know, and put it on at once. Then meet me back where Bel is. Move!"

Roic, face set, moved. Miles used the precious seconds to run to the galley and scoop a plastic waste bin full of ice, and drag it back to the infirmary on the float pallet to dump in the tub. Then a second bin full. Then his wrist com buzzed.

"Found a suit, m'lord. It'll just fit, I think." Roic's voice wavered as, presumably, his arm moved about. Some rustling and faint grunting indicated a successful test. "Once I'm in, I won't be able to use my secured wrist com. I'll have to access you over some public channel."

"We'll have to live with that. Make contact with Vorpatril on your suit com as soon as you're sealed in; be sure his medics can communicate when they bring their pod to one of the outboard locks. Make sure they don't try to come through the same freight nacelle where the quaddies have taken refuge!"

"Right, m'lord."

"Meet you in Small Repairs."

"Right, m'lord. Suiting up now." The channel went muffled.

Regretfully, Miles covered his own wrist com with the biotainer suit's left glove. He tucked his stunner into one of the sealable outer pockets on the thigh, then adjusted his oxygen flow with a few taps on the suit's control vambrace on his left arm. The lights in the helmet faceplate display promised him he was now sealed from his environment. The slight positive pressure within the overlarge suit puffed it out plumply. He slopped toward the lift tube in the loose boots, towing the float pallet.

Roic was just clumping down the corridor as Miles maneuvered the pallet through the door of Small Repairs. The armsman's pressure suit, marked with the *Idris*'s engineering department's serial numbers, was certainly as much protection as Miles's gear, although its gloves were thicker and more clumsy. Miles motioned Roic to bend toward him, touching his faceplate to Roic's helmet.

"We're going to reduce the pressure in the bod pod to partially deflate it, roll Bel onto the float pallet, and run it upstairs. I'm not going to unseal the pod till we're in the ward with the molecular barriers activated."

"Shouldn't we wait for the *Prince Xav*'s medics for that, m'lord?" asked Roic nervously. "They'll be here soon enough."

"No. Because I don't know how soon too late is. I don't dare vent Bel's pod into the ship's atmosphere, so I'm going to try to rig a line to another pod as a catchment. Help me look for sealing tape, and something to use for an air pipe."

Roic gave him a rather frustrated gesture of acknowledgment, and began a survey of benches and drawers.

Miles peered in the port again. "Bel? Bel!" he shouted through faceplate and bod skin. Muffled, yes, but he should be audible, dammit. "We're going to move you. Hang on in there."

Bel sat unchanged, apparently, from a few minutes ago, still glazed and unresponsive. It might not be the infection, Miles tried to encourage himself. How many drugs had the herm been hit with last night, to assure its cooperation? Knocked out by Gupta, stimulated to consciousness by the ba, tanked with hypnotics, presumably, for the walk to the *Idris* and the scam of the quaddie guards. Maybe fast-penta after that, and some sedatives to keep Bel quiescent while the poison took hold, who knew?

Miles shook out one of the other pods onto the floor nearby. If the residue of Solian lay therein, well, this wasn't going to make it any *more* contaminated, now was it? And would Bel's remains have escaped notice for as long as Solian's, if Miles hadn't come along so soon—was that the ba's plan? Murder and dispose of the body in one move. . . .

He knelt to the side of Bel's bod pod and opened the access panel to the pressurization control unit. Roic handed down a length of plastic tubing and strips of tape. Miles wrapped, prayed, and turned assorted valve controls. The air pump vibrated gently. The pod's round outline softened and slumped. The second pod expanded, after a flaccid, wrinkled fashion. He closed valves, cut lines, sealed, wished for a few liters of disinfectant to splash around. He held the fabric up away from the lump that was Bel's head as Roic lifted the herm onto the pallet.

The pallet moved at a brisk walking pace; Miles longed to run. They maneuvered the load into the infirmary, into the small ward. As close as possible to the rather cramped bathroom.

Miles motioned Roic to bend close again.

"All right. This is as far as you go. We don't both need to be in here for this. I want you to exit the room and turn on the molecular barriers. Then stand ready to assist the medics from the *Prince Xav* as needed."

"M'lord, are you sure you wouldn't rather we do it t'other way around?"

"I'm sure. Go!"

Roic exited reluctantly. Miles waited till the lines of blue light indicating that the barriers had been activated sprang into being across the doorway, then bent to unzip the pod and fold it back from Bel's tensed, trembling body. Even through his gloves, Bel's bare skin felt scorching hot.

Edging both the pallet and himself into the bathroom involved some awkward clambering, but at last he had Bel positioned to shift into the waiting vat of ice and water. Heave, slide, splash. He cursed the pallet and lunged over it to hold Bel's head up. Bel's body jerked in shock; Miles wondered if his shakily theorized palliative would instead give the victim heart failure. He shoved the pallet back out the door, and out of the way, with one foot. Bel was now trying to curl into a fetal position, a more heartening response than the open-eyed coma Miles had observed so far. Miles pulled the bent limbs down one by one and held them under the ice water.

Miles fingers grew numb with the cold, except where they touched Bel. The herm's body temperature seemed scarcely affected by this brutal treatment. Unnatural indeed. But at least Bel stopped growing hotter. The ice was melting noticeably.

It had been some years since Miles had last glimpsed Bel nude, in a field shower or donning or divesting space armor in a mercenary warship locker room. Fifty-something wasn't old, for a Betan, but still, gravity was clearly gaining on Bel. *On all of us.* In their Dendarii days Bel had taken out its unrequited lust for Miles in a series of half-joking passes, half-regretfully declined. Miles repented his younger sexual reticence altogether, now. Profoundly. *We should have taken our chances back then, when we were young and beautiful and didn't even know it.* And Bel had been beautiful, in its own ironic way, living and moving at ease in a body athletic, healthy, and trim.

Bel's skin was blotched, mottled red and pale; the herm's flesh, sliding and turning in the ice bath under Miles's anxious hands, had an odd texture, by turns swollen tight or bruised like crushed fruit. Miles called Bel's name, tried his best old *Admiral Naismith Commands You* voice, told a bad joke, all without penetrating the herm's glazed stupor. It was a bad idea to cry in a biotainer suit, almost as bad as throwing up in a pressure suit. You couldn't blot your eyes, or wipe your snot.

And when someone touched you unexpectedly on the shoulder, you jumped as though shot, and they looked at you funny, through their faceplate and yours.

"Lord Auditor Vorkosigan, are you all right?" said the *Prince Xav's* biotainer-swaddled surgeon, as he knelt beside him at the vat's edge.

Miles swallowed for self-control. "I'm fine, so far. This herm's in a very bad way. I don't know what they've told you about all this."

"I was told that I might be dealing with a possible Cetagandan-designed bioweapon in hot mode, that had killed three so far with one survivor. The part about there being a survivor made me really wonder about the first assertion."

"Ah, you didn't get a chance to see Guppy yet, then." Miles took a breath and ran through a brief recap of Gupta's tale, or at least the pertinent biological aspects of it. As he spoke, his hands never stopped shoving Bel's arms and legs back down, or ladling watery ice cubes over the herm's burning head and neck. He finished, "I don't know if it was Gupta's amphibian genetics, or something he did, that allowed him to survive this hell-shit when his friends didn't. Guppy said their dead flesh *steamed*. I don't know what all this heat's coming from, but it can't be just fever. I couldn't duplicate the Jacksonian's bioengineering, but I thought I could at least duplicate the water tank trick. Wild-assed empiricism, but I didn't think there was much time."

A gloved hand reached past him to raise Bel's eyelids, touch the herm here and there, press and probe. "I see that."

"It's *really important*"—Miles took another gulp of air to stabilize his voice—"it's really important that this patient survive. Thorne's not just any stationer. Bel was . . ." He realized he didn't know the surgeon's security clearance.

"Having the portmaster die on our watch would be a diplomatic disaster. Another one, that is. And . . . and the herm saved my life yesterday. I owe—Barrayar owes—"

"My lord, we'll do our best. I have my top squad here; we'll take over now. Please, my Lord Auditor, if you could please step out and let your man decontaminate you?"

Another suited figure, doctor or medtech, appeared through the bathroom door and held out a tray of instruments to the surgeon. Perforce Miles moved aside, as the first sampling needle plunged past him into Bel's unresponsive flesh. No room left in here even for his shortness, he had to admit. He withdrew.

The spare ward bunk had been turned into a lab bench. A third biotainer-clad figure was rapidly shifting what looked a promising array of equipment from boxes and bins piled high on a float pallet onto this makeshift surface. The second tech returned from the bathroom and started feeding bits of Bel into the various chemical and molecular analyzers on one end of the bunk even as the third man arranged more devices on the other.

Roic's tall, pressure-suited figure stood waiting just past the molecular barriers across the ward door. He was holding a high-powered laser-sonic decontaminator, familiar Barrayaran military issue. He raised an inviting hand; Miles returned the acknowledgment.

Nothing further was to be gained in here by dithering more at the medical squad. He'd just distract them and get in their way. He suppressed his unstrung urge to explain to them Bel's superior right, by old valor and love, to survive. Futile. He might as well rail at the microbes themselves. Even the Cetagandans had not yet devised a weapon that triaged for virtue before slaughtering its victims.

I promised to call Nicol. God, why did I promise that? Learning Bel's present status would surely be more terrifying for her than knowing nothing. He would wait a little longer, at least till he received the first report from the surgeon. If there was hope by then, he could impart it. If there was none . . .

He stepped slowly through the buzzing molecular barrier, raising his arms to turn about beneath the even stronger sonic-scrubber/laser-dryer beam from Roic's decontaminator. He had Roic treat every part of him, including palms, fingers, the soles of his feet, and, nervously, the insides of his thighs. The suit protected him from what would otherwise be a nasty scorching, leaving skin pink and hair exploded off. He didn't motion Roic to desist till they'd gone over each square centimeter. Twice.

Roic pointed to Miles's control vambrace and bellowed through his faceplate, "I have the ship's com link relay up and running now, m'lord. You should be able to hear me through Channel Twelve, if you'll switch over. T'medics are all on Thirteen."

Hastily, Miles switched on the suit com. "Can you hear me?"

Roic's voice sounded now beside his ear. "Yes, m'lord. Much better."

"Have we blown the tube seals and pulled away from the docking clamps yet?"

Roic looked faintly chagrined. "No, m'lord." At Miles's chin raised in inquiry, he added, "Um . . . you see, there's only me. I've never piloted a jumpship."

"Unless you're actually jumping, it's just like a shuttle," Miles assured him. "Only bigger."

"I've never piloted a shuttle, either."

"Ah. Well, come on, then. I'll show you how."

They threaded their way to Nav and Com; Roic tapped their passage through the code locks. All right, Miles admitted, looking around at the various station chairs and their control banks, so it *was* a big ship. It was only going to be a ten-meter flight. He was a bit out of practice even on pods and shuttles, but really, given some of the pilots he'd known, how hard could it be?

Roic watched in earnest admiration while he concealed his hunt for the tube seal controls—ah, there. It took three tries to get in touch with station traffic control, and then with Docks and Locks—if only Bel had been here, he would have instantly delegated this task to . . . He bit his lip, rechecking the all-clear from the loading bay—it would be the cap on this mission's multitude of embarrassments to pull away from the station yanking out the docking clamps, decompressing the loading bay, and killing some unknown number of quaddie patrollers on guard therein. He scooted from the communications station to the pilot's chair, shoving the jump helmet up out of the way and clenching his gloved hands briefly before activating the manual controls. A little gentle pressure from the side verniers, a little patience, and a countering thrust from the opposite side left the vast bulk of the *Idris* floating in space a neat stone's throw from the side of Graf Station. Not that a stone thrown out there would do anything but keep on going forever . . .

No bio-plague can cross that gap, he thought with satisfaction, then instantly thought of what the Cetagandans might do with spores. *I hope.*

It occurred to him belatedly that if the *Prince Xav*'s surgeon sounded an all-clear from the biocontamination alert, docking once again was going to be a critically more delicate task. *Well, if he clears the ship, we can import a pilot then*. He glanced at the time on a wall digital. Barely an hour had passed since they'd found Bel. It seemed a century.

"You're a pilot, as well?" a surprised, muffled female voice sounded.

Miles swung around in the pilot's chair to find the three quaddies in their floaters hovering in the control room's doorway. All now wore quaddie-shaped biotainer suits in pale medical green. His eye rapidly sorted them out. Venn was bulkier, Sealer Greenlaw a little shorter. Adjudicator Leutwyn brought up the rear.

"Only in an emergency," he admitted. "Where did you get the suits?"

"My people sent them across from the station in a drone pod," said Venn. He, too, wore his stunner holstered on the outside of his suit.

Miles would have preferred to keep the civilians safely locked down in the freight nacelle, but there was clearly no help for that now.

"*Which* is still attached to the lock, yes," Venn overrode Miles's opening mouth.

"Thank you," said Miles meekly.

He wanted desperately to rub his face and scrub his itching eyes, but couldn't. What was next? Had he done all he could to contain this thing? His eye fell on the decontaminator, slung over Roic's shoulder. It would probably be a good idea to take that back down to Engineering and sterilize their tracks.

"M'lord?' said Roic diffidently.

"Yes, Armsman?"

"I been thinking. The night guard saw the portmaster and the ba enter the ship, but nobody reported anybody leaving. We found Thorne. I was wondering how the ba got off the ship."

"*Thank* you, Roic, yes. And how long ago. Good question to pursue next."

"Whenever one of the *Idris*'s hatches opens, its lock vid recorders start up automatically. We should ought to be able to access t'lock records from here, I'd think, same as from Solian's security office." Roic cast a somewhat desperate eye around the intimidating array of stations. "Somewhere."

"We should indeed." Miles abandoned the pilot's chair for the flight engineer's station. A little poking among the controls, and a short delay while one of Roic's library of override codes pacified the lockdowns, and Miles was able to bring up a duplicate file of the sort of airlock security records they'd found in Solian's office and spent so many bleary-eyed hours studying. He set the search to present the data in reverse order of time.

The most recent usage was first up on the vid plate, a nice shot of the automated drone pod docking at the outboard personnel lock serving the number two freight nacelle. An anxious-looking Venn scooted into the lock in his floater. He shuttled in and out handing back green suits folded in plastic bags to waiting hands, plus an assortment of other objects: a big box of first aid supplies, a tool kit, a decontaminator somewhat resembling Roic's, and what might be some weapons with rather more authority than stunners. Miles cut the scene short and sent the search back in time.

Mere minutes before that was the Barrayaran military medical patrol arriving in a small shuttle from the *Prince Xav*, entering via one of the number four nacelle personnel locks. The three medical officers and Roic were all clearly identifiable, hastily unloading equipment.

A freight lock in one of the Necklin drive nacelles popped up next, and Miles caught his breath. A figure in a bulky extravehicular-repairs suit marked with serial numbers from the *Idris*'s engineering section lumbered heavily past the vid pickup, and departed into the vacuum with a brief puff of suit jets. The quaddies bobbing at Miles's shoulder murmured and pointed; Greenlaw muffled an exclamation, and Venn choked on a curse.

The next record back in time was of themselves—the three quaddies, Miles, and Roic—entering the ship from the loading bay for their inspection, however many hours ago it had been. Miles tapped instantly back to the mystery figure in the engineering suit. What time . . . ?

Roic exclaimed, "Look, m'lord! He—it—was getting away not twenty minutes before we found t'portmaster! The ba must've still been aboard when we came on!" Even through his faceplate, his face took on a greenish tinge.

Had Bel's conundrum in the bod pod been a fiendishly engineered delaying tactic? Miles wondered if the knotted feeling in his stomach and tightness in his throat could be the first sign of a bioengineered plague. . . .

"Is that our suspect?" asked Leutwyn anxiously. "Where did he go?"

"What is the range on those heavy suits of yours, do you know, Lord Auditor?" asked Venn urgently.

"Those? Not sure. They're meant to allow men to work outside the ship for hours at a time, so I'd guess, if they were fully topped up with oxygen, propellant, and power . . . damned near the range of a small personnel pod." The engineering repair suits resembled military space armor, except with an array of built-in tools instead of built-in weapons. Too heavy for even a strong man to walk in, they were fully powered. The ba might have ridden in one around to any point on Graf Station. Worse, the ba might have ridden out to a mid-space pickup by some Cetagandan co-agent, or perhaps by some bribed or simply bamboozled local helper. The ba might be thousands of kilometers away by now, with the gap widening every second. Heading for entry to another quaddie habitat under yet another faked identity, or even for rendezvous with a passing jumpship and escape from Quaddiespace altogether.

"Station Security is on full emergency alert," said Venn. "I have all my patrollers and all of the Sealer's militia on duty out looking for the fellow—the person. Dubauer *can't* have gotten back aboard the station unobserved." A tremor of doubt in Venn's voice undercut the certainty of this statement.

"I've ordered the station onto a full biocontamination quarantine," said Greenlaw. "All incoming ships and vehicles have been waved off or diverted to Union, and none now in dock are cleared to leave. If the fugitive did get back aboard already—it isn't leaving." Judging by the sealer's congealed expression, she was by no means sure if this was a good thing. Miles sympathized. Fifty thousand potential hostages . . . "If it's fled somewhere else . . . if our people can't locate this fugitive promptly, I'm going to have to extend the quarantine throughout Quaddiespace."

What would be the most important task for the ba, now that the flag had been dropped? It had to realize that the tight secrecy it had relied on for protection thus far was irremediably ruptured. Did it realize how close on its heels its pursuers had come? Would it still wish to murder Gupta to assure the Jacksonian smuggler's silence? Or would it abandon that hunt, cut losses, and run if it could? Which direction was it trying to move, back in, or out?

Miles's eye fell on the vid image of the work suit, frozen above the plate. Did that suit have the kind of telemetry space armor did? More to the point—did it have the kind of remote control overrides some space armor did?

"Roic! When you were down in the engineering suit lockers hunting for that pressure suit, did you see an automated command-and-control station for these powered repair units?"

"I . . . there's a control room down there, yes, m'lord. I passed it. I don't know what all might be in it."

"I have an idea. Follow me."

He levered himself from the station chair and left Nav and Com at a sloppy jog, his biotainer suit sliding aggravatingly around him. Roic strode after; the curious quaddies followed in their floaters.

The control room was scarcely more than a booth, but it featured a telemetry station for exterior maintenance and repairs. Miles slid into its station chair, and cursed the tall person who'd fixed it at a height that left his boots dangling in air. On permanent display were several real-time vid shots of critical portions of the ship's outlying anatomy, including directional antenna arrays, the mass shield generator, and the main normal-space thrusters. Miles sorted through a bewildering mess of data from structural safety sensors scattered throughout the ship. Finally, the work suit control program came up.

Six suits in the array. Miles called up visual telemetry from their helmet vids. Five returned views of blank walls, the insides of their respective storage lockers. The sixth returned a lighter image, but more puzzling, of a curving wall. It remained as static as the vistas from the suits in storage.

Miles pinged the suit for full telemetry download. The suit was powered up but quiescent. The medical sensors were basic, just heart rate and respiration—and turned off. The life-support readouts claimed the rebreather was fully functional, the interior humidity and temperature were exactly on-spec, but the system appeared to be supporting no load.

"It can't be very far away," Miles said over his shoulder to his hovering audience. "There's zero time lag in my com linkup."

"*That's* a relief," sighed Greenlaw.

"Is it?" muttered Leutwyn. "Who for?"

Miles stretched shoulders aching with tension, and bent again to the displays. The powered suit had to have an exterior control override somewhere; it was a common safety feature on these civilian models, in case its occupant should suddenly become injured, ill, or incapacitated . . . ah. There.

"What are you doing, m'lord?" asked Roic uneasily.

"I believe I can take control of the suit via the emergency overrides, and bring it back aboard."

"Wit' t' ba inside? Is that a *good* idea?"

"We'll know in a moment."

He gripped the joysticks, slippery under his gloves, gained control of the suit's jets, and tried a gentle puff. The suit slowly began to move, scraping along the wall and then turning away. The puzzling view resolved itself—he was looking at the outside of the *Idris* itself. The suit had been hidden, tucked in the angle between two nacelles. No one inside the suit fought back at this hijacking. A new and extremely disturbing thought crept up on Miles.

Carefully, Miles brought the suit back around the outside of the ship to the nearest lock to Engineering, on the outboard side of one of the Necklin rod nacelles, the same lock from which it had exited. Opened the lock, brought the suit inside. Its servos kept it upright. The light reflected from its faceplate, concealing whatever was within. Miles did not open the interior lock door.

"Now what?" he said to the room at large.

Venn glanced at Roic. "Your armsman and I have stunners, I believe. If you control the suit, you control the prisoner's movements. Bring it in, and we'll arrest the bastard."

"The suit has manual capacities, too. Anyone in it who was . . . alive and conscious should have been able to fight me." Miles cleared a throat thick with worry. "I was just wondering if Brun's searchers checked inside these suits when they were looking for Solian, that first day he went missing. And, um . . . what he's like—what condition his body might be in by now."

Roic made a small noise, and emitted an undervoiced, plaintive protest of *M'lord!* Miles wasn't sure of the exact interpretation, but he thought it might have something to do with Roic wanting to keep his last meal in his stomach, and not all over the inside of his helmet.

After a brief, fraught pause, Venn said, "Then we'd better go have a look. Sealer, Adjudicator—wait here."

The two senior officials didn't argue.

"Would you like to stay with 'em, m'lord?" Roic suggested tentatively.

"We've all been looking for that poor bastard for weeks," Miles replied firmly. "If this is him, I want to be the first to know." He did allow Roic and Venn to precede him from engineering through the locks into the Necklin field generator nacelle, though.

At the lock, Venn drew his stunner and took position. Roic peered through the port on the airlock's inner door. Then his hand swept down to the lock control, the door slid open, and he strode in. He reappeared a moment later, half-dragging the heavy toppling work suit. He laid it faceup on the corridor floor.

Miles ventured closer and stared down at the faceplate.

The suit was empty.

Chapter 15

"Don't open it!" cried Venn in alarm.

"Wasn't planning to," Miles replied mildly. *Not for any money.*

Venn floated closer, stared down over Miles's shoulder, and swore. "The bastard's got away already! But to the station, or to a ship?" He edged back, tucked his stunner away in a pocket of his green suit, and began to gabble into his helmet com, alerting both Station Security and the quaddie militia to pursue, seize, and search anything—ship, pod, or shuttle—that had so much as shifted its parking zone off the side of the station in the past three hours.

Miles envisioned the escape. Might the ba have ridden the repairs suit back aboard the station before Greenlaw had called down the quarantine? Yes, maybe. The time window was narrow, but possible. But in that case, how had it returned the suit to the hiding place outside the *Idris*? It would make more sense for the ba to have been picked up by a personnel pod—plenty enough of them zipping around out there at all hours—and have prodded the suit back to its concealment with a tractor beam, or had it towed there by someone in another powered suit and tucked out of sight.

But the *Idris*, like all the other Barrayaran and Komarran ships, was under surveillance by the quaddie militia. How cursory was that outside guard? Surely not that inattentive. Yet a person, a tall person, sitting in that engineering control booth manipulating the joysticks, might well have walked the suit out this airlock and quickly around the nacelle, popping it away out of sight deftly enough to evade notice by the militia guardians. Then risen from the station chair, and . . . ?

Miles's palms itched, maddeningly, inside his gloves, and he rubbed them together in a futile attempt to gain relief. He'd have traded blood for the chance to rub his nose. "Roic," he said slowly. "Do you remember what this," he prodded the repair suit with his toe, "had in its hand when it went out the airlock?"

"Um . . . nothing, m'lord." Roic twisted slightly and shot Miles a puzzled look, through his faceplate.

"That's what I thought." *Right.*

If Miles was guessing correctly, the ba had turned aside from the imminent murder of Gupta to seize the chance of using Bel to get back aboard the *Idris* and do—what?—with its cargo. Destroy it? It would surely not have taken the ba this long to inoculate the replicators with some suitable poison. It might even have been able to do them twenty at a time, introducing the contaminant into the support system of each rack. Or—even more simply, if all it had wanted was to kill its charges—it might have just turned off all the support systems, a work of mere minutes. But taking and marking individual cell samples for freezing, yes, that could well have taken all night, and all day too. If the ba had risked everything to do that, would it then leave the ship *without* its freezer case firmly in hand?

"The ba's had over two hours to effect an escape. Surely it wouldn't *linger* . . ." muttered Miles. But his voice lacked conviction. Roic, at least, caught the quaver at once; his helmet turned toward Miles, and he frowned.

They needed to count pressure suits, and check every lock to see if any of the vid monitors had been manually disabled. No, too slow—that would be a fine evidence-collecting task to delegate if one had the manpower, but Miles felt painfully bereft of minions just now. And in any case, so what if another suit was found to be gone? Pursuing loose suits was a job that the quaddies around the station were already turning to, by Venn's order. But if no other suit *was* gone . . .

And Miles himself had just turned the *Idris* into a trap.

He gulped. "I was about to say, we need to count suits, but I've a better idea. I believe we should return to Nav and Com, and shut the ship down in sections from there. Collect all the weapons at our disposal, and do a systematic search."

Venn jerked around in his float chair. "What, do you think this Cetagandan agent could still be aboard?"

"M'lord," said Roic in an uncharacteristically sharp voice, "what t'matter with your *gloves*?"

Miles stared down, turning up his hands. His breath congealed in his chest. The thin, tough fabric of his bio-tainer gloves was shredding away, hanging loose in strings; beneath the lattice, his palms showed red. Their itching seemed to redouble. His breath let loose again in a snarl of "*Shit!*"

Venn bobbed closer, took in the damage with widening eyes, and recoiled.

Miles held his hands up, and apart. "Venn. Go collect Greenlaw and Leutwyn and take over Nav and Com. Secure yourselves and the infirmary, in that order. Roic. Go ahead of me to the infirmary. Open the doors for me." He choked back an unnecessary scream of *Run!*; Roic, with an indrawn breath audible over the suit com, was already moving.

He dodged through the half-dark ship in Roic's long-legged wake, touching nothing, expecting every lumping heartbeat to rupture inside him. Where had he collected this hellish contamination? Was anyone else affected? Everyone else?

No. It had to have been the power-suit control joysticks. They'd slid greasily under his gloved hands. He had gripped them tighter, intent upon the task of bringing the suit back inboard. He'd taken the bait . . . Now, more than ever, he was certain the ba had walked an empty suit out the airlock. And then set a snare for any smartass who figured it out too soon.

He plunged through the door to the infirmary, past Roic, who stood aside, and straight on through the blue-lit inner door to the bio-sealed ward. A medtech's suited form jumped in surprise. Miles called up Channel 13 and rapped out, "Someone please . . ." then stopped. He'd meant to cry, *Turn on the water for me!* and hold his hands under the sluice of a sink, but where did the water then *go*? "Help," he finished in a smaller voice.

"What is it, my Lord Audi—" the chief surgeon began, stepping from the bathroom; then his glance took in Miles's upraised hands. "*What happened?*"

"I think I hit a booby trap. As soon as you have a free tech, have Armsman Roic take him down to Engineering and collect a sample from the repair suit remote controller there. It appears to have been painted with some powerful corrosive or enzyme and . . . and I don't know what else."

"Sonic scrubber," Captain Clogston snapped over his shoulder to the tech monitoring the makeshift lab bench. The man hastened to rummage among the stacks of supplies. He turned back, powering on the device; Miles held out both his burning hands. The machine roared as the tech ran the directed beam of vibration over the afflicted areas, its powerful vacuum sucking the loosened detritus both macroscopic and microscopic into the sealed collection bag. The surgeon leaned in with a scalpel and tongs, slicing and tearing away the remaining shreds of gloves, which were also sucked into the receptacle.

The scrubber seemed effective; Miles's hands stopped feeling worse, though they continued to throb. Was his skin breached? He brought his now-bare palms closer to his faceplate, impeding the surgeon, who hissed under his breath. Yes. Red flecks of blood welled in the creases of the swollen tissue. *Shit. Shit. Shit. . . .*

Clogston straightened and glanced around, lips drawn back in a grimace. "Your biotainer suit's compromised all to hell, my lord."

"There's another pair of gloves on the other suit," Miles pointed out. "I could cannibalize them."

"Not yet." Clogston hurried to slather Miles's hands with some mystery goo and wrap them in biotainer barriers, sealed to his wrists. It was like wearing mittens over handfuls of snot, but the burning pain eased. Across the room, the tech was scraping fragments of contaminated glove into an analyzer. Was the third man in with Bel? Was Bel still in the ice bath? Still alive?

Miles took a deep, steadying breath. "Do you have any kind of a diagnosis on Portmaster Thorne yet?"

"Oh, yes, it came up right away," said Clogston in a somewhat absent tone, still sealing the second wrist wrap. "The instant we ran the first blood sample through. What the hell we can *do* about it is not yet obvious, but I have some ideas." He straightened again, frowning deeply at Miles's hands. "The herm's blood and tissues are crawling with artificial—that is, bioengineered—parasites." He glanced up. "They appear to have an initial, latent, asymptomatic phase, where they multiply rapidly throughout the body. Then, at some point—possibly triggered by their own concentration—they switch over to producing two chemicals in different vesicles within their own cellular membrane. The vesicles engorge. A rise in the victim's body temperature triggers the bursting of the sacs, and the chemicals in turn undergo a violently exothermic reaction with each other—killing the parasite, damaging the host's surrounding tissues, and stimulating more nearby parasites to go off. Tiny, pin-point bombs all through the body. It's"—his tone went reluctantly admiring—"extremely elegant. In a hideous sort of way."

"Did—did my ice-water bath treatment help Thorne, then?"

"Yes, absolutely. The drop in core temperature stopped the cascade in its tracks, temporarily. The parasites had almost reached critical concentration."

Miles's eyes squeezed shut in brief gratitude. And opened again. "Temporarily?"

"I still haven't figured out how to get rid of the damned things. We're trying to modify a surgical shunt into a blood filter to both mechanically remove the parasites from the patient's bloodstream, and chill the blood to a controlled degree before returning it to the body. I think I can make the parasites respond selectively to an applied electrophoresis gradient across the shunt tube, and pull them right on out of the bloodstream."

"Won't that do it, then?"

Clogston shook his head. "It doesn't get the parasites lodged in other tissues, reservoirs of reinfection. It's not a cure, but it might buy time. I think. The cure must somehow kill every last one of the parasites in the body, or the process will just start up again." His lips twisted. "Internal vermicides could be tricky. Injecting something to kill already-engorged parasites within the tissues will just release their chemical loads. A very little of that micro-insult will play hell with circulation, overload repair processes, cause intense pain—it's . . . it's tricky."

"Destroy brain tissue?" Miles asked, feeling sick.

"Eventually. They don't seem to cross the blood-brain barrier very readily. I believe the victim would be conscious to a, um, very late phase of the dissolution."

"Oh." Miles tried to decide whether that would be good, or bad.

"On the bright side," offered the surgeon, "I may be able to downgrade the biocontamination alarm from Level Five to Level Three. The parasites appear to need direct blood-to-blood contact to effect transference. They don't seem to survive long outside a host."

"They can't travel through the air?"

Clogston hesitated. "Well, maybe not until the host starts coughing blood."

Until, not *unless*. Miles noted the word choice. "I'm afraid talk of a downgrade is premature anyway. A Cetagandan agent armed with unknown bioweapons—well, unknown except for this one, which is getting too damned familiar—is still on the loose out there." He inhaled, carefully, and forced his voice to calm. "We've found some evidence suggesting that the agent still may be hiding aboard this ship. You need to secure your work zone from a possible intruder."

Captain Clogston cursed. "Hear that, boys?" he called to his techs over his suit com.

"Oh, great," came a disgusted reply. "Just what we need right now."

"Hey, at least it's something we can *shoot*," another voice remarked wistfully.

Ah, Barrayarans. Miles's heart warmed. "On sight," he confirmed. These were *military* medicos; they all bore side-arms, bless them.

His eye flicked over the ward and the infirmary chamber beyond, summing weak points. Only one entry, but was that weakness or strength? The outer door was definitely the vantage to hold, protecting the ward beyond; Roic had taken up station there quite automatically. Yet traditional attack by stunner, plasma arc, or explosive grenade seemed . . . insufficiently imaginative. The place was still on ship's air circulation and ship's power, but this of all sections had to have its own emergency reservoirs of both.

The military-grade Level Five biotainer suits the medicos wore also doubled as pressure suits, their air circulation entirely internal. The same was not true of Miles's cheaper suit, even before he'd lost his gloves; his atmosphere pack drew air from the environs, through filters and cookers. In the event of a pressurization loss, his suit would turn into a stiff, unwieldy balloon, perhaps even rupture at a weak point. There were bod pod lockers on the walls, of course. Miles pictured being trapped in a bod pod while the action went on without him.

Given that he was already exposed to . . . whatever, peel-ing out of his biotainer suit long enough to get into something tighter couldn't make things any worse, could it? He stared at his hands and wondered why he wasn't dead yet. Could the glop he'd touched have been only a simple corrosive?

Miles clawed his stunner out of his thigh pocket, awkwardly with his mittened hand, and walked back through the blue bars of light marking the bio-barrier. "Roic. I want you to dash back down to Engineering and grab me the smallest pressure suit you can find. I'll guard this point till you get back."

"M'lord," Roic began in a tone of doubt.

"Keep your stunner out; watch your back. We're all here, so if you see anything move that isn't quaddie green, shoot first."

Roic swallowed manfully. "Yes, well, see that you *stay* here, m'lord. Don't go haring off on your own without me!"

"I wouldn't dream of it," Miles promised.

Roic departed at the gallop. Miles readjusted his awkward grip on the stunner, made sure it was set to maximum power, and took a stance partly sheltered by the door, staring up the central corridor at his bodyguard's retreating form. Scowling.

I don't understand this.

Something didn't add up, and if he could just get ten consecutive minutes not filled with lethal new tactical crises, maybe it would come to him. . . . He tried not to think about his stinging palms, and what ingenious microbial sneak assault might even now be stealing through his body, maybe even making its way into his brain.

An ordinary imperial servitor ba ought to have died before abandoning a charge like those haut-filled replicators. And even if this one had been trained as some sort of special agent, why spend all that critical time taking

samples from the fetuses that it was about to desert or
maybe even destroy? Every haut infant ever made had its
DNA kept on file back in the central gene banks of the Star
Crèche. They could make more, surely. What made *this*
batch so irreplaceable?

His train of thought derailed itself as he imagined little
gengineered parasites multiplying frenetically through his
bloodstream, *blip-blip-blip-blip. Calm down, dammit.* He
didn't actually know if he'd even been inoculated with the
same evil disease as Bel. *Yeah, it might be something even
worse.* Yet surely some Cetagandan designer neurotoxin—
or even some quite ordinary off-the-shelf poison—ought
to cut in much faster than this. *Although if it's a drug to
drive the victim mad with paranoia, it's working really well.*
Was the ba's repertoire of hell-potions limited? If it had any,
why not many? Whatever stimulants or hypnotics it had
used on Bel need not have been anything out of the ordinary, by the norms of covert ops. How many other fancy
bio-tricks did it have up its sleeve? Was Miles about to personally demonstrate the next one?

*Am I going to live long enough to say good-bye to Ekat-
erin?* A good-bye kiss was right out, unless they pressed
their lips to opposite sides of some really thick window of
glass. He had so much to say to her; it seemed impossible to
find where to start. Even more impossible by voice alone,
over an open, unsecured public com link. *Take care of the
kids. Kiss them for me every night at bedtime, and tell them I
loved them even if I never saw them. You won't be alone—my
parents will help you. Tell my parents . . . tell them . . .*

Was this damned thing starting up already, or were the
hot panic and choking tears in his throat entirely self-
induced? An enemy that attacked you from the inside
out—you could try to turn yourself inside out to fight it,

but you wouldn't succeed—filthy weapon! *Open channel or not, I'm calling her now. . . .*

Instead, Venn's voice sounded in his ear. "Lord Vorkosigan, pick up Channel Twelve. Your Admiral Vorpatril wants you. Badly."

Miles hissed through his teeth and keyed his helmet com over. "Vorkosigan here."

"Vorkosigan, you idiot—!" The admiral's syntax had shed a few honorifics sometime in the past hour. "What the hell is going on over there? Why don't you answer your wrist com?"

"It's inside my biotainer suit and inaccessible right now. I'm afraid I had to don the suit in a hurry. Be aware, this helmet link is an open access channel and unsecured, sir." Dammit, where did that *sir* drop in from? Habit, sheer old bad habit. "You can ask for a brief report from Captain Clogston over his military suit's tight-beam link, but keep it *short*. He's a very busy man right now, and I don't want him distracted."

Vorpatril swore—whether generally or at the Imperial Auditor was left nicely ambiguous—and clicked off.

Faintly echoing through the ship came the sound Miles had been waiting for—the distant clanks and hisses of airseal doors shutting down, sealing the ship into airtight sections. The quaddies had made it to Nav and Com, good! Except that Roic wasn't back yet. The armsman would have to get in touch with Venn and Greenlaw and get them to unseal and reseal his passage back up to—

"Vorkosigan." Venn's voice sounded again in his ear, strained. "Is that you?"

"Is what me?"

"Shutting off the compartments."

"Isn't it," Miles tried, and failed, to swallow his voice back down to a more reasonable pitch. "*Aren't you in Nav and Com yet?*"

"No, we circled back to the Number Two nacelle to pick up our equipment. We were just about to leave it."

Hope flared in Miles's hammering heart. "Roic," he called urgently. "Where are you?"

"Not in Nav and Com, m'lord," Roic's grim voice returned.

"But if we're here and he's there, who's doing *this*?" came Leutwyn's unhappy voice.

"Who do you *think*?" Greenlaw ripped back. Her breath huffed out in anguish. "Five people, and not one of us thought to see the door locked behind us when we left—dammit!"

A small, bleak grunt, like a man being hit with an arrow, or a realization, sounded in Miles's ear: Roic.

Miles said urgently, "Anyone who holds Nav and Com has access to all these ship-linked com channels, or will, shortly. We're going to have to switch off."

The quaddies had independent links to the station and Vorpatril through their suits; so did the medicos. Miles and Roic would be the ones plunged into communications limbo.

Then, abruptly, the sound in his helmet went dead. *Ah. Looks like the ba has found the com controls. . . .*

Miles leapt to the environmental control panel for the infirmary to the left of the door, opened it, and hit every manual override in it. With this outer door shut, they could retain air pressure, although circulation would be blocked. The medicos in their suits would be unaffected; Miles and Bel would be at risk. He eyed the bod pod locker on the wall without favor. The bio-sealed ward was already functioning on internal circulation, thank God, and could remain so—as long as the power stayed on. But how could they keep Bel cold if the herm had to retreat to a pod?

Miles hurried back into the ward. He approached Clogston, and yelled through his faceplate, "We just lost our ship-linked suit coms. Keep to your tight-beam military channels only."

"I heard," Clogston yelled back.

"How are you coming on that filter-cooler?"

"Cooler part's done. Still working on the filter. I wish I'd brought more hands, although there's scarcely room in here for more butts."

"I've almost got it, I think," called the tech, crouched over the bench. "Check that, will you, sir?" He waved in the direction of one of the analyzers, a collection of lights on its readout now blinking for attention.

Clogston dodged around him and bent to the machine in question. After a moment he murmured, "Oh, *that's* clever."

Miles, crowding his shoulder close enough to hear this, did not find it reassuring. "What's clever?"

Clogston pointed at his analyzer readout, which now displayed incomprehensible strings of letters and numbers in cheery colors. "I didn't see how the parasites could possibly survive in a matrix of that enzyme that ate your biotainer gloves. But they were microencapsulated."

"What?"

"Standard trick for delivering drugs through a hostile environment—like your stomach, or maybe your bloodstream—to the target zone. Only this time, used to deliver a disease. When the microencapsulation passes out of the unfriendly environment into the—chemically speaking—friendly zone, it pops open, releasing its load. No loss, no waste."

"Oh. Wonderful. *Are* you saying I now have the same shit Bel has?"

"Um." Clogston glanced up at a chrono on the wall. "How long since you were first exposed, my lord?"

Miles followed his glance. "Half an hour, maybe?"

"They *might* be detectable in your bloodstream by now."

"Check it."

"We'll have to open your suit to access a vein."

"Check it now. *Fast*."

Clogston grabbed a sampler needle; Miles peeled back the biotainer wrap from his left wrist, and gritted his teeth as a biocide swab stung and the needle poked. Clogston was pretty deft for a man wearing biotainer gloves, Miles had to concede. He watched anxiously as the surgeon delicately slipped the needle into the analyzer.

"How long will this take?"

"Now that we have the template of the thing, no time at all. If it's positive, that is. If this first sample shows negative, I'd want a recheck every thirty minutes or so to be sure." Clogston's voice slowed, as he studied his readout. "Well. Um. A recheck won't be necessary."

"Right," Miles snarled. He yanked open his helmet and pushed back his suit sleeve. He bent to his secured wrist com and snapped, "Vorpatril!"

"Yes!" Vorpatril's voice came back instantly. Riding his com channels—he must be on duty in either the *Prince Xav*'s own Nav and Com, or maybe, by now, its tactics room. "Wait, what are you doing on this channel? I thought you had no access."

"The situation has changed. Never mind that now. What's happening out there?"

"What's happening in *there*?"

"The medical team, Portmaster Thorne, and I are holed up in the infirmary. For the moment, we're still in control of our environment. I believe Venn, Greenlaw, and Leutwyn are trapped in the Number Two freight nacelle. Roic may be somewhere in Engineering. And the ba, I believe, has seized Nav and Com. Can you confirm that last?"

"Oh, yes," groaned Vorpatril. "It's talking to the quaddies on Graf Station right now. Making threats and demands. Boss Watts seems to have inherited their hot seat. I have a strike team scrambling."

"Patch it in here. I have to hear this."

A few seconds delay, then the ba's voice sounded. The Betan accent was gone; the academic coolness was fraying. "—name does not matter. If you wish to get the Sealer, the Imperial Auditor, and the others back alive, these are my requirements. A jump pilot for this ship, delivered immediately. Free and unimpeded passage from your system. If either you or the Barrayarans attempt to launch a military assault against the *Idris*, I will either blow up the ship with all aboard, or ram the station."

Boss Watts's voice returned, thick with tension, "If you attempt to ram Graf Station, we'll blow you up *ourselves*."

"Either way will do," the ba's voice returned dryly.

Did the ba know *how* to blow up a jumpship? It wasn't exactly easy. Hell, if the Cetagandan was a hundred years old, who knew what all it knew how to do? Ramming, now—with a target that big and close, any layman could manage it.

Greenlaw's stiff voice cut in; her com link presumably was patched through to Watts in the same way that Miles's was to Vorpatril. "Don't do it, Watts. Quaddiespace *cannot* let a plague-carrier like this pass through to our neighbors. A handful of lives can't justify the risk to thousands."

"Indeed," the ba continued after a slight hesitation, still in that same cool tone. "If you do succeed in killing me, I'm afraid you will win yourselves another dilemma. I have left a small gift aboard the station. The experiences of Gupta and Portmaster Thorne should give you an idea of what sort of package it is. You *might* find it before it ruptures, although I'd say your odds are poor. Where are your thousands now? Much closer to home."

True threat or bluff? Miles wondered frantically. It certainly fit the ba's style as demonstrated so far—Bel in the bod pod, the booby trap with the suit-control joysticks— hideous, lethal puzzles tossed out in the ba's wake to disrupt and distract its pursuers. *It sure worked on me, anyway.*

Vorpatril cut in privately on the wrist com, in an unnecessarily lowered, tense tone, overriding the exchange between the ba and Watts. "Do you think the bastard's bluffing, m'lord?"

"Doesn't matter if it's bluffing or not. I want it *alive*. Oh, God do I ever want it alive. Take that as a top priority and an order in the Emperor's Voice, Admiral."

After a small and, Miles hoped, thoughtful pause, Vorpatril returned, "Understood, my Lord Auditor."

"Ready your strike team, yes . . ." Vorpatril's best strike force was locked in quaddie detention. What was the *second* best one like? Miles's heart quailed. "But *hold* it. This situation is extremely unstable. I don't have any clear sense yet how it will play out. Put the ba's channel back on." Miles returned his attention to the negotiation in progress—no— winding up?

"A jump pilot." The ba seemed to be reiterating. "Alone, in a personnel pod, to the Number Five B lock.

And, ah—naked." Horribly, there seemed to be a smile in that last word. "For obvious reasons."

The ba cut the com.

Chapter 16

Now what?

Delays, Miles guessed, while the quaddies on Graf Station either readied a pilot or ran the risks of stalling about delivering one into such a hazard, and suppose none volunteered? While Vorpatril marshaled his strike team, while the three quaddie officials trapped in the freight nacelle— well, didn't sit on their hands, Miles bet—*while this infection gains on me*, while the ba did—what?

Delay is not my friend.

But it was his gift. What time was it, anyway? Late evening—still the same day that had started so early with the news of Bel's disappearance? Yes, though it hardly felt possible. Surely he had entered some time warp. Miles stared at his wrist com, took a deep, terrified breath, and called up Ekaterin's code. Had Vorpatril told her anything of what was happening yet, or had he kept her comfortably ignorant?

"Miles!" she answered at once.

"Ekaterin, love. Where, um . . . are you?"

"The tactics room, with Admiral Vorpatril."

Ah. That answered that question. In a way, he was relieved that he didn't have to deliver the whole litany of bad news himself, cold. "You've been following this, then."

"More or less. It's been very confusing."

"I'll bet. I . . ." He couldn't say it, not so baldly. He dodged, while he mustered courage. "I promised to call Nicol when I had news of Bel, and I haven't had a chance. The news, as you may know, is not good; we found Bel, but the herm has been deliberately infected with a bioengineered Cetagandan parasite that may . . . may prove lethal."

"Yes, I understand. I've been hearing it all, here in the tactics room."

"Good. The medics are doing their best, but it's a race against time and now there are these other complications. Will you call Nicol and redeem my word for me? There's not *no* hope, but . . . she needs to know it doesn't look so good right now. Use your judgment how much to soften it."

"My judgment is that she should be told plain truth. The whole of Graf Station is in an uproar now, what with the quarantine and biocontamination alert. She needs to know exactly what's going on, and she has a right to know. I'll call her at once."

"Oh. Good. Thank you. I, um . . . you know I love you."

"Yes. Tell me something I don't know."

Miles blinked. This wasn't getting easier; he rushed it in a breath. "Well. There's a chance I may have screwed up pretty badly, here. Like, I may not get out of this one. The situation here is pretty unsettled, and, um . . . I'm afraid my biotainer suit gloves were sabotaged by a nasty little Cetagandan booby trap I triggered. I seem to have got myself infected with the same biohazard that's taken Bel down. The stuff doesn't appear to act very quickly, though."

In the background, he could just hear Admiral Vor-patril's voice, cursing in choice barracks language not at all consonant with the respect due to one of His Majesty Gregor Vorbarra's Imperial Auditors. From Ekaterin, silence; he strained to hear her breathing. The sound reproduction on these high-grade com links was so excellent, he could hear when she let her breath out again, through those pursed, exquisite warm lips he could not see or touch.

He began again. "I'm . . . I'm sorry that . . . I wanted to give you—this wasn't what I—I never wanted to bring you grief—"

"Miles. Stop that babbling at once."

"Oh . . . uh, yes?"

Her voice sharpened. "If you die on me out here, I will not be grieved, I will be *pissed.* This is all very fine, love, but may I point out that you don't have *time* to indulge in angst right now. You're the man who used to rescue hostages for a living. You are *not allowed* to not get out of this one. So stop worrying about me and start paying attention to what you are doing. Are you listening to me, Miles Vorkosigan? Don't you dare die! I won't have it!"

That seemed definitive. Despite everything, he grinned. "Yes, dear," he sang back meekly, heartened. This woman's Vor ancestoresses had defended bastions in war, oh, yes.

"So stop talking to me and get back to work. Right?"

She almost kept the shaken sob out of that last word.

"Hold the fort, love," he breathed, with all the tenderness he knew.

"Always." He could hear her swallow. "Always."

She cut her link. He took it as a hint.

Hostage rescue, eh? *If you want something done right, do it yourself.* Come to think of it, did this ba have any idea of what Miles's former line of work had been? Or did it assume Miles was just a diplomat, a bureaucrat, another frightened civilian? The ba could not know which of the party had triggered its booby trap on the repair suit remote controls, either. Not that this biotainer suit hadn't been useless for space assault purposes even before it had been buggered all to hell. But what tools were available here in this infirmary that might be put to uses their manufacturers had never envisioned? And what personnel?

The medical crew had military training, right enough, and discipline. They also were up to their collective elbows in other tasks of the highest priority. Miles's very last desire was to pull them away from their cramped, busy lab bench and critical patient care to go play commando with him. *Although it may come to that.* Thoughtfully, he began walking about the infirmary's outer chamber, opening drawers and cupboards and staring at their contents. A muddy fatigue was beginning to drag at his edgy, adrenaline-pumped high, and a headache was starting behind his eyes. He studiously ignored the terror of it.

He glanced through the blue light bars into the ward. The tech hurried from the bench, heading toward the bathroom with something in his hands that trailed looping tubes.

"Captain Clogston!" Miles called.

The second suited figure turned. "Yes, my lord?"

"I'm shutting your inner door. It's supposed to close on its own in the event of a pressure change, but I'm not sure I trust any remote-controlled equipment on this ship at the moment. Are you prepared to move your patient into a bod pod, if necessary?"

Clogston gave him a sketchy salute of acknowledgment with a gloved hand. "Almost, my lord. We're starting construction on the second blood filter. If the first one works as well as I hope, we should be ready to rig you up very soon, too."

Which would tie him down to a bunk in the ward. He wasn't ready to lose mobility yet. Not while he could still move and think on his own. *You don't have much time then. Regardless of what the ba does.* "Thank you, Captain," Miles called. "Let me know." He slid the door shut with the manual override.

What could the ba know, from Nav and Com? More importantly, what were its blind spots? Miles paced, considering the layout of this central nacelle: a long cylinder divided into three decks. This infirmary lay at the stern on the uppermost deck. Nav and Com was far forward, at the other end of the middle deck. The internal airseal doors of all levels lay at the three evenly spaced intersections to the freight and drive nacelles, dividing each deck longitudinally into quarters.

Nav and Com had security vid monitors in all the outer airlocks, of course, and safety monitors on all the inner section doors that closed to seal the ship into airtight compartments. Blowing out a monitor would blind the ba, but also give warning that the supposed prisoners were on the move. Blowing out *all* of them, or all that could be reached, would be more confusing . . . but still left the problem of giving warning. How likely was the ba to carry out its harried, or perhaps insane, threat of ramming the station?

Dammit, this was so *unprofessional* . . . Miles halted, arrested by his own thought.

What were the standard operating procedures for a Cetagandan agent—anyone's agent, really—whose covert mission was going down the toilet? Destroy all the evidence: try to make it to a safe zone, embassy, or neutral territory. If that wasn't possible, destroy the evidence and then sit tight and endure arrest by the locals, whoever the locals might be, and wait for one's own side to either bail or bust one out, depending. For the really, really critical missions, destroy the evidence and commit suicide. This last was seldom ordered, because it was even more seldom carried out. But the Cetagandan ba were so conditioned to loyalty to their haut masters—and mistresses—Miles was forced to consider it a more realistic possibility in the present case.

But splashy hostage-taking among neutrals or neighbors, blaring the mission all over the news, most of all—*most* of all, the public use of the Star Crèche's most private arsenal . . . This wasn't the modus operandi of a trained agent. This was goddamned *amateur* work. And Miles's superiors used to accuse *him* of being a loose cannon— hah! Not any of his most direly inspired messes had ever been as forlorn as this one was shaping up to be—for both sides, alas. This gratifying deduction did not, unfortunately, make the ba's next action more predictable. Quite the reverse.

"M'lord?" Roic's voice rose unexpectedly from Miles's wrist com.

"Roic!" cried Miles joyfully. "Wait. What the hell are you doing on this link? You shouldn't be out of your suit."

"I might ask you the same question, m'lord," Roic returned rather tartly. "If I had time. But I had to get out of t' pressure suit anyway to get into this work suit. I think . . . yes. I can hang the com link in my helmet. There." A slight chink, as of a faceplate closing. "Can you still hear me?"

"Oh, yes. I take it you're still in Engineering?"

"For now. I found you a real nice little pressure suit, m'lord. And a lot of other tools. Question is how to get it to you."

"Stay away from all the airseal doors—they're monitored. Have you found any cutting tools, by chance?"

"I'm, uh . . . pretty sure that's what these are, yes."

"Then move as far to the stern as you can get, and cut straight up through the ceiling to the middle deck. Try to avoid damaging the air ducts and grav grid and control and fluid conduits, for now. Or anything else that would make the boards light up in Nav and Com. Then we can place you for the next cut."

"Right, m'lord. I was thinking something like that might do."

A few minutes ran by, with nothing but the sound of Roic's breathing, broken with a few under-voiced obscenities as, by trial and error, he discovered how to handle the unfamiliar equipment. A grunt, a hiss, a clank abruptly cut off.

The rough-and-ready procedure was going to play hell with the atmospheric integrity of the sections, but did that necessarily make things any worse, from the hostages' point of view? And a pressure suit, oh bliss! Miles wondered if any of the powered work suits had been sized extra-small. Almost as good as space armor, indeed.

"All right, m'lord," came the welcome voice from his wrist com. "I've made it to the middle deck. I'm moving back now . . . I'm not exactly sure how close I am under you."

"Can you reach up to tap on the ceiling? Gently. We don't want it to reverberate through the bulkheads all the way to Nav and Com." Miles threw himself prone, opened his faceplate, tilted his head, and listened. A faint banging, apparently from out in the corridor. "Can you move farther toward the stern?"

"I'll try, m'lord. It's a question of getting these ceiling panels apart . . ." More heavy breathing. "There. Try now."

This time, the rapping seemed to come from nearly under Miles's outstretched hand. "I think that's got it, Roic."

"Right, m'lord. Be sure you're not standing where I'm cutting. I think Lady Vorkosigan would be right peeved with me if I accidentally lopped off any of your body parts."

"I think so too." Miles rose, ripped up a section of friction matting, skittered to the side of the infirmary's outer chamber, and held his breath.

A red glow in the bare deck plate beneath turned yellow, then white. The dot became a line, which grew, wavering in an irregular circle back to its beginning. A thump, as Roic's gloved paw, powered by his suit, punched up through the floor, tearing the weakened circle from its matrix.

Miles nipped over and stared down, and grinned at Roic's face staring up in worry through the faceplate of another repair suit. The hole was too small for that hulking figure to squeeze through, but not too small for the pressure suit he handed up through it.

"Good job," Miles called down. "Hang on. I'll be right with you."

"M'lord?"

Miles tore off the useless biotainer suit and crammed himself into the pressure suit in record time. Inevitably, the plumbing was female, and he left it unattached. One way or another, he didn't think he would be suited up for very long. He was flushed and sweating, one moment too hot, the next too cold, though whether from incipient infection or just plain overdriven nerves he scarcely knew.

The helmet supplied no place to hang his wrist com, but a bit of medical tape solved that problem in a moment. He lowered the helmet over his head and locked it into place, breathing deeply of air that no one controlled but him. Reluctantly, he set the suit's temperature to chilly.

Then he slid to the hole and dangled his legs through. "Catch me. Don't squeeze too hard—remember, you're powered."

"Right, m'lord."

"Lord Auditor Vorkosigan," came Vorpatril's uneasy voice. "What are you doing?"

"Reconnoitering."

Roic caught his hips, lowering him with exaggerated gentleness to the middle deck. Miles glanced up the corridor, past the larger hole in its floor, to the airseal doors at the far end of this sector. "Solian's security office is in this section. If there's any control board on this bloody ship that can monitor without being monitored in turn, it'll be in there."

He tiptoed down the corridor, Roic lumbering in his wake. The deck creaked beneath the armsman's booted feet. Miles tapped out the now-familiar code to the office door; Roic barely squeezed through behind him. Miles slid into the late Lieutenant Solian's station chair and flexed his fingers, contemplating the console. He drew a breath and bent forward.

Yes, he could siphon off views from the vid monitors of every airlock on the ship—simultaneously, if desired. Yes, he could tap into the safety sensors on the airseal doors. They were designed to take in a good view of anyone near—as in, frantically pounding on—the doors. Nervously, he checked the one for this middle rear section. The vista, if the ba was even looking at it with so much else going on, did not extend as far as Solian's office door. Whew. Could he bring up a view of Nav and Com, perhaps, and spy secretly upon its current occupant?

Roic said apprehensively, "What are you thinking of doing, m'lord?"

"I'm thinking that a surprise attack that has to stop to bore through six or seven bulkheads to get to the target isn't going to be surprising enough. Though we may come to that. I'm running out of time." He blinked, hard, then thought *to hell with it* and opened his faceplate to rub his eyes. The vid image unblurred in his vision, but still seemed to waver around the edges. Miles didn't think the problem was in the vid plate. His headache, which had started as a stabbing pain between his eyes, seemed to be spreading to his temples, which throbbed. He was shivering. He sighed and closed the faceplate again.

"That bio-shit—the admiral said you got t' same bio-shit the herm has. The crap that melted Gupta's friends."

"When did you talk to Vorpatril?"

"Just before I talked to you."

"Ah."

Roic said lowly, "I should've been t' one to run those remote controls. Not you."

"It had to be me. I was more familiar with the equipment."

"Yes." Roic's voice went lower. "You should've brought Jankowski, m'lord."

"Just a guess—based on long experience, mind you . . ." Miles paused, frowning at the security display. All right, so Solian didn't have a monitor in every cabin, but he had to have private access to Nav and Com if he had anything . . . "But I suspect there will be enough heroism before this day

is done to go around. I don't think we're going to have to
ration it, Roic."

"'S not what I meant," said Roic, in a dignified tone.

Miles grinned blackly. "I know. But think of how hard it
would have been on Ma Jankowski. And all the not-so-little
Jankowskis."

A soft snort from the com link taped inside Miles's helmet apprised him that Ekaterin was back, listening in. She
would not interrupt, he suspected.

Vorpatril's voice sounded suddenly, breaking his concentration. The admiral was sputtering. "The spineless
scoundrels! The four-armed bastards! My Lord Auditor!"
Ah, Miles was promoted again. "The goddamn little
mutants are giving this sexless Cetagandan plague-vector a
jump pilot!"

"What?" Miles's stomach knotted. Tighter. "They found
a volunteer? Quaddie, or downsider?" There couldn't be
that large a pool of possibilities to choose from. The pilots'
surgically installed neuro-controllers had to fit the ships
they guided through the wormhole jumps. However many
jump pilots were currently quartered—or trapped—on
Graf Station, chances were that most would be incompatible with the Barrayaran systems. So was it the *Idris*'s own
pilot or relief pilot, or a pilot from one of the Komarran sister ships . . . ?

"What makes you think he's a volunteer?" snarled Vorpatril. "I can't bloody *believe* they're just handing . . ."

"Maybe the quaddies are up to something. What do they
say?"

Vorpatril hesitated, then spat, "Watts cut me out of the
loop a few minutes ago. We were having an argument over
whose strike team should go in, ours or the quaddie

militia's, and when. And under whose orders. Both at once with no coordination struck me as a supremely bad idea."

"Indeed. One perceives the potential hazards." The ba was beginning to seem a trifle outnumbered. But then there were its bio-threats . . . Miles's nascent sympathy died as his vision blurred again. "We *are* guests in their polity . . . hang on. Something seems to be happening at one of the outer airlocks."

Miles enlarged the security vid image from the lock that had suddenly come alive. Docking lights framing the outer door ran through a series of checks and go-aheads. The ba, he reminded himself, was probably looking at this same view. He held his breath. Were the quaddies, under the mask of delivering the demanded jump pilot, about to attempt to insert their own strike force?

The airlock door slid open, giving a brief glimpse of the inside of a tiny, one-person personnel pod. A naked man, the little silver contact circles of a jump pilot's neural implant gleaming at mid-forehead and temples, stepped through into the lock. The door slid shut again. Tall, dark-haired, handsome but for the thin pink scars running, Miles could now see, all over his body in a winding swathe. Dmitri Corbeau. His face was pale and set.

"The jump pilot has just arrived," Miles told Vorpatril.

"*Dammit.* Human or quaddie?"

Vorpatril was really going to have to work on his diplomatic vocabulary. . . . "Downsider," Miles answered, in lieu of any more pointed remark. He hesitated, then added, "It's Lieutenant Corbeau."

A stunned silence: then Vorpatril hissed, "Son-of-a-bitch . . . !"

"H'sh. The ba is finally coming on." Miles adjusted the volume, and opened his faceplate again so that Vorpatril could overhear too. As long as Roic kept his suit sealed, it was . . . no worse than ever. *Yeah, and how bad is that, again?*

"Turn toward the security module and open your mouth," the ba's voice instructed coolly and without preamble over the lock vid monitor. "Closer. Wider." Miles was treated to a fair view of Corbeau's tonsils. Unless Corbeau harbored a poison-filled tooth, no weapons were concealed therein.

"Very well . . ." The ba continued with a chill series of directions for Corbeau to go through a humiliating sequence of gyrations which, while not as thorough as a body cavity search, gave at least some assurance that the jump pilot carried nothing *there*, either. Corbeau obeyed precisely, without hesitation or argument, his expression rigid and blank.

"Now release the pod from the docking clamps."

Corbeau rose from his last squat and stepped through the lock to the personnel hatch entry area. A chink and a clank—the pod, released but unpowered, drifted away from the side of the *Idris*.

"Now listen to these instructions. You will walk twenty meters toward the bow, turn left, and wait for the next door to open for you."

Corbeau obeyed, still almost expressionless, except for his eyes. His gaze darted about, as if he searched for something, or was trying to memorize his route. He passed out of sight of the lock vids.

Miles considered the peculiar pattern of old worm scars across Corbeau's body. He must have rolled, or been rolled, across a bad nest. A story seemed written in those fading hieroglyphs. A young colonial boy, perhaps the new boy in camp or town—tricked or dared or maybe just stripped and pushed? To rise again from the ground, crying and frightened, to the jangle of some cruel mockery . . .

Vorpatril swore, repetitively, under his breath. "Why Corbeau? Why *Corbeau*?"

Miles, who was frantically wondering the same thing, hazarded, "Perhaps he volunteered."

"Unless the bloody quaddies bloody sacrificed him. Instead of risking one of their own. Or . . . maybe he's figured out another way to desert."

"I . . ." Miles held his words for a long moment of thought, then let them out on a breath, "think that would be doing it the hard way." It was a sticky suspicion, though. Just *whose* ally might Corbeau prove?

Miles caught Corbeau's image again as the ba walked him through the ship toward Nav and Com, briefly opening and closing airseal doors. He passed through the last barrier and out of vid range, straight-backed, silent, bare feet padding quietly on the deck. He looked . . . cold.

Miles's attention was jerked aside by the flicker of another airlock sensor alarm. Hastily, he called up the image of another lock—just in time to see a quaddie in a green biotainer suit whap the vid monitor mightily with a spanner while beyond, two more green figures sped past. The image shattered and went dark. He could still hear, though—the beep of the lock alarm, the hiss of a lock door opening—but no hiss when it closed. Because it did not close, or because it closed on vacuum? Air, and sound, returned as the lock cycled. The lock, therefore, had opened on vacuum; the quaddies had made their getaway into space around the station.

That answered his question about their biotainer suits—unlike the *Idris*'s cheaper issue, they were vacuum-rated. In Quaddiespace, that made all kinds of sense. Half a dozen station locks offered refuge within little more than a few hundred meters; the fleeing quaddies would have their pick, in addition to whatever pods or shuttles hovered nearby able to swoop down on them and take them inboard.

"Venn and Greenlaw and Leutwyn just escaped out an airlock," he reported to Vorpatril. "*Good* timing." Shrewd timing, to go just when the ba was both distracted by the arrival of its pilot and, with the real possibility of a getaway now in hand, less inclined to carry out the station-ramming threat. It was exactly the right move, to leak hostages from the enemy's grip at every opportunity. Granted, this use of Corbeau's arrival was ruthlessly calculated in the extreme. Miles could not be sorry. "Good. Excellent! Now this ship is entirely cleared of civilians."

"Except for you, m'lord," Roic pointed out, started to say something else, intercepted the dark look Miles cast over his shoulder, and ran down in a mumble.

"Ha," muttered Vorpatril. "Maybe *this* will change Watts's mind." His voice lowered, as if directed away from his audio pickup, or behind his hand. "What, Lieutenant?" Then murmured, "Excuse me," Miles was not certain to whom.

So, only Barrayarans left aboard now. Plus Bel—on the ImpSec payroll, therefore an honorary Barrayaran for all mortal accounting purposes. Miles smiled briefly despite it all as he considered Bel's probable outraged response to such a suggestion. The best time to insert a strike force would be before the ship started to move, rather than to attempt to play catch-up in mid-space. At some point, Vorpatril was probably going to stop waiting for quaddie permission to launch his men. At some point, Miles would agree.

Miles returned his attention to the problem of spying on
Nav and Com. If the ba had knocked out the monitor the
way the passing quaddies just had, or even merely thrown a
jacket over the vid pickup, Miles would be out of luck . . .
ah. Finally. An image of Nav and Com formed over his vid
plate. But *now* he had no sound. Miles gritted his teeth and
bent forward.

The vid pickup was apparently centered over the door,
giving a good view over the half dozen empty station chairs
and their dark consoles. The ba was there, still dressed in
the Betan garb of its discarded alias, jacket and sarong and
sandals. Although a pressure suit—one—abstracted from
the *Idris*'s supplies lay nearby, flung over the back of a station chair. Corbeau, still vulnerably naked, was seated in
the pilot's chair, but had not yet lowered his headset. The ba
held up a hand, said something; Corbeau frowned fiercely,
and flinched, as the ba pressed a hypospray briefly against
the pilot's upper arm and stepped back with a flash of satisfaction on its strained face.

Drugs? Surely even the ba was not mad enough to drug
a jump pilot upon whose neural function it would shortly
be betting its life. Some disease inoculation? The same
problem applied, although something latent might do—
Cooperate, and later I will let you have the antidote. Or pure
bluff, a shot of water, perhaps. The hypospray seemed altogether too crude and obvious as a Cetagandan drug
administration method; it hinted at bluff to Miles's mind,
though perhaps not to Corbeau's. One had no choice but to
turn control over to the pilot when he lowered his headset
and plugged the ship into his mind. It made pilots hard to
effectively threaten.

It did rather put paid to Vorpatril's paranoid fear that
Corbeau had turned traitor, volunteering for this as a way

to get a free ride out of his quaddie detention cell and his dilemmas. Or did it? Regardless of prior or secret agreements, the ba would not simply trust when it could, it would think, guarantee.

Over his wrist com, muffled as from a distance, Miles heard a sudden, startling bellow from Admiral Vorpatril: "*What?* That's impossible. Have they gone mad? Not *now...*"

After a few more moments passed without further enlightenment, he murmured, "Um, Ekaterin? Are you still there?"

Her breath drew in. "Yes."

"What's going on?"

"Admiral Vorpatril was called away by his communications officer. Some sort of priority message from Sector Five headquarters just arrived. It seems to be something very urgent."

On the vid image in front of him, Miles watched as Corbeau began to run through preflight checks, moving from station to station under the hard, watchful eyes of the ba. Corbeau made sure to move with disproportional care; apparently, from the movement of his rather stiff lips, explaining each move before he touched a console. And slowly, Miles noted. Rather more slowly than necessary, if not quite slowly enough to be obvious about it.

Vorpatril's voice, or rather, Vorpatril's heavy breathing, returned at last. The admiral appeared to have run out of invective. Miles found that considerably more disturbing than his previous naval bellowing.

"My lord." Vorpatril hesitated. His voice dropped to a sort of stunned growl. "I have just received Priority One orders from Sector Five HQ to marshal my escort ships, abandon the Komarran fleet, and head for fleet rendezvous off Marilac at maximum possible speed."

Not with my wife, you don't, was Miles's first gyrating thought.

Then he blinked, freezing in his seat.

The *other* function of the military escorts Barrayar donated to the Komarran trade fleets was to quietly and unobtrusively maintain an armed force dispersed through the Nexus. A force that could, in the event of a truly dire emergency, be collected rapidly so as to present a convincing military threat at key strategic points. In a crunch it might otherwise be too slow, or even diplomatically or militarily impossible, to get any force from the homeworlds through the wormhole jumps of intervening local space polities to the mustering places where it could do Barrayar some good. But the trade fleets were out there already.

The planet of Marilac was a Barrayaran ally at the back door of the Cetagandan Empire, from Barrayar's point of view, in the complex web of wormhole jump routes that strung the Nexus together. A second front, as Rho Ceta's immediate neighborly threat to Komarr was considered the first front. Granted, the Cetagandans had the shorter lines of communication and logistics between the two points of contact. But the strategic pincer still beat hell out of the sound of one hand clapping, particularly with the potential addition of Marilacan forces. The Barrayarans would only be marshaling at Marilac in order to offer a threat to Cetaganda.

Except that, when Miles and Ekaterin had left Barrayar on this belated honeymoon trip, relations between the two empires had been about as—well, cordial was perhaps not quite the right term—about as unstrained as they had been

in years. What the *hell* could have changed that, so profoundly, and so quickly?

*Something has stirred up the Cetagandans around Rho
Ceta*, Gregor had said.

A few jumps out from Rho Ceta, Guppy and his smuggler friends had off-loaded a strange live cargo from a
Cetagandan government ship, one with lots of fancy markings. A screaming-bird pattern, perhaps? Along with one,
and only one person—one survivor? After which the ship
had tilted away, on a dangerous in-bound course for the
system's suns. What if that trajectory hadn't been a swing
around? What if it had been a straight dive, with no return?

"Sonuvabitch," breathed Miles.

"My lord?" said Vorpatril. "If—"

"*Quiet*," snapped Miles.

The admiral's silence was shocked, but it held.

Once a year, the most precious cargoes of the haut race
left the Star Crèche on the capital world of Eta Ceta. Eight
ships, bound each for one of the planets of the Empire so
curiously ruled by the haut. Each carrying that year's
cohort of haut embryos, genetically modified and certified
results of all the contracts of conception so carefully negotiated, the prior year, between the members of the great
constellations, the clans, the carefully cultivated gene-lines
of the haut race. Each load of a thousand or so nascent lives
conducted by one of the eight most important haut ladies
of the Empire, the planetary consorts who were the steering committee of the Star Crèche. All most private, most
secret, most never-to-be-discussed with outsiders.

How was it that a ba agent could not go back for more
copies, if it lost such a cargo of future haut lives in transit?

When it wasn't an agent at all. When it was a *renegade*.

"The crime isn't murder," Miles whispered, his eyes widening. "The crime is *kidnapping*."

The murders had come subsequently, in an increasingly panicked cascade, as the ba, with good reason, attempted to bury its trail. Well, Guppy and his friends had surely been planned to die, as eyewitnesses to the fact that one person had not gone down with the rest on the doomed ship. A ship hijacked, if briefly, before its destruction—all the best hijackings were inside jobs, oh, yes. The Cetagandan government must be going *insane* over this.

"My lord, are you all right—?"

Ekaterin's voice, in a fierce whisper: "No, don't interrupt him. He's thinking. He just makes those funny leaking noises when he's thinking."

From the Celestial Garden's point of view, a Star Crèche child-ship had disappeared on what should have been a safe route to Rho Ceta. Every rescue force and intelligence agent the Cetagandan empire *owned* would have been flung into the case. If it were not for Guppy, the tragedy might have passed as some mysterious malfunction that had sent the ship tumbling, out of control and unable to signal, to its fiery doom. No survivors, no wreckage, no loose ends. But there *was* Guppy. Leaving a messy trail of wildly suggestive evidence behind him with every flopping footfall.

How far behind could the Cetagandans be, by now? Too close for the ba's comfort, obviously; it was a wonder, when Guppy had popped up on the hostel railing, that the ba hadn't just died of heart failure without any need for the rivet gun. But the ba's trail, marked by Guppy with blazing flares, led straight through from the scene of the crime to the heart of a sometimes-enemy empire—Barrayar. What were the Cetagandans making of it all?

Well, we have a clue now, don't we?

"Right," breathed Miles, then, more crisply, "Right. You're recording all this, I trust. So my first order in the Emperor's Voice, Admiral, is to countermand your rendezvous orders from Sector Five. That was what you were about to ask for, yes?"

"Thank you, my Lord Auditor, yes," said Vorpatril gratefully. "Normally, that would be a call I would rather die than disregard, but . . . given our present situation, they are going to have to wait a little." Vorpatril wasn't self-dramatizing; this was delivered as a plain statement of fact. "Not too long, I hope."

"They are going to have to wait a lot. This is my next order in the Emperor's Voice. Clear copy everything—*everything*—you have on record here from the past twenty-four hours and squirt it back on an open channel, at the highest priority, to the Imperial Residence, to the Barrayaran high command on Barrayar, to ImpSec HQ, and to ImpSec Galactic Affairs on Komarr. And," he took a breath, and raised his voice to override Vorpatril's outraged cry of *Clear copy! At a time like this?* "marked from Lord Auditor Miles Vorkosigan of Barrayar to the most urgent, personal attention of ghem-General Dag Benin, Chief of Imperial Security, the Celestial Garden, Eta Ceta, personal, urgent, most urgent, by Rian's hair this one's real, Dag. Exactly those words."

"*What?*" screamed Vorpatril, then hastily lowered his tone to an anguished repeat, "What? A rendezvous at Marilac can only mean imminent war with the Cetagandans! We can't hand them that kind of intelligence on our position and movements—gift-wrapped!"

"Obtain the complete, unedited Graf Station Security recording of the interrogation of Russo Gupta and send it along too, as soon as you possibly can. Sooner."

New terror shook Miles, a vision like a fever dream: the grand façade of Vorkosigan House, in the Barrayaran capital of Vorbarr Sultana, with plasma fire raining down upon it, its ancient stone melting like butter; two fluid-filled canisters exploding in steam. Or a fog of plague, leaving all the House's protectors dead in heaps in the halls, or fled to die in the streets; two almost ripe replicators running down unattended, stopping, slowly chilling, their tiny occupants dying for lack of oxygen, drowning in their own amniotic fluid. His past and his future, all destroyed together . . . Nikki, too—would he be swept up with the other children in some frantic rescue, or left uncounted, unmissed, fatally alone? Miles had fancied himself growing into a good stepfather to Nikki—that was called into deep question now, eh? *Ekaterin, I'm sorry . . .*

It would be hours—days—before the new tight-beam could get back to Barrayar and Cetaganda. Insanely upset people could make fatal mistakes in mere minutes. Seconds . . . "And if you are a praying man, Vorpatril, pray that no one will do anything stupid before it gets there. And that we will be believed."

"Lady Vorkosigan," Vorpatril whispered urgently. "Could he be hallucinating from the disease?"

"No, no," she soothed. "He's just thinking too fast, and leaving out all the intervening steps. He does that. It can be very frustrating. Miles, love, um . . . for the *rest* of us, would you mind unpacking that a little more?"

He took a breath—and two or three more—to stop his trembling. "The ba. It's not an agent on a mission. It's a criminal. A renegade. Perhaps insane. I believe it hijacked the annual haut child-ship to Rho Ceta, sent the vessel into the nearest sun with all aboard—probably murdered already—and made off with its cargo. Which trans-shipped through Komarr, and which left the Barrayaran Empire on a trade ship belonging to Empress Laisa *personally*—and just how incriminating *that* particular detail is going to look to certain minds inside the Star Crèche, I shrink to imagine. The Cetagandans think *we* stole their babies, or colluded in the theft, and, dear God, murdered a *planetary consort*, and so they are about to make war on us by *mistake!*"

"Oh," said Vorpatril blankly.

"The ba's whole safety lay in perfect secrecy, because once the Cetagandans got on the right trail they would never rest till they tracked this crime down. But the perfect plan cracked when Gupta didn't die on schedule. Gupta's frantic antics drew Solian in, drew you in, drew me in . . ." His voice slowed. "Except, what in the world does the ba want those haut infants *for?*"

Ekaterin offered hesitantly, "Could it be stealing them for someone else?"

"Yes, but the ba aren't *supposed* to be subornable."

"Well, if not for pay or some bribe, maybe blackmail or threat? Maybe threat to some haut to whom the ba *is* loyal?"

"Or maybe some faction in the Star Crèche," Miles supplied. "Except . . . the ghem-lords do factions. The haut lords do factions. The Star Crèche has always moved as one—even when it was committing arguable treason, a decade ago, the haut ladies took no separate decisions."

"The *Star Crèche* committed treason?" echoed Vorpatril in astonishment. "This certainly didn't get out! Are you sure? I never heard of any mass executions that high in the

Empire back then, and I should have." He paused, and added in a baffled tone, "How could a bunch of haut-lady baby-makers commit treason, anyway?"

"It didn't quite come off. For various reasons." Miles cleared his throat.

"Lord Auditor Vorkosigan. This is your com link, yes? Are you there?" a new voice, and a very welcome one, broke in.

"Sealer Greenlaw!" Miles cried happily. "Have you made it to safety? All of you?"

"We are back aboard Graf Station," replied the Sealer. "It seems premature to call it safety. And you?"

"Still trapped aboard the *Idris*. Although not totally without resources. Or ideas."

"I urgently need to speak to you. You can override that hothead Vorpatril."

"Ah, my com link is sustaining an open audio link with Admiral Vorpatril now, ma'am. You can speak to both of us at once, if you like," Miles put in hastily, before she could express herself even more freely.

She hesitated only fractionally. "Good. We absolutely need Vorpatril to hold, repeat, *hold* any strike force of his. Corbeau confirms the ba *does* have some sort of a remote control or deadman switch on his person, apparently linked back to the biohazard it has hidden aboard Graf Station. The ba is not bluffing."

Miles glanced up in surprise at his silent vid of Nav and Com. Corbeau was seated now in the pilot's station chair, the control headset lowered over his skull, his expressionless face even more absent. "*Corbeau* confirms! How? He was stark naked—the ba is watching him every second! Subcutaneous com link?"

"There was no time to find and insert one. He undertook to blink the ship's running lights in a prearranged code."

"Whose idea was that?"

"His."

Quick colonial boy. The pilot was on their side. Oh, but that was good to know. . . . Miles's shivering was turning to shudders.

"Every adult quaddie on Graf Station not on emergency duty is out looking for the bio-bomb now," Greenlaw continued, "but we have no idea what it looks like, or how big it is, or if it is disguised as something else. Or if there is more than one. We are trying to evacuate as many children as possible into what ships and shuttles we have on hand, and seal them off, but we can't even be sure of *them*, really. If you people do anything to set this mad creature off—if you launch an unauthorized strike force before this vicious threat is found and safely neutralized—I swear I will give our militia the order to shoot them out of space myself. Do you copy, Admiral? Confirm."

"I hear you," said Vorpatril reluctantly. "But ma'am—the Imperial Auditor himself has been infected with one of the ba's lethal bio-agents. I cannot—I will not—if I have to sit here and do nothing while listening to him die—"

"There are fifty *thousand* innocent lives on Graf Station, Admiral—Lord Auditor!" Her voice failed for a second; returned stiffly. "I am sorry, Lord Vorkosigan."

"I'm not dead yet," Miles replied rather primly. A new and most unwelcome sensation struggled with the tight fear grinding in his belly. He added, "I'm going to switch off my com link for just a moment. I'll be right back."

Motioning Roic to keep still, Miles opened the door to the security office, stepped into the corridor, opened his faceplate, leaned over, and vomited onto the floor. *No help for it.* With an angry swipe, he turned his suit temperature back up. He blinked back the green dizziness, wiped his mouth, went back inside, seated himself again, and called his link back on. "Continue."

He let Vorpatril's and Greenlaw's arguing voices fade from his attention, and studied his view of Nav and Com more closely. One object had to be there, somewhere . . . ah. There it was, a small, valise-sized cryo-freezer case, set carefully down next to one of the empty station chairs near the door. A standard commercial model, no doubt bought off the shelf from some medical supplier here on Graf Station sometime in the past few days. All of *this*, this entire diplomatic mess, this extravagant trail of deaths winding across half the Nexus, two empires teetering on the verge of war, came down to *that*. Miles was reminded of the old Barrayaran folktale, about the evil mutant magician who kept his heart in a box to hide it from his enemies.

Yes . . .

"Greenlaw," Miles broke in. "Do you have any way to signal *back* to Corbeau?"

"We designated one of the navigation buoys that broadcasts to the channels of the pilots on cyber-neuro control. We can't get voice communication through it—Corbeau wasn't sure how it would emerge, in his perceptions. We are certain we can get some kind of simple code blink or beep through it."

"I have a simple message for him. Urgent. Get it through if you possibly can, however you can. Tell him to open all the inner airseal doors in the middle deck of the central nacelle. Kill the security vids there, too, if he can."

"Why?" she asked suspiciously.

"We have personnel trapped there who are going to die shortly if he doesn't," Miles replied glibly. Well, it was true.

"Right," she rapped back. "I'll see what we can do."

He cut his outgoing voice link, turned in his station chair, and made a throat-cutting motion for Roic to do the same. He leaned forward. "Can you hear me?"

"Yes, m'lord." Roic's voice was muffled, through the work suit's thicker faceplate, but sufficiently audible; they neither of them had to shout, in this quiet, little space.

"Greenlaw will never order or permit a strike force to be launched to try to capture the ba. Not hers, not ours. She can't. There are too many quaddie lives up for grabs. Trouble is, I don't think this placating approach will make her station any safer. If this ba really murdered a planetary consort, it'll not even blink at a few thousand quaddies. It'll promise cooperation right up to the last, then hit the release switch on its bio-bomb and jump, just for the off chance that the chaos in its wake will delay or disrupt pursuit an extra day or three. Are you with me so far?"

"Yes, m'lord." Roic's eyes were wide.

"If we can get as close as the door to Nav and Com unseen, I think we have a chance of jumping the ba ourselves. Specifically, *you* will jump the ba; I will supply a distraction. You'll be all right. Stunner and nerve disruptor fire will pretty much bounce off that work suit. Needler spines wouldn't penetrate immediately either, if it comes to that. And it would take longer than the seconds you'll need to cross that little room for plasma arc fire to burn through it."

Roic's lips twisted. "What if he just fires at you? That pressure suit's not *that* good."

"The ba won't fire at me. That, I promise you. The Cetagandan haut, and their siblings the ba, are physically stronger than anyone but the dedicated heavy-worlders, but they're not stronger than a power suit. Go for his hands. Hold them. If we get that far, well, the rest will follow."

"And Corbeau? The poor bastard's starkers. Nothing's gonna stop anything fired at him."

"Corbeau," said Miles, "will be the ba's last choice of targets. Ah!" His eyes widened, and he whirled about in his station chair. At the edge of the vid image, half a dozen tiny images in the array were quietly going dark. "Get to the corridor. Get ready to run. As silently as you can."

From his com link, Vorpatril's volume-reduced voice pleaded heartrendingly for the Imperial Auditor to please reopen his outgoing voice contact. He urged Lady Vorkosigan to request the same.

"Leave him alone," Ekaterin said firmly. "He knows what he's doing."

"What *is* he doing?" Vorpatril wailed.

"Something." Her voice fell to a whisper. Or perhaps it was a prayer. "Good luck, love."

Another voice, somewhat offsides, broke in: Captain Clogston. "Admiral? Can you reach Lord Auditor Vorkosigan? We've finished preparing his blood filter and are ready to try it, but he's disappeared out of the infirmary. He was right here a few minutes ago . . ."

"Do you hear that, Lord Vorkosigan?" Vorpatril tried somewhat desperately. "You are to report to the infirmary. Now."

In ten minutes—five—the medics could have their way with him. Miles pushed up from his station chair—he had to use both hands—and followed Roic into the corridor outside Solian's office.

Up ahead in the dimness, the first airseal door across the corridor hissed quietly aside, revealing the cross-corridor to the other nacelles beyond. On the far side, the next door began to slide.

Roic started trotting. His steps were unavoidably heavy. Miles half-jogged behind. He tried to think how recently he had used his seizure-stimulator, how much at risk he was right now for falling down in a fit from a combination of bad brain chemistry and terror. Middling risky, he decided. No automatic weapons for him this trip anyway. No weapons at all, but for his wits. They seemed a meager arsenal, just at the moment.

The second pair of doors opened for them. Then the third. Miles prayed they were not walking into another clever trap. But he didn't think the ba would have any way of tapping, or even guessing, this oblique line of communication. Roic paused briefly, stepping behind the last door edge, and peered ahead. The door to Nav and Com was shut. He gave a short nod and continued forward, Miles in his shadow. As they drew closer, Miles could see that the control panel to the left of the door had been burned out by some cutting tool, cousin, no doubt, to the one Roic had used. The ba had gone shopping in Engineering, too. Miles pointed at it; Roic's face lightened, and a corner of his mouth turned up. *Someone* hadn't forgotten to lock the door behind them when they'd last left after all, it appeared.

Roic pointed to himself, to the door; Miles shook his head and motioned him to bend closer. They touched helmets.

"Me first. Gotta grab that case before the ba can react. 'Sides, I need *you* to pull back the door."

Roic looked around, inhaled, and nodded.

Miles motioned him back down to touch helmets one more time. "And, Roic? I'm glad I didn't bring Jankowski."

Roic smiled. Miles stepped aside.

Now. Delay was no one's friend.

Roic bent, splayed his gloved hands across the door, pressed, and pulled. The servos in his suit whined at the load. The door creaked unwillingly aside.

Miles slipped through. He didn't look back, or up. His world had narrowed to one goal, one object. The freezer case—there, still on the floor beside the absent communication officer's station chair. He pounced, grabbed, lifted it up, clutched it to his chest like a shield, like the hope of his heart.

The ba was turning, yelling, lips drawn back, eyes wide, its hand snaking for a pocket. Miles's gloved fingers felt for the catches. If locked, toss the case toward the ba. If unlocked . . .

The case snapped open. Miles yanked it wide, shook it hard, swung it.

A silver cascade, the better part of a thousand tiny tissue-sampling cryo-storage needles, arced out of the case and bounced randomly across the deck. Some shattered as they struck, making tiny crystalline singing noises like dying insects. Some spun. Some skittered, disappearing behind station chairs and into crevices. Miles grinned fiercely.

The yell became a scream; the ba's hands shot out toward Miles as if in supplication, in denial, in despair. The Cetagandan began to stumble toward him, gray face working in shock and disbelief.

Roic's power-suited hands locked down over the ba's wrists and hoisted. Wrist bones crackled and popped; blood spurted between the tightening gloved fingers. The ba's body convulsed as it was lifted up. Wild eyes rolled back. The scream transmuted into a weird wail, trailing away. Sandal-clad feet kicked and drummed uselessly at the heavy shin plating of Roic's work suit; toenails split and bled, without effect. Roic stood stolidly, hands up and apart, racking the ba helplessly in the air.

Miles let the freezer case fall from his fingers. It hit the deck with a thump. With a whispered word, he called back the outgoing audio in his com link. "We've taken the ba prisoner. Send relief troops. In biotainer suits. They won't need their guns now. I'm afraid the ship's an unholy mess."

His knees were buckling. He sank to the deck himself, giggling uncontrollably. Corbeau was rising from his pilot's chair; Miles motioned him away with an urgent gesture. "Stay back, Dmitri! I'm about to . . ."

He wrenched his faceplate open in time. Barely. The vomiting and spasms that wrung his stomach this time were much worse. *It's over. Can I please die now?*

Except that it wasn't over, not nearly. Greenlaw had played for fifty thousand lives. Now it was Miles's turn to play for fifty million.

Chapter 17

Miles arrived back in the *Idris*'s infirmary feet first. He was carried by two of the men from Vorpatril's strike force, which had been hastily converted to, mostly, a medical relief team, and as such cleared by the quaddies. His porters almost fell down the unsightly hole Roic had left in the floor. Miles seized back personal control of his locomotion long enough to stand up, under his own power, and lean rather unsteadily against the wall by the door to the bio-isolation ward. Roic followed, carefully holding the ba's remote trigger in a biotainer bag. Corbeau, stiff-faced and pale, brought up the rear dressed in a loose medical tunic and drawstring pants, and shepherded by a medtech with the ba's hypospray in another biotainer sack.

Captain Clogston came out through the buzzing blue barriers and looked over his new influx of patients and assistants. "Right," he announced, glowering at the gap in the deck. "This ship is so damned befouled, I'm declaring the whole thing a Level Three Biocontamination Zone. So we may as well spread out and get comfortable, boys."

The techs made a human chain to pass the analyzing equipment quickly to the outer chamber. Miles snared the chance for a few brief, urgent words with the two men with medical markings on their suits who stood apart from the rest—the *Prince Xav's* military interrogation officers. Not really in disguise, merely discreet—and, Miles had to allow, they *were* medically trained.

The second ward was declared a temporary holding cell for their prisoner, the ba, who followed in the procession, bound to a float pallet. Miles scowled as the pallet drifted past, towed on its control lead by a watchful, muscular sergeant. The ba was strapped down tightly, but its head and eyes rolled oddly, and its saliva-flecked lips writhed.

Above almost anything else, it was essential to keep the ba in Barrayaran hands. Finding where the ba had hidden its filthy bio-bomb on Graf Station was the first priority. The haut race had some genetically engineered immunity to the most common interrogation drugs and their derivatives; if fast-penta didn't work on this one, it would give the quaddies very little in the way of interrogation procedures to fall back upon that would pass Adjudicator Leutwyn's approval. In this emergency, military rules seemed more appropriate than civilian ones. *In other words, if they'll just leave us alone we'll pull out the ba's fingernails* for *them.*

Miles caught Clogston by the elbow. "How is Bel Thorne doing?" he demanded.

The fleet surgeon shook his head. "Not well, my Lord Auditor. We thought at first the herm was improving, as the filters cut in—it seemed to return to consciousness. But then it became restless. Moaning and trying to talk. Out of its head, I think. It keeps crying for Admiral Vorpatril."

Vorpatril? Why? Wait— "Did Bel say Vorpatril?" Miles asked sharply. "Or just, *the Admiral?*"

Clogston shrugged. "Vorpatril's the only admiral around right now, although I suppose the portmaster could be hallucinating altogether. I hate to sedate anyone so physiologically distressed, especially when they've just fought their way *out* of a drug fog. But if that herm doesn't calm down, we'll have to."

Miles frowned and hurried into the isolation ward. Clogston followed. Miles pulled off his helmet, fished his wrist com back out of it, and clutched the vital link safely in his hand. A tech was making up the hastily cleared second bunk, readying it for the infected Lord Auditor, presumably.

Bel now lay on the first bunk, dried off and dressed in a pale green Barrayaran military-issue patient tunic, which seemed at first heartening progress. But the herm was gray-faced, lips purple-blue, eyelids fluttering. An IV pump, not dependent upon potentially erratic ship's gravity, infused yellow fluid rapidly into Bel's right arm. The left arm was strapped to a board; plastic tubing filled with blood ran from under a bandage and into a hybrid appliance bound around with quantities of plastic tape. A second tube ran back again, its dark surface moist with condensation.

"'S balla," Bel moaned. "'S balla."

The fleet surgeon's lips pursed in medical displeasure behind his faceplate. He edged forward to glance at a monitor. "Blood pressure's way up, too. I think it's time to knock the poor bugger back out."

"Wait." Miles elbowed to the edge of Bel's bunk to put himself in Bel's line of sight, staring down at the herm in wild hope. Bel's head jerked. The eyelids flickered up; the eyes widened. The blue lips tried to move again. Bel licked them, took a long inhalation, and tried once more.

"Adm'ral! Portent. 'S basti'd hid it in the balla. Tol' me. Sadist'c basti'd."

"Still going on about Admiral Vorpatril," Clogston muttered in dismay.

"Not Admiral Vorpatril. Me," breathed Miles. Did that witty mind still exist, in the bunker of its brain? Bel's eyes were open, shifting to try to focus on him, as if Miles's image wavered and blurred in the herm's sight.

Bel knew a portent. No. Bel was trying to say something important. Bel wrestled death for the possession of its own mouth to try to get the message out. Balla? Ballistic? Balalaika? No—ballet!

Miles said urgently, "The ba hid its bio-bomb at the ballet—in the Minchenko Auditorium? Is that what you're trying to say, Bel?"

The straining body sagged in relief. "Yeh. Yeh. Get 's word out. In the lights, I thin'."

"Was there only one bomb? Or were there more? Did the ba say, could you tell?"

"Don' know. 'S homemade, I thin'. Check. Purch'ses . . ."

"Right, got it! Good work, Captain Thorne." *You always were the best, Bel.* Miles turned half away and spoke forcefully into his wrist com, demanding to be patched through to Greenlaw, or Venn, or Watts, or *somebody* in authority on Graf Station.

A ragged female voice finally replied, "Yes?"

"Sealer Greenlaw? Are you there?"

Her voice steadied. "Yes, Lord Vorkosigan? Do you have something?"

"Maybe. Bel Thorne reports the ba said that it hid the bio-bomb somewhere in the Minchenko Auditorium. Possibly behind some lights."

Her breath drew in. "Good. We'll concentrate our trained searchers in there."

"Bel also thinks the bomb was something the ba rigged itself, recently. It may have made purchases on Graf Station in the persona of Ker Dubauer that could give you a clue as to how many it could have devised."

"Ah! Right! I'll get Venn's people on it."

"Note, Bel's in pretty bad shape. Also, the ba could have been lying. Get back to me when you know something."

"Yes. Yes. Thank you." Hastily, she cut her com. It occurred to Miles to wonder if she was locked down in protective bio-isolation right now too, as he was about to be, trying to shape the critical moment at a similar frustrating remove.

"Basti'd," Bel muttered. "Paralyzed me. Put me in s' damn bod pod. Tol' me. *Then* zipped it up. Left me to die, 'magining . . . Knew . . . it knew about Nicol 'n me. Saw my vid cube. Where's m' vid cube?"

"Nicol is safe," Miles assured Bel. Well, as much as any quaddie on Graf Station at the moment—if not safe, at least *warned*. Vid cube? Oh, the little imager full of Bel's hypothetical children. "Your vid cube is put away safely." Miles had no idea if this last was true or not—the cube might be still in Bel's pocket, destroyed with the herm's contaminated clothes, or stolen by the ba. But the assertion gave Bel ease. The exhausted herm's eyes closed again, and its breathing steadied.

In a few hours, I'm going to look like that.

Then you'd better not waste any time now, eh?

With a vast distaste, Miles suffered a hovering tech to help him off with his pressure suit and underwear—to be taken away and incinerated, Miles supposed. "If you're tying me down here, I want a comconsole set up by my bunk immediately. No, you can't have that." Miles fended off the tech, who was now trying to pry loose his com link, then paused to swallow. "And something for nausea. All right, put it around my *right* arm, then."

Horizontal was scarcely better than vertical. Miles smoothed down his own pale green tunic and gave up his left arm to the surgeon, who personally attended to piercing his vein with some medical awl that felt the size of a drinking straw. On the other side a tech pressed a hypospray against his right shoulder—a potion that would kill the dizziness and the cramping in his stomach, he hoped. But he didn't yelp until the first spurt of filtered blood returned to his body. "*Crap*, that's cold. I *hate* cold."

"Can't be helped, my Lord Auditor," Clogston murmured soothingly. "We have to lower your body temperature at least three degrees. It will buy time."

Miles hunched, uncomfortably reminded that they didn't have a fix for this yet. He stifled a gush of terror, escaping under pressure from the place he'd kept it locked for the past hours. Not for one second would he allow himself to believe that there was no cure to be had, that this bio-shit would drag him under and this time he wouldn't come back up . . . "Where's Roic?" He raised his right wrist to his lips. "Roic?"

"I'm in the outer chamber, m'lord. I'm afraid to carry this triggering device through the bio-barrier till we're sure it's disarmed."

"Right, good thinking. One of those fellows out there should be the bomb disposal tech I requested. Find him and give it to him. Then ride herd on the interrogation for me, will you?"

"Yes, m'lord."

"Captain Clogston."

The doctor glanced down from where he fiddled with the jury-rigged blood filter. "My lord?"

"The moment you have a medtech—no, a doctor. The moment you have some qualified men free, send them to the cargo hold where the ba has the replicators. I want them to run samples, try to see if the ba has contaminated or poisoned them in any way. Then make sure the equipment's all running all right. It's *very important* that the haut infants all be kept alive and well."

"Yes, Lord Vorkosigan."

If the haut babies were inoculated with the same vile parasites presently rioting through his own body, might the replicators' temperature be turned down to chill them all, and slow the disease process? Or would such cold stress the infants, damage them . . . he was borrowing trouble, reasoning in advance of his data. A trained agent, conditioned to the correct disconnect between action and imagination, might have performed such an inoculation, cleaning up every bit of incriminating high-haut DNA before abandoning the scene. But this ba was an amateur. This ba had another sort of conditioning altogether. *Yes, but that conditioning must have gone very wrong somehow, or this ba wouldn't have got this far . . .*

Miles added as Clogston turned away, "And give me word on the condition of the pilot, Corbeau, as soon as you have it." The retreating suited figure raised a hand in acknowledgment.

In a few minutes, Roic entered the ward; he had doffed the bulky powered work suit, and now wore more comfortable military-issue Level Three biotainer garb.

"How's it going over there?"

Roic ducked his head. "Not well, m'lord. T' ba has gone into some sort of strange mental state. Raving, but nothing to the point, and the intelligence fellows say its physiological state is all out of kilter as well. They're trying to stabilize it."

"The ba *must* be kept alive!" Miles struggled half-up, a vision of having himself carried into the next chamber to take charge running through his head. "We have to get it back to Cetaganda. To prove Barrayar is innocent."

He sank back and eyed the humming device filtering his blood hung by his left side. Pulling out parasites, yes, but also draining the energy the parasites had stolen from him to create themselves. Siphoning off the mental edge he desperately needed right now.

He remarshaled his scattering thoughts, and explained to Roic the news Bel had imparted. "Return to the interrogation room and give them the word on this development. See if they can get any cross-confirmation on the hiding place in the Minchenko Auditorium, and especially see if they can get anything that would suggest if there is more than one device. Or not."

"Right." Roic nodded. He glanced over Miles's growing array of medical attachments. "By the way, m'lord. Had you happened to mention your seizure disorder to the surgeon yet?"

"Not yet. There hasn't been time."

"Right." Roic's lips screwed up thoughtfully, in an editorial fashion that Miles chose to ignore. "I'll see to it then, shall I, m'lord?"

Miles hunched. "Yeah, yeah."

Roic trod out of the ward on both his errands.

The remote comconsole arrived; a tech swung a tray across Miles's lap, laid the vid plate frame upon it, and helped him sit mostly up, with extra pillows at his back. He was starting to shiver again. All right, good, the device was

Barrayaran military issue, not just scavenged from the *Idris*. He had a securable visual link again now. He entered codes.

Vorpatril's face was a moment or two coming up; riding herd on all this from the *Prince Xav*'s tactics room, the admiral no doubt had a few other demands on his attention at the moment. He appeared at last with a, "*Yes, my lord!*" His eyes searched the image of Miles on his vid display. He apparently was not reassured by the view. His jaw tightened in dismay. "Are you all—" he began, but edited this fatuity on the fly to, "How bad is it?"

"I can still talk. And while I can still talk, I need to record some orders. While we're waiting on the quaddies' search for the bio-bomb—are you following the latest on that?" Miles brought the admiral up to the moment on Bel's intelligence about the Minchenko Auditorium, and went on. "Meanwhile, I want you to select and prepare the fastest ship in your escort that has a sufficient capacity for the load it's going to be carrying. Which will be me, Portmaster Thorne, a medical team, our prisoner the ba and guards, Guppy the Jacksonian smuggler if I can pry him out of quaddie hands, and a thousand working uterine replicators. With qualified medical attendants."

"And me," put in Ekaterin's voice firmly from offsides. Her face leaned briefly into range of Vorpatril's vid pickup, and she frowned at him. She'd seen her husband looking like death on a plate more than once before, though; perhaps she wouldn't be as disturbed as the admiral clearly was. Having an Imperial Auditor get melted to steaming slime on his watch would be a notable black mark, not that Vorpatril's career wasn't in a shambles over this episode already.

"My courier ship will travel in convoy, carrying Lady Vorkosigan." He cut across Ekaterin's beginning objection: "I may well need *one* spokesperson along who isn't in medical quarantine."

She settled back with a dubious "Hm."

"But I want to make damned sure we're not impeded by any hassles along the way, Admiral, so have your fleet department start working immediately on our passage clearances in all the local space polities we're going to have to cross. Speed. Speed is of the essence. I want to get away the moment we're sure the ba's devil-device has been cleared from Graf Station. At least with us carrying all these biohazards, no one is going to want to stop and board us for inspections."

"To Komarr, my lord? Or Sergyar?"

"No. Calculate the shortest possible jump route directly to Rho Ceta."

Vorpatril's head jerked back in startlement. "If the orders I received from Sector Five HQ mean what we think, you'll hardly get passage *there*. Reception by plasma fire and fusion shells the moment you pop out of the wormhole, would be what I'd expect."

"*Unpack*, Miles," Ekaterin's voice drifted in.

He grinned briefly at the familiar exasperation in her voice. "By the time we arrive there, I will have arranged our clearances with the Cetagandan Empire." *I hope.* Or else they were all going to be in more trouble than Miles ever wanted to imagine. "Barrayar is bringing their kidnapped haut babies back to them. On the end of a long stick. I get to be the stick."

"Ah," said Vorpatril, his gray brows rising in speculation.

"Give a head's-up to my ImpSec courier pilot. I plan to start the moment we have everyone and everything transferred aboard. You can start on the everything part now."

"Understood, my lord." Vorpatril rose and vanished out of vid range. Ekaterin moved back in, and smiled at him.

"Well, we're making some progress at last," Miles said to her, with what he hoped seemed good cheer, and not suppressed hysteria.

Her smile twisted up on one side. Her eyes were warm, though. "Some progress? What do you call an avalanche, I wonder?"

"No arctic metaphors, please. I'm cold enough. If the medicos get this . . . infestation under control en route, perhaps they'll clear me for visitors. We'll want the courier ship later, anyway."

A medtech appeared, drew a blood sample from the outbound tube, added an IV pump to the array, raised the bed rails, then bent and began tying down the left arm board.

"Hey," objected Miles. "How am I supposed to unravel all this mess with one hand tied behind my back?"

"Captain Clogston's orders, m'lord Auditor." Firmly, the tech finished securing his arm. "Standard procedure for seizure risk."

Miles gritted his teeth.

"Your seizure-stimulator is with the rest of your things aboard the *Kestrel*," Ekaterin observed dispassionately. "I'll find it and send it across as soon as I transfer back aboard."

Prudently, Miles limited his response to, "Thank you. Check back with me before you dispatch it—there may be a few other things I'll need. Let me know when you're safely aboard."

"Yes, love." She touched her fingers to her lips and held them up, passing them through his image before her. He returned the gesture. His heart chilled a little as her image winked out. How long before they dared touch flesh to warm flesh again? *What if it's never . . . ? Damn, but I'm cold.*

The tech departed. Miles hunched down in his bed. He supposed it would be futile to ask for blankets. He imagined little tiny bio-bombs set to go off all through his body, sparking like a Midsummer fireworks display seen at a distance out over the river in Vorbarr Sultana, cascading to a grand, lethal finale. He imagined his flesh decomposing into corrosive ooze while he yet lived in it. He needed to think about something else.

Two empires, both alike in indignation, maneuvering for position, massing deadly force behind a dozen wormhole jumps, each jump a point of contact, conflict, catastrophe . . . that was no better.

A thousand almost-ripe haut fetuses, turning in their little chambers, unaware of the distance and dangers they had passed through, and the hazards still to come—*how* soon would they have to be decanted? The picture of a thousand squalling infants dropped upon a few harried Barrayaran military medicos was almost enough to make him smile, if only he wasn't so primed to start screaming.

Bel's breath, in the next bunk, was thick and labored.

Speed. For every reason, speed. Had he set in motion everyone and everything that he could? He ran down checklists in his aching head, lost his place, tried again. How long had it been since he'd slept? The minutes crawled by with tortuous slowness. He imagined them as snails, hundreds of little snails with Cetagandan clan markings coloring their shells, going past in procession, leaving slime-trails of lethal biocontamination . . . a crawling infant, little Helen Natalia, cooing and reaching for one of the pretty, poisonous creatures, and he was all tied up and pierced with tubes and couldn't get across the room fast enough to stop her . . .

A bleep from his lap link, thank God, snapped him awake before he could find out where *that* nightmare was going. He was still pierced with tubes, though. What time was it? He was losing track altogether. His usual mantra—*I can sleep when I'm dead*—seemed a little too apropos.

An image formed over the vid plate. "Sealer Greenlaw!" Good news, bad news? *Good.* Her lined face was radiant with relief.

"We found it," she said. "It's been contained."

Miles blew out his breath in a long exhalation. "Yes. Excellent. Where?"

"In Minchenko Auditorium, just as the portmaster said. Attached to the wall in a stage light cell. It did seem to have been put together hastily, but it was deadly clever for all of that. Simple and clever. It was scarcely more than a little sealed plastic balloon, filled with some sort of nutrient solution, my people tell me. And a tiny charge, and the electronic trigger for it. The ba had stuck it to the wall with ordinary packing tape, and sprayed it with a little flat black paint. No one would notice it in the ordinary course of events, not even if they had been working on the lights, unless they put a hand right on it."

"Homemade, then. On the spot?"

"It would seem so. The electronics, which were off-the-shelf items—and the tape, for that matter—are all quaddie-make. They match with the purchases recorded to Dubauer's credit chit the evening after the attack in the hostel lobby. All the parts are accounted for. There seems to have been only the one device." She ran her upper hands through her silver hair, massaging her scalp wearily, and squeezed shut eyes bounded beneath by little dark half-moons of shadow.

"That . . . fits with the timetable as I see it," said Miles. "Right up until Guppy popped up with his rivet gun, the ba evidently thought it had gotten away clean with its stolen cargo. And with Solian's death. Everything calm and perfect. Its plan was to pass through Quaddiespace quietly, without leaving a trace. It would not have had any reason before then to rig such a device. But from that botched murder attempt on, it was running scared, having to improvise rapidly. Curious bit of foresight, though. It can't have *planned* to be trapped on the *Idris* the way it was, surely."

She shook her head. "It planned something. The explosive charge had two leads to its trigger. One was a receiver for the signal device the ba had in its pocket. The other was a simple sound sensor. Set to a fairly high decibel level. That of an auditorium full of applause, for example."

Miles's teeth snapped shut. *Oh, yes.* "Thus masking the pop of the charge, and blowing out contaminant to the maximum number of people at once." The vision was instant, and horrifying.

"So we think. People come in from other stations all over Quaddiespace to see performances of the Minchenko Ballet. The contagion could have spread back out with them through half the system before it became apparent."

"Is it the same—no, it can't be what the ba gave to me and Bel. Can it? Was it lethal, or merely something debilitating, or what?"

"The sample is in the hands of our medical people now. We should know soon."

"So the ba set up its bio-bomb . . . after it knew real Cetagandan agents would be following, after it knew it would be compelled to abandon the utterly incriminating replicators and their contents . . . I'll *bet* it put the bomb together and slapped it out there in a hurry." Maybe it was revenge. Revenge upon the quaddies for all the forced delays that had so wrecked the ba's perfect plan . . . ? By Bel's report, the ba was not above such motivations; the Cetagandan had displayed a cruel humor, and a taste for bifurcating strategies. If the ba hadn't run into the troubles on the *Idris*, would it have retrieved the device, or would it simply have quietly left the bomb behind to go off on its own? Well, if Miles's own men couldn't get the whole story out of their prisoner, he damned well knew some people who could.

"Good," he breathed. "We can go now."

Greenlaw's weary eyes opened. "What?"

"I mean—with your permission, Madame Sealer." He adjusted his vid pickup to a wider angle, to take in his sinister medical setting. Too late to adjust the color balance toward a more sickly green. Also, possibly, redundant. Greenlaw's mouth turned down in dismay, looking at him.

"Admiral Vorpatril has received an extremely alarming military communiqué from home . . ." Swiftly, Miles explained his deduction about the connection of suddenly increased tensions between Barrayar and its dangerous Cetagandan neighbor to the recent events on Graf Station. He talked carefully around the tactical use of trade fleet escorts as rapid-deployment forces, although he doubted the sealer missed the implications.

"My plan is to get myself, the ba, the replicators, and as much evidence as I can amass of the ba's crimes back to Rho Ceta, to present to the Cetagandan government, to clear Barrayar of whatever accusation of collusion is driving this crisis. As fast as possible. Before some hothead—on either side—does something that, to put it bluntly, makes

Admiral Vorpatril's late actions on Graf Station look like a model of restraint and wisdom."

That won a snort from her; he forged on. "While the ba and Russo Gupta both committed crimes on Graf, they committed crimes in the Cetagandan and Barrayaran empires first. I submit we have clear prior claim. And worse—their mere continued presence on Graf Station is dangerous, because, I promise you, sooner or later their furious Cetagandan victims will be following them up. I think you've had enough of a taste of their medicine to make the prospect of a swarm of *real* Cetagandan agents descending upon you unwelcome indeed. Cede us both criminals, and any retribution will chase after us instead."

"Hm," she said. "And your impounded trade fleet? Your fines?"

"Let . . . on my authority, I am willing to transfer owner-ship of the *Idris* to Graf Station, in lieu of all fines and expenses." He added prudently, "As is."

Her eyes sprang wide. She said indignantly, "The ship's *contaminated.*"

"Yes. So we can't take it anywhere anyway. Cleaning it up could be a nice little training exercise for your biocontrol people." He decided not to mention the holes. "Even with that expense, you'll come out ahead. I'm afraid the passen-gers' insurance will have to eat the value of any of their cargo that can't be cleared. But I'm really hopeful that most of it will not need to be quarantined. And you can let the rest of the fleet go."

"And your men in our detention cells?"

"You let one of them out. Are you sorry? Can you not allow Lieutenant Corbeau's courage to redeem his com-rades? That has to be one of the bravest acts I've ever witnessed, him walking naked and knowing into horror to save Graf Station."

"That . . . yes. That was remarkable," she conceded. "By any people's standards." She regarded him thoughtfully. "You went in after the ba too."

"Mine doesn't count," Miles said automatically. "I was already . . ." he cut the word, *dead*. He was not, dammit, dead yet. "I was already infected."

Her brows rose in bemused curiosity. "And if you hadn't been, what would you have done?"

"Well . . . it *was* the tactical moment. I have a kind of gift for timing, you see."

"And for doubletalk."

"That, too. But the ba was just my job."

"Has anyone ever told you that you are quite mad?"

"Now and then," he admitted. Despite everything, a slow smile turned his lips. "Not so much since I was appointed an Imperial Auditor, though. Useful, that."

She snorted, very softly. Softening? Miles trotted out the next barrage. "My plea is humanitarian, too. It is my belief—my hope—that the Cetagandan haut ladies will have some treatment up their capacious sleeves for their own product. I propose to take Portmaster Thorne with us—at our expense—to share the cure that I now so desperately seek for myself. It's only justice. The herm was, in a sense, in my service when it took this harm. In my work gang, if you like."

"Huh. You Barrayarans do look after your own, at least. One of your few saving graces."

Miles opened his hands in an equally ambiguous acknowledgment of this mixed compliment. "Thorne and I both now labor under a deadline that waits on no committee debate, I'm afraid, and no one's permission. The present palliative," he gestured awkwardly at the blood filter, "buys a little time. As of this moment, no one knows if it will buy enough."

She rubbed her brow, as if it ached. "Yes, certainly . . . certainly you must . . . oh, hell." She took a breath. "All right. Take your prisoners and your evidence and the whole damned lot—and Thorne—and go."

"And Vorpatril's men in detention?"

"Them, too. Take them *all* away. Your ships can all go, bar the *Idris*." Her nose wrinkled in distaste. "But we will discuss the residue of your fines and expenses further, after the ship is evaluated by our inspectors. Later. Your government can send someone for the task. Not you, by preference."

"*Thank* you, Madame Sealer," Miles sang in relief. He cut the com, and collapsed back on his pillows. The ward seemed to be spinning around his head, very slowly, in short jerks. It wasn't, he decided after a moment, a problem with the room.

Captain Clogston, who had been waiting by the door for the Auditor to complete this high-level negotiation, advanced to glower at his cobbled-together blood filter some more. He then transferred his glower to Miles. "Seizure disorder, eh? I'm glad *someone* told me."

"Yes, well, we wouldn't want you to mistake it for an exotic new Cetagandan symptom. It's pretty routine. If it happens, don't panic. I come up on my own in about five minutes. Usually gives me a sort of hangover, afterwards, not that I'd be able to tell the difference at the moment. Never mind. What can you tell me about Lieutenant Corbeau?"

"We checked the ba's hypospray. It was filled with water."

"Ah! Good! I thought so." Miles smiled in wolfish satisfaction. "Can you pronounce him clear of bio-horrors, then?"

"Given that he's been running around this plague-ship bare-ass naked, not until we're sure we have identified all possible hazards that the ba might have released. But nothing came up on the first blood and tissue samples we took."

A hopeful—Miles tried not to think, *overly optimistic*—sign. "Can you send the lieutenant in to me? Is it safe? I want to talk to him."

"We now believe that what you and the herm have isn't virulently contagious through ordinary contact. Once we're sure the ship's clear of anything else, we'll all be able to get out of these suits, which will be a relief. Although the parasites might transfer sexually—we'll have to study that."

"I don't like Corbeau *that* much. Send him in, then."

Clogston gave Miles an odd look, and moved off. Miles wasn't sure if the captain had missed the feeble joke, or merely considered it too feeble to merit a response. But that *transfer sexually* theory kicked off a whole new cascade of unpleasant, unwelcome speculation in Miles's mind. What if the medicos found they could keep him alive indefinitely, but not get rid of the damned things? Would he never be able to touch any more of Ekaterin than her holovid image for the rest of his life . . . ? It also suggested a new set of questions to put to Guppy about his recent travels—well, the quaddie doctors were competent, and receiving copies of the Barrayarans' medical downloads; their epidemiologists were doubtless already on it.

Corbeau pushed through the bio-barriers. He was now somewhat desultorily arrayed in a disposable mask and gloves, in addition to the medical tunic and some patient slippers. Miles sat up, pushed away his tray, and unobtrusively twitched open his own tunic, letting the paling spiderweb of old needle-grenade scars silently suggest whatever they might to Corbeau.

"You asked for me, my Lord Auditor?" Corbeau ducked his head in a nervous jerk.

"Yes." Miles scratched his nose thoughtfully with his one free hand. "Well, hero. That was a very good career move you just made."

Corbeau hunched a little, mulishly. "I didn't do it for my career. Or for Barrayar. I did it for Graf Station, and the quaddies, and Garnet Five."

"And glad I am of it. Nevertheless, people will doubtless be wanting to pin gold stars on you. Cooperate with me, and I won't make you receive them in the costume you were wearing when you earned them."

Corbeau gave him a baffled, wary look.

What was the matter with all his jokes today, anyway? Flat, flatter, flattest. Maybe he was violating some sort of unwritten Auditor protocol, and messing up everyone else's lines.

The lieutenant said, in a notably uninviting voice, "What do you want me to do? My lord."

"More urgent concerns—to put it mildly—are going to compel me to leave Quaddiespace before my assigned diplomatic mission is quite complete. Nevertheless, with the true cause and course of our recent disasters here finally dragged out into the light, what follows should be easier." *Besides, there's nothing like the threat of imminent death to force one to delegate.* "It is very plain that Barrayar is overdue to have a full-time diplomatic consulate officer assigned to the Union of Free Habitats. A bright young man who . . ." *is shacked up with a quaddie girl,* no, *married to,* wait, that wasn't what they called it here, *is partners with,* yes, very likely, but it hadn't happened yet. Although Corbeau was thrice a fool if he didn't grab this opportunity to fix things with Garnet Five for good and all. "Likes quaddies," Miles continued smoothly, "and has earned both their respect and gratitude by his personal valor, and has no objection to a long assignment away from home—two years, was it? Yes, two years. Such a young man might be particularly well placed to argue effectively for Barrayar's interests in Quaddiespace. In my personal opinion."

Miles couldn't tell if Corbeau's mouth was open, behind his medical mask. His eyes had grown rather wide.

"I can't imagine," said Miles, "that Admiral Vorpatril would have any objection to releasing you to this detached duty. Or at any rate, to not having to deal with you in his command structure after all these . . . complex events. Not that I'd planned to give him a Betan vote in my Auditorial decrees, mind you."

"I . . . I don't know anything about diplomacy. I was trained as a pilot."

"If you went through military jump pilot training, you have already shown that you can study hard, learn fast, and make confident, rapid decisions affecting other people's lives. Objection overruled. You will, of course, have a consulate budget to hire expert staff to assist you in specialized problems, in law, in the economics of port fees, in trade matters, whatever. But you'll be expected to learn enough as you go to judge whether their advice is good for the Imperium. And if, at the end of two years, you do decide to muster out and stay here, the experience would give you a major boost into Quaddiespace private-sector employment. If there's any problem with all this from your point of view—or from Garnet Five's, very level-headed woman, by the way, don't let her get away—it's not apparent to me."

"I'll"—Corbeau swallowed—"think about it. My lord."

"Excellent." And not readily stampeded, either, good. "Do so." Miles smiled and waved dismissal; warily, Corbeau withdrew. As soon as he was out of earshot, Miles murmured a code into his wrist com.

"Ekaterin, love? Where are you?"

"In my cabin on the *Prince Xav*. The nice young yeoman is getting ready to help carry my things to the shuttle. Yes, thank you, that too . . ."

"Right. I've just about cracked us loose from Quaddiespace. Greenlaw was reasonable, or at least, too exhausted to argue any more."

"She has all my sympathy. I don't think I have a functional nerve left, right now."

"Don't need your nerves, just your usual grace. The moment you can get to a comconsole, call up Garnet Five. I want to appoint that heroic young idiot Corbeau to be Barrayaran consul here, and make him clean up all this mess I have to leave in my wake. It's only fair; he certainly helped create it. Gregor *did* specifically ask that I assure that Barrayaran ships could dock here again someday. The boy is wobbling, however. So pitch it to Garnet Five, and make sure that *she* makes sure Corbeau says yes."

"Oh! What a splendid idea, love. They make a good team, I think."

"Yep. Her for beauty, and um . . . her for brains."

"And him for courage, surely. I think it might work out. I must think what to send them for a wedding present, to convey my personal thanks."

"Partnering present? I don't know, ask Nicol. Oh. Speaking of Nicol." Miles glanced aside at the sheeted figure in the next bunk. Crucial message delivered, Thorne had fallen back into what Miles hoped was sleep and not incipient coma. "I'm thinking that Bel really ought to have someone to ride along and take care of it. Or of things for it. Some kind of support trooper, anyway. I expect the Star Crèche will have a fix for their own weapon—they'd have to, lab accidents, after all." *If we get there in time.* "But this looks like something that's going to involve a certain amount of really unpleasant convalescence. I'm not exactly looking forward to it myself." *But consider the alternative . . .* "Ask her if she's willing. She could ride in the *Kestrel* with you, be some company, anyway." And if neither he nor Bel got out of this alive, mutual support.

"Certainly. I'll call her from here."

"Call me again when you're safe aboard the *Kestrel*, love." *Often and often.*

"Of course." Her voice hesitated. "Love you. Get some rest. You sound like you need it. Your voice has that down-in-a-well sound it gets when . . . There *will* be time." Determination flashed through her own audible fatigue.

"I wouldn't dare die. There's this fierce Vor lady who threatened she'd kill me if I did." He grinned weakly and cut the com.

He drowsed for a time in dizzy exhaustion, fighting the sleep that tried to overtake him, because he couldn't be sure it wasn't the ba's hell-disease gaining on him, and he might not wake up. He marked a subtle change in the sounds and voices that penetrated from the outer chamber, as the medical team switched over to evacuation-mode. In time, a tech came and took Bel away on a float pallet. In a little more time, the pallet was returned, and Clogston himself and another medtech shifted the Imperial Auditor and all his growing array of life-support trappings aboard.

One of the intelligence officers reported to Miles, during a brief delay in the outer chamber.

"We finally found the remains of Lieutenant Solian, my Lord Auditor. What there was of them. A few kilograms of . . . well. Inside a bod pod, folded up and put back in its wall locker in the corridor just outside the cargo hold where the replicators were."

"Right. Thank you. Bring it along. As is. For evidence, and for . . . the man died doing his job. Barrayar owes him . . . debt of honor. Military burial. Pension, family . . . figure it all out later . . ."

His pallet rose again, and the corridor ceilings of the *Idris* flowed past his blurred gaze for the last time.

Chapter 18

"Are we there yet?" Miles mumbled muzzily.

He blinked open eyes that were not, oddly enough, gluey and sore. The ceiling above him didn't waver and bend in his vision as though seen mirage-like through rising desert heat. Breath drawn through his flaring nostrils flowed in coolly and without clogging impediment. No phlegm. No tubes. No tubes?

The ceiling was unfamiliar. He groped for memory. Fog. Biotainered angels and devils, tormenting him; someone demanding he piss. Medical indignities, mercifully vague now. Trying to talk, to give orders, till some hypospray of darkness had shut him down.

And before that: near desperation. Sending frantic messages racing ahead of his little convoy. The return stream of days-old accounts of wormholes blockaded, outlanders interned by both sides, assets seized, ships massing, telling its own tale to Miles's mind, worse for the details. He knew too damned much about the details. *We can't have a war now, you fools! Don't you know there are children almost present?* His left arm jerked, encountering no resistance except for a smooth coverlet beneath his clutching fingers. " . . . there yet?"

Ekaterin's lovely face bent over him from the side. Not half-hidden behind biotainer gear. He feared for a moment that this was only a holovid projection, or some hallucination, but the real warm kiss of breath from her mouth, carried on a puff of laughter, reassured him of her present solidity even before his hesitant hand touched her cheek.

"Where's your mask?" he asked thickly. He heaved up on one elbow, fighting off a wave of dizziness.

He certainly wasn't in the Barrayaran military ship's crowded, utilitarian sickbay to which he'd been transferred from the *Idris*. His bed was in a small but elegantly appointed chamber that screamed of Cetagandan aesthetics, from the arrays of live plants through the serene lighting to the view out the window of a soothing seashore. Waves creamed gently up a pale sandy beach seen through strange trees casting delicate fingers of shade. Almost certainly a vid projection, since the subliminals of the atmosphere and sounds of the room also murmured *spaceship cabin* to him. He wore a loose, silky garment in subdued gray hues, only its odd accessibilities betraying it as a patient gown. Above the head of his bed, a discreet panel displayed medical readouts.

"Where *are* we? What's happening? Did we stop the war? Those replicators they found on their end—it's a trick, I know it—"

The final disaster—his speeding ships intercepting tight-beamed news from Barrayar of diplomatic talks broken off upon the discovery, in a warehouse outside Vorbarr Sultana, of a thousand empty replicators apparently stolen from the Star Crèche, their occupants gone. Supposed occupants? Even Miles hadn't been sure. A baffling night-mare of implications. The Barrayaran government had of course hotly denied any knowledge of how they came to be there, or where their contents were now. And was not believed . . .

"The ba—Guppy, I promised—all those haut babies—I've got to—"

"*You* have got to lie still." A firm hand to his chest pushed him back down. "All the most urgent matters have been taken care of."

"Who by?"

She colored faintly. "Well . . . me, mostly. Vorpatril's ship captain probably shouldn't have let me override him, tech-nically, but I decided not to point that out to him. You're a bad influence on me, love."

What? What? "How?"

"I just kept repeating your messages, and demanding they be put through to the haut Pel and ghem-General Benin. Benin was brilliant. Once he had your first dis-patches, he figured out that the replicators found in Vorbarr Sultana were decoys, smuggled out of the Star Crèche by the ba a few at a time over a year ago in prepara-tion for this." She frowned. "It was apparently a deliberate sleight of hand by the ba, meant to cause just this sort of trouble. A backup plan, in case anyone figured out that not everyone had died on the child-ship, and traced the trail as far as Komarr. It almost worked. Might have worked, if Benin hadn't been so painstaking and levelheaded. I gather that the internal political circumstances of his investigation were extremely difficult by then. He really put his reputa-tion on the line."

Possibly even his life, if Miles read between these simple lines. "All honor unto him, then."

"The military forces—theirs and ours—have all gone off alert and are standing down, now. The Cetagandans have declared it an internal, civil matter."

He eased back, vastly relieved. "Ah."

"I don't think I could have gotten through to them without the haut Pel's name." She hesitated. "And yours."

"Ours."

Her lips curved up at that. "*Lady Vorkosigan* did seem a title to conjure with. It gave both sides pause. That, and yelling the truth over and over. But I couldn't have held it together without the name."

"May I suggest that the name couldn't have held it together without you?" His free hand tightened around hers, on the coverlet. Hers tightened back.

He started up again. "Wait—shouldn't you be in biotainer gear?"

"Not any more. Lie *down*, drat it. What's the last thing you remember?"

"My last *clear* memory is of being on the Barrayaran ship about four days out from Quaddiespace. Cold."

Her smile didn't change, but her eyes grew dark with memory. "Cold is right. The blood filters fell behind, even with four of them running at once. We could see the life just *draining* out of you; your metabolism couldn't keep up, couldn't replace the resources being siphoned off even with the IVs and nutrient tubes running flat out, and multiple blood transfusions. Captain Clogston couldn't think of any other way to suppress the parasites but to put you, Bel, *and* them into stasis. A cold hibernation. The next step would have been cryofreeze."

"Oh, no. Not again . . . !"

"It was the ultimate fallback, but it wasn't needed, thank heavens. Once you and Bel were sedated and chilled enough, the parasites stopped multiplying. The captains and crews of our little convoy were very good about rushing us along as fast as was safe, or a little faster. Oh—yes, we're here; we arrived in orbit around Rho Ceta . . . yesterday, I guess it was."

Had she slept since then? Not much, Miles suspected. Her face, though cheerful now, was drawn with fatigue. He reached for it again, to lightly touch her lips with two fingers as he habitually did her holovid image.

"I remember that you wouldn't let me say good-bye to you properly," he complained.

"I figured it would give you more motivation to fight your way back to me. If only for the last word."

He snorted a laugh, and let his hand fall back to the coverlet. The artificial gravity probably wasn't turned up to two gees in this chamber, despite his arm feeling as though it were hung with lead weights. He had to admit, he didn't feel exactly . . . chipper. "What, then, am I all clear of those hell-parasites?"

Her smile returned. "All better. Well, that is, that frightening Cetagandan lady doctor the haut Pel brought with her has pronounced you cured. But you're still very debilitated. You're supposed to rest."

"Rest, I can't rest! What else is happening? Where's Bel?"

"Sh, sh. Bel's alive too. You can see Bel soon, and Nicol too. They're in a cabin just down the corridor. Bel took . . ." She frowned hesitantly. "Took more damage from this than you did, but is expected to recover, mostly. In time."

Miles didn't quite like the sound of that.

Ekaterin followed his glance around. "Right now we're aboard the haut Pel's own ship—that is, her Star Crèche ship, that she brought from Eta Ceta. The women from the Star Crèche had you and Bel carried across to treat you here. The haut ladies wouldn't let any of our men aboard to guard you, not even Armsman Roic at first, which caused the most stupid argument; I was ready to slap everybody concerned, till they finally decided that Nicol and I could come with you. Captain Clogston was very upset that he wouldn't be allowed to attend. He wanted to hold back giving them the replicators till they cooperated, but you can bet I put my foot down on *that* idea."

"Good!" And not just because Miles had wanted those little time bombs off Barrayaran hands at the earliest possible instant. He could not imagine a more psychologically repugnant or diplomatically disastrous ploy, at this late hour. "I remember trying to calm down that idiot Guppy, who was hysterical about being carried back to the Cetagandans. Making promises ... I hope I wasn't lying through my chattering teeth. Was it true he was still harboring a reservoir of parasites? Did they fix him, too? Or ... not? I swore on my name that if he'd cooperate in testifying, Barrayar would protect him, but I expected to be conscious when we arrived...."

"Yes, the Cetagandan doctor treated him, too. She claims the latent residue of parasites wouldn't have fired up again, but really, I don't think she was sure. Apparently, no one has ever survived this bioweapon before. I gathered the impression that the Star Crèche wants Guppy for research purposes even more than Cetagandan Imperial Security does for criminal charges, and if they have to arm wrestle for him, the Star Crèche will win. Our men did carry out your order; he's still being held on the Barrayaran ship. Some of the Cetagandans aren't too pleased about that, but I told them they'd have to deal with you on the subject."

He hesitated, and cleared his throat. "Um ... I also seem to remember recording some messages. To my parents.

And Mark and Ivan. And to little Aral and Helen. I hope you didn't . . . you didn't send them off already, did you?"

"I set them aside."

"Oh, good. I'm afraid I wasn't very coherent by then."

"Perhaps not," she admitted. "But they were very moving, I thought."

"I put it off too long, I guess. You can erase them now."

"Never," she said, quite firmly.

"But I was babbling."

"Nevertheless, I'm going to save them." She stroked his hair, and her smile twisted. "Perhaps they can be recycled someday. After all . . . next time, you might not have time."

The door to the chamber slid aside, and two tall, willowy women entered. Miles recognized the senior of them at once.

The haut Pel Navarr, Consort of Eta Ceta, was perhaps the number-two woman in the strange secret hierarchy of the Star Crèche, after the Empress, haut Rian Degtiar herself. In appearance, she was unchanged from when Miles had first met her a decade ago, except perhaps for her hairstyle. Her immensely long, honey-blond hair was gathered today into a dozen braids, hanging from a level running around the back of her head from one ear to the other, their decorated ends swinging around her ankles along with her skirt hem and draperies. Miles wondered if the unsettling, faintly Medusa-like effect was intended. Her skin was still pale and perfect, but she could not, even for an instant, be mistaken for young. Too much calm, too much control, too much cool irony . . .

Outside the innermost sanctuaries of the Celestial Garden, the high haut women normally moved in the privacy and protection of personal force bubbles, screened from unworthy eyes. The fact that she strode here unveiled was alone enough to tell Miles that he now lay in a Star Crèche reserve. The dark-haired woman beside her was old enough to have streaks of silver in the hair looping down her back among her long robes, and skin that, while unblemished, was distinctly softened with age. Chill, deferential, unknown to Miles.

"Lord Vorkosigan." The haut Pel gave him a relatively cordial nod. "I am pleased to find you awake. Are you quite yourself again?"

Why, who was I before? He was afraid he could guess. "I think so."

"It was quite a surprise to me that we should meet again this way, although not, under the circumstances, an unwelcome one."

Miles cleared his throat. "It was all a surprise to me, too. Your babies in their replicators—you have them back? Are they all right?"

"My people completed their examinations last night. All seems to be well with them, despite their horrific adventures. I'm sorry that the same was not so for you."

She gave a nod to her companion; the woman proved to be a physician, who, with a few brusque murmurs, completed a brief medical examination of their Barrayaran guest. Signing off her work, Miles guessed. His leading questions about the bioengineered parasites met polite evasion, and then Miles wondered if she were physician—or ordnance designer. Or veterinarian, except that most veterinarians he'd met showed signs of actually liking their patients.

Ekaterin was more determined. "Can you give me any idea of what long-term side-effects we should watch for from this unfortunate exposure, for the Lord Auditor and Portmaster Thorne?"

The woman motioned for Miles to refasten his garment, and turned to speak over his head. "Your *husband*," she made the term sound utterly alien, in her mouth, "does suffer some muscular and circulatory micro-scarring. Muscle tone should recover gradually over time to near his prior levels. However, added to his earlier cryo-trauma, I would expect greater chance of circulatory mishaps later in his life. Although as short-lived as you people are, perhaps the few decades difference in life expectancy will not seem significant."

Quite the reverse, madam. Strokes, thromboses, blood clots, aneurysms, Miles supposed was what this translated to. Oh, joy. Just add them to the list, along with needler guns, sonic grenades, plasma fire, and nerve disruptor beams. And hot rivets and hard vacuum.

And seizures. So, what interesting synergies might be expected when this circulatory micro-scarring crossed paths with his seizure disorder? Miles decided to save that question for his own physicians, later. They could use a challenge. He was going to be a damned research project, again. Military as well as medical, he realized with a chill.

The haut woman continued to Ekaterin, "The Betan suffered notably more internal damage. Full recovery of muscle tone may never occur, and the herm will need to be on guard against circulatory stress of all kinds. A low- or zero-gravity environment might be the safest for it during its convalescence. I gathered from its partner, the quaddie female, that this may actually be easy to provide."

"Whatever Bel needs will be arranged," Miles vowed. For such a debilitating injury in the Emperor's service, it shouldn't even take an Imperial Auditor to get ImpSec off Bel's neck, and maybe rustle up a little medical pension in the bargain.

The haut Pel gave a tiny jerk of her chin. The physician favored the planetary consort with an obeisant bow, and excused herself.

Pel turned back to Miles. "As soon as you feel sufficiently recovered, Lord Auditor Vorkosigan, ghem-General Benin begs the opportunity to speak with you."

"Ah! Dag Benin's here? Good! I want to talk to him, too. Does he have the ba in his custody yet? Has it been made crystal clear that Barrayar was an innocent dupe in your ba's illicit travels?"

Pel replied, "The ba was of the Star Crèche; the ba has been returned to the Star Crèche. It is an internal matter, although we are, of course, grateful to ghem-General Benin for his assistance dealing with any persons outside our purview who may have aided the ba in its . . . mad flight."

So, the haut ladies had their stray back. Miles suppressed a slight twinge of pity for the ba. Pel's quelling tone of voice did not invite further questions from outlander barbarians. Tough. Pel was the most venturesome of the planetary consorts, but his likelihood of ever getting her alone, face-to-face, after this moment was slight, and her likelihood of discussing the matter frankly in front of anyone else even slighter.

He forged on. "I finally deduced the ba must be a renegade, and not, as I'd first thought, an agent of the Star Crèche. I'm most curious about the mechanics of this bizarre kidnapping. Guppy—the Jacksonian smuggler, Russo Gupta—could only give me an exterior view of events, and that only from his first point of contact, when the ba off-loaded the replicators from what I assume was the annual child-ship to Rho Ceta, yes?"

Pel inhaled, but conceded stiffly, "Yes. The crime was long planned and prepared, it now appears. The ba slew the

Consort of Rho Ceta, her handmaidens, and the crew of the ship by poison just after their last jump. They were all dead by the time of the rendezvous. It set the ship's auto-navigation to take the vessel into the sun of the system thereafter. To the ba's credit, this was intended as a befitting pyre, of sorts," she conceded grudgingly.

Given his prior exposure to the arcana of haut funeral practices, Miles could almost follow this evident point in the prisoner's favor without his brain cramping. Almost. But Pel spoke of the ba's intention as fact, not conjecture; therefore, the haut ladies had already had more luck in their interrogation of the deranged ba in one night than Miles's security people had gained on their whole voyage here. *Luck, I suspect, has nothing to do with it.* "I thought the ba should have been carrying a greater variety of bio-weapons, if it had any time to loot the child-ship before the vessel was abandoned and destroyed."

Pel was normally rather sunny, as haut planetary consorts went, but this elicited a freezing frown. "*These* matters are *altogether* not for discussion outside the Star Crèche."

"Ideally, no. But unfortunately, your . . . private items managed to travel quite a way outside the Star Crèche indeed. As I can personally testify. They became a source of very public concern for us, when apprehending the ba on Graf Station. At the time I left there, no one was certain if we'd identified and neutralized every contagion, or not."

Reluctantly, Pel admitted, "The ba had planned to steal the complete array. But the haut lady in charge of the consort's . . . supplies, although dying, managed to destroy them before her death. As was her duty." Pel's eyes narrowed. "*She* will be remembered among us."

The dark-haired woman's opposite number, perhaps? Did the chilly physician guard a similar arsenal on Pel's behalf, perhaps aboard this very ship? *Complete array*, eh. Miles filed that tacit admission silently away, for later sharing with ImpSec's highest echelons, and swiftly redirected the conversation.

"But what was the ba actually trying to do? Was it acting alone? If it was, how did it defeat its loyalty programming?"

"That is an internal matter, too," she repeated darkly.

"Well, I'll tell you *my* guesses," Miles burbled on, before she could turn away and end the exchange. "I believe this ba to be very closely related to Emperor Fletchir Giaja, and therefore, to his late mother. I'm guessing this ba was one of the old Dowager Empress Lisbet's close confidants during her reign. Her bio-treason, her plan to split the haut into competing subgroups, was defeated after her death—"

"Not *treason*," haut Pel objected faintly. "As such."

"Unsanctioned unilateral redesign, then. For some reason, this ba was not purged with the others of her inner cadre after her death—or maybe it was, I don't know. Demoted, perhaps? But anyway, I'm guessing this whole escapade was some sort of misguided effort to complete its dead mistress's—or mother's—vision. Am I close?"

The haut Pel eyed him with extreme distaste. "Close enough. It is truly done now, in any case. The emperor will be pleased with you—again. Some token of his gratitude may well be forthcoming at the child-ship landing ceremonies tomorrow, to which you and your lady-wife are invited. The first outlanders—ever—to be so honored."

Miles waved aside this little distraction. "I'd trade all the honors for some scrap of understanding."

Pel snorted. "You *haven't* changed, have you? Still insatiably curious. To a fault," she added pointedly.

Ekaterin smiled dryly.

Miles ignored Pel's hint. "Bear with me. I don't think I've quite got it, yet. I suspect the haut—and the ba—are not so post-human yet as to be beyond self-deception, all the more subtle for their subtlety. I saw the ba's face, when I destroyed that freezer case of genetic samples in front of it. Something shattered. Some last, desperate . . . something." He had slain men's bodies, and bore the mark, and knew it. He did not think he'd ever before slain a soul, yet left the body breathing, bereft and accusing. *I have to understand this.*

Pel was clearly not pleased to go on, but she understood the depth of a debt that could not be paid off with such trivialities as medals and ceremonies. "The ba, it seems," she said slowly, "desired more than Lisbet's vision. It planned a new empire—with itself as both emperor *and* empress. It stole the haut children of Rho Ceta not just as a core population for its planned new society, but as . . . mates. Consorts. Aspiring to even more than Fletchir Giaja's genetic place, which, while part of the goal of haut, does not imagine itself the whole. Hubris," she sighed. "Madness."

"In other words," breathed Miles, "the ba wanted children. In the only way it could . . . conceive."

Ekaterin's hand, which had drifted to his shoulder, tightened.

"Lisbet . . . should not have told it so much," said Pel. "She made a pet of this ba. Treated it almost as a *child*, instead of a servitor. Hers was a powerful personality, but not always . . . wise. Perhaps . . . self-indulgent in her old age, as well."

Yes—the ba was Fletchir Giaja's sibling, perhaps the Cetagandan emperor's near-clone. Elder sibling. Test run, and the test judged successful—and decades of observant service in the Celestial Garden thereafter, with the question always hovering—so why was not the ba, instead of its brother, given all that honor, power, wealth, fertility?

"One last question. If you will. What was the ba's name?"

Pel's lips tightened. "It shall be nameless now. And forevermore."

Erased. *Let the punishment fit the crime.*

Miles shivered.

The luxurious lift van banked over the palace of the Imperial Governor of Rho Ceta, the sprawling complex shimmering in the night. The vehicle began to drop into the vast dark garden, laced with veins of lights along its roads and paths, which lay to the east of the buildings. Miles stared in fascination out his window as they swooped down, then up over a small range of hills, trying to guess if the landscape was natural, or artificially carved out of Rho Ceta's surface. Partly carved, at any rate, for on the opposite side of the rise a grassy bowl of an amphitheater sheltered in the slope, overlooking a silky black lake a kilometer across. Beyond the hills on the lake's other side, Rho Ceta's capital city made the night sky glow amber.

The amphitheater was lit only by dim, glowing globes lavishly spread across its width: a thousand haut lady force bubbles, set to mourning white, damped to the barest visible luminosity. Among them, other pale figures moved softly as ghosts. The view turned from his sight as the driver of the van swung it about and brought it down to a gentle landing a few meters inward from the lake shore at one edge of the amphitheater.

The van's internal lighting brightened just a little, in red wavelengths designed to help maintain the passengers' dark adaptation. In the aisle across from Miles and Ekaterin, ghem-General Benin turned from his window. It was hard to read his expression beneath the formalized swirls of black-and-white face paint that marked him as an Imperial ghem-officer, but Miles took it for pensive. In the red light, his uniform glowed like fresh blood.

All in all, and even taking into account his sudden close personal introduction to Star Crèche bioweapons, Miles wasn't sure if he'd have cared to trade recent nightmares with Benin. The past weeks had been exhausting for the senior officer of the Celestial Garden's internal security. The child-ship, carrying Star Crèche personnel who were his special charge, vanishing en route without a trace; garbled reports leaking back from Guppy's scrambled trail hinting not only at breathtaking theft, but possible biocontamination from the Crèche's most secret stores; the disappearance of that trail into the heart of an enemy empire.

No wonder that by the time he had arrived in Rho Cetan orbit last night to interrogate Miles in person—with exquisite courtesy, to be sure—he'd looked as tired, even under the face paint, as Miles felt. Their contest for the possession of Russo Gupta had been brief. Miles certainly sympathized with Benin's strong desire, with the ba plucked from his hands by the Star Crèche, for *someone* to take his frustrations out on—but, first, Miles had given his Vor word, and secondly, he discovered, he could apparently do no wrong on Rho Ceta this week.

Nevertheless, Miles wondered where to drop Guppy when this was all over. Housing him in a Barrayaran jail was a useless expense to the Imperium. Turning him loose back on Jackson's Whole was an invitation for him to return to his old haunts, and employment—no benefit to the neighbors, and a temptation to Cetagandan vengeance. He could think of one other nicely distant place to deposit a person of such speckled background and erratic talents, but was it fair to do that to Admiral Quinn . . . ? Bel had laughed, evilly, at the suggestion, till it had to stop to breathe.

Despite Rho Ceta's key place in Barrayaran strategic and tactical considerations, Miles had never set foot on the world before. He didn't now, either, at least not right away. Grimacing, he allowed Ekaterin and ghem-General Benin to help him from the van into a floater. In the ceremony to come, he planned to stand on his feet, but a very little experimentation had taught him that he had better conserve his endurance. At least he wasn't alone in his need for mechanical aid. Nicol hovered, shepherding Bel Thorne. The herm sat up and managed its own floater controls, only the oxygen tube to its nose betraying its extreme debilitation.

Armsman Roic, his Vorkosigan House uniform pressed and polished, took up station behind Miles and Ekaterin, at his very stiffest and most silent. Spooked half to death, Miles gauged. Miles couldn't blame him.

Deciding he represented the whole of the Barrayaran Empire tonight, and not just his own House, Miles had elected to wear his plain civilian gray. Ekaterin seemed tall and graceful as a haut in some flowing thing of gray and black; Miles suspected under-the-table female sartorial help from Pel, or one of Pel's many minions. As ghem-General Benin led the party forward, Ekaterin paced beside Miles's floater, her hand resting lightly upon his arm. Her faint, mysterious smile was as reserved as ever, but it seemed to Miles as though she walked with a new and firm confidence, unafraid in the shadowed dark.

Benin stopped at a small group of men, glimmering up out of the murk like specters, who were gathered a few meters from the lift van. Complex perfumes drifted from their clothing through the damp air, distinct, yet somehow not clashing. The ghem-general meticulously introduced each member of the party to the current haut governor of Rho Ceta, who was of the Degtiar constellation, cousin in some kind to the present Empress. The governor, too, was dressed, as were all the haut men present, in the loose white tunic and trousers of full mourning, with a multilayered white over-robe that swept to his ankles.

The former occupant of this post, whom Miles had once met, had made it plain that outlander barbarians were barely to be tolerated, but this man swept a low and apparently sincere bow, his hands pressed formally together in front of his chest. Miles blinked, startled, for the gesture more resembled the bow of a ba to a haut than the nod of a haut to an outlander.

"Lord Vorkosigan. Lady Vorkosigan. Portmaster Thorne. Nicol of the Quaddies. Armsman Roic of Barrayar. Welcome to Rho Ceta. My household is at your service."

They all returned suitably civil murmurs of thanks. Miles considered the wording—*my household*, not *my government*, and was reminded that what he was seeing tonight was a *private* ceremony. The haut governor was momentarily distracted by the lights on the horizon of a shuttle dropping from orbit, his lips parting at he peered up into the glowing night sky, but the craft banked disappointingly away toward the opposite side of the city. The governor turned back, frowning.

A few minutes of polite small talk between the haut governor and Benin—formal wishes for the continued health of the Cetagandan emperor and his empresses, and somewhat more spontaneous-sounding inquiries after mutual acquaintances—was broken off again as another shuttle's lights appeared in the wide predawn dark. The governor swung around to stare again. Miles glanced back over the silent crowd of haut men and haut lady bubbles scattered like white flower petals across the bowl of the hillside. They emitted no cries, they scarcely seemed to move, but Miles felt rather than heard a sigh ripple across their ranks, and the tension of their anticipation tighten.

This time, the shuttle grew larger, its lights brightening as it boomed down across the lake, which foamed in its path. Roic stepped back nervously, then forward again nearer to Miles and Ekaterin, watching the bulk of it loom almost above them. Lights on its sides picked out upon the fuselage a screaming-bird pattern, enameled red, that glowed like flame. The craft landed on its extended feet as softly as a cat, and settled, the chinks and clinks of its heated sides contracting sounding loud in the breathless, waiting stillness.

"Time to stand up," Miles whispered to Ekaterin, and grounded his floater. She and Roic helped hoist him out of it to his feet, and step forward to stand at attention. The close-cut grass, beneath his booted soles, felt like thick fine carpeting; its scent was damp and mossy.

A wide cargo hatch opened, and a ramp extended itself, illuminated from beneath in a pale, diffuse glow. First down it drifted a haut lady bubble—its force field not opaque, as the others, but transparent as gauze. Within, its float chair could be seen to be empty.

Miles murmured to Ekaterin, "Where's Pel? Thought this was all her . . . baby."

"It's for the Consort of Rho Ceta who was lost with the hijacked ship," she whispered back. "The haut Pel will be next, as she conducts the children in the dead consort's place."

Miles had met the murdered woman, briefly, a decade ago. To his regret, he could remember little more of her now than a cloud of chocolate-brown hair that had tumbled down about her, stunning beauty camouflaged in an array of other haut women of equal splendor, and a ferocious commitment to her duties. But the float chair seemed suddenly even emptier.

Another bubble followed, and yet more, and ghemwomen and ba servitors. The second bubble drew up beside the haut governor's group, grew transparent, and then winked out. Pel in her white robes sat regally in her float chair.

"Ghem-General Benin, as you are charged, please convey now the thanks of Emperor the haut Fletchir Giaja to these outlanders who have brought our Constellations' hopes home to us."

She spoke in a normal tone, and Miles didn't see the voice pickups, but a faint echo back from the grassy bowl told him their words were being conveyed to all assembled here.

Benin called Bel forward; with formal words of ceremony, he presented a high Cetagandan honor to the Betan, a paper bound in ribbon, written in the Emperor's Own Hand, with the odd name of the Warrant of the Celestial House. Miles knew Cetagandan ghem-lords who would have traded their own mothers to be enrolled on the year's Warrant List, except that it wasn't nearly that easy to qualify. Bel dipped its floater for Benin to press the beribboned roll into its hands, and though its eyes were bright with irony, murmured thanks to the distant Fletchir Giaja in return, and kept its sense of humor, for once, under full control. It probably helped that the herm was still so exhausted it could barely hold its head upright, a circumstance for which Miles had not expected to be grateful.

Miles blinked, and suppressed a huge grin, when Ekaterin was next called forward by ghem-General Benin and bestowed with a like beribboned honor. Her obvious pleasure was not without its edge of irony either, but she returned an elegantly worded thank you.

"My Lord Vorkosigan," Benin spoke.

Miles stepped forward a trifle apprehensively.

"My Imperial Master, the Emperor the haut Fletchir Giaja, reminds me that true delicacy in the giving of gifts considers the tastes of the recipient. He therefore charges me only to convey to you his personal thanks, in his own Breath and Voice."

First prize, the Cetagandan Order of Merit, and what an embarrassment *that* medal had been, a decade ago. Second prize, *two* Cetagandan Orders of Merit? Evidently not. Miles breathed a sigh of relief, only slightly tinged with regret. "Tell your Imperial Master from me that he is entirely welcome."

"My Imperial Mistress, the Empress the haut Rian Degtiar, Handmaiden of the Star Crèche, also charged me to convey to you her own thanks, in her own Breath and Voice."

Miles bowed perceptibly lower. "I am at *her* service in this."

Benin stepped back; the haut Pel moved forward. "Indeed. Lord Miles Naismith Vorkosigan of Barrayar, the Star Crèche calls you up."

He'd been warned about this, and talked it over with Ekaterin. As a practical matter, there was no point in refusing the honor; the Star Crèche had to have about a kilo of his flesh on private file already, collected not only during his treatment here, but from his memorable visit to Eta Ceta all those years back. So with only a slight tightening of his stomach, he stepped forward, and permitted a ba servitor to roll back his sleeve and present the tray with the gleaming sampling needle to the haut Pel.

Pel's own white, long-fingered hand drove the sampling needle into the fleshy part of his forearm. It was so fine, its bite scarcely pained him; when she withdrew it, barely a drop of blood formed on his skin, to be wiped away by the servitor. She laid the needle into its own freezer case, held it high for a moment of public display and declaration, closed it, and set it away in a compartment in the arm of her float chair. The faint murmur from the throng in the amphitheater did not seem to be outrage, though there was, perhaps, a tinge of amazement. The highest honor any Cetagandan could achieve, higher even than the bestowal of a haut bride, was to have his or her genome formally taken up into the Star Crèche's banks—for disassembly, close examination, and possible selective insertion of the approved bits into the haut race's next generation.

Miles, rolling his sleeve back down, muttered to Pel, "It's prob'ly nurture, not nature, y'know."

Her exquisite lips resisted an upward crook to form the silent syllable, *Sh*.

The spark of dark humor in her eye was veiled again as if seen through the morning mist as she reactivated her force shield. The sky to the east, across the lake and beyond the next range of hills, was turning pale. Coils of fog curled across the waters of the lake, its smooth surface growing steel gray in reflection of the predawn luminescence.

A deeper hush fell across the gathering of haut as through the shuttle's door and down its ramp floated array after array of replicator racks, guided by the ghem-women and ba servitors. Constellation by constellation, the haut were called forth by the acting consort, Pel, to receive their replicators. The Governor of Rho Ceta left the little group of visiting dignitaries/heroes to join with his clan, as well, and Miles realized that his humble bow, earlier, had not been any kind of irony after all. The white-clad crowd assembled were not the whole of the haut race residing on Rho Ceta, just the fraction whose genetic crosses, arranged by their clan heads, bore fruit this day, this year.

The men and women whose children were here delivered might never have touched or even seen each other till this dawn, but each group of men accepted from the Star Crèche's hands the children of their getting. They floated the racks in turn to the waiting array of white bubbles carrying their genetic partners. As each constellation rearranged itself around its replicator racks, the force screens turned from dull mourning white to brilliant colors, a riotous rainbow. The rainbow bubbles streamed away out of the amphitheater, escorted by their male companions, as the hilly horizon across the lake silhouetted itself against the dawn fire, and above, the stars faded in the blue.

When the haut reached their home enclaves, scattered around the planet, the infants would be given up again into the hands of their ghem nurses and attendants for release from their replicators. Into the nurturing crèches of their various constellations. Parent and child might or might not ever meet again. Yet there seemed more to this ceremony than just haut protocol. *Are we not all called on to yield our children back to the world, in the end?* The Vor did, in their ideals at least. *Barrayar eats its children*, his mother had once said, according to his father. Looking at Miles.

So, Miles thought wearily. *Are we heroes here today, or the greatest traitors unhung?* What would these tiny, high haut hopefuls grow into, in time? Great men and women? Terrible foes? Had he, all unknowing, saved here some future nemesis of Barrayar—enemy and destroyer of his own children still unborn?

And if such a dire precognition or prophecy had been granted to him by some cruel god, could he have acted any differently?

He sought Ekaterin's hand with his own cold one; her fingers wrapped his with warmth. There was enough light for her to see his face, now. "Are you all right, love?" she murmured in concern.

"I don't know. Let's go home."

Epilogue

Epilogue

They said good-bye to Bel and Nicol at Komarr orbit.

Miles had ridden along to the ImpSec Galactic Affairs transfer station offices here for Bel's final debriefing, partly to add his own observations, partly to see that the ImpSec boys did not fatigue the herm unduly. Ekaterin attended too, both to testify and to make sure Miles didn't fatigue himself. Miles was hauled away before Bel was.

"Are you sure you two don't want to come along to Vorkosigan House?" Miles asked anxiously, for the fourth or fifth time, as they gathered for a final farewell on an upper concourse. "You missed the wedding, after all. We could show you a very good time. My cook alone is worth the trip, I promise you." Miles, Bel, and of course Nicol hovered in floaters. Ekaterin stood with her arms crossed, smiling slightly. Roic wandered an invisible perimeter as if loath to give over his duties to the unobtrusive ImpSec guards. The armsman had been on continuous alert for so long, Miles thought, he'd forgotten how to take a shift off. Miles understood the feeling. Roic was due at least two weeks of uninterrupted home leave when they returned to Barrayar, Miles decided.

Nicol's brows twitched up. "I'm afraid we might disturb your neighbors."

"Stampede the horses, yeah," said Bel.

Miles bowed, sitting; his floater bobbed slightly. "My horse would like you fine. He's extremely amiable, not to mention much too old and lazy to stampede anywhere. And I personally guarantee that with a Vorkosigan liveried armsman at your back, not the most benighted backcountry hick would offer you insult."

Roic, passing nearby in his orbit, added a confirming nod.

Nicol smiled. "Thanks all the same, but I think I'd rather go someplace where I don't *need* a bodyguard."

Miles drummed his fingers on the edge of his floater. "We're working on it. But look, really, if you—"

"Nicol is tired," said Ekaterin, "probably homesick, and she has a convalescing herm to look after. I expect she'll be glad to get back to her own sleepsack and her own routine. Not to mention her own music."

The two exchanged one of those League of Women looks, and Nicol nodded gratefully.

"Well," said Miles, yielding with reluctance. "Take care of each other, then."

"You, too," said Bel gruffly. "I think it's time you gave up those hands-on ops games, hey? Now that you're going to be a daddy and all. Between this time and the last time, Fate has got to have your range bracketed. Bad idea to give it a third shot, I think."

Miles glanced involuntarily at his palms, fully healed by now. "Maybe so. God knows Gregor probably has a list of domestic chores waiting for me as long as a quaddie's arms all added together. The last one was wall-to-wall commit-tees, coming up with, if you can believe it, new Barrayaran bio-law for the Council of Counts to approve. It took a year. If he starts another one with, 'You're half Betan, Miles, you'd be just the man'—I think I'll turn and run."

Bel laughed; Miles added, "Keep an eye on young Cor-beau for me, eh? When I toss a protégé in to sink or swim like that, I usually prefer to be closer to hand with a life preserver."

"Garnet Five messaged me, after I sent to tell her Bel was going to live," said Nicol. "She says they're doing all right so far. At any rate, Quaddiespace hasn't declared all Barraya-ran ships *non grata* forever or anything yet."

"That means there's no reason you two couldn't come back someday," Bel pointed out. "Or at any rate, stay in touch. We are both free to communicate openly now, I might observe."

Miles brightened. "If discreetly. Yes. That's true."

They exchanged some un-Barrayaran hugs all around; Miles didn't care what his ImpSec lookouts thought. He floated, holding Ekaterin's hand, to watch the pair progress out of sight toward the commercial ship docks. But even before they'd rounded the corner he felt his face pulled around, as if by a magnetic force, in the opposite direction—toward the military arm of the station, where the *Kestrel* awaited their pleasure.

Time ticked in his head. "Let's go."

"Oh, yes," said Ekaterin.

He had to speed his floater to keep up with her length-ening stride up the concourse.

Gregor waited to greet Lord Auditor and Lady Vorkosi-gan upon their return, at a special reception at the Imperial Residence. Miles trusted whatever reward the Emperor had in mind would be less disturbingly arcane than that of the haut ladies. But Gregor's party was going to have to be put off a day or two. The word from their obstetrician back at Vorkosigan House was that the children's sojourn in their replicators was stretched to nearly its maximum safe extension. There had been enough oblique medical disapproval in the tone of the message, it didn't even need Ekaterin's nervous jokes about ten-month twins and how glad she was now for replicators to get him aimed in the right direction, and no more damned interruptions.

He'd undergone these homecomings what seemed a thousand times, yet this one felt different than any before. The groundcar from the military shuttleport, Armsman Pym driving, pulled up under the porte-cochère of Vorkosigan House, looming stone pile that it ever was. Ekaterin bustled out first and gazed longingly toward the door, but paused to wait for Miles.

When they'd left Komarr orbit five days ago he'd traded in the despised floater for a slightly less despised cane, and spent the journey hobbling incessantly up and down what limited corridors the *Kestrel* provided. His strength was returning, he fancied, if more slowly than he'd hoped. Maybe he would look into getting a swordstick like Commodore Koudelka's for the interim. He pulled himself to his feet, swung the cane in briefly jaunty defiance, and offered Ekaterin his arm. She rested her hand lightly upon it, covertly ready to grab if needed. The double doors swung open on the grand old black-and-white paved entry hall.

The mob was waiting, headed by a tall woman with roan-red hair and a delighted smile. Countess Cordelia Vorkosigan actually hugged her daughter-in-law first. A white-haired, stocky man advanced from the antechamber to the left, face luminous with pleasure, and stood in line for his chance with Ekaterin before turning to his son. Nikki clattered down the sweeping stairway and into his mother's arms, and returned her tight hug with only a tinge of embarrassment. The boy had grown at least three centimeters in the past two months. When he turned to Miles, and copied the Count's handshake with dauntingly grown-up resolve, Miles found himself looking *up* into his stepson's face.

A dozen armsmen and servants stood around grinning; Ma Kosti, the peerless cook, pressed a splendid bunch of flowers on Ekaterin. The Countess handed off an awkwardly worded but sincere message of felicitation for their impending parenthood from Miles's brother Mark, at graduate school on Beta Colony, and a rather more fluent one from his Grandmother Naismith there. Ekaterin's older brother, Will Vorvayne, unexpectedly present, took vids of it all.

"Congratulations," Viceroy Count Aral Vorkosigan was saying to Ekaterin, "on a job well done. Would you like another? I'm sure Gregor can find you a place in the diplomatic corps after this, if you want it."

She laughed. "I think I have at least three or four jobs already. Ask me again in, oh, say about twenty years." Her glance went to the staircase leading to the upper floors, and the nursery.

Countess Vorkosigan, who caught the look, said, "Everything is waiting and ready as soon as you are."

After the briefest of washups in their second-floor suite, Miles and Ekaterin made their way down a servitor-crowded hallway to rendezvous with the core family again in the nursery. With the addition of the birth team—an obstetrician, two medtechs, and a bio-mechanic—the small chamber overlooking the back garden was as full as it could hold. It seemed as public a birth as those poor monarchs' wives in the old histories had ever endured, except that Ekaterin had the advantage of being upright, dressed, and dignified. All of the cheerful excitement, none of the blood or pain or fear. Miles decided that he approved.

The two replicators, released from their racks, stood side by side on a table, full of promise. A medtech was just finishing fiddling with a cannula on one. "Shall we proceed?" inquired the obstetrician.

Miles glanced at his parents. "How did *you* all do this, back then?"

"Aral lifted one latch," said his mother, "and I lifted the other. Your grandfather, General Piotr, lurked menacingly, but he came around to a wider way of thinking later." His mother and his father exchanged a private smile, and Aral Vorkosigan shook his head wryly.

Miles looked to Ekaterin.

"It sounds good to me," she said. Her eyes were brilliant with joy. It lifted Miles's heart to think that *he* had given her that happiness.

They advanced to the table. Ekaterin went around, and the techs scrambled out of her way; Miles hooked his cane over the edge, supported himself with one hand, and raised the other to match Ekaterin's. A double snap sounded from the latches. They moved down and repeated the gesture with the second replicator.

"Good," Ekaterin whispered.

Then they had to stand out of the way, watching with irrational anxiety as the obstetrician popped the first lid, swept the exchange tube matting aside, slit the caul, and lifted the pink squirming infant out into the light. A few heart-stopping moments clearing air passages, draining and cutting the cord; Miles breathed again when little Aral Alexander did, and blinked his blurring lashes. He felt less self-conscious when he noticed his father wipe his eyes. Countess Vorkosigan gripped her skirts at her sides, forcibly making hungry grandmotherly hands wait their turn. The Count's hand on Nikki's shoulder tightened, and Nikki in his front-and-center viewpoint lifted his chin and grinned. Will Vorvayne bobbed around trying to get better vid angles, until his little sister put on her firmest Lady Ekaterin Vorkosigan voice and quashed his attempts at stage directing. He looked startled, but backed off.

By some tacit assumption, Ekaterin got first dibs. She held her new son and watched as the second replicator yielded up her very first daughter. Miles leaned on his cane at her elbow, his eyes devouring the astonishing sight. A baby. A *real* baby. *His*. He'd thought his children had seemed real enough, when he'd touched the replicators in which they grew. That was nothing like this. Little Aral Alexander was so small. He blinked and stretched. He breathed, actually breathed, and placidly smacked his tiny lips. He had a notable amount of black hair. It was wonderful. It was . . . terrifying.

"Your turn," said Ekaterin, smiling at Miles.

"I . . . I think I'd better sit down, first." He half-fell into an armchair brought hastily forward for him. Ekaterin tucked the blanket-wrapped bundle into his panicked arms. The Countess hovered over the back of the chair like some maternal vulture.

"He seems so small."

"What, four point one kilos!" chortled Miles's mother. "He's a little bruiser, he is. You were half that size when you were taken out of the replicator." She continued with an

unflattering description of Miles at that moment that Ekaterin not only ate up, but *encouraged*.

A lusty yowl from the replicator table made Miles start;
he looked up eagerly. Helen Natalia announced her arrival
in no uncertain terms, waving freed fists and howling. The
obstetrician completed his examination and pressed her
rather hastily into her mother's reaching arms. Miles
stretched his neck. Helen Natalia's dark, wet wisps of hair
were going to be as auburn as promised, he fancied, when
they dried.

With two babies to go around, all the people lined up to
hold them would have their chances soon enough, Miles
decided, accepting Helen Natalia, still making noise, from
her grinning mother. They could wait a few more
moments. He stared at the two bundles more than filling
his lap in a kind of cosmic amazement.

"We *did* it," he muttered to Ekaterin, now perching on
the chair arm. "Why didn't anybody stop us? Why aren't
there more regulations about this sort of thing? What fool
in their right mind would put *me* in charge of a baby? Two
babies?"

Her brows drew together in quizzical sympathy. "Don't
feel bad. I'm sitting here thinking that eleven years suddenly seems longer than I realized. I don't remember
anything about babies."

"I'm sure it'll all come back to you. Like, um, like flying
a lightflyer."

He had been the end point of human evolution. At this
moment he abruptly felt more like a missing link. *I thought
I knew everything. Surely I knew nothing.* How had his own
life become such a surprise to him, so utterly rearranged?
His brain had whirled with a thousand plans for these tiny
lives, visions of the future both hopeful and dire, funny and

fearful. For a moment, it seemed to come to a full stop. *I have no idea who these two people are going to be.*

Then it was everyone else's turn, Nikki, the Countess, the Count. Miles watched enviously his father's sure grip of the infant on his shoulder. Helen Natalia actually stopped screaming there, reducing the noise level to one of more generalized, desultory complaint.

Ekaterin slipped her hand into his and gripped tightly. It felt like free falling into the future. He squeezed back, and soared.

Miles Vorkosigan/Naismith: His Universe and Times

Chronology	Events	Chronicle
Approx. 200 years before Miles's birth	Quaddies are created by genetic engineering.	*Falling Free*
During Beta-Barrayaran War	Cordelia Naismith meets Lord Aral Vorkosigan while on opposite sides of a war. Despite difficulties, they fall in love and are married.	*Shards of Honor*
The Vordarian Pretendership	While Cordelia is pregnant, an attempt to assassinate Aral by poison gas fails, but Cordelia is affected; Miles Vorkosigan is born with bones that will always be brittle and other medical problems. His growth will be stunted.	*Barrayar*
Miles is 17	Miles fails to pass physical test to get into the Service Academy. On a trip, necessities force him to improvise the Free Dendarii Mercenaries into existence; he has unintended but unavoidable adventures for four months. Leaves the Dendarii in Ky Tung's competent hands and takes Elli Quinn to Beta for rebuilding of her damaged face; returns to Barrayar to thwart plot against his father. Emperor pulls strings to get Miles into the Academy.	*The Warrior's Apprentice*

Miles is 20	Ensign Miles graduates and immediately has to take on one of the duties of the Barrayaran nobility and act as detective and judge in a murder case. Shortly afterwards, his first military assignment ends with his arrest. Miles has to rejoin the Dendarii to rescue the young Barrayaran emperor. Emperor accepts Dendarii as his personal secret service force.	"The Mountains of Mourning" in Borders of Infinity *The Vor Game*
Miles is 22	Miles and his cousin Ivan attend a Cetagandan state funeral and are caught up in Cetagandan internal politics.	*Cetaganda*
	Miles sends Commander Elli Quinn, who's been given a new face on Beta, on a solo mission to Kline Station.	*Ethan of Athos*
Miles is 23	Now a Barrayaran Lieutenant, Miles goes with the Dendarii to smuggle a scientist out of Jackson's Whole. Miles's fragile leg bones have been replaced by synthetics.	"Labyrinth" in *Borders of Infinity*
Miles is 24	Miles plots from within a Cetagandan prison camp on Dagoola IV to free the prisoners. The Dendarii fleet is pursued by the Cetagandans and finally reaches Earth for repairs. Miles has to juggle both his identities at once, raise money for repairs, and defeat a plot to replace him with a double. Ky Tung stays on Earth. Commander Elli Quinn is now Miles's right-hand officer. Miles and the Dendarii depart for Sector IV on a rescue mission.	"The Borders of Infinity" in *Borders of Infinity* *Brothers in Arms*

Miles is 25	Hospitalized after previous mission, Miles's broken arms are replaced by synthetic bones. With Simon Illyan, Miles undoes yet another plot against his father while flat on his back.	*Borders of Infinity*
Miles is 28	Miles meets his clone brother Mark again, this time on Jackson's Whole.	*Mirror Dance*
Miles is 29	Miles hits thirty; thirty hits back.	*Memory*
Miles is 30	Emperor Gregor dispatches Miles to Komarr to investigate a space accident, where he finds old politics and new technology make a deadly mix.	*Komarr*
	The Emperor's wedding sparks romance and intrigue on Barrayar, and Miles plunges up to his neck in both.	*A Civil Campaign*
Miles is 32	Miles and Ekaterin's honeymoon journey is interrupted by an Auditorial mission to Quaddiespace, where they encounter old friends, new enemies, and a double handful of intrigue.	*Diplomatic Immunity*

The following is an excerpt from:

The Vorkosigan Companion

Edited by
Lillian Stewart Carl
and John Helfers

Available from Baen Books
December 2008
Hardcover

Preface

"Gosh, is it midnight already?"

There are many memorable firsts in a writer's career. First story started—first finished. First submission. First rejection. First sale! First review, good/bad. First public speech about one's writing, urk. First fan letter! First time meeting one's editor face-to-face. First award nomination—first win! Maybe, a first film option. First time on a genre bestseller list—first time on a *general* bestseller list, though this is a much rarer prize. First career award—what, already? but I'm not finished yet! First book *about* one's books.

I'm not just sure where we've arrived, but we're definitely here.

Head down and pedaling as hard as possible, it's not often that working writers have a chance to look back and see just how far they've traveled. Much of my biography and literary biography are covered in the articles and interview that follow, so I won't linger to recap it all here. But in this year, 2007, and in 2008 upcoming, have fallen a couple of firsts that force me to pause and put it in perspective.

My first career award came last month from the Ohio-ana Library Association. Literary awards generally, by nature intrinsically subjective, are mysterious gifts bestowed upon writers; it is something done to us, not something like finishing a novel—that we do. Career awards seem to be awards for winning awards, a suspicious circularity. (That said, this year's Ohioana memento takes the prize for being the prettiest ever, a gorgeous piece of art glass looking like a transparent blue jellyfish. Lead glass apparently looks extremely strange on airport x-ray machines, however. Someone could write a whole essay on the sometimes-deadly designs of the various awards and the challenges of getting them home.)

Next year, as I write this (though it will be a done deal by the time this book is published) I have been invited to be Writer Guest of Honor at the 2008 World Science Fiction Convention in Denver, Colorado, which is very much a career award in its own right. I put pencil to paper for my first science fiction novel in 1982; from there to this in a mere 26 years. Seems . . . fast.

Writing stories, using words to sculpt other people's thoughts, would appear to be the most evanescent of arts. Writers make and sell dreams; the vast publishing industry that conveys those dreams between the writer's head and the reader's seems a lumbering vehicle for such a light load. And yet, of all the many tasks I've undertaken in my life—apart from bearing and raising my children—it's my books that have best lasted and carried forward, the main thing I have to show for all my efforts. The line-up of first editions on my office bookshelf seems a procession of captured years, my basement full of books like an array of vintages laid down in a wine cellar.

A certain branch of linguistics and culture studies has a catch-phrase—"time-binding"—to tag those inventions, including writing, that allow humans to carry their culture and achievements forward, through time that otherwise destroys all things each instant. I would quibble a little with the phrase, since it's not actually time that is bound. "We can neither make, nor retain, a single moment of time," as C. S. Lewis remarks somewhere. But for a little while, time's grinding teeth may be eluded. Most of my life's labors were consumed almost as soon as committed—all that housekeeping plowed under, all those meals I cooked gone in a day, all the forgettable daily tasks duly forgotten. But "Words," as another writer said, "can outlast stones." I'm not sure mine will go that far, but they definitely outlast meals.

I'm a bit bemused by this present volume. Why spend precious time reading *about* books—or worse, about the author—when you could be reading the *actual* books? But I presume the main audience here will be those who have read parts or all of the Vorkosigan saga already, a reflection which allays my writerly anxiety. For you all, I trust that many amusements and some lively discussion follow. So I will get out of the way of the text—as writers should—and bid you all have fun.

Lois McMaster Bujold
Edina, Minnesota, November 2007

(This is the preface from *The Vorkosigan Companion*, edited by Lillian Stewart Carl and John Helfers.)

A Conversation with
Lois McMaster Bujold

By Lillian Stewart Carl

Lillian Stewart Carl: Your father was a remarkably patient man, letting us use his recording equipment and his typewriter for our own projects. Or we'd just sprawl in his chairs and read.

Lois McMaster Bujold: I fell in love with reading early, but hit my stride in third grade when I discovered that I wasn't limited to the thin "grade level" picture books they laid out for our class during library periods, but could take any book from the shelf. I fell ravenously on Walter Farley and Marguerite Henry (this was my horse-obsessed period), and never looked back. I started reading science fiction when I was nine, because my father read it—he used to buy *Analog* magazine and the occasional paperback to read on the plane during consulting trips. With that introduction, no one was ever going to fool me into thinking SF was kid stuff!

LSC: Kid stuff?

LMB: Well, one must admit, SF has roots in boys'-own-adventure genres; I dimly remember reading SFnal tales in my older brother's copies of *Boy's Life* (a Boy Scout magazine) back then. But the term "adolescent" when applied to SF is not necessarily a pejorative, in my later and wider view. The great psychological work of adolescence (in our culture, anyway) is to escape the family, especially the mother but in some families the father, depending on which parent is more intent on enforcing the social norms, in order to create oneself as an autonomous person. This is why, I theorize, so much fantasy and SF is so hell-bent on destroying the protagonist's family, first thing, before anything else. Villages must be pillaged and burned, lost heirs smuggled off to be raised elsewhere, Sfnal social structures devised that eliminate family altogether—because before anything at all can happen, you have to escape your parents. It's their job to prevent you having adventures, after all.

When I was a kid, my favorite writers included Poul Anderson and James H. Schmitz—who had great female leads in his tales—the usual Heinlein (the juveniles, not his later work), Asimov, and Clarke, Fritz Leiber, L. Sprague de Camp, Mack Reynolds, Eric Frank Russell, Zenna Henderson; toward the end of that period there was Anne McCaffrey, Randall Garrett, Roger Zelazny, Tolkien, Cordwainer Smith, and so on. There was a lot less SF on the library shelves in those days; you could read it all up, and I did.

I discovered the SF sections at the public libraries I could occasionally get to. Since we lived on the outer edge of the suburbs, and there was no public transportation, getting to a library involved getting my mother to drive me the 10 or 20 miles there, which became easier when I reached age 16 and could drive myself.

LMB: We didn't know fandom existed till after high school. In junior high we shared our love of books, watched favorite television shows and fell in love with their heroes together (*The Man From U.N.C.L.E.! Star Trek!* The shortlived TV version of *The Wackiest Ship in the Army!*), and became each other's first readers for the (mostly highly derivative) stories, scripts, and poetry that boiled up in both our heads—we were inspired to write because we loved to read, and because stories poured through our heads, welling up uninvited from wherever these thoughts come.

I introduced you to SF and fantasy, and you introduced me to history and archeology. This was the early 1960's, and American television was filled with World War II shows. It was all around in the culture. We shared books like *Escape from Colditz*, which was about WW II prisoner of war camp escapes in Germany by American soldiers. I think it is because we were trapped in high-school and the idea of breaking out of the prison camp was a very captivating idea. "Maybe if we dig a tunnel we could get out of the classroom. . . ."

LSC: One of our history teachers was a big fan of the movie *Stalag 17*, so I suppose the thought of breaking out wasn't exclusive to the students. I well remember writing a brief piece where I was magically transported from the crowded halls of the high school to the Pelennor Fields, hearing the horns of Rohan in the dawn.

LMB: My Tolkienesque epic, embarked upon at age fifteen and never finished, at least has the dubious distinction of having been written in Spenserian verse, the result of having read *The Lord of the Rings* and *The Faerie Queene* twice that year.

LMB: I bought an Ace pirated edition of *The Fellowship of the Ring* on a family vacation to Italy, and found the ending to be a huge disappointment; it just sort of trailed off. Oh, lord, I thought, it's one of those darn dismal British writers... There was nothing on the cover, spine, blurb, nor after the last page that indicated there was more, except for a brief reference buried at the end of the "about the author" paragraph to it being a heroic romance published in three parts. Marketing was more primitive in those days, I suppose.

Half a year later, it was with overwhelming joy, still remembered vividly, that I found its two sequels. I don't remember the names of most of my high school teachers, mind you, but I can still remember where I was sitting when I first opened up *The Two Towers* and read, with a pounding heart, "Aragorn sped on up the hill . . ." My father's home office, the air faintly acrid with the scent of his pipe tobacco, in the big black chair under the window, yellow late afternoon winter light shining in through the shredding silver-gray clouds beyond the chill bare Ohio woods to the west. Now, that's imprinting.

The chair, the room, the man, the world are all gone now. I still have the book. It has stitched itself like a thread through my life from that day to this, read variously, with different perceptions at different ages; today, my over-trained eye even proofreads as it travels over the lines, and sometimes stops to re-arrange a sentence or quibble with a word choice. Is it a perfect book? No, doubtless not. No human thing is. Is it a great book? It is in my heart; it binds time for me, and binds the wounds of time.

"And he sang to them . . . until their hearts, wounded with sweet words, overflowed, and their joy was like swords, and they passed in thought out to regions where pain and delight flow together and tears are the very wine of blessedness" is no bad epitaph for a writer. I could crawl on my knees through broken glass for the gift of words that pierce like those.

LSC: How did you get started?

LMB: I count the beginning of this effort as Thanksgiving Day, 1982, when, visiting my parents, I wrote a paragraph or two on my Dad's new Kay Pro II to try out the toy. I dimly recall that the fragment of description actually had its genesis from a writing exercise done for a couple of visits to a local Marion writer's group. They were mostly middle-aged and elderly women who met in a church basement and wrote domestic and religious poetry; after a hiatus, I found them again the following year when they'd moved to a bank basement, and inflicted much early SF on them. They were a very patient, if wildly inappropriate, audience. The fragment generated, the following month, my first story, a novelette eventually titled "Dreamweaver's Dilemma", although the actual paragraphs were cut from the final version.

Later, I found a much more useful (and younger) group of aspiring writers farther away in Columbus, including some SF, fantasy, and mainstream people. Another influence that certainly deserves mention is Dee Redding, the wife of the minister of my parents' church. She used to let me come and read to her from my scrawled penciled first drafts while she darned socks, and say encouraging things. Lots of people were willing to tell me things. Dee was one of the few who was willing to listen.

Even though I never did formal workshops or took a degree in literature, I still found the honest and competent feedback I needed to test and hone my skills. Which was fortunate, because no editor then or now has time to be a writing teacher.

LSC: Meanwhile, at the 1982 Chicago Worldcon, I met another new fantasy writer, Patricia C. Wrede, who lived in Minneapolis. Her first novel had just been published, I had at that time sold only short stories. She said she'd be glad to critique my work, and anyone else's I happened to know— she's teased since then that *your* manuscript arrived in her mailbox at approximately the speed of light.

LMB: The three of us fell into a sort of writer's workshop by mail, sending chapters of our assorted novels back and forth to each other for critique. With your and Pat's help and encouragement, I finished my first novel and started on my second, *The Warrior's Apprentice*.

LMB: In the fall of 1984, I finished my second novel and started on the third, in the meanwhile sending the first two off to New York publishers, where they languished on assorted editors' desks for what seemed to me very long times. It was a difficult period, financially and otherwise, and as a get-rich-quick scheme writing did not seem to be paying off. But in the summer of '85, my second novel *The Warrior's Apprentice* had returned rejected. You suggested I send it next to the senior editor at Baen Books, Betsy Mitchell. Tell again where you met?

LSC: Standing in line for the bar at the 1983 Baltimore Worldcon. Although it was at the Austin NASFiC in 1985 that I suggested to her she might enjoy your work.

LMB: Your Worldcon attendances have proved awfully useful for my career, I think. So I followed your advice. That October, Jim Baen called and made an offer on all three finished manuscripts.

LSC: And you immediately called me, asking me to use my resources as a SFWA member to determine just who these people were and if they were legit! Admirable caution, considering you were tap-dancing on the ceiling at the time.

LMB: Baen Books actually started at nearly the same moment I first set pencil to paper on my first novel, and were still new in 1985, so I may perhaps be forgiven for having barely heard of them. I had no idea how long or if the company would last, but hey, they wanted my books. Through a succession of phone conversations—me bewildered and slightly paranoid, Jim very patient—I gradually learned the ins and outs of how editing was done, how royalty reports were done, how books were marketed, how cover art happened, and a host of other professional skills.

I first met Jim face-to-face in an elevator crush in the lobby of the Atlanta Marriott at the '86 Worldcon. I rather hastily introduced myself, and as he was borne away into the elevator with the fannish mob he called back something like, "If you can write three books a year for seven years, I can put you on the map!" To which my plaintive reply was—and I can't now remember if I voiced it or not— "Can't I write one book a year for twenty-one years?" I don't know if he ever knew how much he alarmed me with that.

(The rest of this interview can be found in *The Vorkosigan Companion*, edited by Lillian Stewart Carl and John Helfers.)